ALPHA ONE SECURITY

HARRIS
THRESH
DUKE

JASINDA WILDER

HARRIS

ALPHA ONE

Protect at any cost.

SECURITY

New York Times and USA Today Bestselling Author
Jasinda Wilder

1

A FANTASY FULFILLED

IT WAS WAY TOO COLD OUTSIDE FOR WHAT I WAS ABOUT TO DO, but fuck it. This was going to be fun. After months of snooping around I'd finally found Nick's secret hideout where he kept all his guns and ammo. Ever since he'd first mentioned his fantasy of me naked in a bandolier with his M4 assault rifle strapped across my not-insubstantial breasts, I'd had it in mind to surprise him. But until now I hadn't had the chance.

Nicholas Harris was fastidious about anything to do with his company, Alpha One Security, and keeping his armory well stocked, well protected, and well hidden was part of that. He'd had a bunker built under our compound in the mountains of Colorado, and while I knew it existed, he'd never actually shown me the location itself or how to get into it. Not because it was a secret, however, or because Harris didn't trust me, but mainly because I had no real reason to ever go in, since I had my own Beretta, my own stash of ammo and clips, and my own safe for everything.

I had gone into Nick's office to get a book off his shelves when, quite by chance, my fingers touched something unusual when I pulled out a thick book way up near the top of the built-in bookshelf.

I smiled to myself. I knew in an instant that I had inadvertently stumbled upon the thing I had been looking for for months—the entrance to Nick's underground bunker.

I turned the handle of a thick metal door. The door opened slowly and heavily, admitting me into a small, narrow chamber blocked by yet another door. This one had an electronic screen and a camera mounted on the side. I put my palm on the screen thing and the green light flashed, scanning my hand. A while ago I remember Nick bringing me a tablet computer and asking me to place my palm on it and then speak my name after an electronic prompt. I hadn't thought much of it at the time, knowing it was for some kind of security measure or another, and I had never thought about it since. Now it all made sense.

After scanning my palm, a robotic female voice demanded that I say my full name. I did, and low and behold the door swung open to reveal a long, steep staircase leading down to the underground bunker.

The room was silent but well lit, and the walls were covered with rack after rack of weapons. Some of the guns were locked behind glass cases; others were neatly clipped into specially-made racks. Everything was pristine, not a speck of dust or dirt anywhere.

Harris had…well, more guns than the US Army it seemed to me, and certainly more than many tin-pot dictators. Racks of M4s, M-249s, every kind of assault rifle and submachine gun Heckler and Koch made, not to mention shelves and glass cases full of every kind and size of handgun ever made. There were rocket launchers and grenade launchers, even a flamethrower in one corner. If it shot a projectile, Harris had at least six of them. When Nick told me he'd built an armory into our home, I had never imagined anything like this. AK-47s, little assault rifles he called "bullpups", sniper rifles longer than I am tall, smaller hunting style rifles, revolvers, and crates full of boxes of ammo for everything.

And all this was hidden behind a bookcase in his office.

After staring in numb, dumb shock at the contents of the bunker for a full minute, I smiled to myself again—It was obvious that he had an M4 and a bandolier of shells which would be suitable for my purposes.

I went to one of the racks of M4s and chose one. It was empty, no clip, no shell in the chamber. Nick had spent months teaching me everything he knew about weapons so I could safely and accurately shoot just about everything in this room with the notable exception of the grenade and rocket launchers, the flame thrower, and the SAW. I was a damn good shot, too. No eagle-eye, but good. I was about to leave the bunker when I noticed a lone M4 hanging on the wall above the rack of identical weapons, all by itself in a place of honor. It was older, this M4. Scratched, dented, the black paint scraped off in places. Where the other weapons had serial numbers, this one had the serial number plate replaced by a plate engraved with Nick's initials: NH. This must be his personal rifle from his Army days, then. His favorite. *His* M4. So I placed the one in my hands back on the rack and gently, carefully, took down Nick's rifle. I made sure it was unloaded and then I slung the bandoliers over my shoulder—and you know something? Bandoliers are *heavy*.

Having got what I came for I left the bunker quickly and quietly, closing and locking everything behind me. Nick was going to be in for one hell of a surprise, but I was pretty sure he wouldn't be too upset when he realized what I had done…and why, most importantly. Like I said, the armory wasn't exactly a secret from me, I'd just never had reason to go looking for it or want in until now.

Back in the house I peeked out the kitchen window to make sure Nick was still in the barn, working on his latest project: restoring a World War One biplane. He was there, of course, because it was Sunday, and Sundays, when he was home from a mission, were sacred to him. He spent his free time on his small but impressive collection of vintage aircraft. Some rich guys collected cars, Nick collected aircraft. He had several vintage World War One biplanes and a World War Two Supermarine Spitfire, a Vietnam-era Huey, a jet from the Korea/Vietnam era he called a MiG, an F-4 Phantom, and several private planes, both twin and single engine, and a small private passenger jet. All of this meant the compound had its own airfield, with a beautifully paved runway long enough for him to be able to take off and land the jets. The compound was our home, of course, but it was also the base of operations for Alpha One Security.

Now that Nick's most important clients, Kyrie and Roth Valentine, were snugged down in their private Caribbean island fortress with Sasha and Alexei heading up their security operations, Nick was free to hire out his services to other clients. And considering his resources and expertise Nick was in demand, *a lot*, and rich celebrities paid his fees gladly, and without a second thought. Much of his work consisted of single events or brief trips, but there were at least two billionaires out there who had round-the-clock security provided by Alpha One Security—which we all referred to as A1S.

In a relatively short period of time, A1S had become a pretty mammoth operation, actually. It employed dozens of security contractors plus resource staff, with operations bases in LA and New York, as well as the main base here in the wilds of Colorado. The staff here consisted of Nick and Thresh, myself, and four other highly trained security experts: Puck Lawson, Duke Silver, Lear Winter, and Anselm See—his last name was pronounced *Zay*. Yes, those are their real names. I know it sounds unlikely, but they're all real; I've seen their passports—except Thresh, who's just stubborn about revealing his real name. And each of them is as infinitely badass as their names suggested. More on them later, though.

For now, let's get back to the fun stuff. Namely, my quest to fulfill Nick's fantasy.

I stripped naked, leaving my clothes in a pile on the floor in the kitchen, and then draped the bandoliers of shells over my shoulders. And holy fuck, are bullets cold against your skin. And heavy. But if all went according to plan, I wouldn't have them on for very long. I hefted the M4, opened the back door, and stepped outside.

And fuck me running, it was *way* too cold for this. April in the mountains: not even forty-five, with snow still on the ground in some places. I pulled up my metaphorical big-girl panties and ignored the cold. I gripped the stock of the rifle with one hand and rested the barrel on one shoulder in what I hoped was a casual, sexy, badass pose. Then I walked over to the barn with as much sultry sway to my hips as I could manage without popping a joint.

I approached the barn, which was huge. It had been constructed to look like a classic barn, bright red with white accents, but it was a full hangar capable of housing multiple aircraft. The main set of doors were open, revealing the cavernous interior with a loft up near the top and an open space beneath. Workbenches lined the perimeter of the outside walls, tools hanging on the walls and resting on the surfaces. As well, there were several red Craftsman tool chests beneath the workbenches. It seemed that every available surface was covered with parts of one description or another—on a long metal table near the plane he was working on, bigger ones on the floor, some in the corners or stacked along the walls.

Nick was shirtless, wearing a pair of tight, faded blue jeans and a pair of old, scuffed, battered tan combat boots, and a black A1S ball cap. Fuck, he was gorgeous. Ripped, lean and hard. Toned muscle, shredded abs, a wicked V-cut that I absolutely loved to lick, thick biceps, corded arms. He'd let his beard grow a little lately, because I loved him in a beard. It made him look a little older, but that was fine. He was just goddamned sexy with a beard. Not real long or thick, what I would call extreme scruff. A month or two worth of growth, at most, and he trimmed it to stay at that length. His hair was a little longer too, no longer the close military buzz he'd always had. Now his dark brown hair had enough length to it that he could actually style it if he wanted, which he rarely did. Usually it was just messy, maybe finger-combed so it didn't stick up. If he was working an event, he could clean up really well, but I liked him casual and messy. Just like this.

He had the radio on blasting Led Zeppelin, the hood part of the airplane engine open, twisting a wrench by feel, his cheek resting against the side of the cowl, eyes unfocused. The muscles in his back rippled as he worked the wrench, and I took a second standing in the doorway just to watch him and stare at him. I let myself work up a nice burning yearn for him.

He'd come back from a mission just yesterday, late. He'd still had enough energy to have a quickie with me, but then he'd crashed, leaving me…unfulfilled. He'd been gone for two weeks, which meant I hadn't had cock in two weeks, hadn't had an O I hadn't given myself in two weeks. That's an eternity by my standards, especially now that I'm used to getting it from my man on the regular. And by "regular" I mean pretty much every day he's home, and often twice a day. The man is a *stallion*, I'm telling you. Extreme stamina, and even more extreme sex drive. Which is good, because mine is off the charts.

So yeah, it didn't take much to work myself up. All I had to do was watch him work, watch his muscles flex and ripple, think about his mouth on my pussy, my hands on his long, thick cock…

Fuck yeah—I got all drippy just thinking about his cock.

"Ahem." I actually said the word, didn't just clear my throat. Only he had the music too loud, so I had to try again, louder. "AHEM."

He glanced at me distractedly, and then went back to turning the wrench. And then he did a double take, like a cartoon character. Pretty sure his jaw actually hit the ground and his eyes turned to big red pulsing hearts.

"Jesus, Layla." He slowly withdrew his arm from the engine cowl, his hand black with grease, holding a huge wrench. "What the hell is this?"

"I found your armory." I hauled the M4 off my shoulder and let the barrel grip slap into my open palm.

"Obviously. I was wondering how long it would take you." He pointed at the weapon in my hands. "That's not loaded is it?"

"Did you or did you not personally teach me to use firearms?"

"I did."

"Then do you really think I'd come out here like this with a loaded machine gun?"

"Assault rifle," he corrected. "Just making sure," he added.

He took a step toward me, his jade-green eyes blazing. He was prowling, that slow, sleek, predatory way he had, like a puma stalking through the grass. I held my ground, letting him come to me. His gaze raked over me, top to bottom, twice. And then fixed on my tits, visible in glimpses through the brass of the shells. Down to my core, also just barely but not quite covered by the bandoliers. And then to the M4 in my hands.

"That's the one from the wall, right?" he stated more than asked.

I nodded. "Yep. Figured it only counted as fulfilling your fantasy if I was carrying your special *assault rifle*." I emphasized the correct term.

"My fantasy?"

"Yeah, don't you remember? São Paulo? The car chase? You told me you had a fantasy involving me in nothing but a bandolier, with your M4." I swept a hand at myself in a Vanna White style gesture. "Well, here it is, me, naked, in a bandolier of bullets, holding your own very special M4."

Nick hands flexed, tightened, released. Now he was within arm's reach, but he still hadn't touched me. He was just staring at me, as if memorizing the sight of me like this. Cold as I was, I let him look. This was about fulfilling a fantasy, after all.

He must have noticed me shivering. "Cold?"

I shrugged. "A little. It is April, and I am outside naked." I let my desire burn in my eyes. "Can you warm me up?"

"I might be able to." He reached past me and pushed a button on the wall beside the open doorway, and a motor hummed quietly, sliding the twenty-foot tall doors closed. When the doors were shut, lights flickered on automatically, bright LEDs suspended from industrial hanging fixtures.

He moved back a step. "Go sit on the wing of the plane."

I did as he asked, propping my ass against the cold metal of the lower wing, rearranging the bandoliers for optimal visual affect. Instead of coming closer, though, he stayed where he was, pulled his cell phone out of his pocket, and took several photos of me from various angles. Fine by me; I knew he was the only one who would ever see them, so let him have photographic evidence.

Besides, this was fun, drawing it out.

I removed a layer of bandoliers, and struck a different pose. Another layer, another pose. Yet another layer, and now there was only one bandolier, which I hung around my neck. It covered nothing, so I was completely bare for his perusal. And peruse he did, both with his eyes and his cell phone camera.

Finally, I knew he'd taken enough photographs because he tossed the phone into the open cockpit.

"What else did your fantasy involve, Nick?" I asked in my best sultry voice.

He took the gun from my hands—yes, I know it's a *rifle* rather than gun, but I'm a girl, and guns are guns—and set it aside, leaning it butt-down against the side of the airplane.

"Well, in the original fantasy, you kept all the bandoliers on and sucked me off wearing them. And then I returned the favor, and then we fucked. Although usually I didn't get as far as us fucking before I blew my load." He gestured at me. "But I think I like this version better."

"I can put them back on," I said, reaching for the pile on the floor at my feet.

He grabbed me by the wrist, stopping me. "No, like I said, I like this better. I can see more of you."

I sank to my knees. "In that case, let's make the rest of the fantasy a reality."

Staring up at him, I unbuttoned the fly of his jeans. Unzipped him slowly. Tight black CK briefs, huge bulge behind the stretchy, slinky material. I tugged the elastic waistband down to bare his cock, which sprung free in front of my face. One hand went to that lovely organ of his, stroking slowly, gently, and the other untied his combat boots, sliding them off his feet one by one, leaving his socks on because sex in socks is funny. I mean, think about it: a dude, no matter how hot, is just inherently funnier if he's wearing nothing but a pair of socks. Bonus-funny if they're white, and knee high, like Nick's were. He stepped out of his jeans, and then his underwear, and then thank god, Nick was naked for me.

"Tell me," I said, teasing the tip of his cock with my lips, "how exactly did I suck your cock? Slowly? Quickly? Did I swallow? Or did I take it on my tits?"

"Fuck—" Nick swallowed hard, took a deep breath and sighed it out. "You're killing me, Layla."

I took him into my mouth, just a little bit. A short, light suckle, and then backed off. Kept my eyes on his. "Well? You're gonna have to talk me through this, Nick-baby. Tell me what to do."

He buried his fingers in my hair, pulled me toward his body. "Take it into your mouth. Take it deep and slow."

I stroked the hard globe of his ass with my hands and plunged my mouth down on his erection. He groaned as I took him deep. Deeper. I opened my throat and took him all the way, until my nose nudged his belly. He was fucking enormous, both long and thick, so there was a lot of cock to swallow. My eyes watered, and by the time I backed away, I was breathing hard through my nose. But Nick? His chest was rising and falling hard, his fists bunched in my hair.

"Like that?" I asked.

"Just like that. Do it again. But this time do that swallowing thing with your throat."

So I deep-throated him again, this time swallowing so my throat muscles rippled around his cock. I didn't wait for instructions, now, instead backed away, letting him fall out of my mouth, a string of saliva connecting his beautiful cock to my lips. I glanced up at him, took him again, and this time gave him three long, slow, deep strokes of my mouth and throat.

"How's that?" I asked, wrapping my hand around the head of his dick and squeezing, then caressing his length.

"God, so good."

"Now what?"

"Now you massage my balls. Touch my taint. Go down on me until I make you stop."

And that is exactly what I did. Cupped his heavy sack in my hand and massaged it with gentle fingers, using my other hand to press a finger against his taint, taking him into my mouth and blowing him with all the skill I possessed. I bobbed down slowly at first, and then faster, faster, and then slowly again. I pulled back, licked it from top to bottom, took him into my mouth again, stroked the base and bobbed and sucked around the head.

When he started to grunt and shift his hips, I stopped. "You're getting close, aren't you?"

He nodded. "Yeah, babe. I'm real close."

"Now what?"

He hesitated, which told me what he wanted next he wasn't sure about, because Nick never hesitated. "Out with it, hon. What is it you want now?"

"It's just a stupid fantasy I jerked off to."

"You want to come on me, don't you?" I stroked him while I spoke, keeping him going, keeping him right on the edge. "Where do you want to come? On my face? Or my tits? You want me to kneel in front of you with my mouth open like a porn star, waiting for the cum-shot?"

"Layla—" He growled my name, his abs tensing.

He was close, so close. I mouthed the tip, swirled my tongue around him, taking him deep, bobbing hard, pulling at his ass to get him to move. And move he did, fucking my throat. I let him fuck for the space of a dozen thrusts, and then I felt him falter, felt him tense again, pulling back.

"Give it to me, baby," I said, staring up at him.

I sank down low, kept my eyes on him, put my mouth in front of his cock and stroked him hard and fast with both hands, switched to a hand-over-hand stroke until he was pumping into my fists, then I cupped his balls in one hand, middle finger against his taint, the other hand stroking him from root to tip, hard and slow sweeps of my fist down his length.

We'd done a lot of stuff, but he'd never come on me before,

mainly because I didn't know he wanted to. He'd never mentioned it. And actually, no one ever has.

"Fuck, Layla. I'm coming—Jesus fuck, I'm coming," he grunted.

"Give it to me, Nick. Come all over me. Let me feel you all over my face." I gazed up at him, stroking him fast now, pumping him to climax.

He tilted his head back, closed his eyes and groaned long and loud, and then, in the moment of his orgasm, he returned his eyes to mine, watching as he exploded. A thick stream of come shot out of his cock and splashed into my mouth, tasting thick and salty and smoky, splattered onto my upper lip and chin. I kept stroking, lifted up and squeezed my tits together with my arm, took another load of his sticky, warm, white seed all over the slope of my tits.

Nick was cursing up a storm, grunting, thrusting into my pumping hand, watching himself come on me.

"You like this, baby?" I asked. "You like coming on my face?"

"Fuck yeah. So hot."

"Good. Because I've never let anyone else do that before. You're the first, and the only."

"First for me too." He said, reaching down and pulling me up.

There was a rag hanging off the end of a propeller blade, which Nick snagged and used to wipe my face clean. And then, with a hungry, feral grin he wrapped his strong hands around my hips and lifted me effortlessly onto the wing of the plane. I knew what would come next, and I was eager for it. I hooked my heels over his shoulders as he knelt in front of me. He turned his cap brim around to face backward, and then tugged me down the wing so I was all but sitting on his face. I braced my hands on his shoulders, lay back against the wing, let my knees fall open, and gave myself over to his talented tongue.

And god, that tongue of his lashed me to a frenzy. He didn't use his fingers at all, this time. Only his tongue. Spearing into me, flicking and flitting with the stiffened tip, licking and suckling the hard, aching, throbbing, tingling bud of my clit.

I reached down, stole his cap from him and stuffed it onto my head over my thick mass of black curls, pulled the brim low, leaned on my elbows so I could watch him eat me. I buried the fingers of one hand into his dark brown hair. Felt my O brimming, felt it boiling. I tucked my feet up on his shoulders and spread my knees wide, rode his face, using my palm against the back of his head to jerk him harder against my slit, gyrating madly against his lapping tongue until I lost it completely, screaming like a banshee as he licked, nipped, and flitted me to climax and beyond.

And my man, my Nick, he ate me out so good for so long that he was hard and ready for me by the time I was done. And god, was I ready.

Holy fuck, was I ready; I'm never so horny and ready to fuck hard and long as when I'm fresh on the heels of a ripping orgasm.

Nick stood up, gliding his palms up the back of my thighs to hold me in place, slid his erection against my slit, grinding teasing slides of his cock against my clit. I let him tease me, and then when I was done being teased, I reached between us and grabbed a handful of dick, nestled the broad, soft, plump head against my opening, and fluttered my hips, teasing him back.

He slid the single remaining bandolier of bullets off me, tossed it aside, and pushed into me, eliciting a long groaning sigh of bliss from me. He leaned against me, palming my breast. He licked my nipple, kissed my throat, then my chin, then my lips.

"Yum," I said, smiling against his lips. "I love when your beard smells like my pussy."

"Me too," he murmured. "Thanks for this, by the way."

"For what?" I was being driven delirious by the teasing, fluttering thrusts he was giving me, so I wasn't exactly my sharpest at that moment.

"Making my stupid fantasy come true."

"It's not—oh god, oh fuck, I'm close again already—it's not stupid. I like the thought of you jerking off thinking about me." I reached down between our bodies and circled my clit with two fingers, hard and fast motions with a light, deft touch, the way I come the fastest.

"You know I jerk off thinking about you when I'm away, right?"

"You do?"

"Fuck yeah." Nick slid a single finger against the rosebud muscle of my asshole, pressed, teased, and finally slid the tip of his finger in. "Every morning, or whenever I can. Multiple times a day, some days. Those pictures I took? That's highest quality spank bank material right there, baby."

"Next time you're jerking off thinking about me, take pic. Or better yet, a video. Best would be if you can FaceTime me while you're jerking it. I'd love to watch." I was there, on the edge, keeping myself on the edge but not letting myself fall over until Nick was there. "You ready to come, baby?"

In answer, Nick pulled out and let me slide down off the wing, spun me around, pressed a hand against my head to bend me over. I assumed the position, legs spread wide—in the words of the song, face down booty up—hands braced on the wing.

I felt Nick press against me, fitting himself to my entrance, and then he rammed in. God, I loved it when he did that, fucked in hard without warning, knowing I'd take it, knowing I'd be ready for him. He grabbed hold of my hips and pulled me back into his thrusts, which were manic, wild, primal, grunting, pounding slams of his cock as deep into me as he could get, his hips slapping against the juicy meat of my ass. And fuck, it felt good. Especially when I put my fingers to my clit and got myself really going.

"Let me feel it, Nick. Give it to me."

He could only grunt in reply, fucking furiously. "Take it—fucking take it, Layla. Take it all."

"Oh fuck, I'm coming Nick. Come with me."

We both ran out of words then, both of us coming, exploding in unison, orgasming in sync. Nick shouted and I screamed and we kept up the frantic pounding pace, me pushing back into him and Nick slamming in, over and over, until he started to go limp and my thighs shook.

I collapsed against the wing, metal cold against breasts and belly, breathing hard.

And that's when Nick's phone rang.

He gently tugged himself free of me, reached up and into the cockpit to retrieve his jangling handset. "Harris." He was using his curt business voice. It was Sunday, and everyone who had his direct number knew not to call him on Sundays unless it was important.

I flipped over, sat on the wing, resting on my elbows, watching my naked, beautiful fox of a man.

"Went missing, or was taken?" Nick asked, pausing to listen, and then he spoke again. "Have they contacted the police? No? Good. Tell them to leave everything as is, I'll send Puck over with his kit ASAP. Yes, we'll take the case. No, I'll handle this one directly. Lonigan is too high profile to hand this one off to a B team. Usual fees apply, and since it might come to a retrieval situation, make sure they know about the hazard rates. Get the paperwork started and send everything you have to Layla. All right, bye." He ended the call, letting out an unhappy sigh.

"What's going on, babe?"

He spun the phone between thumb and middle finger. "Jon Lonigan and Callie MacPhereson's daughter was kidnapped. He's tapped Alpha One to bring her back."

I grabbed a tablet from the nearby workbench and called up the basics on those two while Nick made a few calls.

Jon Lonigan and Callie MacPhereson were one of the most high profile Hollywood celebrity-couples in the world, married after a whirlwind romance that had been on the front page of every gossip rag in the world. Despite both of them having been married to other people at the time of their romance, they seemed to be making it work, since they'd been together for a good six years already and married for four, which in Hollywood terms is an eternity. They'd recently had their first child together, a beautiful little girl they'd named, in classic Hollywood style, Cleopatra. Yes, Cleopatra Lonigan. I mean, it's got a ring to it, but…Cleopatra? Really?

"So you're leaving again?" I asked, only pouting a little.

"Seems like it."

"You just got back." I sounded a little petulant, but then I felt a little petulant.

I knew I'd signed up for this and all, getting together with a man like Nick Harris, but it still sucked.

"I know. But this is a big case. Huge."

"You're huge," I joked, and then reached for Harris, pulling him to me using his cock as a handle. "Think you can go again? I need to stock up, if you're leaving again already."

"Jesus, woman. I've come twice in the last thirty minutes. Give a guy a minute to recuperate." Yet, despite his protests, I felt him stirring a little.

"Can't help it if I'm starved for your loving. You were gone for two weeks. Two weeks! That's fourteen days without your dick. Fourteen days of my vibrator, which just doesn't cut it."

"You're insatiable, babe." He leaned against me, pressing me back against the wing, kissing me.

"Like you're any better?" I asked.

Oh yeah, definitely stirring. I stroked some life into it.

"No, I'm not better. Can't get enough of you. Never will, I don't think."

"So how about this time you bring me with you? I can help with the case *and* keep your bed warm."

He was hard by this time. Still perched on the edge of the wing, I slid him home, wrapped my arms around his neck and a leg around his waist so he hit the angle I liked best. This time I did the work, grinding my hips on him.

Seriously, Nicholas Harris was a beast, an absolute animal. Insatiable, unstoppable, wickedly virile. I couldn't have custom designed a better man to meet my own unquenchable sexual thirst if I'd tried.

"You're not coming with me," Nick said, cupping my tits in his hands.

"Yes I am."

"No, you're not. Holy hell, don't stop. I'm close."

"I'm so coming with you." I kept doing what I was doing, rolling my hips with Nick's cock buried deep. His thick shaft hit me just so, which meant he was making me come too. "And I'm coming, like right now. Oh god, that's good. How can it get better every single time, no matter how many times we fuck?"

"I don't know, but it does. Jesus, you feel good. So fucking good." He held onto both my thighs now and took over the thrusting, pumping himself to climax for the third time, and me for the...fifth? Sixth? I'd lost count. "And you're staying here. If whoever took Cleo Lonigan was willing and able to snatch her right out of their Malibu mansion in broad daylight, they're at least reasonably professional and likely very dangerous. I'm not risking you."

I let him pull free, holding onto his neck until he was out of me, and then I pressed my face into his chest. "I'm not staying here again, Nick. I'm just not. I've stayed back almost every mission. I want to go. I'm getting bored here."

Nick paced away from me, running his hand through his hair in frustration. He jerked his jeans off the floor and shoved his feet into them, not bothering with underwear. Then he grabbed his boots off the floor, but didn't put them on. Walking over to the control panel, he jabbed the button to open the bay doors, stopping it when they were open just wide enough to admit a body.

Paused in the opening. "Layla—god, you're so fucking stubborn. I'm telling you, you can't come on this one. I'll bring you on the next one, I promise."

I scooped up the bandoliers and draped them over my neck, snatched up the rifle, and followed him out of the barn. Once we were outside, he used the keypad on the outside to close and lock the doors, arming the alarm.

I stalked past him toward the house. "You say that now, that you'll bring me on the next one. But you won't. That one will be too dangerous, too. I'm not fucking helpless, Nick. Or have you forgotten

Brazil?"

He was right on my heels, probably staring at my ass despite our disagreement. "No, I haven't forgotten about fucking Brazil. My job is to keep you safe. Putting you in harm's way is doing the exact opposite."

I stopped in my tracks, spun around and jabbed a finger into his chest. "No, Nick, your job is *not* to keep me safe. Your job is keep me happy and to love me. I love it here; I love being an information analyst. It's challenging, and rewarding. It's the best job I've ever had, and not just because it's with you. But I'm fucking *bored*. I don't need you to babysit me, to keep me shut up in the compound like some fainting daisy prima donna. I can hold my own and take care of myself, and you fucking know it. I can be an asset...I *am* an asset."

Nick snarled, a rare expression of extreme frustration and anger. "We're not having this conversation right now, Layla." He shoved past me and into the kitchen via the back door. I followed him.

And, of course, who should be sitting at our kitchen table, sipping a cup of coffee but Puck Lawson. Five-nine, barely, but what he lacked in height he more than made up for in breadth. He was built like a wrestler, barrel-chested, arms thick as my thighs—which, let me tell you, is fucking *thick*. Trim waist, quads so massive it was ridiculous. Bald as an egg, naturally swarthy skin tanned darker by the sun, and sporting a black beard so long and thick it spread across his chest. Gimlet, intelligent brown eyes that never missed a thing. He reminded me of one of the dwarves from *The Hobbit*, actually, and not at all in a comical way. He was dangerous. Liked to drink a little too much, and liked to fight when he drank. Liked to gamble, and won more than he lost. Quick with his fists, quick with comebacks, and quicker yet with a trigger. I'd seen him perform feats of sharpshooting that shouldn't be possible, pinging a nail head with a handgun from seventy yards, one-handed, without even really trying. Of course, his skill with firearms was tertiary to his real talent: forensics. He had a Ph.D. in forensic science, actually, which came after a tour of duty in Iraq, and eight years as a special agent with the FBI before being lured away by Harris with the promise of a massive salary and a don't-ask-don't-tell policy regarding Puck's wild ways.

Puck liked his women, too. I'd seen him down in town on several occasions with more than one woman on his arm, and never the same one twice. And now he was in my kitchen. The men weren't allowed in our home, as a general rule. When Nick was home, I was naked more often than not, either post-fuck or ready for another round. Which meant the guys stayed out.

Because of situations like this. I hadn't bothered to arrange the bandoliers at all, so they were all just hanging around my neck, not covering diddly-squat. And Puck being Puck, he wasn't shy about staring.

I scooted over to hide behind Nick. "Puck, what the hell are you doing in here?"

He grinned over the rim of his coffee mug. "Waiting for the boss." He gestured at Nick with the mug.

"Well couldn't you have waited out front?" I glared at him from around Nick's back.

"Could've," Puck drawled, "But then I'd have missed this little treat. Got yourself a fine-ass woman, Harris."

Nick's voice was colder than ice and sharp as razors. "Get out, Puck, and stay the fuck out."

"I'm going, I'm going." Puck stood up and moved to the front door, taking the mug with him, walking backward, and still trying to get another glimpse at me.

"Puck." This came out as a whip-crack. "Talk about Layla like that again, look at Layla like that again, enter this house again—I'll fucking bury you. Got it?"

Puck didn't seem fazed. Just winked at me. "I didn't mean no harm, boss. I just can't help admiring a work of art."

"Puck!" Nick actually took a step forward, fists clenching.

And Puck? His eyes widened and he moved back a step. You do *not* fuck with Harris, and all his men knew it. Puck, being a gambler, liked to push buttons. He was the sort who would take a tiger by the tail, just to see what it would do. But even Puck knew when to back off when it came to Harris.

"I'll meet you outside. Need you to brief me on this Lonigan SNAFU." Puck left then, whistling a tune under his breath.

Nick shook his head in disbelief. "I swear to god, if that man wasn't the best goddamn forensic scientist I've ever seen, I'd put a bullet in his thick skull. He's absolutely incorrigible."

"He's an asshole," I said.

"Yes he is. But he's a loyal and talented asshole. If you're his friend, he'll take on Hell itself with a squirt gun for you. And god help you if you get on his bad side." Harris poured a mug of coffee for both of us. "Plus, he makes a hell of a cup of coffee."

"Is he really that good at forensics?"

Nick nodded. "Hell yes. He graduated high school at sixteen, had a Master's by twenty, got recruited by the FBI at twenty-one and had his Ph.D. by twenty-three. And the only reason he didn't move up the ladder at the FBI is because he's too much of a wild card. He's got the intelligence and the skills to run the whole show if he wanted, but he'd rather drink, fight, and fuck than sit behind a desk in Washington." A quick grin. "Plus, he'd have to shave his beard, and that's not happening."

"That beard is out of control." I sipped at the coffee; it was exceptionally good. Which is puzzling, because it's not like he used different water, beans, or brewer. He used everything we have here in our kitchen, but the coffee just tasted better than when Nick or I made it. What was his secret?

"That beard has it's own Facebook page. Legit. Look it up sometime: Puck's Beard. It's crazy. He has as many products for that fucking beard as you do for your hair. You have no idea."

I laughed out loud. "A Facebook page? You're joking. You've got to be joking."

"Truth, babe." He pulled his cell phone out of his pocket, opened the Pages app, and tapped on, yes, Puck's Beard. "Take a look."

And there it was in all its glory, the beard itself in dozens of different photographs. Selfies of Puck, close-ups, pics of women touching it, a little boy tugging on it out on the street somewhere, and even a photograph of a cockatoo peeking its head through the middle of the beard.

"That is the craziest thing I've ever seen."

"You should see him groom it in the morning. He's got special shampoo, balms, oils, brushes, combs, and all sorts of shit. We all rag on him for how long it takes him to get ready in the morning. Thresh won't room with him when we're on assignment. Says it's too much like having a bitch around, the amount of time it takes to get Puck out the door." At my raised eyebrow at the "bitch" comment, Harris held his palms up defensively. "Thresh's word, not mine."

"I really don't know where you dig up these guys, Nick," I said.

Thresh was...another rather unique individual. Standing a full seven feet tall, with a bodybuilder's physique—acres of muscles piled on mountains of more muscle. White-blond hair cropped into a Mohawk three inches wide and spiked an inch or so tall, with permanent blond scruff on his cliff-sharp jawline, as if he never shaved but couldn't grow an actual beard. Scariest motherfucker I've ever seen. Spoke four languages, deadly with any weapon and even more so with his bare hands, and was a proficient hacker, although Lear Winter was the resident tech expert. But Thresh was just...ungodly gargantuan. I watched him deadlift a Ford Taurus right off the ground, once. And not just lift it, but haul the vehicle a half a dozen feet away. The owner of the Taurus had parked too close to Thresh's pickup, and that was his way of dealing with the situation. The owner, being still in the car when Thresh moved it, had learned his lesson, I imagined.

"Put the bandoliers and M4 back, yeah?" Nick said, gesturing at me with his mug. "And keep that shit secret, okay? You're the only person aside from myself that has access, or even knows about it. I'd like to keep it that way."

I shot him a two-finger salute. "Yes sir!"

He tossed back the rest of his still-scalding coffee. "I've got to throw on some clothes so I can brief Puck."

"When are we going?"

Nick closed his eyes, visibly counting down from ten. "Layla. You're staying here. End of discussion."

"End of discussion for you, maybe."

He was in front of me, suddenly. He had my chin in his fingers, and his eyes were blazing. Not with sex, this time, but with irritation. "Do not test me, babe. I will tie you to the bed, I swear to god."

I brightened at this suggestion. "Really? I've always wanted to try a little light bondage."

"Let me clarify: I will tie you to the bed and then I'll leave. And you'll be stuck there until I send someone to let you out."

I knew he wasn't joking. But then, I don't listen.

And Nick tying me up sounded like fun. He may leave me there, but not before he had his way with me first.

Or better yet...I knew he was heading to the LA office, since Jon and Callie lived in Malibu. I could let him think I was going to actually listen to him, and then surprise him in LA...

Now my wheels were spinning, I went upstairs to shower while Nick briefed Puck and sent him ahead to LA to work the scene. I'd have to plan this carefully, as it wasn't easy to surprise Nick—as I'd just learned. He didn't miss much.

2

TROUBLEMAKER

Layla was planning something. I knew it. She had that look in her eye that she only gets when she's scheming. It was the same look she'd had whenever she used to casually refer to the location of the bunker—I knew all along she was driving herself crazy trying to find it and it was kinda funny when she actually managed it. Of course, I wasn't about to tell her that.

Which means she'll be trying to find a way to get in on this Lonigan op, and that I'm going to have to figure something out because I really don't want her in L.A.. She does a great job on the information analytics side of things and, while she knows a lot, I don't tell her everything about my work, especially when I'm personally called in. When it gets to that point, things have gotten gnarly and I just don't want her in harms way.

In this case, Jon and Callie had been swimming in their pool when they heard a scream, and a gunshot. In the space of a few short minutes their nanny had been shot and critically injured and their daughter had been kidnapped. The kidnappers had left a ransom note. No cops, obviously. Fifty million dollars within a week, or they'd get Cleo back in pieces. The note wasn't handwritten. It had been sent digitally, encrypted, the signal bounced all over the place, and it had included a photograph of a masked and hooded man holding the point of a knife to Cleo's throat.

Cleo was three.

Who the fuck kidnaps a three-year old?

Sick fucks, that's who.

By the time Jon and Callie had made it out of the pool and into the house, their nanny was near death in a pool of her own blood, and Cleo was gone. The ransom note had appeared as an email in both Jon and Callie's inboxes before they'd had a chance to make the first phone call. They hadn't called the cops. Instead they called a friend of theirs to get my number, and then they had called me. I'd done security for this friend of Jon's, and he had said I was the *only* one to call. He also stated flat-out that it would cost them a tidy sum. They called me five minutes later asking if I would be willing to go after their daughter.

Willing? Try to stop me.

I'd take the fee, of course, but the kind of scum who would kidnap and threaten to kill an innocent three-year old girl? They're dead men, they just don't know it yet. That's the thing about my guys: you won't see us coming, and when you do, it's too late.

I watched Puck straddle his Harley and fasten his Kaiser-style helmet onto his head. I hit a speed dial on my phone and it rang three times, and then a quiet, accented voice answered. "*Ja.* I have heard of the kidnapping. I am on route to the compound for briefing."

"Actually, Anselm, I have a different assignment for you."

"Which is what?" His accent rendered this *vich isss vat?*

"I need you to keep an eye on Layla for me. She's bound and determined to get in on this case, and I have a bad feeling about things. This is going to get worse before it gets better, and I don't want her involved. But you know how she is."

"She is very strong-minded, this is true." A pause. "And if she does something not so wise?"

"Just watch her. If she goes off the wire, do what you gotta do to keep her safe. Yeah?"

"*Ja*. Is no problem."

I hung up, and dialed another number. While it rang, I wondered to myself if having a man like Anselm See shadow my woman was a good idea. He was a ghost, that man. He didn't exist in any official sense, anywhere. He wasn't a technical citizen of any country, didn't have any official documentation. I knew very little about him myself, only that he was the single best shadow in the world. He operated in darkness as easily as you or I do in broad daylight. He blended utterly into any crowd, and was a master of the subtle disguise. All I really knew was that he'd been raised somewhere remote, way, way off the grid in the backwoods of Europe or Scandinavia or something. Like, out in the wilderness, where there was nothing but trees for thousands of clicks in every direction. I knew this because he'd often talk about how he missed it there, the peace, the simplicity, and how he plans to retire back there someday. But how he got his skills, I don't know. He'd probably worked as a spy for some government or another, doing the kind of ops that are so far off the books that even the black-ops guys don't know about them. Anselm See was, in his quiet, unassuming way, the scariest of all my guys which, all things considered, is saying something that makes even my blood run a little chilly.

As I expected, this next call rings for a solid minute. Knowing Lear's habits, I let it ring. Finally, he answers. "Yo."

"Lear, I need you at the compound."

"I'm in the middle of running this program, so could it wait, I dunno, an hour?"

"Lear."

He clears his throat. "Got it. I'll just…let it run then."

"Good plan. Get your ass up here."

"Got an op?"

"Why else would I be calling?"

A pause. "Oh. Good point."

Lear Winter was, in some ways, a quintessential computer geek. He'd made a fortune as a white-hat hacker, and still moonlighted doing that when he wasn't on assignment for me. At first glance he looked the part of a computer geek, too—tall, wiry, with a curly, unruly mop of sandy blond hair, a few days of growth on his chin and his thick black-rimmed glasses perpetually sitting on the tip of his nose. But the thing is, this was a look he intentionally cultivated. It kept people underestimating him. He'd made his fortune as a hacker, and then had been recruited by the NSA.

Mainly for fun, he'd tried to hack into the NSA servers. They'd caught him and kept him out, of course, because you can't actually hack the NSA. But he'd tried, and he'd gotten farther than anyone else had ever managed, so they snatched him up and taught him some new tricks. He enjoyed the work, but had tired of that gig, as well.

Somewhere along the way he'd been bitten by the adrenaline junkie bug. Free-climbing, wingsuit flying, homemade jet packs, HALO diving, motorcycle racing. Real *Pointe Break* stuff. He could and would jump off the top of a skyscraper in a wingsuit and insert himself into a moving convertible. I'd seen him do it: I'd dared him, doubting he could actually do it. He'd proved me wrong, which had cost me a hundred grand.

So if I needed someone to get in somewhere difficult while doing some *Mission Impossible* style fancy computer shit, I'd send Lear. He wasn't a combat specialist, though. The only man I trusted who hadn't killed anyone—that I knew of, anyway. Didn't mean he was soft, though. He could take care of himself, this I knew. But those were skills he kept deep under wraps. He didn't care for violence, much. He was content to let the rest of us do the dirty work, and considering Lear's prowess in other areas, the arrangement worked for us just fine.

I had one last call to make. I hit the speed dial and let it ring. "Harris. What's happening?" This was Duke Silver.

"I need you and Thresh to come in."

"I heard some rumblings. Some celeb's kid got snatched?"

"Yeah."

"If they're calling you, it must be a good one."

"I don't know if 'good' is the operative word, here. They kid-napped a three-year old girl, Duke. And they're threatening to kill her and send her home in pieces if Jon and Callie don't pay up. They're willing to pay, but they want their daughter back in one piece."

"A three-year old girl?" His voice took on a low growl.

"Cutest you've ever seen."

Duke was Thresh's best friend, and suited to the position. Almost as big, and just as deadly. And they both, despite being stone-cold killers, had soft spots for little kids. Didn't want any of their own— they claimed— but if you put a cute little girl in front of Thresh or Duke, they turned into big ol' puppy dogs. They'd play tea-time and blow bubbles and do their best dancing bear impressions. So I was sort of blatantly pushing his buttons. Not that I needed to—if I told him to suit up, Duke suited up. I sure as fuck paid him enough, so he'd better.

"Thresh is with me," Duke said. "We'll be there in forty."

"Make it thirty."

"See what we can do." He ended the call, and I pocketed my phone.

I didn't want to know what Duke and Thresh got up to when they were off-duty. Probably bench-pressing Hyundais and deadlift-ing entire buildings and eating entire cows, hooves and all, raw. You know the old cartoons where a big beefy guy would pick up a horse-shoe and eat it because he was so badass? Duke and Thresh were like that.

The crew called in, I decided it was time to pack. And see what my dear, stubborn, mischievous Layla was up to.

Not much, it turned out. I found her sitting at her iMac, brows-ing through the info Michelle had sent over from LA. She was doing it naked though, because that was Layla. She got me off three times before noon, and now was prancing around naked hoping for more. Yeah, I'm a lucky-ass man. I mean, just fucking look at her:

Thick black hair in an explosive mass of springy ringlets hang-ing loose down her back. Mocha skin stretched tight and toned and flawless over a body that had curves for goddamn days. Didn't matter how recently I'd blown my load, didn't matter how many times we went at it, I always wanted more. She just had that effect on me. She also had the effect of driving me to my actual wit's end. Stubborn, impossible, difficult, high-maintenance. Not because she was needy or clingy, but because she was just so goddamn determined to do everything her way, and never ever listened to a fucking word I ever said.

"Hey babe." She heard me, felt my presence behind her. Turned, smiled at me. "Got the troops rallied?"

"They're all on their way in, with bells on." I gestured at the computer. "Whatcha got?"

"Not much, yet. Profiles on Jon and Callie, mostly. What you'd expect. Insanely rich, though not quite up to Roth's standards. House in Malibu, one in the south of France, another in the Caribbean. Both are A-list actors, six Oscars and five Golden Globes between the two of them, with the numbers being in her favor, actually. She's got four Oscars and three Globes, he's got two and two. Both divorced three times each, to high profile A-listers. Had affairs, left their respective spouses, dated for a while before finally getting married in a quintessential Hollywood wedding, millions spent, a who's-who guest list, the works. Had Cleo three years ago, and Callie actually Insta'd the whole thing, no filters, no hair or makeup, just her raw experience giving birth. Kinda crazy, actually, and pretty impressive. By all accounts, they're both well-liked and well-respected in the industry, to the point that even their exes don't really hold grudges."

"So no motive that we can see? No obvious enemies?"

Layla shook her head, curls bouncing and swaying—and other bits too. Yum. Mesmerizing. I had to focus on her words rather than the way her body swayed and jiggled with every twitch.

"...They're fucking actors, you know? How would they have enemies who would hate them enough to do something like this? Puck hasn't worked the scene yet, so we don't have his report to look at, but this looks financially motivated. I mean, duh, right? Two rich-as-fuck A-list actors? Of course they have the cash to pay a fat ransom. But the fact that whoever did this was willing to shoot the nanny? They mean business."

"Which is why you're staying here." I grabbed the back of her desk chair and spun it around, stopping it when she was facing me, looking up at me. "Right, Layla?"

"Yes?" Her expression was...worrisome She was going for soft and seductive. Which meant she had a plan up her sleeve.

"Layla."

"Harris?"

Dammit. She's definitely planning something hugely stupid.

I bent over her, took her cheeks in my palms, and kissed her. Went for soft and sweet. "Baby, please. I'm going to ask you one last time, as nicely as I know how. *Please* stay here. Please? I have a bad feeling about this case. Like you said, they've already shed blood. You get in the way, they won't hesitate to drop you."

She didn't answer. Instead, she reached for my pants. Dug her hand in. Got a good grip.

"Fucking hell, woman. Isn't three times in the morning enough for you?" I pulled away, reluctantly, because it wasn't enough for me either, and if I let her distract me again, I'd never get packed and out of here.

"You know it's not," she said, putting on a fake pouting moue. "Come back over here. Give me something to remember you by."

"I just did. Not twenty minutes ago." I held up my cell phone. "I'll send you some pics when I get to LA."

"You better."

"Promise me you'll stay here?"

And fucking goddamn Layla, she just blinked at me, eyes wide and innocent, legs crossed at the knee, arms folded under her big beautiful tits. Seductive, enticing. Jesus, how could I possibly want her again? But I did. Ten more seconds in the room with a naked and mischief-planning Layla and I'd have her sitting on my cock again, fucking a promise out of her.

Thing about Layla is, she'll never lie to me directly. Which is why she's not answering me.

I know this, and she knows I know this, and I know she knows I know.

I just confused myself, I think.

Or actually, I'm pretty sure that made sense.

Point is, she's gonna pop up at the most inopportune time.

Hopefully my ghostly friend Anselm will keep her out of too much trouble.

I turned away before I gave in to temptation. I did actually have to leave. I promised Puck I'd be in LA by three, which meant I didn't have much time.

I made short work of packing. Duffel bag full of clothes, another full of gear, plenty of cash on hand. Then I went out to the landing strip and got the jet warmed up, going through pre-check a few times and then got it ready to taxi to the head of the runway. I logged the flight plan and did a final check of the cockpit. At which point Lear, Duke, and Thresh were all on the compound and shoving their shit into the cargo hold of the jet.

While they got situated, I grabbed a Gator and headed back to the house to pay Layla one last visit.

I found her in a loose, thin robe, watching some idiotic reality show. Women arguing, it looked like. What fun.

I knelt on the carpet in front of her and took the remote from her hand, putting her show on pause. Then I kissed the ever-loving hell out of her. "I'll miss you," I told her.

"I know." She returned the favor, kissed me dizzy. "I'll miss you, too."

"Stay here." I grabbed the back of her neck, squeezing gently. "Or I swear to god I'll tie you up and leave you somewhere safe."

"You keep promising to tie me up like it's a deterrent, Nick." She grinned up at me. "You should know me better than that."

"I do. But I gotta try, you know? I know you won't listen. And I've taken certain…precautions."

"Which means you've got Anselm out there somewhere, watching me?"

"I've gotta go. Jet's warmed up and the guys are on board. I'm due in LA. Got a little girl to rescue."

"You do. You totally have Anselm out there watching me." She got up, went to the front door and shouted out. "ANSELM! YOU MIGHT AS WELL COME IN! I KNOW YOU'RE OUT THERE!"

I just chuckled. "I have no idea where he is, babe. Save your breath." That was the truth, too. Anselm did things his own way. You never knew where he was until it was too late.

I kissed her again, and then head down the steps.

"Nick?" I heard her voice call out from the doorway.

"Yeah, babe?" I turned back.

"I love you. Come back safe."

"Love you too, sweetheart. Try to stay out of trouble, okay?"

"Never."

I laughed as I trotted back to the Gator, which I drove over to the runway on the far edge of the property. As I'd told Layla, the guys were all onboard the jet, strapped in, and shooting the shit. Making bets about something.

I left the door open between the cockpit and the main cabin and shouted back as I took off. "What are you louts betting on?"

Duke, all six foot six and two hundred and eighty pounds of him, slumped into the co-pilot chair and tugged the headphones on. He was a certified pilot too, but only on fixed wing propeller aircraft. I'd trust him to pilot one of these in a pinch, but he's not licensed on them. He was a true orange-as-carrots ginger, had his hair undercut and pulled back into a ponytail. Being the youngest of the group at twenty-eight, he could actually get away with a punk hairstyle like that. Clean-shaven, bright cornflower-blue eyes. He was a pretty sonofabitch—could be a model if he wanted to. He was built like a goddamn tank, though, spent as much time in the gym bulking up as Thresh did, if not more. Gave Thresh a run for his money in terms of sheer muscle mass, despite Thresh's four-inch height advantage.

Duke is a seriously massive individual, on top of being stupidly good looking. Like, you think of one of Tolkien's elves, they're supposed to be ethereally beautiful, otherworldly. That's Duke. It's honestly horrifying the amount of tail the man pulls down on a nightly basis, just based on a single grin. That's all he has to do, give any girl that smirk of his, and they're all but falling at his feet, begging him to plunder them.

Duke hesitated to answer. "You know the guys. They'll bet on anything," he hedged.

I snorted at that. "Out with it, bub."

Duke straightened in the seat, gripped the second set. "Can I have it for a minute?" he asked nodding at the controls.

I let go. "All yours. Nice and steady." I watched him feather the yoke a bit, testing the response. He had a soft touch, that was for sure. I eyed him. "Duke. What were you guys betting on?"

He adjusted the throttle slightly. "Layla." He cut me a glance. "Whether she would show up or not."

"Who's got what?"

"Lear thinks Anselm will keep her in line. Thresh and I think she's going to show up and make trouble before this show is over, and I've got a text from Puck putting money on her staying put."

I chuckled. "Lear and Puck are suckers, if that's the bet. I call a ten percent cut when you and Thresh clean house."

Duke laughed, glancing at me. "That a fact?"

I laughed again. "Buddy, it's not a matter of *if*, it's a matter of *when*, and how bad it'll be. Anselm is just...insurance that her pretty head stays in one piece. Besides, I like having him out there in the shadows, where he does his best work, you know? It's reassuring."

"I hear that loud and clear." Duke took a hand off the yoke. "Back to you, boss."

"I've got it." I took back the controls when Duke released them.

He left the cabin, and I was alone with my thoughts.

Which, of course, returned to Layla...and all the ways she could cause trouble.

3

A GIRL WITH A PLAN

CREEPY AS FUCK IS WHAT IT WAS, KNOWING ANSELM WAS OUT there and not being able to see him. I mean, I *felt* him watching me. It's not like he's weird or anything…I don't like it. Just…he's a ghost. Here I was in LA, prancing up and down Rodeo Drive, spending my man's money, yet knowing that Anselm was in the shadows. Knowing he was watching my every move put a real damper on things.

Now, here's the thing. Nicholas Harris has done well for himself—Roth paid *really* well, apparently, and since starting A1S, things had only gotten more flush for us. Which meant I could blow a G or ten and he wouldn't even care—in fact, he wouldn't even notice. He wasn't in the same stratosphere as Valentine Roth, of course, but few men on the planet were. I mean, you had guys like the Koch brothers, Bill Gates, that Sultan of wherever, and Roth. Top tier of the whole word. But Nick? He was down a few pegs, down with the lowly Hollywood set in terms of overall wealth. Not quite a buy-his-own-island kind of guy, but he was doing well enough that he could hit an auction on a weekend and buy a vintage fighter jet—on a whim.

So a pair of Manolos and a Gucci handbag? Pssshhh. That was nothing to Nick.

Plus, Nick had me on the payroll, took off taxes and deductions and made me log my hours and everything, so really, technically, I'm spending my own money, which makes this feel even better.

The only thing that's harshing my mellow right now is fucking creepy invisible Anslem goddamn See.

Finally, I got sick of it. I couldn't handle it anymore. So I found a little café with a nice shaded outdoor eating area, ordered a mug of coffee and sat my ass down. Seeing as I'm not the type to sit around idle, I took matters into my own hands.

In my purse—the old one, since I hadn't switched my things over yet—I had two cell phones. One was a big white iPhone in a sparkly case—Swarovski-sparkly, not diamond-sparkly, sadly—the other was more like the prepaid one I'd used in Brazil, an ancient plain black Razr, no case, no bling, no features, not even a smart phone. One of those phones was my every day cell, and the other was for use in case of emergencies. Can you guess which is which? Yeah, duh. I'd never used the Razr, seeing as Nick had gone all Scary Harris on me when he gave it to me, told me it was not for fun, not for needing a ride home from the bar because I'd had too much too drink. It was only for real, serious, life or death emergencies.

Yes sir, I'd said, all doe-eyed and innocent.

Ha. Has he met me? Since when do I do what I'm told? Never, that's since when.

Thusly, I pulled out that old Razr, flipped it open—and god, what a marvelously nostalgic sensation that was!—and hunted laboriously through the contact list. Laboriously, I say, because I had to use actual buttons, not just swipe. I mean, there was only what, seven contacts in there? Harris, Duke, Lear, Puck, Anselm, Alexei, and Sasha. The heavy hitters of Alpha One Security. The kind of men you were really glad were your friends, whom you knew you really didn't want to know too terribly much about, because the details of their lives tended be a little…gnarly, shall we say. Even sweet, geeky Lear had his secrets, and he was as vanilla as you could get and still work for Nick.

I found the entry I was looking for: Anselm See.

Before I could remind myself that this was a bad idea and certain to get me in trouble with Scary Harris, I dialed him.

It rang three times.

"You should not be calling me. You know this."

"I know, but it's creepy, knowing you're out there. Can't you just…hang out with me?"

"I do not…*hang out*." Anselm's voice contained a sarcasm so potent it almost hurt. "And certainly not somewhere like Rodeo Drive."

"They have really good espresso here," I said.

I'd seen the break room at A1S headquarters. There was a fridge stocked with craft beer, a bar stocked with bottles of expensive scotch and bourbon, a humidor full of cigars, a cabinet full of junk food and Mountain Dew—I'm sure you can guess who that's for—and… an espresso machine. And not just a rinky-dink Mr. Coffee plastic piece of shit, but a full size, chromed-out, two-brewer-handle monster installed by the contractors who built the HQ because it wasn't the kind of espresso machine you just plunked down and turned on.

Anselm took his espresso *very* seriously.

"Bah. American piss water." He hung up without warning, because that's what spooks and soldiers do, apparently.

Knowing he was watching from somewhere, I flagged down a waitress and ordered a double shot of espresso. A few minutes later the waitress set down a cute little white ceramic mini-mug full of espresso. It was thick and rich, with a frothy golden *crema*, just the way it's supposed to be. I slid the *doppio* espresso across the table to the empty chair and waited.

It was like baiting a bear with honeycomb; I didn't have to wait long.

I was looking in my compact, checking my makeup—the seat across from me was empty. I touched up my eyeliner, reapplied my lipstick, closed the compact—and there he was, Anselm See in the flesh.

I jumped a foot, and clapped a hand to my chest in a vain attempt to slow the thudding of my heart. "Jesus, Anselm. Make some noise, would you?"

He lifted the espresso to his lips, inhaled. Lowered it, peered with extreme scrutiny at the contents, swirled the liquid the way a sommelier would a glass of fine wine. Finally, he took a sip.

"Not bad. Not so good, but not piss." He eyed me. "What do you want?"

I shrugged. "I don't want anything. I just don't liked being watched. If you're going to babysit me, do it in person, not from far away with a telescope or whatever. That's just creepy."

Anselm smirked. "Telescope? You are not a star in the space for me to use a telescope."

"Then what do you use?"

He laughed, a quiet chuckle. "My eyes, *Frau* Campari."

"I always pictured you watching people from the top of a building with a rifle or something, muttering to yourself in German the whole time."

He snorted. "I am not from one of your Hollywood movies. If I have a rifle, I am going to shoot you. If I am watching you, then I just…watch. And I do not mutter."

Anselm was, at first glance, utterly unremarkable. Medium stature, perhaps five-ten, five eleven. Not short enough to be called short, but not tall enough to attract notice either. His hair was somewhere between dark blond and light brown, side-parted in the kind of classic haircut that never really went out of style. Shaved jaw, with a day or two worth of stubble. Brown eyes. Dressed in dark-wash blue jeans, a collared black polo shirt, only the front hem tucked in under his belt, the rest left untucked, and sensible hiking boots. If he put on a blazer, he could sit down at a nice restaurant. You'd never notice him in a crowd.

But look again. He was actually rather handsome, if you took a moment to really notice. Sharp, hard jawline. Piercing, intelligent eyes. And his arms stretched out the sleeves of that polo, not to mention the pull of the fabric across his shoulders. In fact, the more I looked at him, the more I realized he was actually pretty damn hot. It was almost as if he had some kind of ability to will himself into the background, will you to not quite notice him. But now that he was in front of me…yummy.

"Why are you staring at me?" He took a sip of his espresso, a slight smirk on his lips, his eyes betraying a faint humor.

"Nothing. I just…nothing."

"You cannot offend me. What is it?"

"I just always thought of you as…unremarkable looking. Like, you blend in, no matter where you go. Just kind of fade into the background. Even with the other guys in a room, we all sort of forget you're there until you speak. But now I'm sort of realizing that you're not unremarkable at all."

"No? Then what am I, would you say?"

"Kinda hot, actually. I just had to actually look to see it."

"A kind sentiment, *Frau*. In my life, in my training, it was always better to be unremarkable, to go unnoticed. It is a habit I will always have."

"What is your training?"

Almost imperceptibly, he moved his head side to side. "Many and much."

"Well, no shit, Sherlock. Like where? For who?"

"It would only bore you if I told you. Lots of boring days doing boring things for boring people."

I rolled my eyes. "You're not very good at evading direct questions, Anselm."

"I haven't told you anything of a specific nature."

"No, but you're being very obvious about it." I grinned. "Would you tell me if I were to torture you?"

Anselm did not return my smile. "That isn't funny." He leaned forward on his forearms, then rolled one arm over so the inside of his forearm was face up. The skin was…I don't even have a word for what it looked like. As if it had been ripped away, and then healed over. "They peeled my skin off in strips. Hot needles under my fingernails. Other things even less pleasant. And no, I did not tell them what they wished to know."

"Fuck me running, Anslem. I'm sorry, I had no idea." Talk about awkward. But then, when you're surrounded by super-soldiers and ex-spies, I guess jokes about torture might not be funny.

But then he grinned at me and snickered. "I am teasing with you. That was from a motorcycle accident."

I laughed it off, but there was a hardness to his gaze, a faraway look to the way he stared into the dregs of his espresso. Motorcycle accident? I don't think so. Methinks the spy doth protest too much.

"The truth is I am not at liberty to disclose many of the things I did, or for whom. What I can say is that I specialize in the gathering of information and the…acquisition, shall we say, of personnel who may possess such useful information."

"I see. So you watch people, and sometimes make them disappear."

"Essentially, yes."

"And do you kill them?"

"Not if I can help it. A dead person cannot tell you their secrets, after all, and there is always a way to pry a secret from someone."

"And what way is that for you?"

He shook his head from side to side again. "Good espresso."

I snorted at that. "A likely story."

Anselm rose. "*Danke* for the espresso, *Frau* Campari. Now, shall we go?"

"Go where?"

He gestured at the street. "Shopping? Unless you are finished?"

"I'm never finished shopping." I left some money in the tray and followed him out onto the street. When he walked beside me, and even offered to carry my bags, I gave him a quizzical expression. "Wait, you're really coming with me?"

He shrugged. "Why not? I am here, and I was told specifically to keep watch over you. I can do that so easily from here as back there." He waved behind us.

"So let me get this straight. You really just…follow me?"

"Yes. It is not so hard."

"But I looked behind me all the time. I knew you were back there, and I still never spotted you."

He gave me that smirk of his, a tipping up of one corner of his mouth, a sly, small grin. "That is because I am exceptionally good at it, *Frau*."

I turned to look behind us, scanning the crowd, not sure what I was looking for. "So, if I was to try and spot someone who was following me, what would I look for?"

He thought for a moment. "Well, it depends on their skill. I can follow a professional like myself and he probably won't spot me. It is what I do, what I'm best at. But a civilian? They would have no chance of spotting me. But to have any kind of hope of spotting someone, you always have to be watching your surroundings. Watch for patterns. Look for someone who seems to be near you all the time. Doing different things. Paying for gas, maybe, or tying a shoe, or checking a cell phone. The little things. The details." He turned around, ever so briefly, and glanced behind us, then looked at me. "There is a woman behind us. The blonde. Take one quick look, like I just did, and tell me everything you can see about her."

I looked back: a dozen feet behind us there was a blonde woman. On the shorter side of medium height, hair cut in a cute bob, streaked with reddish highlights. Business clothes, tailored slacks, blouse, and blazer. She was talking on a cell phone, carrying a paper cup of coffee with which she gestured while talking. She was upset about something, which was obvious, berating the person on the other end.

I only looked for maybe two or three seconds, and then turned back to Anselm and relayed my observations.

He nodded. "Very good. More than some would see. Where does she work, can you tell me?" When I shook my head, he shot me that smirk again. "She works for Gaines Technology Systems. Her name is Theresa Crane. She is married, and on a lunch break. She is talking to who I suspect is a man she's having an affair with. She is planning to meet him later. He's pushing her to leave her husband and she is not ready to do so yet."

I stared at Anselm. "Okay, what the actual fuck?"

He shrugged. "I have excellent hearing, and she is being loud, which is how I can relay to you the content of her conversation. She is wearing a security badge with her name on it, and she is wearing an engagement ring as well as a wedding band. She does not have her purse with her, and she is still wearing her badge, so I know she is on a break from work."

"How do you know she's planning on meeting him later?"

"She has a hotel key card with her security badge."

I frowned at him. "How do you know?"

"Her ID badge is the kind you show to a guard. It is in a clear plastic envelope with a clip, you know this kind, *ja*? Fastened to her coat lapel. Some badges you must scan. They have a stripe on the back, for magnetic readers, and those are usually on a string which retracts, *ja*? To easily pull and scan and return. But hers, being in an envelope and fastened to her coat, it would not be practical to take it out and scan it all the time. But the back of the security badge has a magnetic strip. It is an assumption, one that I could be wrong about, but I don't think I am. Why would she need some kind of extra card? It is a great hiding place for a hotel key. No one would think twice about it."

"So the affair, what makes you think that's going on?"

"She said 'no, Tom, I'm not going to tell him yet. I'm not ready. I'm just not.' And then he said something, and she replied with 'you're not the one leaving your husband. I am, and I'll do it when I'm ready.' And the whole time, she was using her ring finger to tap against the side of her coffee. A nervous habit, which makes me think she feels guilty."

"Damn, Anselm. That's a lot of detail to notice in one glance."

"I deal in information. It is what I do."

While shopping during the rest of the afternoon, Anselm and

I played a game wherein he tried to teach me the art of noticing details. Walk by a car, and without stopping to look, memorize the contents of the interior. What clothing was the mannequin wearing in the window display we just passed? What brand of shoes is the man, about to turn the corner, wearing? The woman sending a text, passing us right now, what is she typing? Look as we pass by.

It was a fun diversion. I didn't notice as many things as he did, of course, but it was a fun game all the same.

And it served another purpose: it put Anselm at ease. It made him think I'm an easy mark. I'm not, though. I learn fast. Case in point? I asked him how to vanish when someone is watching you, and the silly man told me.

My plan was probably not going to work, but it was worth a shot. I knew the address of Nick's office here in LA. I asked Anselm to run into that bakery there real quick and get me a muffin. In a stroke of perfect timing, a cab stopped a few feet away and a woman got out. I hopped in, slammed the door and told the cabbie to step on it. Which was fun, because I'd always wanted to do that: slide into a cab and tell the driver, in an impatient voice, to step on it. Once we were moving, I gave him the address of the A1S LA office.

Thirty minutes later I was paying the cab driver and heading into the cool, marble-covered lobby. I took the elevator up to the tenth floor, suite C.

Michelle was at her desk, typing a million words a minute, a headset on, talking at the same time. After a minute, she ended the call and removed the headset. "Layla, what a surprise. I didn't know you were going to be joining us. Can I offer you a cup of coffee? Mr. Harris is out at the moment, but he should be returning any minute."

"No thanks. I'll just wait in his office." I moved past her desk to the double doors of Nick's office.

Michelle shot to her feet and followed me. "Oh, I, um, don't think I can let you go in there alone."

I stopped, my hand on the knob. "Why not? I'm his girlfriend. I live with him. I work for him. What am I going to do?"

She blinked at me, clearly uncomfortable and unsure. "It's just I've got standing orders that no one is allowed in there but him unless he's expecting them and sends them in. He's very territorial about that kind of thing. I'm sure you understand."

I put on a certain...*knowing*...expression. "I get that. But he doesn't know I'm here, and I just want to...surprise him. Know what I mean?"

Michelle, bless her heart, blushed. "Oh. *Ohhhhh*. I—I see. I guess it would be okay. Just..."

"If he gets mad at you, I'll take the blame. I could punch you, and say I overpowered you, if you want."

Michelle backed up quickly. "No, that's...that's fine. It's fine."

"Don't tell him I'm in here, 'kay?"

"Sure, no problem."

I went in, then, closing the door behind me. God, this office was fucking bland as hell. He was never here, though, so it made sense. It was just a space to work in if he had to be in LA for some reason. Big desk, a filing cabinet, a computer, some pens, a couch, a view of a suburban park. Nothing special.

This, too, was all a part of my plan. I was sick of being left out and left behind. I could help Nick out in the field if he would just trust me and stop treating me as if I were helpless. Don't get me wrong, I love that he protects me. That he doesn't want anything like what happened in Brazil to ever happen again. I don't want that either. At least not the kidnapping and almost being raped part. But the car chase and the shooting and all that? It was...fun. Exciting. The adrenaline rush was like nothing I'd ever experienced before. And I didn't panic, you know? Which means I could do it again, with practice, and get better at it. Learn soldiering, spying, and driving techniques. Be like one of Charlie's Angels.

It'd be cool.

But I have to play my cards right. Nick specifically told me to stay in Colorado, which I didn't do, obviously. Now I'm here, and he'll be pissed unless I can get him, shall we say, in a more vulnerable state of mind. By which I mean, he's always more amenable to my crazier ideas when I've just made him come a few times. So now that I'm here, I'll give him a killer BJ under his desk, and maybe he'll bring me along.

Crazy?

Probably.

Bound to backfire?

Most likely.

Stupid, foolish, and in every way unwise?

Absolutely.

Nick will be *pissed*. He might even spank me, or better yet, actually tie me up.

A girl can hope, right?

4

CHANGE OF PLANS

I WAS ON THE ELEVATOR UP TO OUR OFFICES IN LA, FRESH FROM the scene of the abduction, where Puck was still working, gathering evidence. I had Lear working his computer magic: scouring video feeds across the city for matches of the van caught on Jon and Callie's security camera. Thresh and Duke were pumping their sources from among the less savory elements of the mercenary community, hoping to shake loose some info on who could or would attempt this abduction. Because even among mercenaries, it takes a special kind of sick to fuck with little kids. So the pool of candidates with the skills necessary to get past the kind of security Jon and Callie had, plus the lack of morals necessary to shoot women and kidnap children was, in fact, fairly small.

The elevator doors opened, admitting me into the hallway outside our suite of offices and just then my phone rang.

"Anselm," I answered, after checking the caller ID. "What's going on?"

"Your woman, she is a tricky one."

"What does that mean, exactly?"

"It means she gave me a slip."

"Gave *you* the slip?" I asked. "You're a professional spook, man.

How did she get away from you?"

"It was pretty simple, actually. She could be a very good spy, I think. She lulled me into…what is the word? Complaint? Compliance? Something like that. Made me think she was content to only shop, *ja*? She asked me to get her a muffin, and when I returned with it, she was in a cab, and gone."

"And you followed her?"

"No, there was no point. I tagged her purse with a tracker. She is in your office."

"I can't believe she gave you the slip, Anselm."

"I told you, she is very good. You should get her out of the office more. She could be of much use in the field, I think."

"She's a loose goddamn cannon. You don't even know. She never listens."

"But a woman with her intelligence and skills, left to her own boredom? Not so good."

I laughed. "No, you're probably right. Okay, well, I'm about to go into my office now. Gotta deal with this."

"Very well. I'll find Thresh and Duke."

"No, stay out in the shadows. I need you as insurance."

"This is LA. There are no shadows."

"Don't be so literal. You know what I meant."

He chuckled. "Yes." A pause. "Complacence, that is the word I was thinking of. Anyway, *auf wiedersehen*."

"Yeah, talk to you later."

I stood outside the door to my office, mentally preparing myself to go to war with a Layla determined to have to her own way. I couldn't let her seduce me into giving in; that was her main M.O., and fuck me if she wasn't damned good at it, too.

Stay strong, Nick. No matter what she does, keep telling her no. Promise her you'll train her to go on more field ops. But do not allow her to think she can just do whatever she wants and get away with it.

I blew out a breath and shot a glance at Michelle, who was working a little too hard on appearing innocent. "Go take lunch, Michelle.

And lock the door behind you."

Michelle took off her headset, shut down her computer, shouldered her purse, and stood up. "Mr. Harris, I—"

"You're cool, Michelle. No worries. Just go, and don't come back for…an hour or so, I'd say."

"Yes sir." She ducked her head and scurried out of the suite, locking the glass door behind her.

I took another breath.

Let's be clear, here: I'm not afraid of Layla.

But she *does* have a hell of a temper, and she *does* have a talent for verbally thrashing anyone who gets in her way, including me.

And she *does* have a way of fucking with my head until I don't know which way is up or even what I was originally trying to accomplish. I mean, she gets those goddamn soft hands on me, puts those plump, sweet, fuckable lips on me, and I lose all sense. It's a fucking problem.

I shoved open my door, opened my mouth to berate her, and promptly lost all capacity for thought.

Mainly because the second I set eyes on Layla all the blood left my brain and went down into my cock. In the words of the late, great Robin Williams: "God gave men both a penis and a brain, but unfortunately not enough blood supply to run both at the same time."

She was leaning back in my desk chair, feet propped up on the edge my desk. Leaning way, way back, almost to the tipping point. Knees splayed apart. Stark naked. Hair loose and wild and all in her face. Fingers working her clit like mad, hips gyrating. Making this quiet, subdued, but intensely erotic sighing noise as she got closer and closer. I know when my woman is close to coming, and she was right *there*, riding that razor edge. Tits thrust into the air, lower lip caught between her teeth in an effort to keep quiet. She had her pussy lips spread apart with one hand, two middle fingers working herself with the other.

Fuck.

Fuck.

Fuck.

How does she manage this shit? How did she know exactly when I'd be walking in? How the *hell* does she do it?

Instantly, I was hard as a goddamn rock. Stomping across the office, breath coming hard and fast. Fingers working my fly, pulling myself out.

She knew I was there, but she ignored me until I was right beside her and then she cut me a look, shifted her gaze from my stormy expression to my rigid cock gripped in one fist.

"Yeah, baby," she murmured. "Jerk it hard. Watch me come."

"I have a better idea," I told her. "How about you keep doing what you're doing, but put that sexy mouth of yours to work?"

Layla leaned further back yet in my chair, which was, fortunately, one of the expensive ones that could recline almost horizontal. She stretched her body out, feet kicking the paperwork off my desk. She turned her head to the side, fingers of one hand still circling madly around her clit. She shot a look up at me, opening her mouth for me. I fed her my cock, inch by inch, and she took it all. God, it should be impossible, but she does it. She takes every last fucking inch of me, every time. And god, does it feel good. Too good.

Talk about multi-tasking. My girl was working both of us hard and fast now. Flicking herself and sucking me.

And then, abruptly, she lost the ability to multi-task. She started coming and nearly bit down on my cock. I pulled out of her mouth, straddled the chair, sucked her nipple into my mouth, pinched the other one hard enough to elicit a flinch from her even as she screamed through her release.

I kicked off my shoes, shoved my pants and underwear off and stepped out of them while Layla kept coming, wave after wave wracking her, fingers still circling crazily. Grabbing her heels, I wrapped them around my waist, cupped her big beautiful ass in my hands, and shoved myself in, slamming into her pussy hard and deep.

Pretty sure whoever was on the floors both above and below us heard her scream.

I moved with her, thrusting into her slowly, sinuously, taking my time. Keeping her on the edge. Keeping her hot and wild. She hung her head backward, hair draping onto the floor, one of her hands now playing with her nipples, the other going crazy between her legs.

Surreptitiously, I reached into a drawer of my desk and pulled out a handful of zip-ties. Yes, I keep zip-ties in my desk drawer—don't ask. I grabbed her hand quick as a striking snake and zipped a tie around her wrist and the arm of the chair, tugged it tight enough to bind, but not so tight it would hurt her. That caught her attention.

She instantly stilled. "Nick?" She wiggled her wrist. "What the fuck are you doing?"

I ignored her question, securing her other wrist.

"What are you doing here, Layla? I told you to stay in Colorado."

She glared at me, testing the strength of her bonds. "Yeah, well, I didn't listen, did I?"

"And now look at you, tied to my chair."

I was still hard, and she was flushed and flustered, frustrated from having been right on the edge of orgasm. I thrust into her, feeling the need to come surging inside me and holding it back.

"Let me go."

"Not a chance, babe." I kept moving, slow, shallow, teasing thrusts, not enough to get her off.

"Then at least help me come." She lifted her hips against mine, trying to get more of me.

I flicked at her erect nipple. "I might. Eventually." I pulled out, gripped my cock, and used the head of it like a dildo, smearing it in circles against the rigid little pearl of her clit until she was writhing and gasping, jerking at the zip-ties, hips gyrating.

"God, Nick, please—yes, right there, just like that, god, please don't stop, Nick—"

I felt her clenching, tensing. Watched the way her hips rose involuntarily off the chair, watched the way her breathing went hoarse and ragged, making her goddamned perfect tits bounce and sway in the sunlight streaming in through the open windows.

When I judged her to be seconds from coming, I pulled away completely. "You need to learn to listen to me, Layla."

She went crazy, jerking upright, planting her feet on the floor, tugging ferociously at the bonds. "Nick, you bastard! I was right there!"

I moved us, swiveling the chair so we were parallel with the desk and the wall. Knelt down, threw her feet over my shoulder. "How close were you, Layla?"

She moaned as I kissed the inside of her thigh. "Right the fuck there, baby. I was—Jesus, please, keep going. I was so close. So fucking close."

I kept kissing upward, teased the swollen, wet lips of her pussy with my tongue, and then kissed down the other thigh, eliciting a series of increasingly frantic whimpers from her, culminating in a crazed, wild shriek of frustration when I moved away.

"You're such a dick, Nicholas," she snarled. "You can forget about getting any more BJs out of me, if this is the game you're gonna play."

I stood up, then. "Oh yeah?"

"Yeah."

I stood directly in front of her, cock hard and upright, swaying in front of her face. I moved closer, so it was centimeters from her mouth. "I know you better than that," I said, leaning in to whisper in her ear. "You love the taste of my cock, don't you?"

She shook her head, closed her eyes. "No."

"You love it best when it's been inside you, first. You love tasting yourself on my cock, you dirty girl." I backed away, cupped the back of her head with one hand, pulling her closer. I gripped my cock in the other hand and traced her lips with the tip. "You smell your juice on me? I was close, you know. Probably a little pre-come on there."

Layla's nostrils flared. Her lips parted. "You asshole."

"I know you, baby. I know what you like. I know what you love. You want it, right now, don't you?"

"No..." she said, but her mouth opened. Her tongue flicked out. Touched the groove. She whimpered. "Fuck you. God, fuck you for being right," she whimpered.

She slid her lips around the head of my cock, tongue swirling, bobbing down, backing away. She licked up the side and went to pull me back into her mouth again, but I had other plans.

"Ah ah ah. Not so fast," I scolded, backing away.

I grabbed her ankle and tipped her and the chair backward, so far back she was off-balance. Helpless, tied to the chair, whimpering and moaning. I gripped my cock again and plunged into her. Hard, fast. One thrust. Two. Three. A fourth. No mercy, no gentility. Just hard, rough fucking, the way she loved it best. I kept going until she was into it, moving with me as best she could while bound to the chair.

And then I stopped. Pulled out. Ignored her curses, ignored the names she called me—*bastard, cocksucker, dickhead, motherfucking asshole*. Worked the head of my dick against her clit again, slow and soft, smearing her juices around her.

"You're fucking soaked, Layla," I said. I slid two fingers into her slit, scooped her essence out and touched it to her lips. "Taste that? That's all you, baby. That beautiful smell is all you."

I let her fall forward again and then I moved in so I was straddling her knees, cock close to her face. She was frantic now, eyes wide and wild, breathing hard, tits rising and falling. I cupped the back of her head and put the crown of my cock to her lips.

"Taste it, baby."

She tasted it. Fuck, did she taste it. Moaned as she sank her mouth on me greedily. Turned her head sideways and mouthed the girth of my shaft, one side and then the other, licked it like an ice cream cone, and then sank her mouth on me, worked me, bobbing slowly, tongue moving, swirling, tickling.

I let this go on until I was riding the edge, and then pulled away.

"Fucking hell, Nick. What game are you playing?" she tossed her head to get the hair out of her face, spat strands out of her mouth.

I knelt between her thighs, brushed the hair away. "I've got you tied up, babe. I'm getting all the mileage out of this I can. You're helpless, and Michelle won't be back for an hour. I might just tease you and I both for the whole time. Make us both a little crazy."

I dove in, then, not bothering to listen to her response as I sucked her clit between my teeth. Teased her with my tongue, plied her clit with kisses, stroked the seam with licks, worked her into a frenzy, got her right at the edge, and then...

Stood up.

Thrust my cock into her mouth, once. Let her taste us on her tongue, and then pulled free.

I notched myself against her entrance, tilted her and the chair back, and slid in. Slowly, this time.

Taking my time. Pushed in deep, pulled out gradually. Feathered a slow, stuttering thrust back in.

No rhythm. No pattern.

Slow.

Slow.

And then once, hard; Layla shrieked at that one.

"What do you want, Nick?" She was close to sobbing, so close to coming she would have agreed to anything if I would just let her come. "Tell me what you want!"

I leaned in and slashed my mouth across hers, kissed her hard, kissed her breathless. "Are you getting desperate, Layla?"

"Fuck yes, I'm desperate. Quit teasing me, and let me come. Or let me make you come. Something, anything! Please!"

I pulled out, let her fall forward, brushed her lips with the tip of my cock. Teased her with it until her mouth was open and hunting for it, seeking it. I played keep away, never letting her get her mouth on me. It was almost funny, actually. Would have been, if I weren't going a little crazy from my own game. Teasing her was teasing myself.

Only, I was the one in control; Layla hated being helpless, hated not being in control.

"You want it?" I asked.

"Yeah, I fucking want it."

"What are you going to do if I let you have it?"

"Suck you so hard you'll come for a week." She stared up at me, and the look on her face was so fierce with crazed need I nearly lost it right then, just from the erotic, seductive look she was giving me. "I'll make love to your beautiful cock with my mouth. Fuck you with my mouth until you can't take it anymore."

"Show me," I told her.

And holy hell, did she ever.

She did exactly what she promised, and did it without the use of her hands. Honestly, I think not having her hands available made her all the more talented and inventive with her mouth. The things she did to my cock with her mouth over the next few minutes were… probably the most unbearably erotic moments of my life. Watching her very literally make love to me with nothing but her lips and tongue was almost too much to handle. I held back, wanting to enjoy this for as long as I could, never wanting it to end.

But it had to.

When I was at the point of having to exert effort to hold back, I pulled away.

"Goddammit!" Layla seemed almost near tears, now.

"Will you promise me something?"

"Yes, Nick, goddammit, yes, I'll fucking stay back!" She shouted. "I'll fucking do as I'm told."

"Swear?"

A groan escaped her. "Yes. Fucking fine. I promise."

I knelt between her thighs. "Then let me hear you scream."

I plunged my face against her slit and went to work, and this time it only took her a few seconds to reach the peak. No toying around, now. I let her fall over, let her break apart on my mouth, screaming for all she was worth. At the crest of her climax, I slid up her body, wedged my hips in the V of her thighs, plunged myself home inside her.

No games here anymore, either. I came almost instantly, exploding inside her in a matter of half a dozen hard thrusts.

When we were both done, and I was capable of motion, I pulled away. I snatched a handful of tissues from the box on Michelle's desk and returned to kneel between Layla's thighs once more, this time cleaning her, carefully, gently, and reverently. She watched me do this with an unhappy expression on her face.

I rocked back on my heels when she was clean and shot her a look. "What? What's that look for?"

She planted a heel in my chest and kicked me backward, forcefully but not with the intent of hurting me. "I'm pissed off at you, that's what."

"Because I turned the tables on you?" I stood up. "You were planning on seducing an agreement out of me, were you not?"

"Yeah, I'm ticked about that too, but that's not why I'm mad."

I scrutinized her face; she wasn't just mildly irritated about being bested at her own game, she was genuinely angry with me. "Then what?"

"You don't trust me. You don't want me in the field with you."

I paced away, jerking my hand through my hair. "Goddammit, Layla, that's not—"

My phone rang at that moment. I dug it out of my pants and answered it. "Talk to me, Puck."

"I think between Lear and me, we've got a lead. And plugging it in to the intel Thresh and Duke came back with, it's not looking good, Boss."

"What's that mean?"

"It means we need to meet up. Should we all head to the office?"

"Did you get everything you could from the scene?"

"There wasn't much, but yeah, we did."

"Don't come to the office. Meet me at the airfield."

"Gotcha."

I hung up, sent Anselm a text updating him, pocketed the phone, and returned my attention to Layla. "Look, I've gotta go. We've got to follow up on this lead while it's hot."

"Whatever."

I jerked my pants on, stuffed my feet back into my shoes. Buttoned and zipped and tucked. Moved to kneel in front of Layla, withdrawing my knife from my pocket. Snicked the blade across the zip-ties, freeing her. As soon as she was free, she pushed past me and started dressing.

"Thought you had to go?" she asked, when I didn't immediately leave.

"It's not that I don't trust you, Layla. I do, its—"

"I thought we were partners, Nick. I thought that's why you taught me how to shoot. I thought—" she shook her head. "You know what? It doesn't matter. Guess I was wrong."

"I'm not saying never, Layla, I'm just saying not this one. Puck just said that this isn't looking good, and you know Puck's not given to worrying. You can shoot, yeah, but there's more to it than that. I'll train you, I promise. I'll bring you on more ops. But this one? This one isn't a game, Layla. There's a three-year-old girl's life at stake."

"But you can take the time to tie me to the chair and fuck me?"

Ouch.

"Without a lead, it's a non-starter. Now that we have a lead, we have to move on it." We were both dressed, now. I gestured at the door. "Let's go. I'm putting you on a flight back to Colorado."

I led the way out of the office, Layla trailing behind me, looking morose.

The drive to the airfield was silent.

I had a bad taste in my mouth. Despite knowing I was doing the right thing by keeping Layla out of this one, I still hated the way things were shaking out.

"Layla—"

"Save it...*Harris.*"

Shit.

I hated this. Telling her no, and being frozen out for it, despite it being the safest thing for her. Most of all I hated being put in this position.

I parked beside my private jet, and I wasn't even out of the driver's seat when Lear came jogging down the stairs and trotted over to me.

"Bad news, Harris. Timetable got bumped up. They found out Jon called you in." Lear had an iPad Mini in his hands, turned it to face me, and touched the screen to start a video message.

A camera jiggled, showing a ceiling, part of a couch, and a window, and then pivoted and settled to frame a large man dressed in basic black BDUs. A strap crossed his chest, and while whatever was attached to the strap was out of frame, I would have bet my 1917 Albatross D.III that it was an assault rifle of some kind. He was broad-shouldered, had a bit of a belly, and sharp brown eyes visible behind a tactical balaclava which hid his identity. An adorable little girl with straight, long black hair stood in front of him, and the man had a long, wicked, serrated knife held to her throat. The little girl, obviously, was Cleo, and I was impressed by her composure given the circumstances. She wasn't fighting or sobbing, but rather was just standing there, hands at her sides, tears running down her face, although she clearly was trying to be brave.

"Nicholas Harris." The man, his voice muffled by the balaclava, spoke with a thick accent, Eastern European, maybe. "I hear that our mutual friend Mister Lonigan has hired you to retrieve his little girl."

The edge of the knife wasn't quite touching the skin of Cleo's throat, but was only a hair's-breadth away. With exquisite control, the man lifted the knife and deftly sliced free a lock of her hair, caught it as it fluttered free, and held it up for the camera. "I am a patient man. I told Lonigan one week, but now that you are involved, I have revised our timetable. Anyone else, and this little girl would already be fish-bait. But me? I am willing to forgive stupid decisions. I have given him twelve hours to arrange for the money. I know you, Nicholas Harris. I have sent Lonigan another email with the details of the transfer, where to bring the cash so he may get his daughter back. And you, Harris, will do the transfer. Not Lonigan, not his wife, not his assistant, not any of your hired guns. You, and only you. My men are at the location already, and they will know if you try anything. One wrong move, and this pretty little thing here—" he paused, looked down, flicked the point of the knife against the shell of Cleo's ear, drawing a single welling drop of blood. He returned his gaze to the camera. "I think you get the point. Twelve hours." The message ended.

I turned to Lear, who had been joined by Puck and the others by then. "Do we know who this guy is, yet?"

Lear shook his head from side to side, saying softly "I think it's Cain."

I tilted my head to one side. "Cain? Rings a bell, but I can't place him."

"Not much is known about him. Your average, nefarious underworld scum. Comes from somewhere in Europe, specializes in the most evil shit you can imagine. Human trafficking. Prostitution. Drugs. Murder, by which I mean assassinations, as well as good old fashioned he just-likes-to-kill-people murder."

"He said he knows me. I've never met a Cain."

Lear frowned at me. "Dude, think—of course his name isn't actually Cain." He peered at me, as if I'd grown a second head. "Got your head in the game, boss?"

After taking a long breath in and letting it out slowly, I shot a look at Layla. "On the plane—*now.*"

She frowned at me. "Excuse me? You want to rephrase that?"

"No. Get your ass on the plane, Layla."

"But I thought—"

I gestured at the iPad. "This changes the plan. You're involved, like it or not. Now…GET. ON. THE. PLANE."

She caught the tone in my voice, the one that says I'm no longer tolerating her bullshit. When she was aboard, I took another deep breath, and then refocused on my men.

"Lear. We know the location?"

He shook his head. "Lonigan is freaking out, obviously. Not answering his phone. He's probably at the bank getting the money."

I turned to Puck. "Get him. Callie too. They don't leave your sight again. No cell phones, no purses, no wallets. Stop on the way here and get them new outfits from head to toe, skin out. Assume these guys are watching our every move. Assume they've got Jon and Callie tracked somehow."

I turned back to Lear. "Get into Jon's email and get those coordinates. If you can wrangle some aerial or satellite on the location, that would be a bonus. At the very least, I need to know what I'm walking into."

"You're going through with this?" Duke asked, skeptical.

I nodded. "Yes. We're giving him the money, I'm going in alone and unarmed, and you all are staying well back. That's the plan. Getting Cleo back unharmed is our only goal."

Thresh spoke up, his voice rumbling up from somewhere just above the center of the earth. "If he says he knows you, and wants you alone, it's a trap."

"No shit, man." I gestured at the stairs up to the jet. "Everyone, get on board. Puck, get Jon and Callie. Make sure they're clean. Drive north, we'll meet up somewhere. Sacramento, maybe."

"Got it." Puck turned away.

"And Puck? Haul ass."

He just waved a hand as he slid behind the wheel of an H2. A screech of tires, and then he was across the tarmac and gone. Everyone else was on the jet. Layla was in the very back, buckled in already, earbuds plugged into her ears, staring out the window with a petulant expression on her face. She felt me board the aircraft, swiveled her head to glare at me balefully. I jerked my head at the cockpit once, sharply, and then took my place at the controls.

After a minute, she joined me, closing the cockpit door behind her. She'd tied her hair into a tight bun at the back of her head, as she always did before flying. I'd taught her to fly a while we were still traipsing the world with Roth and Kyrie, but in the year since moving to Colorado, I'd spent even more time honing her skills, personally supervising her official flying lessons. A few more official hours and she'd have her certification, even though she already had enough unofficial hours to qualify. I'd even shown her the basics of piloting a chopper, although it would be a while before I was ready to let her attempt a take off or landing on her own.

A basic Learjet, though? No problem. We went through preflight together, working as seamlessly as ever, despite the crackling tension between us. Preflight done, I let Layla radio the tower for permission to take off. When it was granted, she glanced askance at me, and I nodded my permission; she taxied us to the runway, spent a moment breathing, focusing, and then, squaring her shoulders and stiffening her spine, she feathered the throttle to get us moving. Slowly, gradually, she increased power until we were hurtling down the runway at speed. Softly she tugged the yoke toward herself, and then we were airborne, angled high into the broad blue of the sky. I called out the heading I wanted her to put us on, and once she'd done so I took over the process of bringing us to cruising altitude.

Finally, I muted the radio input and keyed the mic so she'd hear me in her headset. "Layla, we need to talk."

"The fuck we do," she snapped. "Nothing to talk about."

"Yes there is. Look at me, please."

She shook her head, staring ahead, arms crossed. "Nothing to say, nothing I want to hear."

"Too fucking bad." I put it on autopilot and turned to face her. "You know I love you. You know I respect your strength and independence."

"Sure as fuck didn't feel that way a little bit ago."

"Which part are you angry about, babe? Being tied to the chair? Or being told no?"

"Neither, you idiot." She finally swiveled to look at me, and I saw a tear sliding down her cheek. "I *liked* being tied up. It was hot. But that scene in your office? That hurt."

"You use sex to get your way all the time, Layla, so don't—"

"Yeah, but I never undermine you or us in the process. I use sex to get you to take me flying or shooting, or let me go with you guys on cute little security jobs. What you did? It was—you manipulated me. You fucked me, and you used me. You fucked compliance out of me, and then you were going to just send me home like your little booty call."

"Now hold on just a goddamn second, that's not fair."

"I'm a slut, Nick. I always have been. I own it. I like men. I like sex. I like dick. I've never been above using sex to get what I want from guys. I had no problem being some guy's booty call. I had no problem with some dude being my sugar daddy. But no sugar daddy ever paid my bills. I never lived with them. I let them buy me luxury shit, things I'd never spend my own money on."

"Layla—"

"No, you shut the *fuck* up and listen to me." She paused after that outburst, sucked in a breath, blinked the tears away. "You've always had this way of making me feel…I don't know—like none of that mattered anymore. Like I wasn't that girl anymore. Like I was worth—*more*. As hot as it was, that sex in your office—and I do not deny enjoying every second of that, being teased and edged and fucked the way only you can, I *loved* that— you used it to put me in my place. You got what you wanted—me agreeing to go home like a good little wifey—and then you were done. Back to the important shit, to manly man stuff, saving the world. No girls allowed in this macho club."

"That is not what this is about, Layla."

"No?" The expression on her face cut me to the bone. "I think it is."

"How do you figure?"

"I know I'm not as badass as the rest of your guys. I don't have years of combat experience. I don't have mad hacker skills or a forensics degree or—any of that shit. But I thought you saw something in me. I thought, after Brazil, I thought that we'd be a team. That eventually I'd come to be more than just a glorified secretary for you. That's all I am, you know. I sit around, sort through paperwork and intel, collate it, and pass it on to you and your guys. That's cool, it's work I don't mind doing. It's fun, actually. And more challenging and mentally stimulating than waitressing or answering phones or whatever other bullshit jobs I used to work, and it's certainly better than going to fucking college. I'm not cut out for any of that shit. I don't mind what you've got me doing, Nick, I really don't. But I want *more*. And I thought you were going to give me more. I thought that's why you were teaching me to fly and to shoot and all that. Turns out you were just humoring your little girlfriend. You don't trust me."

I groaned, slid back in the pilot's chair, scrubbing my face. "Fuck. Fucking goddammit, Layla." I sat up and leaned across the space between the pilot and copilot chairs. I took her hands. "I told you when we agreed that this thing between us was a real relationship, which was a first for both of us, I told you I was going to have a hard time with it. I don't do relationships. I never have. I never judged you on your past because I was never any better. I don't know *how* to trust you, Layla, but I'm trying. And the thing you have to understand about me is that I'm one thing, and one thing only: a mercenary. A soldier. That's all I've ever known. And all the guys on my team, all those guys back there, that's what they are too, except Lear, really. And even he gets the basic tenet that makes the team work: *I'm* in fucking charge. I started this company. I own it. I pay the checks. I make the calls. They all do what I tell them because they trust me to make the right calls, and I trust them to speak up if they have a legitimate concern with a decision. We're all ex-military. We've all learned the importance of trusting your C-O, of obeying orders, when those orders are thoughtfully, rationally, and intelligently issued."

"I may not have been in the army or whatever, but I get that, too. I can follow orders."

"No, Layla, you can't!" I shouted this, a little more loudly than I should have. Her eyes widened—I rarely raised my voice. "You never do what you're told. You say this yourself all the time. It's part of who you are, and I get that. And in private life, it's cool. It's fine. It's cute and endearing and utterly maddening. But professionally, it's not cool or cute or endearing. It's dangerous. On a security job, escorting some highfalutin A-lister to a red carpet event? Fine. There's not likely to be any real danger. Bringing you along, letting you sit in the command center and be part of things, it's fine, then. But situations like this? We're dealing with someone very much like Vitaly. Smart, vicious, and deadly. Playing for keeps. In a combat situation, when lives are on the line, Layla, I *have* to be able to trust, on an instinctive, blood-and-guts level, that the people around me will number one, follow orders, number two, not panic or freeze, and number three, react calmly, efficiently, and intelligently to the circumstances. I have to trust the people around me. And yes, Layla, I trust you. I trust you in my life, I trust you with my heart. But do I trust you with an assault rifle when the bullets are flying at us? I—I can't say that I do. Not yet, anyway. And that's not because you're not capable of it, but because it takes training and experience to get to that point. And me trusting you aside, I don't want to ever put you in that kind of scenario ever again. I *love* you. I couldn't handle it if something happened to you. Thresh, Duke, Puck—they all understand the danger, and they've signed up eyes wide, head up, knowing what they're signing up for, because they've each been there. Lear is different, but even he's not a vanilla civilian who's never seen combat."

Oops. That was the wrong thing to say, and I realized it as soon as it left my mouth.

Layla, however, didn't give me a chance to correct myself. "Vanilla civilian? VANILLA CIVILIAN? Never seen combat?" She went shrill, deafening.

"Layla, I'm sorry, that wasn't what I meant. I know you've—"

"I killed Cut with my bare hands. I planned and executed an ambush with you. I kept my shit together. I followed your orders. I stayed in place, didn't shoot until after you did, and I took down my target. Not once in the entire time I was in Brazil, with you or alone, did I *ever* freeze or panic or falter." She turned away from me. Took a deep breath. "Nick, I just—I want to be beside you. In everything. I want to fly with you. I want to jump out of airplanes with you. I want to go on car chases and shoot bad guys with you. And I *can*. That's the thing. I *can*. How many women do you think are out there that are capable of understanding exactly what it is you do, on a personal, visceral level? From experience? I've been shot at. I've seen you get shot. I've almost lost you. And no, I never want to go through *that* again, but if anything happened to you, and I was just sitting around at home, on my ass? I couldn't deal with that. I'm not a sit-at-home girl, Nick. And if that's what you expect of me, what you want from me, then this isn't going to work. Either you accept me as I am, you trust me, train me, and let me walk beside you no matter the situation, or..."

I swallowed hard. "Or what, Layla?"

"Or I'm gone. I can't do this with you if you can't trust me all the fucking way."

"So it's all or nothing?"

"I'm not saying you put me in BDUs and give me an HK right *now*, Nick. I'm not saying put me point next time you're sweeping a building. I'm saying—get me to that point. In time, with training."

I sat back, brushed the headset off. Tried to process what she was asking of me.

Could I do that? Not just teach her to shoot at targets and clay pigeons. Not just teach her to fly biplanes and Learjets for takeoffs and landings now and again, for fun. But really *train* her to be part of the tactical team? Put her next to Thresh and Duke, in combat gear, knowing someone can and will shoot at her?

It was fucking loony.

She was from the suburbs. She was a waitress, a secretary. She was my *girlfriend*; she was more than that, although I hadn't taken any steps yet to make us more. Emotionally, the boyfriend/girlfriend thing didn't cut it or even begin to describe us. We were *more*. So much more.

And she wanted to go into combat with me?

I mean, fuck. How could I agree to that?

But if I didn't agree, I'd lose her.

Did I think she was capable of it?

I stared out at the clouds beneath us, an eye as always on the readouts—thinking. Considering.

Back to Brazil. What she'd been through. Cut. The ambush. The car chase. She was right: she'd never hesitated, never let fear get the better of her. And in life-or-death situations, she did what I told her.

She was capable of doing this, I realized.

I didn't like it, though. But the thought of Layla in BDUs, an HK in her gloved hands, hair braided back, clearing a room, pivoting, swiveling, running with the guys? Layla at my side, everywhere I went. Never having to leave her behind, because she was part of the team in every way.

A woman in my life who didn't just let me go on missions, but who went with me? Did it get any better than that? Except for the whole part where we both risked death, risked watching the other die. That scared me a little. Or, actually, a lot.

But after the way we fell in love, was it fair of me to deny her this? Deny her the opportunity to at least try?

No.

I turned to her. "There'd be a lot more to it than just weapons training, Layla. I wouldn't let you on the team unless you passed an evaluation by someone other than me. There'd be physical conditioning. Close-quarters combat training. Hand-to-hand. Room clearing. Someone that's not me has to do the training, or nothing will ever get done, and I can't always be objective. And above all, when I give an order, you listen. No questions asked."

"If we're working, I can agree to that. In our private life, I reserve the right to tell you to go fuck yourself."

I stifled a smirk. "You listening has to start with this mission, Layla. When I tell you to stay put, you *stay fucking put*."

She faked a salute. "Yes sir, Mister Harris, sir."

"I'm willing to try," I said. Made sure she was looking into my eyes, saw how serious I was. "I don't like it. It's going to be hard. You're going to hate the physical conditioning part. I'm probably the world's biggest idiot and sucker for even considering this. And if you get hurt, it'll ruin me. But I love you, and—"

"If you say I've left you no choice, I'll never speak to you again."

"You *are* capable of this. I believe that, Layla. I wouldn't agree to this if I didn't think you were." I fixed her eyes with mine. "But I'm serious when I say you have to go through every phase of the requisite training and pass an evaluation before you join the team full-time. You don't pass, you don't go. Just like Thresh and all the others, you have to go through refresher courses, pass yearly check-ups and evals. This isn't a static thing where you just suddenly have the skills and then you're done. It takes a fuckload of work to stay sharp all the time, to be on your game every day, no matter what."

She was wiggling in her seat. "I get it, Nick. I hear you. I can do this."

"Prove me right, babe. Please. Don't make me regret this."

"You won't—I won't, I mean." The grin on her face was ear-to-ear.

"I've got to be out of my mind," I said with a groan.

"You are. But I love you anyway." She got out of the chair, leaned close to me, careful to not bump any switches, buttons, or the controls. "Thank you, Nick."

"I can't lose you, Layla. You're too important to me."

She took my face in her soft, warm palms. "I know. And you won't." She kissed me, then. Slowly, deeply. But then she pulled away. "You owe me an apology, you know."

"I do, don't I?"

"You do." She grinned at me, lips curling against mine. "I've got some ideas for how you can apologize."

"Oh yeah? How's that?"

She resumed her seat, switched off the autopilot, and took the controls. "Oh, you'll see. But it involves a lot of you on your knees. Possibly a lot of me riding your face."

"Apology cunnilingus?" I asked with a smirk. "I can do that."

She quirked an eyebrow at me. "Oh, you'll apologize with words too. Don't think you'll get off that easy, Mister. I haven't forgotten the move with the zip-ties."

Shit. Layla was crafty enough that I had a feeling I'd wake up hogtied at some point. If I knew Layla, she'd find a way to make me beg her for forgiveness. I intended to make her work for it, but I'd do it.

5

FIREFIGHT

I WONDERED, WITH NOT A LITTLE BIT OF FEAR, WHAT I'D GOTTEN myself into.

I was hot.

I was uncomfortable.

I was bored.

I understood the plan, and the plan made sense. Didn't mean I *liked* the plan, though. But I was in no position to complain…about anything. Nick had been as good as his word: a complicated rescue plan had been formulated on the flight to Nevada and Nick made it perfectly clear that I would be part of it. To their credit, the guys never spoke a word of disagreement, and I saw, firsthand, what it meant to take orders without question, and to raise logical, respectful disagreements. Each person on the team had the full respect of everyone else, and it showed.

They were all tight, they were brothers. Tighter than brothers, as only men who have faced combat together can be. And now…*I* was going to be a part of that. It made me a little giddy, as well as more than a little afraid, which I felt was reasonable and expected.

I'd listened to the men formulate the plan and kept my thoughts to myself, knowing I needed to sit back and learn by listening.

We were in the desert somewhere in Nevada, waiting. Miles and miles and miles from anything. I was in the back of an ex-military Humvee, one of the huge wide mammoth ones. Tan, with gargantuan tires. Armored to withstand bullets. No creature comforts. No AC, no music, no diet Coke.

The plan was that Nick would bring the duffel bags full of cash in the back of an old Jeep Wrangler from his location a few miles on the opposite side of the drop-point from where we were. Exchange the cash for the girl, and then haul ass to us. Thresh and Duke would cover Nick's approach to us, which they'd dubbed the "EZ" for extraction zone, Puck would be behind the wheel of the Humvee, and I would be in the back of the Humvee to be with Cleo. Once Puck had Cleo and I clear, Thresh, Duke, and Nick would cover our retreat, making sure Cain and his goons weren't following us, or trying to double-cross us.

Nick was going in alone, unarmed, only a walkie-talkie to coordinate with the others. Just the bags of cash and the Jeep—which didn't even have a top—and the clothes on his back. We knew from Lear's surveillance that Cain had the drop location covered from every direction, and that we were outnumbered, and that his guys were all heavily armed. There would be at least a dozen cross-hairs on Nick at any one time. Sure, we had both Lear and Anselm with big old rifles covering Nick the entire time, but what could a couple of guys with rifles do against twelve or fifteen guys with machine guns? Sorry, assault rifles. Or submachine guns, or whatever. Anselm and Lear couldn't keep them from shooting Nick. If someone got an itchy trigger finger, Nick would be dead, and no one could do anything.

What assurance did we have that Cain wouldn't have his guys shoot Nick as soon they had the cash?

None, I was told.

That was the biggest risk.

It could turn into a firefight.

In fact, I think Thresh and Duke were planning on that eventuality. Planning? Hoping? With those two, it might equal the same thing.

As for me? I was wired, and bored out of my mind. And scared for Nick.

I had my Beretta 9mm in a black tactical holster on my right thigh, the belt going around my waist and the bottom of the holster itself fastening around my thigh. The holster also contained two extra clips of ammunition. I felt kind of like a legit member of the team, although I was under strict orders to not pull the pistol out unless my life was directly in danger and I had no other choice. No matter what happened, I was to leave the gun-slinging to the professionals.

Soon, that would be me!

No time to think about that now. Focus on the op, Layla.

Except, there was absolutely nothing happening. Not a goddamn thing. Puck was in the front of the Humvee, the engine rumbling with a deep diesel clatter, the door propped open, his feet crossed and propped in the V-gap where the door met the frame at the hinge. He had a laptop on his belly and was playing poker on it, a cigar between his teeth, lit and curling acrid smoke.

"Is it always like this?" I asked.

"What? Ops? Yeah. Boredom is part of the gig. Lots of sitting, lots of waiting."

"Being wired and full of adrenaline and all that bullshit while bored at the same time is a weird feeling."

Puck chuffed a laugh as he pulled a mouthful of smoke off his cigar. "Yeah, it's a shitty feeling. You wanna go, go, go, but you gotta wait, wait, wait. It fuckin' sucks." He tapped at his laptop, playing a hand, and then returned his attention to me. "This feels a lot like my TOD in Iraq, actually. Sitting in a Humvee, bored out of my skull, waiting for shit to hit the fan. Kind of wigging me out a little, actually."

"You don't look like you're wigging out," I said.

"Yeah, well, fear happens on the inside. It's what you do on the outside that determines the kind of person you are." He didn't look at me as he dropped that little nugget of wisdom.

"That was deep, Puck."

"Nah." He pulled on his cigar, blew out a stream. "It's experience. My first firefight, I fuckin' froze. Hid in a doorway ignoring my L-T's orders to return fire. Bullets whippin' past, buzzing and shit. They make this sound when they pass right by your ear, a kind of buzz—"

"Sometimes they make a...snapping sound," I said, remembering Brazil, being in that old Defender, bullets going past my face. "Sometimes they snap, sometimes they buzz."

Puck looked at me, a piercing stare that contained a new element of respect. "Yeah. The snap is when they're not as close. You hear 'em buzzin', you best fuckin' duck."

"That first firefight, what happened?"

He returned his attention to his online poker game. How he was getting signal out here was beyond me, since my cell phone said *no service*. "Like I said, I froze. By the time I got my balls back, the fight was over. L-T reamed me a new asshole, made me pull latrine duty for three days. All the guys ragged on me. Next time shit went FUBAR, I refused to let myself freeze. I was still pissin' in my boots, but I didn't freeze. After that, it got easier. Never is exactly easy, though, you just...deal."

"When I was running from Vitaly's men, I kept telling myself I had to hold it together. I promised myself I could freak out later."

Puck puffed again, sending a thick mushroom cloud skyward. "I've heard bits and pieces of that story, but never the whole shit and shebang."

"It's a long story, but here's the Spark's Notes version: Vitaly Karahalios had me kidnapped as a ploy to get back at Roth and Kyrie. I was bait, and he told me as much. Had me brought down to Brazil—and that trip is it's own fun story, let me tell you. I spent three days with Vitaly, never sure if he was going to kill me, rape me, or both. He ended up leaving on business, and his second in command tried to rape me. I stabbed him in the eye with a pen, stole his clothes and gun, then hijacked a car from a one of the valets that worked in the building. I bought a burner phone, called Kyrie, which got me

Nick—Harris, I mean. I was supposed to find somewhere and wait for Harris to find me, but Vitaly's guys found me first. I stole their truck and took off like a bat out of hell. Eventually I managed to cross paths with Harris. We took down some of Vitaly's guys in an ambush, hooked up with Thresh, who got us a flight out of South America."

Puck just stared at me. Then, after a few processing blinks, he burst out laughing. "Jesus, woman. You stabbed a man in the eyeball with a pen?"

I snickered. "That's not the worst part."

He raised his eyebrows. "What is, then?"

"When they'd first kidnapped me, they'd kept me locked up in this little room in the bottom of an old fishing boat. There was an old, dirty ink pen lying on the floor. So I cleaned it off and—hid it."

He frowned at me. "Hid it? Where?"

I quirked an eyebrow at him. "Best hiding spot a woman has, Puck. Up my hoo-ha."

"You gotta be shittin' me."

"That's not something I'd make up," I said. "I called it 'Mr. Papermate the Pussy Pen.'"

This got me another disbelieving belly laugh. "And you shoved it so far into the dude's eye that he died?"

I couldn't quite suppress a shudder at the visceral memory. "Not…immediately. I had to sort of…" I mimed slamming the heel of my palm down, over and over, "drive it…in a little. And even then, it took him a while to—you know. Die."

"Fuuuuck." He wiped at his face, still laughing. "That has got to be the most hard core thing I've ever fuckin' heard." The awe in his voice sent thrills of pride through me.

"I was in survival mode. I would have done anything to stay alive. I don't go down easy."

Puck snickered. "I think our boy Harris might disagree."

I glared at him. "Don't be a cock-waffle, Puck."

He held up his hands, palms out. "Sorry, sorry. I'm an ass. I ain't ever really had a filter. It's why I never made it very far in the FBI.

They don't appreciate a man calling his superior a 'pencil-dick wea-sel-fucker', apparently."

I snickered. "I would imagine not."

Puck grinned. "He was, though. Typical desk jockey, you know? Couldn't find his balls with both hands if you gave him a map and a flashlight." He checked his watch, the same type that all the guys wore, thick rubber chronographs that looked like they could survive a direct nuclear blast. "Shit should be happening soon."

He snagged a handheld walkie-talkie from the seat beside him. "Anselm. Report?"

"He is making the trade off now. He has the little girl in the Jeep, and he's giving them the bags of money." There was pause, and then a crackling as Anselm keyed his mic again. "Be ready. I have a bad feeling, you know? In my stomach. Shit! I knew it, I knew it!"

"Anselm, talk to me, what's happening?"

"I cannot, I cannot. Go to him. Drive east and be ready to pro-vide assistance. It has gone, as you say, off the rails." There was a loud *BOOOOM* that echoed weirdly, coming loudly from Anselm's end of the line, cut off as his radio went silent, a sound which we also heard in the distance, the report of a rifle.

Immediately after the echoing boom of Anselm's rifle we heard automatic fire crackling from multiple locations, and another long rifle report.

Puck had closed and tossed his laptop aside as soon as Anselm cursed, and by the time the first rifle report echoed, he had his door closed and the Humvee in gear.

"Hang the fuck on, Layla!" he shouted as he gunned it and slewed the truck around, the tires spitting sand and dirt and rocks.

I heard the radio crackle, heard Nick's voice: "I'm heading to-ward you, coming in hot." I heard gunfire in the background, a girl's screams.

I was hanging on, leaning into the turn, trying to see out the window and failing. All there was to see was desert flying by. We hit a ditch and went flying, my head hitting the ceiling, and then the Humvee bottomed out with a nasty scraping crunch, and immediately we pitched down, sliding partially sideways down a steep, short hill. My heart was pounding in my chest, and my head was throbbing, but none of that mattered, buried as it was beneath the adrenaline and the fear.

Gunfire echoed from a thousand different directions, assault rifle fire, Anselm's rifle—a deep, distant, basso concussion—overlapped by a different rifle report, this one louder, closer, and sharper.

"Puck!" the radio crackled. "Where the fuck are you! We need cover!" That sounded like Duke.

Puck, in a lightning fast movement, snatched the radio off the seat and tossed it back to me, putting his hand back on the wheel as fast as possible. "You talk," he barked at me. "I drive."

I keyed the radio. "This is Layla. We're on the way to you."

"Well you'd better haul ass," Duke snarled. "We're taking heavy fire and there ain't shit for cover out here."

"Is anyone hurt?"

"Not yet."

"Any sign of Harris?"

"No. Should be seeing him any minute, though." I heard gunfire batter across the radio, either Duke or Thresh.

"What's happening?"

"The op went FUBAR, that's what. It was a fuckin' trap, like I fuckin' said."

"Leave the interrogation for later," Puck told me. "Let him focus on what he's doing. We're almost at their position."

The transfer had taken place in a canyon between two tall ridges. It was an old riverbed or something like that, Nick had said, and it made sense. The middle of the canyon had walls a good fifty feet high, and the land stretched away in either direction for dozens of miles as high ground, with lower elevations approachable from either end of the short canyon. This meant both parties could approach the meet from a neutral direction. It also meant the location was easily defensible for Cain's men. The land rose sharply away from the end of the canyon, leveled off, and then bucked up again sharply. Puck and I had waited at the highest possible point, out of sight of the actual transfer location, but still fairly easy to get to with an off-road vehicle like the kitted-out Wrangler. Duke and Thresh had been positioned a good half-mile closer, where the ground had briefly leveled off, so they could rush forward and lay down covering fire for Nick as he drove away from the transfer. This meant they were exposed to a certain degree, but only to any gunmen on a high enough elevation to see them, not from the canyon itself.

We didn't have far to go, a little over half a mile, but it seemed to me in that moment that it took forever to reach Thresh and Duke's position—time was moving like taffy, stretching out, and then re-tracting to snap too fast, leaving me with still images of Puck's hands on the wheel, utterly focused, and then a jumbling, jouncing, too-fast flash of the desert moving past the window, brown and blue and brown, rocks, dirt, reddish stone slicing into the sky.

Abruptly, Puck threw the Humvee sideways into an arcing skid, shoving me hard against the wall, and then he had the big vehicle in park and his door open, and he was standing in the doorway, an HK MP-5 to his shoulder, kicking in three-round bursts over the wind-shield. I heard his submachine gun rattling, at once too loud and not loud enough. And then I saw Duke throw himself around the hood, taking cover behind the Humvee, ejecting a magazine from his M-4 and replacing it. I heard Thresh's voice, and then the rear door flew open, slammed against the apex of its hinges, and Thresh was there, all seven feet and three hundred plus pounds of him. Sweat poured down his face, and blood reddened the outside of his right bicep from a thin, shallow scratch. He had an M-4 too, and was using the momentary reprieve of hiding behind the door to reload, like Duke.

Thresh winked at me. "Hi-ya, Layla." He rolled out, peering around the edge of the door, cracked off a few rounds, and then rolled back. "Having fun yet?"

I couldn't swallow. "No. Not really."

"Hey, this is where the party's at, babe. Got your nine?"

I patted the holster. "Should I...I don't know. Help?"

I had to wait for a response, as Thresh had rolled out and fired, and was now ducking back in behind the door. "No. Just be ready. I don't know what state Harris will be in. Might need extra cover." He eyed the radio in my hands. "See if Anselm can report."

I thumbed the mic. "Anselm, can you see Harris?"

"*Nein. Er ist nicht*—he is not in my line of sight. He had pursuit, however. Expect them at any moment."

I peered through the window, and saw a starburst of fire from a muzzle somewhere in the distance, and then a second, and then a third. I wasn't sure where the shooters were hiding. I wasn't sure of anything. Why were they pursuing Nick? He'd given them the money. I wasn't sure who we were shooting at, or why they were shooting at us, or why anything was happening.

I jumped as something slammed loudly into the side of the Humvee, on the other side of the metal from me, jarring me. The impacts reverberated across the length of the Humvee toward Thresh, who was rolled out to return fire.

"Thresh! Get back!" I shouted.

He moved instantly, threw himself down to the ground and scrambled onto his back behind the Humvee, out of the line of fire. I saw the glass in the back door of the Humvee, which Thresh had just been hiding behind, crack and then spider web as bullets hit it—it was bulletproof, however, and held.

I heard an engine roaring, then. I shuffled across the bench seat and peered tentatively out the door. The ridge rose up behind us, and the ground fell away in front, the top of the canyon walls in the distance. It sounded like the engine noise was coming from the lower ground, from the canyon, which would mean it was Nick in the Wrangler.

Gunfire echoed, distorted, cracked, chattered, rattled. Duke was returning fire, Puck was shooting, Thresh was shooting. The Humvee was rattling and banging from multiple impact points, making me feel like a mouse under a metal bell, with someone hammering on the bell. I moved back away from the door, covering my ears, fighting the urge to scream. I couldn't think, felt only panic stuffing my brain, freezing me. This wasn't like Brazil, not at all. I didn't know who was shooting at me, or why, or where from. I didn't know where Nick was.

I wanted nothing more than to hide in the furthest corner I could find until this all blew over.

But I couldn't.

I'd asked for this.

"FUCK!" I heard Thresh shout, sounding pained.

That shook me back to reality. "Thresh! You okay?" I hauled myself to the doorway again.

Thresh was on the ground just around the corner of the Humvee, leaning against the side of the vehicle. I couldn't quite see him without leaving the vehicle, and I'd been told not to do that under any circumstances. But Thresh was hurt. I couldn't just sit here. I inched further out the door. Craned my head around the corner.

Thresh was a bloody mess, cradling his left arm against his body, grimacing, heels digging in the dirt. I wasn't sure where else he was hit besides his arm, but just that looked bad enough. I saw bits of white bone, gristle, gore. His M-4 was on the ground beside him.

"Thresh? Can you climb in here with me?"

He swiveled his head to glare at me. "I'll be fine. Just—gimme a second."

I hopped out of the truck and crouched behind the door. "You're hurt. You need to get in there. Let me help you."

More impacts thudded into the dirt, into the side of the Humvee. The engine roaring was louder now, closer, about to crest the verge. I scrambled out of cover and threw myself to the dirt beside Thresh, behind the Humvee.

"You're not supposed to leave the Humvee," Thresh said through clenched teeth.

I ignored him, because he was right. Tossed his M-4 by the strap over my shoulder, grabbed his uninjured shoulder under the armpit.

"Come on. Get in there, you big idiot. Move."

"I need to cover Nick. That's his Wrangler coming up the hill. He needs cover." Thresh lumbered to his feet, released his hurt arm, reached for the rifle on my shoulder with his bloody good hand. "And you need to get back in the damn truck."

Fuck, that wound was nasty. It looked like the bullet had broken his forearm and then that same round or another one had torn through his bicep.

"I'll get in if you do," I said. "You can't shoot with that wound."

He yanked the rifle from me, shouldered the strap, grabbed me around the middle, and tossed me bodily into the back of the Humvee. He was handling the M-4 with just his right hand. And then, with a grimace, uncurled his left arm from against his chest, and tried to grab the front grip of the assault rifle. But he couldn't do it.

Yet, despite this, he popped off a round. The rifle bucked up, almost out of his grip, eliciting a curse from him.

"Fucking goddammit, Thresh!" I shouted.

But then the Wrangler dove over the ridge, front tires going airborne and then burying in the sand, hauling the rest of the vehicle over the hill. The Wrangler, once black, was now brown with dirt and sand, and bullet holes punctured it in dozens of places. It had huge wheels and a lift kit, no doors, no roof. Meant for off-roading. The windshield was spider webbed, shattered in places. I couldn't quite see Nick through the shattered glass.

Even as the Wrangler heaved up over the crest, I heard multiple other engines roar in the distance, smaller, thinner sounds, dirt bikes probably. Thresh was still trying to fire with one hand, and making a horrible mess of it, bracing the gun against the edge of the door, reaching for it with his bloody left hand, cupping the grip just long enough to pop off a shot or two before the kick sent what had to be excruciating agony through his injured arm.

The Wrangler didn't manage the jump over the crest very well, going airborne, slamming down, and then tipping forward, taking its weight on the front left wheel, bottoming that corner out against the ground. Pitching forward. I heard Nick's voice and then heard a thin, high, female shriek.

And then the Wrangler rolled. I saw it happen in slow motion, the way it just sort of…toppled forward and to one side, wheels still spinning.

Duke was out from behind cover, firing while running toward the Wrangler; Puck not far behind him.

It looked from what I could see that Nick was pinned under the Wrangler, the vehicle tipped onto its side, driver's side down, the open cab facing us; I couldn't see the little girl, but I heard her voice, crying hysterically.

Thresh was trying to reload.

He looked pained, not physically so much as emotionally wrecked by the knowledge that he was hurt and unable to help fast enough. I watched through the door, feeling helpless, as Puck hid behind the rolled-over Wrangler and laid down covering fire over the top while Duke tried to wrestle Nick free, tried to lift the Wrangler enough to free whatever was caught.

"THRESH!" Duke shouted, "I NEED YOU!"

I thought, stupidly, of that scene in *The Princess Bride* where Inigo is trying to get through the locked door so he could follow the Six-Fingered Man, and Fezzik comes lumbering up to smash it down with one kick—*FEZZIK, I NEED YOU!*

Thresh shouldered his M-4 and left cover, running faster than any man his size had a right to run. Crouched beside Duke, he placed both hands—the idiot, *both* hands—on the frame of the Wrangler at the bottom, between the vehicle and the sand. Then he shouted, a guttural, rage-filled roar.

And…

He *lifted*. The Wrangler left the ground, and Duke's hands flashed, slicing something, and then he was hauling Nick free. Or trying to. Puck was firing nonstop, reloading.

And I was just sitting there.

Doing nothing.

Watching.

And then I spotted the little girl. Strapped in a five-point harness into the front passenger seat. Tiny, so small your eyes skipped right over her. Trapped by the seatbelt, suspended. Puck was shooting. Thresh was holding the Wrangler off the ground as Duke tried to extricate Nick from whatever was trapping him.

No one had the girl.

Fuck it.

I didn't think, I just acted. I ran, hauling my big ass across the dirt, slamming bodily into the Jeep, rocking it. I ignored Nick, who was shouting at me.

Ignored Puck, who was also shouting at me.

Ignored Thresh, who was doing something utterly superhuman, and also shouting at me.

Duke was the only one not shouting at me.

Bullets were still snapping overhead.

The motorcycles were somewhere close by. There was one, off to the left, the rider skidding over the crest of the hill, submachine gun dangling from a strap. I didn't think again—my hand yanked my Beretta out of the holster, and I drew a bead on a T-shirt covered torso, and then the pistol bucked in my hand, and the rider slumped, and the bike tipped, hit sand, and skidded.

I holstered my weapon and returned my attention to the little girl. "Cleo? Hi, sweetie." I tried to keep my voice soft, despite the circumstances. "I'm gonna unbuckle you now, okay? You're gonna have to grab on to me real quick, and we're gonna get out of here, okay?"

Cleo just howled.

I took that as an okay. I jabbed at the red button that released the five buckles with one hand and grabbed the girl around the middle with the other. I caught her weight as the buckles released her, and yanked her body against mine. God, she was so small. Like a little doll, made out of porcelain. Had a hell of a set of pipes on her, though, piercing my eardrums with her screams.

Not that I blamed her one bit.

As soon as I had the girl in my arms, I got my ass moving again, running as fast as I could back to the Humvee, hearing bullets going *snap-snap-snap*, hearing the reports from everywhere. No buzzing, though, no angry-bee sounds of bullets coming too close. I hit the edge of the open back door of the Humvee with my stomach and hips, effectively tossing Cleo in, and then I jumped in after her. She was on the floor, crawling away from me, finding a corner and huddling in, staring around her, screaming, sobbing. Fine black hair. Brown eyes. Dirt track tears on her cheeks. Shaking uncontrollably, staring around her, confused, terrified. I wanted to comfort her, but had no idea how.

I heard another motorcycle engine, but this one was coming from the wrong direction. I crouched in the opening of the Humvee's back door, pistol in both hands. I saw the front wheel of a motorcycle spitting rocks and dirt, flying up from the canyon, the rider leaning forward to take the slam of the landing. Seeing the Humvee, seeing me, he braked hard then gunned the throttle, spinning the dirt bike in a circle so he could arc around the back end of the Humvee and go for me—and Cleo.

He was another casually dressed guy, dark hair, jeans, a T-shirt, Chucks on his feet. A big ol' silver handgun tucked into the front of his waistband, hauled free as soon as the dirt bike was level once more. Spitting and sliding to a stop, the rider sitting back, lifting the gun. To shoot me? Threaten me? Take Cleo back? I don't know.

Fuck that.

I don't even remember drawing the gun, I just popped off a shot without thinking. *BAM!* The gun bucked in my hands, and a dark spot spread on the rider's chest. He looked confused, the barrel of his hand-cannon of a pistol drooping. I shot again, a little higher, and this time I saw the spray. Bile rose in my throat as his neck just beneath his chin turned into a smear of red, and spray blasted out behind him. He rocked back, slid to one side, toppled backward, and then he and the bike collapsed.

Cleo was screaming bloody murder, hands over her ears.

I holstered my Beretta and moved in a crouch closer to her. I hated kids. I was no good with them, and they never liked me. They were always scared of me, no matter what I said or did. This was no different as Cleo shrank, away from me, further into the corner.

"Hey, it's gonna be okay," I murmured, going for a calm, soothing voice and only managing to sound like I was talking to a little puppy or something, "We're going to bring you back to Mommy and Daddy, okay?"

"M-m-m-Mama?" Cleo whimpered.

"Yeah, Mama. We're gonna go see Mama. Can you sit on the bench, there?"

Cleo nodded and scrambled onto the bench, and I sat beside her, facing the opening, effectively shielding her. I hauled out my pistol again and kept it pointed at the opening, reminding myself to make sure I knew who was in the opening before shooting.

The gunfire was dying down, and I heard voices.

Thresh, first, his arm a bloody wreck, his face strained. Puck, jumping behind the wheel, slamming the door closed. Duke, next, his arm around Nick's middle, helping him inside.

Suddenly, the back of the Humvee was crowded, smelling like man-sweat and something acrid, and blood.

We were moving, bumping, jouncing over hills.

It was silent, but only for a moment.

"Goddammit, Layla—" This was Nick.

"That was fucking badass, Layla!" Duke shouted, at the same time as Nick. "You nailed that fucker while he was *moving*!"

"Duke." Nick, voice low, threatening. "Shut it."

Duke went quiet, eyeing Nick. "You are *not* gonna bitch her out right now, man. If she hadn't grabbed the girl when she did, we'd still be there. She was an asset. That's why she's here; it's what she wants. And I gotta say, she's pretty damn good."

"We all heard you two in the jet, you know," this was Thresh, through clenched teeth. "Heard you arguing. I'm with Duke on this one."

Nick's eyes cut to mine. I could see he hated that I'd disobeyed him, that I'd risked myself. But I could also see the grudging respect my actions deserved.

"Good job, babe," he growled.

"I just have one question," I said, keeping my voice quiet until the last second. "WHAT THE FUCK JUST HAPPENED?"

6

FUCKIN' SNACKS

I'D BEEN FUCKING LUCKY. SERIOUSLY FUCKING LUCKY. I WAS banged up, and had at least one bruised rib, but I had somehow avoided getting shot, and Cleo was unhurt. When that Jeep rolled, man, I thought I was done.

But my people came through. Puck covered us, Duke cut me free, and Thresh, Jesus Christ, Thresh had lifted the Jeep free so Duke could cut the tangled, trapped seat belt free. With a broken forearm. Fucker was inhuman.

And my baby. My woman. Layla. She'd disobeyed orders. Rushed through incoming fire, gotten Cleo, and rushed back with her. She'd taken down two tangos in the process. My girl was a badass. All the guys were eyeing her with renewed respect. And me? I was torn between wanting to ream her a new asshole for disobeying orders and being insanely proud of how she handled herself in a gnarly situation.

I took stock of my crew, examining all of them. Thresh was the only one hurt, miraculously, but he was seriously fucked up. A bullet had hit his ulna and shattered it, lodging in his bicep. Looked like maybe he'd taken another round to the shoulder, but with the way he was cradling his arm against himself, it was hard to tell. I knew from experience, though, to just leave Thresh alone. He'd survive, and wouldn't let anyone help him. If he were conscious, he'd do what needed to be done. Even now, in the state Thresh was in, I'd still have chosen him to back me over just about anyone else on the planet—except maybe Duke. Speaking of whom, Duke was still on alert, watching out the window for pursuit, unconsciously toying with the safety of his HK, thumbing it back and forth. Dusty, dirty, and unfazed. Puck was driving.

And that was when I noticed it. Giving Puck a once over while he drove, I noticed two big black duffel bags on the seat beside Puck.

Two awfully familiar duffel bags. Full bags.

"Puck." I kept my voice low and even.

"Yeah?" He didn't turn around, kept his eyes on the…well, we weren't on a road, but on the ground ahead.

"What exactly the *fuck* is that on the seat?"

Puck shot me a grin. "That, my friend, is fifty million dollars. *And* the girl."

"How?"

"One of the fuckers on the dirt bikes had 'em strapped to the back of his bike. I happened to see 'em, and figured there was no sense in leaving fifty mil just laying around in the desert, you know?"

"Fuck." I leaned my head back against the wall. "FUCK!"

Puck frowned at me. "What's the issue?"

"I figured out who Cain is: Ledion Dushku. And he's not just some minor league drug runner; he's a major threat. Albanian by birth, former Russian Special Forces. Mercenary turned assassin, Mafioso, and all around bad, bad, bad dude. He and I crossed paths a few years back. I was with the Rangers, he was with Spetsnaz. My unit and his were supposed to be working together to take down a terrorist cell in Pakistan. Turned out, though, that Ledion was working with the terrorists. Feeding them intel and supplies and warning them of raids, and taking bribes. I found out, reported him, and got him in major shit. He's never forgiven me, obviously."

"So what does that have to do with the money?" Puck asked.

"It means he's going to be extra pissed. His ambush failed, thanks to Anselm's quick rifle work. We shot his guys, took his money, and took the girl. He's got a chip on his shoulder, and being shown up, made to look like a fool? He won't take it well."

"It was kind of a poorly-planned ambush," Duke pointed out. "They had the high ground, they had the numbers, and they chose the location. You block off one end of that canyon, post a couple guys with SAWs on the high ground? You could hold off an army with a couple of squads. We should all be dead."

I nodded. "That's Ledion's problem: he's not a great tactician. But what he lacks in tactical know-how, he more than makes up for in brutality, vengefulness, and utter lack of morals. He's the type that'll set off a car bomb to take out what he perceives as an enemy, without sparing a single thought for the collateral damage. He just doesn't care. He shoots first and doesn't stop to ask questions."

Layla was listening to all this. "Did you not hear me? I asked what happened. Someone explain to me what just happened."

I probed my ribs, wincing as I found the bruises. "Whoever Ledion's second in command was, the guy running the show, he had the girl right out in the open, waiting as I approached. I stopped the Jeep, left it running. Told him I'd give him the money once I had the girl. I got her buckled in and then handed him the money. That should have been it, and I thought it was, honestly. I got in the Jeep, pulled a U-turn, and that was when I heard Anselm start shooting. Apparently Ledion had ordered his guys to wait until they had the money, and then just…cut us down. Anselm obviously suspected as much, and took out the gunners on the canyon wall, him and Lear together. That's the only reason I'm here. It took them by surprise, which gave me time to get out of the canyon and away. Of course, they couldn't just let us go. Ledion obviously told them to make sure I didn't survive, so they gave chase."

"What I don't get is…and don't take this the wrong way, but— there was so much shooting." Layla pointed at Thresh. "Only, no one but Thresh got hurt. How is that possible? I mean, I'm glad, but I don't get it."

Duke answered for me. "That's the statistic of a battle. Hundreds, if not thousands of rounds are fired in the average exchange, but only a few ever hit anyone. It takes a lot of training, a fucking assload of hours on the range and in battle to learn how to make every shot count, especially when you're under fire yourself. And even then, a lot of the shots you lay down are meant as suppression, to keep the other guy's head down, and they're doing the same. And that's assuming the guys shooting at you are trained. If they're just thugs with guns who've never received real combat training, then they're honestly lucky as fuck to have even hit anything, much less caused any real damage."

"So, the guys shooting at us," Layla asked. "Were they trained, or not?"

Duke shook his head side to side. "Some yes, some no. The guys on the bikes, the guys you took down, I think they were higher rank-ing, and thus had some experience or training. The tangos in the canyon, they were just foot soldiers. Hired cannon fodder, basically. There were a couple who knew what they were doing. Somebody had the Humvee locked down pretty good, laid down some fairly effective suppressing fire."

"Was Ledion himself there?" Layla asked.

I shook my head. "I didn't see him. He might have been watch-ing from a distance, but he wasn't in the canyon. He wouldn't have been, though. He went in and snatched Cleo, and he's likely the one who shot the housekeeper. But if he was planning an ambush like this one, he would have made sure he was well clear. He's not going to risk his own neck in case things go south, and in any op, there's al-ways a chance shit can go south. Especially when you're dealing with the kind of soldiers the Russian mafia or whoever he's working with or for can field. Those guys are vicious, but when you put them up against a unit like us, tight, trained, and tactically superior? They're cannon fodder, and he knows it. He'd never go into a situation per-sonally unless he had people he trusted with him, and babe, I think you shot at least one of them."

Layla closed her eyes, rested her head back. "This is starting to sound like Vitaly all over again."

I reached across the space between us and took her hand. "Not even close. It's not good, but Ledion, or Cain as he's calling himself now, isn't on the same scale as Vitaly was. We'll have to be on our toes, and expect retaliation, but for one thing, Ledion doesn't have the resources Vitaly did. And, honestly, he's not as smart. Still dangerous, I don't want to give you the wrong impression, he's fucking dangerous. But he's not on the level of Vitaly. Not in any way."

"'Sides," Duke said, "now you got us."

It was quiet for several minutes as Puck drove us back across the desert to the main road.

A tiny, hesitant little voice piped up, unexpectedly. "I hungry."

"Me too, little boo," Duke said. "Come sit with Uncle Duke. I think I've got some candy here somewhere."

And wouldn't you know it, tiny little Cleo, all of two feet tall, if that, weighing maybe thirty pounds soaking wet, hopped down, scooted past Layla, and climbed up onto Duke's lap. Never mind the M-4 on his shoulder, never mind the smell of cordite, never mind the fact that he's a monster of a man that can scare grown men into pissing their pants.

Little girls love him. I don't get it.

He swept his black A1S ball cap off his head, revealing his ginger undercut man-bun hair—fucking man-buns, man, fucking stupid—and plopped the hat on Cleo's head. It slid down and covered her face.

"Eeew. Stinky hat. Get it off!" She knocked the hat off her head, grabbed it in her pudgy little hands, and reached up to stuff it onto Duke's head.

"It is kind of sweaty, I guess," Duke said. He dug in the cargo pocket of his BDU pants, producing a handful of fun-size bags of M&Ms. "You don't like M&Ms, do you?"

"YEAH!" Cleo shouted. "Neminems!"

"Yo, I like neminems too," Thresh said, extending his paw.

The hand on his uninjured arm was black-red with dried blood, and he was still oozing blood from his arm and shoulder. Not that he seemed to care. You wouldn't know Thresh was even feeling pain, unless you looked for the tension lines in his forehead and at the corners of his eyes. Other than that, he could be right as rain.

Duke ripped open a bag of M&Ms and dumped them into Thresh's palm, and the crazy fucking giant ate them, bloody residue and all.

Layla made a disgusted face. "That's gross, Thresh."

"What?" Thresh asked, through a mouthful of candy.

"Your hand, it's all messy. And now you're eating from that hand?"

Thresh shrugged. "Hey, it's my blood."

"Do you want me to look at that arm?" Layla asked.

Thresh grunted a negative. "Needs surgery. Got a round lodged in my shoulder, too. I'll be fine."

Layla looked at me. "Do we have a doctor waiting?"

I nodded. "Yeah. Anselm and Lear should be a few minutes ahead of us. They'll have a medic waiting."

"Don't want a fuckin' medic," Thresh grumbled.

I sighed. "Listen, you hard-ass. You need medical attention. We're not having this conversation. You can't just take some fucking Ibuprofen and sleep this one off."

"I know I need a doctor, I'm not stupid." Thresh tossed another M&M in his mouth. "I got a specific doctor I want to see."

Duke and I exchanged puzzled glances. "What are you talking about?"

"That hot doc down in Miami. The one at Jackson Memorial? When you were laid up after that shit with Karahalios? She was fine as hell."

I rolled my eyes. "Thresh. You can't pick a doctor halfway across the country just because she had a nice pair of knockers, man. We're taking you to a hospital in Vegas."

"You can try," Thresh said. "But good luck. I'm going to Miami."

"You're bleeding!" Layla shouted. "You have a broken bone. You have a bullet in your shoulder."

"I noticed," Thresh deadpanned, "seeing as it's my arm and my shoulder."

"Thresh." I stared him down. "Make sense. Please."

"I am making sense. It's not just 'cause she's hot. I mean, yeah, she is, but she's also a good doctor. I watched her take care of you. She's good. Plus, I think she likes me."

I sighed. "This is the dumbest thing I've ever heard."

"I never claimed to be the sharpest crayon in the tool drawer," Thresh said, looking peeved. "You know how I feel about fuckin' hospitals and fuckin' doctors, Harris. If I've got to have a goddamn doctor poke at me, might as well be a doctor of my choosing. And the one I choose happens to be in Miami, Florida, and happens to have the most bangin' hourglass figure I've ever seen. On top of which, she's not afraid to get in my face, and I like that shit. She's got balls."

"Okay, fine. Whatever. It's your broke ass that's gonna bleed all the way there." I rubbed at my face with both hands.

"You'll fly me down there?"

"Well you can't very well walk, can you?" I said.

"Cool. Thanks, boss." Thresh nudged Duke with his hand. "Got anymore candy? I'm still hungry."

Duke, with a playful, long-suffering sigh, dug into his cargo pocket and pulled out a protein bar. "You never bring your own snacks, man. You're always hungry after a firefight. You think you'd learn to bring some fuckin' snacks once in a while."

"I want some fuckin' snacks too!" Cleo shouted. "I like fuckin' snacks!"

Duke snorted. "Now look what you fuckers did. Taught her to say fuckin'."

That drew laughter from everyone, including Cleo, who I don't think quite understood the joke, but knew everyone was laughing at her. "Fuckin', fuckin', fuckin'!" She shouted it, chanting, over and over, until everyone was in stitches.

Layla swatted at Duke. "Tell her not to say that!"

"Why? She ain't my kid. I think it's funny." He ruffled her platinum hair. "I'm getting paid to rescue her, not teach her manners."

Thank god kids are resilient. Although, I had a feeling the poor thing would be having nightmares for a while. I made a mental note to make sure Jon and Callie put her in therapy; shit like what Cleo went through is the kind of shit that'll scar you for life if it's not addressed. She was laughing and seemed fine for now, but PTSD tended to manifest when you least expected it, especially in children.

I'd tried to downplay the threat Ledion posed when explaining it to Layla. But the truth was, fear niggled in the back of my head. Ledion—Cain—was just smart enough to be dangerous, but dumb enough to worry me. He wouldn't care who else he hurt in the process. He would feel slighted and, to save face, he'd go after me. He'd go after all of us. Jon and Callie I wasn't too worried about; I'd put guards on them 24/7, tell them to move, take proper measures. But Cain's attention was on me, now, and my crew. On Layla.

We might have just started a war.

But I wasn't about to say that, not until I knew for sure.

7

PAYBACK

IHADN'T EXPECTED NICK BACK IN COLORADO FOR A FEW DAYS yet, but it seemed Thresh had told him to get lost, his life wasn't in danger, and Nick's presence would just be a cock-block.

So Nick came home early from Miami.

He slept lightly that first night. Probably a good thing, because I had nightmares. I kept hearing gunfire in my dreams. Kept seeing that guy's throat explode, kept feeling the pistol buck in my hands. Nick woke me up, comforted me. Held me. Stroked my skin and let me be weak and vulnerable.

The next night was better. No nightmares, no dreams. Just deep, peaceful sleep in Nick's arms.

There was tension simmering between us, still, though. Nick had tied me up, and without asking me first. And yes, I'd been so turned on I hadn't known which way was up and, in the moment, certainly hadn't remembered that I'd intended to seduce him. I'd waited in his office for fifteen, twenty minutes, and then I'd heard him on the phone just outside. I still don't know what possessed me, but the second I heard his voice, I'd stripped naked. I don't know if I've ever shucked my clothes that fast. And then, when I heard the knob twist, I'd started touching myself. Naughty, naughty girl, I know. Right there in his office. Stark naked, flicking my bean. Blinds open, no less.

And the bastard had turned the tables on me.

That pissed me off.

And the way he'd intended to just…send me home like a bad little disobedient wifey? Oh *hell* no. I was hurt, deeply. Beyond hurt, beyond pissed.

Duke and the others had come through for me, and Nick had come around.

But still. I hadn't forgotten.

So now I was awake, at four thirty in the morning, waiting for Nick to wake up.

I may or may not have roofied his scotch. Just a little, so I could tie him up without having to fight him.

Yes, I'm a terrible person, I know.

I heard him stir. Groan.

"Fuck. What the hell happened?" He sounded groggy, scratchy voiced. Then I heard him yank on the neckties I'd used to spread-eagle him to the bed. "What? Shit. Layla? Very funny. Untie me."

I didn't answer right away. I wanted him to sweat.

"Layla?"

More struggling. But I'd been practicing my knots, so I was reasonably sure he couldn't get free.

"Layla? Where the hell are you, woman?"

The room was dark enough still that he couldn't see me. I was about eight inches to his left, but he didn't need to know that. I was breathing as quietly and softly as I could.

"I fucking hear you breathing, Layla. I can *smell* you. Untie me."

"Oh, I don't think so." I stood up. Moved forward exactly one step; I'd practiced. Reached a hand out, trailed my fingers along his skin, from toe to hip. "You had to know I'd find a way to get even, Nick."

"When did I fall asleep? And how did I stay asleep while you did this to me?"

"Oh, I roofied your scotch last night."

"You *roofied* me?" He sounded utterly incredulous. Admittedly, it was a pretty extreme length to go to.

"How else was I supposed to get you tied up? You'd have woken up and overpowered me otherwise."

"So you ROOFIED me?"

"Yep."

"And now what?" He sounded…hesitant.

"And now?" I slid my palm along his belly. Walked my fingers up his chest, found his lips. Used my thumb to pull his lower lip down. "And now, stud, I have my way with you."

I skated my hand back down, slithered my palm down his belly, skirting around his cock from hip to hip, teasing him. Leaned in, kissed him. Bit his lip so hard he grunted in surprised pain, a sound that turned to a moan as I took his burgeoning erection in my fist. One, two, three slow strokes and I felt him thicken, lengthen, harden in my hand.

When he was appropriately hard, I crouched down and picked up the tube of lube from where I'd left it, just under the chair I'd been sitting on. I squirted some into my palm, and smeared it all over Nick's partial erection, glopped it on and stroked him a few times to make sure his length was coated. And then I crouched once more and grabbed the cock ring I'd ordered.

Small, tight. Perfect. I guided the ring to the broad tip of his dick and fitted the ring on and slid it down. Carefully, I worked it on, further and further. Nick grunted as I seated the cock ring home, as far down his shaft as I could get it. And good lord was it tight.

"Fuck, Layla. What the hell is your game?"

"My game? My game is pretty simple, Nick: I'm going to use you as an experiment. I've always said I don't have an orgasm threshold, right? But we've never tested it. I turned off all the phones, locked the doors, and told the guys we're out of commission until we contact them. I've got you all trussed up like a Christmas present to my pussy, and I'm gonna have myself a good old time, riding your cock and sitting on your face. I'm gonna use you like a flesh-and-blood dildo to make myself come as many times as possible, until I either get sick of the game, pass out, or stop being able to come, whichever comes first."

"We've had all-night marathon fuck sessions, and you've still been raring to go afterward."

"Exactly. I've got supplies, Nick. I brought snacks and juice boxes and several bottles of lube, and even some Viagra. Just in case, you know—you're not up to the task."

He snarled. "Oh I'm up for the fucking task, woman. Don't you doubt that."

I reached out and petted his penis. "I figured you would be. But men have their limits. Even you'll need some refractory time at some point."

"This is going to be a long night, isn't it?"

"I very much hope so, babe." I climbed onto the bed, straddled his chest. I grabbed the headboard between his outstretched hands and slid my pussy over his face. I crouched above him, holding onto the headboard for balance. "Get lickin', stud. I'm keeping count."

His tongue flicked out, eagerly. Found my clit, circled it. Stabbed in, flattened. His lips pinched the bud, and he suckled. Then he returned to licking, a quick, steady rhythm, just how I loved it best.

Within seconds, I was on the edge, gasping. The man had a wicked tongue, knew just how to lick me to get me there fastest. Usually he would draw it out a little, play with me, edge me, use his fingers. But this time, it was only about getting me to climax. And god, did he ever. That motherfucker hit like a ton of bricks, an orgasm blasting through me like a tidal wave, spurred on by his tongue.

"One," I gasped.

I slid down his body, straddling him still then reached down, took hold of his rock hard cock, and brought the plump, springy head against my clit, rubbing in circles. Planting my hand on his chest for balance, I used that beautiful dick of his like a dildo on my clit. But it was better than any sex toy, because this was Nick, my man, my love. And while this whole thing was to get back at him—I didn't intend to let him come until the last possible second, and as few times as possible—it was still about us, about me and him and the bond between us.

He just had to remember that he couldn't pull that kind of bondage bullshit on me and expect to get away with it.

Number two seared through me within minutes of the first, and while the orgasm crested, I sank down on him, impaled his thick cock into my throbbing pussy. And fuck, fuck, fuck, that sent number three tumbling through me, because that first thrust, when he pushed into me for the first time, filled me, stretched me, sinking so deep our hips bumped together and his balls gently slapped against me and he couldn't' possibly get any deeper. That's the fuck best feeling in the world, isn't it? I fucking love that. I love it so much sometimes I come from that feeling alone.

I leaned back, found my balance. Lifted up, way up, and then slammed down, and Nick shouted a curse. He yanked at the bonds, wanting to grab my hips and jerk me down, lift me up, work me hard to get himself deeper. But this wasn't about him. This was about me. And I wasn't ready for hard and fast yet.

Oh, no.

I sank deep, rolled my hips. Relished the feel of him inside me. Fluttered a few shallow thrusts, just to tease him. Lifted up, sank down. Every time I pressed down, I rolled my hips, spread my thighs as wide as they would go, so he shoved in deeper and deeper. Fuck, so deep.

So good.

I felt a tremor then so I flicked my fingertips against my clit and began to rock on him, fingers circling my clit, fingers pinching my nipples, one and then the other. I moved harder, faster. Harder, faster.

And when number four ripped through me, I leaned forward and buried my face in his neck, then kissed his bearded jaw, his cheekbone, and his eyelids. I found his lips and kissed him as I rode him through numbers five and six.

God, with that cock ring keeping him from coming, there was no need to hold back or worry about technique. I rode him, then, long and hard. Slow, then fast. Shallow, shallow, teasingly shallow until number seven hit, and a shallow-thrust orgasm is a wild thing, fierce and fiery and subtle. And then hard, fucking-like-animals hard. Slamming down, flesh slapping. Number eight. Jesus, number eight was a doozy.

I'd only been on top of Nick for twenty minutes, maybe, and I was going slow and hard as numbers nine and ten broke through me.

"Jesus, Layla. Fuck....It hurts. I need to come, it hurts so bad."

"No way, babe. I'm just getting started."

"I need to come."

"Oh, you will. When I let you."

I pulled off him, crawled up to his face, and rode his tongue across numbers eleven through thirteen.

I hadn't been kidding about the snacks: I took a long drink of water and fed some to Nick, fed us both some power bars.

Then I climbed on, turned around, and rode him reverse cowgirl style for numbers fourteen through twenty. Six, baby, count 'em *six* orgasms in reverse cowgirl. And Nick was a wild man by this point, snarling, grunting, thrusting up with his hips, trying to get more, and trying to do anything that would let him come.

Time to tease.

I'd purchased a flavored lube, for this exact purpose. I teased him with my mouth. Licked him, top to bottom. Mouthed him, bobbing only shallowly. Stroked him at the root, just above the cock ring, and sucked on the head. Got him so worked up I thought he might explode despite the cock ring.

But no, he couldn't.

And he was crazy.

"How does that feel, sweetheart? Needing to come, wanting to come, but not being able to?"

He snarled at me, wordless.

"That's what I thought." I slid off him, biting his lip in passing.

"Don't go anywhere."

I grabbed the third and last item off the floor underneath the chair: a little silver bullet vibrator with a remote. Turning it on, I touched it to Nick's cock, tracing his length with it.

"Know what this is for, Nicky-baby?" I gestured with the vibrator as I straddled his stomach and sat on him. I squirted some lube onto my fingers and leaned over so I was resting my torso on his chest, my lips to his ear. Then I applied the lube to my asshole. "It's going inside me. Remember that night I let you fuck me back there? That still counts as the hardest I've ever come, you know. I'm not planning on breaking *that* particular record, but I'm going to get close, I think." I pressed the cold, buzzing vibrator to the lubed-up knot of muscle, exhaled and relaxed.

I whispered in Nick's ear the whole while. "God, this feels good. It'd be better if it was you putting it in there, but…oh god, fuck, there it goes. Oh Jesus. Fuck!" Number twenty-one speared through me like lightning, before I was even ready. And then I turned up the power of the vibrator and slid Nick's erect cock into me, and came again, and again, and again. So hard, so many times, coming on each down stroke, the vibrator going wild in my back door, Nick thick and hard inside me, his big beautiful body beneath me, his lips at my ear, his voice grunting, his beard tickling me, the sweat on his skin mingling with mine.

I'm pretty sure I passed thirty. I may have lost count, lost track of time, just laid collapsed forward on Nick, my tits crushed against his chest, kissing him wherever my lips touched, holding onto his neck and shoulders and arms, riding him like a charging stallion for all we were worth.

I was beginning to feel it, now. Not doubting, exactly, but feeling the toll. And Nick was a mess.

"Are you ready to come, Nick?" I gasped in his ear.

"Fuck…please. Yes, Layla."

"Will you beg me?" I rode him slow, now. "I think I need to hear you beg."

"Layla…" he murmured my name. "Please, Layla. Please, please, *please* let me come. I need it, so bad. I'm begging you." He whispered this in my ear. Desperate, earnest, intent. A ragged whisper.

"I think you've earned it."

I slid him out of me. Moved to the foot of the bed, untied his right ankle. His left ankle. And then I lay down on my back beside him, putting my lips to his ear. "I'm going to untie your left hand now."

"Bad idea," Nick growled, sounding more like Scary Harris than anything. "Really bad idea. I have zero control."

I bit his earlobe, reaching up to work free the knots of the necktie binding his right wrist to the bedpost. "Don't you know me well enough by now, sweetheart?" I freed the last of the knots. "That's what I want most."

As soon as his wrist was free, Nick moved like a pouncing lion. He ripped the cock ring off and hurled it viciously across the room. Something smashed. He yanked open the bedside drawer—I heard the snick of a knife unfolding, and then I knew he was free.

No lie, my heart was pounding. I was a little scared of the monster I'd created. I'd lost track of time, but I think I had Nick tied up and helpless beneath me for, oh, at least three hours, if not more. An eternity, for a man accustomed to utter control. An eternity of needing to come, being on the edge, and not being able to cross over.

He moved like a predator, pouncing on me like a lion grabbing a gazelle. He snatched my wrists, both of them in one hand and used his other hand to knock my thighs open, one, then the other. He traced the opening of my wet, throbbing pussy, guiding his cock to the entrance, holding himself there, just the wide head notched inside me. He leaned down, breathing hard, shaking all over and put his lips to my ear.

"You got me back, babe." He whispered in a guttural, barely-controlled snarl in my ear. "You got me back good."

And then, without warning, he let go of my wrists, grabbed my hips and flipped me over. He shoved my face into the mattress, jerked my hips up, so my ass was high in the air.

Then he slapped my ass so hard I squeaked, rocked forward away from the spank, more out of surprise. But Nick grabbed me and put me back in place. Then he reached down and guided himself back in, just the tip nestled in the very outer limits of my cunt. He held himself there, as if gathering himself. Focusing.

And then, with a feral roar, he slammed in, deep, hard. Fucked in mercilessly. Flesh slapped, and his cock buried itself in me, and I cried out. He gave no quarter, then, but began fucking me in earnest, harder than he'd ever fucked me the entire time we'd been together. Almost brutally hard.

And I loved every single second of it, rocked with his battering thrusts, rocked back into them. Cried out in bliss as he fucked more orgasms out of me. No more counting.

Lies: Thirty-five—thirty-six…fuck, fuck, fuck, how many more could I take? They hurt, now. Ripping, plundering, scattering climaxes, one after another, because Nick was fierce and wild and insatiable.

And then he came, slammed home once more, and then buried himself to the hilt and ground his hips against me, ground himself inside me, fingers gripping my hips with bruising force, keeping me jerked hard against him. He came, exploding in me so hard I felt it like a geyser.

"Layla! Fuck—fuck, oh fucking Christ—" and then he was just shouting incoherently as he literally blew his brains out through his cock inside my throbbing, well-used cunt.

Over and over and over, he came. So long, so hard. A seemingly endless orgasm.

And then he collapsed.

I was done.

So done.

"How—how many?" Nick gasped.

"Thirty…thirty-nine, I think. I lost track toward the end there."

I was seeing stars, feeling dizzy and faint.

The vibrator was still buzzing madly inside my ass.

Nick could feel it, too. He reached back there, levering himself over me. "Thirty-nine?" He found the pull-string, and gently tugged. His other hand was busy, too, swirling against me. "Might as well make it a nice round forty."

"I don't know…" I grated out, teeth clenched. Fighting it, now. "I don't know if I—if I can."

"I thought you didn't have a threshold?"

"I think we…oh fuck, oh fuck, oh fuck! I think we found it." I sounded desperate. Panicked. The pressure inside me was unbearable. Volcanic. Sharp. Cutting. I couldn't take it. This one would be too much. Too much. One over the line.

"Can't stop now, isn't that right?" Nick's voice was pleased, because he was once again in control.

And the truth was, I'd known all along I'd never find the edge, never find my limit without Nick to take me there.

I was not a woman who submitted, not to anyone, not ever. But when I gave in to Nick, that's when shit got the most intense.

I gave over, then.

Abandoned myself to it. His fingers worked hard. He gradually drew the vibrator out, and then pushed it back in. Out, and then back in. Further out, and then in. Fingers circling me wildly all the while.

I found the crest, and I reached it sobbing. Actually sobbing, the searing, painful heat of the breaking climax was so much, too much, so completely too much for me to handle. And when it crested, when I fell over that edge, sobbing too hard to even scream, Nick pulled the vibrator free and the orgasm detonated within me, a white-hot nuclear spasm washing through me, overtaking me.

And then I literally passed out.

When I woke up, I was in Nick's arms—I was home. I let out a contented sigh before I even opened my eyes. I knew he was awake already, from his breathing.

"I love you, Layla Campari." His voice was muzzy; he hadn't been awake long, then.

"Even though I'm stubborn, reckless, and refuse to ever do what

I'm told?"

He rolled over, my head cradled on his forearms, his body over mine, nestling into me, gliding in where he belonged, lips kissing mine, whispering. "Especially because of that."

"You know I'll listen to you when it counts, right?" I said, between gasps of bliss.

"Yeah, babe. I know. And I promise I'll never take it easy on you. Out there, you're one of the guys." He plunged, bucked, rocked, but slowly, smoothly, lovingly. "In here, though—"

"I'm all yours."

"Forever."

"Promise?"

He pressed his forehead to mine. "Yeah, I promise."

"You know I still expect a romantic proposal one day, right?"

"You'll get it. Someday."

That's all the promise I needed. I didn't really need a ring or a proposal, I just needed this man, no matter what.

BONUS SCENE:

VALENTINE'S DAY

I WASN'T EXPECTING MUCH FROM ROTH BY WAY OF A VALENTINE'S Day celebration.

We were parents, now, after all. Corinna Abigail Roth was six months old, and demanded pretty much every moment of our attention. My man had gotten his baby girl, which irritated me on some level. I mean, he'd decided he was having a girl, so we had a girl? How fair was that?

Rinna, as we called her, was easily the most adorable human being ever born. She had my blond hair and her father's mesmerizing blue eyes. She was always hungry, never sleepy, and hated being put down even for a second. Which I blamed entirely on her father, seeing as he never put her down. Never. He'd sit out on the deck with his laptop on a table nearby, working one handed while holding Rinna on his lap and playing with her with his other hand. She'd fall asleep on his chest, and he'd stay where he was until she woke up. If she woke up crying, he'd be there in a flash to soothe her.

Which meant when I put her on the floor every once in a while to play or practice rolling over or sitting up, she would freak out. Mama was the bad guy, Mama put me down. Bad Mama.

I honestly worried she'd never learn to crawl if Valentine didn't put her down to play. But I didn't bring it up too much, because he loved her to pieces. Shit, the man adored her. He was absolutely crazy for her. And that was heart melting.

Panty-melting, too. But that was something that had suffered a bit: it's hard to find time for sex when you're raising a baby that needs you every moment and refuses to sleep more than four hours in a row.

What I mean to say is Corrina Roth is outrageously, absurdly adorable, but impossibly difficult.

Valentine claims stubbornness and being difficult is a hallmark of the intelligent, but I think he's just saying that because she's a perfect little angel for him. Not so much for me. I get the Rinna that won't latch onto the nipple and gets angry, smacks me in the tit with her little fists, snuffling at my breast and screaming and acting like a brat. And then, when Valentine comes over and strokes her cheek and says something soothing in that hypnotic voice of his, she just latches on without a problem and goes to town.

It's ridiculous and maddening and I love it.

Even when I hate it.

Don't get me wrong: I love being a parent, but it's hard, so, so, so hard. I worry all the time that we're doing it wrong, that we're going to mess her up. I miss being able to sleep in until whenever I want—shit, I miss being able to sleep through the night. I miss being able to hop onto Roth's monster cock and ride him whenever the mood takes me, and I miss being able to cut loose and scream as loud as I want when we do catch a few minutes to fuck. I miss Roth's mouth on my tits.

But the thing is, it's all worth it. Because when Rinna is at my breast and gazing up at me, suckling and scratching at my skin with her fingernails, blueblueblue eyes wide and so intelligent and so full of personality, I just...I sometimes feel like my heart can't be any fuller. When she's cradled in my arms, fighting sleep, drowsing and jerking awake and dropping off again, going limp in my arms, utterly helpless, and all mine...I'm happier and more complete than I ever thought I could be. And when Roth has our daughter on his chest, her chubby little cheek smushed against his bare skin, a contented smile on her sleepy face, Roth's palm covering her back protective-ly…I just melt.

So, yeah, Valentine's Day. It's never been a huge occasion for me. If I was seeing someone when Valentine's Day came around, it was nice when he did something thoughtful. But if he forgot, I wouldn't wig out over it. It was a stupid Hallmark holiday, created to sell choc-olate and greeting cards. I didn't need a special holiday to celebrate love. And with Roth, every day we spent together was a day to cel-ebrate our love. Our anniversary was a day to celebrate our love. When Rinna decided to take a long afternoon nap Roth and I would sneak in a quickie—*that* was a day to celebrate our love.

Valentine's Day. An arbitrary holiday? Meh.

So when Valentine's Day came around I didn't really spare it a second thought. It passed like any other day, slow and lazy, Roth working on his laptop, doing what he did, and me spending time with Rinna, prepping for dinner, reading when Rinna went down for a short nap. An average, domestic day. Honestly, it was the kind of day I loved most.

I never thought domestic life would be for me, but I absolutely love it. I'm a mom. A wife. I have a home which words like beautiful and stunning don't even begin to describe. I have the world's best husband, and the world's most amazing daughter. I've even learned to cook and, surprisingly, I'm really good at it. I like finding a recipe and using it as a starting point, finding interesting ways to person-alize it. I like experimenting, trying weird and new and fun things.

Before Rinna I felt at loose ends, like I didn't know what to do with myself. Roth would always have his businesses to run, because even though we have enough money that we'll never have to worry, Roth is driven to work. He has to. Sitting around doing nothing all day isn't an option for him. But he works from home, now, so I still get him to myself all day every day. It's the best of all possible worlds. Like I said, though, before Rinna, I didn't know what my purpose was, what I was meant to do. I'd always just worked to survive, one dead-end job after another. Honestly, I didn't have a particular skill or passion or talent, and that was a weird and disconcerting thing to realize about myself.

And then I had Rinna, and my life had meaning. I'm a mother; that's my purpose in life. To love Rinna, to take care of her, to nurture and cherish and protect her—and her beautiful, incredible father, of course.

It's not for everyone. Some people are driven to succeed, some have a talent that demands expression, and some just need to be busy, to be out there working and doing and going. Me? I'm content to be at home with my husband and daughter.

And that, right there? Husband and daughter? That never gets old. Never.

God, I'm really digressing, aren't I?

Valentine's Day. Six p.m.

I was just about to put dinner in the oven. Roth had just finished his work for the day, and Rinna was, for once, playing on the floor quietly and contentedly, lying on her back on a little play-mat that dangled toys over her face, making sweet cooing noises and batting at the toys.

I heard a boat, in the distance, but paid it no mind. Boats passed by all the time, and we received frequent deliveries via boat. But then I heard voices, Roth's, and a female voice. One I'd heard before, but couldn't place. The voices were approaching the house so I, curious, tucked Rinna onto my hip and went out onto the beach to see who was visiting us.

Roth was walking toward the house and I could see a boat anchored a ways out. Alexei was standing on the beach in the distance, assault rifle dangling from a strap, head constantly swivelling and scanning. Walking beside Roth was a small female figure, her features silhouetted by the setting sun. I stood curling my toes in the warm sand, Rinna tugging at a strand of my hair while Roth and the woman approached us.

Roth saw me waiting and he lifted a hand. "Kyrie, come say hello to Ella."

I moved toward them, finally realizing whom it was: Ella, the dressmaker, and the elder sister of Eliza, Roth's former housekeeper whom had been killed as retribution during a kidnapping attempt on me. Ella was in her fifties, short and thin and beautiful, with caramel skin and long black hair going silver near the temples.

I leaned in to hug Ella with one arm. "Hi, Ella! So good to see you."

I was puzzled, though. Why would Ella be here? Why would we need a dressmaker? And if we did, why wouldn't we just go see her on St. Thomas? Roth wasn't giving anything away, though.

He led the way back inside, and took Ella on a guided tour of our home, which was situated at the center of our privately owned island. She was suitably impressed by the scope of our home, which, Roth being Roth, was immense. It wasn't a colossal, echoing monstrosity, though. It was something near thirty-thousand square feet all total, but that was spread out in a vast sprawl over the island, with all the various rooms and sections perfectly placed to have the best views, connected to each other by covered walkways—which had storm shutters that could be deployed at the touch of a button. So while the square footage of the home was immense, each room was designed to feel cozy and comfortable and elegant.

I contained my questions until Ella scooped Rinna up in her arms and took her out onto the beach, cooing in her rhythmic island voice.

And then I pounced. "Not that I'm not glad to see her, Roth, but why is Ella here?"

Roth smirked. "Well, it's Valentine's Day. We haven't had any time alone together since Rinna was born, so I invited Ella over to spend the night with Rinna. You and me, love, are going on a date."

I actually squealed. "We are? Holy shit! Where are we going? Should I change? What do I do with dinner? I was just about to put it in the oven? We have to tell Ella that Rinna can't sleep without her floppy pony, and did you show her where the formula is? I should—"

Roth's mouth slammed down on mine, silencing me with a short, powerful kiss. "Kyrie, shush. I've got it covered."

"But Rinna—"

"Is in the best possible hands, I promise. Ella has five children of her own, and each of those five children has at least two children apiece. Ella is a grandmother to thirteen children, and she babysits them all the time."

"Oh."

"And yes, I've run her through Rinna's bedtime routine, showed her where the formula is, as well as the backup breast milk you pumped. She knows where the diapers and wipes are, and she has both of our phone numbers in case something comes up. But nothing will come up." He grabbed me by the hips and spun me around, gave me a gentle but insistent shove toward the docks where our boats were moored. "Now, get your sexy ass onto the baby yacht. I want as much time alone with you as I can get."

"But where are we going? I'm not wearing anything very nice, and—"

He kissed me again, and this time he spanked my ass hard enough to make me jump. "You're fine. We're not going anywhere where it'll matter what you're wearing." He leaned in, murmured in my ear. "In fact, where we're going, the less you wear, the better."

I grinned broadly, heat and excitement flushing through me. "Oh. Well, in that case…" I glanced around, making sure no one was watching.

I was wearing a loose, ankle-length skirt made of light, flowy, breathable cotton, so thin it was nearly—but not quite—sheer, and a spaghetti-strap tank top. With Roth's eyes on me, I reached up under my skirt and tugged off my panties and stepped out of them. I leaned up against Roth and kissed him, while tucking my panties into the hip pocket of his shorts.

Roth's smile was wide, and hungry. "Come on. Let's get out of here."

What Roth, my dear, silly, out-of-touch-with-reality husband, called the "baby yacht" was in fact a totally normal-sized luxury yacht, the kind of thing you'd see tied up at any harbor anywhere in the world—it was just that in comparison to the ocean-going mega-yacht we'd sailed the world in, it did seem a little small. Although, at a hundred and fifty feet long, I wouldn't exactly classify it as small. But when you put it up next to the *Eliza*, our mega-yacht, it did seem like a little baby thing.

It's small, but blinged out to the max. Custom built as private cruiser just for Roth and me. It had so many goodies and bells and whistles it would take a week to list them all.

We boarded the mini-yacht, which Roth had dubbed the *Rinna*. We had Sasha with us, piloting the yacht, but otherwise we were alone on the ship. We sat in the lounge area built into the very bow, sipping wine and nibbling on a cheese-and-cracker tray Roth had produced. Since the *Rinna* was meant as a short-cruise, island-hopping vessel there wasn't a big galley like we had on the big yacht . It had a small galley, just enough to keep some snacks and beverages, and a few staples so we could throw together a quick meal if we wanted to. The sun was lowering into the water, bathing everything in a golden light. I'd spent long enough down here in the Caribbean that I knew we weren't heading for any of the major ports or islands, but rather somewhere more remote. Which made sense, given Roth's innuendo-laced statement.

It took us over an hour and half, but Sasha finally slowed the *Rinna* to a stop and lowered the anchor, and then let the skiff down over the side and lowered the ladder. I was intensely curious, now, since we were in the middle of nowhere, no populated islands within several nautical miles, just a little atoll with a long, wide, sandbar extending out for hundreds of yards. I let Roth help me down into the skiff, and then sat in the bow, trying to figure out what his plan was. Roth powered up the outboard motor, and then got us moving toward the atoll in the drowsing golden light of early evening.

It didn't take long before I understood.

Roth skirted the outside edge of the sandbar, following it around to the far side of the atoll from where the *Rinna* was anchored. He cut the motor and angled the skiff so the nose slid up onto the sandbar, and then planted an anchor deep in the sand. He hopped out into the water, which was knee-deep. He reached for me, intending to lift me out into the water.

"I'm still wearing my dress," I pointed out.

"Tuck the ends into the waistband."

I lifted the hem of my dress and tucked it into the waistband, as Roth suggested, so it was short enough that it wouldn't get wet. Which meant it was just barely above my hoo-ha.

"Is Sasha watching?" I asked.

Roth shook his head. "No. Well, yes, but he's not watching *us*. He's just keeping watch. Scanning the horizon, making sure we're left alone."

"Am I going to have to be quiet?" I asked, as Roth lifted me down into the water, which came up to mid-thigh.

Roth smirked, eyes sparking. "He's got earbuds in, and music cranked. He won't hear a thing."

"Good," I said, "I'm not sure I have it in me to keep quiet any more."

"You're never quiet, love."

I swatted at him. "I am, too."

"You woke up Rinna the other night, and I'd even turned on a fan for cover noise."

"Well…you did that thing with your finger. You know what that does to me."

We were wading through the water, and Roth's hand drifted down, under the edge of my skirt, and brushed the seam of my ass. "This thing?" He wiggled a finger against me, just so.

I sucked in a breath. "Yeah, that thing." I knocked his arm away.

"Don't you dare start that. If you start that, we'll end up fucking right here in the water, and I'm hungry. I hope you have some way to feed me all the way out here."

He gestured. Just ahead of us, a dozen tiki torches had been planted in the sand in a wide circle, surrounding a square table with two chairs that had been planted right in the water. It was a high-top style table and chairs, so that when sitting down in them, the water would be just beneath the bottom of the seat, lapping against your knees as you dined. There was a single candle on the table, and a single red rose in a crystal vase. Another, smaller table had been set up a short distance away, on which were several covered dishes, two bottles of wine and a pair of wine glasses.

The sun was setting, bathing everything in a crimson-golden light, turning the water molten. A gentle, warm breeze blew, just enough to make the torches flutter and dance, and toss my hair playfully.

I took in the scene, amazed. "I know I shouldn't be surprised by the things you manage, but I still am, every time."

He shrugged, smiling at me as he guided me to my seat. "It wasn't hard. I just arranged for this to be set up, and had Sasha let them know when we were a certain distance away so they could deliver the food and have it still be hot when we got here."

He uncorked a bottle of wine first, poured me a glass, and then uncovered the dishes and brought them to the table two at a time.

Dinner, at sunset, literally in the water? Pretty damn romantic.

We sat, ate leisurely, and just…talked. Which, when you have kids, is a delightful luxury. A rarity, even. Especially when you have a baby that's as high-maintenance as Rinna.

It wasn't dramatic. There were no fireworks or a magical proposal or extravagant gifts. What could Roth possibly give me that I didn't already have? There was nothing. The best gift he could give me was exactly this, a night out alone, a romantic setting, good food, good wine, and a chance to just enjoy the company of my husband.

I do confess, however, that I was glad when dinner was done and

Roth suggested we take the last bottle of wine and our glasses and wade to the atoll itself. He'd been touching me all throughout dinner. Nothing sexual, nothing overt, just brief, teasing brushes of his hand on my hand, a thumb across my cheek, his knee glancing against mine. And now, strolling through the water, he had an arm around my waist, his hand resting on my hip.

God, I wanted more.

Not that the sex isn't always good, but when you're keeping an ear out for your baby, or when you know she's only going to be asleep for another twenty or thirty minutes, it's just the not same. I wanted him alone, all to myself, for a whole night.

No rush, no baby monitor, just him and me.

He'd thought of everything, of course. There was another torch planted and lit on the beach of the atoll, shedding a small circle of orange light on the sand, illuminating a blanket laid out on the sand.

I was excited, flushed with need, vibrating with anticipation. Just waiting, waiting, waiting for Roth to make his move.

I took a moment to absorb the scene: water rippling black and warm around my ankles, moon glow shed from a full moon bathing and illuminating and silver-washing all the world, torches flickering in a light breeze, flames bent sideways and dancing straight for a breath or two and then bending once more, sand white and cool and arcing off into the distance, the far small bobbing yellow-orange light of the yacht, close enough to be a familiar comfort, but far enough to afford us total privacy. And the torch gave off just enough light that Valentine could see me, that the orange glow could bathe my skin and my curves for him to enjoy, just bright enough to set the mood. The blanket was, of course, a specially made beach blanket with stakes at all four corners and slight lip around the perimeter to keep the sand away. It was made of soft blue fleecy cotton, and was large enough that Valentine could stretch out.

Perfect.

I turned away from the setting and back to my husband, only to discover him staring at me, his gaze raking over me, taking me in. As if he didn't see me every single day. As if he didn't see me in the morning, with gnarly morning breath, hair a rat's nest. As if he hadn't seen me burgeoning with baby, waddling and feeling like a whale, emotional and prone to unpredictable outbursts of tears and craziness and manic nesting-phase obsessions. As if he didn't know there were stretch marks on my belly, which I couldn't get rid of no matter much how Shea butter I put on, no matter how much yoga I did; as if he didn't see the few extra pounds I still carried, no matter how faithfully I hit the elliptical machine and the kettlebells. He was gazing at me as if he didn't see any of that.

"Do you want to walk some more, love?" he asked, taking a slow step closer to me.

I closed the last few inches between us, gazed breathless and wide-eyed up at him. "No. I don't want to walk some more."

"What do you want to do, then?" He was smirking, azure eyes twinkling; he knew exactly what I wanted.

I wasn't in a playful mood, I was in a needy mood. But I pushed the franticness down, wanting to take my time with this, wanting to enjoy every single millisecond. Roth was wearing a pair of khaki shorts and a white short-sleeve button-down, barefoot, the top three buttons of his shirt unbuttoned. Casually decadent, easily perfect, deliriously delicious. I flicked open a button, pressed a soft kiss to the V of skin between the edges of his shirt. Slid open the next button, and followed the widening gap of skin with more kisses, button by button, until the garment hung open. I carved my palms over his shoulders, brushing it off to bare his upper body. And god, what an upper body it was. He wasn't as razor-cut as he used to be, and I loved his body all the more for it. He still worked out regularly, but he was less rigorous about it, and focused more on bulk than definition, lifting weights and running several miles every day. Thicker, broader, harder slabs of muscle outlined his chest and he still had that trim waist and wicked V-cut, abs so rock-hard you could smash open coconuts against them. I tossed the shirt aside onto the sand, scouring skin and muscle with greedy hands. He stood and held me and let me touch him, let me kiss his body until I'd had my fill; or, more accurately, until I couldn't keep my hands from exploring. I tugged open the fly of his shorts and slowly slid the zipper down, feeling him harden as I did so. I felt him harden even further as I let his shorts fall to the sand. He kicked them away, buried his big, strong hands in my hair as I sank to my knees in front of him. I pulled the elastic of his underwear away from his waist, slowly lowering them until his massive erection was bared. A step, and he was naked for me, standing bare and godlike on the sand and in the moonlight.

"Kyrie, you don't have to—" he started, and then stopped as I took him into my mouth.

I ran my tongue in swirling circles over the tip, and then looked up at him. "I haven't tasted you in—I don't know how long," I said, and then sank my mouth around him once more.

"God, Kyrie."

"One and the same," I joked, and then went back to tasting his cock.

I sucked and licked at him until I felt him beginning to breathe hard and struggle for control. And then I stood up and reached for the hem of my tank top.

Roth's hands grabbed my wrists, stopping me. "Let me."

I dropped my hands, and let him take over. Instead of peeling off my shirt first, as I'd expected, he reached around behind me and unhooked my bra, and then stripped both shirt and bra off in one move, yanking them up and off, tossing them onto the growing pile of clothes. And then it was his turn to fall to his knees in front of me, burying his face against my breasts, nuzzling, flicking, and licking, groping and caressing and squeezing. Worshipping. Paying homage. Loving.

I feathered eager, shaky fingers through his thick blond hair as he caressed my breasts with lips and tongue and fingers and palms, gasping at the new sensitivity of my nipples. And then he curled his fingers in the waistband of my skirt, gave it one sharp tug, and it was off. And now my fingers tightened in his hair as he drew his face down my belly, nuzzled the opening of my pussy, and drove his tongue in against me. I gasped, and clutched him closer, widened my stance, and clung to him. Gasped as he lapped at my clit, groaned when he slid two fingers into me, curling them in high, and then added a third as he began to slide them in and out of me, mimicking in miniature the grinding, penetrating friction I so badly craved.

He worked me into a frenzy, suckled my clit and worked his fingers in and out and licked and flicked until I was humping his face unashamedly, holding him against me and rocking into his mouth until I came…and came and came.

I felt my knees give out as the climax rocketed through me, and Roth was there to catch me. He lay me down on the blanket, cradled my face in his palms and kissed me as if this was our first time together, kissed me with all the fervor and tenderness of a brand-new lover.

Good thing I was laying down already, or I would have fallen down from the intensity of that kiss.

I had to break the kiss so I could suck in a whimper as he slid into me, burying himself home inside me. He held himself motionless, our hips crushed against each other, his breath coming in gusting drafts, brows lowered, eyes fixed on mine. There was no looking away, now. No blinking, no breathing. Only him and me, only the sizzling connection between us, the fire that never seemed to die, but only ever grew hotter and hotter.

I squeezed around him as hard as I could; thankful for all the Kegels I'd been doing when his eyes widened and his hips gyrated as if by impulse, instinct. I ground my hips against his, lifted my feet and hooked them around his waist, held onto his shoulders and took control of our movements. I set a slow-burning pace, lifting up to drive him deep, lowering to let him glide almost out. He planted his fists in the sand on either side of me and let me have the control for a while, just watched us, just stared at me, his chest heaving as he kept himself reigned in tight.

And then, when he could cede control to me no longer, he reared back and tucked my heels against his shoulders. Leaned in between my thighs, lifting up on his knees, and pushed deep, thrusting hard, now. No more slow. He took me, then, drove against me until I was writhing and helpless in his grip, feeling him thicken as he neared his release even as I reached my own.

I held back, though, wanting to wait for him. I was so close, teetering on the edge. Watching him move, watching sweat dot his skin and slide through the crevices of his muscles, watching his trim, hard hips pivot and flex and drive. His eyes fluttered as his thrusts stuttered, and then he leaned over me, letting my heels drape over his shoulders, kissing me as he came. His release seared into me, blasting any hold I had on my own climax.

I clung to him through my orgasm, bit his lip and snaked my hands in his hair and demanded more kisses, ground my hips against his and milked our releases, both of us gasping and grunting and groaning and whispering *I love you* and murmuring each other's names and the kind of sweet silly nothings that are drawn out of you in the heat of passion.

When were finished, both of us spent, he collapsed to the blanket and drew me against his chest.

We spent long minutes in silence, staring up at the scintillating wash of stars overhead, his heart beating under my ear, the breeze cooling the sweat on our skin.

At some point in the night, Roth drew me on top of him and I rode him like the powerful stallion he was, rode him until I was screaming his name into the Caribbean wind.

We dozed in each other's arms, drowsed and snuggled and kissed lazily, murmured of idle things.

With dawn sprinkling pinks and grays on the horizon, I lifted up on my elbow and stared down at the man I'd come to love so much I'd lost track of where I ended and he began—a cliché I was only now beginning to truly fathom.

"I think we just made baby number two," I said.

He toyed with the fall of my hair. "It will be a boy, this time."

"You're calling it already?"

He nodded, a sleepy, contented smile on his handsome features. "I can feel it, the way I felt it with Rinna."

"You know what I feel?"

"What's that, love?"

I reached between our bodies, found him ready. "I'm feeling you inside me once more before we go home."

He rolled on top of me, pierced me, and kissed me through my gasp as he filled me. "Only once more?"

I laughed. "How long can Ella stay?"

He didn't answer, because his mouth was on mine and his hands were seeking my skin in the dawn haze.

I didn't demand an answer, because I was too busy being loved senseless by Valentine Roth.

Turns out every day is Valentine's Day.

THRESH

ALPHA ONE

Protect at any cost.

SECURITY

New York Times and *USA Today* Bestselling Author

Jasinda Wilder

1

DAMN THAT MAN

Experience paradise in exotic St. John! I flipped through the brochure, staring somewhat longingly at the pictures—not that Miami wasn't beautiful, because it was, but Miami was home, and I needed a change of scenery, even if just for a few days.

Beautiful Belize! I tossed this one in the "no way" pile; Central America didn't entice, for whatever reason.

Come see Thailand! Nope. No way. I'd heard stories, and Thailand seemed a little too…adventurous, for my first vacation in more than three years.

I picked up the St. John brochure again, and as I was flipping through it for a third time, a colleague plopped down beside me on the couch in the ICU doctor's lounge.

"St. John, huh?" she said, reading over my shoulder. Lizzy was several years older than me, married, and had three young kids. "Sounds good, let's go!"

I laughed. "Just you and me, huh?"

"Sure, why not? John can handle the kids for a few days."

I quirked an eyebrow at her. "What about the time he sent your oldest to school wearing two different shoes and without a lunch?"

"She's been wearing two different shoes ever since. Says it's her style statement. And the school gave her hot lunch. It was fine."

I laughed. "Lizzy, you didn't talk to him for three days afterward!"

She shrugged. "Yeah, well, I tend to overreact." She tapped the brochure in my hand. "For real, though, Lola. You need to take a vacation. You haven't taken a single day off in three years. I know we're not exactly close, but even I can see you work too hard."

I nodded, sighing. "I know, I know. I just..." I waved a hand in frustration. "I don't know where, and I don't know what I'd do."

Lizzy stared at me like I'd sprouted a second head. "Sit on the beach, drink too many Mai Tais, and find a hot beach bum to shack up with."

I didn't even know where to start. The drinking too much sounded like fun, and the sitting on the beach sounded like fun, but after what happened—

The hospital PA system crackled over the speakers at the same time as my pager buzzed in my lab coat pocket. "*Paging Dr. Reed to the ER. Dr. Reed to the ER.*"

Saved by the pager, apparently. Going down that mental road when on shift was a recipe for disaster.

My pager confirmed what the PA had just announced: I was needed in the ER.

I'm not an ER doctor. I hated the pressure and the pace of the ER, and vowed after doing my med school rotation that I'd never work in the ER again. I like the peace and relative quiet of the ICU, and I like being able to track the progress of my patients. In the ICU there's none of the wild bustle and manic, frenetic insanity of the ER, paramedics shoving crash carts through the doors, ambulances coming and going, nurses on the run, doctors bustling from patient to patient, never a moment to yourself, never a moment to breathe.

Nope. The ER is not for me.

So being paged to the ER was kind of unusual. I wondered what they wanted?

I hustled at a quick clip to the elevators, my shoes squeaking on the tile floor. I traveled down to the first floor and across the hospital to the ER department. I found the triage desk, and the brusque, gray-haired man working it.

"Hi, I'm Dr. Reed. I was paged to the ER."

He didn't look up from the computer screen. "Waiting room. Patient asking for you."

"Pardon me?" It wasn't that I didn't comprehend what he'd said, it was just that…what he said may as well have been a *non sequitur*.

He finally turned his attention to me. "The waiting room." He enunciated each syllable, speaking to me as if I was either stupid or hard of hearing. "There's a patient asking for you by name."

Who in the world…?

Anyone who knew me would come up to the ICU looking for me. Or call me. Or text me. Or find me at home. Who would come to the ER and ask for me?

I tugged on the ends of the stethoscope looped over the back of my neck, a nervous habit of mine. I blinked a few times, and then pushed through the door and out into the waiting room.

I scanned the crowd—it was a Saturday night, so the Jackson Memorial ER was a hopping place. The waiting room was packed and there were people everywhere, bleeding, holding makeshift bandages, moaning, leaning on loved ones. At first, I didn't see anyone I knew.

And then…there he was. The man I'd privately nicknamed Atlas was sitting right next to the admissions desk.

Oh, I remembered him all right. Seven feet tall, probably somewhere in the neighborhood of three hundred pounds, maybe three twenty. A real monster. But…a ridiculously gorgeous monster, if you went in for mountains of muscle wrapped around tectonic plates of bone, all sheathed in rolling acres of tan skin.

But, holy hell, those eyes. Pale, pale, pale ice blue. Almost white, they were so blue. An odd, piercing shade. And his hair—platinum blond, shaved on the sides to create a short but wide mohawk that resembled a Roman helmet crest, perfectly trimmed and shaped. The kind of hair that on anyone else would look stupid, or at least juvenile. But on this man? It just suited him. Made him look even scarier. Thick blond scruff on his jaw. God, that scruff was delicious looking.

He'd been in here a little over a year ago, standing guard for a friend or co-worker who had been shot. Nicholas Harris? I thought that was his name. Older guy, good-looking in a lean and sharp and rugged way. Shot four times, or five? Lived, and walked out to tell the tale. Damnedest thing I ever saw, and I'd seen a lot.

And now, here was Atlas again, asking for me by name?

Two things were immediately evident—the blood from his injuries made him look even scarier and, despite the crowded waiting room, everyone was giving him a wide berth.

I could see his left arm was a bloody wreck. His whole torso was covered in blood, but I think the worst of it was coming from his arm, and possibly his shoulder. Some of the blood was dried, and the blood on his black T-shirt was crusted stiff, which meant he'd been injured a while ago.

That shirt was so big I could probably fit into it two times over, yet it was tight on him, stretched across his chest, and bursting at the biceps.

I took a deep breath and walked over to him.

"You again." I kept my voice sharp. "How can I help you?"

He shrugged his shoulder, indicating his wounded arm. "This."

"I'm not an ER doctor." I gestured at the waiting room. "This is the ER, you have to—"

"Been waiting a while, Doc. I want *you* to fix it."

"I'm not a triage physician, Mr.—?"

"Name's Thresh." He stood up, slowly, carefully. Woozily. Instinctively, I moved closer to him, put my shoulder under his good arm to prop him up. Not that I could do much to support him if he were to pass out. "Don't care what kind of doctor you are. Just…fix it."

"You'll have to go through the appropriate channels, Mr. Thresh."

"Then I'll just bleed out here, I guess. Been bleeding for awhile, now." He leaned into me, and his weight nearly crushed me.

I bore up under it, tensed, and straightened. Lifted. "You can't guilt me into seeing to your injuries, Mr. Thresh."

"Just Thresh." His head flopped back on his neck. His weight increased as he lost the ability to stand up on his own. I'm a pretty buff girl, but there was no way I could hold him up for much longer. "I'm getting faint, Doc."

I stared up at him, at his sculpted, brutally beautiful features. He really did look peaked and pale. I wondered how long he'd been bleeding—how long he'd been waiting here. What had happened to him? I shook those thoughts away; it didn't matter.

"First things first: we need to get you processed." I glanced over my shoulder at the male nurse behind the desk. "Can I get his paperwork, please?"

The nurse, once again, didn't look up. "Wouldn't fill it out."

"Can I have the blank forms, then, please?"

He heaved a sigh, as if I'd asked him to sell his firstborn child, or a kidney, but he brought me a clipboard with the intake forms. "Here. Good luck." He glanced at Thresh warily, and possibly a bit derisively. "You're gonna need it."

Thresh growled, a sound not unlike the warning rumble you might get from, oh, say, a displeased grizzly bear. "Hey, pal, watch it. I can still crush you like a fuckin' bug."

The nurse paled, shuffled backward a step. "I—I'm sorry. I just—"

"Piss off, pissant," Thresh said.

The nurse fairly ran back to his desk. I hated how it made me feel, seeing Thresh put that unpleasant person in his place. I fought to keep the grin off my face. I handed Thresh the clipboard. "Fill this out, please."

He just lifted an eyebrow. "Fuck paperwork. I ain't gettin' a lung transplant, here. No allergies, no relevant medical issues. Just the gunshot wounds."

"You still have to fill it out, Thresh. At least the basics."

With an irritated sigh, Thresh took the clipboard and pen from me. His hand was big enough that he could almost span the width of the clipboard between his thumb and pinky. When he pinched the pen between his fingers, it nearly vanished, swallowed whole by the size of his hands. It was ridiculous. He was so huge it boggled the mind and defied comprehension.

I watched him scribble the most basic of information—name: Thresh; age: 37; height: seven feet and one-half inch; weight: 328 pounds; sex: *Yes please*.

I rolled my eyes and sighed. "Really? You're Austin Powers, now?"

He just chuckled and handed me the clipboard. "There. Now, can we go?"

I eyed him. "Thresh…no last name?"

"Nope. Just Thresh."

"You have to have a last name, Thresh."

He shrugged. "Sure, I've *got* one. But I don't use it."

"And is *Thresh* your given name?"

He stared me down. "It's the only name you're getting, Doc, so best quit while you're ahead."

"Ahead? How am I ahead? You won't give me your real name, won't give me your last name—I'm beginning to wonder about you. What do you have to hide?"

"Got shot more'n four hours ago, Doc," Thresh said. "Not sure how much longer I can hold out."

"Four *hours*?" I shouted this, exasperated. "What the fuck have you been doing since then?"

"Flying here."

"*What?* You flew here yourself?"

"No, my boss did. Harris. You were his doc, year or so ago."

"I remember that," I said as I moved with him toward the doors that led into the triage area. "Where were you that there were no hospitals closer than four hours away?"

He tripped, and we nearly went down, but he righted himself, barely. I had to bend at the knees and use my deadlifting form to get him upright again. Good thing I work out.

"Jesus, Doc, you're a real beast, ain'tcha?" His voice was low, meant only for me, rumbling in my ear.

I glanced up at him, not sure of his meaning. "Excuse me?"

He reached down with his good hand—which was black-red with caked blood—and squeezed my bicep. "You got some guns under that lab coat."

I flushed, but worked hard to keep my tone neutral, even a little sharp. "Hands off, Atlas."

He chuckled. "Atlas?"

"You're big enough that you could probably carry the weight of the world on those shoulders so, yes. Atlas."

"He's from mythology or some shit, yeah?"

"Or some shit, yes. Greek mythology, to be specific." I couldn't help but laugh. "A Titan, son of Æther and Gaia, if you listen to Hyginus. God of the moon, in some cases, and generally known as the Titan tasked with holding up the sky."

I felt his gaze on me. "No shit? And if you don't listen to Hyginus?"

"Some scholars say his father was the Titan Iapetus, and his mother was Asia, the Oceanid. Some say Clymene. Opinions vary. I like to go with Æther and Gaia. Makes the most sense to me."

We were in the triage area, now, and I was desperately looking for a bed to deposit Thresh onto. I couldn't prop him much longer and I don't think he was faking the weakness—he'd clearly lost a hell of a lot of blood. There was one bed, sitting in the hallway, freshly remade. I angled him toward it, backed him up to it, and he collapsed gratefully onto it, releasing his arm from around my shoulders. I felt light, free, as if I could float away, now that his weight wasn't bearing down on me. I rolled my shoulders, straightened my back.

And I didn't miss the way his gaze focused like lasers on my chest as I stretched. Not like you could see much, since I was wearing a sports bra as well as a tight camisole under my button-down.

I liked to keep my girls well contained while I worked, as I didn't appreciate the attention I received if I revealed too much cleavage. I actually dressed conservatively since I wanted to be respected for my talent, skill, and worth ethic as a doctor, not because of my DD-cup breasts.

But still, he looked.

I made sure he caught my gaze, made sure he knew that I'd caught him staring. He just smirked, quirked an eyebrow, not looking apologetic whatsoever.

Nor did he look as faint as he'd acted just a moment ago.

But he was still rather pale, and it was clear he'd lost a lot of blood, and he had to be in an enormous amount of pain.

I nudged his uninjured shoulder. "Lie down."

He moved to comply, but slowly, stiffly. As if he wasn't used to lying down, as if it hurt to do so. He lay on his back, looking uncomfortable, and unsure. "How's that?"

"It's just a bed, Thresh. Try to relax."

"You try to relax with a shattered ulna." He rolled his injured shoulder, hissing. "Or a couple of rounds in your shoulder."

As gently as I could, I pried his arm away from his body; he'd been keeping it clutched close for so long, it was probably cramped in that position. And yes, he was right in his assessment: his ulna was in pretty bad shape, although I wouldn't classify it as shattered. More like a severe fracture. I peered at his shoulder, noting two entry wounds in the meat of his shoulder and pectoral muscle.

"Can you rock to the side for me? I need to look for exit wounds." I tugged at him, indicating the way I wanted him to move.

He remained motionless. "No point, Doc. There aren't any exit wounds, 'cause the rounds are still in there. This ain't my first rodeo. I know when it's a through-and-through, and when they're lodged in there."

I sighed. "Well, how about since I'm the doctor I'd like to see for myself so, again, please—let me have a look." And, as I suspected, there were two clean exit wounds. So much for his medical expertise.

"I don't know if you're going to be happy or sad about this but, the fact is, you have two clean exit wounds."

"Hmmph," was all he said.

I unlocked the wheels to the gurney. "Let's find you to a room so I can get to work. I have other rounds to make, you know."

"I know I could use some fuckin' pain killers. You got any Tylenol in that sexy lab coat of yours?"

I stared at him, a blank expression on my face. "Doctors don't keep medication in their lab coats, Thresh." I couldn't stop my eyebrows from scrunching down. "And what do you mean by *sexy* lab coat?"

"What? Nobody's ever told you you're sexy in that lab coat?"

I stiffened. "No. Not that I can remember."

"Then whoever you've been hangin' around with needs to get their eyes checked. That shit is *sexy*." He lifted up on his good elbow, a sly expression on his face. "You ever walk around wearing just that lab coat? Maybe some black knee socks and a pair of high heels? Get that thick fuckin' hair of yours out of that stupid bun, let it loose around your shoulders. Fuck, man." He slumped back down. "Shit…I popped a semi just thinkin' about it."

We turned a corner, and I pushed the elevator call button.

I flushed again, and then my eyes, of their own traitorous accord, slid down, down, down. Damn it, damn it, damn it. Do *not* check out his package, Lola.

I checked out his package; that big bulge was a *semi*?

I went a little faint.

And then I got angry, both with him for making me look at his crotch and think about how huge his dick must be, and at myself for being so weak and easily manipulated.

I was not going down *this* road again.

"No," I snapped. "I've never done…what you said. It's stupid."

"You should. You could give a man a heart attack, if you did that. Real spank bank material, right there."

"Spank bank?" I felt my cheeks going even more flame-red than they already were—not that he would be able to tell, not with my Samoan skin tone, but *I* knew I was blushing, and that only pissed me off even more. "Jesus, you're a real pig, aren't you?"

"More of a bear than a pig, I'd say."

I ran my gaze over his body, unwillingly—God, he was massive. Very much like a bear. Kodiak, maybe, or a polar bear, what with his blond hair and pale eyes.

And shit, shit, *shit*, he caught me checking him out. But he didn't say anything, just smirked and covered his eyes with his good arm as the elevator doors opened.

"I don't even own any knee socks," I said, and I wasn't sure why I said that, or where that admission came from.

The doors closed, and Thresh spoke without looking at me. "You should get a pair. Nice, thick, muscular legs like I picture you having under those damn baggy-ass pants of yours? They'd look fuckin' bangin', Doc. *Bangin'*. Pair it with a short skirt and some heels? Man, I'd be done. Stick a fork in me, done like dinner."

"Stop talking to me like that," I said, and I admit I fairly snarled.

"What? Can't a man appreciate a beautiful woman?"

I hated the curling warmth in my heart, the way part of me wanted to sit up and beg for more of the way he was talking about me. "No. I'm a doctor and you're my patient. Plus, you're objectifying me, and I don't appreciate it."

His voice was sharp, now. "Hey. I don't care for that statement. I ain't objectifying shit. I flew here from fuckin' Nevada, Doc, just to have you, specifically, look at my little booboos. Because I respect your *skill* as a doctor."

"Thank you."

"And because you're fuckin' hot as hell."

I sighed. "You're incorrigible."

"A woman can be both beautiful *and* successful based on her skills and education, and I'm perfectly capable of recognizing that. Don't be so fuckin' uptight."

"I am *not* uptight," I snapped. I hated being called that, with a passion. "I'm *reserved*, and *private*. I am *not* uptight."

He chuckled. "All right, all right. Calm your tits."

"Excuse me?" I snarled.

The elevator doors opened, but I didn't move. I was so irritated. "*Calm…*my *tits*?" I got in his face. "If you want me to see to your wounds then I suggest you keep a civil and respectful tongue in your head. Do…you…*fucking*…understand me?"

His eyebrows lifted, and I think he fought a grin. "Yes, ma'am. Read you loud and clear."

"And I wouldn't classify your injuries as 'little booboos.'"

He waved his hand dismissively. "Bah. I've had worse and kept fighting."

I didn't want to think about that statement too closely. Or, at least, that's what I tried to tell myself. I couldn't help wondering, though, what it was he did. An army guy, or someone from the armed forces, would be seen to at a military base, not at a civilian hospital. So what was he doing here?

The idea that he'd come to Jackson Memorial from Nevada just to see me made my head spin, made me woozy and faint and made certain things ache and throb that had no business aching or throbbing—and I wasn't talking about my yoo-hoo. My heart had been closed down and shut off for a long, long time, and for good reason. Without even trying, Thresh had pried open and breathed life into some long-dormant part of me I had kept firmly closed and shut off.

When we got to a room and I cut his T-shirt off, I could see that he hadn't been lying: his body was a maze of scars, old and new, thin lines and puckered bullet wounds and jagged gashes.

Jesus, what had this man been through in his life to accumulate such extensive scarring?

I met his eyes, and for a moment his expression was full of world-weariness, followed by a hardness, a cold, calculating cunning that terrified me to my core, but it disappeared as quickly as it had appeared, buried and layered under a scrim of warmth and humor.

I put my emotions away, shoving them deep down in the place

where I knew they were protected.

I called for help. We gave him some local anesthetics, and I went to work on his arm, first. I cleaned the wound, set the bone, checked for muscle damage, stitched it closed and wrapped it. He wouldn't need plates or screws, thankfully, as it was a fairly clean break and the bullet wounds were through-and-through, with clean entrance and exit wounds.

Before I sent the nurses away I had them give him a tetanus shot as well as a bunch of antibiotics and painkillers. I watched him for a moment, sitting on the foot of his bed. He was awake, but out of it and fading fast.

He was staring at me. Woozy. Tired.

"Rest, Thresh." I hated how tender my voice sounded.

He was a pig. A bastard. The biggest, roughest, toughest man I'd ever encountered. Huge, hard, and beyond bad.

But the really bad news, the worst news, was that he was the kind of man I'd spent my entire life avoiding.

And very successfully, I might add…up until now.

Why did I feel so…

Drawn to him?

I shot to my feet, bustled out of his room without a backward glance, tugging on the ends of my stethoscope, unreasonably angry.

I heard a chuckle behind me.

Damn that man. Damn him to hell.

2

IN DENIAL

I DIDN'T GET A CHANCE TO CHECK ON THRESH AGAIN THAT ENTIRE shift. I was kept busy with patient after patient up in the ICU, until finally my shift was over and I was so exhausted I couldn't think. I was so tired I could barely keep putting one foot in front of the other. I got my stuff out of my locker, said goodbye to the nurses on the night shift and then walked over to catch the Metrorail home. When it let me off at my stop I trudged my ass the four blocks home to my third-floor condo.

My home. My sanctuary. My escape from everyone and everything.

The second I was through the door I tossed my pager onto the kitchen counter, kicked off my shoes, and shrugged out of my scrubs. By the time I was in my bedroom, I was naked. By the time my head hit the pillow, I was asleep.

I didn't have a dreamless sleep, though. I dreamed of a pale giant with a mohawk and ice-blue eyes and hands so big he could span my waist—and I'm not a dainty girl. I dreamed about the way he looked at me. I dreamed I was standing in the dark, and he flicked on a light, and then suddenly I realized I was naked, except for my lab coat, with my stethoscope around my neck, and a pair of white knee-high socks. He reached for me, in the dream, and I let him. In the dream, I wore my lab coat, the socks, and nothing else…and felt no embarrassment.

Which was how I knew it was a dream.

I don't have body-image issues—I just…don't feel comfortable putting myself out there like that. And with damn good reason.

When I woke up, I was out of sorts. I was angry at Thresh for invading my dreams, and…if I didn't know any better, I'd say I was horny. But that couldn't be possible—that part of myself had shut down long ago.

I shoved it all away, the anger, Thresh…and the empty, hungry-but-not-for-food, wanting *something*, fragile, delicate, internal throbbing. Whatever that stupid feeling was, I shoved it down deep and locked the trapdoor on it, where I kept all the feelings I didn't know how to deal with, or even want to deal with.

Which was most of them.

I rummaged through my pajama drawer, pulled out my favorite T-shirt, my dad's old Florida State University shirt, several sizes too big for me, older than me, soft as silk, with tiny pinprick holes here and there. It hung just long enough to cover my ass, with the maroon fabric just barely stretching around my tits, which, left unconfined and unsupported, were big enough that they strained the ancient cotton nearly to breaking point. There were actually holes right over my nipples where the fabric was starting to give out, so my nipples played peek-a-boo. Or, more apropos, peek-a-boob.

Not a single living soul had ever seen me wearing this shirt, and no one ever would. It was my secret. Wearing it was only time I ever felt even remotely attractive, or sexy. It was for me, and no one else.

So why was I wondering what Thresh would think, if he could see me now?

He'd probably pop an erection so big he'd split his pants open.

Alone, in my own apartment, I found myself blushing.

And, yes, thinking about Thresh…or more accurately, wondering how big his man-part really was.

Plenty big, I'd say.

His hands, after all, were simply *enormous*.

That old saying, about the relationship between the size of a man's feet and his...*you-know*? It's not true. There's no real correlation. But it *is* true if you're using the size of his hand as comparison: the span from a man's wrist to the tip of middle finger provides a pretty good approximation of how big he'll be, down there, when fully erect.

You learn a lot of odd things in medical school.

I fixed some breakfast, watched the news, and tried gamely to stop thinking about Thresh. I succeeded, mostly.

I took a shower, and it was all business. Get in, get wet, get clean, and get out. No funny business for me. Certainly not while thinking about Thresh.

God, what was wrong with me?

I hadn't so much as touched myself, hadn't even had a dirty thought of any kind, in three years. No sexual activity of any kind in three years.

And here I was, in the shower, thinking about Thresh, a perfect stranger and a uniquely terrifying human being, as well the sexiest man I'd ever seen. I didn't *do* anything about it, but I thought about him plenty.

I was distracted enough that I forgot to rinse the conditioner out of my hair, and had to get back in the shower.

For more than three years, I'd thought my libido was just...broken. Useless. Dead.

Maybe, just *maybe*...it wasn't.

Didn't mean I'd ever trust a man again, but at least I knew I wasn't broken.

Or, probably not. Not totally, at least.

Right?

It was almost time to head to work, and I knew that once I had that lab coat on, I'd be back in control. No emotions, no odd or out of place thoughts. Strictly business. I was a doctor, and a good one.

Curiously, though, while getting dressed, it was the first time since being hired at Jackson Memorial that I'd forgone a super-tight and constricting sports bra in favor of a lacier, push-up bra from Cacique. Totally coincidental.

Had nothing to do with Thresh.

Nope.

I'd meant to check on Thresh a lot earlier, but I was swamped the minute I arrived in the ICU. Lizzy had car problems and she was several hours late, which left me covering the entire ICU alone. I had no time to even stop to pee, much less take lunch, *much* less take time to visit ER patients. As it was, I didn't get over to see him until my shift was over.

My plan was to check in on him, make sure he was doing okay, and then go on my way. Make sure he knew this was it, buh-bye. No more Thresh. There was no point. Nothing good would come of it, or from him. Nothing whatsoever.

When I walked into his room he was sitting up in the hospital bed. He had six paper take-out bags on his lap, five of them unopened, and a 32oz cup on the table near at hand. The TV was on, tuned to a UFC bout, and he had a double cheeseburger in his good hand. He devoured half of one burger in a single bite, swallowed after chewing three times, and then finished it in another bite. The second was gone just as fast. He dug into the bag, producing two more double cheeseburgers, and made short work of those, as well.

At which point I realized that all *six* paper bags were likely full of burgers.

My mind wobbled at the amount of calories and the sheer amount of *food*.

"Jesus, Thresh! Are you trying to give yourself a heart attack?"

He glanced at the doorway, noticed that it was me, and grinned. "What?"

I gestured at the bags. "Looks like you have enough artery-clog-ging bullshit there to feed an army."

He wadded up the wrappers, tossed them into the bag, and opened the next one. And, sure enough, he produced two more burgers. "I'm hungry," he said around a mouthful.

"Clearly." I crossed the room and pulled out a chair near his bed. "How many burgers is that, anyway?"

He blinked at me, glanced at the bags, then back to me. Clearly, a little sheepish. "Thirty-six."

I coughed in surprise. "Thirty-six? You're planning on eat-ing thirty-fucking-six double cheeseburgers? By yourself? In one sitting?"

He bristled. "Have you seen me? One or two ain't gonna cut it. Not with the blood I lost. Takes a fucking hell of a lot of calories to power a body as big as mine."

I gestured at the bags. "But...*that* kind of food?" I wrinkled my nose in disgust. "That shit is horrible for you."

He narrowed his eyes at me. "Doc, I don't know if you've no-ticed, but I'm not really in any position to be choosy. If you know where I can get a crate of fresh salmon and a grill to cook it on, let me know. Or maybe you have a blender and a bucket of whey protein in your lab coat?"

I sighed. "I guess you have a point there. But the cafeteria here surely has some salad you could eat, or—"

"Doc. Again, take a good look at me. You think an itty bitty little styrofoam container of wilted lettuce and rubbery chicken is gonna cut it? I did call down, but when I asked for a dozen burgers and a whole pizza, they hung up on me. So I said fuck 'em, and had my boss get some food delivered to me."

I shook my head. "A dozen burgers and a whole pizza?"

He sighed. "I eat a lot, okay? I lost a shitload of blood, and slept for a good sixteen hours. I was in a good bit of pain for four hours before all that, and I'd been in a firefight before *that*. I need a *lot* of calories. Yes, I know fast food burgers ain't exactly the healthiest choice out there, but when you got a hunger as big as mine, you do what you gotta do."

I raised my hands in surrender. "As long as you don't eat that way on a regular basis."

He eyed me with amusement. "Why, Dr. Reed, I do believe it sounds as if you just might care."

"Don't flatter yourself, Atlas." I was betrayed by my stomach, which chose that moment to re-enact Mufasa's hyena-scaring roar from *The Lion King*.

Thresh smirked at me, dug a burger out of the sack, and handed it to me. And, fuck me, but it did smell good, and I hadn't eaten anything in over twelve hours. I eyed the wrapped burger.

"Damn you." I took the burger, unwrapped it, and took a bite. It was as good as it smelled. I ate it in four bites, which earned me a sarcastic grin from Thresh. "Shut up. I haven't eaten since breakfast."

He dug in the sack. "Have another. I've got plenty." He eyed me. "Got a first name, Doc?"

I finished my bite. "Lola." Took another, swallowed, and returned his gaze. "And you? Got a real first name?"

"Told you. My name is Thresh."

I didn't believe him, but there was a hint of warning in his eyes, so I let it go. I'd get it out of him, one way or another.

Wait, no, I wouldn't. I was done with him, remember?

Gah. Apparently I wasn't.

Which was how I ended up sitting in Thresh's room, eating shitty-for-me but delicious double cheeseburgers and watching UFC. I considered UFC barbaric and savage, but damn me if it wasn't fascinating.

When I checked my watch, I realized I'd spent two hours with Thresh, chatting about UFC, about popular movies and TV shows, music, sports—he'd played linebacker for FSU, which meant we had Florida State football in common.

What we didn't do was share any meaningful personal information of any kind.

But it wasn't weird. We just…hung out. He didn't make any lewd comments, didn't hit on me. Not what I was expecting. It was a decidedly unexpected, but pleasant visit. I hadn't hung out and shot the shit with anyone in…I didn't even know how long. I didn't really have any close friends, or…*any* friends, actually. I had colleagues I was friendly with, like Lizzy, and I had my dad, but he was holed up in his shack deep in the Everglades, so I only saw him on occasion.

Which meant I spent most of my time either at work, at the gym, or at home. Sometimes I'd go see a movie by myself, or have a nice dinner. Alone.

By choice.

Sort of.

My train of thought was making me morose, so I stood up, brushed the crumbs off and said, "Thank you for the company, Thresh. I actually enjoyed myself."

And now his gaze finally did what I'd been expecting all evening: raked down my front, and fixated on my chest. He swallowed hard, blinked, ripped his eyes up to mine, and tried like hell to keep them there, but…it was futile. I glanced down too, and then allowed a tiny smile. I mean, I could see why he'd stare. It's hard not to, after all. When you're sporting puppies as big as mine, on a frame like mine? They don't need much help to stand out. When you prop them up in a push-up bra? God help any hetero man with eyesight. He'd be trapped, pulled into the orbit of my colossal, all-natural breasts.

Thresh cleared his throat, plucked at the sheet covering his legs, and turned his eyes to the TV. With great effort, I noted. "Don't sound too surprised," he said. "I can be good company, sometimes."

"I didn't mean it to sound like that—"

He grinned at me. "Don't worry about it. People make assumptions about guys that look like me. And, plus, you brought your girls, and you didn't trap them in some stupid sports bra."

I laughed. "I typically bring my girls with me everywhere, since they're sort of attached to me."

"Yeah, well, I think I might be getting attached to them, too." He paired this statement with a blatant ogling.

"You can't even really see anything! I'm just wearing a regular bra."

"I can see the general shape, and I've got a vivid imagination." He winked at me, and then turned his attention back to the TV.

"Oh? And what does your imagination tell you about my breasts?"

He very slowly swiveled his head to look at me, shutting off the TV with the remote wired to the bed without looking at it. "Not sure you want to ask me that question, Doc. Not unless you're ready for the answer." His voice was a guttural bass rumble, husky, dark, ripe with lascivious promise.

I swallowed hard, my gut roiling and my blood pounding in my veins; the look in his eyes was positively feral. It did something to my insides, made my knees watery. I never backed down from a challenge, though, and he was daring me.

"I wouldn't have asked if I couldn't handle the answer."

He pivoted on the bed, brushing monitor lead cords and IV tubes aside. He should have been in pain, still. Should have been weak. Instead, he radiated power. Oozed sensuality, and dominance. Strength. Sexy, masculine charisma. Sitting on the edge of a hospital bed, dressed in a hospital gown way too small for him, connected to monitors and IVs—he shouldn't have been capable of turning me to mush, of making my palms sweat and my knees shake and my skin tingle.

But he did.

He reached out his good arm, snagged the ends of my stethoscope and hauled me toward him. I didn't *let* him, per se, I just…I was helpless to resist.

He hauled me closer and closer, inch by inch, until I was standing between his knees, staring up at him. Breathing hard, which made my breasts—already prominent—swell even further. His gaze went to my chest and stayed there, watching me suck in deep breaths, watching my button-down strain against the buttons.

Like most girls as well endowed as I was, no button-down shirt ever fit me right. They were either shapeless, or too big everywhere, or too small. Or even if they did fit my shoulders and waist properly, the buttons over my boobs would be strained to capacity, and there'd be boob-gap, where the edges of the shirt didn't quite meet. The shirt I was wearing was of the latter variety, which meant that from the right angle, he'd be able catch glimpses of skin and lace.

He was at the right angle, clearly.

His raised his eyes, impressively enough, to meet mine, and they stayed there. Now he was looking at me. At *me*. Not just *at* me, either, but seeing into me. I wondered what he saw, what he read in my eyes. God knows I was confused enough that I myself had no idea what I was thinking or feeling.

His eyes on mine, he reached up with his hand, slid his fingertip down the front of my throat. Where his fingertip touched, my skin burned; his touch was electric, setting me on fire. Down, down, past the collar, to the uppermost button. I'd buttoned all but the top button, which meant his finger only traveled a short distance. But then, when he reached that top button, he didn't stop. He did something impossibly dextrous with his huge fingers, and the button slid free.

"Thresh?" My voice was thin, weak.

"Yeah, Doc?" His was firm, strong, but low.

"What—*ahem*. What are you doing?"

He unbuttoned a second button, and now cleavage was visible. Not a lot, but some. And god, that third button…it was fighting valiantly to contain my boobs. One deep breath, and it might just pop free.

Thresh to the rescue…of the button. He flicked it open, and now my tits spilled out of the opening, a huge expanse of dark caramel skin mounding over the bra. Thresh's eyes widened almost comically, and a monitor beeped at the sudden spike in his heart rate.

"Jesus fucking Christ on a bicycle, Doc," he breathed. "That is the most fantastic thing I've ever seen."

"I'm still completely covered," I pointed out.

"And better than all the other naked tits I've ever seen, combined."

"The hell you say." I tried for in charge, casual, and ended up just sounding stupid and argumentative.

He met my eyes again, and now maybe he did see my insecurity.

Wait, no. I'm not insecure. I'm just...conservative. Private. I don't like dressing for attention.

My internal scolding did nothing for me. I stepped out of reach, buttoned my shirt back the way it belonged, all but one button fastened. "Thanks for the burgers, Thresh." I turned away, and made it to the door before he spoke up.

"I told you so."

I stopped, hand on the doorknob, and glanced back at him. "Told me what?"

"You wouldn't like the answer."

"Your imagination told you to unbutton my shirt?"

"My imagination told me to do a fuckuva lot more, Doc." His voice was that lewd snarl again, the one that made my knees quaver. "But I won't do any of that 'til we've been on at least one date."

"Date?"

"Yeah. A date. You know, where a guy an' a gal go out and spend time together doing various sorts of vertical activities?"

"Vertical activities?" My intelligence, which was usually rather prodigious, seemed to have deserted me.

"As opposed to the horizontal variety." He paused for effect, pale blue eyes fierce and hot and piercing. "By which I mean, fucking each other's brains out."

"Goddammit, Thresh...you can't say shit like that to me." I barely got the words out.

"Oh no?"

I shook my head, and my hair, long, black, wavy, insanely thick, bound in a loose braid hanging past my shoulder blades, bounced back and forth. "No."

"Why not?"

"Because we're not going on a date, much less...what you said."

I was rather proud of how steady my voice was.

"What'samatter, Doc? Can't talk dirty?" He sounded amused.

"I swear all the time."

"Big difference between cussing and talking dirty, Doc." He smiled at me, but it wasn't a sweet smile, or an innocent one, or even reassuring. Far from it, as a matter of fact. It was a smile that reminded me of a lion with easy prey in sight.

"True. But, regardless, none of that is happening. No activities, vertical or horizontal."

He didn't seem fazed by my rejection. "Doc. Why you lyin'?" He said this with a cocky grin.

I turned toward the door and grabbed the door handle. "I'm not lying. I'm not going out with you, and I'm not sleeping with you." I managed to actually sound as if I believed this.

I did believe it, mind you. I had zero intention of doing anything with a bad news monster-man hunk of beefcake like Thresh, horizontal, vertical, or otherwise.

But one's intentions and what one does are often very different.

Nonetheless, I told myself it was true. I meant it. Dammit, I wasn't—

He was right behind me, stretching the IV tubes and monitor leads as far as they would go. I felt him. "Lola." He growled my name.

It was the first time he'd said it, and the sound made my heart flip and my stomach drop out and my knees go watery.

"What, Thresh?" I refused to turn around.

"When do I get out of this joint?"

"I'll check your charts. Tomorrow, though, would be my best guess."

"Tomorrow is Thursday, so..." he sidled closer, and I could feel his body behind mine, pressing up against me.

I felt a tug on my hair, and realized he was wrapping my braid around his fist. Then he tugged my head back, gently but firmly. My face tipped upward, and I felt his hot breath on my ear and heard— no, *felt*—his voice like the tremors of a distant earthquake.

"Friday. Six p.m. I'll pick you up at home." He released me, then, and I heard him shuffling back to the bed.

I heard the bed protest as he lowered himself onto it, and then I heard the TV click on, the sounds of the UFC fight resuming.

I finally managed a breath, my first in almost a minute.

I totally ran from that room like a scared little gazelle. Not that I'm built like a gazelle, but whatever.

I fled without looking back, fled so fast my head spun.

And as I fled, I chanted internally: *NOPENOPENOPENOPENOPE.*

Call it a pep talk.

3

'ROID-HEAD

I HAUL DOWN A LOT OF PUSSY. A *LOT.*

Not as much as my buddy and partner-in-arms, Duke, simply because, very honestly, I'm not as pretty as that motherfucker. That's not the point, though. Duke and I don't compete, never have and never will. No need. We're wingmen. Brothers. I back his plays, he backs mine, no questions asked. If he asked me to storm Fort Knox with a Daisy BB gun, I'd do it and wouldn't bother to ask why.

Back to my point, though. I haul down pussy wherever I go, and I don't have to try. *Walk into a club like what up, I got a big cock—* sorry, sorry, that song is stuck in my head. The line is true for me, though. Girls take one look at me and assume, correctly, that I'm packing as much between my legs as I am everywhere else. I crook my finger, and I've got fun for the evening, or the weekend, or the week. Never longer than a week, because I'm never in the same place longer than a week, except when I'm at the compound in Colorado.

But ever since Harris and Layla got hitched that damn place is always echoing with Layla's screams, and that's not something I care to hear. Harris is sacrosanct, and so is Layla. Duke and I have swung threesomes together, or foursomes. No problem there. I got no problem listening to him make his latest conquest scream. But Harris is the *BOSS*, and Layla is the *BOSS LADY*. And the boss's lady. So, no, I'm not sticking around to listen to her howl. And, Jesus fuck, does she scream loud.

For real, though, I swear I have a point to all this.

My point is Dr. Lola Reed, M.D. is a little…tricky. I want her. She wants me. But she's closed off and shut down. Yet, I catch glimmers of fire in her every once in a while. She's sexy as fuck, and exotic looking. Islander, or Filipino, or something like that. Mixed, maybe? I don't know. Tall, closing in on six feet, maybe five-nine, five-ten. Skin like caramel only a little darker, smooth and flawless. Fuckin' *bangin'* figure. Like…I get all emotional and choked up and horny just looking at her fully clothed; I wouldn't stand a chance if I ever got to see her naked. Girl's got *curves*. Toned, though. Fit. She clearly spends time in the gym and eats healthy, but she's got no problem indulging now and again. I don't know sizes or anything like that because I don't give a fuck, so I couldn't tell you if she was a nine or a nineteen, I just know she's got an ass that don't quit, and tits that—I don't even have words…they're huge. Perfect. Round, delicious-looking globes of sweet, sweet flesh. I have yet to see enough of her legs to say what they look like, but if what I have seen so far is any clue, they'll be thick, strong, curvy and muscular.

When I first showed up at the ER, I really was close to passing out. I was playing it up only a very little bit, but she actually supported my weight. Half-carried my heavy ass, and that's no easy feat. Strong girls are sexy as hell, if you ask me. But she's not all muscle, like a body builder. She's soft. Womanly. Shit, that may have come across chauvinistic or whatever, but that's how I like a woman. Strong, but still soft and curvy and girly.

And Lola has all that in spades.

Yet she hides that killer body under conservative clothes. Loose dress slacks, loose flowy blouses, a tight sports bra, sensible, comfortable shoes for a woman on her feet all day.

Except yesterday. She showed up in my room at the end of her shift looking exhausted, hungry, stressed…and wearing a push-up bra that had her tits just begging to be set free. Begging to licked and sucked and fucked and seen and worshipped.

She's not immune to me, I've seen her stealing glances, and I've watched her breath catch. But she always rallies, and shoots me down.

Good for her.

Doesn't mean I'm going to let her get away. It just poses a challenge and, honestly, when it comes to women, they've never really been a challenge for me.

And sweet goddamn, do I love a challenge.

Lola was off the next two days, so the ER doctor on call was a dude, an old dude, and a surly one. But he told me I was good to go and worked up the papers to discharge me that morning, Friday. He fitted me with some kind of experimental forearm-bracing cast, which was supposed to be waterproof, removable, breathable, and less of an impediment to movement than a traditional cast. I was happy about that because I had too much shit to do to be stuck with a big plaster or fiberglass monstrosity; plus, Harris was paying the hospital bill. The doctor bound my arm against my torso in a tight sling, with extensive bandaging around my shoulder and chest.

Fortunately it was my left arm and shoulder, not my right, as I'm right-handed. I could still use a handgun if necessary, and in the direst of circumstances I could work a sawed-off one-handed, or shoot an assault rifle from the waist one-handed. Wouldn't be accurate for shit, but it'd make the bad guys think twice, at least.

I signed the discharge papers, left the hospital, and caught a cab to a nearby hotel and booked a room. I was assuming the good doctor didn't live far from work.

I settled onto the hotel bed, pulled up Lear, my high-tech friend, on my cell. It rang and rang and finally went to voicemail. I didn't bother leaving a message because, knowing Lear, he'd call me back in…five…four…three…two…

Brrrrring. I hit *accept.* "Lear, buddy. Can you do me a quick favor?"

Lear Winter was the tech expert at Alpha One Security, a hacker of the highest order, former NSA and scary fucking good with anything electronic. He could do the kind of spy-in-the-sky bullshit they show in the movies; like track someone across the world with a hacked satellite while sitting in his damn living room. Just to show off once, he'd hijacked a satellite and zoomed in on a nude beach in Canada somewhere, Wreck Beach in Vancouver, I think it was. He zoomed in so close you could practically touch the naked babes sunbathing. It was freaky, is what it was.

"For the last time, Thresh, *no*, I'm not hacking the D.C. Madam's client list for you."

"Funny, Lear, really funny. Why would I—wait. You can do that?"

He snorted. "In my sleep. In a drunken stupor, while vomiting. Point is, you'd have to be willing to blackmail the entire U.S. government. Which, having worked for them, I'm not." I heard tapping in the background, as well as the rhythmic thudding of some kind of electronic music. "What do you need, Thresh?"

"I need the home address for one Lola Reed, M.D. She's a doctor in Miami. Works for Jackson Memorial—"

"Got her," Lear interrupted, and read off her address. "It's a condo, third floor, couple miles from the hospital."

"That's freaky, Lear. Seriously. That was like, what, thirty seconds?"

I could almost see his shrug. "Child's play, Thresh. Finding someone who doesn't want to be found is easy enough, unless they're a pro. Someone with no conception of staying off the grid? Please." The phone rustled, as if he was changing hands. Meaning, he'd done that in under thirty seconds, one-handed. "I've got her profile, if you're interested. Went to FSU—"

"No, thanks. Just her address is fine. I'll find out the rest the fun way. Thanks, nerd-boy."

"No problem, 'roid-head. Hey, how's the arm?"

"Arm and shoulder, actually, but…well, I mean, it's not fine, but it's fine. Know what I mean?"

He laughed. "Not really. Never been shot."

"You're missing out, man, it's the most fun you'll ever have, I swear. Fractured ulna, shredded shoulder muscles. I'll be out of com- mission for a while, except for emergencies. But I'll heal. I've been shot worse."

"Really?"

"You don't want to know. You really don't."

"Probably not. Okay, well, get better. And if you need anything else on your doctor lady, let me know. Give me a couple minutes, I can probably tell you what kind of toothpaste she uses, and where she buys her lingerie."

"Freaky, nerd-boy. Freaky as fuck. But that's why I'm glad you're my friend."

"If you only knew how easily I could erase or hijack your entire identity, you'd stop calling me a nerd."

"Yeah, well, the 'roids have scrambled my brain, you know?"

"True. All right, I'll talk to you later, meat-head."

"Bye." I hung up, laughing.

I call Lear nerd-boy because it's funny, and it's true, although Lear does have an adrenaline-junkie aspect to his personality that's entirely un-nerd-like. He's freaky smart, freaky-fast with the com- puter magic, and entirely lacking in any common sense when it comes to doing stupid-dangerous shit that can get him killed just for the shits and giggles of it. I mean, I'm a mercenary—I get into gun battles for a living. But that's different, since I get paid to risk my neck. That crazy asshole does it for fun. Fuckin' weirdo nerd.

And, for the record, I don't use steroids. That's all part of the in- side joke between Lear and me. Just…you know, to be clear. People take one look at me and assume that either I use steroids, or I'm stu- pid, and usually both. Truth is I don't and never have used 'roids, no matter how big I am, and I'm far from stupid, although I'm nowhere near as smart as guys like Puck or Lear.

I pulled her address up in Google Maps on my phone—a thirty-minute walk from here, and there were several good restaurants in the area.

I decided to grab some shut-eye; I don't sleep well in hospitals, never have.

It was barely noon, so I slept for a few hours, then headed out to hunt down some clean clothes, came back for a shower, and then it was time to start wooing the good doctor.

Or maybe 'seducing' was the more apropos term…

4

JUST ONE KISS

FRIDAY WAS MY DAY OFF, AND IT WAS ALSO LAUNDRY DAY, AND heavy lifting day at the gym. This meant I slept in late—till eight a.m, which, in a doctor's world, is late—ate a big breakfast, gathered up every last stitch of clothing I owned, except for a pair of skin-tight workout shorts, my tightest sports bra, and a long, loose tank top.

I started a load of laundry and then headed over to the gym. I worked the free weights until I was jelly all over, hit Jamba Juice for a big protein shake, switched loads...and headed to lunch. Usually on Fridays I caught a movie between lunch and the rest of the laundry, but today I didn't feel like it.

I was restless.

I worked out harder than I ever had, pushing myself until I couldn't physically bang out even one more rep, even if my life had depended on it.

The whole time I was tossing clothes from washer to dryer and folding dry clothes, I was conflicted mentally. I've had a rule since my residency that I never ever think about work when I'm off—I don't ever bring work home with me. It's the only way to stay sane. The problem today, though, was that if I didn't think about work, I'd be thinking about Thresh.

And that was a *bad* idea.

I didn't dare think about what his torso had looked like, after I cut his bloody shirt off. How massive his biceps were, how thick his pectorals were. How flat and hard and defined his abs were. God, definitely do *NOT* think about that stupid, beautiful V where his abs grooved in and angled under his desert camo military pants. I don't know what they're called, camos? Uniform pants? Whatever. The V disappeared under that waistband like an arrow pointing the way to the Promised Land.

Only... I DON'T WANT TO GO THERE.

I don't.

Really fucking *really*, I don't.

But I just couldn't stop thinking about him.

That growl, his voice in my ear...so full of sexual hunger and lascivious promise. His eyes on me. The fact that his expression, never mind his words, tells me he really does find me attractive.

Okay, fine, so I've got a bit of an issue with self-confidence. There's a reason, though, and it's not really about how I'm built. I work my fucking ass off to stay in shape. I'm strong as hell—I'm just not small. No part of me is small. I've got thick thighs, thick arms, and my waist isn't waif-thin. But my arms are thick with muscle, and my thighs too. My tits are pretty much perfect, which even I can admit—assuming you like huge knockers. And my ass is—yes, big—but also round and taut and pretty damn firm, but with just enough jiggle and sway to it to remind you that I'm all woman.

I work *hard* to look the way I do.

I'm just...not thin.

But this is not the problem I have, mentally and emotionally, with myself. I don't care about being thin, I swear. I love myself, I love my body, and I have no desire or need to lose weight.

The real reason for my insecurity is...complicated. Delves deep into the most traumatic part of my past, to things I don't think about, and certainly don't ever, ever, *ever* talk about.

But Thresh didn't know any of this. All he knew is that he liked what he saw. And he *wanted* what he saw.

But…what did I do about it?

Three years ago I swore that I'd never trust a male again. And I haven't. There's been interest. I've been asked out and hit on, guys at the gym trying to bring me home for casual sex, fellow doctors looking for more than casual sex…I rejected them all out of hand, didn't even think twice. None of them so much as made me hesitate. Just no. Nope. No way. Not interested, thanks anyway.

But Thresh, god…he does something to me. To my head, to my body. Even my cold, dead heart seems to feel some kind of *something* when he's around.

But how could I trust him? Even for something casual? God, perish the thought. I could never do casual. Never ever. Even before everything that happened to make me the way I am, I couldn't have done casual. But now? Fuck no. Hell no, fuck no, oh my fucking god…*NO.*

So then where does that leave me, in terms of Thresh's interest in me? No way is a guy like him looking for anything more than quick and casual. He flew in to Miami just to get me to fix him, which means he's mobile. He can and will go anywhere, anytime, on a whim. I'm tied here, to Miami, to the hospital; it's home, and I have no reason to leave.

Plus, he's just bad news. Everything about him screams *player*, and it'll be a cold day in Hell before I get played by another player.

Also, he treated getting shot *twice* like it was a common occurrence. More of an inconvenience than anything else, really, is how he acted. I got the feeling I could have treated his wounds without anesthetic if I'd had to, and he wouldn't have flinched. A man only gets that kind of tough from long experience, and the scars I saw on his body told the story clearly enough.

He is, to put it in precise terms, a very, very dangerous man. I don't need to know anything else about him to know that. He just exudes danger and threat, and it's not just because of his size. I mean, yeah, he's seven feet tall and over three hundred pounds of pure muscle, but he just…it's just his very essence. He's deadly. It seeps from his very pores.

And that scares the spit out of me.

Literally, it leaves me dry-mouthed.

But then…the dry-mouth could also be from the potency of my attraction to him.

Which presents the problem.

I'm terrified of him. Attracted to him so powerfully that it scrambles my brain and leaves my hormones in turmoil.

But…I can't trust him. He's a man, for one thing. And he's obviously a player used to getting what he wants on his own terms, and my feelings and my future won't factor into that. Plus, he's not from Miami, which means it doesn't matter what either of us want or intend, it can't amount to anything anyway.

All the evidence tells me to stay clear of him, keep away, shut him down, close him out, do what I do and don't give him another thought.

But my brain doesn't seem to be paying any attention to wisdom.

Because all damn day, my thoughts kept returning to goddamn Thresh.

By the time all of my laundry was washed and dried and folded, it was quarter to six in the evening and I was carrying my clothes home, lost in thought, fighting to keep Thresh off my mind. I was still in my workout shorts and tank top, and I never took a shower at the gym, so I stank like old sweat, my hair was a messy rat's nest pulled back in a frizzy ponytail. I hauled my laundry up the stairs, because I vowed years ago to never use the elevator and that's a vow I've kept.

By the time I reached my door, I was already looking forward to stripping off, taking a shower, pouring a bottle of wine into my favorite holds-a-whole-bottle wine glass, and watching stupid TV. I was sweating again, because I just carried six loads of laundry up three flights of stairs, and the strap of my tank top was coming off my shoulder, leaving pretty much my entire left breast exposed. I was juggling the laundry basket and my purse, trying to get my keys out without setting down the basket, not really looking where I was going, because why would I? My door was at the end of the hallway, so there wouldn't ever be anyone coming toward me.

I bumped into something, bounced away, dropping my laundry basket, my purse, and my keys. My laundry exploded, everything unfolding and scattering all over the fucking floor, panties, bras, shirts, pants, dresses, skirts, blouses, all over the place. And my purse…upended. All my shit rolled over the floor. Tampons, pads, keys, wallet, gum, receipts, sunglasses, all the shit a woman keeps in her purse.

And me? I landed on my ass on the floor, stunned, confused, and pissed.

When I looked up and saw Thresh leaning back against my door, arm in a sling across his body, good hand stuffed into the hip pocket of a pair of dark blue jeans, that hair of his in the ridiculous, amazing fucking mohawk, eyes like ice chips glinting amusement, and a black polo stretched across his chest and around his arms…god…dressed casually but so fucking sexy, almost preppy for a guy like him.

I just gaped at him for several seconds, staring, mouth working, brain spasming, trying and failing rather significantly to come up with something to say, some kind of appropriate response.

He beat me to it. "Evenin', Doc." He said this with a cocky grin, as if he knew exactly the effect he was having on me.

Bastard.

That got my cylinders all firing again. "What the fuck, Thresh?"

He had a massive watch on his wrist, a huge black rubber-encased thing, expensive looking, some kind of fancy tactical military chronograph, probably. "Just shy of six, and it's Friday. We have a date."

My mouth flapped open and closed a couple times. "No. We don't."

"Yes, we do. I told you before you left my room the other day that I'd pick you up today at six."

I finally stood up, brushed my butt off, and then stomped over to stand in front of Thresh, staring up at him angrily. "That's not how asking a girl out works, Thresh. You don't *tell* her you're going out. You ask, politely, and if she says yes, then you have a date. You gave orders, and I declined to respond. That means we *don't* have a date."

He just stared down at me, holding his ground, unperturbed. "You didn't say no. You didn't answer, and don't make it out like you did that shit on purpose. You ran off like a skittish pony. Couldn't handle the intensity of the moment."

Fuck him and his truth.

I turned away, knelt down and started replacing the contents of my purse. "I didn't—I wasn't—" I cut myself off with an angry huff, and then started over again. "So I'm a horse, now?"

"What I said was 'like a skittish pony', actually, which isn't the same. But if you want to take it that way, sure."

I stood up abruptly, whirling to face him, ready to deck him, foot of height difference and hundred and fifty pounds of muscle difference be damned. "Are you fucking serious?" I even went to slap him, but missed, on account of the fact that he was crouched a couple feet away, re-folding my clothes and putting them in the basket.

His big, rough, callused, powerful paws—clean, albeit, and yes, I noticed that his hands were clean—were all over my clothes. Rolling my size twelve panties into messy balls, stuffing one cup of my bra inside out and folding it in half...but not before checking the tag: 34DD. Folding my yoga pants into thirds, and folding my blouse sleeves in first, hem up, then collar down.

Folding my female clothes as if he knew exactly how to fold a woman's clothes. An odd skill for a man like him to have. And kind of impressive, especially considering he was doing most of it one-handed, only occasionally using the hand of his wounded arm.

I watched in puzzled wonder for a moment, then remembered that I was angry at him, and also pissed and embarrassed that he was handling my clothes and checking the tags for sizes...

"Fuck off, Thresh. Get your dirty paws off my clothes, and quit checking the fucking tags, you goddamned asshole." I snatched my favorite pencil skirt out of his hands and shoved him away. "You have the balls to call me a fucking horse, and then you're gonna look at the tag on my bra? What the fuck is wrong with you?"

He stood up, unfolding himself like a tree growing in time-lapse. "You mistake me, Doc. Or, more accurately, you assume that being compared to a horse is a negative, that I'd mean it as an insult." He stalked toward me on feet entirely too quiet, entirely too lithe and graceful for a man of his size. He stood in front of me, snatched the skirt from me, and folded it deftly, then stood towering over me, eyes fierce and serious. "Horses are incredible animals, Lola. They're powerful, graceful, intelligent, and beautiful. It's a compliment, to be compared to a horse. Yes, horses are bigger than people, but a horse is one of the most beautiful animals there is, Doc. So even if that's what I *had* said to you, it would have been a compliment, not an insult."

"I—" Fuck him again, for having a point. But I didn't manage to respond, even if I had known what to say, because he wasn't done.

"As for checking the tags? Sure, I'll cop to that." He managed to move even closer to me, and his gaze was…hypnotic. Fierce and fiery and glittering with a wealth of emotions. He seemed…angry. With me? For me? It was hard to tell. "You embarrassed, Lola?" He waited until it was clear he expected a response. "You embarrassed that I know what size bra you wear?"

"Yes, Thresh, I'm embarrassed. I don't even know you, and you're folding my fucking underwear?"

A brief smirk broke his serious expression for a heartbeat. "You swear as much as I do, you know that? And I'm a soldier."

"That bothers you?"

He shook his head. "Not at all. It's sexy." He touched my chin with one finger. "But that's not what I meant. Yeah, sure, be embarrassed that a dude you just met is folding your underwear. I get that. But I don't think that's why you're pissed."

"Then enlighten me, if you know so much." I regretted the challenge as soon as it left my mouth, because somehow I had no doubt he would proceed to do exactly that, and do it far too accurately.

"You're pissed I looked at the tags. And not even because it was a rude, nosy, asshole thing to do, but because you're embarrassed about the numbers on the tags."

"Fuck you." This was said in a small voice, though.

"Funny part is, you don't really seem insecure." The genuine confusion in his voice brought my eyes up to his. "That's what I can't figure out."

"You figure that out, let me know. Then at least one of us will be in the know." I took the folded skirt from his hands and placed it in the basket.

His hand latched onto my wrist, and he brought me back around. "You're fucking sexy as hell, Lola." He touched my chin again, and I forced myself to look up at him, to meet his gaze. "You're seriously beautiful. In every way there is, from head to toe."

"Thanks." I pulled away from him, tossed the rest of the unfolded clothes back into the basket in a wadded-up ball, then turned away from him to unlock my door. "Still not going out with you." I shoved open my door and went in, kicking my laundry basket in ahead of me.

"Why not? Tell me that much, at least." He had the balls, of course, to follow me into my condo.

I whirled on him, shoved him backward, using all my strength to do so. "Because I don't *want* to, you fucking ogre!"

To my credit, and my very great surprise, he actually stumbled backward a couple of steps; he seemed legitimately shocked himself.

He barely made it past the threshold before I tried to slam the door on him. The door ended up hitting his foot and his injured arm, eliciting a narrowing of his eyes and a tightening of his jaw.

"You're a shitty liar, Doc," he growled.

I sighed. "Fine. You want me to spell it out for you? I don't want to go out with you for a lot of reasons. I don't want to go out with you because you never *asked*. You *told* me, and assumed I'd say yes. You show up at my house unexpected—and how the *hell* do you know where I live, anyway? That's fucking creepy. Third—or is it fourth? I've lost count." I waved a hand in dismissal. "I don't want to go out with you because you scare me. You make me nervous. You're dangerous, in a *lot* of ways, and I live a safe and simple life. That's how I want it, and that's how I like it, and you'd mess that all up."

He nodded, his face pensive and thoughtful. "That's a lot of reasons. I guess I can respect that thinking." He sidled closer to me, in that predatory way he had, standing close enough that his heat radiated against me and I could smell cologne, spicy and silky and dizzyingly delicious. "But you're still a shitty liar."

"I'm not—" I had to back up, away from him, away from the intoxicating scent, away from his massive, overwhelming presence. "I'm not lying."

He had the gall to smirk. "Are too. You *want* to go out with me, but you don't want to want to. Just like you want *me*, but you don't want that desire. It makes you uncomfortable. It scares you. You said it, Doc: *I* scare you."

"Thresh—"

He backed away from me. "But you said you don't want to, and I've never pushed myself on a woman. She says no thanks, I back off. Just...do yourself a favor, Lola."

I swallowed hard. "What's that?"

"Try to be honest with *yourself* about why you don't want to go out with me, if you can't be honest with me."

I shook my head, irritated at his insight and his persistence. "You're impossible." I was the one to move closer to him, this time, letting the welter of emotions I was feeling flare up into my voice and my expression. "Yes, I'm attracted to you. You're an attractive man, Thresh. I don't deny the effect you have on me. But you're a risk I'm just not willing to take. And *that* is the honest truth."

Respect filled his features. "All right then." He backed up a step, then two, and then put his hand on my doorknob. "You're somethin' else, Lola Reed."

He twisted the knob and opened the door. He seemed to be...

hesitating, or going slow, maybe hoping I'd change my mind. And, honestly, part of me wanted to. Part of me was screaming at me, telling me a man like Thresh didn't come along very often, and a man genuinely interested in me didn't come along very frequently either. I'd be a fool to let him go.

But my fear, my years of conditioning myself against men, against trust, against relationships of any kind…that part was winning out. I just couldn't make myself let go. Wanting him, wanting… everything that would come along with a relationship with him, however brief it may be—that wasn't strong enough to overcome my deep-seated fear.

But I still felt the disappointment as he turned away from me. I'd hoped maybe he'd push a little, try a little harder to get past my walls. Maybe it's stupid storybook nonsense, but I'd kind of hoped he'd try to force me past my fear, you know?

But that was stupid.

I'd told him no, and he was listening. That's the gentlemanly, respectful, thoughtful thing to do.

I was about to turn around. He was outside, closing the door behind himself. With more than a little regret bubbling inside me, I watched that sliver of light from outside narrow as he closed the door, vanishing from my life forever.

Then something happened in the blink of an eye. I honestly couldn't comprehend how a seven-foot-tall, three-hundred-pound mountain of muscle could move that fast, so swiftly I didn't even register his movement until I was in his embrace, his arm wrapped around my waist, lifting me clear off the ground, spinning me around, and pinning me back against the wall. One second I was three feet from the doorway, the next I was flat against the wall beside the door, his knee between my thighs, his huge paw gently cupping my cheek, thumb brushing over my lips. I stopped breathing. My heart stopped beating. My stomach fell away.

"Just one kiss, Doc." His voice was a whisper, his breath on my lips.

I couldn't speak. Couldn't think.

He was everything, overwhelming all my senses, engulfing every aspect of my universe. I felt him, a mammoth wall in front of me, flesh and bone and muscle and heat and spices and so, so *male*, so powerful, making me feel tiny, fragile, delicate…

Safe.

I felt safe, here, his impossibly broad shoulders erasing the whole world, his hand on my cheek, his lips millimeters from mine.

Damn it.

My face tilted up, my lips parted: silent permission.

He kissed me then, and I utterly melted.

He kissed me with skill and passion; he kissed me as if I was the only thing that existed, as if to kiss me was…

A moment of desperation.

His tongue slid across my lips, tasting me, and then I was lost to it, because I tasted him, his breath. He tasted clean, like mint toothpaste and mouthwash and spearmint gum. He smelled like heaven and felt like raw rugged male perfection. I kissed him back, damn me, I did. I couldn't help it.

You don't get kissed like Thresh kissed me and not kiss him back. It's just impossible.

How long did that kiss last? I have no clue. A minute? An hour? Long enough to make me dizzy, to make me delirious, to send a pang of deep, throbbing desire pounding through me, a sensation so foreign to me I didn't know what it was at first, other than a *need*, a hunger I couldn't sate.

Only I *did* know how to sate it:

Keep kissing Thresh—

But he pulled away, stepping backward away from me. Hand outstretched, as if losing that final contact with my skin was physically painful.

Fuck, I wanted more.

And so did he. I could see it in his eyes. The bulge behind his zipper told the story clearly enough, if nothing else did.

He was true to his word, though. One kiss. He was gone before I could regain my bearings, ducking to fit under the lintel, gone before I could recalibrate.

He was gone, and I felt empty.

My head spun, my lips trembled, and I felt myself doubting everything I thought I knew.

Dammit, Thresh.

5

GOING DARK

IF I DIDN'T LEAVE HER THEN, I WOULDN'T LEAVE HER AT ALL. THAT one kiss, man…it straight fucked me up. She just tasted so damn sweet, and she was so damn responsive, once she gave over and started kissing me back, man…I was done in. I've never been much of a kisser, I usually just used kissing as a tool for getting a girl worked up and turned on so we could get to the fun stuff, but that kiss with Lola…

It was its own entity. It was beautiful by itself, made me dizzy, made me want to run back up those three flights of stairs and break down that flimsy-ass door of hers and kiss her until neither of us could breathe, until our clothes came off and—

Fuckfuck*fuck*—I stopped at the bottom of the stairs, trying to get my raging libido under control.

When I was sure I wasn't going to either bust the zipper of my jeans or charge back up to Lola's condo and ravage her senseless, I left her building, moving on foot back toward my hotel.

The thing about being a soldier your whole life is it hones your senses. Even distracted, my mind and body are attuned to my surroundings. Which means when I felt that nebulous sense of unease in the pit of my stomach, I shook all thoughts of Lola out of my head and started paying attention. Something was up. Someone was either watching me or following me, or something was about to happen.

I kept moving, didn't slow my pace or give off any signal that I suspected anything. Took two or three blocks before I spotted him: he was good, keeping twenty or so feet behind me, nondescript, talking on a cell phone, or pretending to. Average height, average build, black hair, jeans and a T-shirt. But the way he walked, the way he held himself...a hunter can always recognize his peers. He was discreet, staying at a distance, stopping here and there so he didn't get too close or seem to be too obviously following me. But what he had no way of knowing is that Anselm taught all of us who work for Harris how to spot a tail, and how to lose them.

I hauled out my cell phone and dialed Anselm See, our resident spook. We weren't exactly sure where Anselm had got his skills, except in the employ of some European government or another. He was a ghost, in every way. I don't think he existed in any official capacity, and oh yeah...he could put a bullet dead center in a target at a thousand yards with laughable ease.

He answered on the first ring. "*Ja? Was geht ab, Bruder?*"

"I've picked up a tail."

"If there is one you see, there is certainly at least one more you do not see. Keep walking, and do nothing yet."

"I shouldn't take him out?"

"*Nein.* That would tip them off that you have made them, as my American counterparts like to say."

"I was just visiting a...*friend.* You think it's possible they've got someone on her?"

"That is your doctor friend, Lola Reed?"

"Yeah. Lear tell you about her?"

"Naturally. But, back to your question, it seems likely they would have her covered."

"Fuck. I can't let her get pulled into whatever this is."

I worked for a company called Alpha One Security, and our last operation had gone distinctly sideways. We'd been hired to rescue a little girl who'd been kidnapped for ransom. We'd done so, but in the process had managed to seriously piss off an eastern European crime boss who went by the code name "Cain". He was a ruthless, merciless, well-connected kingpin with a veritable army of thugs, most of whom were of the unskilled variety. A few, however, seemed to be significantly well-trained. Word was Cain was after every last of one of us who worked for Harris at A1S, and was willing to use any tactics necessary to get to us. Which meant Lola, having met me—however briefly—was probably in danger.

"I think that ship has set sail." Anselm was quiet for a moment. "I will contact Harris."

"I've got a bad feeling about this, Chewie."

"What? I do not understand your meaning."

"*Star Wars*? Whatever. I don't like this. I just left Lola's condo. I'm circling back. I have to make sure they don't bring her into this."

"If you go back, you will lead them to her, and there is still a chance she is not on their radar."

"Who do you think this is? Cain's guys?"

"*Ja*, Cain is the most likely option."

"I need Duke."

"As I said, I will contact Harris. Keep calm, and do nothing rash."

I snorted. "Have you met me?"

Anselm sighed. "You don't know their plan. You don't even know for sure this is Cain's doing. It could be a coincidence. There are many potential scenarios, my friend."

"You taught me to tag a shadow yourself, Anselm. He's fucking following me. He's good, but this is no mistake."

"I believe you, *ja*? But if you go off the rails halfway cocked, you could make things worse."

I laughed. "You just mixed your metaphors, man."

"Your American sayings are stupid, and I cannot ever seem to get them right."

I'd gone another couple blocks in the time I'd been on the phone with Anselm, and the guy was still back there, despite the fact that I'd taken several turns at random.

I felt the stirrings of something vicious inside me, and it all centered around Lola, around the thought of Cain's fucking goons getting their hands on her. Even if nothing ever happened between us, I couldn't let her get pulled into my fucked-up world. Not like this, unaware and innocent.

"If they're tailing me, they're probably looking for the rest of you, too."

He must have heard the coldness entering my voice. "Thresh, please, think through every step, every action."

"I'm going dark, Anselm. Get shit moving." I ended the call, and then turned off the phone.

I kept walking, and started mentally planning. I was low on cash, and only had my holdout pistol, a Sig Sauer P238. It was holstered at the small of my back, hidden under the tail of my shirt. One clip. No wheels. No backup for several hours at best. And oh yeah, my left arm was out of commission.

But even one-handed, I'm more than a match for most.

I didn't think much of my tail's chances, now that I was committed to going on the offensive. But...as Anselm had pointed out, if you see one tail, there's probably another you don't see, plus their backup, and whoever they're reporting to.

I needed more gear.

In a moment of sheer luck, I found myself passing an army/navy surplus store. I ducked in, started browsing, keeping an eye on the door. I chose a rucksack, a roll of para cord, a four-inch folding knife, and a KA-BAR tactical blade with a sheath, some MREs, a flashlight, a pair of tactical shooting gloves, and a lightweight sleeping bag. Paid for it all with cash, which nearly depleted my limited liquid funds. I strapped the KA-BAR to my belt, stuffed the folding blade into my pocket, and left the store.

My tail was across the street, leaning beside a doorway, pretending to be absorbed in his cell phone. As soon as I started moving, so did he.

Time to lose him.

I reached an intersection, slowly increasing my pace until I was moving at a fairly brisk walk. I spotted a bus stop around the corner, with a bus approaching. I took off at a sprint, darting between cars, earning honked horns and middle fingers, and barely made the bus. I caught a surreptitious glimpse of my shadow, jogging across the street, running his hands through his hair in consternation. I had to force myself to sit down and not look at him, not make eye contact. I was just a guy catching a bus.

I rode the bus for two stops, got off, walked two more blocks up and took a bus going a different direction, along a different route, transferred twice more at random, keeping my eyes peeled for the tail. Once I was sure I'd lost him, I walked until I found a bank with an ATM inside the lobby and used it to withdraw as much cash as I could, then walked until I found another ATM and did the same, repeating until I'd hit my daily withdrawal limit, but at least I had a few thousand dollars in my pockets and in my backpack. Next, I found a convenience store and bought a burner phone, a few liter bottles of water, some protein bars, a few packages of beef jerky, and a box of condoms, just in case things went my way with hot as fuck Dr. Reed.

The next part was something I regretted having to do, but my choices were limited; I needed wheels, and badly, but I couldn't risk renting, didn't have the time or liquid resources to buy. Which meant I had to…liberate…something. Call it a borrow.

I ambled slowly along the street—I wasn't sure which one, but it didn't really matter. Once I had a ride, I'd use GPS to find Lola's place again.

There, across the street, was the perfect target—a faux-hipster douche, wearing tight pale red pants with the hems rolled up to his ankles, stupid pre-scuffed leather boots, a tight plaid button-down with the sleeves rolled up to mid-bicep, long stringy curly hair left long on top and undercut to the skin on the sides. He was in the process of loading a few bags of groceries into the trunk of a sweet-looking Jeep Grand Cherokee SRT, deep crimson with huge black rims and red calipers…a quick, rugged, powerful vehicle, but not so flashy as to attract attention, or be super noticeable.

I sidled up behind him, drew the KA-BAR—seven inches of black carbon steel, razor sharp, vicious looking, intimidating, and eminently valuable as a tool for the deletion of human life. I love me a good KA-BAR, man.

I touched the point to the hipster-douche's spine, blocking anyone's view with my body. "Don't shout, don't flinch, and don't fight. I got no plans to do you any harm, if I can help it. I just need to borrow your ride for a while."

"Fuck, man. Not my car!"

"Yes, my man. Your car. It's a sweet ride, so I'll take nice care of it." I dug the point a little deeper into his spine, just enough to make it hurt a little. "If I had another choice, believe me, I'd go for it. Now, give me the key—*don't* turn around."

"Fuck." He reached into his pocket—very slowly—and brought up a set of keys, unhooked the key fob for his Cherokee and extended it behind his back. "Just…try not to wreck it, okay? I'm still making payments on it."

"I'll do my best to make sure you get it back in one piece. Like I said, I just need to borrow it." I took the key fob, but kept the blade against his spine. "You wanna keep your groceries?"

Hipster-douche snorted a laugh. "Seriously? This is the weirdest carjacking ever, man."

"Don't I know it. Get your groceries, set them on the ground. No sudden movements."

He set the paper bags on the ground, and then turned his head to look at me.

I jabbed the point into his skin. "*Don't* look at me, man. You want plausible deniability. You never saw me—you don't know what I look like. Don't report this stolen, and it'll go better for you, yeah?"

"Meaning what?"

"I'm trying to stay under the radar. Give me a couple days, and I'll make sure you're taken care of, okay? I'm serious, I don't mean you any trouble, I just…I need wheels, and fast. This is easiest, and honestly, I picked you 'cause you've got a sick ride and you dress like a douchebag."

"Wow, that was a little harsh." He grinned though. "It is a sweet ride, isn't it?"

"Yeah. Now take your groceries back into the store, and don't look back at me."

He did as he was told, albeit a little stiffly. There may or may not have been a wet, red spot on his shirt where I'd pricked him with my knife. As soon as he was inside, I closed the trunk hatch, hopped into the driver's seat, tossing the backpack onto the passenger seat. I had to move the seat back as far as it would go, and lean it back, and even then, I didn't really fit. But then, at my size, I don't fit in many vehicles.

Damn, this was a slick-ass set of wheels. Silky black leather, GPS, upper end stereo…when I hit the ignition, the engine burst into a snarling purr, the sound of a powerful, well-tuned engine. I set out, punching Lola's address in as I drove.

Ten minutes later, I was parking my temporary SUV a block and a half away from Lola's place. I left the backpack on the floor in front of the passenger seat, donned the tactical glove on my right hand. Circled the block on foot twice, scanning rooftops and passers-by, looking for someone sitting in a car, seemingly idle.

There he was—across the street from Lola's condo building, sitting in an older model Mercedes, ostensibly occupying himself with an e-reader, but I noticed his attention tended to drift constantly back to the doorway of Lola's building. He had the window open, one arm hanging out, the other propped up to hold the e-reader in front of his face.

Fifty yards away, with a clear profile of his head…he would be an easy shot if I had both hands. One-handed, my accuracy drops enough that I didn't like the chances of getting him in one. Plus, a gunshot attracts attention, which was something I wanted to avoid and minimize as much as possible.

Since his attention was on Lola's building, though, maybe I could use this opportunity to…elicit, shall we say…information?

I crossed the street, hugging the building on my left, approaching the Mercedes at a casual stroll. Reached behind my back, drew my P238, and kept it low against my right thigh, so it wasn't readily visible. This could be tricky, one-handed—damn this useless fucking arm.

I slowed down as I reached the front passenger door, tucked the gun into my hip pocket, jerked open the door, sat down in the passenger seat, closed the door, and drew the pistol again, all in one swift movement. He never even saw me coming, the stupid bastard.

I aimed the Sig Sauer across my torso, steadying it in the crook of my sling-bound left arm. "Hands on the wheel, asshole."

He moved slowly, setting down the e-reader—which was turned off—and put both hands on the steering wheel. "Can I help you? My car is not so new, not very useful to you, I don't think. But you may have it, if you wish." He had a thick accent, Eastern European. Czech, Ukrainian, something like that.

"Cut the shit. You're watching that condo." I thumbed back the hammer with a *click*.

"Ah." He eyed me, and I saw recognition dawn. "You are him. The mark."

"Guess so. You work for Cain?"

He shrugged. "He pays me, yes."

"What's the job with the girl? Watch her? Snatch her?"

"Watch. If I can grab her without trouble—" Another shrug to finish the thought.

"How many others are here in Miami? The dumbass trying to tail me, you, who else?"

That shrug again. "That is it, only. Two, no more." His eyes cut away, though, as he said it.

I sighed. Holstered the pistol behind my back…

And drew the KA-BAR, lightning-fast, gripping the handle so the blade faced down. Slammed it into his right thigh, burying the blade to the hilt. He gritted his teeth and screamed through them. I left the blade in his leg and re-drew the pistol.

"Now—let's have the truth. How many?"

He sucked in a ragged breath, swearing under his breath in his native tongue, whatever it was. "Three more. One more to watch this girl, I don't know where he is, and the others are in a car, a few blocks away, in case—*hovno*, it hurts—in case something like this should happen. A few more on call if they should be needed."

I checked the side-view mirror, scanned the street around us: empty, except for a bus slowly trundling toward us, "out of service" on the route screen.

It sure would be easier overall if I could just pop this guy in the head, quick and easy, but that'd be a mess, and Harris would be pissed if it got back to him. So I lashed out with the butt of the gun, catching him right at the base of his skull. He groaned, swayed forward—damn it…I had to hit him once more to put him under. They make that look so simple in the movies, but in reality, it's actually pretty tricky.

I checked the unconscious man's body, found a Glock and a spare clip, and stuffed the extra pistol behind the holster at the small of my back and the clip in my hip pocket. I withdrew my knife, cleaned the blade on his pants leg, left the car, trotted across the street to the condo building. It was an older building, with an intercom system; I used the same trick I had last time, pressing an intercom button at random.

"Hello?" A gruff male voice, older.

"Delivery." I barked it, brusque, as if in a hurry.

"All right, yeah."

The intercom buzzed and the lock clicked. I ran up the stairs, taking them three at a time until I reached the third floor, gun still drawn. I scanned the hallway as I left the stairwell, then jogged to Lola's door. I put my shoulder to it, ear to the door, listening—all I heard was the TV.

I knocked, twice, softly.

She opened the door after a second, but with the safety chain drawn, showing only a sliver of her face, and her body clad in a thin purple robe sticking to her wet body. Her hair hung in long damp black strings beside her face.

"Thresh? What are you doing here? I thought—I thought you left?"

"Can you let me in? We need to talk."

"Is everything okay?"

I shook my head. "Not really. Let me in, and I'll explain as best I can."

She hesitated, eyeing me. Her gaze slid down, lit on the pistol in my fist. "Um…you're armed?"

I frowned at her. "You treated me for double gunshot wounds. Is the fact that I'm carrying really a surprise?" I leaned close to the cracked-open door. "I know this is going to sound like a Tom Cruise movie or something, but you're in danger, Lola."

"You're right, that does sound like a line from a bad action movie."

"Go to your front window, look out. There's a car across the street."

She closed the door, was gone for a few seconds, and then I heard the chain slide and she opened the door, looking pale and shaken. "Who—who is—who was that?"

I pushed in past her, did a quick, thorough sweep of her condo, and then returned to where she was still standing in shock by the door. "Someone was watching you, with orders to kidnap you when the opportunity presented itself. Next time you went to work, probably. He's not dead, though. Just rendered temporarily unconscious."

"Kidnap me? Why would anyone want to kidnap me?"

I tapped my chest with the barrel of the gun. "Because of me. I sort of got you pulled into some shit, babe."

"Pulled into some shit?" She staggered backward, caught up against the door. "What…what does that mean?"

"It means you're in trouble just for meeting me."

"With whom?" Unsurprisingly, she sounded faint.

"Bad guys. European gangsters, mercenaries. Short version is this: the guy you treated last year, Harris—he owns a security company called Alpha One Security. We usually do personal bodyguarding type shit, but sometimes we take more dangerous assignments, and the last one put us afoul of a pretty nasty character named Cain. We pissed him off, and now he's going after me. Seeing as you know me, that puts you in his sights. He's the type that's not going to have any qualms about hurting you if it gets my attention, and since I kind of like you, I'm not willing to allow that."

Her big brown eyes met mine, reflecting a welter of fear and confusion. "So you're…a mercenary?"

I shrugged. "Sort of." I holstered the pistol behind my back, and then cupped her shoulder. "I can explain later, but right now we need to get you out of here. That guy out there wasn't alone."

"Where are we going?"

"Not sure, immediately. Anywhere but here. I have car close by, we just need to put some distance between us and the guys looking for us."

"I still don't get why they'd want me. I barely know you." She tugged the edges of the robe tighter, which didn't help my concentration any, since it only served to mold the thin, damp cotton to her breasts.

I forced my gaze away from her tits—there'd be time for that later…hopefully. "Leverage. If they can get you, they can use you to get to me."

"Would it work?" she asked, staring up at me. "Could they get to you through me?"

"Absolutely. Which is why I'm here, to make sure that doesn't happen. I can protect you, but you have listen to me. Right now, you need to get dressed."

"How do I know this isn't some game to get me naked and in bed?"

I gestured at the window. "Did that look like a game to you?" I moved closer to her until I was in her space, filling her vision. God, she smelled incredible, fresh out of the shower, still damp, shampoo and soap and lotion. "And besides, Doc, when I decide to get you naked and in bed, I won't need games to do it." I tugged her lower lip down with my thumb, watched her pupils dilate, her nostrils flare, her chest swell. "When I want you naked, Lola, it'll be my hands stripping your clothes off. And when I want you in bed, it'll be me tossing you where I want you."

"Oh." It was a breath, a whisper.

I trailed my index finger down her breastbone, between the edges of her robe, tugging it open just a little, down to the knotted belt. I tugged the end to untie it, and then I was treated to a widening gap of bare caramel flesh, the V of cleavage, the upper slopes of her incredible tits, a sliver of belly—I didn't allow myself to look any lower. Save that for later. Savor it. I let myself breathe in her scent, memorizing the precious glimpses of her body…

And then I pushed her toward her bedroom. "Get going, Lola. Put some clothes on."

She moved toward her bedroom, and I had to bite my lip and force myself to stay in place as the robe billowed open. A tug, and she'd be naked, facing me. All that flesh, all those sweet curves, bare for me.

I growled from the effort necessary to keep myself where I was, hands to myself.

Lola paused, glancing at me over her shoulder as she reached her bedroom door. "Why are you growling?"

"Because we don't have time for what I want, and you're pushing the limits of my self-control."

She frowned. "I'm not doing anything."

"You don't have to *do* anything. You tempt me just by existing, Doc."

Skin as dark as hers didn't really flush, but I could see it in the way she looked at me, in the pause, in the confused, pleased light in her eyes. Her mouth opened, but then closed again and she shut the door between us. Probably safest for her. Within a few minutes she emerged dressed in a pair of skin-tight black yoga pants and a tight orange tank top that highlighted the exotic shade of her skin and the unbelievable perfection of her tits, hair in a tight French braid, wearing a pair of old, worn, comfortable looking, and—most importantly—sensible Chucks. No makeup, she was dressed in ten minutes flat, including that fancy French braid.

"Damn, girl, that was fast."

She shrugged. "You gave me the impression that time is of the essence."

"Sure as hell is, honey." I glanced out the window again, but didn't see anything amiss outside. "Grab your purse and any necessities. I'm not sure when we'll be coming back here."

She unplugged her phone from the charger cord on the kitchen counter, tossed it in her purse, and slid the purse over her shoulder cross-body. "I have to work tomorrow."

"Well...you'll have to call in sick or something. Not now, though. Once we're clear of immediate danger.

"A couple things you need to understand before we really get started, okay? Number one, when we're on the move, in a hot situation—and I don't mean sexy hot, I mean people trying to hurt us hot—you do as I say, when I say, and you do not ever hesitate. That's most important." I cupped my hand around the back of her neck, drawing her closer to me. Let her see the truth in my eyes. "Second, just as important, is that no matter what you see me do, know that I'll never ever hurt you, or let anyone hurt you. Okay? You don't need to be afraid of me."

She frowned. "You're scaring me a little, Thresh."

I drew my Sig Sauer. "You should be a little scared. I'll get you through this, but...it ain't gonna be a walk in the park. Now, yank open your door, but don't put yourself in view of the opening. As soon as it's open, get behind me and stay tight on my ass. We're live, baby."

Adrenaline was pumping, shooting through me, pulsing in my

veins. Lola stood to the left of the door, leaned over, twisted the knob and, on my nod, jerked it open, staying out of the opening. As soon as she had the door open, I was through, pistol aimed through the frame; the hallway was empty, but I heard a voice echoing in the stairwell, speaking in low tones in the same Eastern European language the guy in the car had used.

I motioned for Lola to stay where she was, replaced my gun in its holster, drew my knife—no sense making more noise than I had to, or using rounds that might come in useful later.

The hallway was clear to the elevator, so I motioned for Lola to join me at the doorway to the stairwell. I had her open the stairwell door for me, listened, heard nothing.

We descended, Lola close behind me, down to the first floor.

Something warned me. That unease.

I held the KA-BAR so the cutting edge was facing up, easing forward on silent feet to stand beside the stairwell exit. I waited, tensed, barely breathing. I blocked out Lola, blocked out my own nerves; if you're not a little nervous, a little scared going into a fight, then you're either crazy or a liar, and I'm neither.

I watched as the doorknob to the stairwell door twisted, and then the door swung inward, and a body appeared in the doorway.

He saw me, I saw him…

I struck first, and I struck hardest. There's a spot, on the left side of the body, midway up the torso. Angle the blade to slide in under the ribcage….

He hit the ground like a sack of meat, blinking, gasping, dying.

I wiped the blade on his clothes, hauled him fully into the stairwell out of view of the thankfully-empty lobby, and then straightened.

Lola had seen the whole thing. When someone with the kind of dark, exotic skin that Lola had went pale as a ghost…ugh, not good. Not good at all.

I sheathed the knife, kept my hands visible, and approached her slowly. "Lola. He had a gun, okay? These guys aren't playing around."

She backed away from me. "You—you just…" She jabbed her fist upward in a parody of the move I just used. "It was…like…*easy*. So fast. You just—killed him. He never even had a chance."

"That's the point, babe." I got a little closer, keeping my voice low and smooth and soothing. "No point in giving him an opportunity to hurt me, or you. My job is to keep you alive, and out of the hands of the bad guys. I'm not gonna fuck around."

She just blinked at me. "You've done that before. Lots of times."

I sighed. "Yes, Lola. I'm not gonna lie about it. It's part of my job."

"That's why you told me I don't need to be afraid of you."

I nodded, and she let me get within touching distance. I put my hand on her arm, then slid it up to cup her neck, which seemed to calm her nerves for some reason. "I can do bad things, but only to people who deserve it, okay? You really don't want to know what could happen to you if these guys get hold of you. Now…we gotta move. I know there are at least two more out there, and I got no time to deal with the cops once the body gets reported."

She started shaking when she passed the corpse on the floor, with the pool of blood spreading beneath him.

"Don't look, Lola," I said, drawing my Sig. "You don't need to see that."

She shook her head, and looked away, and then we were trotting down the stairs. "I'm a doctor, Thresh. I did my rounds in the ER, and I work in the ICU. I've lost patients before. I've seen dead people before."

I beckoned for her to follow me across the lobby. "Yeah, I get that. But it's different when you watched the person get killed in front of you. Even fixing gunshot wounds like you did for me is different than fixing gunshot wounds you watched occur. Dealing with the aftereffects of violence is not quite the same thing as being involved in the violence."

She shuddered. "So I'm learning."

Once we hit the street, I put away my pistol and draped my shirt tail over it, then took Lola's hand in mine, threading our fingers together. There was no sign of cameras, which meant hopefully, given the fact that I'd worn gloves and that there hadn't been any witnesses, there wouldn't be any way to trace either the unconscious guy in the car or the dead guy in the stairwell back to me. What I did see was a Range Rover a couple blocks away inching around the corner toward us with two men in it; one of them lifted a cell phone, dialed a number, and held the phone to his ear; he spoke briefly, and then ended the call.

"Shit." I tugged Lola into a power walk, away from the scene, toward the Jeep.

"What is it?" Her voice was surprisingly even and steady, considering the events of the last few minutes.

"We've been made."

"What does that mean in normal person lingo?"

"It means that Range Rover over there is a very bad thing, and those two guys in it are very bad men."

"What about the good guys? Does the man you work for, Harris, does he know you're in trouble?"

We reached the Jeep, and I gestured for Lola to get in. "I'm assuming he does by now. I made a call of my own. We should have help at some point, but for now…we're on our own."

Once in the Jeep, I started the engine and pulled away, resisting the impulse to floor it. We didn't need attention, just now. The Range Rover followed closely behind us.

Things were about to get fun, and quick.

I turned left at the nearest intersection, and as soon as I was around the corner, I buried the pedal. The engine roared, torque kicked in, and we were both pressed back into the bucket seats as the powerful SUV leaped forward, hauling ass past the slower-moving cars. I had to do a bit of creative driving, jinking and swerving into oncoming traffic, back into the proper lane, then far right, left again…I chanced a glance in my mirrors, and saw the Rover following close behind, wending its own route through the traffic.

"Which way to a freeway?" I asked.

She blinked, hesitating a split second to think. "Left here," she said, giving me just barely enough time to hit the brakes and drift around the corner, tires squealing, smoke curling, the suspension doing its damnedest to keep us level as centripetal force fought to push us into a roll.

Two blocks passed in a matter of seconds, but it felt like minutes as I constantly swerved and braked to avoid cars and pedestrians and buses. Then she indicated left again, and then a right after another few blocks, and then the on-ramp was angling away and down. I hit the gas hard and we barreled down the on-ramp and onto the freeway, which one I wasn't sure and I really didn't care. *Away*, that was all I cared about.

It was oddly calm and quiet for a minute despite the fact I was doing 110mph and was still accelerating. The Rover was behind us, seemingly content to merely follow us for now. No shootouts on the freeway, I guess? I wasn't complaining. Hitting anything from a moving vehicle is hard enough as it is, much less trying to manage it one-handed. God, seriously, fuck this gimpy arm.

I kept an eye on our pursuers, who stayed a couple of car lengths back. When it became obvious they weren't going to mount a mobile assault, I backed off the accelerator until we were back to legal speeds.

Once we were cruising smoothly, Lola dug out her cell phone and called the hospital, claiming an unexpected family emergency that would keep her occupied for several days. After that, we drove in silence for a while, passing out of Miami and away from the urban and suburban areas.

"Where are we going?" Lola asked.

I shrugged. "No idea. They're just following us for now." I eyed her, noting her thoughtful expression. "Why? You got an idea?"

She bobbed her head side to side in a *maybe* gesture. "Well, there is a place, but...I'm hesitant for a couple of reasons. First, it's hard to get to, which is part of the reason I'm even considering it, but when I say hard to get to, I'm really not kidding. Remote doesn't even begin to cover it. Second, I really don't like the idea of leading anyone there, because it's…it's my dad's place. I don't want to pull him into this mess, too. He's…kind of a hermit."

I considered. "Where are we talking?"

"He's got this place way down in the Ten Thousand Islands area, the kind of place you have to know exactly how to get into and out of, or you'll be totally lost forever."

"And you know how to get there?"

She nodded. "Yeah. I half grew up there. It was our summer getaway. We'd pack up as soon as school let out and take his boat out there, and we wouldn't come back until the day before I started school again. Then, when Mom died, Dad moved out there full-time. Hasn't left since. He has this friend who delivers supplies, and I visit him sometimes when I can." We were nearing an exit ramp for a different freeway, and she directed me to take that exit, which put us on a smaller, two-lane highway heading south and west out away from Miami.

"So I'm assuming it's not accessible via a vehicle," I said.

She snorted. "Yes, Thresh, there's a nice highway leading right up to my dad's handmade cabin deep in the Everglades." Not only did I get the snort and the sarcasm, I also got an eye roll. Bonus points. "That's the tricky part." She looked at me sidelong, chewing on a thumbnail. "I'm kind of assuming you didn't just happen to purchase this vehicle since arriving in Miami…"

I twisted my fist around the leather of the steering wheel. "Not… exactly, no. I more…borrowed it. Firmly."

She snickered. "Which means you bashed some poor asshole over the head and stole his very nice Jeep?"

I pretended to bluster as if I was offended. "I would *never* bash some poor asshole over the head and steal his very nice Jeep." I affected an arch tone. "I have *standards*, I'll have you know. For your information, I held him up at knifepoint and stole his Jeep. But I was polite."

She raised both eyebrows. "You *politely* stole a vehicle at knifepoint?"

"Yep. Didn't even hurt him—" I tipped my head to the side with a shrug of one shoulder, "—much. Just a little tiny, itty-bitty spot where I pricked him with the knife. Won't even need a Band-Aid."

She eyed me. "Well. I certainly wouldn't like to know what it looks like when you're *not* being polite about something."

I shot a glance in the mirror, checking for our pursuers; they looked a tad bored. I'd have to make things interesting for them, at some point.

"You've seen it," I said. "It can get…messy."

That silenced her for a moment. "I see. I guess I can understand why you'd be upset, all things considered."

I laughed outright. "Upset? I'm not upset at all. This is a bit of fun, so far. It'd be better if I hadn't gotten shot, but then these are the same guys who put the bullets in me in the first place, and I did a number on them during the last op, so I'm kind of looking at this as…retribution, for both sides."

A few more moments of silence went by, and then she glanced at me again. "What was the op? I mean, if I'm gonna get dragged into some shit out of a Jason Bourne movie, I might as well know why."

I debated about what to tell her, and then figured she deserved to know the truth for the reasons she gave. "First, when I said I was a security contractor, I really did mean that. We generally provide personal security for high-profile clients on an event-by-event basis. Like when some A-list celebrity is doing some big flashy event and they want to beef up their normal security, they'll hire us. My job is usually to be big and scary and intimidating, honestly. So, for the most part, I'm not a mercenary, I'm a security contractor." I paused to change lanes, accelerating around a slow-moving RV. "But some-times a job comes our way that's…not as simple."

"Like killing people?"

I didn't have to affect the offended tone of voice. "I'm not a fuck-ing assassin, Lola."

"Well shit, Thresh, I know next to nothing about you, so how am I supposed to know? You killed that guy with laughable ease. You don't even seem affected. I didn't mean to offend you but, if you look at it from my perspective for a second, it's not a completely outlandish assumption."

"I guess you have a point," I said. "The jobs I'm talking about are things that go beyond the bounds of basic security. We're not contract killers, we're a threat-removal team. An insert-and-extraction team. If someone needs security against an active threat, where there's real possibility of danger, you call us. The job that caused all this fuckery was…different, even for us."

Lola pivoted in her seat so she was partially facing me, openly and avidly listening, now.

I sighed and drove with my knee while I rubbed the back of my neck, then re-took the wheel. "You know the actors Jon Lonigan and Callie MacPhereson?"

Lola snorted. "Um, duh?"

"Right. Well, they have a daughter, three years old. Cleo. Cute little thing, blond hair, blue eyes, innocent, and sweet as sugar." I let out a breath. "She got kidnapped. It was…messy. The guys who snatched her did it in broad daylight, nearly killed the nanny in the process. Sent a ransom note with a photograph of some asshole with a big fuck-off knife to this little girl's throat. Harris did security for a friend of Lonigan's, so Harris got the call. Go get the girl. Cost was no object, and he didn't want to know the details of how we did it. Just get his little girl back. So we did what we do: we got the girl back.

"Only, it wasn't exactly simple. The tangos who snatched Cleo weren't just some hack thugs. It was a professional job—people Harris ran into back in his black-ops days. Evil fuckers, and smart ones to boot. Coordinated, well-armed, trained, and with serious numbers. The guy in charge found out Harris was involved, and it turns out the two had bad blood between them. They planned to ambush us, so we set up a counter ambush—" I waved a hand, not wanting to go too heavy on the details, for both our sakes. "Things got hot, and fast. The whole thing went sideways. We barely got away, and we took out most of Cain's guys in the process, but not Cain himself, *and* Cain never got his ransom money. So now we have one seriously pissed-off European mobster, and this guy...he has money, he has connections, and he's just arrogant enough to think he can take on Harris and win."

Lola was taking all this in stride, so far, but then she was proving herself to be fairly unflappable. "Can he? Take on Harris and win, I mean."

I laughed, hard. "Sweetheart, Harris makes both Rambo and Chuck Norris look like pussies. Put them together, and they're still pussies compared to Harris. Cain doesn't stand a chance. And now that he's gone after me? Shit, the motherfucker's signed his death warrant, and I ain't even pissed off yet."

"Just out of curiosity...what would happen if you got pissed off?"

I thought for a second, trying to figure out how to answer that. "I've only lost my temper once in my life. I've always been bigger than everyone, and my old man, sadistic fuck though he may have been, made sure I knew I had to keep a lid on my shit. He drilled self-control into me from a very young age. So...I don't get pissed off too easily."

Lola frowned. "It happened once, though?"

I sighed. "Yeah. But that's...not something I like to talk about. It was a bad time."

Lola turned back in her seat to face the front. "I see. Well, I'm sorry it happened, whatever it was."

"So. This plan of yours, to disappear into the swamp..."

"First, it's not really a swamp, it's a wetland forest. It's a very complicated and very special place."

I rolled my hand in a *keep-going* gesture. "Okay, so how do we get into this very complicated and special wetland forest of yours?"

She sighed. "It's actually one of only three locations in the world to be declared—"

I cut her off. "Tell me when we're in there, babe. Let's get to the part of the explanation where I can plan how to lose these two assholes behind us without getting you killed."

"Or you. We don't want you killed."

I guffawed. "Sweetheart, there's only two of them. They couldn't kill me if they had a goddamn bazooka. Pretty sure I can handle two little Euro wanna-be thug fucks."

Lola rolled her eyes at me. "Okay, tough guy. Point is, you're my protection, so I need you in one piece." She eyed my cast-wrapped, sling-bound arm. "Or, at least, in the number of pieces you're already in."

"I'd like that too. Despite what you may believe, getting shot ain't fun, so I'd like to avoid it if I can."

"So the plan is to use Dad's extra boat."

I gaped at her. "Extra boat? Why didn't you say so?"

"Because you distracted me with your *I politely stole a Jeep* nonsense."

"*You* started that, honeybuns."

"Honeybuns? What the fuck is that supposed to mean?"

"It means tell me where this fucking boat is so we can go get it."

She hesitated. "Well, the thing is, getting *to* it is the easy part. Actually getting into the boat and on the water? A little more difficult." She gestured behind us. "Especially since I'm relatively certain they'll try to stop us."

"Relatively certain," I echoed. "Yeah, I'd agree with that."

She tapped at the GPS, inputting an address on Plantation Island, wherever that was—*what*ever that was. "First stop, Uncle Filipo's."

"What's at Uncle Filipo's?"

"The boat."

"I'm confused."

She rolled her eyes at me. Seemed like she did that a lot. "I know, it's complicated. Further complication is that Uncle Filipo isn't really my uncle. He's the friend of my dad's who brings him supplies. He has a boat—well, actually it's *Dad's* boat if you want to be technical about it, but he's letting Uncle Filipo borrow it more or less permanently, so Filipo can bring Dad food and propane and whatever else."

I frowned. "So it's Filipo's boat?"

She shook her head. "Filipo is very particular on this point. It's not his boat, he's just using it."

"And what does this have to do with our plan to borrow the boat?"

"Well, it's next to Filipo's trailer." She did that hesitation again, the one that meant I wouldn't like what she was about to say. "It's on a trailer, and we have to tow it to the water."

"Which means we have to lose the dudes behind us."

"That would make it easier, yes."

"This place of your dad's…is it listed? Like, is he on the grid?"

"On the grid?"

"Searchable. Utilities, address, cell phone records, credit cards?"

"Oh. No, he's off the grid, then. No electricity or running water, no cell phone, obviously. He has a bank account with his savings in it, but he doesn't use it. He'd have to leave the mangroves, and that's not happening. I can't think of anything that would lead to him. To the world at large, after Mom died, he just disappeared. I even changed my last name to Mom's maiden name after she died, so it's not easy to tie me to Dad that way. Only Filipo and I know how to find him, or that he's even still alive."

I nodded. "That's good. You might be able to hide out there until I can get you off Cain's radar."

"How are you going to do that?"

"By being charming and persuasive, of course." I said it with a grin, hoping she got my meaning without having to have it spelled out.

She shook her head with an amused sigh. "I see." She held up her fists, shook the left, "Charm…", then the right, "…and Persuasion?"

I laughed. "Exactly. You get me, Doc."

She twisted in her seat to look back at the Range Rover, still following two car lengths behind. "Any ideas how to take care of them?"

I drove with my knee, pulled my Sig out, and laid it on my lap. "Yeah—shoot 'em."

She glanced out the windows at the freeway. "What, here? Now?"

I shrugged. "Now that we're out in the country and away from traffic, we'll switch seats, and I'll take care of the assholes behind us."

"That easy, huh?"

I bobbled my head side to side. "Easy? I wouldn't say *easy*, exactly. I'd say it's simple. Which ain't the same as easy."

She sighed. "I have a feeling this *is* going to get interesting."

I grinned. "Lola, babe, when you're with me, everything is interesting."

Yet again, she rolled her eyes at me. "So I'm discovering. Funny thing is, I was perfectly content with my boredom."

To prove a point, I used my knee on the steering wheel, reached out, traced my fingertip over her knee, down to the inside of her thigh, then dragged my finger slowly up the length of her thigh, slowing as I neared the juncture of her thighs. "Lola, sweetheart. You suck at lying."

"I—I…I'm not lying," she stammered as I drew my touch to within an inch of her pussy, and then backed away. "What would I lie about?"

"You were so not content with your boredom." I teased closer again, and her breath caught. "You were dying for someone to force you out of your rut."

"I wasn't in a rut."

"Were too." I moved my finger to the other thigh, teased up the inside from knee to pussy and back.

"Well if I *was* in a rut, there was a reason for it." She was trying to act casual, as if she was unaffected.

She wasn't, though. She was squirming. Fighting to keep breathing normally, to stay in her seat.

"Oh? What reason would that be?" I trailed my hand over her core, a light, teasing touch.

"Stop that." She grabbed my wrist, but didn't apply any pressure to stop me as I cupped my hand over her, rubbing the heel of my palm against where her clit would be, beneath the yoga pants and the underwear.

"Stop?" I kept rubbing, a little harder now, in slow circles, and her hips began to mirror the movement. "You sure you want me to stop?"

"Yes…" she said, but her hand told a different story, doing more to guide my motions than halt them. "God…you're an asshole…you have to stop—"

I pulled my hand away, then. "If you insist."

She moaned, writhing in the bucket seat. "Damn it, Thresh."

"What?" I cupped her again. "Maybe you'd like to revise your request that I stop?"

I rubbed against her clit in slow deliberate grinding circles, just enough to get her going, to hint at what I *could* do.

She leaned her head back against the seat rest, flexing her hips in time with my movements. "I hate you."

"Do not."

"Do too."

"Why?" I moved a little faster, now. "Why do you hate me, Lola? Is it because you like the way I'm touching you, but you don't *want* to like it?"

"What are you doing, Thresh?" She gasped as my touch sped up. "God, what are you *doing* to me?"

Fuck, she was so goddamned responsive. I was barely touching her, not even touching bare flesh. She was moments away from coming and I'd only touched her over her clothes. Jesus, the things I could do to this woman if I had her naked and the time to do them all. I found myself wondering if she was a screamer. If she'd rake her nails down my back. What kind of a gag reflex she had.

I realized that we had little or no traffic behind us. The Rover was right behind us now, but still staying fifty or so yards back. Now was the time, if I was going to make a move.

Problem was, now I had Lola all worked up.

What's a guy to do?

I glanced at Lola. "Take the wheel, babe. We're switching spots."

"NOW? You do this *now*?" She released her seat belt and grabbed the steering wheel, even as she shouted at me.

I grinned at her. "What?"

"You know damn well what! You can't leave me like this!"

"Like what?"

"All…you know. Worked up." She seemed sheepish, for some stupid reason. Embarrassed. Which was weird, considering how shamelessly she was into it only moments ago.

"You gotta trust me, Doc. I'll take care of you, don't you worry." I levered the seat back as far as it would go, set the cruise control, and then worked my bulk across the console, behind Lola, and into the passenger seat. Which makes it sound a lot easier than it actually was. "I'll take such good care of you, you'll be begging for more. Now…drive. Keep it floored, and hold it steady."

I hung out the window, the stolen Glock in my good hand, angling backward, drew a bead on the driver, squeezed the trigger twice—*BANG-BANG!*—the windshield spiderwebbed as my bullets smashed through, but the Rover kept on after us—I'd missed. I sent two more rounds at the windshield, aiming for where the passenger would be, if he was idiot enough to still be sitting there. I didn't think he was an idiot, necessarily, but it never hurt to try.

There was return fire then, a hand gripping a pistol appearing out the passenger window, bucking, gunshots echoing, and the Jeep shuddered as bullets thunked into the rear bumper; they were trying for our tires, I realized.

Hell no.

I drew a bead on the hood this time, and squeezed a few more shots off. Smoke billowed from under the hood, the Rover swerved, skidded, slewed sideways, and then juddered to a halt.

"Pull over," I told Lola, and she obeyed immediately.

As soon as we were stopped, I shoved open the door and leapt out, leveling my gun at the Rover. A gun barked from the driver's side, and I returned fire, sending the round at the windshield, which shattered completely, then. The driver was slumped over, still alive but bleeding, and the passenger was nowhere to be seen.

I moved forward in a low crouch, reached the hood, circled around to the passenger side, crouching low automatically, keeping my barrel trained on the passenger window. I inched closer, lifting up to peer over the lip and in, intending to plug him sudden-like.

A shot blasted at me and the round buzzed past my ear, missing me by a matter of centimeters, if that. When a bullet goes *snap* past your head, you'd better duck; if a round goes *buzzzzzz* like an angry bee, you'd better thank sweet baby Jesus, 'cause that one almost had your name on it.

I cursed under my breath, took a second to slow my heartbeat, and then crouched, inched forward, peered around the side of the Rover. Squatting, I put my back to the Rover, waited another couple seconds…raised up a few inches to peer into the windows, caught a glimpse of him in the rear of the Rover, trying to flank me via the trunk. I ducked back down, waited for the sound of the hatch opening. Waited for the sound of feet on concrete. He appeared from around the rear; I pulled a bead on his chest, and squeezed off a round.

He took the round dead center mass, red blooming on his shirt. He stumbled backward, his grip on his pistol going slack, and then he sat down hard, clutching his chest in confusion. I waited until I was relatively certain he was past the point of being dangerous, and then moved out from beside the Rover. I kicked his gun away and kept mine trained on him as he toppled to his back, clutching his chest with one hand, gasping, blinking.

He had a cell phone in his hand. He was fading fast, beyond talking already. His hand unfurled, showing the screen of the smartphone. The name at the top read "Cain", and listed the duration of the call as being just over five minutes…and counting.

Cain was still on the line.

I crouched, tucking my pistol away, and caught up the phone. "Cain."

"Ah, Thresh, I assume?" His voice was smooth as silk, lightly accented, venomously cold. "My men are dead, then?"

"What do you want?"

"We are beyond that, which I think you know." There was a moment of silence. "You may keep running. I will find you. Your friend Mr. Winter is not the only one with skills of a certain technological type, you know. Nor is Anselm the only one adept at the finding of people. Have fun with Dr. Reed, Thresh."

The line went dead, then.

Shit, shit, shit.

Did he know where we were going? How could he, though? *I* didn't even know exactly where we were going.

Not good, not good, not good. I dropped the phone on the ground and crushed it under my heel, just for good measure. I wasn't sure how Cain intended to find us, which meant my only real option was to continue with the plan and hope either Cain wasn't as good as he seemed to think, or that I'd be able to handle whatever he sent our way.

Didn't like our odds either way, but hey…you do what you gotta do.

When I turned around, Lola was staring at me, at the two dead men. Pale, trembling, hand over her mouth.

Then she bent over double and vomited, collapsed to her knees, and started sobbing.

6

FOUR-WORD WRECK

WITHOUT THE BANTER THRESH HAD KEPT UP—INTENTIONALLY, I surmised, to occupy my mind—it all just kind of crashed down on me. The guy in the car, knocked out. The guy I'd watched Thresh kill with a knife in one move, as easily as I'd administer an injection. Then these two guys…the danger became all the more real when guns started going off and bullets hit the Jeep. Thresh had handled it calmly enough, which was freaky in itself.

Top that with the fact that I was running for my life with a man I knew nothing about, someone who was clearly, utterly capable of bloodshed without even flinching.

And only minutes ago, he'd been touching me…touching me in ways I'd not been touched, even by myself, in years. Making me feel things I hadn't felt in years. I'd nearly had an orgasm, and he hadn't even been touching my flesh.

And then he just stopped, leaving me on the edge…to kill people.

I don't know why I vomited, honestly. I don't have a weak stomach. I've seen some ugly shit in my career. I think it was the shock of it, really. It was just so sudden. The noise, the abrupt mess.

And then the tears? God, I hate crying. *Hate* it. HATEHATEHATE. I don't cry. Haven't since…since everything that happened. I swore I wouldn't cry, after all that, and I hadn't.

And now, in front of Thresh, I was sobbing, and I couldn't seem to stop. I felt Thresh come up beside me, more hesitantly than usual. Worried I was going to be afraid of him, I guess. And I should have been, shouldn't I? He could kill without compunction. But, I felt no fear of him. I expected it, was prepared for it, but it never came. I just knew, deep down, that he wouldn't ever hurt me. Maybe I was being naive, or stupid, or maybe my ability to judge people was just broken—god knows that wouldn't be a shock—but the fact was, I trusted Thresh.

It seemed stupid to trust him, though. Wasn't it? Who would trust a killer? Stupid-ass Lola Reed, M.D., clearly.

Hormonal, emotionally unstable, sexually fucked up on an epic scale, and stuck in the middle of nowhere with a giant, terrifying, deadly brute of a human being...one who also was stupid sexy. He just...did things to my head, to my hormones, to my body. I just...*reacted* to him. I had no control over it. He got close to me, touched me, spoke in my ear in that throbbing bass rumble of his, and I just... went to pieces. Everything I thought I knew, everything I thought I wanted and didn't want went out the window.

Even now, as his arm slid around my waist and pulled me against him, I reacted. The sobs quieted, and my breathing evened out, and...he was just...*there*. Huge and solid and reassuringly powerful. Just holding me.

He looked down at me and asked, "Can you make it back to the Jeep?"

All I could do was nod.

He turned me toward the Jeep, opened the passenger door, waited till I was in, and then closed it behind me. He got in the driver's side, turned over the engine, looked at me and said, "Let's get the fuck outta here."

We continued on our way south and west toward Plantation Island, neither of us speaking for several miles.

"You all right, Lola?" he asked, eventually.

I shrugged. "I don't know."

"I didn't want you to see that."

"The shooting stopped, so I thought…" I paused to take a deep breath, and to wipe my eyes.

He touched my chin, lifted my face so I was looking up into his pale blue eyes. "Remember what I told you, back at your condo?"

I nodded. "I remember. It just doesn't make it any easier watching you do those things. Even if I can recognize that you're only doing it to protect us, it's…ugh. Horrible."

"It's not pretty, no. But it's what I do. And for what it's worth, I'm sorry I got you into this."

I shrugged. "Who was on the phone?"

A growl of unhappiness. "Cain. He hinted that he'd be able to find us as easily as Lear or Anselm can."

"Who are they?"

"Lear is a hacker. Works for Alpha One with me. He's the one who got your address for me. And, by the way, that's the only piece of information about you I let him give me."

"There was more?"

He laughed. "Babe, if he went looking, Lear could tell you things about yourself even you didn't know."

"Well, that's unnerving." I looked over at him. "And you didn't let him tell you anything about me? Why not?"

He grinned over at me for a second. "Because, as I told Lear, I intend on finding all that out the fun way."

I swallowed hard. "Oh, yeah? How's that?"

His eyes on the road, his grin faded into something fiercer, hungrier. "You'd be surprised what you can find out about someone after a couple orgasms."

"A—a *couple*?" Like, in one day? I'd read about that, but didn't think it was real.

His eyes narrowed and his features reflected suspicion.

"You've never had a multiple O before, have you, Lola?"

"You have any idea how long it's been since I've even had a single

O?" Now why the hell did that come out of my mouth?

"How long?"

I tried to stop myself from answering, but apparently I had conflicting ideas about what I wanted. "Three years."

He just blinked at me for several seconds, his expression utterly blank. "You—you haven't had an orgasm in *three years*? Jesus, Lola, what kind of losers are you dating?"

"The nonexistent kind?"

He tilted his head to the side, understanding beginning to filter in. "Um. So...you're saying you haven't had any sex at all in three years?" I shook my head, not looking at him. "What about your fingers? Or a vibrator? You haven't tried to make yourself come, either?"

This was getting dangerously close to topics I'd studiously avoided even thinking about, much less talking about, for many years. I decided it was time to move the conversation away to safer, less painful topics. "And Anselm? Who's that?"

He sighed. "Avoiding the subject. Sure sign there's something fucked up you don't want to talk about."

"Sort of like why you lost your temper that one time?"

He winced. "*Touché.* I'll let it go, but not for long." He paused, letting out a short breath, then went on, "Anselm is...uh...well... it's hard to talk about Anselm with any accuracy. He's a spook. A former spy, you know? Nobody knows dick about his past, who he worked for, what exactly he did, where he came from, nothing. He can blend into any crowd, disappear like smoke in the wind, and find anyone anywhere, anytime. Combine his spy skills with Lear's hacking abilities? Those two scare the fuck out of me. I mean, I can lay out major damage with any weapon created, including my bare hands. But...I'm not exactly the subtlest of dudes, obviously. I can sneak around, do urban combat and woodcraft and shit like that, but what those two are capable of? It's freaky. It's on another level. And Anselm is just...cold. You think I'm cold? I'm like a warm, fuzzy little puppy compared to that fucker. But he's my friend, and I trust him with my life. All the guys I work with, I trust that way. Which is why the thought of Cain going after my buddies? Oh, no. Fuck that. Shit's gonna get hot real fucking fast."

I reflected on what it might mean if a man like Thresh claimed to be freaked out by something—the thought made me shudder. To ignore those shudder-inducing thoughts, I decided to push Thresh, a little, about his past. See what I could get out of him.

"So…in the hospital you mentioned you played football for Florida State. Did you graduate from there?" I wasn't just pushing for info, though, I was honestly curious. What shaped a man like Thresh?

He didn't respond very quickly, and when he did, it was obvious he was choosing his words with care. "No, I didn't. I…pursued other opportunities."

"Like what?"

He glanced at me. "Well, I got recruited, if you really want to know. NFL. Made it through training camp, played an entire season with the Carolina Panthers."

I gaped at him. "You played pro football?"

He wouldn't look at me. "Yep. I had the size, strength, speed, and talent. That season, man…I wrecked shit right up. It was a good year. Lots of fun, lots of money, lots of bitches—women, I mean."

I rolled my eyes at him. "Why censor yourself now, Thresh? It's not like I'm unaware of your status as a professional-grade player."

He shrugged. "I'm not trying to censor myself, I just—"

"You want in my pants, and you think I'm less likely to let that happen if I'm constantly being reminded that you've probably perfected the art of the hump and dump?"

He frowned at me. "Okay, now hold the fuck on a second. That's not entirely fair. It's not like that, okay? *I'm* not like that. Can I say I've never humped and dumped before? No. I was an animal in college, and that year with the pros. But things changed. *I* changed. I don't play it that way. Do I do monogamy? No. Not even really serial monogamy. I'm a soldier, and I have been my whole life. I travel too much, and I'm constantly in and out of gnarly situations. It would be stupidity of the highest order for me to try to saddle some poor chick with my freight train of shit."

He sounded genuinely upset at the accusation I'd leveled at him. "I lay it out before I even step up to the plate with a girl. You don't get to first base with me until you understand the game. It's not that I don't want to stick around, and it's not that the girl isn't worth it, or anything like that. It's the nature of my job. Just the way my life is right now. I'm gonna move on. We can have fun until I'm called away, but that's it. It ain't gonna be more than that. Can't be. Won't be. Even if it could be—and Doc, there's been a few times where it could have been something—that *can't* happen. I won't let it. No point. No chick is ever gonna be fine with me hopping all over the damn globe getting shot or stabbed or whatever. But I don't fuck and chuck, okay? I don't play that way."

I met his eyes. "I'm sorry, Thresh, I didn't mean to insult you. It's just…how you come across, I guess."

A shrug. "I get that."

"So, only the one season, huh? What happened? Injury?"

His expression shuttered, just shut down. "No. I could've kept playing. Probably should've." He twisted the leather of the steering wheel. "I felt the call to serve my country, that's what happened."

"You left the NFL to join the Army?"

He glanced at me. "Hell the *fuck* no. I left the NFL to join the goddamn Marine Corps. Shit was going on in Iraq, and I was having drinks after a game in the hotel bar with this guy. He was Recon. Real deal badass, hard as fuck, and made it seem cool. Told some sick stories, and got me thinking. He didn't make it seem all honor and glory, you know? He told it like it was."

A moment of silence.

"Never told anyone this. You got one hell of a bedside manner, Doc, if you're getting me to talk about this bullshit. He told me I wasting my potential playing football. 'Sure, you're a monster,' he said. 'Sure, you're fast and tough and can sack QBs like nobody's business,' he told me. 'But is that what you really want to use your size and strength and toughness on? Football? A goddamned game?' And the shit of it was, I realized he was right. So I finished the season, joined the Marines at twenty-one. I played for FSU my freshman, sopho- more, and junior years. Got recruited to play for Carolina my junior year, played with them the next season. Joined the Marines. Made Recon by the time I was twenty-three. Never looked back."

"So you were a Recon for…what, fifteen years?"

He laughed. "You're really fishing, Doc. No. I was Recon for four, five years? Then I got recruited onto a black ops team. Real hush-hush sort of shit. Did that for a while, and then—" He let out a slow, pensive breath. "Then I got out. Some shit happened that made it obvious it was past time to get out. I'd done a few missions with my current boss, Harris. He'd gotten out before I did, worked private security for Valentine Roth. Ended up starting his own security firm, and hired me the second I turned civvie."

"Civvie?"

"Civilian."

"Oh."

I watched him, watched the way his brow tightened, the way his fist clenched the wheel. "I've upset you, haven't I?"

He made a visible effort to shake it off. "No, Doc. You just… brought up memories I usually keep in the box, is all."

I huffed. "Yeah, well, then that's two of us." I shot him a grin. "So have you met Valentine Roth?"

He tipped his head side to side. "Yeah, a few times. He's cool. Richer than all fuck, but he's cool about it."

"I've read a few articles about him. He seems like an interesting person."

He laughed. "Interesting is one word for it. Honestly, there's not many people like him. He's a real one-of-a-kind. He's no pussy rich- boy who's inherited his daddy's money even though, from what I understand, he did come from serious money."

"Tell me about the rest of your team."

"All right. But you gotta answer some questions in return."

I swallowed hard. "Fair enough. But…don't lead with the hard stuff, okay?"

"Now would I do that to you?"

I scowled at him. "Yeah, I think you might."

He laughed. "Actually, you're right. But I'll be nice." He reached out, tugged the end of my braid; and no, I didn't like it, not one bit. "How about family, is that a safe enough opening topic?"

I sighed. "Not really, but then, I'm not sure what would be, so we'll go with it." I took a moment to gather myself, and my thoughts. "My mom died when I was sixteen. She was in a car accident, and she should've recovered, but she got an infection and…she never left the hospital. Dad always swore it was negligence on the part of the hospital, and talked about suing, but he was just too lost without her. So that's when he turned into a hermit."

"Jesus, Lola, I'm sorry. That's rough."

I nodded. "It was. She suffered for two weeks before she finally passed and, when she did, it was kind of a relief in some ways, because finally the agony was over. That feeling of helplessness, watching her suffer…that was what made me want to be a doctor. If I could help anyone, lessen anyone's suffering, help them heal, bring families back together when mine was ripped apart…"

"What was your mom like?"

I stared out the window, watching the green fields pass by. "She was…amazing. She was a therapist. She could make you feel better just by being in the same room as her. She could get anyone to talk about anything, and when you were done talking, everything just… made more sense."

"And your dad?"

"Oh, Dad. Dad is something entirely different. He's Samoan. He grew up there, lived there until he was…thirty? Moved to the States on a scholarship to FSU in ecology. Met mom at FSU, had me when he was…thirty-five? Thirty-six? Spent most of my childhood studying the ecology of the Everglades. It was always an obsession with him, part of the reason we always spent the summer down here. He loved it. Mom used to joke that he'd retire to the Everglades, and never come back out. Well…when Mom passed, he did just that. Couldn't handle life out here, the people, the questions. He's this massive guy, you know? Like your typical huge Samoan guy? That's my dad. Not quite as big as you, but close. I guess that's partly why I'm so attracted to you, if you want the real psychology behind it. You're nothing like my dad, but the sense of size, being close to you, it makes me feel safe. Comforted.

"My dad is…private. Hates people, hates crowds, hates civilization. When he speaks, it's softly, and you listen, because he's got this way of just…cutting to the heart of things. He's this big guy, but he's painfully shy. Mom was really the only person he ever actually got close to, but that's how Mom was. That's why they worked together, I guess."

I had to stop, because it was just so hard to think about Mom, and how Dad just sort of fell inward after she died. "Dad taught me to lift, taught me to love working out. I look like him. I'm nothing like Mom, physically. She was small, petite, like five-five and thin. She was so tiny next to Dad. I'm like her in personality in some ways, though. People like to talk to me, but I'm more like Dad in that I don't really want to talk to them."

"You lift?"

I laughed. "It figures. Out of everything I just spilled, that's what you seize on." I patted his bicep, which was sort of like patting a tree trunk. "Dad loves to lift. He was religious about the gym until Mom died, and I'm the same way, even still. It's all that keeps me sane, some days. Can't handle people anymore, and if I can't deal with the bullshit—I go to the gym."

He nodded. "Damn straight. Gym is life."

I extended my fist and he tapped his knuckles against mine. Honestly, I was grateful he'd let most of the painful shit go without comment.

"Gym is life," I repeated. "So, it's my turn. Your family, go."

He twisted the steering wheel leather with his fist again, which I was starting to recognize as a nervous gesture. "Well, Dad was a sick fuck, let's just get that out of the way first. I say 'was' but, as far as I know, he could be alive somewhere. I just got no fucking desire to lay eyes on the evil bastard ever again.

"I had one of those stereotypical abusive childhoods, I guess you might say. Got beat on the regular, but it sometimes went beyond a mere beating. Got my size from him, and he never pulled his punches with me, starting from when I was just a kid in diapers. He'd break bones on bad days, but there wasn't ever money for a hospital, and he wasn't about to let me go anyway, since I might talk.

"Mom had been a nurse, so she'd set my bones when he broke 'em. Mom was my…she was the only light in my life. The one thing I ever had that wasn't pain and despair. We lived in a trailer in the middle of nowhere in Buttfuck, Mississippi. Wasn't nothing but nowhere, nothing, and nobody. Surprising I even got any schooling, to be honest. But I did, and I got scouted by FSU for football, and you know the rest."

"You're skipping a lot."

He snorted. "No shit, Doc. Not much worth repeating. Dad beat me every single damn day and Mom kept me alive. That's it."

I felt the pain, the things he'd never say, not to anyone. The shit he'd buried way down deep, long ago. "So the one time you ever lost your temper…"

He sighed—or actually, it wasn't really a sigh, it was more of a growl, a rumble so deep I didn't know a human could produce such a sound. "The one time I went back. After I made Recon. I was shipping out, knew I wasn't going back, not ever. So I showed up to see Ma, and…he'd ruined her. Without me to take the brunt, she just…" He shook his head. "He'd ruined her."

"I tore that trailer apart, every stud, every board, every stick, I wrecked the whole damn thing. Tore the old man apart too. Took ten deputies, four tasers, pepper spray, and a baton to the back of the head before I went down. Nearly killed that fucker, and I wish I had. Got Mom out—just took her away. Used every cent I'd ever saved and put her up in Florida. When I went pro, I gave her all my money. Every cent."

I blinked back tears. "Fucking hell, Thresh."

He winked at me. "Hey, baby, it's all in the past, now. It ain't worth revisiting, so I don't do it all that much." For the most part, his voice was fairly accent-free, smooth and intelligent and clearly educated—but sometimes, like right then, I could hear the Mississippi in his voice.

"I'm sorry."

He rested his hand on my thigh. "Don't even think on it, Doc."

I didn't dare ask about his mom again. I had a feeling it wasn't a good answer.

As the miles continued to mount, we shared a few minutes of silence. I ruminated on my past, and on his, and...mostly, the attraction between us. But I did have one more question, which I wasn't sure I was going to get an answer to.

"So...Thresh—"

"Nope." He cut me off. "I'm not telling you my real name, Doc. One person on this earth knows it, and that would be my miserable, no good, evil, abusive, sick fuck of a father, and he's probably dead drunk in a ditch somewhere in the backwoods of Mississippi, where he belongs."

"How can I get you to tell me your real name?" I asked.

He shot me a lecherous grin. "Well, if you're so determined, I can think of a few trades."

My stomach flip-flopped, and my blood raced. "Oh? Such as?"

He checked the rearview mirror, then pulled off the road, shoved the shifter into park, left the engine on and the A/C blasting against the blazing south Florida heat. His gaze burned into me, hot with lust. "You say that, Doc, but you're all kinds of standoffish when it comes to me touching you. Something bad happened to you, and I ain't gonna push you to tell me what it was. But it ain't no secret that I want you. I want you six ways to Sunday, and every moment I spend with you I'm thinking up new ways I could make you scream my name."

He unbuckled himself and then me, and then reached out, dragged his palm up my thigh, and this time he didn't stop to tease me, he just cupped his huge hand over my core, covering me completely, and then began rubbing the heel of his palm over me in such a perfect way that I felt it in my gut, in the quivering of my thighs, in the shortness of my breath, in the way my eyes wouldn't quite stay open. "You want this with me, you're gonna have to let go of some of your mental blocks, sweetheart."

"I—I don't have mental blocks," I lied.

He grinned at me. "Oh no? Then tell me what I'm doing to you, right now?"

He drew his fingers up, found the waistband of my yoga pants and underwear, and slid his fingertips under, against my skin, and then began slowly worming them down, closer, closer, through my neatly trimmed thatch of pubic hair—yeah, I wasn't shaved bare, and I wasn't about to apologize.

He'd read my mind, it seemed. "Mmmm, Doc…you wanna know something? I really like that you ain't shaved bare down there. I don't like feeling like I'm messing around with some girl not old enough to grow pubes."

"I—I trim it."

He leaned closer to me, pressed his lips to my neck, and kept working his way down between my thighs, centimeter by centimeter, in no rush at all. "I can feel that Doc. It's perfect. Just how a woman should be, if you ask me." He finally reached the apex of my core, and his long middle finger found the beginning of my opening. He began teasing his way in. And I—I couldn't breathe. Not at all. "So now, Doc, on the subject of mental blocks. What am I doing to you, right now?"

I swallowed hard, but my mouth was dry and my throat was seizing, and my gut was doing its best impression of a roller coaster. "You're—you're touching me."

"No shit, Doc." He found my clitoris, then, and any breath I had left was gone in a sharp gasp. "Where?"

"Between my thighs."

"Say it, Doc. Tell me where I'm touching you."

"My—oh, oh, oh god—" His fingertip pressed lightly, delicately, perfectly against my clitoris, and everything inside me started whirling and zinging and tightening and heating. "My—my vagina."

He laughed outright. "Well, yeah, but that's not really the sexiest word there is. Try again." He moved his fingertip away just enough that the wild frenzy of sensations subsided, leaving me aching and empty. "Or I'll stop."

"No, no. Please don't."

"You like it, don't you, Lola?" He whispered this in my ear, his voice thick, his breath hot. "You like it when I touch your pussy?"

I writhed, seeking the touch, the pulse of heat, the pressure. "Yes...god, yes. I like it."

"What is it you like, Lola? Say it for me. Let me hear you. Whisper it to me."

He bent closer, twisted his head, and now my lips were brushing against his ear. He touched me again, pressing a single fingertip to my clitoris, giving me a bolt of intense sensation that left me breathless and aching. And then, swiftly, abruptly, he slid that finger through my opening and penetrated me with it, slid through my slickness—god, I was wet, hot, pulsing...and his finger filled me, making me feel tight. Then out again, and now as he smeared my own essence over my clitoris, all the sensations were heightened.

And god, fuck, I was no virgin, not by a long shot, but I didn't remember anything feeling this good. Nothing had ever felt like this. No one had ever touched me like this. Made me feel this so strongly. God, it was good. It was addictive. It felt like an illicit drug high, like I was spiraling out of the universe and into some alternate dimension where all that existed was—*pleasure*. And that word wasn't enough, didn't encapsulate even partially how good this felt. His finger, sliding back into my channel and gathering my essence and smearing it against my clit, and then circling a light even touch against my clit—

"Tell me what I'm doing to you, Lola. Say it."

He drew his touch away, and this time I moaned in protest and my hips flexed, driving my core forward, seeking the touch, needing it. I needed it. *Needed.* It had been so long and it felt so good, better than anything I'd ever felt, and I wanted more, I was aching, drowning in the ache, years and years of built up, pent-up, denied sexual frustration long buried now boiling up and all focused on my hard, throbbing clitóris, on his touch, and he kept *stopping* because he wanted me to say—

What? I didn't even know what he wanted.

"What am I supposed to say, Thresh? Tell me what to say and I'll say it. Just—god, please don't stop touching me again."

I felt his grin, triumphant and hungry. He nipped my earlobe, and then I felt his voice. So powerful, so strong, so deep, so smooth and hot and wild. "You want me to tell you what I want to hear?"

"Yes, Thresh. Please."

"Beg me a little more."

Fuck him and his games. "*Please*, Thresh. Please. Tell me what to say."

He put his finger back where I needed it: against my clit. But he didn't move it, just…touched. And it wasn't enough. Nowhere near enough. "You know what I'm doing to you, Lola? I'm touching your pussy. I'm fingering your clit." He slid his finger inside me, gathered wetness and smeared it over me, circled, and I gasped in equal parts relief and renewed need. "That's what I'm doing. And that's what I want you to say. Tell me what I'm doing to you, Lola."

"You're—oh god…" He stopped, and I whimpered. "Fuck, don't stop, please!"

"Then stop thinking and start talking dirty to me."

"You're touching my pussy." He circled faster then, a reward for me saying a dirty word, apparently. "You're gonna—you're gonna make me come."

Faster and faster then, and all thoughts flew out of my head; all capacity for speech left me. "That's right, Lola. I'm gonna finger your tight wet pussy until you come all over my hand."

Oh god, oh god, oh god, why was that so fucking hot, hearing him talk like that? Why did it make my pussy throb even harder, even hotter? Why did it make his swift light circling touch all the more delicious?

"And when you come, you're gonna scream my name."

"Thresh..." I panted.

So much. So fucking much. My hips were driving, thrusting, my clitoris pulsing under his finger, and my tits ached and felt heavy and my nipples were hard and I couldn't breathe and I was going to—oh, oh....*ohhhh*—

"Louder, Lola. Let go."

"More...god—more—don't stop, Thresh...please don't stop, now. It feels so good." I couldn't stop the words, now. They were flowing like a river. "I love the way you touch my pussy. Oh—oh god, I want—I want—"

"What, baby? Tell me what you want. Ask me for anything, and I'll give it to you."

I couldn't help arching my back to thrust out my tits. "More. I need...more. I need you to touch me here." I reached up, wrapped my hand around his head, feeling the soft smooth skin of his shaved scalp and the soft yet prickly stripe of his mohawk.

"Say it, and I'll do it." His finger was flying in mad circles and then pausing to slide into my tight wet channel and gathering dew and smearing it against my clit and circling again, and each time he stopped even for a second I panted and whimpered, but when he started up again it only felt all the more intense, better, deeper, and the building climax was a force inside me waiting to be unleashed, so much pressure, so much heat it was unbearable. "Say what you want, Lola, and I'll give it to you."

I tugged down the strap of my tank top, heart pounding, palpitating uncontrollably, and then the other strap. I hesitated, because I was crossing a line, somehow, baring myself for him. Touching me under my clothes was one thing, but letting him *see* me? I was scared even through the need, even though I needed to feel his touch on my bare flesh so insanely much, even though my nipples ached and throbbed and begged to be included, to be touched, to be licked and sucked and whatever other wonders Thresh might work on me…

To both say what I wanted in so many words, *and* to expose myself to him? Even in the heat of the moment, it was almost too much to ask.

What I'd been through had ruined me. I could admit that, deep down in my soul, in that moment, I could finally admit that what Jeremy had done to me had ruined me.

But maybe Thresh could fix it.

I wanted to be fixed.

I wanted to *feel* again.

I wanted to enjoy…my *self* again. My body. Sensations. Emotions. I'd shut them all down for so long, and Thresh just yanked them all out of me unbidden, and he did it so easily.

"You're thinking, Doc." His voice ripped through my internal war. "Stop thinking. Just feel."

I slid aside one bra strap, and then paused to take a fortifying breath…then pushed away the other. "I want your mouth on my breasts, Thresh."

"Thank *fuck*," he breathed. He withdrew his hand from between my thighs, and I whimpered in protest. "Don't worry, baby, I'm not stopping."

"I need it, Thresh."

"Need what?" he asked as his hands reached into my top, be-tween bra and flesh, and tugged down one cup and then the other, letting my tits fall free with an ample bounce, my dark flesh mound-ing over the top of the bra, nipples puckered and hard and standing tall and dark against the lighter brown of my palm-sized areolae.

"I need to come. I need to come so bad."

"You will, honey." He murmured this in my ear, and then pulled back and ducked to meet my gaze. It was difficult to hold those eyes of his, palest blue and seeing so much, too much, not just my body but my soul, my heart, my fears, my insecurity, the knowledge of my flaws. "I'll make you come so hard you'll see stars. I'll make you come so hard you'll be left crying from it. I promise you."

"I hate crying."

"You won't be able to help it, by the time I'm done with you."

"Stop talking and do it, then." God, that sounded bossy, rude.

But Thresh only grinned. "Mmm. Tell me what to do, Lola. Tell me what you want. Make me give it to you." Now that my breasts were bared, he returned his hand to the waistband of my pants. Dug his fingers under the elastic, but then stopped. "Let's move these out of the way, shall we?"

He started tugging them down, but I caught his wrist. "No, Thresh. Not yet. That's too much. Okay? Please? This is as much as I can take right now. Any more and I'm liable to panic."

He searched my eyes, and seemed to see the truth there. "Whatever you need, Lola."

"Just…touch my tits. You seem to like them, and I need to—" I had to cut myself off to take a breath as he simultaneously slid his fingers under my panties and between my thighs and into my pussy, and lowered his mouth to my left breast, tongue flicking against my nipple, lapping flat against my areola.

"You need to what? Say it, baby."

I couldn't. It was too much. Making me too vulnerable. I shook my head, arched my spine to press my breast into his mouth, and let my knees fall apart to grant him better access to my core. God, who was this, doing this? In a car, on the side of the road, with a man I just met. A killer. A warrior. A mammoth, insanely powerful, self-admitted player.

But fuck, a sexy one. A goddamned gorgeous human being. A primal beautiful man, and one who seemed to know *exactly* how to touch me. How to draw me out of myself, how to draw me past my fears and insecurities.

"I need—"

He worked his finger against my clit hard and fast now, and

covered my nipple with his mouth, and then—oh, oh, ohhhhh, started suckling the hard, sensitive nipple. Jesus, oh Jesus—

"Thresh, oh my god Thresh—"

"Does that feel good?" he asked, then leaned across me to suck
my other nipple into his mouth and flick it with his tongue in light
fluttering flickers that had me gasping staccato breaths.

"So good…so fucking good."

"Finish what you were going to say, Lola."

"Just let me come, Thresh. No more talking." I was already ex-
posing my body; no way I could expose my vulnerability to him, too.
It was too much. Too much. He was too much. This was too much.

He circled my clit a few more times, and now my hips were rolling against his touch, and I was aching all over—and then he slid that
finger inside me, curled it and touched me somewhere deep and high
inside and I just—shit, I just lost it completely, sank back against the
chair, fumbled with one hand for the lever on the side of the bucket
seat and lowered the back until I was lying down, crying out loud,
wordless breathless whimpers as he rubbed that magic spot inside
me. And then he withdrew that finger, tapped it against my clit,
once, twice, quick sharp taps, and I—already breathless—couldn't
even manage a whimper. But oh, he wasn't done, no ma'am. He slid
his finger back inside me, but this time it was…*more*. Stretching me
wider; god, two fingers? Holy shit. Holy shit. Oh god. Two fingers,
sliding in and out of my channel, and each time he worked those
thick strong fingers into me, he bumped my clit with his fingers and
then it happened… Lightning. Fireworks. Heat blasting through me,
making me twitch, making me jerk and jolt and writhe.

And *scream*.

God, I was screaming.

He was licking my nipples and suckling them and biting them,
and then gently and reverently kissing my areolae and the upper
slopes and the undersides…

He was…god, everything inside me curled up and tightened
and tensed.

He was making love to my breasts with his mouth.

And it was enough to make my eyes prick. To make my gut churn. To make my heart palpitate and my chest tighten.

Because with his hands, his mouth, his eyes raking over me and meeting my eyes as he passed from one breast to another—he made me feel beautiful.

Like a desirable *woman*.

I was coming apart and he was suckling my left nipple into his mouth—the more sensitive one—and then he added a *third* finger to the sliding driving penetrating rhythm, and my hips were driving, and I was fighting to breathe, trying to scream, and holding at bay the tears he'd promise I'd shed.

Tears that meant so much.

Joy, that I wasn't broken.

Relief, because three years worth of repressed sexual frustration were finally coming to an end, and he was about to break it open, burst it apart, shred it all to pieces.

And tears of pure, unadulterated ecstasy, because nothing in my life had ever felt this good. Nothing, not ever.

My eyes were squeezed shut, my hips were writhing and rolling and pistoning uncontrollably, unashamedly riding his fingers.

When it began to pass through me and wash over me, I clenched my jaw tight and my eyes tighter and screamed past my teeth and my body went taut as a piano wire, feet pressed against the floor boards and shoulders and neck against the seat back, the rest of my body arched up and suspended, hips flexing involuntarily as everything inside of me burst open, detonated.

But he wouldn't let me just ride it out. Oh no. He had to *talk*. "Open your eyes, Lola."

My eyes flicked open. And god, his eyes were so fucking blue, so fierce and piercing.

"Don't you fucking dare take your eyes off me." He kept fingering me as the orgasm continued to expand, but now his attention was solely on me. "Look at me, Lola."

"I'm—oh god, oh god, oh *god!*" The last *god* was sobbed, because I couldn't help it anymore. It felt so good, so perfect, as if the universe was aligning to make me feel this bliss for the first time in my life. "I'm looking at you—oh, oh, *ohhhhhh* fuck—I'm looking at you, Thresh."

He suckled my nipple. "You—"

Flicked the other with tongue-tip. "Are—"

He rubbed that spot inside me with his fingers and ground his thumb against my clit, and I was wracked and gasping and couldn't look away from his mesmerizing pale ice blue gaze. "So—"

And then, damn him, damn him, damn him…he kissed me. Once, a soft, brief, searing kiss, tongue feathering against mine, scouring my lips and my teeth and my tongue, a single kiss that rocked me to the bottom of my ruined heart.

"—Beautiful," he said, pulling away enough to whisper the word against my lips.

And that was it.

I couldn't hold out anymore.

The climax was blasting through me in endless waves of ecstasy, yanking screams out of me and pushing sobs out of me and making me thrash and writhe on his fingers, and then when he spoke that phrase, each word punctuated with a touch meant to drive me wilder and wilder, I lost it.

Everything.

Every last vestige of my hold on the sobs.

I came, and I did it sobbing.

And his gaze wouldn't release me, wouldn't let me look away.

Because, goddammit, he *meant* it.

And that was what wrecked me. More than the orgasm, even though it was the most intense, brutally powerful, erotic, thrilling, beautiful, perfect sensation I'd ever experienced, those four words he spoke, with his open blue gaze luminous with the truth of his statement…that was too much.

Because it was exactly what I'd almost said.

Touch my breasts, I'd said.

You seem to like them, I said.

—*And I need to feel beautiful*—that's what I'd almost said.

I came, and I came, and I came. It seemed like it would never end, the waves of climax. He milked every wave out of me, kissing my breasts all over throughout it.

And when I finally stopped orgasming, he withdrew his hand from my core and cupped my breast in his huge palm, rolling the heavy weight in his palm, thumbing the nipple—which made me gasp and sob and flinch all over again—and then weighed the other breast in his hand. He was playing with my breasts for himself, I realized. Not for me, not to make me feel good, but for his own enjoyment.

I couldn't breathe, and I was still sobbing.

Which he, somewhat belatedly, realized.

"Lola?"

"You told me I'd cry," I said.

Trying to angle away, trying to shrug my bra straps back up and my shirt back on and trying to tuck my breasts back into the cups and not look at him and not think about anything and not feel anything, because it was all bashing down on me, all the feelings I'd been pushing away for so long, plus the orgasm and what he'd said and how it had made me feel and the *orgasm*, Jesus the orgasm, still quavering inside me, making me shake and shiver and shudder as after quakes struck one after another.

"Well, here I am, crying." I was trying to do everything at once, and managed none of it.

Except the crying.

"Well shit, Lola, I didn't mean like this."

7

ENDURE THE ACHE

SHITSHITSHITSHIT.

When I said I'd make her cry, I meant the kind of crying a girl does when an orgasm is just so powerful she doesn't know how else to express it.

Not these shuddering, wracking sobs that shook her whole body.

These weren't good tears.

These were the tears of someone who'd had something so seriously hardcore done to her in the past that it had fucked her up. Something serious enough to make her shut down and refuse any kind of sexuality whatsoever. Something that left her unable to even talk dirty.

She wouldn't look at me.

Her breasts were still hanging out of her shirt—and Jesus fuck and holy shit, those tits were pure perfection. More perfect than I'd even fantasized about. Huge, juicy, softer than anything I'd ever felt, quivering with every movement she made. God, I couldn't get enough of them.

But she was having a full-on panic attack, made worse by the fact that she was bare from the waist up and had just had her first orgasm in three years, and couldn't seem to make her hands work because she was sobbing and trying to get away from me, or herself, or just everything.

"Lola."

She shook her head, and god, god, those tits bounced and shimmied, and my already painfully hard, diamond-hard cock hardened even more.

No time for that, though.

I touched her jaw with my index finger, and tilted her face to me. "Look at me, Lola. Please. Just…look at me."

She twisted her head, peering at me through partially closed, tear-wet eyelids. Heaving, fighting sobs, teeth clenched, hands shaking. "Don't, just—don't."

"Look at me, Lola."

"I AM!" she shouted.

I held her gaze, steady and even and calm. "Breathe."

She shook her head again. "I—I can't. I can't." She began to shudder and convulsing sobs wracked her body. "I can't catch my breath—" Beneath the hurt or whatever it was I'd caused, was the panic attack fear of not being able to breathe.

I leaned close to her, slowly, cupped the back of her neck, pulled her face to mine. "Then take my breath." And I kissed her. Softly, gently, slowly.

I'd never kissed anyone the way I kissed Lola Reed in that moment. With every emotion inside me, with everything I had, I kissed her.

She sank into it after a moment of surprise, and her sobs slowed, and she slowly began to lose herself in the kiss, and god, I could lose myself too, because her lips were so fucking soft, so wet and warm and pliable and she kissed me desperately, beyond passion, beyond desperation, as if kissing me could fix whatever was wrong with her.

I didn't let myself get lost, though.

Usually when I kissed a girl and she started to get into it, that's when I'd make my move, slide her straps off so I could get to her tits. But in that moment, that kiss with Lola, I did the opposite.

I tugged one bra strap into place, and then the other. Tucked one breast into the lacy red cup of the bra, and then the other. Pulled up the straps of her tank, and then she was covered.

Sad, but necessary.

I broke the kiss, and she rested her forehead against mine and sucked in long, deep breaths, held them for three or four seconds each, and then let them out slowly. Her fingers knotted in my shirt over my chest as she fought to calm herself. Then, after a minute or so of breathing, she backed away, rubbed my chest, then slid her hands around to the back of my neck and the back of my head, and her eyes met mine, finally, still tear-hazed, but calmer and clearer.

"Thank you," she whispered.

I frowned. "For what?"

She huffed a disbelieving laugh, shaking her head. "I don't know. I don't know, Thresh. Everything? For making me come? For telling me you think I'm—" she stopped, shook her head, ducking. "For telling me you think I'm—"

She couldn't even say it?

"Beautiful, Lola. That's the word you're looking for." I touched her chin, lifted her face to mine. "More than beautiful. You're sexy. You're gorgeous."

"Stop, Thresh."

"Incredible. Delicious. Fine as hell. Foxy as fuck."

She chuckled at that last one. "Oh my god. Stop!"

I held her jaw so she couldn't look away. "Not stopping, Doc, so you'd best pay attention." I leaned in, teased a kiss. "You're the most beautiful woman I've ever met, Lola."

She jerked out of my grip, turning away. "Almost had me until that one, Thresh."

"Look me in the eyes and tell me I'm bullshitting, Lola."

She hesitantly turned back to look at me, and I gave her as much honesty in my eyes as I could muster. I meant what I said. She really was the most alluring, beautiful, sexy woman I'd ever met. She just didn't believe it.

"I've met Hollywood A-list actresses, models, porn stars, pop stars." I held up a hand to forestall the protest I saw forming. "And yeah, those chicks were all pretty gorgeous. But they all had one fault."

She rolled her eyes at me. "Let me guess: they weren't me." She turned away again. "Nice try, Thresh."

"That's not what I was gonna say, as a matter of fact."

This got her curiosity. "Oh? Then what? What could I possibly have that models and porn stars don't?"

"None of them turned me on. They didn't make me crazy." I palmed her cheek. "You...Lola, you make me crazy. You make me think, and say, and do things that are utterly unlike me. You make me so fucking horny it hurts, and that was *before* I got to see your tits. I nearly creamed my pants just touching you. I'm still so fucking hard I'll have blue balls for a week."

"Thresh—" Her voice was small, hesitant.

"And Doc, let me reassure you, that is not normal for me. At all."

Her gaze flicked down from my eyes to my crotch, which was bulging to comical proportions. I had to adjust in the worst way, but I didn't dare. If I so much as brushed my cock, I'd either spurt all over myself—which I hadn't done since I was fucking twelve—or I'd be begging her to finish me off.

And she was in no way ready for that.

But once her eyes fixed on my groin, she couldn't seem to look away. "Jesus, Thresh." Her hand reached tentatively toward me. "That looks...uncomfortable."

"You have no idea." I snagged her wrist. "But I'll be fine. And I didn't say that just to get you to do anything about it. You're not ready for that. I just want you to understand how crazy you make me. You haven't even touched me, and I'm about to explode. That's how much you turn me on, just by fucking *existing*, Lola."

This got her attention. "Thresh..."

"Someone fucked you over. Made you feel...I'm not sure exactly what. Ugly? Maybe they size-shamed you? I don't know. Something horrible. And if I could get my hands on him—"

She jerked her hand out of my grip. "Don't tell me what I'm not ready for, Thresh." Her gaze was fierce, determined.

"I'm not trying to, I just—you—" I lost track of what I was saying, because she had her palm cupped over my bulge.

"You're right," she said. "Someone did something really horrible to me, and it fucked me up."

"And I don't want to push you into anything you're not ready for."

She laughed. "If that was true, then I wouldn't have just had the most incredible orgasm of my entire life. You do want to push me."

"But not—"

She cut me off. "And I want you to, if I'm gonna be honest about this. You make me…feel things. You make me feel things I thought I'd never be able to feel again." Her gaze went to mine, her bright brown eyes unwavering, rife with a flurry of emotions too numerous for me to sort out. "That's scary, especially because I know you won't be sticking around. But I like the way you make me feel. And I want more of it. Whatever I can get out of you, I want it."

"Lola—" I started, but she had other ideas.

She put her finger over my lips. "Shut up. I have no idea what I'm doing right now, but I'm going to do it, and you're going to let me." She kept her finger over my lips to keep me quiet. "Just…sit there. Don't move. Don't talk. Just…let me do whatever it is I'm going to do, and—hopefully—you'll enjoy it."

"Lola, wait." She lifted an eyebrow in question. "Don't do anything for…for me. I don't need anything. I didn't make you come expecting anything."

She smiled at me, and I saw that determination in her expression, as well as fear and nerves…and desire. "Thresh?"

"Yeah, Doc?"

"Shut up." She brushed both sets of straps off her shoulders, tugged the cups down to set her tits free, and then did a sultry little shimmy that set them bouncing and swaying. "The fact that you covered me while I was having a panic attack, and the fact that you were able to help me breathe again, just by kissing me—that does something to me. Makes me crazy. And you make me want things. Want more. I want more. Of you. Of this. Of…whatever this is we've got going on. And I like the way you look at me, the way you make me feel when you look at me. I like the way you make me feel when you touch me. That orgasm, god, Thresh. That was the most incredible thing I've ever felt. Honestly, it was."

"And now you want to touch me?"

She still had her hand on my bulge. Not doing anything, just holding, cupping, feeling. And I know she felt me twitch, and then harden even more when she bared her huge gorgeous tits for me. God, I was so hard it was all-consuming. Every drop of blood in my body was rushing to my cock, and I couldn't think, couldn't feel anything but the need for relief, and she was just cupping over my zipper, tits hanging out lush and luscious and tasty-looking, huge perfect globes of dusky flesh with wide areolae a few shades darker than her tits, and the tight hard darker-yet nipples…fuck, I was ready to pop, but I couldn't, because I was all twisted in my pants, folded and bent and unable to harden to my full length, no matter how hard I got, and fuck did that hurt. And those tits…Jesus, they just made it worse, by which I mean so much better—and fuck I wanted her to touch me. I needed it. I needed it *so* bad.

But if she'd been messed up by a guy so bad she wouldn't even touch herself—for *three years*? She was finally getting through all that shit, and I was honored that she was letting me help her past it, and I wasn't about to mess it up for her by pushing her too fast.

So I'd do what she instructed: just sit here and endure the ache, and let her do what she wanted.

"Yes, Thresh. I want to touch you. But I'm not letting myself think about it, because if I do, I'll panic, or freeze, or I don't know what. And I do want this, but I just—" She shook her head. "See? I'm overthinking. Just stop talking, okay? Please? Just sit there and be huge and beautiful and let me…let me do what I want without interference."

I leaned my seat back enough that I could recline, hooked my hand behind my head. "I'm all yours, Lola. Not a word, and I won't move a muscle."

Her eyes went hot, and dark, and fiery. "Perfect."

8

MORE THAN A BLOW JOB

PART OF ME COULDN'T BELIEVE I WAS DOING THIS.

Part of me was screaming to get a move on because, holy hell, I might never get my hands on a man like this ever again.

All of me was nervous and excited and scared all at once.

I felt him under my hand. HUGE doesn't begin to cover the scope of what I felt straining beneath that dark-wash denim. He had the seat back so he was partially reclining, his right hand under his head, trying to look casual. But I saw through it. He wanted to pounce. He was in pain, actual physical pain. And he *wanted* me; he wanted *me*.

He thought I was beautiful.

Sexy.

He'd made me come so hard I did indeed see stars. So hard I cried. For the first time in three years, I had an orgasm. That was no small feat.

And...for the first time in three years, I felt desire. I felt the yawning aching emptiness of need. I felt the yearning hunger, the excited thrill.

I wanted him.

I didn't care about anything but this moment. I refused to let my fears hijack this for me. We were utterly alone, on the side of a desolate highway, far, far from anyone or anything. It was safe. *He* was safe.

This wasn't then.

Thresh wasn't…*him.*

To shake that train of thought away, I refocused on Thresh. With his arm behind his head, the improbable size of his bicep was highlighted, the girth, the round hard-veined scope of it, the curve of his shoulder and the angle of his trapezius…god. He was so well developed. Perfectly sculpted.

Having grown up being tutored in the art of weightlifting by my father, watching him sculpt his own body, I'd come to deeply appreciate the beauty of a well-developed male physique. And Thresh? He was the most beautiful man I'd ever seen. Not too much, not pro body builder over-done, just…hugely muscled, sculpted, broad, hard. But I'd also watched him move, seen him strike faster than a serpent, seen him move on silent feet, as graceful and predatory as a jaguar stalking a deer.

I needed to see more of him; I caught his eyes, pushed up at the hem of his black polo shirt. He quirked an eyebrow at me, shrugged the sling off, and then ripped the shirt off in one lithe movement, grabbing the back of the collar and jerking it off, tugging it carefully past his cast—and…holy Jesus, the way his muscles shifted under his tan skin when he did that? I shuddered, my core—my *pussy*—clenching and quavering. God, his body. So fucking glorious.

And all those scars? I wanted to lick each one, kiss each one, and discover the story behind each one. He'd been shot so many times, stabbed, cut, and burned, along with other scars whose causes were less obvious.

I carved my hands over his body, running them up the hard planes and ridges of his grooved abdomen, cupping his sides, and then skating up his pecs, circling the flat disks of his nipples, moving across his shoulders. Just touching him. Watching his face as I did so, watching his expression shift, eyes narrow, jaw tighten.

Oh, and that bulge. No way I'd forgotten about that.

I was just…working up the courage to do something about it.

Once upon a time, I'd been…voracious. Courageous. Fearless.

And then—

NOPENOPENOPE.

Shut that shit down, ASAP.

I pushed away those whirling thoughts, and cursed again my inability to shut down my thoughts like guys seemed to be able to. I wanted to just shut them down and enjoy Thresh's body, but I couldn't. I couldn't forget, couldn't totally block it all out.

All I could do was push through it.

Who had I once been? I let myself feel it, remember it.

I'd been young, sheltered, and horny. When I finally got out on my own, I'd gone a little wild, but I'd always preserved my sexuality, kept it under wraps, kept it private. Drink, party, do stupid shit with my friends, sure. Get a little wasted at a kegger and maybe dance on a table, or flash some frat boys? Sure. What's the harm in that? Typical college girl shenanigans. But I'd felt it, though, the desire, the hunger, the raging hormones. The NEED. So much of it, so fierce, so hot, so primal and wild. But I'd kept it back, kept it private, kept it shut down. Tamped and bridled.

Until I met—

NOPE. Still couldn't go there.

Back to Thresh. Touch him. Feel him. He was real. He was strong, and he was safe. He'd kept me safe. I knew he'd never do anything to hurt me. The opposite was true: he'd do anything to keep me safe. I felt that truth in my bones.

Try it again.

I'd been young, wild, and horny.

I met someone I wanted so much I'd let my guard down, let him in, let him bring all that up and out of me, and I'd discovered an insatiable animal waiting inside me, lurking deep down—and when it finally got free? I was voracious. Unstoppable. Nothing could satisfy me. There was never enough. He couldn't keep up, truth be told.

Then I'd been betrayed and had lost it all. Buried it all back down so deep I'd been sure it would never surface again.

That was as close as I could get and stay in control of my emotions.

Thresh was watching me, and seemed to know I was working through things, and was patiently allowing me to do what I needed.

Damn the man, and how he always seemed to know exactly what I needed.

Because right now? Inexplicably, something about Thresh was bringing that insatiable, voracious, hormone-saturated wild animal out of me again. I was remembering her, finding her again.

And man, oh man...did she feel *good*. Powerful. Primal. Possessive. Full of need and hunger and desire and all those emotions I'd thought I'd lost...I was getting them back, and in spades... Thresh was giving them to me.

I ran my hands over his body, letting myself roam the broad expanse of his rugged male beauty. I traced each muscle, each scar. The bullet holes low on his right side, two of them side by side; those had to have barely missed vitals. A six-inch-long knife-slice wound going from left nipple diagonally down to his ribs on the right side, a thick ropy knot of scarred flesh. I was a sucker for a six-pack, and good goddamn, did Thresh have that. They weren't the kind of razor-sharp abs you see on the lean, rangy sort of dudes; Thresh's six-pack was the huge, heavy slabs of iron-hard muscle that was more like armor plating than human flesh.

God, I couldn't help myself, then. I leaned over him, and pressed my lips to his chest. Right in the center, between his pecs. My palms scoured his abs, roamed down closer to the waist of his jeans. I felt his abs tighten, and I knew he wanted more, wanted me to unbutton him, unzip him, take him out. And god, I wanted that.

I let that feeling percolate:

Desire.

I tried to remember how much I'd loved my sexuality, once it had been unleashed; I wanted that part of myself back.

Once I'd had a taste of Thresh's flesh, I needed more. I kissed across his chest, climbing closer to lave my mouth up his throat, under his chin, across his jaw, letting my hands roam further and further south along his abs, around his waist, back to his abs, up his chest, and back to his abs. God, they were so hard, so thick, so perfect.

Finally, I felt ready.

I let myself look at the bulge.

It was mountainous. Straining.

I cupped my hand over it again, feeling the straining power behind the denim. Rubbed a little, just to test it out, and felt Thresh shift under me.

I glanced up at him; his eyes were heavy-lidded, his jaw tensed, his breath coming in deep drafting gusts, his fist clenched behind his head.

A moment, then, with my eyes locked on his as I finally caught hold of the button snap of his jeans. Popped it open. He sucked in a breath, held it, and let it out slowly, watching me closely.

I had to break away from his gaze, then, because it was so intense, so intent. And also, because I desperately wanted to see what I was unleashing.

I pinched the tab of his zipper between finger and thumb and drew it down. Black stretchy cotton/rayon blend bulged out between the edges of the zipper, a thick fat rod bending against the fabric. Oh Jesus. His penis was curled sideways, pressing against the elastic waistband, and now that the jeans were opened, it was starting to straighten, the outline clearly visible. In a few seconds it would be peeking up over the top of his underwear, regardless of what I did next.

Which was to tease myself, and him.

I cupped the ridge, followed the curve, stroked up and down the curled length of him a few times, which made him harden, made the unfurling monster straighten all the faster.

I glanced up at him, biting my lower lip, then tugged at his jeans with both hands. He lifted his ass up, and I tugged the jeans down past his butt, to his knees. By the time I returned my attention upward, a bit of pink was showing over the top of his tight black boxer briefs.

No more wasting time. I wanted to feel flesh in my hand.

I wanted to feel *Thresh* in my hand.

I curled my fingers in the waistband of his underwear, an inch on either side of his now straight and still-burgeoning erection, glanced up at him, and then pulled down. He lifted up, let me pull the underwear away and down past his erection, past his knees.

And then, oh....fuckfuckfuck*fuck*—he was bared for me.

And I went literally faint-headed at the sight of him.

Fucking twelve inches long and nearly as thick as my wrist, or I was a size-zero white girl.

"Jesus Christ, Thresh." I glanced up at him, dizzy, shocked, and now...feeling decidedly ravenous.

He smirked. "No part of me is small, babe."

"No shit."

It was wreathed at the base by a neat crown of blond hair trimmed tight against his skin. Balls the size of plums, heavy. And the cock itself—oh god. I spent a few moments just staring at it. Straight as an arrow, standing up against his belly, a little paler than the rest of his sun-golden skin. Fat, plump, broad head, circumcised. Those veins, standing out dark against his pale skin.

I glanced up at him again, nervous all over again. It was just... *so—much—cock*. I wasn't sure what to do with it all.

"I'm not moving a muscle, Lola," he said, his voice tight with restraint. "I promised. This is all you. Say the word, and I'll be dressed and we can go on our way."

"No!" I protested. "I just...it's been a long time, and..." I looked down at his enormous, straining erection, "—you know what? Fuck it."

I reached over, wrapped my hand around his cock; he sucked in a breath, and I felt his abs tense again. "Okay?" I asked, darting a glance up at him.

"Lola. You've got your hand on my cock, and you're asking if I'm okay?"

"Yeah, I'm asking."

"I'm better than okay."

"You seem tense, is all." I added my other hand, and there was still more of him peeking out above my fist and below.

"I've had a hard-on for you since the moment I walked into that hospital, Doc." His voice was a deep bass rumble, thick with need and lust. "And I haven't exactly had time to do anything about it, if you know what I mean."

I slid both fists up, and then back down, slowly, gingerly, hesitantly, and dear sweet heaven, he felt so good in my hands. So good. Back, before…I used to love this, the feel of a cock in my hands. The power of it, as any woman will tell you, is knowing you can make him lose control, make him feel so good just with your hands, or your mouth—and I loved using both. Yeah, there was that. But I also just…I loved the *cock* itself. It was a beautiful organ, when erect. Soft, yet hard. Warm, and smooth. Erotica books liked the phrase "silk on steel", which was cliché and cheesy and stupid, but so apt.

I got accused of teasing more than once simply because I would take my time, just playing, toying, feeling, enjoying. Playing with his cock just for my own enjoyment. Which, apparently, wasn't cool. I wasn't in a rush to get the guy I was with to orgasm, I just liked feeling him in my hands, touching him, stroking him. And yeah, I'd taste him too. Kisses, and licks, and maybe some sucking, but again, that was usually not for him, but for me.

And that's what I found myself doing with Thresh, just touching him, toying with him. Stroking his length with one hand, then the other, then both. Not really pumping or jerking or caressing with any rhythm, just…touching. Memorizing the feel of his monster cock in my hands, the veins rubbing against my palm, the head squeezed in my fist, his huge balls in my hands, toying with them ever so gently, carefully.

I lost track of time, lost myself in the sheer pleasure of just feeling this again, of finding enjoyment in the physical. I'd lived in my head for so long, lived just for work, keeping everything else at bay that now, reveling in physical sensation, and finding pleasure in something I'd lost…

I didn't ever want it to stop.

"Fuck, Lola. You're making me crazy." He growled this, his voice rough, low, taut.

I looked up at him, and he was visibly tensed, straining. Jaw clenched, gripping the back of his neck with his good hand, staring at me. Every line in his body was hardened, tensed, tautened.

"I'm sorry, Thresh, I just—I don't mean to tease you."

"Don't apologize," he growled. "I told you this was about you. You want to just touch me and nothing else, then I'll sit here and let you. I won't always be this passive or accommodating, just so you're aware, but for right now? This is only for you. Whatever you want. I know you're not teasing me on purpose."

"I'm not, I swear—I'm just…reacquainting myself with my own desires, I guess you could say."

"Reacquaint away, then. But if you keep doing that, eventually I'm going to blow my load—you know that, right?" He groaned quietly as I stroked his length from tip to root slowly, squeezing and twisting my fist on the way down. "Fuck, Lola. I really do love watching you touch me, feeling your hands on me. I'm counting sheep like crazy over here."

"Counting sheep?" I paused and glanced at him, confused.

"To hold back."

I frowned. "I thought that was for falling asleep?"

He shrugged. "Never did shit to help me fall asleep, but it does wonders for keeping me from coming too soon."

"So you're actively holding back right now?" I asked.

I glided my fist up to the head of his cock, squeezed, twisted, and rubbed my thumb across the top. Stroked down again, pumped my fist at the base, then took his balls in my other hand, cupped them, massaged them. He groaned, and then, when I caressed his length in a slow rhythm, began to flex his hips, the only movement he'd allowed himself, thus far.

"It comes and goes. I can hold it back, then it starts rising up again and I push it back, and then you do—holy shit, *that*—you do something like that…and I—oh fuck—fuuuuuuuuck, Lola, that feels *so* good."

His eyes closed and his head tipped back, but he quickly wrenched his eyes open and watched as I began to stroke him more rhythmically. Slow, long, leisurely trips of my fist up his length, toying in soft squeezes and caresses around the head, then back down to the root, where I would twist, stroke back up. I added my other hand, stroked him hand over hand, faster and faster until he couldn't help the way his hips flexed into my touch.

God, he was so fucking gorgeous. His abs tensed and hardened as he flexed into my fists, and his jaw clenched and loosened, and god, his cock, that beautiful perfect organ, it throbbed in my hands. I knew I'd been playing with his cock for a long time at that point, and I knew he had to be dying for the orgasm. I knew I had to give it to him—I *wanted* to bring him his release.

Because I remembered how much I'd loved that, too, once upon a time. Watching the guy lose control, go animal, pumping, going wild, shouting, grunting, cursing, sweating, all just because I was touching him. A big, strong guy, and he was a slave to my two little hands, and my mouth.

I wanted to feel Thresh lose it. Watch him come apart. Know I could level a giant like him, know I had that power, still. Know that my hands could give him pleasure, that my lips and my tongue could make him crazy.

Could I do that to him? Right now? Did I dare?

Fuck yes, I dared.

Something about Thresh made me feel brave. Made me feel in charge. Made me want to put my fears out on the street, face them and triumph over them. Not let the past get in the way of my present or my future. Yes, I really liked Thresh. I was really attracted to him, both physically and for who he was as a person. But while that was true, I had no illusions that this thing between us was going any-where serious. I knew the score. But he brought things out in me, he elicited strong emotions and desires, things I hadn't felt in a long time and had truly believed were dead and ruined. So I was abso-lutely prepared to let him help me past my issues, especially since he seemed willing to do so without knowing the details.

I just couldn't look too closely, or think too hard about what it was we had or where it was going. I couldn't let myself get attached.

But I could enjoy the hell out of what I had when it was in front of me.

And right now, I had a twelve-inch cock—at *least* twelve inches, if not more—in front of me, and it was hard and beautiful and just begging for more than my hands.

It was begging for my lips. For my tongue.

I clutched his rigid erection in both hands, leaned across the space between us, pressed a kiss to his chest. Another, lower, tucking my legs under me. Again. And then I was kissing his abs, each ridge and groove, flicking my tongue over and between each delineated muscle. Lower, and lower, closer with every kiss to his cock, to my fists, which were stroking him leisurely, slowly, both of them at once, gliding up and down.

"Lola?" He sounded pained, speaking past grinding teeth.

I was there, guiding his cock against my cheek, across my closed lips, tilting my face to look up at him. "Thresh?"

"You don't—"

"Hush," I said, and squeezed him hard enough that he listened. "You didn't think I'd leave you aching, did you? I just had to work up to this."

"But I don't want you to think—"

I caressed his cock at the base, and nuzzled the upper portion of his erection with my face. "Let's get one thing straight, Thresh. I'm doing what I want. I lost this part of me for a long time, and you've somehow managed to give it back to me. So make no mistake: I'm doing what I want to, for *me*. And what I want right now is for you to stop holding back, and let me make you feel better than you've ever felt in your life. No more holding back. Just let go."

I emphasized my statement by taking him in my mouth, and holy shit, I had to stretch my jaw to cracking to fit him. I couldn't take much, and didn't try. That's not my thing. I enjoyed the feel of him in my mouth, the taste of his flesh, the tang and smoke of his leaking essence on my tongue. I kissed him, lips to the broad springy beauty of his cock-head, as if I was making out with him. Licked up the side, slowly, long fat licks along his length, then turned my head sideways and took his length in my mouth horizontally and slid up to the tip and moved my head back upright to take his head between my lips. Let him slide into my mouth until he pushed against my cheek, widened my jaw enough that I could slide him in and out in quick strokes, tongue fluttering against him.

"I can't—I'm—shit, *shit*, Lola—I ain't gonna last much longer, babe. It's too good. So fucking good, the way you do that."

I gave him another look as I slid my tongue up his length, watched him as I made love to his cock with my mouth. That's what I was doing, the way he'd worshipped my tits, I was doing that to his cock.

And I couldn't help a thought from popping into my head, and then out my mouth. "When we get somewhere private, will you—"

I didn't get the rest out. He interrupted me, his voice feral, like the rumbling of a grizzly bear. "Lola, sweetheart, the moment I've got you somewhere we've got privacy, I'm gonna do so many things to you—god, you have no idea. I'm gonna make you scream so loud they'll hear you in fucking Miami."

"What will you do?" I asked, feeling bolder by the second.

His hand left the back of his head, finally—I'd been wondering how long he'd last. He gripped my braid, a light but firm hold, and didn't apply pressure, just held it as I took him into my mouth and worked back and forth, slowly at first but faster with each stroke of my lips and tongue.

"Oh…fuck. Fuck. I'll—oh god*damn*, Lola—I'm gonna strip you naked and kiss every single perfect inch of your fucking glorious body. I'm gonna start at your hands and then your feet and work my way in to all the best parts, and I'm gonna save your sweet pussy for last. By the time I get there, you'll be begging me to lick your pussy. And I will, baby, I'll lick you until—oh fuck, oh fuck, god, Lola, don't you fucking stop now."

I took him from my mouth and grinned up at him. "No? Don't stop? Like you did, earlier? Got me to the edge, and then chose that particular moment to ambush the bad guys?"

He slammed his head back against the headrest. "Knew I'd pay for that."

I caressed his length again, the upper few inches now wet with my saliva. I gathered a mouthful of spit and, making sure he was watching, let it drop into my palm, and then smeared it onto his head and used both hands to spread it all over him, top to bottom—only there was so much of him that I had to spit into my hand again just to coat his entire massive, lovely length. And when he was fully coated, I wrapped both hands around him at the base, one atop the other, and started pumping his length. No more fucking around, now. No more teasing. No more playing.

He groaned long and loud, then, when I started caressing him faster, with long smooth strokes up and down his unbelievable cock.

"Tell me what else you're going to do to me, Thresh." I lowered my face to his cock, smirking up at him. "Tell me what you're going to do to my pussy."

Ohhhh, I was twisting in desire, just thinking it, just saying it. Dirty talk was never something I'd done, it was new, and it was sexy and erotic and I could have come again right then if I'd let him touch me.

"God, Lola. I'm gonna eat you out, baby. I'm gonna lick you and fuck you with my fingers and make you scream, and I'm gonna do it until you come so hard so many times you'll beg me to stop.

I'm gonna teach you the meaning of multiple orgasms, Lola. And then—"

He halted, then, because I'd taken him into my mouth and was stroking him at the root and bobbing my mouth up and down on his crown, licking the glans each time I went down, sucking as I moved up, and I was giving this to him hard and fast and without mercy.

He throbbed between my lips, and I knew he was close, knew it from the way he gasped, from the way he couldn't quite fully thrust, but was pulsing his hips in taut, tensing movements, from the way he tasted in my mouth, from the helpless grunts he was making.

I paused just long enough to murmur around his cock, "What? What else?"

"I'm gonna come, Lola. I'm gonna come so fucking hard—oh Jesus..."

I asked it again. "What else will you do, Thresh?"

As soon as I heard his voice, I gave him my mouth, gave him the stroke of my fists.

"I'm gonna put my cock inside you."

"Gonna fuck me hard?" I couldn't help asking. And god, did I want that too—in that moment, at least.

"No."

I paused in surprise, shot him a shocked look. "No?"

He wrapped my braid around his fist, but still didn't try to push me onto his cock. He gave me a look so hungry, so fierce, and so intense I had to look away or risk being scorched to cinders from where I sat. "No. I'm gonna fuck you *slow*. So slow it's not gonna be fucking." At this, I couldn't make him wait any longer. I wrapped my lips around him, stroked his length with one fist and cupped his balls with the other, massaging them I caressed his length and sucked and licked his crown. "Oh...*oh*—oh *fuck*, Lola, yes, yes, god yes, please don't stop. I've never begged for anything in my life, but I'm begging now, baby, Lola—*please* don't stop."

I hummed around him: *mmmm-mmm*, meaning no, I wasn't going to stop.

He kept talking; bless the beautiful giant with the perfect cock. "I'm gonna show you how it should feel to be worshipped, Lola, 'cause woman, you are a Polynesian goddess, and you deserve to be worshipped, and that's what I'm gonna do, Lola, that's what I'm— fuck, fuck, I'm right there, I'm so close."

Worshipped?

Polynesian goddess?

It was an effort to not cry.

I wanted that, *so* fucking bad.

I wanted to be worshipped.

I wanted to be shown how that feels. More than I'd ever wanted anything in my life, I wanted *that*. And I wanted it from Thresh.

I felt his fist jerk my braid twice, and I remembered that signal too.

I hummed an affirmation around his cock—*mmmmm-hm-mm*—but that turned into moans of pleasure, because god, yes, it did feel that good to have him lose it, to feel his loss of control, to know I could drive this man past his breaking point and take him into ecstasy, and god, yes, I did love the feel of his cock in my mouth sliding against my tongue and in and out of my fist.

Now…

It was time to taste him.

I kept moaning, because I felt that good, and I knew he loved it when I moaned on him.

And I kept sucking, stroking his enormous length, massaging his balls.

"Oh—*ohhhhhhhhh—fuck*…" he gasped.

Mmmmmmmm….mmmmm…mmmmm, from me, high-pitched, each moan timed with the furious bobbing of my head and the stroke of my fist around his root, my bare tits draped against his thighs.

I was fucking his cock with my mouth.

When I felt him tense, then, I slowed. Switched from fucking his cock to making love to it. Slow, taking him to the back of my throat and then just kissing the tip, like I had before, sucking it and licking it and stroking him with both fists now, from top to bottom, chin to root, sucking—

"*Lola—*"

It's all he said when he came.

Salty, wet, hot, thick warmth splashing on my tongue—god, I loved his taste, that hint of sweetness, the musk. I swallowed it and kept sucking, kept caressing, fondling his cock with both hands, milking his orgasm from him, moaning until he spurted into my mouth again, and I swallowed that, and moaned and fondled and sucked and stroked him through a third spasm, and then I let him fall out of my mouth. I looked up at him. Loose, limp, his hand resting on my back, still panting.

And his cock was still so hard I could climb on and ride him to orgasm—

"Lola, holy shit, Lola." He groaned this, helpless, breathless.

He brought me up to his face by my braid, whispered against my lips. "Lola, that was—fuck, I don't even know how to explain what that was."

"Good?" I breathed.

Would he kiss me after he'd come in my mouth?

"Honey, good isn't the word."

I whispered back, my breath on his lips. "What is the word, then?"

He did kiss me, slowly, deeply. Thoroughly. Plundering my mouth, showing me where his words failed. "Best. Ever."

"Best blowjob ever, huh?" I tried for casual, and failed.

He pulled my face back so I was looking at him. "Lola. That was so much more than a blowjob. For you, and for me." He wiped at my lips with his thumb. "So don't pretend it wasn't."

He was so right, and the fact that he could see and recognize the significance of what I was doing…that sent something hot and sharp twisting through my heart, something so potent it worried me, scared the fuck out of me.

Because now, out of the moment, the heat having abated, I knew

I'd have to tell him what had happened to me.

I wanted more.

I wanted what he'd promised me, that he'd worship me.

Didn't every girl want to be shown what it felt like to be worshipped?

Goddammit, but I wanted that so fucking bad. After what had happened to me, what was *done* to me…I needed that. I needed that affirmation.

I just wasn't sure I could get through telling him about it without losing it.

And I also knew I was probably going to have a major freak-out when he tried to get me naked, when we went to have actual sex. Touching him, kissing him, and sucking his gorgeous cock, those were all breakthroughs for sure, but the real emotional landmines were all buried around the act of sex. The intimacy. The trust. And how completely I'd had those ruined for me.

I wasn't sure I could go through with it, no matter how much I needed and wanted it.

At least, not without having a serious panic attack before, possibly during, and definitely afterward.

And Thresh deserved to know, deserved fair warning, if and when we ever got to that point.

He rubbed his thumb across my lips, and his eyes were piercing, knowing. "I'm losing you, ain't I? You're falling into your own head."

I shrugged. "Yeah, sort of."

"Care to share?"

I shook my head, shrugged, but couldn't manage either. "Just… there's a lot."

"That you haven't said."

"Right."

He nodded. "I get that. But, babe, don't even think on it. We'll cover it when the time comes."

I shook my head. "No, you don't get it—you don't *get* it. I'm going to freak out on you. If we ever get around to—all the things you promised you'd do to me, how you'd fuck me long and slow, that you'd worship me? There's a lot of shit to get through between us and that point, Thresh."

He cupped my face in his palm, tilted me so I had to look at him, and fuck me if the expression on his face didn't wreck me. "Maybe so, Doc. But I'll take it all, every bit of it, if it means I get you at the end. 'Cause baby, you're worth it."

I fell against his chest. "You did not just quote Fifth Harmony at me."

"Maybe I did. So what?" He chuckled. "Don't mean it ain't truth."

Well…shit.

That plan to just enjoy what Thresh was offering in the moment? Shot all to fucking hell.

9

INTO THE EVERGLADES

S HE WAS QUIET THE REST OF THE WAY TO OUR DESTINATION, which turned out to be a trailer park on the edges of somewhere called Plantation Island. It was a tiny oasis of civilization in the middle of the Ten Thousand Islands area of the Everglades, on the far southwestern edge of Florida. Mainly occupied by Everglades tour guides, it was…well, remote wasn't quite the word, as Lola had pointed out earlier. A whole lot of not much—it occupied not even four hundred acres, and had a population of less than two hundred….

Yeah, if you liked your space and privacy, this was where you went.

And this was the *starting* point for getting to her dad?

Yeesh. Hermits are weird, man. I mean, I like my space. I like a few miles between me and the next fella, but I also like to be able to pop into town and grab a Starbucks and a burger, or pop a squat in a dive bar and have a glass of bourbon with Duke, check out the selection of ladies. But out here? There wasn't anything.

And I hated it. *Hated*.

Because it reminded me of how I grew up. Home for me had been a ramshackle, dilapidated single-wide in the middle of literal nowhere. Just plopped down in a little holler a good twenty miles from fuckin' anything. Only reason we even had running water or electricity was because there happened to be a freight depot not too far from our trailer, so whoever had originally occupied the spot where we lived had somehow convinced the powers that be to run a line and some pipe to the holler. Hell if I know how, or why. I just know it was fuckin' *remote*.

I had a six-mile walk to the nearest bus stop, and another forty minutes one way on the bus to the school, and I considered that a blessing, because it got me out of the fuckin' trailer and away from my old man. It meant being out from under his drunken stare, away from his swinging fist and boot. It meant I got fresh food in the afternoon, from people who seemed to give at least half a shit about me.

I don't mean Ma, when I say that. Ma cared, probably too much. She'd always try to step in between the old man and me, try to get his attention on herself, to spare me the beating, but once I was old enough to figure out the way of things—when I was four or so—I'd make sure he went after me. I couldn't bear to see him take after her. She was a tiny little thing. Frail. Weak. But she was my angel, the only good thing in my life, the only reason I had for existing, so I had to protect her. *Had* to. Which meant I'd learned to take a vicious motherfuck of a beating without a peep by the time I was five or six. He broke my forearm with an empty whiskey bottle once, and I don't think I even cried; I was barely seven.

Lola shot me a few glances as we slowly meandered down the road onto Plantation Island. Finally, she spoke up. "You're awful quiet all of a sudden, Thresh."

"This place reminds me of where I grew up, is all."

"The trailers?"

I nodded. "That, and the remoteness of it. The silence. The emptiness." I glanced out the window at the trailered boats and scrap heaps and makeshift porches. "Takes me back."

"And that's not a good thing, is it?"

"Not so much, no."

"Well, if all goes well, Uncle Filipo will have us in the water pretty fast, and we can get you out of here."

I didn't say it, but I'd be grateful for that. My hands were getting twitchy, and that never boded well for anyone.

Lola gestured at a trailer indistinguishable from any of the others. "Here."

I snorted when I saw the…watercraft, I guess you could *sort of* call it…on the front lawn. "Boat? Sweetheart, that's a tin cup with a trolling motor attached to it."

She eyed me. "Ever been out there?"

"No," I admitted.

"One, there's a no-wake law. Two, you can't go fast anyway, or you'll miss a turn, hit something, get snared, any number of things. Trust me, this is the best option."

I eyed the boat skeptically. "Will it hold me? I ain't exactly dainty, don't know if you've noticed."

She rolled her eyes at me. "If it can hold my dad, Filipo, and me, I'm sure it can manage you."

"And you know where we're going?"

She eyed the sky; it was early evening. "It's gonna get dark soon and I, for sure, don't fancy making the trip at night. Filipo could do it, and so could Dad, but if I'm navigating? We'd best get moving."

"That's not exactly inspiring my confidence, Doc."

She just shrugged. "Yeah, well, I'm what you got."

"Getting lost in the 'Glades isn't going to help our case any, Lola."

A man appeared in the doorway of the trailer. Older, tall, obviously was once powerful, but age had stripped him of his muscle mass. Long hair pulled back in a ponytail, shading his eyes against the sun with one hand. The other hand clutched a sawed-off shotgun.

"Who that out there?" he called out.

Lola exited the Jeep, waving. "Hi, Uncle Filipo!"

"Lola? What'chu doing out here? *Talofa*, baby girl, *o a mai oe*?"

"I—" She halted, obviously struggling with what to say. "I need to see Dad."

"He been askin' 'bout you. Been a while."

"I know, Uncle. I just…it's been busy, you know?"

Filipo shrugged. "Not so busy 'round here, baby girl." He ducked, trying to see more of me. "Fancy new wheels, huh? Who that wit' you?"

She shot me a glance, jerked her head to indicate I should get out too. I shut off the engine, snagged my backpack, unfolded from the vehicle.

Filipo's eyes widened as I reached my full height. "*O'ai oe*?"

Lola gestured for me to join her as she moved toward the house. "Uncle Filipo, this is my—this is Thresh."

Filipo didn't move, didn't relax, but he also didn't level the scattergun at me. "What kinda name is that?"

I lifted a shoulder. "The one I go by."

"Not what your mama gave you, though." That didn't seem to require a response, so I didn't offer one. Filipo turned his attention back to Lola. "Tai don't like strangers, baby girl. You know that. 'Specially not a big fuck-off *alelo* like that."

"No shit, Filipo. Think I don't know that? I wouldn't have brought him this far if it wasn't important."

Filipo considered. "You ain't ever been *valea*, so I guess it's all right. But you gotta come in and tell me what trouble you got into." He stood in the doorway as Lola and I made our way inside, and I know the wary, sharp-eyed old man didn't miss the knife on my belt, or the gun at my back.

The inside of the trailer matched the outside. Cluttered, dirty, old. He'd been here a long-ass time, and didn't give much of a shit about appearances. Beer bottles and soda cans were clustered on a coffee table, along with an overflowing ashtray, contractor bags full of more empty bottles, takeout containers, dishes, and more than anything else, fishing gear. Tackle boxes, lures, flies, rods, reels, and waders. If there was anything that helped catch fish, Filipo had several of them of varying ages and qualities.

He cleared off the couch by sweeping his arm across it to knock the detritus to the floor, and then kicking it aside. Lola sat beside him, while I did my best to hunker near the door. The trailer was small enough that I barely cleared the ceiling if I stood upright, which only served to make me feel all the more conspicuous and claustrophobic. The smell of cigarettes and old booze, the fake panel walls, the threadbare couch, the shit everywhere, the oppressive heat and humidity…I was back in the trailer in Mississippi again. I hooked my thumb in my hip pocket and focused on keeping my breathing even.

Filipo focused on Lola. "Why you here, Lola? Real talk."

"I'm just…there's trouble. I need to get away for a while. I thought I could go in and see Dad for a few days." She looked at me. "He's helping me."

"Help you do what?"

"Keep away from the trouble."

"What's the trouble?"

"Less you know, better for you," I said.

Sharp dark eyes fixed on me. "That kinda trouble, huh? So you're runnin' into the 'Glades to get away?"

"I'm taking her in there, make sure she gets there, and then I'm gonna go handle things."

"Problem with that is you go in, you don't come out unless you know the way."

I hadn't considered that aspect.

"I'll figure something out. Just gotta get her somewhere safe. So we need the boat, so Lola can get us in there."

Filipo tapped the shotgun barrel against his palm, eyeing me thoughtfully. "Your trouble…it gonna find its way down here?"

I bobbed my head side to side. "Maybe. Seems likely, honestly." I jerked my chin at his shotgun. "Anyone shows up that ain't me or her, shoot first and ask questions later."

Filipo nodded. "Got'chu. Got no hold up 'bout that. My girl, here." He nodded at Lola. "You and her—"

"*Ua lava*, Filipo. That's my business."

"That *susopoki* what done you over—"

Lola's eyes blazed. "I said *enough*, Filipo. That's…*my*…business."

He raised his hands. "Fine, fine." A thumb jerked at me—"But this *pukio*, if he—"

"*Filipo!*" Lola hissed.

He let out a breath, stood up, and patted the air placatingly. "You know I'm gonna worry. But you take care of it. Whatever. I'll get the boat in the water."

He left the trailer with a slam of the screen door, and that sound, the *bang* of the door...fuck, man. Shoot a fucking cannon next to me, I won't flinch. Grenades going off every which way? No problem. That slam of the screen door? I jumped half a foot.

And bet your ass Lola noticed. "Thresh, you okay?"

I shook my head. "This fucking trailer, man. Keep expecting to see my old man stumble outta that bathroom." I had to shut my eyes and shake my head to clear the thought. "Sooner we're gone, the better."

I shoved open the screen door, exited the trailer, careful to not let the door slam—old habit. Lola wasn't far behind me, her hand on my shoulder as I moved toward the Jeep.

She didn't say anything, which was fine, since there wasn't much to be said.

Eventually, she glanced up at me, digging a toe in the dirt. "Where we're going, there's no signal of any kind. You want to get hold of your guys, you'd best call them now."

I nodded, dug my burner phone out of my pocket, dialed Duke. It rang, and rang, and rang...which wasn't like him. He always answered on the second ring, always. Especially if it was me calling. Worry seared through me. I dialed Puck.

"Who's this?"

"This is Thresh. Burner phone."

He'd answered on the fourth ring. "Hey, Thresh, can't talk long, man. Got some shit going on."

"That shit come in the form of Euro-trash thugs?" I asked.

"Got it in one. You too?"

"Yeah. I'm about to go way off the grid and wanted to check in.

You hear from Duke?"

"Negative. He's been radio silent for a few days. Anselm called me, though, gave me a head's-up. Problem is, these guys aren't the typical bone-headed thugs Cain usually hires. These dudes know their shit. Watch your tail, big man."

"This is what he wants, you know." I let out a frustrated breath. "Separating us, keeping us off-balance."

"Got that right, and it's working." I heard rustling in the background, the blare and roar of a train. "Gotta go, my ride's here and I'm gonna lose you. Listen, you remember the spot I showed you? The Ozarks? Where we shot cans and got shitfaced?"

"Yeah," I answered.

"Meet me there. Soon as you can make it. We gotta coordinate, take these fuckers down and go after Cain. This shit ain't gonna fly. I got plans, and they don't include running around this damn globe ducking bullets."

"Hear that, Puck, I hear that. Can't say when I'll make it, but I'll be there."

"Check you later."

"Right." I ended the call, dialed another number.

Three rings, and Anselm answered. "Thresh. Did you lose your tail?"

I wondered if I wanted to know how Anselm knew it was me, since I was on a burner. "And a couple others."

"They are on Puck's tail, and Duke is not responding to communication. I am in search of his last known whereabouts."

"Yeah, I just talked to Puck." I lowered my voice, even though there was only Lola nearby. "I spoke to Cain himself, briefly."

A stunned pause. "I see... and?"

"I think Cain might be a little smarter than Harris gives him credit for. He's going after all of us in A1S. At once, I think."

"I wondered about this." Anselm paused for a moment. "I have not noticed a tail, but then, I think anyone would have a difficult time finding me anyway, even if they knew where to look. I will stay out of their purview as long as I can, see what I can do."

"I'm getting Lola somewhere safe. You need to make sure everyone else knows what's going on."

"What is this safe place?"

"Her dad is a hermit, lives deep in the Everglades somewhere. I figured she could chill with him till we get this sorted out."

"I think you should stay with her, Thresh. I know you will disagree, but you are recently injured already—"

"I lost one tail and took out three others. I think I'll be fine."

"We must begin assuming Cain is a very real threat, with a reach further than what we had originally considered."

"You've got a point, but—"

"*Thresh.*" Anselm cut me off, his voice hard, which got my attention. Anselm was unfailingly polite under all circumstances, and never raised his voice. So for him to snap at me...

"Anselm?"

"You have never, in the years I've known you, expressed interest in any female to the extent which you have toward this Dr. Reed. This means something, for me. You must protect her. If they found her, when none of us even knew her name, then I think this danger goes beyond our scope of understanding. Stay with her. Protect her. I will have Lear begin tracking you, and then arrange an extraction. For her to be safe, and for us to have the use of your skills in your full capacity, then she must be in a place which we can control."

"Fine. Agreed."

"*Das ist gut.* Expect a call from Lear."

"Thanks, Anselm." I was about to hang up, when I remembered a promise I'd made, back in Miami, to a certain hipster-douche. "Anselm, one other thing. I sort of borrowed a car. It's parked outside a trailer in Plantation Island, Florida. I'd like it returned to its original owner if possible, or have the guy recompensed, if not."

"Consider it done."

"Thanks, again."

"*Es ist nichts.*"

I hung up, then, and Lola leaned against me.

"What's going on?" she asked.

"Just making plans," I said.

"Which are what?"

"Well, for now, we continue with our original plan to go see your pops, and then we hang tight. My boy Lear is going to use his hacker magic to track us, and someone is going to pop in for an extraction."

"An extraction? What does that mean, exactly?"

I shrugged. "I dunno. A helicopter, probably."

"There will be nowhere to land, and the backwash could cause major damage," Lola pointed out.

"It won't be that kind of an extraction, babe. Harris will swing by with a helicopter, pop into a hover a hundred or so feet up, and someone will be in the back to lower down a cable which we'll hang on to while they haul us in."

Lola stared at me, looking skeptical. "That sounds…fun?"

I laughed. "Don't worry, Doc, I'll keep a good hold on you." When she only frowned harder, I rolled my eyes at her. "You'll be clipped to the cable. It'll be fine. I've done it dozens of times."

"If you say so."

I gestured at the nearby river, which I assumed led out to the channels and canals into which we were soon to be venturing. "I'm trusting you to get us in there, you trust me to get us out, okay?"

She nodded. "Fine. But I'm not super keen on helicopters."

"And I'm not super keen on riding in a tin pot through a vast wetland. Times like this, you do what you gotta do."

My burner phone rang just then. I accepted the call. "Lear, talk to me."

"Got to make this fast, Muscles. Just stay on the line for me while I run the triangulation…" The line went quiet for several moments, and then I heard Lear snap his fingers on the other end. "Gotcha. Damn, you are *way* the hell out there, man."

"Just getting started, my friend. I won't have signal where I'm going."

"That doesn't matter. Now that I've got your location pinged, I can keep a close eye on you. Harris is getting a bead on a helo down that way, and then he'll scramble one of his faster rides to get down there."

"Is everyone else accounted for? I spoke to Anselm and Puck, and now you, and you've spoken to Harris."

"Duke is the only one we can't get hold of. Layla is with Harris, obviously."

"Can you do anything to find Duke?"

"That's why I'm trying to get you sorted as fast as possible. Either he's intentionally gone dark, or something happened, because I'm having trouble pinning him down. I know Anselm is working things on his end, too. We'll find him."

"I'm not worried about him," I lied. "I'm worried he'll have all the fun without me."

"He would never." Lear was tapping at a keyboard in the background. "Okay, Harris is en route to you. He said to expect him in a few hours."

"Great. See you soon, little buddy."

"Oh fuck off, you damn tree." He clicked off with an amused chuckle.

I stuffed the phone back into my pocket, and ran my palm over my mohawk with a frustrated huff. "Goddammit, Duke."

"Someone is missing?"

I didn't bother trying to hide the worry in my voice; something told me Lola wouldn't see it as a weakness. "Yeah, my buddy Duke. He's never out of communication. He's permanently attached to that fucking iPhone of his. He's even got this bulletproof case he had custom made, so he can take it out on ops without risking it getting blasted. For him to not answer *anybody*, let alone me? Not like him. Even if he's in the middle of getting it on with a girl, if one of us calls, he answers. Even if just to say he'll call back when he's done. Even Anselm and Lear are having a tough time getting a lock on him. It's worrying, and I don't worry easily."

"I'm sure he'll be fine. He's probably just doing the same thing we are."

"Yeah, but you don't know Duke. Subtlety is even less his strong suit than it is mine. And he may not even stop to check in with anyone before he goes on a rampage if he were to catch wind of someone following him. The dude is my equal in every way when it comes to wreaking ruin, but once he gets his ire up, it's almost impossible to rein him in. I learned early how to shut my shit down. Duke... doesn't have that off button. And it can blind him."

Lola's eyes were soft on mine. "You're really close to Duke, aren't you?"

I had to look away, because the expression on her face was doing something weird to my heart, and my worry for Duke was putting a lump in my throat. "Yeah. Everybody at A1S is family, and the only family I got, but Duke...he's the brother I never had."

"He'll turn up. He'll be fine."

Filipo was approaching on foot, waving for us to join him.

"He better, or Cain is gonna see a side of me he'll wish he'd left buried." I nodded at Filipo. "Time to go."

Since it was nearing sundown, Filipo insisted on taking us in himself, and I noticed Lola didn't argue very much.

The trip was slow, oppressively hot, and stultifying. Bugs bit me nonstop, and every channel looked the same as the last. Oh sure, it was beautiful enough, but not my thing. Give me mountains or white sand beaches and, preferably, the snow bunnies and beach bunnies to go with them. This endless slog through one identical waterway and channel after another, the banks sliding past on either side in sludge-slow increments, the motor buzzing weakly, our bow barely causing a ripple...?

No thanks.

I understood within ten minutes what Lola had meant by having to know exactly where you were going, though, because that's how fast I was lost. Filipo, however, obviously knew exactly where he was going, because he never hesitated when it came to turning into a minor offshoot, or cutting across a larger bay and into another tiny canal. When we hit larger, more open areas, Filipo would gun the motor a bit, which always caused me relief but, for the most part, he stuck to tiny, narrow channels, meandering our way slowly south and west. At least, that's how I interpreted our overall vector. It was hard to keep track.

After what I reckoned to be over an hour, and probably closer to two, Filipo slowed to a crawl, scanning the bank on our left side. When I say bank, I mean a wall of mangrove trees, unbroken, thick boughs waving softly in a slow hot breeze, the occasional tree arching out over the water. I don't know what Filipo was looking for, since there didn't seem to be anything to find, even as I scanned the same bank, looking for any kind of irregularity. Filipo just trawled along slow enough that I could have gotten out and crawled on my hands and knees faster, bum arm and all.

And then, seemingly at random, he swung the tiller of the boat to angle the bow toward the bank. As we got closer, I saw it: an opening in the trees, so narrow and so well obscured by low-hanging branches that you'd miss it if you weren't looking for it very carefully, and knew what to look for ahead of time.

As we cut toward the opening, Filipo cut the outboard motor and tilted it up out of the water, and then pulled a long, thick pole from a set of hooks spot-welded to the inside lip of the boat along the right side. The trees concealing the opening were swiftly approaching, despite our slow pace, and it wasn't until Filipo spoke up that I realized exactly how low those were.

"Best duck, *uso*," he called up to me, "or you get a nasty whack on the head."

I ducked, just in time, and even then the branches scraped and grabbed at my head as we slid under them. Once past, we found ourselves in a tree-shrouded tunnel, the water so shallow it was a wonder we didn't run aground. Filipo dug the pole into the water, still sitting, and used it to push us forward, pulling at the pole until he reached the end of it, when he would extend his grip, plant the end in the bottom of the waterway and push/pull us along.

"This little inlet is invisible from the air," Lola said. "Dad showed me once, when I was a kid. He had a friend take us on a helicopter ride, and we passed right over this spot. You wouldn't even know it was there."

I snorted. "Babe, when you said your dad lived remote, you weren't kidding."

She grinned. "Thresh, honey, just wait until you see this place. We still have a good ways to go yet."

She called me honey.

I tried not to read too much into that, but it was tough. I called her all sorts of stupid names, but that was just how I was. Words like honey and baby and sweetheart just sort of popped out when I was talking to a girl I was digging on, and I dug Lola *hard*. Anselm was right on that score.

We traveled via pole-driven locomotion for another ten or twenty minutes, and then the channel just sort of dead-ended in a copse of huge, ancient-looking mangrove trees whose roots extended away from the bank and into the water. Filipo just kept poling us toward the bank, and then when the prow scraped sand, he hopped out.

"Haul us in, yeah?" Filipo murmured. "I gotta see if Tai is around."

"Meaning, you'd best stay here until he finds Dad. Unannounced visitors, even me and Filipo, make Dad antsy." Lola had taken off her shoes and socks and was rolling her yoga pants up to her knees, and then she hopped out of the boat and into the water, helping me haul the boat up onto the bank.

There was another boat there on the bank, a long, narrow, shallow-draft dugout-style canoe, hand-carved from the trunk of a tree, with an outrigger float extending off to one side.

"That your dad's boat?"

Lola glanced at it. "Yeah. It's called a *paopao*." She smiled. "Dad showed me how to build them, actually. We made one together, one summer. It was fun. I did an essay on the process and got extra credit the next year."

I chuckled. "Suck-up."

She pulled a face. "Dad made me, as a matter of fact. Despite the fact that I have an M.D, I actually hated school."

"I still have the one you made, you know," came a honey-slow, cavernously deep voice, from off to my left. He had an accent, but it was soft, arching his vowels, only barely making his words sing-song, unlike Filipo's accent, which was pronounced and thickly Polynesian.

Lola glanced past me, and her face lit up. "Dad!"

She jogged past me and into the arms of a truly mammoth individual. Coming from me, that's saying a lot. He wasn't much over six-three, maybe six-four, but what he lacked in height, he made up for in sheer bulk. Lola had said he'd been a bodybuilder, and I believed it. Dressed in a pair of knee-length cut-off khakis and a pair of water shoes and nothing else, I could see he'd lost the ultra-sharp definition of a bodybuilder, but had clearly packed on additional mass in the form of sheer muscle.

Every inch of his upper body from wrist to wrist, across his shoulders and down his chest to his diaphragm was covered in intricate tribal tattoos done in thick black lines and angles and whorls, and the designs continued down beneath the waist of his shorts, and reappeared on his calves, ending at his ankles. He had a scuffed and battered kukri in one hand, and a modern fishing rod and a string of more than a dozen huge fish in the other.

His voice as he spoke to his daughter was even, calm, affectionate.

But when his gaze fixed on me...

He was *not* happy to see me.

"Who is *this*, Lola La'ei Solomon?" His voice, now, was cold. Still quiet, still calm, but...frigid.

"I go by Reed, now, and you know it." Lola put herself between me and her father. "And he's a friend of mine. I know how you feel about visitors, but I…well, I didn't have much choice. You know I wouldn't have brought him here if I could avoid it."

"I get you changed your name, baby girl, but you'll always be a Solomon." He glared at me past his daughter's shoulder. "You haven't even visited me yourself in over six months, and now you bring a stranger?"

"I know, Daddy. I just…it's complicated, okay?"

His gaze flicked down to hers. "Complicated?" He looked from me over to Lola. "You're in trouble."

"In a word, yes."

He eyed me again, assessing. It was hard to endure that piercing gaze. It was harder yet to feel as if I measured up to his standards. "You're involved with him?" He returned his gaze to Lola, and now his expression was openly disapproving.

"Again, it's…complicated." Lola turned away. "Can we not do this, Daddy? Please?"

If I didn't know better, I'd say that was almost a smirk on his face. "Daddy? You never call me that. Not since you were six years old."

"Yeah, well…it's been a long day." She seemed to visibly wilt, as if the exhaustion from everything we'd gone through to get here was settling on her shoulders. "I just want to rest, okay?"

Tai rested his hand on her shoulder. "Go. I want to talk to your… *friend.*" He flicked a look at Filipo. "I have some carvings for you to bring back with you, since you're here, so don't go yet."

Filipo nodded. "I'll see Lola to the *fale* and gather more wood."

When we were alone, Tai ambled over to me, moving with that slow, easy grace men of our size and power seem to have. "What's your name?"

I held out my hand. "Thresh."

We shook, and his grip was firm, but he wasn't trying to intimidate me by crushing my hand. Good luck with that, anyway. "Tai Solomon." He released me, and then handed me the string of fish. "You know how to clean fish?"

I nodded. "Sure."

He gestured at my knife. "Then get to it."

There was a flat wooden board in the sand near the outrigger dugout, so I tossed the fish onto the plank and got to work gutting them.

Tai just watched. "Last time my daughter got herself in any kind of trouble, it changed her, and not for the better." There was an accusation in that statement, and a warning, as well as a question.

I chose my words carefully. "I haven't known your daughter very long, sir, but I've gotten a couple hints at what happened to her. And I can assure you of a couple things. One, the trouble that brought us here isn't that kind of trouble, and two, whatever it was that happened, I'd never allow anything like it to ever occur. I don't need to know the details to know that I'd do anything to protect her from whatever might have happened, or anything else."

"From what I understand, since all that trouble Lola hasn't done much but go to work and to the gym. I'm having a hard time understanding how she got herself into trouble." A pause. "Which leads me to wonder about your involvement in all this."

I set aside one cleaned fish, and placed another on the plank, sliced open its belly with my KA-BAR. "It wouldn't be inaccurate to say I sort of got her into this, but it wasn't anything I could have predicted or prevented, I can promise you that. I'd never knowingly bring anyone else into my problems."

"You have a gun, and you use that knife like you're comfortable with it." He leaned against a nearby tree and crossed his massive arms over his broad, heavy chest. "I'm not liking what that says about you."

"This shit came to me, sir, and Lola got dragged into it just for associating with me—and trust me, she was doing a bang-up job of sending me on my way. I'm doing everything I can to get her out of it and make sure it stays that way."

"My daughter has issues with forming relationships."

I couldn't help a laugh. "No shit. I caught that part."

"But yet she brought you here. She knows I wouldn't be happy to see someone new, but she brought you here anyway." And thick, meaningful pause. "And she left you alone with me."

"I can only venture to guess that I've earned a little bit of her trust, then."

"How?"

"How much truth do you really want, here, Tai?"

He lifted his chin. "Tell it like it is."

"This is a work thing. There's a group of people who really don't like the company I work with, and they're…aggressively taking steps to demonstrate that. Anyone involved with any of us is fair game, it looks like, only the true extent of the prejudice wasn't apparent until I'd already come into contact with Lola." I didn't see the need for details, but I had a feeling Tai wouldn't be content until he understood the lay of the land.

And I wasn't one to dissemble.

"And how did that come about?"

"My boss went through the ICU when she was on shift, and she and I…well, I wouldn't say hit it off, but it felt like there was something there. So when the opportunity presented itself, I…decided to see where things might go."

"If you had asked me, I would have told you things wouldn't go very far. She was hurt very badly by someone she once trusted, and the experience closed her off. For good, I'd thought."

"So I gathered. And it didn't seem like things between us were going to go too far, but then this trouble cropped up, and when you go through something hairy with someone you're attracted to…barriers tend to fall faster than they otherwise might."

Tai was quiet as I finished gutting the fish. When I was done, I handed them to him.

He caught my eye and held it. "My daughter can make her own decisions. She brought you here, so she must trust you, but that doesn't mean I do. So all I will say is this: I haven't been to the mainland in sixteen years, and I have no plans to ever go back. But if I find out you let anything happen to my daughter, I'll find you. Got it?"

I nodded. "I'd say that's fair, sir."

He turned away from me and headed deeper into the mangrove forest. As we walked, he spoke over his shoulder. "Hope you like fish, and don't mind sleeping in the open."

I hiked my bag a little higher on my shoulder. "Don't mind fish, and sleeping in the open don't bother me all that much. Wouldn't mind some bug spray, though."

That just got me a sarcastic snort. "Nothing like that out here. Bugs get bad enough, you could smear on some mud."

"Figured as much."

We entered a clearing, in the middle of which was a circular domed structure fashioned out of whole tree trunks for upright supports, with a thatched roof and open sides, and a floor suspended a good three feet off the ground. I could see some kind of shades or slats that could be lowered to keep out inclement weather. So craftily fashioned was the dwelling that until I realized what I was looking at, I didn't immediately recognize it as human-made structure. It just blended in perfectly with the rest of the surroundings. The roof thatching was woven from palm leaves which, considering all I'd seen on the trip in were mangrove trees, I assumed he must have brought them in himself from somewhere else for this purpose. Having gone to FSU, I'd taken a few filler courses in the history of Florida and the Everglades, and the Seminoles who had once inhabited this area, so I recognized some elements of the structure as being of Seminole origin, but the photographs and drawings I'd seen had shown the Seminole dwellings to be rectangular, whereas this one was more rounded. Something was off about the structure, but I couldn't figure it out.

Tai had noticed that I'd stopped and was staring at the structure. "Can't figure it out?"

I shook my head. "Anthropology ain't really my thing, Tai. I know there's something, but...I can't pin it down."

"No shame there. It'd take familiarity with the traditional dwellings of two different cultures to spot it." He thumped his chest with a huge fist. "I'm Samoan. I was born there and lived there most of my life, and my *tama* was a big believer in the old ways. He taught me how to build the *va'a* and the *paopao*." He indicated the ink decorating his body: "I got the *pe'a* the old way, from a *tufuga ta tatau*. He also taught me to build the *fale*, in the old way. But then I came here, and discovered the mangrove forests, and learned of the Seminole culture. Some twenty years ago, I met an old, *old* Seminole man, who showed me some of their old ways. So, when I decided to make a place for myself out here, I fused the styles of my culture and that of the Seminole. So, what you're seeing is a combination of Seminole and Samoan style dwelling structures."

Now that he explained it, I could see it. I'd also spent a few weeks of leave time in the Polynesian islands, and had come across a few of the old-style houses, which, like this one, were rounded, with the roofs extending down to barely a few feet from the ground, and those were built flat on the ground. The Seminole, living in a wetland, built their rectangular dwellings a couple feet off the ground, and didn't extend the roof quite as much. I shook my head in wonder; the fusion of the two styles was brilliant, blending both cultures to create a home for himself that suited the climate, used local materials, and was practically invisible until you were right on top of it. Plus, when he eventually died and years passed, it would all return to the earth without leaving any permanent mark of his presence.

If you're gonna be a hermit, this was the way to do it.

There was a fire built on the ground near the dwelling, with a few chairs hand-made from lengths of wood and rope-knot webbing. In one of these chairs, barefoot, clad in only her bra and yoga pants, eating fruit from a can with a six-inch boning knife, was Lola.

There was nothing special about the moment. She didn't even notice me. She was lounging in the chair, skewering pieces of fruit from the can with the knife, one leg hooked over the side of the chair, foot kicking. Her hair was loose, taken down out of the braid to flutter in the breeze, gorgeous, beautifully long, draping past her shoulder blades to nearly mid-spine. The yoga pants were shoved up to her knees, baring toned, muscular calves, and her upper body was bare but for the bra, and I just—

I couldn't figure out what was happening to me.

It wasn't the usual feeling I got when I saw a hot woman, which was the urge to rip her clothes off, fuck her sideways, and then have a stiff drink. I mean, yeah, that was there, because Lola was the sexiest damn woman I'd ever seen. Now that I was really looking, and wasn't blinded by lust, I realized how fucking ripped she was. She had serious muscle development going on, from hard, rounded biceps and shoulders to flat, toned, defined abs…it was ridiculous. The girl had serious gym cred. She was fucking stacked, *and* ripped.

Which made her odd insecurity even more inexplicable. Sure, she wasn't a runway model skinny girl. But she was *gorgeous*. Shit, you ask me, she was gorgeous *because* of that. She was muscular, strong, fit, healthy as all fuck. But she was still all woman. Fucking perfect.

So why the hell had she sworn off sex? Why was she so closed off? It couldn't be physical insecurity. She'd stripped off her top easily enough and without qualm, and hadn't tried to cover up. She was also clearly not a novice when it came to sex; the way she'd touched me, the way she'd put her mouth on me…fuck, the girl knew what she was doing. And again, that was a turn-on to me.

But then she'd just…sworn off all sex for three years, including masturbation? What the hell?

Furthermore…what the hell was this twist in my gut when I looked at her? Why did I feel so fucking protective of her? The thought of Cain's goons getting their filthy fucking hands on her, doing something to her to get at me? That made my well-controlled temper flare.

And just looking at her sitting there, completely unselfconscious, hot as fuck, casual and comfortable in a camp in the middle of nowhere, in a place so rustic it was nearly Bronze Age. Everything inside me seemed to just…fuck, I couldn't even find the word.

It was kind of like desire, kind of like need, kind of like protectiveness, and something more, something deeper, harder, stronger…

plus all of that rolled up into a gnarled, tangled ball of seething intensity.

I tried to shake myself out of it, but the unsettling feeling didn't go away. If anything, it intensified.

And that was when I realized Tai was watching me intently. He clapped his hand on my shoulder, and spoke in a tone pitched for my ears alone. "Son, I think you just got hooked."

I flinched and glanced at him. "Wh—um, what?"

He smirked. "Lola. That look you were giving her. You're caught, hook, line, and sinker."

I shook my head. "No, I just—fuck, man, I don't know."

He laughed, then. "No point in fighting it. She's like her mom, got that way of just pulling you in." The humor vanished beneath a wave of old pain at the mention of his wife. "Don't know it's happening till it's done."

I stared at him. "What are you talking about, Tai?"

He clapped my shoulder again. "One word, four letters. Rhymes with dove. And you're scared of it."

Oh.

Ohhhhh.

Well…shit.

10

MEAN SOMETHING

I HAVE A LOVE-HATE RELATIONSHIP WITH DAD'S PLACE. I'VE SPENT so many summers out here, fishing, living by campfire and starlight, eating canned fruit and roasted fish and venison and the various crops Dad cultivated here and there on various islands: sweet potatoes, maize, melons, and even a small patch of pumpkins and a few canes of grapes.

I spent my summers helping him plant and weed his crops, helping him hunt, repairing the home, cleaning fish, cooking, making dugouts. One entire summer was spent replacing the thatch roof, a job which took Dad, Filipo, and me three months working from sunup to sundown to complete, from importing the heavy sheaves of palm leaves to splitting and binding the wood. I was glad to return to Grandma and Grandpa's that fall.

I love it out here. It's peaceful. It's beautiful. It's a whole other world totally removed from the bustle and chaos of Miami. It's a primeval world, and thanks to Dad, I'm still comfortable out here, even though I don't come out very often anymore.

But I also hate it, because this place stole my father. When Mom got sick, he began spending more and more time out here between visits to the hospital. I was the one who sat by her bedside all day every day while she wasted away. Dad couldn't watch it. Just couldn't. So he'd vanish into the mangrove forests in his little *paopao* and fish and hunt until he felt strong enough to face her withered form again. But he wouldn't stay long, and the visits became fewer and fewer, until the doctors told him she was going to die any day, and then he sat on the floor beside her bed, reached up to hold her hand, and told her it was time to go.

So she went.

And so did he.

And then the forest took him.

It was years before he was anything like his old self again. For the first two years, not even Filipo knew where Dad was. I think he just paddled the Ten Thousand Islands in his *paopao* and survived on fish and tubers, and focused on forgetting her. He hasn't spoken her name since—which is why I took her last name, so at least one of us had to remember her—but I know he thinks of her. I catch him staring off at the sunset sometimes, which was always Mom's favorite time of day, and that's when Dad says a prayer for her spirit, as the sun sinks beneath the horizon.

I sat in my favorite chair by the campfire and let my thoughts roam.

I knew Mom would want me to trust Thresh. She'd want me to give him a chance. What that means, what it looks like, I don't know. She'd see the sweet, tender person buried beneath the warrior's tough exterior. She'd get him to talk about his past and the things that make up his personality. She'd ask about each and every scar on his body, and listen to the stories, no matter what they were. She'd understand.

But I'm not sure I'm as strong as Mom.

I'm more like Dad. When something doesn't make sense, or hurts or scares me, it's easier to push whatever it is far away, to run from it, to hide from it, to not face it.

But I can't do that. Not anymore. Not with Thresh. It's...inexplicable, in some ways. It's not like insta-love, where I'm just immediately falling head over heels for him. It's instant chemistry, yes. It's something about him, his size, his strength, his rugged masculine beauty, his bravery, and now, fuck…the way he touched me, the way he kissed me. All that, yeah, it's stronger than anything I've ever felt. But that doesn't mean I'm in love with him.

And what does that mean, anyway? In love?

I thought I was in love, once, and look how that turned out.

Yeah, fuck that.

No way.

But there he was, standing on the edge of the clearing, staring at me with a stunned expression on his face.

And there was Dad, a string of cleaned fish in hand, his kukri sheathed at his side, carrying his favorite fishing rod and reel. He knelt by the fire and got to work getting the fish roasting, and I, out of habit, went over to help.

We worked in companionable silence for a few moments, and then Dad eyed me sidelong. "He's got it bad."

"Dad."

"Just saying."

"Don't just say. I'll handle it."

He worked in silence for a few more moments, filleting the fish and laying them across the roasting stone. "I got a good feeling about him. Won't hear any arguments from me. Maybe he can help you really put everything that you went through fully behind you."

I sat back on my heels. "Dad, for real. Stop, please."

"Why?" he asked, tilting his head to one side.

"Because…it's—because I'm—"

He hid a grin, ducking to fillet another fish. "Ohhhh, I get it. You've got it just as bad, and you're just as freaked."

"Since when are you this nosy?"

He shrugged. "Since my baby girl finally finds a man who's worth half a shit. And that one? Strikes me he's worth a lot more than that, you give him a chance to show it."

"You just met him, Dad."

"So did you. But you're telling me you don't get the same feeling from him? You got my sense about people. Most of 'em aren't worth shit. That's why I stay away, can't stand most of 'em. Filipo, your mom…that was it. Only people I trust. But I have a sense about people, and he's a good one."

"He's a soldier. He's killed people."

"So's Filipo. He fought in Vietnam."

"Really?" I hadn't known that; I knew Filipo was older than Dad, but if Filipo fought in Vietnam, he had to be nearly ten or fifteen years older than Dad. "He never talks about it."

"You've never asked." Typical Dad answer.

"I watched him, Thresh—I watched him—"

"Was it just because? For fun? Did he enjoy it?"

"He was good at it… but no, he was doing it because they were coming after him, or me, or both. I don't know. But he is so fucking good at it, it's scary. He did it so easily. He didn't enjoy it, but he was good at it."

"Doesn't make him a bad person. He just knows what he's good at, and it's something a little scary."

"Killing people?"

"Protecting." He rose from his knees, took a chair near mine, and wiped his hands on his shorts. "And you know it, Lola. Don't act like you don't. You wouldn't have dared bring him here if you didn't know that about him, trust that about him. And you sure wouldn't have left him alone with me, knowing I was gonna go in after him, get his measure."

"Did you? Get his measure?"

Dad chuckled. "Why you think I'm here talking to you about it? I got his measure, and he's not lacking." He lapsed into silence. We were alone; I wasn't sure where Thresh went, or Filipo for that matter. "After we eat, Filipo and I are gonna go check on the crops. I'll stay over at my fishing *fale*, you know the one. You helped build it, remember?"

God, did I. That was another summer of brutally hard work. Dad's "fishing *fale*" was an open-sided hut even more rudimentary than this one. Four pillars, a raised floor, a thatch roof, just big enough for two people to lie down in, over on an island near Dad's favorite fishing spot a few miles from here.

Basically, Dad was saying he was giving Thresh and me privacy. Wonderful.

⁓

Thresh ate a shitload of fish, and even more sweet potatoes, and made idle conversation with Dad and Filipo. It was odd, watching Thresh interact with the two most important men in my life—and, really, my only family since Grandma and Grandpa passed. He was at ease, seemed at home out here, comfortable with my little family, even in this unusual place. I don't know many men whom you could bring to your hermit father's primitive camp in the middle of the wilderness. Thresh just took it all in stride.

Once we'd all eaten our fill, Dad kissed my cheek, and preceded Filipo out of the clearing. They were heading to the other side of the island, where Dad moored his *va'a*, the larger, two-person vessel.

Thresh watched them vanish, and then he looked at me. "Where are they going?"

"Ostensibly to check on Dad's crops."

"And in reality?"

I shrugged, trying to sound a lot more casual than I felt. "To fish, and to give us privacy."

"Privacy?" Thresh's voice sounded strange—strained, tense.

"Dad approves of us, apparently." I smiled at him. "He likes you. That's quite a feat. He hasn't liked anyone since he met Filipo, and that was thirty years ago."

"He's a cool guy. I'm glad he likes me. I don't get intimidated, but if I did, he would do it." He glanced at the house behind us; I still thought of it as a house, even though it wasn't, not in any proper sense of the word—it was home, to me, out here. "Quite a life he's made for himself."

"It really is. I vacillate between envying him for it and resenting him for it."

"Why would you resent him?"

I sighed. Here came the serious talk. "Because I lost him to this place. When Mom got sick, he just…couldn't handle it. I resent him for not having the courage to stay, for me. I needed him, but he couldn't do it. Couldn't face life without her. So I went to live with my grandparents in Fort Lauderdale, until I got into FSU."

"They still around?"

"My grandparents? No. They passed when I was twenty-six, both of them the same year. Grandma first, then Grandpa."

"I'm sorry." He shifted his chair closer to mine. "Sounds like you've lost a lot of loved ones. Your dad's out here, so he's…around, like, alive, but you gotta make that crazy-ass trip just to see him, so…"

"Yeah. Pretty much everyone is gone. Work makes it hard to come out and see Dad, and…honestly, it's hard for me to be out here. I can't just pop out for a weekend, you know? This place, to live here, you have to sort of shift your mental state. Especially the way Dad does it. Totally off the land, the way people survived for thousands of years before civilization took over. It's not easy."

"Yeah, I gotcha."

Thresh added another small stick to the fire—it wasn't large, and it was built from mostly deadfall. Dad refused to cut down trees unless absolutely necessary, seeing as it was illegal, number one, and that the trees were endangered and thus protected. Gathering deadfall branches was another huge daily job, finding it, stacking it, setting it out to dry if necessary.

The other benefit of a deadfall fire is that it gives off very little smoke, and what little there was got dissipated by the trees, so even someone passing directly overhead wouldn't know we were here.

I was fighting an internal battle, at that point. I knew Thresh had questions, and I knew I owed him answers. But that meant dredging up memories I'd done my best to repress, suppress, and otherwise totally block out. But if I felt this intense draw to Thresh, if I felt like he was someone truly trustworthy, and that I was willing to take that risk, then I had to put out all the shit I'd kept buried for so long.

"I was pretty wild in college," I said, by way of opening. Thresh used a long stick to poke at the coals, glanced at me to tell me he was listening. "Typical college stuff, you know? I drank way too much, went to parties, got in trouble. Messed around with college boys.

"But until I went to college, I'd been pretty sheltered. Dad kept a tight rein on me, didn't let me date, and scared off any guys who ever showed interest. That was high school, for me. Sheltered, protected, kept from really finding myself, or that's how I looked at it back then at least.

"I went a little nuts, honestly. I'd make out with guys, flash people from balconies or cars, get just absolutely wasted. But all that was a cover, because I was a virgin. I never let anything go too far with guys, even when I was hammered. Dad never came right out and said so in so many words, but he made it obvious that my virginity was special. Something to be given to the right person, when I was ready. And since I'd never really dated, I didn't know how. I didn't know what I was looking for in a guy. So I messed around, right? What we did in the car today, that was as far as things ever went for me. I guess that's why that was easier for me than…" I blinked hard. "Than sex would be…will be."

"Someone hurt you."

I nodded. "But not like you're thinking." I met his eyes briefly, before turning back to the fire. "It wasn't rape, or assault, or anything like that."

"So what happened?"

I sighed. "I met Jeremy. He was the coolest, sweetest guy I'd ever met. Tall, muscular, enough that I didn't feel like I'd break him. Some guys, they were just…it wasn't about size, it was that I knew I was so much stronger than them, and they knew it, and it intimidated them, and made me feel…" I searched for the word. "I don't know. Like I'd break them, if I got too…excited, you know?"

Thresh nodded. "I know all too well, babe. Guy my size, those teeny tiny little stick-thin chicks? I just can't do that. I feel like if I got really into things, I'd just snap 'em like twigs."

"Exactly. Jeremy didn't give me that feeling, and he made me feel beautiful. I've come to accept and love my body since, but back then, I still struggled with things, sometimes. Being taller and stronger than not just other girls, but some guys too. I knew I had curves, especially then, because I didn't take fitness quite as seriously as I do now, so there were even more curves then. But Jeremy made me feel like he genuinely appreciated the way I looked. He was...god, he was so hot." I glanced at Thresh. "Sorry, I know I shouldn't—"

"Don't apologize, Lola. Doesn't bother me any."

I breathed in relief. "It's part of it, the way he looked. Because there was an element for me like, god, I really don't deserve this guy. He was popular. Everyone at FSU knew him, loved him. Star quarterback, four-point-oh grade average, hot as sin, and just genuinely seemed like a great guy. Didn't come across as arrogant or anything."

Thresh frowned. "You're talking about Jeremy Hofflinger, right?"

I nodded. "Yeah, that's him."

"Kid had a hell of an arm. Great leader, too."

I sighed; figured that Thresh would know who I was talking about. "That's Jeremy. People liked him, people flocked to him. Just... followed him around. He had a crew, all these people who just wanted to be around him, and when he showed interest in me, it put me at the center of that. Made me feel good. I was never unpopular, but I'd never been part of the real in-crowd, you know? It was awesome. I had cool friends, and they'd throw these amazing parties at their parents' fucking dope Miami condos, or out on yachts...and it only got better. I loved Jeremy, and he loved me." I paused.

"I guess it's relevant to point out that I didn't meet Jeremy until I was in my graduate program. So I wasn't some naive nineteen-year old. I was twenty-four when I met him. We dated for four months before I got up the courage to tell him I was still a virgin. He was great about it, too. Didn't make fun of me or anything, and promised we'd take things slowly. And we did. We didn't have sex for another two months, and when we did, it was—well, the very first time wasn't anything to write home about, but I could tell he was holding back, going slow and gentle for me.

"Things got…intense, after that. I really, really, *really* liked it. Like, a fucking lot. I'd always felt this…yearning, or this crazy part of me, but until I had sex with Jeremy, I didn't know what it was, or what it meant. It was just this…*drive*, that I'd kept a hold on. And then Jeremy, and I—" I stopped to laugh, because looking back, it was a little funny. "He was shocked by what he had unleashed, once I got my first taste of sex. I was unstoppable. Insatiable. Things got pretty intense pretty fast. I couldn't get enough. I ran Jeremy ragged, honestly."

Thresh's gaze was unreadable. "Poor Jeremy," he said, his voice dry.

"Yeah, poor Jeremy." I had to pause to gather courage. "We dated for the next five years. All through the rest of my graduate program and my doctorate and into my residency. I thought he was *it*. We talked about marriage, we even talked about kids, once I was done with my residency." I had to stop, choked up, thinking about all those plans, how excited I'd been for our life, how much I'd loved him.

Thresh sensed that this was getting difficult, reached over, scooped me up in his one good arm. I clung to his neck as he lifted me easily and settled back in his chair with me on his lap. God, this was too right. Too good. His heartbeat was under my ear and his arms were around me, and he just made everything okay, and that scared the shit out of me.

"The longer we were together, the better our sex life got. We experimented a lot, tried a lot of things." I burrowed against him. "Again, I'm sorry for bringing this stuff up, but it's relevant."

His voice was something I felt more than heard, with my ear against his chest like this. "And again, I'm saying don't worry about it. I'm not okay with you getting hurt, obviously, but I'm not threatened by your past or whatever. We've all got history, Lola. Can't be tight with someone and not accept their past."

"Right. Good point." I breathed in deeply, let it out slowly. "Then I won't mince words. Jeremy…he liked to watch us. He put a mirror on the ceiling, which I thought was hot. I could look up, and see him, and myself, and…yeah. But then he wanted to record us, and it was weird at first, but I got into it after a while."

"Shit."

"Sensing where this is going, huh?"

"I fucking hope not."

I let it all wash through me, let it well up and burst out. All the hurt, the anger, the confusion, the embarrassment, the betrayal. Let myself just…feel it.

"He would watch our videos. Like, a lot. He got off on it, watching us. I didn't, like, *get* it, totally, but I was fine with it. Better that than porn or cheating or whatever, right? He was getting off to us, to me. So I was fine with it. He had a stash of these SD memory cards. He had a camera set up in our room, and he'd record us, every time we had sex. He'd take it with us if we went somewhere, or convince me to have sex with him outside somewhere. Always recording us. It was weird, I guess, but a harmless fetish, since I knew about it and was okay with it." I paused again, breathing, feeling. "I only said it in so many words once, that he couldn't ever let anyone else watch those videos. I mean, I'd hope it would be obvious, right? I assumed it was."

"He showed someone?"

I nodded against his chest. "Worse." I swallowed hard, tried to keep breathing. "He didn't just, like, show a buddy or something. I would have been pissed and probably would have broken up with him over it, but it wouldn't have…it wouldn't have fucked me up the way what he really did to me fucked me up. Shit, that made no sense, did it?"

"I know what you're saying."

"This is really, really hard, and I'm trying not to cry, and—"

"Feel what you feel, Lola. Don't fight it."

"I hate crying."

"Me too. Only done it once, when my mom died. But I didn't fight it then, because she was worth crying over." He ran his hands in circles over my back. "So tell me what happened, what that fucker did, and if you cry, you cry. Only me around, sweetheart."

I nodded. "He made a movie. Like, with Final Cut. Edited it, put a soundtrack to it. Our entire relationship, from the first time he took a video, which was within the first year after we had sex together, all the way through to the end. Everything we ever did. I was... *wild*, Thresh. I never held back, no inhibitions. I wanted it all, did it all with him. And he videotaped every single thing, and put it into a movie, and uploaded it onto the Internet. All the porn sites picked it up, shared it around."

"Mother*fucker*." Thresh's voice was terrifyingly cold and hard. Vicious. "Why? Why would he do that?"

I shook my head, shrugged. "I have no clue. Then he moved. Just vanished. I don't know why he'd do that. Was it all a long con? Some sick, fucked-up, long-term game? I don't know. I never got an answer. I couldn't afford a lawyer to get it taken down and, honestly, from what the lawyer said, it's like playing Whack-a-Mole. Take it down, and it'll pop back up. Once something is out there on the Internet, it's up there for good—it's nearly impossible to get something removed entirely."

"It's still up there?"

I nodded, tears flowing now, throat tight. "Yep. It's called 'Lola Loves to Fuck', and it's got over a million views, last I checked."

"Jesus," Thresh said, under his breath. "I bet I could have Lear write some kind of program. A phage or something to sift and crawl and take it down. Probably could even make it so it infects the computer of anyone who watches it."

I shook my head. "Then he'd see it."

"Lear is a professional. He wouldn't watch it."

"It doesn't matter."

"It *does* matter," Thresh insisted.

"Why? It's not going to change anything. I still got put out there for everyone to see. It's not going to change anything. Getting it taken down isn't going to fix me." I was crying hard by now. "He even taped me masturbating. Giving him blowjobs, taking it from behind, riding him, outside…*everything*. And the comments, god, the comments. The names people called me. The things guys said they wanted to do to me. I still get recognized every once in a while. 'Hey, you're Lola, from 'Lola Loves to Fuck', and they think because Jeremy put that video out there that I'm a porn star or a whore or something, and they just assume I'm easy. Those moments were fucking *private*. And it wasn't like it was a spur of the moment thing, or a little clip from his phone sent by accident. He worked hard for a long-ass time on that video. He even did fucking dissolves and cuts and an intro and a soundtrack. He did it on *purpose*. It's a forty-five-minute video. Of me, having sex."

"That's…*Jesus*, Lola." He smoothed his fingers through my hair. "That is honestly the most fucked-up thing I've ever heard."

"Yeah." I thought I'd break apart when I told this story. Thought I'd sob. I was crying, but I wasn't a blubbering, ugly-crying mess like I thought I'd be. Of course, all I was doing was talking. "And that is why I haven't had sex in three years. I just couldn't. I stopped wanting it. I shut down. I'd gotten a spot at a private practice, my dream come true job—and they all watched it. They all saw it. That's how I found out, actually, from one of the other doctors at the practice. I left, got the job at the ICU, stopped talking to all my friends, because they all watched it. I couldn't—I could barely talk to people after that. After a while, I healed as much as I could, but I never really made any new friends, and I just couldn't even *think* about sex. Because I just—" I didn't even have words for it. I tried, but nothing came. "I just—*couldn't*."

"Goddamn, Lola. No wonder you seemed so skittish."

"You—there's something about you. You make me feel safe. I just…I don't know, I just innately trust you. But that scares me, because I trusted Jeremy too. I *loved* him. I really did. I thought he loved me, too. So it wasn't just the video being out there, it was the betrayal, the loss of Jeremy, the fact that he'd done it all, out of the blue, and then he just vanished, *poof*, gone. I was heartbroken on top of feeling betrayed. I trusted him. I really did.

"But you—you're different. Jeremy earned my trust over a five-year relationship. There may have been signs I missed, I don't know—" I tilted my head to look up at Thresh. "I *want* to trust you. I like you. You scare me, but I also know I'm safe with you. And we have chemistry, Thresh. We really do. And I—I *like* that. You make me feel like the old me. The Lola who had no inhibitions, who wasn't afraid. Who was…brave, fierce, sexy. You make me want to find that girl again. Be her again."

He cupped my face with his huge, hard, rough yet gentle hand. "I wish it was as easy as me saying you can trust me, but I know it's not. You *can*, though, you know. What that evil little fucker did, if I ever got my hands on him…" The threat in that ellipsis was enough to send a shiver down my spine.

And he *could* find Jeremy, which was the really scary part. The people he worked with, they could find Jeremy in a split second. I tried not to think about whether I wanted that or not. I doubted Jeremy would survive the experience, for one thing, and I wasn't sure I would be all that upset. What he'd done, it was a kind of rape, wasn't it? I would never, ever compare what I'd gone through to what an actual rape victim goes through, because they weren't in any way the same, but…it was still a violation.

"What I'm saying, Thresh, is that I do trust you. It's just scary. Part of me doesn't *want* to trust you. But I do."

"I'll never let anything happen to you."

I shook my head. "You can't say never, Thresh." I looked up and met his pale blue gaze. "That's part of my hang-up, with you. You're not staying in Miami. You'll move on. That's who you are. I don't expect anything but that."

"Don't put expectations on me, Lola. You don't know what's possible. My boss, Harris, he just got married. His wife is on the team, even goes on some jobs with us. And before her? He was as married to the job and the single life as any of us. Anything is possible, okay? That's all I'm saying. Just because I've never settled down, just because I bounce around all the time now, doesn't mean that's how it always has to be."

I blinked at him. "What are you saying, Thresh?"

He groaned, wiped his face with his hand. "I don't know. I don't know, Lola. Just that… Whatever this is between us, it's not casual to me. I've never had anything *but* casual, so I for sure don't know what serious looks like, and I wouldn't know what I'm doing, but…" He paused, thought for a few seconds. "I'm saying I would like to think there's something real between us. That's what they say, right? In the books and movies—that we have something real? That I'd like to try? We could figure something out."

"Thresh." I stood up, paced to the edge of the clearing, faced away from him. "I don't—I don't know what to say."

"Me either."

"Sounds like you're saying plenty."

"Yeah, well, doesn't mean I know what I'm talking about. I'm sort of shooting from the hip, here. I like you. I respect you. I'm fucking insanely attracted to you. I feel like—like with you, I could really be…totally me. What you said about always holding back? That's how I've felt my whole life, with everyone I've ever been with. Holding back. Didn't want to hurt them or scare them. And the full force that is everything I am? Chicks think they can dig it, think they can handle it, but they can't." He was behind me. "I feel like you could. You could handle me, all of me, all of who I am, and you wouldn't be scared of me."

I could barely find my voice. "I feel the same way."

His hand slid across my stomach, and he pulled me backward, so I was flush up against his front. "So why wouldn't we see if…if there could be an *us*?" His lips touched my ear. "Because Lola, baby, I think we could have something amazing."

I couldn't help a little laugh. "I'm honestly not sure the world is ready for what would happen if we got together for real. Global temperatures might rise a few degrees."

"We'd cause tectonic shifts, maybe." There was humor in his voice, but also heat.

I spun in place, and his chest was there, his heartbeat thundering against my cheek. His hand was on my back, low, at the base of my spine and daring lower. I pressed against him, loving far too powerfully the way my breasts felt crushed against his chest, the way his hand felt on my body, slipping daring fingers under the hem of my shirt to find bare skin.

I loved it.

And I knew I wanted more.

I wanted to see all of him. Feel him above me.

I tried to picture it, feel it, Thresh's massive body above me, moving, thrusting—

Panic seized me.

I buried my face against his chest and focused on breathing, the way my therapist taught me.

"Lola?" Thresh, unfortunately, didn't miss my reaction. "What's wrong?"

He tugged me back to the chair, sat down and hauled me onto his lap, snugged me against him, and fuck fuck *fuck*—he felt like *home*, and it scared the everloving shit out of me.

"I picked up this guy at a bar, like three months after Jeremy uploaded the video. The guy—I don't even remember his name—he had no idea, I made sure. We were both half-drunk, but sober enough that I knew what I was doing. I let him take me home, to his place. We made out, and I was fine. He started groping, I was fine. It felt good. He was good with his hands, I remember that. Decent kisser, too. He got me out of my shirt, even got me riled up with his fingers. Then it got serious, and his clothes came off, and so did mine, and he grabbed a condom, and—" I breathed deep, let it out slowly through my mouth. "That was as far as we got. I freaked out. Like, total meltdown. It hit me out of fucking nowhere. I couldn't breathe, couldn't move, couldn't think. It was—it was so fucking weird, and terrifying. I felt—I felt like people were watching me. Like there was a camera live streaming the whole thing.

"I knew, intellectually, that it wasn't true. But knowing something mentally doesn't help when you're wigging the fuck out. The poor guy, he had no clue what to do. He thought it was him, and it wasn't, it really wasn't. As soon as he noticed I was having an issue, he stopped and was trying to help, but I just—I barely made it home. The guy was so nice, got me into my clothes and got me a cab, actually rode in it with me all the way home and made sure I got there okay. I wish I could thank that guy, because he was a real gentleman. Never said anything negative. There are good people out there. I know that. But the second he was on top of me, I just—I freaked. I didn't really get a handle on myself until like twenty-four hours later. I had to call in to work and baby myself all the next day."

"Jesus. No wonder you stopped having sex."

I nodded. "Yeah. I didn't stop wanting it, though. Like, alone, I'd feel the thoughts, the desire, the urge, the need, and the frustration. So I'd try to take care of things myself, and I just—again, even alone, in my own apartment, touching myself, I felt like someone was watching me. Like I wasn't alone. Like Jeremy would pop out from somewhere with that fucking camera. I just couldn't. I tried so many times, and I'd get so angry, so frustrated, because I *knew* there was no reason for it, no one was there, no one was watching, but I couldn't shake the feeling.

"I even tried sex again. This time with this hot kid doing his residency. Super sexy, super sweet, had a serious crush on me. I let him take me out. More than once, because it wasn't some random at the bar—which, by the way, I've never done, before that guy or since. So I let Mike, the hot doctor, take me out a few times, took him back to my place, and again, all through foreplay I was fine. Maybe because Jeremy didn't usually tape that part? I don't know. BJs and when he went down on me, sometimes. Not all the time. But rarely foreplay, usually just the actual sex. So Mike and I were hot and heavy, and it was great. He was super sexy and so sweet and had these super talented surgeon hands. He was planning on being a surgeon, once he was done with his residency, so he had these hands—" I halted my monologue. "Not too much, is it?"

"It's fine." Thresh's expression and words didn't jibe.

I frowned at him. "Thresh."

He huffed. "Getting a little detailed, maybe, but tell your story your way and don't worry about me. It's all past, yeah?"

I nodded. "Yeah. It's all past. So anyway, Mike and I got through the foreplay just fine. And when it came time to get down to real business, I made sure I was on top. I love it like that, or I used to. I thought maybe if I was in more control, I'd—maybe I wouldn't panic."

Thresh made a rumbling sound. "No dice?"

I shook my head. "No dice." I hated the memory of Mike's face when I'd freaked out, rolled off him, huddled in the corner of my room hyperventilating. He'd assumed what someone would logically assume, in that situation. "Poor Mike. He was so clueless."

"Bet that made work awkward."

I laughed. "Yeah, just a little." I tried to sort through the whirlwind of my thoughts and feelings. "I sometimes wonder if maybe part of the issue with the first guy and with Mike was that I wasn't really invested, you know? Like, by the time Jeremy and I had sex, I was pretty much totally in love with him already. It…it *meant* something to me, you know? Maybe you don't. I don't say that to insult you, I swear, but if all you've ever had is casual sex, it might be difficult for you to understand how different casual sex is from when it means something. So I just wonder if I was emotionally invested, if it might be easier. If I might be able to work through it. I think I'd still panic, but I might be able to work through it."

"I get what you mean." His voice was quiet, as soft and gentle as I'd ever heard it. "There was someone, once. After I'd finished Basic, I had like ten days or so of leave time before I had to report to Camp Lejeune for SOI. I had nowhere to be, no one to visit, nothing to do. So I just sort of kicked it around Charleston by myself. Hooked up with this chick I met, god, I don't even remember how. Bar? Beach? Doesn't really matter. She was such a cool chick. Fine as hell, fun to talk to, easy to be around. Marie. It was only ten days, but it felt like a lifetime.

"I met her the first day I hit Charleston, and we never separated that entire week and a half. I'd told her right off I had to report and when, so she knew. Made it all the more intense. We were together every single second, and it was…fucking incredible. We never talked emotions, because we both knew it had an expiration date, but they were there. I've never been good with emotions, so mine sort of freaked me out, and I'd cover it by going in after her, you know? Cover what I was feeling inside with feeling good outside, so I could push it away a bit longer. She was doing the same thing, I think." He was quiet for a moment. "I've always thought, deep down, when I'm feeling introspective—usually after a close call, like when something happens on a job that makes me remember my own mortality—I think about Marie and that maybe I could have fallen in love with her. Or that maybe I did, a little. Point is, sex with Marie did mean something. It wasn't just casual fucking. We didn't, like, use words to say as much, but we both knew, you know?"

I nodded. "So you know what I mean."

"Sure as hell."

I twisted to look up at him. "Do you think—do you think it would make a difference to us? To be invested?"

He let out a long slow breath, and didn't answer right away. I liked that about Thresh, how he always considered his words before answering. "Maybe. If the person you're with understands where you're coming from and sort of expects it, I think it might definitely make a difference, because he could listen and do what you need to help you through it."

I rubbed my palm against his chest. "You know exactly what I'm saying, so quit mincing words."

"I'm trying not to assume anything."

"Which is sweet of you, but I think we're past that."

"We've barely known each other for what, three days? Four?"

I tipped my head to glare up at him. "What's your point? Seems to me like you're working against yourself, here, buddy."

"Just playing devil's advocate. For your sake. Would you be emotionally invested, if you and I had sex?"

I kept my eyes on his, but my glare morphed into something else—something hotter, something darker, something intense. "Would *you*?"

"Sure as hell, Doc." He touched my chin with a fingertip. "If I wasn't invested, I wouldn't have gone back for you. Wouldn't have taken out those guys. Wouldn't be way out here, in the ass-end of nowhere, getting eaten alive by fucking mosquitos. Yes, Lola, I'm invested. Not sure where that's supposed to go, or how I'm supposed to handle it or anything, but shit, yes, I'm invested."

"Even though, like you said, it's only been a few days?"

"I don't claim to know much about this shit, Lola. But I don't think we really get to choose who our emotions latch on to or how fast."

"Who our hearts latch on to, you mean."

"Yeah. That. For reasons I don't really understand, you mean something to me. The thought of anything happening to you makes me see red. Makes me feel all panicky, and Doc, I don't do panic. In my line of work, panic gets you killed.

"But you get these feelings all worked up inside me, and fuck if I know what to do with them. I didn't even really know what it meant, but your dad very helpfully pointed out that it, in his words, rhymes with dove and that I'm scared of it."

"Are you?"

"What?"

"Scared."

He nodded slowly. "Yes ma'am. I sure as hell am. Because I've got no out, this time. Last time I felt anything this strong for a woman, I was a kid only a handful of years out of my teens, and I had an out, something I couldn't and wouldn't get out of. I had no choice but to walk."

He buried his fingers in my hair. "Babe, I ain't young anymore. I'm not old, not by a long shot, but I'm not a kid anymore either. Which makes the potency of this all the more frightening. Because, yeah, we just met, and how can I feel this much for someone I barely know? But I *do* know you, don't I? I mean, there's a lifetime of little shit to learn about each other, but I do think you can know a person, the important stuff, very quickly."

"So you're going into this with your eyes wide open?"

"Very much so. No less scary, but yeah."

"And if we start having sex, and I freak out..."

"I'd stop if you needed to stop, I'd hold you if you needed to be held. I wouldn't let you run, and when you were ready to try again, we'd start slow, and get you through if, if that was what you wanted."

"And if I said I wanted to keep things at the level they were this afternoon?" I didn't, but I wanted to know what he'd say.

"I'm not sure I buy that, but if that's what you wanted, I'd find a way to hold off."

"It would mean a lot of blowjobs."

He grinned and shook his head. "Babe, make no mistake, here. You are officially invited to give me as many blowjobs as you want. The more, the better. I'll never ever get tired of the way you made me feel earlier."

"I sense a 'but' coming," I said.

"But a blowjob is no replacement for the things I want to do with you. The way I want to feel you. You tell me, 'Thresh, all I wanna do right now is suck you off,' I'll sit back and let you go to town, and when you're done, I'll kneel between your sweet caramel thighs and make you scream a thousand times. But it'll never be the same as how I can only imagine it'll feel to sink inside you, to feel you wrap your legs around my waist and scream my name as you come apart in my arms." He whispered in my ear, then, hot dirty secret whispers. "I want to bend you over and fuck you from behind, feel that fucking phenomenal ass of yours slap against me. I want you on all fours, taking me like the animals we are. I want you to ride me and I want to make love to you sweet and slow and gentle, and I want to fuck you rough and hard."

"Oh…" Well fuck me…that sounded *amazing*.

That sounded like my kind of heaven, truth be told.

"And babe, no amount of getting my cock sucked will ever come close to how that'll feel." He tipped my face up to his, and his next words, murmured against my lips, were what pushed me past any possible objections. "Because Lola, connecting with you, giving you a part of me I wasn't sure even existed, much less ever gave anyone else…*that*, sweetheart, is gonna *mean* something."

I palmed his stubble-rough cheek. "Then kiss me like it means something—"

As his mouth lowered to mine, I whispered the deepest truth.

"—And this time, Thresh…don't stop."

11

NOT FIGHTING IT ANYMORE

WHEN SHE SAID THAT, I WAS DONE. STICK A FORK IN ME, DONE. Shit, I was done way before that. Not sure exactly when, but at some point I'd come to realize that I wasn't getting out of this situation with Lola Reed with my heart intact.

Then, she said that: *"And this time, Thresh...don't stop."*

The moment my mouth met hers, I knew I couldn't stop. Wouldn't. Had no capacity to.

But yet, for all her strength, physical and emotional, she was still fragile. She was giving me something special, by trusting me. I had to honor that. I'd never made it with a virgin, but I felt like this was sort of like that—in that same sphere. If I messed this up, pushed her too fast or too hard, said or did the wrong thing...I felt like I had the capacity to destroy her beyond all repair. I felt the weight of that responsibility, and it was a beautiful and precious burden. She had a core of steel, the strength that had helped her go on when her mom was dying and her dad was too fucked up to be there, the strength that had pushed her past the insane fucked-up disaster her cuntbag of an ex had put her through.

God, the bastard who had done this to her...I could flay the fucker. If I got my hands on him, I would, probably.

I knew for a fact, sure as I was breathing, I was gonna sic the boys on him. Lear would ping him, Anselm would track him down, and I'd—well, honestly, the guys knew me well enough that they'd never let me near him. That pussy little shit would pay, as sure as the sun rose in the east and set in the west; that was all that mattered.

The fury I felt told me everything I needed to know, when it came to Lola.

Little secret about soldiering: we're bored a fucking lot. So I've read a shit-load of books, and the fact that I was the first guy in my unit to get an e-reader meant no one was ever the wiser about what I read. I discovered sort of by accident the secret, almost illicit high that comes with those girly erotica books. I'd never admit it, even under torture, but I used to read the hell out of that shit. Long weeks and months surrounded by dudes, yeah, it gets a little lonely. Sure I had magazines, but I like variety. And because I liked to read, it seemed only natural that I'd read the steamy shit to help me alleviate the ache in my poor, neglected balls.

Point here is that I'd read about this, about what I was feeling: Alpha male falls for the girl, gets scared of his own feelings, which he'd always dismissed as being for pussies and weaklings, and when he finally admits he's gone for the chick, gets all growly and protective and sappy and shit.

Yep, that was me:

Big, ripped, alpha male? Check.

Fought my feelings until it was futile to pretend anymore? Check.

Über-protective, and ready to take on Satan with a steak knife if my girl was threatened? Check.

Wait, '*my girl*?' See? Fucked.

I was in trouble. Big fucking trouble.

"And this time, Thresh…don't stop."

So fucked. And I wasn't even fighting it anymore. I was gonna run with this as far as it would go, because once I commit to something, I'm all in, come hell or high water, with every particle of my being.

Her palm was on my cheek, her other hand was stealing under my polo to caress my chest, her big lush tits were pushed out, busting out of her bra, on beautiful display just for me, and her ass was on my thighs, and…fuck. I couldn't kiss her fast enough, hard enough, thoroughly enough. I wanted to smash my mouth against hers and crush her with my kiss. But I didn't. I felt like she might even want that, a hard brutal mouth-fuck of a kiss, but it'd be a dodge for both of us. Hard and fast would push us way too fast past the difficult and intense emotions involved in all this.

We had to go slow. Let ourselves really experience everything, moment by moment.

So instead of slamming my lips on hers and devouring her mouth like a starving beast, I dug my hand in her hair, gathered a fistful of her long, thick black locks, twisted until my grip in that unbelievably long and shimmery, luscious black mass was firm and unbreakable, and I pulled her face closer to mine, bending over her so she was staring up at me, enveloping her with my frame. Drown out the world, block everything out, surround her with myself.

I kissed her slow, sliding my lips gingerly over hers, teasing at first, dodging away when she tried to close in too hard and fast. Softly, tenderly, I kissed her, just lips at first. I kissed her like I'd never kissed anyone, letting my heart lead. Usually my cock was in control of the kiss, but she deserved more than that. I was kissing her—and in that moment I was kissing her only for the sake of the kiss, needing nothing more, wanting nothing more, delirious just to kiss her soft, sweet, wet, warm lips and never stop.

God, it was like drowning and coming alive at the same time. Her breath mingling with mine, her lips gliding across mine, fighting for purchase and dominance, the kiss descending into frantic hunger, her tongue finding mine first, seeking my mouth, slashing and tangling with mine. Both of her hands were on my face now, holding me in place so I couldn't escape this kiss, as if I could, as if I would, as if I wanted to.

And I didn't.

I wanted the kiss to last forever; I wanted to live in this kiss, because it felt like I was finally, for the first time, discovering what a kiss was really meant to be, what it could be. Every other time I'd kissed anyone else was a shadow, a precursor, a pale imitation of this.

Lola broke the kiss first, but she did it with a lost whimper, lips parted, big liquid brown eyes wide and impassioned and frenzied. "Thresh—" Her voice broke.

She was feeling the intensity of it, feeling, like I was, that she'd never be the same, because that kiss had...

Well, it had meant something.

I'm no good with words, never have been, never will be.

But I *am* good at physical things. Like showing her what I had trouble formulating into words. I flung the sling off and tossed it aside, grazed her cheek with those fingers, rubbed my thumb over her kiss-swollen lips. Let myself feel it all, because I knew it'd shine out through my eyes.

She saw it. Oh, she saw it. No mistake there.

"More," she said, curling her hand around the back of my head, pulling me back to her mouth.

More, indeed. I lost track of time, kissing her there by the fire. Holding her, roaming her body with my hands, not caring about the occasional twinge of pain if I jostled or moved my injured arm wrong. Didn't matter. Touching her was all that mattered. Feeling her skin, her curves.

I let her dictate the pace, though, let her decide what came next.

She was the one to pull my shirt off, and then she guided my hand around her back to the clasp of her bra. I did the honors with extreme pleasure, pinching and releasing the clasps, then pulling the undergarment free and tossing it back into the dwelling—the *fale*. And then, my god, the silver light of night bathed her skin and melded with the orange glow of the fire, her huge beautiful tits pushed up toward me, begging for my touch, my kiss, her dark skin glowing. She sighed against my lips, a sigh that was equal part whimper, and god, that sound, it slayed me. Just tore me up, made me crazy. It was such a tiny, fragile, needy sound. Just a breath, a gasp, a whisper of sound past her vocal chords. And it made me absolutely crazy.

I laid her backward across my knees, her legs hanging off the side of the chair, her head cradled in my good arm, index finger and thumb of my cast-wrapped hand pinching her nipples, my mouth descending to devour the soft tender flesh of her exposed throat, kissing down that elegant column to her clavicle, to her breastbone, each kiss of my lips eliciting a gasp from her. Finally, fuck, *finally* I had my lips around her nipples again, licking and lapping at the impossibly silken skin of her breasts, taking her hard dark nipples into my mouth and suckling one and then the other back and forth, and back and forth, until they were taut and erect, and then flicking each of them in turn with my tongue. She writhed on my lap, arching her spine up, bowing, thrusting her tits against my face.

"God, I could come just from the way your mouth feels on my tits, Thresh."

I had something else in mind. I helped her sit up. "Arms around my neck, babe, and hold on." She clung to my neck, burying her nose into my throat and inhaling, shuddering. I stood up with her, hooked my one good arm under her, getting a good grip on her ass.

"You're holding me up with one arm?"

I curled, lifting her higher. "You're light as a feather, sweetheart."

She laughed and buried her nose in my neck again. "Show-off."

I tucked my own nose into her hair, inhaled her scent. "Yeah I'm gonna show off. If this isn't the time to show you what I can do, I don't know what is."

I stepped around the chair, brought her to the edge of the *fale*, set her on the platform. And wouldn't you know, considering how tall I was, the three-foot height of the raised platform—a stylistic element from the Seminole dwelling design—put her perfectly in position for all sorts of beautiful and dirty things.

She kicked her legs and stared up at me, a nervous smile on her lips. "Show me all your tricks, Thresh."

I dragged my palm over her tits, and then cupped her waist. "I plan to, Lola. Every single one."

She bit her lip, brows furrowing as I hooked my fingers in the waistband of her yoga pants. "I bet you know a lot of tricks."

"A few, yeah." Hauled one side of the stretchy cotton down past her hip, then the other side, using my one good hand. One side, then the other, until the pants were at her ankles, and then I yanked them off and tossed them over her shoulder into the *fale* along with her bra and my sling. "You got one of my tricks earlier, a demonstration of my manual dexterity and facility with the female orgasm."

"I award you full marks for that effort," she breathed, and suddenly we were playing a little game. Good idea, make this fun, keep her mind off the nerves. "What is the next demonstration?"

"Oral skills." I cupped the back of her neck, kissed her mouth, and this time I didn't hold back, this time I gave her the full mouth-fuck, tonguing her and scouring her lips with mine relentlessly until she was gasping into my mouth and sagging against me.

"Jesus, Thresh. Where the hell'd you learn to kiss like that?"

I shrugged. "Dunno. You just…bring it out of me."

"Well it's bringing something out of me," she murmured, and then couldn't speak because she was gasping again as I laid her back onto the platform and leaned over her, taking her breast in my mouth, then the other, giving her tits the same thorough attention I'd given to her mouth.

"Good," I said, around a mouthful of lush Samoan tit. "Let it all out."

"I plan to. The way you use that mouth of yours, I don't think I'll have much choice."

I kissed downward then, and felt my heartbeat ratchet up, because although I'd had my fingers in her pussy, I hadn't seen it yet, hadn't really gotten the full experience of it, and I was so fucking excited to see her bare for me, to feel her naked body, to get my mouth on her…I felt like a teenager, I was so giddy.

Fortunately I hadn't lost my adult self-control or stamina,

because as a teenager I'd not really had much of either. Now, though, I had both in spades. Men can and should do Kegels, let me tell you. Works wonders for holding off. That plus counting sheep? I could hold off almost at will, until I was ready to let go. Although I'd never been with anyone like Lola, a woman who turned me on this much, got me this hard without even touching me. So I might not be as in control as I usually was.

She was wearing a thong. Blue as the Caribbean Sea, nothing but an inch-wide strip of lace around her hips and a minuscule triangle over her pussy, and even then, the lace only barely disguised her sex, showed it in tantalizing glimpses and hints. I was already hard as a fucking rock, but when I saw that, I reared back, left her lying on the platform, tits bulging up and swaying to each side, hips wide, bell-shaped, perfect, and those thighs, my god, those thighs, muscular and thick and soft, framing her pussy in a tight wedge…

I immediately began aching. I went so hard I bent in half as the top of my straightening cock hit the ceiling of my waistband.

"Fuck, Lola," I growled.

She lifted her head and glanced at me, perplexed by the fact that I'd stopped touching, and by the tone in my voice.

"What's wrong, Thresh?"

"Wrong? Nothing's wrong, honey." I slid both hands up her shins to her thighs. "Everything's perfect. You're perfect. I swear to god, I've never seen a more perfect woman in my whole life."

She shut her eyes and let her head thump down on the wood platform. "Oh stop."

I growled. "I'm serious. You are so fucking sexy I can't even handle it."

She lifted up to rest on her elbows. Her hair framed her face and partially obscured her breasts, and her expression was…I wasn't sure. So happy, so grateful she was near tears? Let's go with that.

"Thank you, Thresh."

"No, Lola, thank *you*." I ran my hands up her thighs to her waist, hooked my fingers in the strap of lace around her hips. "Thank you for trusting me. Thank you for giving me this gift."

She frowned, puzzled. "What gift?"

I hauled that ridiculously, incredibly erotic thong down, and she lifted her ass to let me take it off; I tossed it on our growing pile of clothing. I knelt, and now she was at perfect face-height.

I met her gaze, leaving my hands on her thighs, then gripped her, shook gently. "This. *You.*" I tugged my hands apart, and she slowly, reluctantly let me open her thighs. "You're the gift, Lola. I've unwrapped you, now let me enjoy you."

"I'm a little scared, Thresh." Her voice was small.

I kept my eyes on hers. "Watch me. Look at me. Don't close your eyes."

"I'll try."

I put my lips to the inside of her knee, then the other. Laved kisses up the insides of her thighs, one side and the other, pushing her legs farther apart with each kiss as I went. Every once in a while I'd look up at her, make sure she was looking at me. And she was, the whole time. Eyes wide but brows drawn, lower lip caught between her teeth. The closer I got to her pussy, the harder she breathed; by the time my breath was soughing over her pussy, she was almost hyperventilating.

"Keep breathing, babe. Slow breaths in and out. And if you want me to stop, all you have to do is say so. I'll stop immediately."

"I'm totally panicking right now, but don't you dare stop. I might strangle you with my thighs, though."

I shifted a little closer to her, nudged her thighs farther apart, pushed her feet closer to her buttocks, and now she was spread wide for me, opened for me. And god, what a gorgeous pussy. Tight, a thin, trimmed scrim of curly black hairs...god. I wanted it. I needed to taste it. I glanced back up at Lola.

"Keep going, Thresh. Just...go slow."

I just touched her at first. One finger, my index finger, trailing from the top of her pussy downward. She shivered as I traced her opening, feathered my touch over the tight firm lips. I gently flicked the beautiful little hard button of her prominent clit and she gasped, and then I circled my fingertip against it, barely touching, and her head fell back on her neck, whimpering.

"Look at me, Lola," I commanded. "Watch me as I finger your pussy."

She lifted up a little more, watching as I ran my finger around her clit. "That feels too good—oh god…"

I moved my finger down, to the entrance of her channel, and slid my finger into her wet tight warmth. Dragged her wetness out of her and smeared it against her clit. "You're wet for me, Lola." I slid two fingers in, then drew them out of her and showed her my slick, glistening fingers. "See how wet you are?"

"It's you, the way you touch me. You make me so wet. You make me ache."

"You're aching?" I asked, sliding my fingers back in, pulling them out and then pushing back in, then going to her clit again, slow circles around the now-lubricated nerve center of her sex. "Aching for what?"

"Oh….mmmmm…" She moved her hips, head lolling back again. "More."

I circled faster, until her hips were gyrating. "More of what?"

"You."

"You can have anything you want, Lola."

She jerked her head up to glare at me. "This again?" She sounded as riled up and turned on as she did frustrated. "You're gonna make me ask, aren't you?"

"Damn right I am," I said. "I like to hear you talk dirty. It's so fucking sexy."

I slowed my touch, ran my tongue along her inner thigh, right along the crease where inner thigh met labia, and she gasped, a breathy, whining sharp intake of air.

"That, Thresh. Your mouth." She shoved her hips at me, seeking more of my lips. "Put your mouth on me."

I kissed around her pussy, over the top, just barely missing her clit, then down the other side. "My mouth *is* on you."

She huffed. "Damn you…" She flopped down, scooted her ass to the edge of the platform, and reached her hands to clutch my head. "Lick my cunt, Thresh. Make me come with your mouth. Don't stop, no matter what I say or do."

I nearly came in my pants, then, but managed to hold it back. "Play with your tits while I lick your cunt, Lola."

I watched as she ran her hands over her breasts, and that too was so erotic I could barely contain myself. I slid my two fingers deep inside her, curled them to finger her G-spot, and when she bucked her hips off the platform, I knew I'd found it, and that's when I dove in, flicking my tongue over her clit, a questing first taste. She gasped, and her grip on my head tightened. I licked again, from the bottom of her pussy to the top, pressing in at the apex to flatten my tongue against her clit, and then I began circling, alternating with side-to-side flicks, changing at random, glancing up now and then to watch her roll her nipples between her fingertips, then squeeze her breasts hard and knead them, then return to flicking and pinching and rolling her nipples.

The more I licked her clit, the breathier and more frantic her breathing became, until she was almost hyperventilating again, each breath in a sob, panicked, frenzied.

"Oh fuck, oh fuck—Thresh, Jesus—" she bit out, and then her head jerked up and she stopped toying with her breasts to lean on her elbows, just watching now. Her eyes darted around, and I realized she was feeling the panic then, feeling the eyes on her.

Time to amp it up. I slid my fingers in and out, curling as I slid them in to brush her G-spot, then sliding out, faster and faster, increasing the pace of my tongue against her clit. She fell back to the platform, and her fingernails dug into my scalp and she was jerking me against her pussy, riding my face, grinding against me, legs around my shoulders and clinging tight. All the while, she was sobbing, gasping, periodically jerking her eyes open to meet my gaze.

"Fuck, fuck, fuck!" she screamed. "Oh god, please, please—"

I didn't know what she was begging for, who she was begging to, but I didn't stop, even as her sobs took over, replacing the gasps and the whimpers. Tears streamed down her face, but she was writhing against me and had my head in a death-grip, holding me so hard against her pussy that I couldn't have stopped even if I'd tried. She was levered up on her elbows, staring at me, watching me, and I saw the fear, the panic, but I also saw that she was working through it, letting herself feel it.

She broke apart on a sob. Her spine left the platform, her shoulders taking her weight, feet digging against my shoulders, pushing away, pushing herself up and away even as she clung to my head with both hands, my tongue moving in a wild frenzy, fingers gliding in and out hard and fast, squelching in her wet channel, bringing her up, up—

"THRESH!"

She arched, paralyzed, spine bowed out, hips fluttering in tiny helpless circles as I licked her past her orgasm, past her climax.

Eventually, she relaxed, letting her spine and ass meet the platform once more, hips still jerking as the after-shocks wracked her, and I laved her through those, too.

She finally pushed me away, panting. "Stop, stop. God, please stop now—it's too much, fuck, it's too much—"

I let her stop me, sank back onto my haunches and watched her pant, chest heaving, tits bouncing with each desperate breath. Eventually, I stood up, licking her essence off my fingers as she watched. "You come so beautifully, Lola," I said. "I think I need to watch you come a few more times."

She shook her head as I bent over her, claiming her mouth. "Mmmm-mmm," she said, and broke the kiss. "My turn. *Your* turn, I mean."

She ripped at the closure of my jeans, opening the button, jerking down the zipper, shoving them down past my hips, freeing my cock to sway and bounce, hardening yet more under her gaze.

"Fuck, Thresh. That cock of yours is just too beautiful." She wrapped her hand around it; glanced at me, then back down at it. "It's so big, so much. It's perfect, and I'm scared it won't fit."

I counted sheep and clenched my PC muscles as she caressed my length. "We'll go slow. You need to come again. The more you come, the looser and more ready for me you'll be."

"I'm not sure I'll ever be ready," she said. "And I'm not sure I can come again."

"Rub me against your clit," I told her. "Use my cock like a dildo."

She pressed the head of my dick against her clit and rubbed in circles, and fuck, fuck, fuck, I had to clench, had to hold back, because she felt so good, just the soft warmth of her clit against my crown felt like heaven. It wasn't taking her long, despite her worry that she wouldn't be able to come again. It was almost too much, watching her use me to make herself feel good, watching her hand around my cock, using me to stimulate her hard little clit until she was writhing against my cock, gasping now, whimpering, gyrating.

I had to close my eyes and clench and focus, because I was on the edge, and if I didn't stop myself now, I'd come all over her belly and pussy and both of our hands, and then she'd be covered in my come—

I had to jerk out of her grip and stumbled backward, breathing through clenched teeth, counting out loud: "One...two...three... four..."

"You're that close?"

"You almost made me come all over you," I said.

"Oh..." This was breathy, aroused. "That would've been pretty hot, I think."

"Goddamn it, don't encourage me, woman."

"You want to come on me?"

I opened my eyes to slits, still breathing hard, even though I'd gotten myself under control by that point. "One of these days I'll come on you. I'll paint your tits with my come, and watch it trickle down your stomach."

She reached for me, palmed my ass and hauled me back between her legs, then wrapped her hands around my erection, her touch on my cock gentle, soft, her eyes impassioned and hooded with erotic heat. "Would you come on my face?" she breathed.

"Only if you told me to."

"I've never done that before," Lola murmured, stroking me slowly. "But I've thought about it. Maybe I'll let you, sometime."

I reached between her thighs and found her clit, gave her the light fast circling touch she liked best. "You want that, baby? You want to wrap both of your hands around my cock and suck me and jerk me off until I shoot my come all over your face?"

"Oh—oh fuck, you and your goddamn talented hands, Thresh!" she said, panting, "How can you get me off so fucking fast? Jesus, Jesus, oh fuck, that's right, just like that, don't stop, don't—fuck, oh fuck, don't stop! Yes! I want that! Ohhhhh—"

I had her riding my fingers again, and this time all I had to do was slide them inside her and press my thumb against her clit and let her writhe against my finger and she did all the work, fucking my fingers hard and fast, her grip on my cock mercifully tight, squeezing hard involuntarily until I hissed at the pain of it, but it was good, because watching her fuck my fingers was the hottest thing yet.

"I'm coming, Thresh, I'm coming again!"

"Come hard for me, beautiful," I murmured, "let me feel you clench around my fingers."

She squeezed her vag muscles hard around my fingers. "Like that? Oh—oh—*ohhhhh*—"

"Fuck me, Lola, you do that around my cock and I won't stand a chance."

I wasn't exaggerating. If she felt that tight around my fingers, and then squeezed even tighter? I'd come so hard so fast it wouldn't even be funny.

She writhed and ground on my fingers, whimpering and gasping through her climax, and then flopped backward, panting.

I stood and stared down at her exotic beauty, made all the more intoxicating in the glow of two orgasms. "You are so goddamned beautiful, Lola."

She sat up all the way. Stared up at me for several long moments, and I couldn't quite read her thoughts, this time.

"You have protection?"

I nodded. "In my bag," I said, indicating the backpack on the ground by the fire.

"Get it."

"You're sure?" I cupped her face, bent down to kiss her. "We can take this as slow as you—"

"I'm scared out of my mind, and I'm more turned on than I've ever been," she said. "I'm torn between wanting to run as far and fast as I can because I'm scared out of my fucking head, and wanting to jump on your cock and ride you like a mustang at the rodeo."

God, when she said shit like that, it was the hardest thing not to grab her hips and start fucking. I needed her so goddamned bad. I'd never wanted anyone this bad, never needed anything this desperately. I *needed* to be inside her. I needed to come. I needed to feel her pussy wrapped around me, clenching, throbbing, coming.

It took every ounce of self-control I had in me right then to keep my hands at my sides, to not seize and take her the way I wanted.

But this wasn't about me, this was about her.

Bad alpha. Down boy.

I sucked in a breath, let it out. "Lola—"

She bent forward and took my cock in her mouth before I could react, shutting me up instantly, fists sliding and fluttering at my base, and then she took me deep, sucked hard and bobbed down on me once, twice, three times, backing away when I hissed through gritted teeth.

"I'm choosing the second option, Thresh," she said, her voice sultry and low, "so get the goddamn condom."

12

SCREAMING IN THE MANGROVES

MY HEART WAS HAMMERING SO HARD IN MY CHEST MY RIBCAGE hurt. I was only barely in control of my panic. I felt the eyes. I felt watched. I was constantly fighting the urge to scan the clearing for hidden cameras. So far, I was winning. And thank fuck for that, because Thresh was…*incredible* wasn't a strong enough word. His fingers, his mouth…the things he could do with them. God, I was shuddering, still feeling it, still quaking from the aftershocks.

But his words?

I don't think he understood how potent his constant praise was. I got the impression he didn't think he was good with words, but he always seemed to know exactly what I needed and wanted to hear. He could get me crazy just by talking, just by telling me what he was going to do.

Had I really told him I wanted him to come on me? That'd always been a hard line for me, with—*before*. One of the few things we'd never done…but now, with Thresh in front of me, with his huge hard thick iron rod of a cock swaying in front of my face, just begging for me to touch it and lick it and suck it and ride it and make him come a dozen different ways, fuck, I wanted to watch him come, wanted to just caress him with my hands as slowly and for as long as I could, until he shot his load all over my hands... I shivered, picturing, imagining how it'd feel, how it'd look, his eyes squeezed shut, rugged, handsome features twisted in ecstasy as I slid my hands up and down that massive, glorious cock of his, that perfect specimen of manhood, and then he'd give me a warning, or better yet, he wouldn't, he'd be so caught up in how good I was making him feel that he'd just come, and it would squirt out of his cock like a fountain, and it would hit my tits, hot and wet and thick and viscous, or maybe—god, maybe I'd aim his cock at my face and take that milk, musky seed on my face, sticky and hot and salty on my lips and down my chin—

I felt heat clenching between my thighs, and I realized I was getting myself worked up just thinking about this. So I went with it. Better than the fear, the panic, the irrational worry.

He stood in front of me, his gaze hot, but full of compassion and concern. I was still flushed and loose from the second orgasm he'd just given me. He'd fingered me, and he'd gone down on me, and fuck, his tongue inside me, fluttering against my clit, that was the stuff of fantasies, his fingers inside me...but using his cock to rub my clit, that was—whatever was better than a fantasy.

I could still barely breathe from the power of how hard I'd come, and now I was aching all over again, throbbing, and he was just standing there, cock hard and at attention, begging for me.

I needed more.

I was ready for more.

The hungry, lust-hot, lascivious gleam in his eyes, there and gone in a quick gleam, told me which option he preferred. The way his cock twitched and straightened, visibly hardened, the way his hands curled into fists, the way his muscles tensed as he fought for control, fighting the urge to ravage me, most likely—

He was holding back, for me, I realized.

He was a rough, take-charge, dominant man, and he was holding those instincts at bay for me. No way I'd have gotten this far, through this much of my own mental fuckery, if he'd just gone for me the way I figured he normally would have, just grabbing and commanding and ordering and taking what he wanted. I was a mess, and required a good bit of finessing.

Oh, I knew once I was in full possession of my old libido, I'd want his dominance, want him to take me anywhere and everywhere and any time. I'd expect that from him. But for now, I was beyond grateful that he was working as hard as I could tell he was to let me set the pace, giving me time to work myself past my barriers and fears.

Fucking hell, watching him hold back like that was sexier than anything I'd ever seen. His jeans were down around his thighs, his balls heavy and taut against his shaft, a hint of tree-trunk-thick thighs.

"Lola," he started protesting, but there was nothing for him to say.

I gripped his shaft, marveling at the way my middle fingers didn't meet my thumbs, stroking him near the root. I bent forward and filled my mouth with him, giving him strokes of my hands around his base as I welcomed more of his goddamn perfect cock into my mouth, rolling my tongue against him, taking him to the back of my throat, sucking, backing away, and then committed to it, bobbed on him, doing my best impression of a porn star, fucking his cock with my mouth a few times, until I felt him tense and heard him hiss, and then I knew I had to stop, because as much as I really truly did want to watch and feel him come like this, it wasn't what I needed.

I needed to be fucked.

No, that wasn't right. Earlier, it had been more than a blowjob, and this…what Thresh and I were about to do…it was going to be so much more than fucking.

I met his gaze. "I'm choosing the second option, Thresh, so put on the goddamn condom."

I didn't have to tell him twice.

He did two things at once, then, kicking off one boot and then toed off the sock, then did the same with the other foot, all the while rummaging in the backpack for a box of condoms—magnums, ob-viously, and that reminded me of just how massive the man was, especially his cock.

He shucked his jeans in a flash, and then he was beautiful-ly, intoxicatingly naked, and good god*damn*, what a man. What a fucking man. Huge, larger than life, massive and exuding power, a real-life colossus, a Titan made flesh. Rippling with muscle, ripped and gnarled with scars, carved out of living marble, but no statue ever carved had ever boasted the dizzying proportions of the man standing proudly before me; I'd certainly never seen a statue with a twelve-inch cock.

I reached up, grabbed his handsome, rugged face in my palms and brought him down to me, sought his kiss, because holy fucking hell that man could kiss like a god, and his kisses never failed to erase any fears, never failed to quiet my panic and never failed to add fuel to my raging libido.

But there was something…missing. Something holding me back.

I pulled back, stared into his eyes and held him and breathed him in, and then, in a flash, it hit me, the one thing I was missing in that moment. "I—Thresh, I need something, before we do this."

"What, baby? Anything, tell me."

"Your name. I need your *real* name."

He ducked his head, pulling his gaze from mine. One breath, two, and I wondered if it was a deal breaker for him, started to won-der if he wasn't going to answer. "I hate my name," he rumbled. "And there's a reason I don't use it, why no one knows it."

"I won't use it, I just—"

He spoke over me. "But because it's you—" He sighed. "Thomas Harding."

I blinked. I was expecting something weird, something embar-rassing. "Thomas Harding?" I frowned up at him. "Your real name is Thomas Harding?"

He nodded. "I was called Tommy up through high school, and

I fucking *hate*, and have *always* hated being called Tommy, and Thomas sounds like some pencil-dick lawyer nerd who goes by three names and wears polos with the collar popped to play a round of golf." A growl of irritation. "Worst part is, technically, I'm a 'Junior', or 'the second', because my dad is Thomas Harding, too. And, really, he's why I refuse to go by that name. I want nothing to do with that man. I'm not him. I'm nothing like him, and I want nothing of his, especially not his fucking name. I don't even want to speak his name, not fucking *ever*."

I caressed his cheek with my fingers. "You're *not* him, and you're *not* like him, Thresh." I made sure his eyes were on mine. "You're *you*. You're Thresh. You're sweet and gentle and smart and kind, and so fucking sexy I can't even handle it."

He let out a breath and looked away from me. "My mom died, I told you that, and I'm guessing my dad has too, but I don't know for sure and I don't wanna know. Which makes *you* the only person who knows my real name, except for a couple of top brass in the military, and they all have top secret security clearance, and I threatened them within an inch of their lives before I left. So, yeah, Lola. You're the only one. Not even Harris knows my real name."

I kissed his jaw, the corner of his mouth, then his lips, a soft sweet brush of my lips across his. "Thank you, Thresh." I tugged at him until he looked at me, really truly saw me. "I mean it. Thank you for trusting me with your name."

He cupped the back of my head so I couldn't escape the kiss. "Only for you, babe." He took my mouth then, claimed me, marked me. "Only for you."

Another kiss, this one hotter, pushing heat through me, reminding me that I needed this man, and the fact that he'd shared his name with me when it was clearly a difficult issue for him…that trust sank into my heart and opened me for him, took what was already building between us and deepened it, strengthened it. And then when he kissed me like that, as if he was starving and only I could sate him… god, that tore me apart, made me crazy, made me delirious for him.

Made me ache for him. And then his hands began moving, seeking, searching, caressing, sliding down my back, across my hips, over my thighs, lifting and kneading my breasts, sending desperation searing through me.

"We done talking now?" he growled, rubbing my nipple between his rough fingertips.

I throbbed between my thighs, and couldn't help that my fingers dove down there, sliding between my legs and finding my clit and, judging by the way he ground his teeth and the way his cock twitched and the way he clawed open the box and tore free a condom, I knew he didn't mind.

I felt a frenzy boil inside me as I fingered myself, felt the bubbling heat, the tension and pressure building as I circled my clit. Adding to the taut fiery madness coalescing inside me I tweaked and pinched my nipples, *hard*, until I was panting and gasping.

As he rolled the condom down his length in three strokes of his bear-paw hand I breathed, "We're done—I need you."

"Lola," he snarled, his voice a thunder-deep boom, his fingers replacing mine, circling my aching clit, driving me higher, closer to climax. "I need you too, baby. I—god, I need you so goddamn bad."

Tears pricked in my eyes, the panic seizing me as he nudged his cock against my opening, panic clamped down around my lungs like constricting bands, even as a third orgasm blasted through me, stealing whatever breath I had left, searing and pulsing and bathing my pussy with slick sluicing need.

Stronger than the panic, however, was the desperation. The fire. The pulsating heat. The ache in my belly and the throb between my thighs. The passion. It was there, boiling, overflowing, that passion, that wildness, that manic, insatiable need. Thresh had brought it all out, brought it all back, and it was blazing through me, a wildfire set off in a tinder-dry forest.

I was on the edge of the platform, exactly at waist height to Thresh, in perfect position to take him inside me just like this. I clawed at his face with one hand, gripped the back of his neck with the other, my lips trembling against his, and then I reached with my one hand between our bodies, found his hard, waiting, rubber-sheathed cock and, oh fuck yes, that condom was studded for pleasure.

My eyes were open, and so were his, and I kept hold of his nape, my mouth open, my lips quivering, looking up at him, into his searing, blue ice-chip eyes, eyes the exact color of the underside of a iceberg. I clutched his cock, wrapped my legs around his waist, hooked my feet together, held my breath and guided him to my opening.

He hissed through his teeth, never blinking, not moving, and letting me do this my way, at my pace.

I felt him, and the tears pricked my eyes again, but these weren't tears of panic or fear, these were tears of relief, of pleasure, of overwhelming ecstasy, a thousand incredible emotions and sensations all mingling into something without a name, something I could only call perfect, could only call finally finding my *home*.

The broad plump head spread open my pussy, stretched me, and I had to wait, breathless, even though I was still shuddering from my last orgasm, because it had been so long and he was so *big*. I inched closer to him, and felt him slide into me a little further, and now I really did gulp and then sob, because he stretched me so *tight*, filled me so far beyond full I couldn't breathe, could only gasp through the burn, the ache, the beautiful searing fullness.

"Lola—" he grunted. "Fuck, you're—"

"Shut up, Thresh, just—please, baby, just shut and up let me feel this."

Baby? I wasn't one for endearments, not ever.

But…calling Thresh *baby*?

That had just…tumbled from my lips, as easily and naturally as breathing.

He had a hand on my waist, holding but not exerting pressure. I looked down at that hand, white against my dark skin, and in that moment I loved that, the size of his hand against my hip, the contrast of his skin against mine, the way his touch felt, just holding me. And then I shifted my eyes to where we were joined, and I felt my chest tighten and my stomach flip and my heart squeeze at how fucking beautiful that was too, how perfect, the first couple inches of his cock swallowed by my pussy, stretching my labia around his shaft as it rubbed against my clit. I watched then as I tilted forward a little more, shifting closer to him, and I loved the sound of my voice whimpering as he slid deeper into me, filling me further, more inches of his cock disappearing into my channel. His grip on my hip tightened then, and he hissed again.

"So tight, Lola, fuck…you're so tight."

I bit his lower lip and whimpered as I slowly closed the space between our bodies, touched my cheek to his so I could watch him enter me, inch by perfect inch. "So beautiful, Thresh. You…*us*, watching you fill me—it's so beautiful."

"*You* are, sweetheart. It's all you."

Impossibly, the more of him I took, the better it felt, and the more I needed, and I was split apart and aching and throbbing and there was still so much of him left, but I couldn't stop, wouldn't stop, because it was perfect. It was everything, it was the whole universe clicking into place with every inch of Thresh I took inside me.

I'd taken as much as I could, in that moment, and all I could do then was fall forward against him and breathe, whimpering, afire from the sheer pleasure of having him inside me at last.

"God, Thresh, I didn't know—I didn't know anything could feel this way," I sobbed.

He breathed against my cheek. "Me either, baby." He growled, hips tensing and shifting. "I need to move, Lola. I can't take it anymore. I need to move."

I clung to his neck with both hands, lifted myself up, legs wrapped around his waist. "Take me, Thresh." I leaned back to gaze into his eyes, felt myself exploding—heart, mind, body, and soul— from the intensity of all of this, of him, of us. "Give me yourself, honey. Let me feel you move."

Every word, every endearment, every exhortation felt as natural as breathing, as familiar and as comfortable as lying down in one's own bed after a long trip away.

He thrust once, slowly, gently on an exhalation of raw shudder-ing relief. "Oh…thank *fuck*."

Another thrust and I was lifted up by him, his hand under my ass, kneading, gripping, and I was kept aloft by his cock impaling me and my arms were around him, and my legs clung to his waist. He was exploring my ass, caressing and touching and loving it with his hand.

This was just him and me, and he sought my eyes as he pushed up into me, thrusting deep, forcing a cry from me. He hiked me higher so I was sitting on his forearm, and his cast-bound hand lifted to touch my face and trace my cheekbone, his thumb arcing across my lips, three fingers brushing my hair away from my face.

And then he flexed his hips; I cried out as he pierced me, and it shook my whole being. This…him inside me, giving me another slow, questing thrust…it was so perfect it hurt, so much ecstasy I couldn't contain it, could only hold onto his neck with both hands and pull myself higher as he slid out of me, and then I released my weight to fall onto him as he pushed up, pivoting his hips and thrust-ing up on his toes. And, oh fuck, oh fuck, oh *fuck* he was so deep now. I was completely filled by his engorged, slick, sliding cock when I felt an earthquake begin inside me, sending tremors through me, eradicating any strength I had. All I could do was cling to his neck, hold on with my legs, and rise and fall as he thrust into me.

I felt dampness on my cheeks as I buried my face in the side of his neck, gasping, sobbing in sync with each slow powerful thrust.

He didn't stop, but leaned back and pushed my face away with his hand, the cast scratchy against my cheek. "All right, baby?"

I nodded, nuzzling against his throat. "So good, Thresh. It's just…you feel so fucking good inside me, I don't know how I've ever…how I've lived without this, without you…"

The earthquake tremors were intensifying: quakes and quivers and shudders and shivers rocking me as each powerful thrust delved deeper inside me. Every tremor had me clinging tighter and writhing harder on him, lifting higher and sinking lower to get him deeper. I looked down to watch, leaning back so I could see him sliding in and out of me, and fuck, he was going so deep, and still I couldn't fit all of him inside me.

He was still holding back.

I felt a climax building up inside me, felt it rising, tautening, and I couldn't fathom how he was still able to hold me up with one arm, even though I was clinging to him for dear life. The power and the strength he possessed were baffling. He was still just thrusting slowly, long gliding strokes that went deeper and deeper with each thrust.

I felt the orgasm seize me, and it made all the others that came before seem pale by comparison. He flexed his body away so he could thrust into me at an angle, his cock sliding along my clit as he pushed in and then, at the very last moment, he tilted forward and hit my G-spot.

I lost it, just absolutely lost it, screaming against his shoulder as spikes of heat and pleasure so acute and all-consuming that my whole being narrowed down to focus on Thresh, on his cock inside me, feeling each inch of him glide over my clitoris and then hit that perfect spot. I could only scream his name.

THRESH!—THRESH!—THRESH!

As I was wracked by tremors, I went weak and limp and loose, and had to interlock my fingers behind his neck to keep from falling. "I can't—Thresh, I can't hold on. Lay me down, baby—I can't hang on any longer."

He pivoted in place, sat down on the edge of the platform, and then laid back, taking me with him so I was able to collapse on his chest. My entire body fit perfectly on top of his, my breasts crushed to his chest, our hips bumping, thighs to thighs, my toes curling as the orgasm shuddered through me. I gasped against his throat, my chest heaving, sweat slicking my skin.

"Lola…" he whispered, tucking my hair behind my ear, tilting my chin up to face him. "You come so beautifully, sweetheart. Watching you come, feeling you shake in my arms, feeling you clench around my cock, that was the most incredible thing I've ever experienced."

I laughed, palmed his cheeks, and kissed him, a sweet intimate brush of lips over his. "And you haven't even come yet."

He ran his hand down my spine and cupped my ass. "Take me there, Lola."

I walked my hands along his torso until I was sitting upright on top of him. Impossible as it had seemed, I'd taken all of him. His hips were flush against mine and I had never seen anything as beautiful as the way we were now connected.

I lifted up, my palms flat against his hard stomach, and leaned forward to let him slide out of me. I drew my feet under me, supporting my weight on his hipbones. He moaned as I swirled my hips around, drawing his cock in wide circles, leaving just his tip inside me.

I met his eyes as I teased him with those circles, and then tilted my hips toward his feet, flexing his cock away from his body as far as it would go, and now he was hard against my clit. I sank down on him, slowly, and he groaned, his palm on my ass, trying to push me down, wanting to be inside me, wanting to be deeper.

"Fuck, Lola."

I smiled at him, a lust-hot, promising grin. "Not enough, Thresh?"

"You're teasing me, woman," he said, trying to thrust into me, trying to push me down onto him. But I wouldn't let him. I was keeping him where I wanted him for now, just the plump head snugged between the aching, wet lips of my pussy.

"Damn right I am, now hold still and let me do everything." I moved, another slow, shallow downward stroke. "I'll take you there, baby. I promise."

He tucked his hand under his head. "For you…anything."

I rewarded him with another stroke, just as slow, just as shallow, only taking an inch or two. He groaned at each one, his stomach tensing with the need to move, the urge to drive up into me. I needed that too, but I wanted to savor this, the absence of fear, the absence of panic.

I wanted to drown myself in the bliss of him, the feeling of us, the decadent joyful rush of being penetrated, filled, flush with an orgasm and still desperate for more. I wanted to revel in the yawning pit in the hollow of my gut that could only be filled by Thresh, a hunger that could only be sated by him. There was nothing bad, nothing scary, nothing to fear, because it was just him and me, and I *trusted* him with every fiber of my being. I felt *safe* and protected and I couldn't get enough of this feeling.

But I couldn't hold back anymore.

I lifted up, pressing on his chest with my hands, thighs tightening as I drew upward. With my eyes on his, neither of us daring look away, we both knew what was next. He caressed my breasts, flicked my nipples as I drew the moment out, hovering with him barely inside me…

And then I slammed down, my ass slapping his thighs, a scream ripping from my lips, a roar from his. I was left breathless, aching, split apart by him, filled with him. Only he existed. He wasn't just *inside* me; he was part of me, mingling with my soul. I lost myself in him, drowning in his gaze, groaning at the wet slick slide of him as I sank down on him over and over, breathless as he penetrated me.

I felt it rising within me *again*, this one hotter and deeper and sharper than the last, and when I felt it start to crash up through me I couldn't control myself. I could only seek it, chasing the high.

It was a million bolts of lightning all searing through me at once as I rose and fell on him faster now, crying out, screaming and shrieking. I sank down on him, faster and faster, harder and harder, until it was an endless beautiful perfect slide of him in and out of me, my thighs burning with the exertion as I flung my ass up and down with utter abandon, feeling the heavy globes bouncing at the upswing and slapping loudly down on him. He was groaning nonstop, growling, snarling, grunting—

And then I came apart on top of him, falling forward, weight on my shins and my arms snaking under his neck to crash my mouth against his, paralyzed and trembling as the orgasm tremored through me, my lips quivering against his, my breath thin and shallow as I drew up slowly, and then I gasped a whimper as I crashed my pussy down around him, a full hard filling stroke, feeling him push so deep I wasn't sure where he ended and I began.

I was at the apex of the climax when, faster than snakebite, he rolled us over, his good arm taking the weight. He was on top of me, above me, his hips forcing my thighs wide open, his wounded hand tucked against my cheek, fingers nuzzling me, motionless for a long moment, staring down at me, buried deep.

He shuddered, let out a jagged breath, and then thrust into me, a slow but powerful thrust.

I clutched his ass and pulled at him. "Harder, Thresh." I curled my legs around the backs of his thighs, cupped his hard ass with both hands. "Give it to me, Thresh. Don't hold back. Let go, baby."

He shook his head, setting a slow pace. But he was shaking all over, and I could tell he was tensed, muscles all hard and taut, each thrust one of measured control. "I don't want to hurt you."

"You won't, Thresh. I can take everything you have. I *want* it. I want everything you are. Stop holding back. Give up control." I flexed my hips up into his, meeting him thrust for thrust, but I pushed him faster, increasing our pace, pulling at his ass, clawing at the iron muscle, using my legs to yank him closer.

He buried his face in my tits, and I moved one hand up to the back of his head, caressing the stubble and the thicker hair of his mohawk, running my palm over his scalp, but keeping his face against my tits. I moaned as he bit my nipples and breathed against my areolae and nuzzled between my breasts, his hips driving harder now.

I arched my back, grinding my hips faster and faster, matching his pace and ramping it up, demanding more.

He groaned, his weight heavy and perfect on me, his face rough and delicious between my breasts, his hips driving his cock into me, deeper and deeper, and it was so far beyond beautiful I was overcome, overwhelmed, not with climax but with emotional overload.

This was almost too much pleasure, too much perfection, too much bliss for one mortal soul to contain. He was still going, but I could tell he was still holding back.

"God, Thresh, yes, just like this," I moaned, "I love it so much, feeling you inside me. More—*more*, fuck me, Thresh, fuck me like you mean it. I want it, I want all of you, baby."

"Lola...*Lola*..." and he moved faster, fucked me harder, his movements losing the smoothness of control.

"YES, Thresh, just like that!" I met him pounding thrust for thrust, taking all of him and gasping for more. "Harder! Harder!"

He growled, then, a feral, primal sound, and I felt the shift in him, felt him lose it, felt him give up the last vestige of control. He pressed himself up on his palm, drew his knees under him and straightened to his full kneeling height. I willingly, eagerly, scooted toward him and wrapped my legs high around his ribs as he thrust once, hard, and then found his rhythm, harder and faster than ever, his face a rictus of desperate abandon, wild pleasure, all control relinquished.

I gave voice to my ecstasy, as much for him as for how incredible it felt. I was screaming as loud as I could with each thrust, each one bringing him closer to his release.

He was growling nonstop, nonverbal sounds somewhere between a snarl and shout as he fucked me so beautifully perfectly hard. It was pleasure I'd never known until then, nothing had ever felt this way, and all I could do was scream through it.

"I'm—" he gasped, "I'm gonna—Lola, *Lola*, fuck—LOLA, I'm coming!"

He pushed in, held it, thrust deep, hips flush against mine, and I felt him jerk, felt him pulse inside me, felt him come, and then he was moving again, fucking me with everything he had, totally lost, eyes on mine, wide and blazing and rife with emotion.

"Holy fuck, Lola...Jesus—"

"Oh *fuck* yes, Thresh, me too! Come with me, come with me right now, come so fucking hard, just for me, baby...please, *please*—harder, baby...god yes, yes! YES! Harder!"

He fucked me just the way I was begging for it, hard, fast, brutally beautiful.

Finally, his movements slowed and he buried his face in my neck, still thrusting sporadically. I clutched the back of his head and his ass and put my lips to his ear and whispered to him. "God yes, that was…god, I don't even have words…so fucking incredible." I bit his earlobe and sighed as he finally went still. "Stay like this, baby. Let me feel you on me, in me."

"I'll crush you," he murmured, but he didn't move, gasping for breath, sweat-slick, heaving, still hard inside me but slackening now.

"No, it's perfect," I whispered. "*You're* perfect. *That* was perfect."

He kissed where his lips were pressed against my throat. "Lola, that was—"

I pushed him to where I could look into his eyes. "The best thing I've ever experienced in my whole life."

"I've never—" He shook his head, as overwhelmed as I was. "Never in my whole life—nothing has ever been—"

I shuddered. "I know. Me too."

He kissed me, and it was another Thresh Special, the kind of kiss that made my toes curl and turned my insides to jelly and had my still-quaking pussy twitching anew.

He rolled off me, pulling out, and tucked me into the crook of his arm. I curled against him…

And felt at home in a way I hadn't known even existed.

13

RUINED

LOLA HAD JUST RUINED ME FOR ALL OTHER WOMEN, FOR SEX with anyone else. I lost control with her in a way that I'd never allowed myself, ever before, with anyone. Not even close. I'd always been in complete control, making sure to give my partner as many orgasms as I could before I finally pushed through to my own. It's always felt good, great, amazing, even as I was careful to measure my thrusts, not going too deep or too hard, even if she was begging for more.

With Lola, I just…let go.

And not only did she take it all, every brutal, pounding thrust I gave her, she demanded more, begged for more, and when I was finished, she was tender and sweet and whispered things to me that made me shiver, made me shudder, made everything inside me twist up, making my throat close and my heart clutch.

God, what was she doing to me?

I was slack, my cock resting against my thigh, the tip of the condom bulging with my come. Lola was curled against me, cheek on my shoulder, breasts smashed against my side, thigh over mine, one hand tucked between us, the other tracing idle patterns on my chest. She traced my pec, my nipple, the hard line of my sternum, then the other side of my chest, and then down the grooves and ridges of my abs, still heaving despite my efforts to get my breathing under control.

And then she reached my groin, glanced up at me with a small mischievous smile, and tugged the condom off me, knotted the end, and tossed it aside. Then she returned her attention to my dick.

I watched her, curious. "Whatcha doing, Lola?"

She shrugged one shoulder. "Just touching you. Playing with you. Getting you hard again."

"And then?"

Another lift of her shoulder. "Whatever I want."

"I can deal with that."

She snickered. "I bet you can." With a sly glance up at me, and then back down to my cock, she took me in her hand. "What if I said all I wanted to do was this?"

"This what?"

She flopped my cock one way and then another. "Just…play with you." She blinked up at me, toying with me. "No mouth, no pussy, just my hand."

I groaned. "I haven't had just a hand job in…god, I don't even know."

Lola laughed. "Thresh, honey…*just* a hand job?"

I shrugged. "How I always thought of it."

"Then allow me to change your mind."

I rubbed my hand up and down her side, cupping her hip. "Do your worst, or your best, or whatever."

She didn't answer in words.

Instead, she kept her focus on my cock, rubbing her thumb over the tip, sliding it back and forth across my belly, making a ring of her forefinger and thumb and sliding it up and down my still-slack length. She shifted, lifting her breast to where I could see it. God, why was that so effective? Maybe it was the worshipful look on her face, the tender, sweet, loving, attentive way she was touching me, as if my cock was a priceless gift meant just for her, as if she meant to lavish me with all the love and affection she possessed, with everything she'd kept pent up and locked down for three years, all bestowed on me, on my cock.

Just a hand job?

Something told me this would be every bit as life-altering as the sex had been.

God, the sex.

That had been so much…*more*…than anything I'd ever experienced. I still couldn't quite wrap my head around it, nor believe that I'd felt it, that I'd gotten to share that with this woman. It wasn't just sex, it wasn't just fucking. I mean, we *fucked*, and hard, but it was so much more than that.

I didn't know what to make of it, or of myself in this new, emotional landscape, where every touch had meaning, where every kiss was a seduction.

I'd always wanted to believe in love, but never had.

I didn't see it growing up as a kid. The NFL certainly hadn't shown it to me, and neither had the military. Shit, I'd watched buddies cheat on their wives with locals and hookers, and then go home and act the part of the loving husband. I'd watched wives leave their faithful men. I'd watched marriage after marriage disintegrate for a wide variety of reasons.

And then I'd met Harris, and Harris had met Layla, and they'd fallen in love, and there was no way I could doubt what they had. I saw it, and I believed in it.

And yeah, deep down, I'd wanted that for myself. I'd just never expected to find it.

And then…I met Lola. From that first time I saw her, from the way she'd stood up to me in the hospital, so determined in her care for Harris that she'd not just stood up to me but had pushed back in a way nobody ever had before. I left, but I'd never forgotten her. A year went by, missions and jobs and off time—and yeah, other girls—but I'd never forgotten her. She was just hooked into my mind, into my soul. Then I showed up at her hospital and met her, really met her, and spent a little time with her, and those hooks had been sunk deeper.

Each moment in her presence dug those hooks deeper.

Watching her come on my fingers in that Jeep on the side of the road…that had been the first realization, when I initially understood that this thing with her wouldn't be a little fun in bed and maybe a little adventure together outside of it. This would be something else entirely.

That she'd been able to push through some kind of fear, some kind of nerves, and she'd touched me back, had gone down on me. That was my second realization. Because that blowjob, it had felt better than anything else before it. Something in her touch had gone beyond mere physical pleasure. It wasn't something I could really put into words. It was just…*better*…somehow.

Then she did…*this*.

The way she'd clung to me, the way she'd urged me to give it to her harder, begging for more, the way she'd looked at me, the things she'd said, the utter abandon I'd seen in her. She'd totally committed to the moment with me. And then she'd gone for more, had gone past her own pleasure to draw more out of me, to bring me to a place I hadn't thought possible. It had been total release, a letting go of everything, for both of us. And that was my third realization.

I knew, even if I had been with her less than a week, that I'd never want another woman again.

Lost in my thoughts, I'd lost track of what was going on or where I was, but Lola brought me back down. I was hardening again, and the sensation wrenched me out of my thoughts and back to the present, to the earth. To her.

She had me going erect in record time, a few scant minutes, fifteen, max—and she wasn't even hurrying. Still curled up against me, she seemed totally content to, as she'd said, just play with me.

It was so unbearably erotic, staring down, watching her toy with my cock, idle strokes, lazy caresses, twisting her fist around the head, tracing the veins along the sides with her fingernail—shit, that tickled. She rarely repeated the same kind of touch twice in a row, which was maddening and incredible.

Time stood still.

Seriously, I had no idea how long she was content to just play with my cock, stroking and caressing and rubbing, never setting a pattern, never really trying to bring me to completion.

It was utterly maddening.

It was beautiful.

It was frustrating.

It was so fucking erotic I couldn't handle it, but time after time I bit my tongue and held still, forced myself to just watch, to just let her do what she wanted for as long as she wanted.

The ache grew.

And grew.

It became a throb in my balls, a tension in my belly, eventually making it difficult to breathe, impossible to hold still. Every touch had me twitching, gyrating, pushing into her hand, but she ignored me and just kept her touch impossible to predict

"You have such a beautiful penis, Thresh," she murmured, after long, long, uncountable minutes of silence.

"Thanks?"

"Would it be weird if I told you I love your cock?"

"No weirder than if I said I love your tits. And your pussy." I pinched her nipple, and then cupped her hip. "And your ass."

She smirked up at me, gripping my cock firmly at the base. "So...not weird?"

I shook my head. "Not at all."

"Good, because god*damn*, Thresh, I *love* your cock. It's the most perfect thing I've ever seen. I feel so fucking lucky to be here, with you, getting to touch you like this." She met my eyes, inquisitive. "Are you sure I'm not teasing you?

"Oh, you're teasing me, all right."

She glided her fist up my length without looking away from me, then stroked back down. "You know I won't leave you hanging, right?"

I nodded. "Of course. Besides, even if you did leave me hanging, just feeling your touch is pleasure enough, Lola. For real, I'm the lucky one here. You, naked, in my arms, touching me? I don't think it could get any better."

She smiled up at me, that small, secret, intimate smile I'd come to crave. "You don't, hmmm?"

"Gonna prove me wrong?" I asked.

"So wrong." She clutched my shaft with both hands and stroked me slow. "So very, very wrong. I can make it so, *so* much better."

I strained to sound casual. "Oh yeah? How?"

She held her hand up to my mouth. "Spit."

I spat into her hand, and then she put her hand to her own mouth and her spit joined mine, and then she smeared it all on my cock, rubbing it over the head and spreading it down, using both hands now, and holy motherfucking shit, she wasn't kidding. It did get better. So much better. I closed my eyes and just threw myself into the sensation, her hands sliding up and down my slick length, her fists pressed together and gliding in unison from root to tip and back down, so slowly, agonizing slow, and when I finally opened my eyes, she was smirking up at me, pleased with herself.

"Better?"

"God, yes. That feels incredible, Lola."

She rolled onto her back, pulling me to my knees, straddling her, staring up at me with those wide brown eyes so full of emotion, so full of desire, so full of affection and…

I wasn't quite ready to go there yet, but it was present. I saw it.

I felt it—

Love.

The way she touched me said it all.

She continued the slow caresses of my length, up and down, up and down, torturously slow. And then she tugged my cock down and fit me between her tits, crushed them together around me, and I couldn't help thrusting between them, feeling the softness of them around me, and as I pushed through, she licked my tip, flicking her tongue against me

She glances up at me. "I'm gonna make you come, now." She stroked my length faster, both hands, sliding and gliding. "But you have to promise me something."

"What's that, babe?"

"Never hold back, not ever again. The way you were at the end? That's what I want all the time. Give me crazy, Thresh. Whatever you want, do it. Take me, however, wherever, whenever."

"What if I want to pull your hair as I fuck you from behind? What if I want to spank that juicy ass of yours until it's raw?"

She moaned. "Are you promising?"

My turn to groan. "Fuck—your hands, Lola, how can just your hands feel so fucking good?"

She was fisting my length hand over hand, adding more saliva now and then, keeping me slick and warm in her hands, and then, when I asked that question, she started pumping my length, root to tip, harder and faster.

"Promise me, Thresh."

"I promise."

"Promise what? Say it? Promise me everything you'll do."

"I won't hold back. I'll give you everything I've got, every time."

Faster, faster, both hands still, sliding my whole length so fast her hands were a blur and I felt my orgasm rising. I couldn't help fucking into her hands, couldn't help grunting.

"Fuck yes, Thresh, be the animal, fuck my hands, give me your come." She stared up at me, dirty words on her lips, tits huge and heavy and beautiful and dark. "Come on me, baby, right now."

She let go with one hand, used it to cup my balls and press a finger underneath to massage my taint, and even inched closer to my asshole, pressing her finger there. I hissed and thrust into her fist. One hand pumping me with blazing speed, our spit lubricating me so her fist slid slick and easy up and down my length, rolling her finger against me back there, massaging my balls, staring up at me with those eyes, god, it was too much. I was lost, I was gone.

"Promise me you'll spank me and fuck me from behind. Promise me you'll pull my hair and fuck my mouth and finger my ass."

"All that and more."

"Promise me you'll make love to me, slow and soft?"

It was hard to talk, the way she was touching me, bringing me closer and closer, her hand a blur along my length. "Promise...so soft, so sweet, so slow. I'll love you all night long, until dawn. All day."

"Promise me you'll fuck me so hard I can't breathe? Promise me you'll fuck me so hard I can't walk the next day?"

"Ohhh fuck, Lola, god, I'm—"

"What, Thresh? Tell me."

"I'm so close. I'm so fucking close."

She slowed, then. "How close?"

I ground into her fist, groaning as she twisted her fist around me, ran her fingers over my tip on the way back down, returning to the slow deliberate strokes. "Fuck—"

"You want it hard or slow, Thresh? Tell me what you want and I'll give it to you."

I gasped, hips pivoting back and forth, fucking her hand, arching and bowing. "This...this, don't stop, Lola, just like this."

She kept up the slow twisting gliding strokes, not hurrying even as I became more and more desperate.

And then it was roaring through me, blood rushing in my ears, heart hammering, skin tingling, balls clenching, cock throbbing as my orgasm ripped through me, so hard and so fast I had no time to warn her.

She moaned as I came, still going slow, smearing my come over my cock and rubbing her thumb over the tip between spurts. "God yeah, baby, just like that. So beautiful, Thresh, you're so fucking beautiful when you come, you big perfect man. Give it to me, let me feel you come on my tits."

I wrenched open my eyes and watched her stroke my cock with slow loving caresses, watched my come shoot out of me and hit her skin, white against her dark flesh, and she just kept stroking me as I came again and again, until my come was a white pool on her tits, dribbling down her nipples and between her tits and sluicing down the inner slopes, and when I was done coming she was still stroking me, until I flopped off her and to my back, shuddering…

And that was when she bent over me and took my still-hard length in her mouth and sucked, then licked the side, fit me sideways in her mouth and licked, then sucked me into her mouth again, sucking another few drops out of me and making me jerk and shudder, until my spine left the platform and I was paralyzed by it, left breathless and trembling.

"Jesus—Lola," I gasped. "Jesus."

She gazed at me, lifted her hand to watch my come dripping through her fingers. She licked it away.

I couldn't move for a few moments, unable to do anything but fight for breath and marvel at what Lola had just done for me.

"That was—" I tried to sit up, and failed, flopped back down. "Fuck, Lola. Just….*fuck*."

She curled up in the sheltering nook of my arm, a pleased smile on her beautiful face. "So?"

"I will never look at a hand job the same way ever again." I angled my arm over her shoulder, across her breasts, threading my fingers in hers. "Or these hands."

She tucked her face into the side of my neck again, a shy but giddy gesture I was very swiftly coming to love.

Shit, did I just think that?

Maybe I was still denying my feelings a little.

Understandable, though, right? It had been less than a week. How was this possible? I always rolled my eyes at how fast things happened in the books I read in secret. Pssshhh, right. Nobody falls in love that fast.

Um…guess I was wrong, huh?

"Tell me what you're thinking right now, no hesitation, no bullshit." She was staring up at me, I realized, examining me closely, trying to read my thoughts.

I let out a nervous breath, forcing my rambling thoughts into words. "I was thinking about how I love it when you put your face in my neck like that, all shy and happy at the same time, and then I realized I'd thought—out loud in my own head, if you know what I mean—that I *loved* that, and it sort of freaked me out, like a lot. Because I've known you less than a week, and it's crazy to think that, to think I could feel that." I blinked up into the darkness, nerves and even fear shooting through me in a way they didn't even during a firefight. "That's...that's what I was thinking."

She kissed the edge of my jawline, midway between chin and ear. "It is crazy. It's totally nuts."

I laughed. "Thanks?"

She laughed with me. "No, I mean, it's crazy, because I was thinking the same thing. Or...similar, at least. I was thinking how much I love it here, with you. How you make me feel more alive and more...more like my old self, except even better. I'm not afraid anymore. I have myself back, my sexuality back. And I have you to thank for that. You just—you just erased all my concerns, and I'm not even sure how you did it, or how you made it seem so easy and effortless."

She paused to kiss my jaw again, then my cheek, then just beneath my eye, and it made everything inside me just...twist, and shiver, the way she kissed me like that. "I don't ever want to go back to that."

"You don't have to," I said.

She sighed. "But we can't stay out here forever. Dad's gonna want his *fale* back, for one thing, and there are people out there hunting us, and your friends, for another. We both have jobs. We can't just hide out in the Everglades forever."

"We'll figure something out."

"Will we? I went into this not expecting anything from you. I knew we had sexual chemistry, and I was really hoping you'd be able to help me past my fucked-up psychological-slash-sexual hang-ups, but I wasn't expecting more than that."

"We've talked about this already, Lola." I shifted so she was lying on my chest, so I could look into her eyes. "I don't know how things will work out, but we'll figure it out. This wasn't just sex, Lola, and we both know it. It's all happening fucking crazy fast, but I've never backed down from a challenge in my life and I'm not about to do it now. I don't know what 'our thing' is going to look like, but I've got no problem not labeling things if it'll make it easier for both of us."

She nuzzled into me. "I guess I'm freaked out by how this got so intense so fast."

"You and me both, babe, that's what I'm saying. But it feels right, though."

A nod. "It does." She let the silence hang for a while, and then she sat up. "Bath time."

I gave her a quizzical look. "There's a bath around here?"

She grinned. "Sort of." Standing up, she took my hand and pulled until I stood up. "Come on, I'll show you."

Lola led me by the hand through the mangrove forest, both of us still naked. The moon was bright overhead, filtering through the branches in silver glints. I lost track of where we were, but Lola seemed to know exactly where she was going.

Eventually, we came across a decent sized stream trickling through the forest, and Lola followed this for a while, until the ground sloped downward toward a clearing, where it plunged over an abrupt edge toward a pool. At first, I thought I was seeing a natural waterfall with a pond at the bottom, but then I looked more closely and realized this was more of Tai's clever handiwork. The slope of the earth was natural, but Tai had carved away part of the hillside and built a rock wall, and then had dug a pool some ten feet across and probably five or so feet deep. On the side of the pool opposite the short waterfall, Tai had allowed the stream to carry on through the forest on its way out to the rest of the waterway. The constant flow of water kept the pool fresh and clean, and even though Tai had artificially created the waterfall and pool, he'd done it in such a way that it looked and felt totally natural. Most importantly, because he'd also cleared away the underbrush around the pool, he'd left no hiding places for snakes. I knew enough about the Everglades to know that cottonmouths, also known as water moccasins, were a problem, one major reason to never enter the water in the 'Glades, especially at night, when the predatory nocturnal snakes were most active.

I grinned at Lola. "Let me guess, another summer project?"

She feigned a dramatic eye-roll. "Actually we did this one over Christmas break." A laugh. "I didn't complain about doing this project at all, because until we created this we had to take baths the hard way, by carting buckets of water across the island by hand, heating them up, and squatting in this tiny little tub, which was actually just a livestock watering tank. It was a super difficult pain in the ass, and I totally understand why people in the olden days didn't bathe very often, if that was the only way to do it."

I eyed her with renewed respect. "So you really did grow up out here, didn't you?"

She nodded. "I spent half my life out here, no plumbing, no electricity. Shit, there weren't even walls. I can hunt, fish with a bow and arrow, I can tell you which plants are edible, and I know how to treat a cottonmouth bite. When I'd go back for the first day of school I went through culture shock all over again."

I nodded at the pool. "So there aren't any snakes in there, right?"

"That's why we built it, for cottonmouth-free bathing."

She picked her way down the hill to the side of the pool, sat down on the edge, and then slipped in. The water was deep enough to cover her breasts, which meant it would probably hit me at waist height, maybe a little higher. I slid in after her, pleasantly surprised to find the water cool enough to be refreshing but not cold enough to make my balls retract.

There are moments in life that you just know you'll never forget. Events that get burned into your mind, good or bad, and you are aware even as it's happening that you'll always be able to recall every detail with perfect clarity for as long as you live.

I don't have many, and most of them aren't...the most pleasant.

But this moment with Lola in the waterfall pool was one of those moments that were instantly burned into my soul. This one was brighter, clearer, sharper, deeper, and it was one I would never want to forget, even if I could.

The scene was a montage of so many arresting images: Lola, illuminated by the silver moon, her breasts not quite covered by the water, her skin gleaming dark caramel, looking sweet enough to eat. The fall of the water, the way it splashed and spread ripples through the pool. The way Lola ducked under the water, her hair spreading across the surface like a spray of ink. Her finding my legs beneath the water, climbing up my body, surfacing, wet, dripping, breathtaking, her arms going around my neck to pull me in for a kiss. The taste of her mouth, the wet slide of her slick skin under my hands.

Each moment of that time in the pool is permanently seared into my memory.

Tai had built a little shelf into the rock wall behind the waterfall, and there was a bar of soap and two small bottles of shampoo and conditioner. We stood beneath the water and washed each other, which turned into more kissing, which turned into Lola up against the rock wall, taking me inside her, bare, smooth, soft, wet, and warm, writhing against me through her orgasm, and then slipping out as she finished me with her hands, my come smearing against her skin and on her hands and belly, washed away by the spray of water.

Which meant washing again, but you'll never catch me complaining about an excuse to get my hands on Lola's skin.

Eventually we had to get out, and it was still warm enough that by the time we reached the *fale*, we were both dry.

We lowered the mosquito netting Tai had installed around the interior of the *fale*, and lay down in the nest of sheets and pillows in the center of the platform. Lola snuggled up against me, her spine to my front, spooning me, tugging my hand tight across her chest. And, for the first time in my life, I was completely and utterly at peace.

14

COMPANY

I WASN'T SURE WHAT WOKE ME UP AT FIRST.

Thresh was a huge warm presence behind me, his cast-bound hand draped over me, his fingers clutching my breast. Despite having given him four orgasms, his cock was erect again and snugged tight between the globes of my ass. I drowsed for a few moments, contemplating idly how if things continued like this with Thresh, I'd need to get on birth control, because I'd finally found a man as sexually insatiable as I was.

I thought about how I could wake him up, rub my ass against him, see if could get him to come before he even woke up.

But then something niggled at me.

What was it?

Something had woken me up.

I blinked, opening my eyes, focusing my senses. The fire had gone out, a thin trail of smoke trickling skyward in the dim gray of early dawn.

Then it hit me: the birds were silent, the frogs had quieted. Around here, it was never silent.

Then I heard it: the low buzz of an outboard motor. Close, and approaching.

Dad would never use a motorboat and, last I knew, Filipo was still with him.

I rolled onto my back, shook Thresh's shoulder. "*Thresh*," I hissed. "*Wake up.*"

He blinked twice, and must have seen something on my face. He tapped his ear twice, then leaned toward me.

"Outboard motor," I whispered. "It's definitely not Dad, and if it's Filipo, there's something wrong. He would never come this early, and that's assuming he ever went back home. Whoever it is, they're too close."

Thresh nodded, rolled to his feet, and crouched beside me. "Stay here."

He dressed swiftly, stepping into his jeans—there was a small holster attached to the back of his jeans, with the butt of his small pistol sticking up from it, and the sheath for that huge dagger of his hung from the belt on his right hip. He tugged his shirt on, then made short work of his socks and combat boots. He ducked out from under the mosquito netting, rummaged in his backpack and produced a larger handgun, two extra clips of different sizes that he stuffed in each hip pocket to keep them separate. I watched as he checked the loads of each pistol, and then replaced the one at his back, his original pistol, and kept in hand the one I assumed he'd liberated from one of the bad guys he'd taken down.

By now the buzzing of the outboard motor was getting louder, meaning the boat was approaching this place.

Thresh was back by the platform. "Change of plans, babe. Get dressed and stay with me."

I was dressed in a flash, and when I left the *fale* to stand beside Thresh, he handed me the smaller gun.

"Know how to use this?" he asked.

"Point it at the bad guy and pull the trigger?" I quipped.

He shrugged. "Essentially. Don't jerk the trigger, though, squeeze it gently, and try not to anticipate the bang. Use both hands, like this—" He adjusted my hands so one hand was clutching the handle, finger along the trigger guard, the other wrapped around front of that hand to brace it. "And don't shoot until you're sure of your target. Could be your dad, or Filipo, or me, if we get separated. But if it's not one of us, and if that person has a weapon, don't hesitate, just shoot. Doesn't matter what they say. 'We just want to talk, we're not going to hurt you, we just want Thresh,' doesn't matter. They're lying. Believe that, and don't hesitate. Aim for center mass, and keep shooting until the person hits the ground."

"What if it's your friends?"

"It's not. They know exactly where we are, and they'll be approaching by helo."

We heard a stick breaking behind us and Thresh reacted instantly, pivoting to put himself in front of me, pistol swinging up. I hadn't bothered reacting, because I'd grown up with Dad. He was a ghost in the forest, utterly silent under all circumstances. So if he broke a twig, it was on purpose, and since the sound of the motor was still a ways off, I knew it was him.

He emerged from the trees, kukri in hand, signaling for quiet. Thresh came up out of the aggressive stance and moved toward Dad.

"Know anything about that boat?" Thresh asked in a low murmur.

Dad shook his head. "Only that it's not friends. Filipo left yesterday evening, and that's not his boat. I know that sound; it's got a tic in the rotation. Whoever they are, they've been heading steadily this way for a while, but not directly."

"Any safe assumptions?"

Dad considered. "I think your problems found Filipo and they're making him show them the way here. But he's too crafty for that and, unless you know this area, you can circle forever and not find the right inlet. He's warning us."

Thresh nodded. "Makes sense." He gestured at Dad's kukri. "You ever use something like that on a person?"

Another shake of Dad's head. "No. But I will, to protect my daughter and my home, although I have no desire to do so."

"I'll try and keep it that way, then. Got somewhere you can hide with her?" He indicated me.

"I'm staying with you, Thresh," I protested.

Thresh ground his jaws together. "Got no time for arguments, honey. I'm going on the offensive, and I can do this faster and more effectively if I know you're hidden. You've got the gun, use it if necessary. You hear me whistle like this," he let out a low, simple, three-tone whistle, "you'll know it's me, and it's clear. You hear me call for you to come out, instead of whistling, you stay put. Got it?"

I nodded, feeling nervous, now. "Why would—"

The sound of the motor was loud enough now that I knew they were close to the inlet that would bring them here. I knew Filipo well enough to know he'd delay things as long as he could, but he also knew Dad wouldn't want him to risk his life to protect this camp. He'd eventually lead them here, and it sounded like that was happening soon.

I closed my teeth over my question. "Go. We'll be fine."

Dad pulled me away, and I knew where we were going: a copse of trees deep in the center of the island, so dense and thick you could barely squeeze between the trees, and at the center of the copse was a small but deep pool, deep enough that you could stand up in it and only your nose and eyes would show over the top of the water.

I turned back to Thresh, and the man I'd been spending time with had vanished. Oh, he was still there physically, in the clearing by the *fale*. But it wasn't Thresh, the man who'd kissed me, touched me, loved me.

It was the version of the man who'd swung a knife once, and killed a man. This Thresh somehow seemed larger, harder, sharper. His stance was different, the way he pivoted his head to scan the clearing, the blank, cold, calculating light in his eyes…he was the predator, the killer.

The last thing I saw him do was stuff the pistol behind his back and withdraw his knife, testing the edge of the blade with his thumb, watching as Dad led me through the forest and out of sight.

15

AMBUSHED

As soon as Tai had Lola moving toward whatever hiding place he had in mind, I crept out of the clearing back toward where the one-man canoe thing was moored, the *paopao*. The motorboat we'd arrived in was gone, and I wondered when Filipo had been here to take it, and if he'd heard anything…

I shut that line of thinking down, hard. No time for that, no headspace for that.

I'm too big to hide, most of the time, but this forest was thick enough that I could pick my way off to the side of the inlet, where I'd be out of sight unless they knew where to look for me. Dawn hadn't fully broken yet, which meant certain parts of the forest were still shadowed, the inlet still and dark. I found a spot where I could see the water and settled in to wait.

After fifteen minutes or so, I heard the slosh of water, saw ripples spreading ahead of a bow, and there was the motorboat, the motor pulled up, Filipo poling slowly. He was scanning the banks, I could see, looking for me. I lifted up just a little, and Filipo's eyes paused on me, only for a split second, but long enough that I knew he'd seen me. He nodded almost imperceptibly.

There were three men in the boat with him, each carrying a

subcompact machine gun, UMP-45s, it looked like, plus side arms.

This made things tricky. Three men, all more heavily armed than me, with Filipo's life in the balance. Not a situation where I could just start shooting and hope for the best.

I waited until Filipo had run the boat aground, stayed put as the three men jumped out first, fanning out to cover the area, scanning for immediate threats; they knew I was here. When they were confident the area was clear, one of them gestured for Filipo.

"Where are they?" he demanded.

Filipo shrugged, gestured toward where the camp was. "That way, I guess. They probably heard us coming, so they could be anywhere. Told you, I bring you here, but I can't make them stand still for you."

The man who'd spoken jabbed the barrel of his subcompact into Filipo's chest. "You better hope we find them, or I kill you."

Filipo must have had balls of steel, because he just laughed. "Go ahead. You won't never find your way out. You be croc and gator bait in a few days. That's *if* that big scary *alelo* don't get you first. You be gator bait sooner, he find you."

"*Where?*" This was snarled, with another vicious jab of the gun barrel.

"*Ufa!*" Filipo said through gritted teeth, and staggered backward under the blow, rubbing his chest. He gestured at the narrow path through the forest. "That way, *susu poki*. Best I can help you, even if you hit me."

Two of them flitted down the path and disappeared, guns raised, creeping slowly. These guys had training, judging by the way they held their subcompacts and crouched, one watching the front, the other covering the rear. The third stayed behind, keeping Filipo covered, so he wouldn't make off with the boat and their only way out of here, I guessed.

Time to make a move.

There was a stick underfoot, which I tossed into the water. At the splash, the guard pivoted toward the sound, ducking into a crouch, leveling his machine gun with both hands, leaving Filipo behind.

I crept as quietly as I could out of cover and, considering my size and bulk, I tend to surprise people by how silent I can be if needed. It just requires intense focus and care, each step measured and slow. Maddening, when time is of the essence. As now, with the guard watching the water, expecting an assault, probably.

Sure, I know, it's the oldest trick in the book to toss a stick to distract the guard left behind, but there's a reason it's a common trope in books and movies: it really does work. The guy left behind is always on high alert, especially if left behind with a prisoner, and he'll be even more on edge if he knows a deadly threat is out there.

Like me, in that moment.

I crept across the forest floor, knife out, making my way up behind the guard. Filipo caught my movement out of the corner of his eye, and when he saw me he grinned. I flattened my hand and pressed my palm toward the ground, a gesture that Filipo, being ex-military, recognized as a command to hit the deck. He did, and with alacrity, flattening himself beside the dugout canoe, where there was less of a chance for a stray round to hit him. The old guy was no dummy.

I made it to within six feet of the guard when he dismissed the noise as incidental, probably thinking it was an animal or something. He pivoted, blowing my plan to take him out silently. As soon as he saw me, he squeezed off a four-round blast, which, if I weren't as good as I was, would've ripped me open stem to stern. As it was, I barely managed to leap to the side as soon as I saw him move. The bullets snapped past me, and then I was lunging forward, blade held hammer-fisted, cutting edge up, jabbing for his gut. No finesse, no technique, just intent to hurt as much as possible as fast as possible. The blade went in, I retracted, plunged it in again, pivoted to the side and dragged the blade along his inside wrist, severing the tendons and immediately compromising his grip on the machine gun. He dropped it, staggering backward, clutching his gut, and I struck again, another upward strike, this one angled to go up under his ribcage to hit his heart. I hit my target, and he blinked twice, gasping, and fell to the ground. He'd be dead in a few seconds. I scooped up his UMP, searched him for extra magazines, and stuffed them in my back pocket.

I glanced at Filipo. "Get out of here."

He rose to his feet, squinting at me derisively. "*Kissi la'u muli, kefe.* That's my best friend and goddaughter out there." He went to his boat, reached under the seat by the outboard, and ripped free a sawed-off shotgun he had taped underneath the seat. "Never had a good chance to go for it."

"These guys are no joke," I warned.

"Good thing I ain't playin' then, yeah?" He jerked his head at the path. "They heard that, I figure. Best get off the path."

I hesitated. "How'd they find you?"

Filipo shrugged. "That Jeep you left, all slick and new. Found that, somehow. Kicked in my door, early. Ain't no fool, so I played along, hoping you might find some way of making the odds more even, know what I mean?"

"I'm sorry you got involved, Filipo."

Another shrug. "Yeah, well, nothing else to do but what we gotta do, huh?"

"Guess so," I said.

I melted into the forest, sheathing my knife now that the element of surprise was gone. Using a UMP one-handed wasn't my notion of ideal, but it was a far sight better than a 9mm, so I went with it. We crept parallel to the path, made it as far as the camp, but the other two were nowhere to be seen. I heard voices, though, two of them, speaking in low tones in a foreign language. They were up ahead, around a curve in the path, which I realized, in the light of day, led to the waterfall.

We left the forest, making our way after the voices.

I never saw it coming.

One second the path was empty, the next it wasn't. They swept out from either side of the path, UMPs blasting.

Every once in a while, I'm granted a moment of pure

unexplainable luck. Or maybe it's fate or God or whoever, whatever, telling me my time here isn't done. Those moments of luck are never free. The luck took me, then. I felt the rounds snap and buzz past my cheek, felt one pluck at the cotton of my shirt, felt another tag the denim of my jeans.

They were less than fifty yards away, well inside the effective range of a UMP-45, especially if the shooter has training. They should have hit me. I should have died.

For whatever reason, they missed me. I didn't even have time to duck or dodge, they just…missed.

Filipo didn't get my luck.

He took three rounds to the chest, *smacksmacksmack*, wet thunks hitting muscle and bone. Filipo stayed upright, leveled his shotgun, knocked one back with a blast, shredding his chest into wet red ribbons, and then he fell.

Another blast of a UMP, and I felt the gun in my hand jerk and then was ripped out of my hands; more luck. That blast should have hit me, but the gun in my hands saved my life.

But now I was out of options. He'd closed the distance between us, UMP leveled at me. "Where is she?"

I just stared at him. No way I'd give her up.

He stuck the gun barrel under my chin, the hot metal searing my flesh. "I'LL KILL HIM! COME OUT, BITCH!"

"Why do you want her? She's not even involved," I asked.

He shrugged. "Orders. Cain wants her. You're protecting her, means she's worth something to you. Means Cain wants her. Leverage, I think."

"Won't work."

Another shrug. "We will see if it works. If not, I'll kill you and be done with it. The bitch can rot out here for all I care." He cast a glance at Filipo, who was writhing and gasping in the dirt. "So can he."

A few moments of silence, and then Lola appeared on the path, my Sig in her hand, held low at her side. "Let him go. You can have me."

A snicker. "Not how this goes. Drop it, or he dies." He dug the gun barrel deeper into the soft flesh under my chin, which, let me say, didn't feel too hot.

Lola didn't drop the gun. Instead, she lifted it, aimed it. "You can kill him. You're probably going to anyway. So you shoot him, I'll shoot you. No way you're gonna get him and then me, not before I get you. Or, let him go and I'll go with you, no fighting."

"Goddamn it, Lola," I said, fear seizing me.

This wasn't happening.

Shoot me. Torture me. Fuck, do anything, but leave her alone. I couldn't say any of that, though, because he'd take it as a challenge.

My captor gave that stupid snickering laugh again. "This bitch, she's got balls, huh?"

"You have no idea," I said. I met Lola's steady stare. "Babe? Whatcha doin'?"

She shrugged. "I figure you'll come after me. No worries."

I couldn't keep anger and fear out of my voice. "Yeah, but—"

"Shut up." The barrel jabbing into my jaw was an effective way to quiet me. "Fine. Count to three, I'll lower mine, let him go, you lower yours and come with me."

Lola nodded. "Fine. One—"

"Don't do it, Lola," I snarled. "These guys don't keep promises."

"I do," said the guy beside me.

"Two—" Lola slowly began lowering the pistol crouching toward the ground as she did so.

"Goddamn it." I tensed, ready to move. "Lola, you can't. You don't know what you're doing."

Panic had me by the throat, had me by the balls. I wasn't about to let her go. Not with these guys. I'd already gotten Filipo killed, I wasn't about to let Lola go too—

But there was something in her eyes as she crouched, a warning? A plea, a meaningful look.

"Three—"

The next several seconds were a blur. I wasn't even sure what happened until it was over.

As soon as Lola said "three", the gun in my chin was lowered, and he stepped toward Lola, reaching for her, for the gun she'd set on the ground. But she hadn't stood up, she was still crouched low. And then there was a blur of something black hurtling through the air, and there was the wet squishing thud of metal slicing into flesh, and my erstwhile captor was staggering backward, Tai's huge kukri buried to the hilt in his chest.

He wasn't dead, though, fumbling with his UMP, gasping, gagging, stumbling. He managed to squeeze the trigger, sending a spray of bullets into the ground at his feet.

I lashed out with my good hand, snatching the UMP away; I plugged a single round through his forehead. He fell backward, hitting the ground hard, dead immediately. I leaned over, yanked the kukri free.

Silence fell thick, like a blanket.

And then Lola vomited, and Tai sagged against a tree trunk, staring at his hands as if he didn't recognize them.

Filipo was on the ground, blood pooling underneath him, eyes blinking rapidly, mouth working. He was gone, his body just hadn't caught on to that fact quite yet.

Tai lurched across the path, fell to his knees beside Filipo. "*Uso…* no, no, no."

I was still holding the kukri, blood on my hands, dripping off the point of the blade into the dirt. "I'm sorry, Tai. They ambushed us, I never…I didn't see it coming."

Guilt. So fucking much guilt. Should've been me. Why did I get away clean and Filipo was dead? Not an unfamiliar feeling. Did a tour in Iraq, and another in Afghanistan, and I've had my share of squad mates go down around me. A bullet slices a couple inches one way, and it's you dead, a couple inches the other, it's your buddy. Why him and not you? That's part of the guilt. The rest is the fact that I'm the professional here, I should've seen this coming, shouldn't have let Filipo go with me, should've been more careful.

Plus, none of this would be happening to these people if I hadn't gotten Lola dragged into my bullshit.

I knelt, wiped the kukri clean on the pants leg of the dead guy, setting it beside Tai. "I—" I wasn't sure what to say. "I'm sorry, Tai."

He just nodded. "Filipo wasn't one to stay behind. It's not your fault."

"It is, though." I retrieved the Sig from where Lola had set it down, replaced it in my holster.

A shrug. "Maybe. What's done is done."

I bent, hefted the messy bulk of the first corpse over my body, hauled it over to the tin boat, tossed him in. The second and third bodies joined the first, and Tai piloted us to a certain lagoon he knew of, where crocs and gators were known to congregate. We heaved the bodies over the side, one by one, and then gunned the motor away. I glanced back, and by the time we were a hundred yards away, the water was a churning, boiling, red-bubbling froth of gore as the scavenging reptiles made short work of an easy meal. Bonus: there was a very, *very* slim chance any part of those three would ever be found. Not that anyone would be looking except Cain, but still, three fewer loose ends to worry about all around.

Tai and I returned to camp to find Lola still sitting by Filipo, staring into space, lost in thought.

I knelt beside her as a helicopter's rotors became audible in the distance. I glanced up, even though the helo was far enough away still that I couldn't see them. "That's my people." I glanced at Lola. "Time to make your choice, honey. Stay here with your dad, or come with me. You'll probably be safe here for a while, but eventually Cain is going to send more, if he knows you're here. I'm not sure how he's tracking us, but if we're here, or you're here, this is just going to happen again. Coming with me is the most effective way to keep your dad safe and protect his privacy. But it's your choice, babe." There was so much else I wanted to say, but none of it really mattered in the moment; apologies were futile.

She took her father's hand. "I don't want to leave you, Dad.

Without Filipo…"

Tai squatted in front of Lola and met her eyes. "You go. Come visit me when you can. I'll be okay."

"No, you won't. After you lost Mom—"

"Enough, *afafine*. You're going. You'll be safer with him. Happier with him. What is there in Miami for you? Nothing. You can get a job at any hospital, anywhere. You don't need me, and if I know you're happy, that someone is taking care of you, I'll be content. I'll have the fish, the mangroves, my *fale*, my *paopao*. You know I'll be fine." Tai finally looked at me, sadness etched in his features. "Bring her back to see me, sometimes, yeah?"

I nodded. "I will, I promise."

Tai closed his eyes, turned back to Filipo. "Go. Filipo is mine to bury."

Lola wrapped her arms around Tai's neck, clinging to him for long, long minutes, sniffling. "I love you."

"Love you too, Lola. Now *go*." He glanced at me again. "End it, Thresh. I don't want any more unwelcome visitors."

I lifted my chin. "With extreme prejudice, Tai. I swear."

We took the tin boat, which I'd rinsed the blood out best I could. Tai poled us out of the inlet and into the main waterway, and by the time we got out to the main waterway, Harris was circling our general location in the helo. He spotted us pretty much right away, angled for us, flared into a hover a good hundred feet up. A cable with a sling was lowered to us, and I secured Lola first, tugged on the cable to signal, watched her twist as she was hauled up by the winch. I was next, but I didn't bother securing myself entirely, just hooked a foot into a strap, stood up in it, and hung on with my good hand.

I waved once at Tai, who held the pole aloft in farewell.

16

NO MAN LEFT BEHIND

THE NEXT SEVERAL HOURS WERE A BLUR. THE HELICOPTER RIDE seemed interminable. Apart from the pilot, there was another man in the back of the helicopter with us, short and squat, stout. Barrel-chested, arms nearly as broad as Thresh's, head shaved bald, sporting a massive black full beard braided into a thick queue, hanging down to his chest. He looked like nothing so much as the dwarf Dwalin from *The Hobbit: Battle of the Five Armies.* And, yes, I know the names of the dwarves from the Hobbit.

The helicopter landed, the two men exiting first, and then Thresh wrapped his arm around my waist and bodily lifted me down to the tarmac.

I slapped at his chest. "I can walk."

He snorted. "You're in shock, babe. You haven't spoken a word in the last hour."

"What am I supposed to say? Filipo was family, and I'm leaving my dad, leaving Miami, leaving everything I've ever known. Not to mention, I've now personally witnessed you kill four men in less than twenty-four hours."

The bearded man shot Thresh a raised-eyebrow look. "That's got to be an off-duty kill-count record."

"Shove it, Puck," Thresh snarled, his voice low with venomous warning. "I'll tell you later."

His name was Puck? Like the character from Shakespeare's *A Midsummer Night's Dream*?

Before I could remark on the man's name, Thresh turned to me. "I'm sorry you've had to witness those things, Lola. If I'd known I was going to drag you into this, pull you through all this—" He sighed, obviously struggling with what to say. "I wish I could have spared you, if nothing else. I can't make myself wish I'd never met you, though. I just can't, as selfish as that is."

I leaned into him. "I don't wish I'd never met you either, Thresh. But I hope you know a good therapist."

"When this is settled, I'll find you the best there is, I swear," Thresh answered.

He guided me to a mobile staircase leading up into a small private jet, waiting until I was buckled into the window seat and then buckled himself in beside me.

I glanced out my window and watched a tall, slender man exit the front of the helicopter, its rotors still slowing. He jogged toward the jet. A moment later he appeared in the doorway. He was on the upper end of average height, slim and lean and hard-looking in a way that reminded me of Thresh's dagger. He had piercing green eyes, messy brown hair shot through at the temples with a little gray, a closely-trimmed beard, somewhere between stubble and a real beard. He exuded danger and confidence and authority.

His eyes fixed on me. "Dr. Reed. Welcome." He stepped toward me, extended his hand, which I took and shook automatically. "My name is Harris. We've met before, I believe."

I nodded. "Yes, you were my patient a year ago."

"Pleased to have you with us, although I'm sorry about the circumstances."

"Yeah, it's been a little less than ideal."

Harris's expression darkened, hardened. "For all of us. I still have one of my men missing, and even my two best assets can't seem to find him. But, I assure you, we will be pursuing this with extreme prejudice."

"That's what Thresh said, 'extreme prejudice.' What does that mean in normal people terms?"

Harris didn't answer right away, but eventually responded, "It means we're going to go after these fuckers with everything we've got, and we're not going to worry overmuch about pesky things like laws. It means we're going in hard and fast and mean."

I nodded. "I can't argue with that. They killed my uncle." I choked up, because that was still more than fresh, so fresh I hadn't really processed the fact that Filipo was dead. "Get them. And if you need a doctor, I'm your woman. Just get me some supplies."

Harris regarded me intently. "We can hide you somewhere until it's over. I have a few strings to pull, but I can make sure you still have a job at the hospital when you're ready to go back. You don't have to throw in with us, Dr. Reed."

"Call me Lola," I said, glancing at Thresh, who was watching me carefully, anticipating my answer but trying not to give too much away. "And I already have, Mr. Harris."

"It's just Harris." He clapped Thresh on the shoulder. "And if you ever need help wrangling this big stubborn son of a bitch, just call me."

I tried to smile, and only partially succeeded. "Once you get past his 'I'm a badass' façade, he's really just a big teddy bear. But, thank you."

Harris gave me a skeptical expression. "Not sure I've ever seen that side of Thresh. But if you insist." He paused for a moment, leaned into the cockpit, opened a cabinet, and produced a notepad and a pen, which he handed to me. "Why don't you spend some time on the flight making a wish list of supplies you'd need to be well-stocked and ready for pretty much anything, and I'll make some calls, see what I can get my hands on."

I just nodded. "All right."

Harris glanced at Thresh. "Talk to you in the cockpit?"

Thresh heaved a sigh, hesitated, then leaned toward me, palmed my cheek with his paw, turned my face to mine. Kissed me long and deep and hard. "Back in a bit," he murmured against my lips.

"Okay," I whispered, still dizzy from the force of the unexpected kiss.

Then, when I saw the expressions on Harris's and Puck's faces... it all made sense. They were staring at Thresh like he'd grown a second head and was reciting Japanese poetry.

Thresh preceded Harris into the cockpit, and then the door to the cockpit closed and I was alone with Puck, who had taken Thresh's seat beside me and was eyeing me with open curiosity.

"Pardon my staring, sweet cheeks, but when you see the impossible done before breakfast, it tends to take a man by surprise."

"Don't call me sweet cheeks, Dwalin. And what's impossible?"

"Dwalin, that's a funny one," he said, with a hearty guffaw, telling me he didn't take any offense. He waved a hand at me, "Thresh... acting like a...shit, I don't even know. Like Harris is with Layla. I'd've sworn Thresh was gonna die a bachelor, with a hot bitch on each arm, and another on his lap. Bitches love Thresh, and he don't even try."

I eyed Puck. "Oh reeeeeally?" I drawled the word, drew it out.

He affected an innocent expression, holding up both hands palms out. "Least, that's how he used to be. Now he's here with you at his side, and he's kissing you like I ain't ever seen him kiss anybody."

"And I bet you've seen that plenty?"

He shrugged. "If you want to know how he used to be, you'd be better off talking to Duke—those two are inseparable. Wingmen, know what I mean?" Puck rubbed a finger along the leather stitching of the seat near his thigh. "'Course, Duke's pretty-boy ass is AWOL at the moment, which isn't doing us any favors."

I noticed Puck's drawl seemed to come and go, and wasn't really an accent so much as what I suspected was an affectation, probably meant to hide or disguise his intelligence. His eyes betrayed him, though. You couldn't look Puck in the eyes and miss the cunning, the calculation. He was big, burly, with a beard any Hell's Angel would be envious of, a half-sleeve tattoo on one arm from shoulder to elbow, but it was obvious he was far from stupid and didn't miss a thing.

"Are you worried about Duke, too?"

"Everybody is. Duke doesn't disappear. Anselm? Sure, dude's a straight-up ghost. Even Lear has a tendency to go to ground for days on end, especially if he's running a program or writing code. But Thresh and Duke? All you ever gotta do to find those two is follow the trail of broken hearts and empty bottles. And maybe a few bodies here and there. Those boys are rough. They ain't hard to find, that's my point. Gym, a dive bar, or the compound. That's it. So for Duke to just…vanish? Not good."

"You think Cain has him?"

Puck bobbed his head side to side. "Possible. Likely, even. But Duke…our boy can hold his own. I'm more worried about the poor, soon-to-be-dead motherfuckers who took him. Duke's a pretty boy, but he's no pussy. He's got an ugly temper." He gestured at the cock-pit. "Thresh keeps his shit under control. He's cool as a cucumber, your man. But Duke, now? He's hot-headed, liable to pop at any moment, especially if you put his back to the wall. Corner someone like Duke? It won't be pretty."

"You'll find him," I said. "Thresh says you guys are like family to each other, and I may not have known Thresh very long, but I know him well enough to know he doesn't leave people behind. He doesn't let them down, and he won't stop until those he considers his own are all safe."

Puck nodded. "Got that right. None of us are the kind of folks you'd write home about. We've all got blood on our hands and skeletons in our closets, and some of us have 'em right in the foyer, know what I mean? But we got one thing most don't: loyalty. Fuckin' un-compromising, no man left behind kind of loyalty. And Thresh is the epitome of that. He's literally carried members of this team out of a bad situation on his back, while wounded, fighting his way out. And now these fuckers have his best friend? This shit is gonna get real fuckin' gnarly, real fuckin' fast."

There was a long pause. When Puck spoke again, I wasn't sure he meant his words for me. "But yeah, I'm worried about Duke. I just hope we get him back in one piece when this is all over."

So did I, if only for Thresh's sake.

After another few minutes, Thresh exited the cockpit took his seat beside me, and jerked his thumb toward the cockpit, addressing Puck. "Boss wants you up front, Stubby."

Puck grinned. "No he don't, you just want to be alone so you can neck this saucy little minx, here." He stood up, winked down at me. "Not that I blame you."

Puck swaggered up to the cockpit, whistling a merry tune. Within seconds, the engines revved up to a roar and I was pushed back into my seat as we took off.

Thresh stared after him, then turned to me. "Puck can be an acquired taste," he started.

"HEARD THAT!" Puck shouted from up front. "I'M WHISKEY, BITCH!"

I laughed. "I like him."

Thresh seemed relieved. "He's a good guy. Or, well, he's a good guy to have on your side, may be a more accurate way to put it."

"So, did you and Harris come up with a plan for rescuing Duke?" I asked.

Thresh nodded. "Although I've got a feeling we're more rescuing Cain's goons from Duke rather than the other way around."

"That's what Puck said."

"Duke doesn't fuck around, and he doesn't have an off switch. But we're not taking any chances. I guess Anselm got a lock on his last known position, and an eyewitness to his abduction. So at least we have somewhere to start."

I unbuckled as the jet straightened out to a cruising altitude. "Well, I'm not sure what help I'll be during the operation or whatever you call it, but if the last twenty-four hours have been any indication, you'll need me on hand to patch up—what was it you called them?

Oh yeah, your little boo-boos."

Thresh grinned at me. "I've got a boo-boo you can kiss right now."

I sat up in my chair. "Yeah? I didn't know you'd gotten hurt."

His grin turned hot, rife with dirty promise. "I didn't get hurt, babe. It's just been a few hours since I've had you, and all the adrenaline has me horny. So I'm feeling a little…achy…if you know what I mean."

"If we're going after Duke," I said, "you're gonna need to be at the top of your game, I'm guessing."

Thresh smirked at me. "I would say that's an accurate statement."

"Well, you can't go into a dangerous situation feeling all…achy… now can you?"

"Nope."

"I'm gonna have to help you out, then, aren't I?"

"I think you are, babe," he murmured.

My heart hammered in my chest as I reached down to unzip him, then tugged his jeans down to his knees. I slid down to the floor, took his erection in my hand, stroked him to writhing readiness, then wrapped my mouth around him, took as much of him as I could, then backed away.

"Holy shit, babe," Thresh grunted. "I didn't mean *now*… goddamn—"

I grinned up at him, pumping at his root. "You'll just have to come quickly, then, won't you?"

I felt daring, felt wild and crazy, going down on Thresh in this tiny little jet, his friend and boss just a few feet away, on the other side of a door. The thought turned me on, knowing they could come out any second. The old fear, the paranoia…it was gone. I wasn't the old Lola again, no, I was someone better, someone stronger. I was more ravenous than ever, and I had a man who could not only handle me as I am, but who challenged me, pushed me, and could match my insatiable sexual appetite.

It didn't take long, not with my mouth around him, my hands

on him. I brought him to orgasm within minutes, swallowed every-thing he had and then demanded a kiss from him.

He gave me the kiss, and then touched his lips to my ear. "Just you wait till I get you really alone, babe."

"Oh yeah?" I smiled for him, met his pale, intense blue gaze. "What are you gonna do?"

"I'm gonna get you on your hands and knees," he answered, "and I'm gonna fuck you so hard for so long you won't know where one orgasm begins and the next ends. I'm gonna do it bare, no stupid condom between us, and when I'm done, I'm gonna pull out and come all over your big beautiful ass."

I writhed, picturing it, wanting it. "Is that a promise?"

He bit my earlobe. "Damn straight it is, Doc."

"Good, because that sounds like the best thing I've ever heard."

"And *then*..." he whispered, "I'm gonna hold you the whole night long, and we're gonna wake up and make love so slow it'll be noon before we're done."

I blinked at him. "Make love, huh?"

He nodded, serious, vulnerable. "Make hot, sweet, messy love."

"I lied," I whispered, "*that's* the best thing I've ever heard."

DUKE

ALPHA ONE

Protect at any cost.

SECURITY

New York Times and *USA Today* Bestselling Author
Jasinda Wilder

1

FANCY

WELL...FUCK.

This sucked.

Woozy from the crowbar I'd taken to the back of the head—which of course came with a splitting headache straight from Satan's own asshole—I was disoriented and sluggish. It was a chemical sluggishness, though, which suggested someone had either roofied me—and if it was a woman, she shouldn't have bothered; I'd have fucked her without the drugs—or someone had tranked me. Which wasn't the brightest idea, because I was slowly coming out of it. And what with the headache, and the fact that I was hungry, it didn't exactly spell rousing games of charades and shuffleboard once I got my bearings and figured out who I had to hit.

I tried to blink, but that didn't accomplish much; either it was pitch black and there wasn't anything to see, or I was blindfolded.

I focused hard, which hurt. Then I tried to subtly flex my muscles. I tested my toes and fingers and wrists, and tried to see if I was simply bound, or drugged into paralysis. I had feeling in my limbs so I knew I wasn't paralyzed. The bad news was that my wrists were tied; the good news was my ankles weren't bound, and they hadn't gagged me, either. Stupid move—I can fuck you up with just my feet, let me tell you. I learned Muai Thai in Thailand, from some seriously scary little motherfuckers, the kind of dudes who go out and kick trees just to toughen their shins.

I kept my breathing slow and steady, something I did out of long habit. I listened hard and I heard nothing that gave anything away. The floor was cold and hard underneath my shoulder, hip, and knee. I was pretty sure it was a cement floor. I was lying on my side, hands bound in front of me—another mistake.

Struggling to push past my haze, I figured I was in a room, cement of some sort. I kept listening, but there wasn't much to hear.

Now that my faculties were returning, I could feel the blindfold around my head and it felt like a folded bunch of cloth. It would be easy enough to remove when I was ready.

Staying still and quiet I kept listening, focusing on breathing slow and steady as if I was still unconscious. The bonds around my wrists were zip-ties, and they were wrenched tight to my skin which, while painful, was actually good news. Zip-ties are plastic, which means their overall tensile strength isn't that great. One hard wrench of my arms, or bashing them against my knee, and they'd be gone. It would take me ten seconds max, a number I quote from experience.

I was about to start the process of determining whether to play this out a bit longer or start my escape when I heard a muffled whimper. Definitely female, close by.

"*Pssst*," I hissed.

"*Gnnnhhh?*" Definitely a chick, definitely gagged.

"Keep still. Pretend you're still knocked out. No matter what you hear, no matter what happens, keep playing possum. Got it, babe?"

"*Ugh-oo, doh gah ee ay.*"

I stifled a chuckle; she sounded *pissed*, and if I was anything like a decent translator of pissed-off, gagged females, she said something like *fuck you, don't call me babe.* Better for her that she had a bit of spark. If she could cuss me out while bound and gagged, it meant she had spark, which meant spirit, which meant whatever was going on, she wasn't as likely to flake out if shit got weird.

I tried to think back and remember; what was the last thing I remembered?

Some shitty dive bar in...Denver? Probably Denver. I remember that after Nevada, Thresh had gone to find that doctor chick he was so hung up on—which I understood because, seriously, that chica had curves for fucking *days*, and she'd pushed back at Thresh, which was the fastest way to get him horny short of reaching into his shorts. Plus, all that exotic Islander skin, and that thick fucking hair? No wonder Thresh wanted to take her for a tumble. I'd hit it, if he hadn't had dibs. And no, we weren't so juvenile as to call dibs out loud, but when you spent enough time hunting tail with your bro, you know when he's interested, and you don't go after that chick, even after he's done.

So...I had been in a Denver dive bar, alone. I remembered that much, at least. I'd been on the prowl, going slow on the drinks, ready for any sign of my two favorite activities: fucking and fighting. I'd gotten a whiff of some kind of sweet floral perfume while exiting the head, and followed the scent to an out-of-place honey with a tight body and a serious attitude problem—in short, exactly my kinda girl.

I hadn't really made a move, not as such, just sort of scoping her out, getting a feel for her. Hadn't even started with the charm-and-flirt routine yet, but she wasn't playing. Shut me down cold, even though she had no wing girls with her, no bling ring, and no sign of a guy, just sort of drinking alone.

Now, I ain't one to buy into the gender stereotypes much, okay? I served with some chicks in the Army, and some of 'em were just as much my bros as BangBang and Gutierrez had been. I may be a shameless manwhore of the worst kind, but I take people as they are. I don't fuck chicks with diamonds on their left hand, and no means no...except when I sniff out that *no* means *chase me*, and that's always obvious.

But there are a few clichés and stereotypes that tend to hold

JASINDA WILDER

true. Like, if you see a dude sitting by himself in a smoky shithole dive bar, you're better off leaving him alone, 'cause he don't want to talk. And the other one that's almost always true is, if you see a lady, like a real-deal *lady*, with Louboutins and Chanel clutch purses and expensive perfume and two-carat diamond earrings, the kind of lady who wears that fancy shit like it ain't no thing, in a LoDo dive bar, no less…well, partner, that shit there spells trouble.

What? I've hooked up with some *ladies* in my time, and I like nice shit, so I know one-percenter name brands when I see them, okay?

Anyway, she'd gotten up and gone outside to smoke. Pall Mall Lights lit with a snazzy looking fancy-ass electric flameless lighter.

You know how they say you are what you eat? And you know how they say curiosity killed the cat? Well, I eat a lot of pussy…

I was curious and went out after her. I lit my one-hitter and took a quick toke of some fine-ass herb I'd picked up—a habit I only indulge in when I'm off-duty. I opened my mouth to talk to her, and then her eyes had gone wide, surprised, but she'd been looking behind me, not at me.

Then, bam, everything went black.

And now, here I am, bound, blindfolded, and fighting a headache and a wicked chemical haze.

So, if I had to guess, that lonely fancy chick was the same person now bound and gagged behind me.

Next question?

Who the fuck would take me prisoner like this? And why?

The events in Nevada floated through my head and I remembered Harris's warning about Cain reappearing and being bent on revenge…and now I have an inkling as to what is going on.

I was still working through the situation in my head when I heard voices in the distance followed by footsteps shuffling down the stairs.

"Play possum, okay?" I hissed, quiet as I could. "Trust me."

"*Nnnnng?*" She sounded less sparky, and more fearful.

"You've got my word, Fancy. I'll get you out of this. But you gotta listen to me real carefully. Breathe like you're still asleep. Relax your muscles. Don't react to *anything*."

"*An-cee?*"

"Yeah, Fancy, that's you. Now shut up and play possum."

I followed my own orders as the voices got closer, the footsteps just on the other side of the wall. I heard a lock twist, then hinges protested, and feet—two pair, three—three, I'd wager—scuffed across the floor. Definitely a cement floor. European voices, thick Eastern Bloc accents. Definitely Cain's group.

"Still out," a voice said, in heavily accented English.

A pair of feet shuffled toward me. "Should be. We hit this big one with enough tranquilizer to take out a pair of elephants." This from a second voice.

"And the girl?" The first guy again.

"Cain said no witnesses, no chances." Third voice, sounding like he had a bit of authority.

"Think we could have some fun, first?" First voice again.

They were baiting me, I realized. They'd be talking in Czech or Ukrainian or whatever if this discussion were meant for their ears only. This was for us, to see if we were awake.

"After she wakes up," said voice number three, the one that sounded in charge. "No hurry. Cain won't be here for a few days yet. We have time for fun later."

The feet shuffled even closer to me. My heart hammered, but I kept my breathing steady and slow, my muscles loose. There was a moment of silence, and then a shock of agony and a loud thud as a big boot slammed full force into my gut. No warning, no way to tense against it, I couldn't breathe, shit—

I forced myself not to react, struggling through the lack of oxygen, the wind knocked so far out of me stars burst behind my eyes and panic clutched at my instincts. I stayed still, as if the tranquilizer was still working in my bloodstream; and when I didn't react they must have assumed, logically, that I was still under.

You don't survive alone on the streets for as long as I did and not learn to take a kick or ten to the gut.

I heard their feet retreat; they were speaking in their own language now. The door closed, the lock turned, boots ascended, and then I heard the floorboards overhead creak, followed by a loud squeal like rusty screen door hinges slamming shut.

Finally, I let myself gulp oxygen, gagging on it as it flooded through me. "Fucker's…gonna…pay…for that," I gasped.

"Oooh oh-kay?"

"Just fine, Fancy, just fine. Gotta catch my breath, and then I'll do some commando shit or something." My head was still thick, aching, my mouth was dry, and now my stomach throbbed.

Thinking was hard.

I gave myself a thirty count, and then I brought my hands up and used my thumbs to rip off the blindfold. Yep: basement, bare concrete floor, metal posts holding up the low ceiling, open rafters and ductwork, an old box fan in one corner, along with a stationary bike. There was an old weight bench with a single barbell bar on it but no weights, a freestanding heavy bag, and a shelving unit with aging canned goods. In short, this was the basement of a tired, old suburban house. I rolled onto my back, then onto my other side.

And there was Fancy, in all her glory. She was on her side too, perpendicular to me, the top of her head near my stomach. Five-six or five-seven, sleek, svelte, tight round ass in a knee-length dove-gray skirt, black wedge heels, and a white blouse cupping a sensational pair of high, plump, firm tits, not super huge, but enough to fill even my big ol' paws. She looked just like I remembered her from last night.

Only now her fine blond hair, which I remembered being done in a casually elegant up-do, was now tangled and messy, lank strings hanging in her eyes and sticking to her neck and cheeks. And holy mother of fucks, the woman's skin…*damn*. Pale as pearls, flawless, enticing. Except her cheeks, which were flushed bright pink. She was glaring at me, and her eyes were…fuck, her eyes were like nothing I'd ever seen before. Cerulean blue shot through with streaks of green and hints of hazel. Wide eyes, full of fierce personality. Beautiful, hypnotizing eyes.

"*Hey, ahh-hoh. Geh a mooh on.*"

Clear enough, I supposed.

I rolled forward to my knees, stood up, worked the kinks out of my stiff joints, then laced my fingers together, flexed my wrists away from each other to put tension on the zip-tie, swung my arms up and then back down hard as I could while swinging my knee up. My wrists hit my knee with crushing force, and the zip-tie snapped, freeing my hands. Ten seconds or less, motherfucker.

I knelt beside the girl who flinched away from me, automatically, it seemed. I frowned down at her. "Hey now, Fancy, don't be hatin'. I'm on your side, okay? I'm not gonna hurt you. I'm gonna get that gag off, and then you can cuss me out all you want, as long as you do it quiet, all right?"

She held still, but kept wary eyes fixed on me as I knelt closer to her, leaned forward, reached around behind her head to untie the knot. Yeah, I could've knelt behind her to do it, and where's the fun in that? She smelled like jasmine; I got a good whiff as I worked at the knot, and good fucking goddamn, that scent, on that woman? Made me dizzy. I swear I could get hard just sniffing her.

I acted like I was having trouble with the knot, pausing, leaning a little closer to peer over her shoulder. It was an act, since it was a fairly simple knot loosely tied, and I could have gotten it free with my eyes closed, but it got me another subtle nose-full of her intoxicating scent, which was its own reward, and well worth the glare of daggers I got from Fancy when I pulled back to work on the knot a bit more.

Once it was free, I tossed the handkerchief aside...

And Fancy promptly set to complaining. "My god, that thing tasted like old sweat. I think I'm going to vomit."

"Breathe in through your nose and out through your mouth, sugar, and it'll pass. The nausea is more from whatever they used to knock us out."

She shot me that patented death-and-daggers glare. "My name is Temple. Not sugar, or babe, or *fancy*." She was breathing in through her nose and out through her mouth, I noticed. "Temple Kennedy."

Damn—that was a name I knew. Hell, *everybody* knew that name. She was one of those "famous for being famous" celebrity honeys. Daddy was a retired rock star and her mom was an A-list actress with multiple Oscar noms and at least one Golden Globe that I knew of. Beyond wealthy, spoiled, she had lived her whole life in the spotlight. Has a reality show where cameras follow her around as she trots the globe and suns herself on yachts in the Mediterranean, yells at servers, and insults her mom and sucks up to her dad. She turned all that into a lucrative career doing…I wasn't sure what. She had an app which did who knew what, clothing lines, makeup, a tell-all book or two, and any number of other bits and pieces of merchandising with her name and likeness on it.

So what the ever-loving *fuck* was a high-class *lady*-lady like Temple Kennedy doing in a dive bar in LoDo?

That was the million-dollar question.

Or, actually, shit—a hundred million dollar question, given how much her parents were worth.

I leaned down and put my face inches from hers, reached out an index finger, brushed her sunshine-and-honey hair out of her face. "So, Temple Kennedy. Think these dick-knobs know who they've got in their basement?"

One plucked eyebrow lowered, the other arched upward. "I would assume so."

She had a little smudge of dirt on her forehead from the floor. I rubbed my thumb over it, gently, wiping it away. She was breathing hard by the time I finished, tension written in every line of her body and face. She did *not* like my proximity. Funny, most honeys are tripping over themselves to get closer to me, to get my hands on them. But then, Temple Kennedy was *way* above even my pay grade.

"See, I don't think they do."

She struggled to sit up, but her hands and feet were both bound, her hands behind her back leaving her helpless. Bound hand and foot, *and* gagged? She must have put up a fight.

"Why wouldn't they? I assume they're kidnappers looking for a ransom."

I laughed quietly, and then lifted her to a sitting position, keeping a grip on her until she was steady. "Oh, sweetpea, not everything is about you. Unfortunately, the situation is a lot worse than that."

"Why is it so hard for you to use my name?" She wavered and I caught her, keeping her upright. "And how could it be worse than me being kidnapped? And can you *please* do something about these restraints? They're beginning to chafe."

I crept from corner to corner, rummaging through the detritus, but found nothing useful for severing her wire bonds. Then I ducked under the stairs, remembering the basement of a foster house I'd stayed in for a bit, and how the drunken old bastard had kept an ancient toolbox under the stairs in the basement. Sure enough, I hit the jackpot. In a corner was a rusting Craftsman toolbox filled with screwdrivers, ratchets, a hammer, loose nails, and a pair of wire cutters. I returned to Temple with the wire cutters and knelt behind her.

"Hold still, Fancy, I'm gonna pop these ties." I clipped between her wrists, and she immediately drew her hands around in front and massaged them. "As for how it could be worse? They didn't snatch me because I was with you, they snatched *you* because you were with *me*."

"I wasn't *with* you. I was outside smoking."

"And I went out after you. They saw you next to me and, as you heard, they had orders not to take chances or leave witnesses." I moved to her feet and clipped her ankles free. "I'm not sure what they want, but I'm gonna go out on a limb and suggest it ain't a tickle fight, princess. They got no problem burying you if you cause trouble, trust me on that.

"And if they were to somehow find out who you are if, say, *someone* was to bust out with a *'do you even know who I am?'*,

Baby-cakes…that would *not* be beneficial to your situation. They'd not only have a witness, but they'd have a hostage, and money to be made. The guy in charge of this whole mess, he ain't a nice guy. He'd be the sort to send severed fingers to your dad until he got his money. So I suggest you keep your mouth shut and follow my lead."

She paled at that, and considering her pearly complexion, that meant she went *really* pale. "They *wouldn't*."

I shrugged. "That's my best guess. This Cain guy isn't really my particular enemy, he's more my boss's enemy. But since I'm connected to him, they snatched me, and got you in a twofer. And, yeah, honey, they would absolutely hack off your pretty little manicured fingers."

She was rolling her ankles, trying to get the feeling back, so I took her foot in my hand, slipped off her wedge sandal, and massaged her foot. A low, sultry groan of pleasure left her lips before she could stop herself, but then she yanked her foot back and shot me that glare again.

I let her go, and squatted next to her, watching her try to massage feeling back into her extremities and admiring her tight, toned body. "I happen to think you've got beautiful hands, and it'd be a shame to see them come to any harm, so you can relax. I won't let anything happen to your fingers, or any other part of your fine-ass body."

"Oh really? There were three of them, in case you didn't notice." She said this as if I should be afraid.

"Yeah, I noticed."

"You were blindfolded, how could you tell?"

I shrugged, smirking. "I counted their voices, and heard their different footsteps."

"And you can take on all three of them, can you?" Skeptical, sarcastic.

I stood up to my full height, which got her attention. I'm six-six and two-eighty, and there's not an ounce of fat on me. And believe me, she fuckin' noticed. There was no mistaking the way her eyes raked up and down my body several times, and then she blinked, shook her head, and looked away, those pretty pale cheeks blushing scarlet.

"Yeah, Fancy. I'm thinkin' they only brought three guys, and that was their second mistake."

"What was the first?"

"Not killing me outright," I said. "'Cause now I'm inconvenienced. I've got a headache, and that makes me cranky. I'm hungry, which makes me hangry, and when I get hangry I tend to lose a bit of rationality and self-restraint. And they only brought three guys? They're going to wish they had a whole lot more."

She stared up at me, and her gaze reflected equal parts attraction, fascination, and revulsion.

I heard the screen door squeal, then footsteps on the floor above us, and then on the stairs.

I winked at Temple. "Fun's about to start, honey-buns. You just sit there and be your pretty, innocent little self. Let them come in, and do *not* look at me. Then, when I give you the signal, you get your sexy ass out of the way."

She looked panicked. "Wh—what's the signal?"

"When I start hitting people, obviously."

I started to turn away.

"Wait!" she called out.

I turned back, quirked an eyebrow. "What's up?"

"What's your name?"

I gave her my signature panty-melter grin. "Name's Duke Silver."

Snagging the barbell from the rack, I hefted it, swung it around a few times, and then positioned myself near the door as the footsteps clomped down the stairs.

The lock clicked, the doorknob twisted.

Temple sat frozen on the floor, like a deer caught in headlights and then, in the moments before the door swung open, she shook her hair out, fluffed it, and unbuttoned her blouse to show a cock-hardening amount of plump ivory cleavage.

A little too effective, since it cost me several seconds delay—I was staring too, right when the three cocksuckers ambled through the door with their guns at the ready.

Great, now I have to fight with hard-on.

2

CATCH ME IF YOU CAN

Dᴜᴋᴇ Sɪʟᴠᴇʀ? Rᴇᴀʟʟʏ?
     The big, gorgeous bastard looked like he'd stepped off a Jerry Bruckheimer movie set, the kind where there were explosions, big tits, and a muscle-bound oaf with more brawn than brains. So far we were batting two for three, because I had big tits and he fit the muscular moron bill to the T. I guess the explosions were still to come.

And then he had to look like a fucking movie star—the angular cheekbones, the craggy, sharp jawline, those cornflower-blue eyes? Then there was his hair. I got all twitchy and weak in the knees for his hair. True natural red hair, a Ron Weasley orange. Except Duke's hair was thick and wavy, almost curly, and he had it been severely undercut, the sides buzzed to the scalp, with the top left long enough to pull back in a ponytail.

And if his hair made me gaga, his body did worse things to me—his body made me flat-out stupid, is what it did. Think Arnold Schwarzenegger in his prime, and you'll have a rough idea of how Duke Silver was built. A little leaner, though, not quite as bulky as Arnie was in his Mr. Olympia days, but only by a hair. Scary thing was, Duke didn't move like a bodybuilder—he moved like a tiger.

Smooth, easy, lithe, graceful, and viciously powerful. And he had…
it. That magnetism, the kind that just draws your attention to him
against your will. I mean, my mom is Jane Kennedy, so I've met some
of the biggest movie stars in the world, and was on first name basis
with a lot of them, sweet old Arnie included. Duke? He just had a
presence that could put any of them to shame.

But there was something else about him that wasn't like the
A-listers I knew. Those guys didn't…scare me. That was it, wasn't
it? Duke Silver made me shudder, and not in a *damn I'd like to fuck
him silly* sort of way, but in the way you'd shudder in terror if you
suddenly found yourself face to face with a full-grown and hungry
Bengal tiger. That kind of shudder. The involuntarily wetting of your
pants kind of shudder.

I should go back and qualify that thought, though. Yes, I really
did want to fuck Duke Silver until he forgot his name. Or, more accurately, until *I* forgot his name and mine both. And that pissed me
off. I was Temple Kennedy. I crooked my finger, and dozens of rich,
beautiful, successful men would drop to their knees and do whatever I told them to, simply because of my name, because of what
I looked like, and who my parents are. I wasn't affected by any of
it. I've walked the red carpet for the Oscars, the Golden Globes,
the Emmy's, the Tony's…I've been interviewed by *Rolling Stone*, *E!*,
Entertainment Weekly, *Vogue*, *People*, and have been on the cover of
US Weekly almost as frequently as Kim Kardashian. No man *ever* left
me feeling weak in the knees.

Yet there were my stupid, traitor knees, getting all wobbly. Good
thing I was sitting down.

Goddammit, he even made my mind wander.

I mentally scolded myself, instructing my lust-ridden libido to
check itself before it wrecked itself, told my knees to stiffen up, and
forced my mind to focus.

*They would absolutely hack off your pretty little manicured fin-
gers*, he'd said. Well that wasn't going to work for me, since I happened to be allergic to having my fingers chopped off. Or anything

else, for that matter.

Focus, Temple, focus.

I unbuttoned my blouse to show a little extra cleavage, and fluffed my hair. And yeah, you bet your ass I noticed Duke noticing me. And, yeah, I also noticed the way his khaki cargo shorts tightened at the zipper just a little when I plumped my tits—good to know I affect him, too.

The footsteps were right outside the door, now.

Duke was standing to the right of the door, so when it swung open he'd be able to swing that weight bar into the opening. The annoying part of the scenario was that Duke was wielding the weight bar like a quarterstaff. Annoying, I say, in that it was a full Olympic bar, weighing 45 pounds, and he could swing it around like a wooden stick.

And, BTW, don't give me that *you're just a spoiled little blonde bimbo so how would you know how much an Olympic barbell weighs* shit; you don't maintain a body like mine without spending almost as much time in the gym as I'm sure Duke does so, yeah, I know how much an Olympic bar weighs. I can clean it with eighty pounds on the bar, too. Not much for Duke, but he's three times my size.

The door opened, and a man stepped through, two more right behind him. The first guy took three steps into the room before he saw me sitting on the floor, gag gone, bonds cut, blouse showing cleavage and a hint of bra, hair mussed like I'd just been fucked— yeah, he stopped in his tracks.

I've still got it, bitch.

The two men behind him bumped into him with a chorus of curses.

"How you are like this?" The man in front asked, confusion mangling his English. "And where is—?"

Whack.

I cringed, and then gagged. Because FUCK. Duke had swung the bar as hard as he could, and it had connected with the poor guy's skull like a baseball bat connecting with a watermelon. Similar red wet spray, too. I vomited on the floor in front of me at the sight of the wreckage that had once been a man's skull, but I didn't have time to even really register that I'd upchucked before Duke was in motion, the bar now held in a wide grip, like a quarterstaff. One end smashed into a belly, and then it was whistling around the other way and taking out a knee with a sickening crunch, and then too many things happened at once for me to track.

One guy managed to gut through his ruined knee to draw a gun from his waistband and squeeze off a round with a deafening report. I heard concrete shatter and saw the wall to Duke's right explode in a spray of slivers and dust—a missed shot, thank god.

"Dumb idea, dipshit," Duke said, his voice as calm and cool as you please, sounding amused, even.

Whack.

This time the bar's tip cracked into the shooter's chest, knocking him backward, then rotated and began arcing downward. I looked away, then, because seeing that once was plenty for me.

I heard the sick wet crunch, though.

I also heard another gunshot, heard Duke grunt in irritation, and then I heard yet another now-distinctive crunch, that of a human head turning into hamburger.

Oh god, I should not have thought that. Should not have—shit.

I puked again.

"You can open your eyes now, Fancy," Duke said. "They're all dead."

"I'll keep them closed, thank you very much," I said, trying my damnedest to sound like I wasn't as traumatized as I felt.

"Suit yourself. Might step in something nasty, though."

I had my eyes squeezed shut and my hand clapped over them; I extended my other hand in front of me for him to take. "Can you… lead me out? I really don't want to see that."

"Oh." A pause. "Right. Guess you're not used to this shit, are you?"

"Used to what, deconstructed human skulls?"

He chuckled. "Deconstructed human skulls. Huh, never heard it put that way before."

"No, for your information, I'm *not* used to that shit. And if you are, then I'm sorry for the life you've lived."

I felt his hand clasp around mine, and I couldn't suppress a shiver. His hand was *huge*, and I could feel his calluses against my skin. "Come on, Fancy. Up you go." He tugged me upright with surprising gentleness, and then his hand was at the small of my back, guiding me forward, nudging me to one side, then the other. "Uh…big step here, got a puddle of—um, just take a big step."

I kept my hand over my eyes and took a big step. My other foot followed, and as I put my heel down, it hit something slippery, so my foot shot out from underneath me. I'd have gone down, but Duke's hand on mine kept me upright. As soon as I slipped, I felt his other hand catch my waist, and I was airborne.

"Let's just do this, huh?" he said, more to himself than to me.

I was in his arms. I could feel the bulge of his biceps, the hardness of his chest, his masculine scent. Nice. This was…very nice.

Only, underneath his scent, I could smell other, less pleasant smells. My puke, and something sharply tangy and queasy-making. Blood, gore. That took the nice right out of the moment, because that scent pushed into my head the all too vivid visual of the bar smashing into the skull.

I groaned, my stomach revolting again.

"Shit, you gonna hork again?"

"Trying not to."

"Shallow breaths through your mouth. Stop thinking about it."

"Can't." I turned my face into his black V-neck T-shirt, the image flashing through me again and again. "Keep seeing it."

We were ascending then, his feet quiet on the stairs. He stopped after maybe ten or eleven steps. "Need you to hang out here a second, okay?" His voice buzzed quietly in my ear. "Gotta be sure that was all of 'em before I take you up there."

He set me on a stair, and I had to open my eyes, then. My gaze, of course, was drawn with morbid curiosity downward. But his hand caught my jaw and he turned my head to look up at him.

"Nope." He didn't smile, but his expression was…understanding, I guess you might call it. "No looking down there, Fancy. Keep your eyes up this way. Sit tight, keep breathing, and try not to think about it."

I got a good look at his ass as he stood up and left the stairwell. And, god, what an ass. Even in those stupid cargo shorts, it was obvious his ass was as hard and round as a pair of cannonballs. I didn't tell myself to focus, then, because thinking about Duke Silver's ass was better than thinking about what was at the bottom of the stairs.

A good minute of silence passed, and then Duke appeared in the doorway at the top of the stairs, an automatic pistol in both hands, held as naturally as if it were an extension of his arms, probably liberated from the now-dead guys back downstairs.

"Come on, Fancy. Time to bust a move."

"My name is Temple, goddammit," I snarled.

"I know." He shot me that grin, the one I just knew he probably used on a regular basis for the melting of female undergarments. "But I like you better all riled up."

I glared at him. "Wipe that stupid grin off your face," I snapped. "You're not going to melt my underwear with it."

He reached down, took my hand, helped me stand up, and drew me up the stairs and out into the main level of the house. And just like that, I was flush against him, staring up at his idiotically beautiful blue eyes and stupidly perfect face.

And then he murmured something truly obnoxious: "Can't exactly melt panties you ain't wearin', can I, Princess?"

"You're a pig." I slapped him across the face as hard as I could and then stepped backward angrily.

Of course, my slap and angry retort were ruined by the fact that I had stepped backward toward the stairs and would have gone down them had Duke's ninja reflexes not sent his hand shooting out to snag me around the waist and pull me back up against him.

"Careful," he murmured, his breath on my lips. "Don't wanna fall down those stairs."

I let out a very unladylike growl and yanked myself out of his arms, this time away from the stairs. "Thank you." I shot him a middle finger. "But you're still a pig."

"I'm a pig for noticing that you're not wearing any panties?" He didn't sound insulted or offended. More…amused, again.

"Yes. And even more so for saying so."

He grinned again. "So I am right? You're not wearing any panties?"

"No! I mean—I'm not telling you!" I went to slap him again, and he just let me, not even flinching when my hand cracked across his cheek. "And stop calling them panties! That's a horrible word."

"You already did tell me, sweetheart." He wiggled one eyebrow suggestively. "But then, that skirt is tight enough I'd have noticed panty lines."

"God," I huffed. "You're a barbarian."

He shrugged. "Meh. Been called worse." He eyed me. "And why is panties a horrible word? What else am I supposed to call them?"

I shuddered when he said the word. "Underwear?" I suggested.

"Boring. Panties is more fun."

"Fun? It's horrible! It's just a gross word. Like moist."

He cringed. "Now *that's* a horrible word."

I rolled my eyes at him. "Yeah, and panties is worse."

"So what do you call 'em, when you wear 'em?"

"Underwear. Or a thong, if that's what I'm wearing."

His eyes actually twinkled, but lecherously, rather than merrily. "Thongs, hmm? You like the G-strings better, or the ones with the wide waistband and the little lace strap between your ass cheeks?"

I goggled at him. "What are you, an underwear aficionado?"

That damn grin again. "Why, yes, yes I am. Duke Silver, underwear aficionado." He scrubbed the stubble on his jaw with his fingertips. "Although, panty-master sounds more badass."

I actually slapped my forehead. "Panty-master? Are you twelve?"

He shrugged and pulled a *why not?* face. "Yeah, sometimes. Especially when it comes to hot women in sexy—*underwear*." He wiggled the one eyebrow again. "And Fancy, you, in a G-string? That's fucking hot."

"Yeah, well...if you want to see me in a G-string, you'll have to go buy last July's issue of *Maxim*." I turned and walked away from him a few steps, cursing myself for saying that.

Sometimes my mouth ran away from my brain.

He wasn't moving, still standing behind me at the top of the stairs. "Wait. You were in *Maxim*?"

I shrugged one shoulder and avoided looking at him. "Yup. Four page article, double-page photo spread."

"How about *Playboy*?"

I whirled on him. "No, I haven't been in *Playboy*!" I shouted. "And do you not possess a filter?"

"Nope." He ejected the magazine of the pistol, looked at it, and replaced it, exactly like they do in the movies. For my benefit, probably. Asshole. "I say what I'm thinking, say what I mean, and mean what I say because, sweetheart, I may be a lot of things and not all of them good, but one thing I'm not is a liar."

I huffed in irritation, because I couldn't exactly find fault with that logic, since I had similar tendencies. "Are we going to stand here bickering all day, or are we going to get out of here?"

He pointed at me with index finger and thumb. "That, hot stuff, is an excellent point."

I let my head hang back on my neck. "Swear to god, you have more misogynistic ways of talking down to me than I can even keep track of."

He led the way through the house, a modern suburbia dump. White pressboard cabinets, warping laminate floor, low popcorn ceiling, claustrophobic floorplan...ugh. Double shudder. Except this place was clearly used by the deceased thugs in the basement as a sex, drugs, and torture den. There were empty forties everywhere, crumpled cigarette packages, overflowing ashtrays, glass drug-smoking pipes, bongs, condoms both used and still wrapped, empty Styrofoam carryout containers, McDonald's bags…a vile, filthy pigsty.

"Hurry up and get me out of here before I catch a disease," I said. "This place is disgusting."

Duke moved through the kitchen, at the back of which were the stairs down to the basement. There was also a side door leading out into a driveway. Instead of exiting the side door, however, he went through the kitchen into the living room, stopping at the front door, a solid wood slab painted white with three small square windows near the top and a heavy glass storm door on the other side.

"Um." I tapped his shoulder, which was kind of like tapping the side of a boulder. "Go?"

"Hush, Fancy."

"I'll hush when you use my fucking *name*."

He glared at me over his shoulder. "Okay, then. Temple, please, *shut* the *fuck* up."

"Well that was uncalled for."

His growl in response was feral enough that I paled, backed up a step, and promptly shut my mouth. "Okay, then. Shutting up."

Duke was just looking out the window in the door, as if the quiet, lower middle class suburban neighborhood was going to suddenly erupt in gunfire in the middle of the morning. Which, now that I thought of it, wasn't entirely out of the realm of possibility, given the events thus far.

And then, as abruptly as he'd halted, he jerked open the door, shoved the storm door out of the way, pistol whipping up and then sweeping side to side as he stepped through, the motion done in one smooth glide. Satisfied that the street was clear, he reached back, grabbed my wrist, and yanked me out of the house. I tripped forward, lost my balance as my toe caught on the transition plate of the doorway, and landed flush against Duke's chest. My hands automatically shot out and wrapped around him as my cheek flattened against his hard chest. And, totally by accident, obvs, my hands might have possibly grabbed onto his ass.

"Not the time for hanky panky, Fancy," he said with a laugh.

I shoved away from him. "I tripped."

"Sure you did. And I've got a Nobel peace prize." He didn't push it though, just trotted down the three short steps of the porch, gesturing at me to follow him. Waiting for me, his eyes flicked up to the eaves of the house, and his expression darkened. "Shit. That complicates things."

"What does?" I asked, turning back to see what he was looking at.

He pointed, and I followed his gesture to see a home security camera pointing down at the front porch. "That."

"Are you going to shoot it out?"

He snorted. "It already saw us."

"Maybe it's not recording?" I suggested.

He sighed. "Unlikely. From what I know about Cain, he's not the type to waste resources. Putting a security camera on a dump like this, in a neighborhood like this? Not only is it definitely recording, but it's probably transmitting to a remote server somewhere that Cain's tech monkeys can monitor the feed." He grabbed my arm and hauled me into a trot. "Which means we need to get scarce, pronto."

"Who even says pronto anymore?" I asked, trying to keep up with Duke's long strides, which was tough seeing as I was at least a foot shorter and wearing Louboutin wedges. "And who, exactly, is this Cain you keep mentioning? Also, can you please slow down? I'm not exactly wearing the right shoes for a run."

"Then take 'em off, princess, because running is what we're doing."

"I'm not running barefoot in a neighborhood like this! Not only will I ruin my brand new pedicure, I'll probably step on a needle or something."

Duke halted again and whirled to glare down at me. "Ruin your pedicure? Are you not hearing what I'm telling you? Did you miss what just happened in that basement? I don't go around killing people for shits and giggles, sweetheart—I kill when I've gotta remove a threat to myself or the person in my care and, in this case, it's both. You're about as helpless as a kitten, which makes you my responsibility, for one, and you're only here because of me, for another. Those guys would have likely raped you six ways till Sunday, and once they found out who you were, it would have only gotten worse. And then, after they killed me in front of you, they probably would've raped you a few dozen more times. And *then* they would've given you to Cain, and Satan himself only knows what would've happened to you then." He put his face up close to mine, and his expression was dark, grim, and scary. "Listen to me, Temple Kennedy. All jokes and bullshit aside, this situation I've gotten you into is life or death. Meaning, if I can't keep you alive, you'll be very quickly and very painfully dead."

"How'd you get me into this? I'm not following."

"Told you already, I went outside after you, back at that bar. I was planning on puttin' the moves on you, see where things led. They wanted me; you were there, so they got you too, thinking having a piece of ass around is never a bad plan. Right? They got their target, but they can't leave witnesses behind, so they knew they'd have to get rid of you eventually, which meant they could do whatever they wanted before putting a bullet in your head." He shrugged. "I couldn't have prevented them snagging you, but you're still here because of me."

"You're out of a bad movie, Duke, seriously. You were going to put the moves on me? Let me guess, you have a tried and true pick up line, too?"

"Don't need pickup lines when you look like me, sweetheart." He pulled a frown. "And you seriously focus on the wrong parts of what I'm saying."

"Yeah, well, call it a coping mechanism." I gestured back at the house. "How else would you like me to handle what I saw back there? Either I'm going to dissolve into a sobbing mess, or I'm going to pretend I didn't see anything. And probably channel all my fear into extreme sass."

"I guess that's fair," he said with a shrug and a nod. "As long as you don't lose sight of that fact that listening to me is going to keep you alive."

He grabbed my hand and pulled me into a trot again, so I kicked off my wedges and held them in one hand by the straps. What followed then was a good thirty or forty minutes of barefoot jogging on cement sidewalks through a run down neighborhood. Block by block the houses got shabbier, the yards smaller and more overgrown, the cars older and more rusted.

Eventually my feet were throbbing, and I had a stitch in my side. I hauled on Duke's arm to stop him. "I need a break...tough guy," I panted. "Running...barefoot here...remember?"

He halted immediately, gave a quick look around at the deserted neighborhood, and then nudged me off the sidewalk and into a clump of trees at the edge of a run-down park a few steps from the curb. "Sit."

The asshole wasn't even winded.

I sat, and he crouched in front of me taking my feet in his hands, and proceeded to give me the single most incredible foot rub in the history of the world. It would have been thrillingly erotic, had I not been in pain.

"Okay, so maybe I'm missing something here, but why are we running? Even if that camera was live and transmitting, how soon can this Cain get here to catch us? I haven't seen a single person in the last half hour, let alone signs of pursuit. Which reminds me, you never told me who Cain is, and why he's after you."

He kept rubbing as he answered me. "Cain won't show up himself, he doesn't work like that. He'll send more guys like the ones back at the house. He's a crime lord, basically. Like Kingpin from *Daredevil*?" He eyed me expectantly. "No? Nothing? Well anyway, he runs a huge, complicated operation which, from what I've learned is drugs, mainly, along with some hardware and other black market shit like underage prostitutes. He operates on a cellular basis like the cells of operatives, terrorist style. Most of them don't interact with each other, so there's an element of overlap and deniability, plus few of them will have ever interacted with Cain directly."

He set my foot down and I flexed my toes, and then poked at the blisters on the bottom of my feet. "And why were you kidnapped by a kingpin?" I asked.

He shrugged. "Because my boss pissed him off. He was probably hoping to use me as leverage to get back at Harris."

"How would he do that?"

"The usual," Duke said. "Videos of me being tortured or having parts hacked off until Harris agreed to give himself up for me." He said this casually, as if the thought didn't bother him a bit.

"You mean that literally, don't you?"

"Oh, very literally."

"Would your boss have traded himself for you?"

A shrug. "If there was no other way, probably. But the rest of the boys wouldn't have let him. Especially Thresh. He'll probably want to go after Cain directly. They're probably mounting a very pissed off rescue operation right about now, which is going to be bad for Cain and his guys. "

"Thresh?"

Duke grinned. "My best friend. Biggest, toughest motherfucker I've ever met, and the only man who's ever beaten me in arm wrestling."

I just stared at Duke. "Bigger than you?"

"By several inches and at least twenty pounds of muscle."

"Jesus."

Duke laughed. "Yeah. Thresh is a monster."

"He sounds terrifying."

"Yeah. He's huge, insanely strong, and knows as many ways to kill you with his bare hands as I do, but…once you get to know him, you'll find out he's pretty much a teddy bear, most of the time. Never seen the man angry, like, not ever. Even in bar fights, he's just…chill. So, yeah, he looks scary, and you should be scared of him if you're not his friend, but…truly scary? Nah." He rocked back on his heels and then sat down in the grass beside me. "Now Anselm...*he's* scary."

"And who is Anselm?"

"The wild card on the team. From Germany, I think, but I could be wrong. Somewhere over in that area, at least. You wouldn't want to get stuck in a dark alley with any of us, but Anselm? I wouldn't want to be stuck on the same *continent* as Anselm if he didn't like me. The problem with Anselm is you never know where he is. You piss off Anselm, he'll put a rifle slug in the back of your head from a mile away, and you'll never even know what happened. Or you might brush up against him walking down the street and you'll just...drop dead. You hear people say, oh that guy's a ghost, you know? Like he's impossible to keep track of? Well Anselm isn't just a ghost, he's a fucking...he's why people are afraid of the dark man. Anselm scares the poop right out of me, and I've known the man for several years."

I let a few beats go by. "So...what exactly is it you do that you know people like Thresh and Anselm?"

"I'm a private security contractor."

"Like Blackwater?"

His eyes narrowed. "Overpaid grunts. No, not like Blackwater. I'm the kind of security that billionaires hire to be their personal Secret Service, except we don't answer to Uncle fuckin' Sam."

"So which billionaires do you work for, then?"

"We don't do long term contracts. We're more...specialized than that."

I frowned. "And what the hell does *that* mean?"

"It means I don't get paid to walk around some rich dick's fancy ass estate with a taser," he said. "We get hired when a billionaire's daughter gets kidnapped for ransom. Let's say you're yachting around the Mediterranean or wherever with your mommy and daddy, and someone like, oh, Cain for example, decides there's money to be made kidnapping your fine ass. So you find yourself locked in the hold of a stinking fishing boat while Cain sends a video to Daddy showing Cain severing your finger and demanding a couple hundred million dollars be transferred into an untraceable Swiss bank account. Your dad, instead of calling the FBI or Interpol, would call my boss, Harris, and hire us. And instead of bargaining with the assholes, we'd go in heavy, shoot their shit up, make off with you, and we wouldn't leave anyone left alive to talk about us afterward, either."

"And there's enough of that kind of thing happening that you have steady work?"

He laughed, and it wasn't exactly a pleasant sound. "Sweetheart, you have *no* idea what goes on in this world."

"Not sure I want to, either."

"Yeah, probably not." He slapped his knees. "Time to move."

"Are we going somewhere in particular?"

"Indirectly, yes."

"Care to elaborate?"

Duke hesitated, eyeing me as I stood up and brushed the grass of my butt. "Well, not really, no. I'm not sure you'll like it."

"I'm not going to faint on you, Duke."

"Okay, well here it goes, then. My plan is to steal a car from a gangbanger, haul ass to my stash spot in downtown Denver, and then figure out some way of getting in contact with Harris. Those assholes back there took my phone and I couldn't find it anywhere in that piece of shit house. There wasn't a car in the driveway or in the garage either, so I'm guessing there was at least one more person in that cell, which in turn means at some point our absence is going to be reported, assuming the camera hasn't already done that. Which means Cain is going to have his guys looking for us. I know Cain has deep pockets and a lot of resources, so the faster I can get in touch with my guys, the faster I can get you somewhere safe. The longer we're out here alone and out of contact, the more likely it is Cain will find us."

I processed what he'd said. "When you say Cain has a lot of resources, what does that mean?"

Duke set off at a brisk walk rather a jog, so I paused and slipped on my sandals to give my feet a rest.

"You ask a lot of questions, Fancy." Duke shot me a glance as I caught up to him. "Someone like Cain has only one way he can get his product across state and international lines, and that is if he has contacts that can facilitate the process. Airspace is monitored, borders are monitored, cargo ships, planes, trains, tractor trailer haulers...all that shit is kept track of. So if he wants to get fifty kilos of coke from South America to Europe, or a load of guns from Europe to the States, he has to grease palms, has to own somebody who'll turn a blind eye to a shipment in exchange for a stack of cash.

"He also has to own well placed cops here and there, because people are going to notice a sudden influx of drugs or guns or whatever, right? Those kinds of contacts, they can do other favors, for the right price. A dirty cop can find someone pretty easily. A cop asks a few questions, puts out an APB, or gets a buddy in tech to do a facial recognition search and then, bam, Cain's target is acquired, and he can send his boys to fetch. And those are just the small-time local cops. If he happens to know someone higher up, there're more possibilities in terms of favors Cain can get done. None of which is good for you and me at the moment, since he's going to be pulling in favors to get eyes on us."

"And why are you going to hijack a car from a gangbanger?"

"Less likely it'll be reported, for one, and I won't feel as bad, for another. I don't like stealing rides from innocent middle class folks. Some little punk slinging dimebags? I just don't feel as bad. Maybe that makes me an asshole, but...fuck it, right?"

"Oh." I made it a few more steps before a thought occurred to me. "But isn't it more likely that a gangbanger will put up a fight?"

"Yeah, but that's half the fun. And besides, if one lonely little thug from the hood can get the best of me, then it's time I retire."

"Retire?" I ask, baffled. "You can't be more than thirty at the most."

"Twenty-eight," he answers. "And in my line of business, you only get old by staying good. You get sloppy, you get iced."

"Iced," I repeated. "You're seriously a commando straight out of Central Casting."

"Not sure if that's supposed to be an insult or not."

"Me either, actually," I said, and I wasn't quite able to hold back a grin.

"Well, at least we agree on that."

We walked a bit longer, turning down this street and another, seemingly at random, until I was thoroughly lost.

We'd been walking for another half hour at least when we stopped at an intersection, Duke glancing around as if deciding which way to go.

A low-slung car pulled up to the intersection, long as a battle-ship and old as the houses around us, with tinted windows and spin-ning rims and thudding bass notes hitting in the trunk. The driver's window slid down slowly, revealing a young black guy wearing a Broncos hat with a flat brim, a long, thick blunt dangling from the corner of his mouth.

"Yo," he said, over the bass. "Ya'll must be lost, rollin' up in this hood."

Duke swaggered over, confident, easy, hands clasped casually behind his back to hide the gun in his right fist. "Got that right," Duke said. "And I think you can help."

The guy in the car just laughed. "Yeah, right. Step off my shit, man."

Duke was a few feet away now, and his hands came around from behind his back. The next several seconds occurred in a blur too fast for me to follow. All I know is, one moment Duke was two or three feet away, hands behind his back, and then he was pressed up against the car, fist through the open window, the other guy's shirt in his fist, pistol against his temple.

"This ain't personal, kid," Duke said. "I just need your ride."

"A'ight, a'ight," the black guy said. "Ease off, man."

"Put it in park and show me your hands, and I'll ease off."

His hands went up, he shoved the shifter into park, and then Duke let go of his shirt, yanked open the driver's door and hauled him out of the driver's seat. Scrambling to his feet, the kid backed away, hands up by his face. "What're you gonna do with my ride?"

"Take it downtown," Duke answered. "Like I said, this ain't personal. I don't even plan to keep it. I'll park it somewhere as safe as I can and put the keys under the mat. It'll be LoDo, somewhere near Decatur Street."

"Man, it's as good as gone, you do that."

"Yeah, well, unfortunately for you, that's the best I can do. I'm trying to be nice, here, kid," Duke said. He glanced at me, and then gestured at the car. "Get in, Fancy."

I quickly rounded the back end of the car and settled into the passenger side. The interior was cloudy with pot smoke, thick and acrid, giving me an instant contact buzz. I rolled open the window and waved at the smoke, trying to clear it before I got totally high.

Duke kept his gun trained on the erstwhile owner of the car as he backed away, toward the open driver's door. He paused halfway there, went back over to the driver and snatched the blunt from his mouth. And, to my stunned disbelief, took a big drag on it, held it, and then let the smoke out in a slow exhale, then handed it back.

"Good shit." Duke turned away, moseyed confidently back to the driver's seat. And, of course, the second Duke turned his back; the owner of our new ride stuck his hand behind his back, reaching for his waistband.

"Duke!" I shouted, meaning to warn him.

I might have saved my breath, though, because Duke didn't even bother turning around. He already had his pistol up without looking, trained on the kid as he opened the driver's door.

"Don't do it, kid," Duke said, settling behind the wheel, right hand aiming the gun across his body, left pulling the car door closed. "You won't even get a shot off." He said this as he pulled the car into gear.

The kid kept his hand behind his back, probably on the butt of his own gun, but he was hesitating, staring down Duke. Or, trying to.

Duke gestured with the barrel of his pistol. "Hands up, kid. You got exactly three seconds or I'll put a hole in your skull."

His hands went up slowly, reluctantly, realizing discretion was, in this case, the better part of valor.

Duke started to lower his gun, but then jerked it back up again. "We really are lost, though. Which way to LoDo?"

"Man, you for real? Jack my shit, and then ask me for directions?"

"Which…*way*?" Duke demanded.

"Crazy white mothafuckas." He pointed behind himself. "That way. Go straight, turn right when that street ends, and then you'll see signs for the highway."

Duke mashed the accelerator so the engine roared and the car bolted forward, pushing me back against the seat.

Thirty, maybe forty minutes of awkward silence later, Duke pulled into a fenced off, pay-to-park lot and paid the fee with cash he'd found stashed in the glove box.

After parking, Duke led the way across the street to the intersection and turned right, then followed that street for two more blocks, shouldering through the occasional groups of pedestrians—most of them locals on their lunch breaks. We entered a nondescript apartment building, four stories, fairly new. It wasn't a nice enough building to have a doorman, but there was a desk with an old, overweight security guard behind it, ostensibly watching the camera monitors.

He looked up, saw Duke and I, and lit up. "Dan Stephens! Nice to see you again, sir."

Duke took the security guard's hand and shook it vigorously, roughly clapping the older man on the shoulder. "Bruce, my man. How's the missus?"

"Ah, you know how it is. She's an ugly old bitch, but I'm too old and fat to upgrade, so I hang on to her."

"Bullshit, Bruce, you know you love her."

"Got me there, Dan, got me there. Thirty-eight years next week I've been married to her, so I guess I like her okay."

"Got any big plans for the big three-eight?" Duke leaned up against the desk as if he had all the time in the world, content to shoot the shit.

"Nah. Been saving my paychecks to take her to Jax's, but that's about it."

Duke managed to work up a surprisingly convincing look of embarrassment. "So, my girlfriend and I popped into town on a whim, you know how it is, and I…well, I sort of forgot my keys back in LA. Can you help a brother out, Bruce?"

"I really shouldn't."

"You know me, Bruce. Ain't like I'm a stranger, right?"

"I know, but—"

"Come on, buddy. We just need to get off our feet for a while, you know what I mean? Been traveling most of the day, we just wanna kick back for a minute."

Bruce eyed us, and then sighed heavily. "All right, I guess I can let you in. Just…don't tell anyone and don't make a habit of it."

"My lips are sealed, buddy," Duke said.

We took an elevator up to the third floor, Bruce ambling and shuffling down the long, low-ceilinged hallway to a unit in the far back corner. He jingled through a huge set of keys, found the correct one, and unlocked the door to what I assumed was Duke's apartment, although he'd called it a "stash spot", whatever that meant. Stash, like drugs? He'd taken a hit of that black guy's blunt but, despite that, he didn't seem like the type to keep an apartment just for stashing drugs.

Bruce unlocked the door and pushed it open, then pocketed the keys. "There you go, kids. Have fun."

Duke clapped Bruce on the shoulder yet again. "You're a real life saver, Bruce, you don't even know."

Bruce waved a pudgy, veiny hand as he shuffled back to the elevator. "I know, Dan, I know. I'll see you around."

Duke pressed a palm to my lower back, gently nudging me into the apartment. I went in, and Duke closed the door behind us.

"So, Dan Stephens." I meandered into the apartment, which was about as sparse and spartan as you might imagine a commando's backup stash spot would be. Meaning, a futon on one wall and a stack of moving boxes in the corner, and nothing else.

He shrugged. "The whole point of a stash spot is that it ain't connected to you. Dan Stephens ain't much but a fake ID and bank account."

I stood in the center of the empty living room and finally asked what was on my mind. "So, um. What exactly do you keep in this stash spot?"

"Nothing much. My collection of women's panties, porn, crack rocks…you know, the usual." The asshole delivered this totally straight-faced, so I wasn't entirely sure he was kidding.

I stared at him, trying to read him. Which should've been easier than it was, but his expression wasn't giving anything away. "I want to assume you're kidding, but I don't know jack shit about you, Duke. Hell, I don't even know if Duke is your real name."

He let out a huff of laughter, shaking his head. "Okay, I get that we don't know each other, but do you really think I'd buy an apartment under an alias just to store drugs and nudie mags?"

"You called yourself the panty-master. How the fuck am I supposed to know?"

He tilted his head to one side, looking perplexed. "That was a joke, Jesus." He took two long steps, which put him in my personal space, his cornflower eyes bright and piercing and vivid…and intelligent. "I know I look—and sometimes act—like…what did you call it? A commando from Central Casting? Yeah, I get why you'd think that. But you don't survive in my line of work by being stupid, so don't make the mistake of underestimating me, Temple."

I searched his eyes, and realized I'd been doing exactly that, underestimating, stereotyping him. He looked like a typical douchebag gym bro with more muscles than brains, and he even talked like one sometimes, but the way he was looking at me right now, something told me I was dead wrong in my estimation of Duke Silver.

"Is Duke Silver really your name?"

He nodded. "Sure is, honey."

"And what do you keep here?"

He ignored my question for a long moment, remaining in my space, towering over me, staring down at me, filling my field of vision with his massive body, his biceps stretching the sleeves of his shirt, chest huge and broad and hard. Goddammit, he was sexy. Too fucking sexy for my good. That hair, fuck me, that hair. I wanted to rip it out of the elastic ponytail holder and run my fingers through it. Shit, I wanted to get a good grip on those kinky red locks and pull that craggy jawline of his between my thighs and ride that sarcastic, arrogant, dirty mouth of his. I wanted to feel those big bear paw hands of his on my bare skin. I wanted to see if he had abs to match his biceps. I wanted to get him out of those stupid fucking cargo shorts.

"You keep lookin' at me like that and you're gonna make me think your sass is all show."

"How am I looking at you?"

"Like you want rip my clothes off and do nasty things to me."

I did my best to wipe my thoughts off my face. "You wish, soldier boy."

He held my gaze as he reached up with both hands and nimbly opened a button of my blouse. The shirt had never exactly been equal to the task of holding in my tits, even with a bra, but then that was the point, wasn't it? Make 'em look without giving 'em anything to actually see. So then, when he flicked open that fourth button from the top, my tits kind of spilled out, only marginally constrained and concealed by a not-quite-sheer lacy maroon bralette. Yes, I know, my boobs are a little too big for a bralette, but dammit, they're comfy and cute and I like them, and I don't care if they don't really do the job a bra is supposed to do. You'll have to pry my bralettes out of my cold, dead hands, along with my yoga pants and my leopard print Tieks.

I felt my nipples harden, and that was when he finally let his gaze break away from mine.

"I'm not just wishing I could do nasty things to you, Fancy, I'm planning to." He undid another button, and then another, and then the shirt was open completely.

I willed myself to unfreeze, to slap him, to back out of his reach, to do *something*, anything. But my body betrayed my brain by remaining still. All I could do was stand there as he slid his palms over my shoulders and down my arms, brushing the blouse off along the way. His eyes were roaming and flicking, fixing on my breasts then moving up to my face. His hands, though. God, those hands were a tease. Hovering at my waist, not quite touching me.

"You're fucking gorgeous," he murmured.

Put your hands on me, goddammit. I stood stock-still and stared up at him, waiting, barely breathing. Willing him to make the move so I could claim all I was doing was going along with it.

He didn't, though. Didn't touch me. He simply looked, his big chest rising and falling a little too quickly for me to believe he was unaffected.

"You take my shirt off for any particular reason?" I asked, working hard at sounding casually sarcastic.

"Yep." He rubbed a thumb over the lace, across my erect nipple, sending a shiver through me. "I wanted to see your tits."

"And do you typically just take what you want without asking?"

He brushed his thumb over the other nipple, sending another shudder through me. "Yeah, for the most part. But I don't think you need to act all pissy, since you didn't exactly stop me, did you?"

"You didn't give me a chance."

"Bullshit, sweetheart. I'm touching you right now, and you're not stopping me. Nothing's preventing you from taking a step backward, is there?" He pressed closer to me, his hand now closing over my lower back, just above the waistband of my skirt. "Even now, you can stop this, if you really want to."

"Implying that I don't want to?"

"I'm not implying anything, Fancy. I'm flat out stating it. You don't want me to stop." He pulled me against him, but he did it slowly and gently, giving me plenty of opportunity to put the lie to his words. Only, I couldn't. Because I'm stupid, and he was right, damn him. "You want me to touch you. You don't want me to stop."

I've always had a weakness for bad boys with an attitude. Some girls have a weakness for diamonds, others for chocolate, or boys in uniform, or dimples. And then there's me. Is he an unmitigated asshole with a superiority complex? I'll take him…for a couple hours. Assuming he can last that long; most can't. If he's shit in bed, he's gone the second he pulls out—buh-bye. I haven't had a guy stay for a second round in more than a year, and it's no one's fucking business how many single rounds there've been. Enough, just leave it at that. Or, maybe not enough. Maybe I just haven't sampled a wide enough range of men to find one worth keeping around for a second fuck.

What? Guys are the only ones allowed to be one-and-done horndogs with a one-track mind and short attention span? Fuck that. I like sex, and I don't like clingy guys who want "more", primarily because they're only pretending to want more so they can get a ride in my private jet, or get stage-side tickets from my dad, or swim in the infinity pool at our place in Malibu they saw on the show. They think they can pretend to be in love with me, and they let me take them on exotic vacations and even buy them expensive cars, and then once they've sampled the perks of dating Temple Kennedy, they're in the wind. Yeah, been there, done that, already burned the T-shirt. No thanks. Worse than the gold diggers are the ones who just want to get a pic of themselves with me so they can sell it to TMZ or whatever. Yeah, that's happened a few times: take a guy home only to discover he snuck a pic or two and sold it. Or if they don't have a pic, they have a story they told their bros and then somehow there's rumors going around that I did anal on the first date (both true and false—true because I do like anal, but false because I'd never give that up on the first date, and nobody ever gets a second date with me, or even really a first, because I don't date, so thus even though I like it, I don't actually ever do it), or that I gave a BJ in the back of a club (false, I don't give BJs, and I certainly don't hang out in clubs), or that I like to ride around topless in my Aston Martin (again, both true and false—true because what's the point in having privacy glass if you're not going to go topless, and false because my car isn't an Aston Martin, it's a Bentley).

Okay, so that was a lot of internal rambling. The point in all this is that Duke is a bad boy. Duh, like, obviously. The problem is that he was clearly created in a laboratory with the single specific goal of tempting me into doing something spectacularly stupid, like fucking him without an NDA. I know, it seems stupid, but I've been screwed by too many selfish assholes. I have a system, and it works. No sex without an NDA, they always bag it, no photos, and no dates. That way, I get the sex I need, and I don't have to worry about the fallout, because if they break the NDA I'll sue them into poverty. My system protects me from myself, because I have absolutely *terrible* judgement in men. Like, the worst. Line up ten guys, all hot, and I will unerringly pick the biggest douchebag in the line-up. My judgement is unerring in this respect.

Thus, I don't trust myself, or anyone else, guys especially.

After the last asshole burned me, I signed off all guys. No boys. No sex. Nothing. I need to reset myself, try to rejuvenate my head and my sex drive and my anorexic sense of morality. Which means no sex. NO sex. NO SEX.

I'm an idiot to think I can go three months without sex.

But I'm sticking to my guns, I'm holding onto my rules, because those rules are keeping me out of trouble.

And Duke threatens this. I *WANT* him. Like, bad. I want to fuck him so many different ways it should be illegal, but I don't dare. The second I give in, he'll turn into a douchebag, like all men turn into douchebags after you fuck them, and sometimes they are douchebags *while* you're fucking them. And I actually like Duke, so far. He's honest to a fault about what he thinks and what he wants, doesn't try to hide or disguise who and what he is, and also, he got me out of that house with the scary foreign dudes.

I let out a breath, and step back; Duke immediately lets go, even though his eyes continue to bounce between my tits and my eyes. "Wrong again," I said, lying through my teeth. "No more touching."

He stuffed his hands in his pockets. "Fine. If that's the way you want to play it."

"It is." Not. My sex drive was really pissed off at me at this point, telling me I'm turning down what's sure to be the ride of my life.

Duke took one last look at my breasts, and then turned around, making for the bedroom. I snagged my shirt off the floor, slid it on, and buttoned it, going as far as buttoning it all the way to the second button from the top, meaning I felt a little choked, but if I didn't show him cleavage, maybe he wouldn't look at my tits as much, which would be good and bad, because I liked it when he looked at my tits, I want him to touch them again but I'm not having sex with Duke because then I'll want to have ALL the sex with him, and that's not going to happen, for the aforementioned reasons.

There was only the one bedroom in this apartment, and the door was closed. Duke stood in front of the door, hand on the knob. He twisted the knob and started to open the door, then stopped and glanced back at me. "Try not to freak out, okay?"

"Why would I—" I started, and then he opened the door and I cut myself off, because holy shit. "Oh. That kind of stash."

Guns.

ALL THE GUNS.

Like, literally, he could put a gun in the hands of an entire fucking army. There are so many different kinds of firearms in this room that I don't even know what to do with myself, other than stare in shock. Machine guns, handguns, rifles, old guns, new guns, big guns, small guns, boxes of ammo, big clips and little clips, at least three different types of grenade, a fucking actual rocket launcher, three machetes, six big knives like Rambo used in *First Blood*...

And a stuffed tiger, old and tattered, the fur worn, one eye replaced with a coat button.

The guns are all in glass cases mounted against the walls, arranged by type. The cases themselves are clearly meant for security as well as display, since they're framed with wrist-thick bars of steel, and the glass is easily an inch thick, and each one is locked with a fingerprint scanner. So even if someone did break in, they'd have to cut the cases out of the wall and carry them out of the apartment, or they'd have to have serious tools to cut them open.

"Um." I blinked a few times. "Wow."

"You didn't really think I have a collection of panties, did you?"

I blinked a few more times. "I wouldn't put it past you."

He laughed. "Actually, neither would I." The laughter turned... lascivious. "I mean, I'd collect your panties, if you wore any."

"I do usually wear them," I said. "I just..."

He turned to face me, arms crossed over his chest, an eyebrow lifted. "Go on. I'm curious. Why aren't you wearing any panties, Temple?"

I glared at him for a few beats, and then crossed my arms under my breasts, giving him my hardest, coldest, I-don't-give-a-shit expression. "Because I was boy-hunting."

He unsuccessfully tried to stifle a burst of surprised laughter. "Boy-hunting? What the fuck is that?"

"The girl version of picking up chicks."

"So you were in that shitty dive bar looking to get laid?"

"Yep."

His shit-eating grin pissed me off. "Well, now, there's honesty for you."

"What were you expecting?"

He shrugged. "I dunno. Trying to drown heartbreak at the bottom of a bottle, maybe? You were giving off some pretty strong leave-me-the-fuck-alone vibes. Didn't even give me the time of day."

"Maybe you're not my type."

"What is your type?"

I hesitated because I didn't really have a type, other than a minimum standard of hotness. "Not you."

Duke chuckled and turned away, putting a thumb to one of the cases. "Piece of advice for you, Princess: don't ever play poker, because you suck at lying."

"I'm not lying!" I huffed.

When the lock beeped, he opened the case and pulled out a gun. It looked like a miniature version of the machine guns you see SWAT guys using on TV. It had a stock that folded and a short barrel. There were several long, curved clips with the gun, which he stuffed into the cargo pocket of his shorts. That also pissed me off, because putting those idiotic pockets to actual use meant I couldn't mentally make fun of him for wearing cargo shorts anymore.

Slinging the machine gun over his shoulder by the strap, he turned and paced over to where I was still standing in the doorway. He stopped when our bodies were almost, but not quite, touching, the tips of my breasts so close to his chest it would have been difficult to slip a piece of paper between us. His proximity did that stupid black magic again, whereby my body completely overreacted, going straight into hyper drive—my nipples hardened, my breath shortened, my brain went to useless goo, and my pussy got all hot and moist.

And you bet your ass Duke noticed.

His breath was warm on my cheek. "Temple, babe, not only are you lying, you're lying poorly." He touched his forehead to mine, and my face tipped up automatically, my lips parting, my breath caught entirely, now. "If I'm not your type, then why can I smell your pussy dripping for me?"

"My pussy is *not* dripping," I lied.

"Oh no?"

"Nope." Gotta maintain the lie, even when neither of us believe me.

He wrapped one hand around the back of my neck, his thumb brushing through the flyaway hairs at the nape escaping from my bun. His other hand, where was his other hand?

OH.

Oh shit.

Ohhhh….

Well…dammit.

His other hand was sneaking beneath the hem of my skirt and

stealing upward. What I should have done was get pissed at his brazenness, walk away, knock his hand down, slap him, or at least pretend to put up a fight. Instead, like a hussy, I let my thighs loosen a little as his fingers drifted slowly up to my slit. Here, again, I should have taken steps to stop his advance but, as established, I am an idiot who can't seem control herself around assholes who only want me for sex, especially when said asshole is a godlike creature so fucking gorgeously sexy he leaves me literally gibbering incoherently.

My legs opened for him. It was like he had some kind of goddamn key, like he knew some magic word or gesture. I really, really, really don't normally behave like this, I swear. But Duke just…*does* something to me. All he had to do was get close to me, look at me with those piercing, intelligent blue eyes and I was done for. My legs just popped open like they were spring loaded or something.

And, oh yeah, I was wet.

Soaked.

He slid his middle finger through the lips of my pussy, making a wet sound we both heard—I cringed, while he looked like the cat who ate the canary. God, that slide of his finger was an entire moment all by itself. A slow, deliberate journey through the dampness of my pussy. His finger moved upward, just barely brushing my clit, and even at that minor, almost accidental contact, I jerked and shuddered, and my hips flexed forward. And then, damn the man, he pulled his hand out from under my skirt and lifted his middle finger up for us both to see. His finger was glistening, wet with my juices, from the tip to the middle knuckle.

"See, Fancy? You're wet for me." He stared me down as he slipped that finger into his mouth and slowly pulled it out. "I'm exactly your type, and we both know it. You just wanna deny it 'cause you like playing games. Fine by me, Princess—I like a nice game of catch me if you can."

"You're an asshole, Duke Silver," I said, but the insult lacked sting, since I was breathless and quaking from a single touch.

"Maybe," he admitted, "but I'm an asshole who can give you an orgasm so fast and so hard you'll pass out."

"Bullshit."

He leaned closer, whispering in my ear. "Is that a challenge, Fancy?"

Yes, god yes, that's a challenge. Make me come, Duke. Make me come so hard I pass out.

I didn't say any of that. Instead, I worked up all the self-control I had left, and took a step backward. "I thought we were on the run from a kingpin who wants to use you as bait?"

"You have a point," he agreed, and took a step back from me, and I breathed a little easier once a few feet separated us.

He turned around and opened the case containing handguns, and I watched him choose several guns, and wondered what I'd do if he put the moves on me again.

Probably compromise my already questionable morals.

Actually, that wasn't a probably or a maybe, that was a guarantee. He was too damn potent, too damn sexy, and I was too damn horny. My libido ran high as it was, then add in the fact that I'm two months into a three-month self-imposed sexual hiatus, and you have a recipe for one insanely horny Temple.

Like…bad.

Really bad.

The sexual hiatus was a dumb idea, wasn't it?

I could break it for Duke, and then go back to no sex. Or maybe I'd have to start over, a whole new three-month break? God.

Why am I such an idiot? And why am I so weak when it comes to sexy bad boys?

HARD TO GET

THIS FUCKIN' GIRL WAS GOING TO BE THE ACTUAL DEATH OF ME. If I don't die trying to rescue her hot yet complicated ass, I'm going to die from blue balls. For fuckin' real, Temple had this capacity to get my cock hard as a rock without so much as touching me. I haven't kissed her, haven't gotten her to come yet, haven't even seen her naked titties, yet I'm already hung up on the woman. I NEED to fuck her. It's instinctive, primal, a physical, mental, and emotional requirement for me to continue functioning as a man. Meaning, if I don't get her naked and riding my dick within the next seventy-two hours, I might very well just combust. My balls will explode, my dick will fall off, and my man card will be permanently revoked. I'll be useless.

And good goddamn, she plays a hell of a game of hard to get.

I'm good at a lot things: I can take an absolutely unreal amount of pain and keep functioning, I'm a vicious, cold-blooded killing machine on the battlefield, but keep my soul and humanity out of it, I can use nearly any weapon ever created, bladed or projectile, ancient or modern, I speak three languages fluently, and I have a master's degree in criminal justice. Plus, I have a ten-inch cock and I've been known to make women come in less than three minutes—faster if

I've got toys at my disposal.

One thing I'm not good at is playing games with women. I don't play games. I don't chase them—they chase me. That's been true for as long as I've been sexually active, and I popped my cherry at twelve. Bitches just want my ass, and I'm sorry if that term offends you, but it's true. It's always been true. A nice little grin, put some promise in my eyes, and I can have any three chicks at the bar fighting over me, and that's a proven fact.

But Temple Kennedy? She's a cipher, man. I just don't get her. She's a reality star, so she should be all vapid and ridiculous, and she is in some ways, but she's not dumb. Not at all. She's spoiled, but she does what has to be done and doesn't complain. She wants me, and she wants me hard, but she's not letting herself. And that's what I don't get. We're both adults, and neither of us is looking for anything serious. Shit, we don't even know each other. But yet she's resisting. I can get her off a dozen times in the same amount of minutes, and that's before I start fucking…and that's a reality most chicks tend to pick up on somehow, without me having to say it. I'm a goddamn champion when it comes to fucking, and nothing gives me more pleasure that making my sexual partner get off hard, fast, and frequent. So…why is she bugging about this? We can fuck, I'll keep her tight, round ass safe and sound, deliver her back to Malibu, and that'll be that. I get to sample a piece of one of the hottest women in the country—legit, she's been in the *GQ* list of sexiest women of the year for like three years in a row. With me she'll get the most and best orgasms of her life, guaranteed. If I was a gigolo, my shit would come with a customer satisfaction guarantee.

But no.

She's playing hard to get. But I also wonder if maybe she's not playing, that she really is that hard to get. I mean, that's fine. Better, even, because then it means she has standards and that I meet them. Or maybe she's scared of getting with me for some reason? I don't know. I just don't know. And the curiosity and doubt is killing me.

What's killing me more is how fucking hot she is. Those tits?

Goddamn. I got a lace-obscured glimpse when I relieved her of her shirt, and that was enough to leave me salivating for more. And that mouth? Her mouth is, literally and metaphorically, something I could get hooked on: literally, her mouth is just beautiful, plump red lips in a perfect cupid's bow, a quick, easy, sassy smile…god, I've got visions of that mouth wrapped around my cock running through my head the longer I'm around her; and metaphorically, her mouth… her sass, her attitude, her comebacks—those turn me on just as hard. I bet she talks dirty, like nasty dirty.

I wonder if she's bossy in bed, or passive? She's got that attitude, that arrogance of a girl who's been beyond spoiled her whole life, so I want to think she's bossy, but sometimes those are the ones who end up being the most submissive when you get 'em naked. I don't mean submissive in a dom/sub way, just as an aside. I don't do that shit; it's just not for me. I don't mind pain, but I don't get off on it, whether receiving or causing. I mean, if a chick begs me to spank her or blindfold her or something, that's one thing, but whips and gags and bondage, shit like that? Nah. I'll take a good old-fashioned fucking, thanks.

She stood behind me as I sorted through my selection of hand-guns. I had any number to choose from, but I had some old standby favorites: the Sig Sauer was great as a hideout, so that one would go on my ankle; the Glock, of course, but I also liked the Beretta, and a nice big fuckoff Desert Eagle was always good for intimidation value…

The Desert Eagle was stupidly enormous, and distractingly loud, and hard to carry enough ammo for, so that's staying behind. The Glock *and* the Beretta in twin shoulder holsters—the Glock in the left holster, Beretta in the right—with the Sig as a backup, and the HK as the main.

Grenades? Um, probably not, since shit was likely to happen in populated areas.

Ah, don't forget the KA- BAR.

Three spare mags for each pistol meant my shorts pockets

were…a little full, plus two backups for the HK in my back pocket…

I got the shoulder holsters arranged, settled the pistols in the holsters, set the HK on top of a case, and turned around to face Temple.

"Think I'm overdoing the weapons?" I asked.

She just blinked at me. "Um." Her gaze flicked from pistol to pistol, then to the HK, then to my sagging pockets, and then the Sig on my ankle, just above my combat boots. "Maybe a little?"

I frown. "Right. Lose the ankle holster, huh?"

She nodded. "Yeah, I mean, it's a little obvious, don't you think?"

I glanced down. "Yeah, maybe a little."

I unstrapped the Sig and put it back, then grabbed the KA-BAR. It'd have to go on my belt, as it was too big for a pocket. I unbuckled my belt and whipped it off so I could thread the leather through the sheath.

Of course, without the belt to hold up my shorts, they sagged, being full of magazines. The sagging of my shorts left me showing…a little skin, let's say. Yeah, I go commando. Easy access, and more comfy. Underwear is stupid. Boxers are too much fabric, too loose, and uncomfortable, and briefs or boxer briefs are just too damn tight. They constrict my shit, and that's just cruel. No underwear? No problem. Just my style, you know? The issue is that I was still rocking a semi hard-on from having my finger inside Temple's pussy.

God, she tasted good.

And bang, that one thought had my dick going all the way hard.

And it was sticking out the top of my sagging cargo shorts, showing the first couple of inches, and my tight T-shirt wasn't doing much to hide it. Or, anything, actually.

Temple's eyes bugged out. "Oh. Um."

I saw the look in her eyes. Saw the way her thighs pressed together, saw the way she grabbed one hand with the other as if to keep herself from reaching for me.

"Like what you see?"

I'd finished threading the belt through the sheath, so I was left holding the belt in one hand, and my shorts with the other. Let go, and the khakis would be on the ground.

"Nope." She said this in a calm, unaffected voice, but her tongue flicked out and ran along her lower lip, and her eyes were locked on my cock.

I sidled over to her. "No?" I let the shorts sag a little further, showing another inch of dick. "You don't wanna see any more?"

She shook her head side to side, but her eyes still hadn't left my cock. "Nope. Don't want to see it."

I stopped when I was a few inches away. "Remember what I said about not playing poker, Fancy?"

Her eyes finally flicked up to mine. "Um. What?"

"You're a shitty liar, Princess."

Those eyes, man. Those fucking eyes. Blue as a clear summer sky, with streaks of green and hazel. They searched my eyes, then went to my cock, and then back up to my eyes.

"Fine," she huffed, managing to be irritated yet breathless at once. "I'm lying through my teeth."

I grinned at her, dropped the belt to the floor and let the shorts slide down another inch. "I like the truth, sweetheart. Good, bad, crazy, the truth is always better than bullshit."

She glanced down at my cock. "So hot."

"What is?"

Her tongue slid along her lips, her eyebrows lowering as her eyes widened. "You. Everything about you."

"You're pretty goddamn sexy yourself, Temple."

She cast a long searching gaze at me, and then back down to my dick. "But this…it's perfect."

"Those tits of yours are perfect."

My first estimation, back in the basement, had been that her tits weren't huge, more of a decent handful. Now, though, having seen them in a little semi see through bra…those beauties were a lot bigger than I'd thought. It wasn't the size of them that made them perfect though, it was their shape. High and firm, yet with enough droop and sway to make me reasonably certain they were all natural. They bounced and jiggled convincingly enough with every movement, and you can be damn sure I noticed.

But this particular moment wasn't about Temple's tits, as perfect as they were, but about my very erect and ready to play cock.

She didn't even hear my comment about her tits, apparently. Or if she did, she didn't respond. She just stared at my cock, tongue sticking out adorably, her considerable and lovely chest heaving as if she was having trouble breathing.

"Temple?"

She glanced up at me. "Hmmm?"

Fuck it. Let's see what she'd do.

I let go of the shorts entirely, and they sank to the floor with a loud thunk. My cock was now on full display, all ten inches of him, hard as a rock, straining toward the ceiling.

"You want to touch it, don't you?" I asked, my voice low.

"No." She said this way too breathily for me to even try to believe her.

I laughed. "Bzzzzt. Wrong answer."

"I shouldn't."

I boggled at her. "And why not?"

She spoke directly to my penis, her hands unclenching from each other, reaching out tentatively. "I'm—I'm taking a break."

"From what?"

"Boys."

I latched onto her wrist, guiding her hand to me. "Well then, there's no problem."

She resisted, but only a little. "There's not?"

"Nope."

Her eyes went to mine. "I made a promise to myself. Three months, no boys."

"I'm not a boy." I loosened my grip on her wrist, and her hand kept drifting toward my cock on its own. "I'm all man, sweetheart."

She blinked slowly, as if giving up the battle with herself.

"Dammit." Her fingers closed around my shaft, and I had to bite down on a hiss of pleasure. "Dammit, Duke."

"I think what you meant to say was 'oh my god, Duke,'" I said.

She ignored my comment, her teeth sinking into that plump lower lip of hers. "So gorgeous," she breathed, but it was to herself, not really meant for me to hear.

I heard though, and my ego swelled a bit. Not that I wasn't pretty well self-assured of the size and generally pleasing aesthetics of my dick, but still, hearing a woman say that, in that tone of voice…it does wonders for any man.

But what her hand was doing…oh my fuck. I can last a hell of a long time, but the way she touched me—goddamn. I was going to blow in a matter of seconds if she kept that up.

Slow, gentle strokes, twisting on the way down, thumb rubbing over the tip when she reached the head. One stroke, two, three. That twist on the way down, the sweet, almost loving way her thumb caressed the very tip? I was clenching my jaw and tightening my ass cheeks within thirty seconds.

Normally I could last most of twenty minutes and be ready again in less than ten, but this girl, she was gonna get me to come like a damn schoolboy getting his first handy.

"Jesus, Temple," I growled, "you got me fuckin'—"

"Shut the hell up," she snapped. "Just…shut up."

I quirked an eyebrow at her, and she met my eyes with an embarrassed blush.

"Oh yeah?" I asked. "Just shut up, huh?"

She stopped with her fist at the root of my cock, her eyes on mine. "Yeah, just shut up." She gave me a hard enough squeeze that I winced. "Your mouth just ruins the moment."

"Funny, since I think your mouth would only improve the moment."

She stared at me in disbelief. "You asshole."

I shrugged. "What? You think I haven't pictured your mouth around my cock? What's wrong with that?"

"I'm not like that."

"Like what?"

"I don't do that. Blow jobs, I mean."

"Your hand on my cock says otherwise."

"Do I like to touch cocks? Yes. Do I like to fuck? Also yes." She resumed her slow strokes. "Do I suck cock? No."

"You don't? Ever?"

She shook her head. "Nope. Never."

"You've never sucked a cock before? Never?"

"I said I *don't*, not that I *haven't*."

"So that's a rule? You don't suck dick?"

Temple nodded. "That's one of my rules, yes."

I focused on the conversation rather than the way her hand felt on my cock, or the way her small pale fingers looked wrapped around me. "*One* of your rules, implying there's more than one?"

"I have…rules, yes."

"Rules," I repeated. "What kind of rules?"

"There's an non-disclosure agreement listing it all. No pictures, no contacting me when we're done, no talking about what we did, no telling your buddies, no selling stories."

Wow. She had rules? For sex?

"And no oral? That's on there?"

She shook her head. "That's not one of the written rules, no. It's just…something I don't do."

"Why not?"

"Men are assholes. They're all jerks and douchebags and walking dickbags. But I get horny as hell, so I need sex. But sex for me is… straightforward." She watched her hand moving on my cock, still going torturously, teasingly slow. "No playing around, no bullshit. Just fuck me and go away."

"You didn't answer my question, but whatever," I said. "You really just…fuck and then you're done? That sounds boring."

She jerked her eyes up to mine. "Boring?"

I nodded. "Boring as hell, princess." I took a moment to pull myself back from the edge, which was getting more difficult with every second. Her hand was so soft, her touch gentle, and I couldn't help watching her hand slide up and down my shaft, traveling all those inches in infuriatingly slow increments. "So when you have sex, you just…fuck? You just go right to riding the dick?"

"For the most part, yes."

We both watch her stroke my cock. "Babe, you're missing out on the best part of sex."

"I like it simple."

"Because you've never been shown how good complicated can be, Princess."

"And that includes me sucking your cock?"

"It could." I was having to focus on holding back now, which was making it hard for me to talk. "It could include a lot of things. Me eating your pussy. You like to have your pussy licked, Fancy?"

She let out a breath. "Yeah."

"How about we make a deal."

"A deal?"

I grabbed her wrist. "Yeah. If I can make you come three times in less than twenty minutes, then you go down on me."

"And if you can't?"

"I'll do anything and everything you ask. Including nothing at all, if that's how you want it."

"What if I want to tie you up and put my finger in your asshole?" She searched my eyes as she said this.

I grinned at her. "Sweetness, when I say anything, I do mean anything. The only hard limits for me are full-on pegging and sick shit like golden showers or whatever. Anything else you can think of, I'll let you do." I released her wrist, and she resumed stroking; I don't think she could help it. "But that's only *if* I can't make you come three times in twenty minutes or less."

I was pretty damn sure I had this one in the bag. Get to watch her come, get to taste her sweet little pussy, *and* I get to have her mouth on my cock. Win-win for me, and I didn't think she'd mind the three orgasms.

The smirk on her face made me pause, though. "What's that look for?"

"Oh, just that I've never had a multiple orgasm in my life. Not on my own, nor has anyone ever given me one."

She had me on the edge; acting normal was impossible now. I was throbbing, aching. My cock was about to burst, my balls were tight and hard and full, and her hand was the most incredible thing I'd ever felt in my life. Just that one hand. I watched her fingers gripping me, watched them slide down my shaft, watched her thumb caress over my tip, across that little slit, and then her fist plunged down again. I don't think she was trying to get me off, she just liked my cock. Fine by me, but things were reaching the point of no return.

"Goddamn, Temple."

Her lips curved; she was pleased with herself. "What?"

"Don't play coy," I said, my voice low and brusque now as I struggled to stop myself from coming. "You know what you're doing to me."

"Obviously."

"Then you have to know how close I am."

She slowed her stroking. "How about I change the deal?"

I growled, tensing and holding back. "To what?"

"If I go down on you now, then you make me come. If you can make me come more than once, you decide what we do next. If you can't give me a multiple O, then I decide."

"I thought you didn't give blow jobs."

"I don't," she said, sinking to her knees. "But I also don't have sex with guys without that NDA, so this whole thing is happening outside my rules."

"Fuck the rules."

"The rules protect me," she whispered.

"From what?"

"Asshole guys."

"Well, honey," I said, "I might be an asshole, but I can make you a couple promises."

She kept her hand on my cock, stroking slowly, then stopped at the top, thumb caressing the tip, and Jesus goddam, that was almost my undoing, that little circle of the pad of her thumb across the top of my cock. But now she was on her knees, staring up at me, her eyes wide, a little nervous, and a lot horny.

"What promises?"

"I will keep you safe or die trying, number one. And number two, you have nothing to worry about from me, in terms of the reasons you have those rules. You don't need an NDA for me to keep everything we might do private."

Her eyes on mine were open and a more vulnerable than I'd have expected. "You swear? No stories? No photos?"

"I swear on my Glock," I said, putting my right hand on the pistol in question, in the shoulder holster strapped to my chest.

She gave me a baffled and irritated look. "You're swearing on your gun?"

I grinned. "Hey baby, I'm a soldier. I take my guns very, *very* seriously."

She shook her head. "Men are so weird."

"Do we have a deal?" I asked.

She plunged her fist down my length, my cock sprouting out of the top of her fist. She lowered her mouth toward my cock, and then hesitated. "I'm an idiot. You're *so* going to screw me over."

I palmed her cheek, turned her face up to mine. "Temple, honey, I'll fuck you like you've never been fucked in your life. I'll fuck you backward and forward and upside down, and I'll make you come so hard you'll see Jesus. But one thing I won't do is fuck you over." I stared down into her eyes, letting her see the honesty in mine. "Because babe, I always keep my promises. Always."

4

BREAKING THE RULES

WHAT THE HELL WAS I THINKING?

I'm an idiot. A moron. A dumbass. Weak and stupid and ruled by lust. You think it's only guys that think with their dicks? Ha, no. I'm proof positive that chicks are just as susceptible to thinking with their pussies. I mean, look at me. On my knees in front of a man I literally just met a few hours ago. I watched him kill three men with a weight bar. I watched him hijack a car. He has an apartment dedicated to a backup weapons stash.

But holy shit, the man is gorgeous.

And his cock…it is, without question, the single most beautiful male organ I've ever seen, and I think I've established at this point that I'm somewhat of an expert, given my one-night-stand-only rule.

It's not the biggest cock I've ever seen either—it's not about the size. I mean, yeah, the dude is legit *hung*. But it's just…beautiful. Thick, straight, well-shaped, with just enough well-trimmed reddish pubic hair to emphasize his manliness; call me weird, but I don't like men who shave their balls bare. It's just…weird. I'm not waxed down under, either, because I equally think a totally bald pussy is just… ick. A cute, sexy little landing strip…yeah, that's all you really need.

Duke's dick is just pretty.

I want it. I like touching it. I like the way it feels in my hand, and I'm seriously eager to feel him inside me. I'd bet the title to my Bentley that fucking Duke Silver will be the best sex of my life…and, in fact, I kind of am betting on that, really. Betting more than a stupid car. I'm betting my self, my pride, and my still-recovering image.

Shit, if I had a heart to lose, I'd be betting my heart. But my capacity to fall in love got stomped on and screwed over one too many times, and is now dead. So no worries there. But still, I'm gambling on the sex being that good.

I slid my fist down his big, beautiful cock as he uttered that sentence: *"Temple, honey, I'll fuck you like you've never been fucked in your life. I'll fuck you backward and forward and upside down, and I'll make you come so hard you'll see Jesus. But one thing I won't do is fuck you over."* My hand froze, and his palm touched my cheek and I was stuck staring up at him, seeing honesty in his eyes that I wasn't expecting from him, which freaked me out. *"Because babe, I always keep my promises. Always."*

And that was it. Done. It was over. How was I supposed to resist a line like that?

So I did something I hadn't done since Trent: I put my mouth on Duke's cock.

Those photos Trent took? Yeah, most of them were taken while I was going down on him. The tabloids loved it. Actual photos of Temple Kennedy sucking a dick? Headline gold. And that, dear friends, was the last time I sucked a dick. Got burned, know what I mean? Like when you drink too much vodka and you can't ever drink vodka again? Kinda like that. Those photos killed me. They pushed the ratings of our show through the roof, and got me offers from all sorts of magazines to do photo spreads, and at least a dozen contracts to do porn. And it was those porn offers that really pushed me over the edge. Porn? Really? Is that how people see me? It hurt. It still hurts. And stupidly, irrationally, I associated it with the one time I went down on a guy. I mean, I actually *liked* Trent. He was cute, sexy, nice, fun, smart, and successful. He didn't need my money, or so I thought, because he was pretty well off on his own, and not from an inheritance either. I trusted him. I let him play me. And the very moment I tried to do something hot for him, he photographed it and sold the pics to the tabloids.

Five grand. That's how much I was worth to him. Shit, I'd have given him that much in cash from what I carried in my damn purse. But no. He had to sell pics of me blowing him.

I gave him a hell of a BJ, too.

So why, oh why, oh why was I doing this with Duke?

I didn't have any good answers for that. Because I wanted to? I liked his cock so much I felt like it deserved to be kissed and licked and sucked? Because he saved my life? Because he seemed to have every intention of risking his life to keep me safe? Because he was fucking gorgeous, and I wanted him to like me? Those two shouldn't be connected, actually. He was fucking gorgeous…stop; I wanted him to like me…stop; I didn't want him to like me because he was gorgeous…right?

Right?

He was a badass, and a lot smarter than I'd originally given him credit for. Actually, I didn't really know whether he was actually intelligent, but he was defying my original stereotype of being nothing more than a rough, gun-toting, F-bomb-dropping commando. I mean, he *was* that, but I got the impression he was also a lot more.

And I wanted him to like me.

The question was *why*? I didn't have an answer for that.

What I did have answer for was the question: *am I going to blow him?* And the answer was yes.

I watched him from the corner of my eye as I wrapped my lips around his dick. He was breathing slowly and deeply, fists clenched at his sides, brows furrowed, eyes on me. Watching, but holding back; this wasn't going to last long, then. Good, because I was out of practice, and his cock was so big I wasn't sure how much of him I could take, or for how long.

He groaned out loud as my lips touched his shaft, and his hands clenched and unclenched. "Ohhhh…shit."

I slid my mouth down his shaft, taking him a little deeper, and then I backed away. Okay, so "a little" may have been an overstatement. Like, maybe two inches of him went into my mouth, but in my own defense, I didn't do this very often, and I was nervous. I mean, I've given like, a grand total of *maybe* four BJs in my life, and the first three were to my one and only serious boyfriend, who is even more responsible for my emotional frigidity than anything else in my life. But I'm not going there. Not going there. Not thinking about Lane. Nope, nope, nope.

I focused on Duke. He was here, he was real, and if I got through this BJ I had an orgasm coming my way. At *least* one. I mean, judging by how hot he got me just from a single touch, I kind of believed him when he said he'd make me come so hard I'd see Jesus.

So I focused on Duke.

Focused on his pretty cock. I licked around the head, and he groaned again, and then the groan turned into a hissing inhalation as I worked my mouth down the shaft an inch, two, three, and that was as much as I could take without gagging. I stole a glance up at him, and his eyes were closed, his mouth open, a blissful expression on his face.

He caught his lower lip between his teeth as I palmed the side of his cock with my hand and licked my way from root to tip—and that, oh, that part I didn't mind at all. He was clean, tasted like skin and man, and the way he shuddered all over, the way his cock twitched in my hand, under my tongue? Oh yeah. I liked that. The gagging I didn't like, but licking him? Mmmmm. Yeah. So I did it again, licked, and then licked more, and then just kept licking, one side, the other, the tip, and his big heavy taut balls.

"Fucking hell, Temple," he growled. "The way you use your tongue…"

"Yeah?"

"Fuck yeah. It's hot as hell."

I swirled my tongue around the head, then licked up the shaft.

"Like that?"

"Ohhh…fuck. Fuck yeah. Just like that."

He liked it, but I wasn't sure he'd come like that. And I wanted to get to the part where he licked my pussy. Call me selfish, but that was my goal from the beginning. I'd blow him in exchange for a nice long session with his gorgeous face between my thighs.

I needed him to come. But what did I do when he came? Did I swallow? I sure as hell wasn't taking it on my face or my tits, especially since we weren't at my house for easy clean up. At my place or his, after we'd fucked a few times, maybe. But here? Now? Hell no. I'd have to swallow, I realized, since it was by far the cleanest and most efficient way of dealing with cum.

First, though, I had to get him there.

Hell—I'll just ask, I decided.

"What do you like, Duke?" I looked up at him, and then licked his plump, broad, soft head. "Tell me how to make you come really, really hard."

He narrowed his eyes and stared down at me. "Use your hands and mouth at the same time."

I wrapped my fist around his cock at the base and stroked him lightly, and then put my mouth around the head. Bobbed shallowly while pumping my fist around the base.

"Like that?" I asked, glancing up at him.

"Fuck. Yeah, Fancy. Just like that."

So I kept doing that. Short, quick strokes around the base, my fist touching my mouth as I plunged him into my mouth. He groaned, and his hands went to my shoulders. He clutched me briefly, and then his fingers drifted up to the back of my neck, brushing against my nape. If he grabbed my head and started shoving me onto his cock, this would be over before it really started because I don't play that game—but I didn't say that. I just kept doing what he said he liked, using my hands and my mouth. Twist my fist around him and bob my mouth on his cock, faster and faster. This was nice, too. Didn't have to try to avoid gagging, but still got to taste his cock *and* feel him in my hand.

More, and more.

He was sighing and groaning, and his hips were flexing, fluttering.

"Goddamn." He hissed this, teeth clenched. "Don't stop."

"Mmm-mmmm," I hummed a negative, and he twitched at the vibrations.

"Shit, shit, shit," he grunted, his hand cupping my nape, now.

I knelt a little lower, tilted him away from his body, and looked up at him from under my eyelashes. "Mmm-hmmm?"

"Fuck, Temple. You hum like that again, I'm not gonna have a chance to warn you. I'll just blow down your throat."

Which was an intriguing idea—more because of the thought of a man like Duke losing control than because I was, like, super excited for an unexpected load of cum down my throat. I increased the pace of my twisting, plunging, stroking fist, and started moving my mouth on him faster. I even took him a little deeper.

He groaned, and his grip on my neck tightened, but he still didn't try to push me onto him.

Smart guy.

A man brought as close to the edge of orgasm as I had Duke in that moment, though…he'd do anything to come. He had no control over his faculties. Yet even like this, Duke was holding back. Not really gripping me as hard as I suspected he could, with those huge, powerful hands. And he wasn't fucking. He was a monster of a man, and I suspected he possessed a libido to match. He liked to *fuck*. But he was holding back.

I kind of liked that. Yet…I wanted to be able to make him lose control. Like, completely. I was a little scared of what he'd do, but I was curious just as much.

So…time to up the ante.

Both hands around his cock, twisting, sliding down and gliding up, spreading my saliva around, I hummed, and it was a hum of my own pleasure. Erotic, a deep, breathy moan. A little faked, sure, because I wasn't getting any sexual enjoyment from this, but I *was* enjoying his reactions. The way he flexed his hips to get deeper, the way his jaw flexed and released, and a long low groan escaped him. The way his hands buried into my hair and gripped tightly, as if fighting the urge to pull me toward him.

Another hum, and his entire body twitched.

"Fuck!" he grunted. "Temple, I—oh...*fuck*."

And that was it. I felt him tense, felt his cock throb.

I fucked him with my mouth, then. Held onto his dick with both hands, tilting it toward my face, and started bobbing hard and fast, not thinking about how deep I took him, just fucking him with my lips as quickly as I was could. I felt him at the back of my throat, and my moan turned to an almost-gag, and then his fingers in my hair jerked twice.

"Temple, goddamn Temple—I'm—oh fuck oh fuck oh fuck."

I'm not a swallower. I never swallowed Lane's cum; the few times I did blow him I'd go down on him until he got close to coming, and then we'd fuck. I never blew him to orgasm. When I went down on Trent, he came into my hands, which was...messy, but better than taking it down my throat, I'd figured at the time. So, even though I've given BJs before, I've never swallowed. I don't really know what cum tastes like, TBH.

I was about to find out.

Duke came with a shouted "*FUCK!*" so loud I was pretty sure they heard it across town. His cock throbbed between my lips, and then I felt something wet and hot and salty hit the back of my throat. A surprised hum left me, and then I had to either swallow or choke, so I swallowed. It was thick and viscous, sliding warm down my throat. Salty, musky, a little tang and a hint of sweetness. Another spurt of cum filled my mouth, and this time I was ready for it. It pooled in my mouth, coated my tongue, and the taste of his cum was strong, potent, but not necessarily unpleasant. I swallowed again while glancing up at him, and discovered his eyes open, watching me. I went down on him once more, taking his cock to the back of my throat and then backed away, opened my mouth so the head of his dick sat on my tongue, and he twitched against my tongue and his abs flexed and his jaw clenched, and he curled forward over himself as he shot one last stream of cum onto my tongue. I grinned up at him, feeling satisfied with my performance, enjoying how spent he was, how rocked he looked. I stuck my tongue out, showing him his own cum. And then I swallowed it.

Duke stood over me, gasping, chest heaving. "Holy motherfucking hell, Fancy," he said, reaching down to lift me to my feet. "That was…"

I gave him a coy look. "It was what?"

He wiped his thumb across my lips. "The hottest blow job I've ever gotten."

I rolled my eyes at him. "Bullshit."

He flicked open a button of my shirt with one hand, and began gathering the fabric of my skirt with his other. "For real."

I stood still, reminding myself to keep breathing. "A manwhore like you? I'm sure you've gotten hundreds of BJs. No way that was the best one."

He frowned. "How do you know I'm a manwhore?"

His fingers traipse up between my thighs, tickling and teasing and touching on the way up. Brush my slit, and I jerk, thighs clenching, and then I relax myself for his touch.

"Aren't you?"

He bobs his head side to side. "I guess, yeah. But why do you assume?"

"You're gorgeous, you have money, you're a badass commando…" I shrug. "Just stands to reason. Maybe it was an unfair assumption on my part, though."

He can't help a pleased look from crossing his features. "Gorgeous, huh?"

I roll my eyes again. "You know you are. No point in fishing for compliments."

"Yeah, but everyone likes to hear it every now and again."

"True," I say, on a sigh, as he slips a finger through my folds. "Just because I'm a reality star and on magazine covers and whatever, most guys I fuck just sort of assume I know what I look like and that I don't need to be told that they think I'm pretty. So then no one ever—oh…*ohmygod*—no one ever says it."

He slipped that finger through my slit again and again, not quite going in, not quite touching my clit. But still, it felt good. The teasing made me needier than I already was, made me unsure of what he was going to do next.

"You're not pretty," Duke says.

I stare at him. "Excuse me?"

He steps back, using both hands to open my shirt the rest of way, letting go of my skirt. The gray fabric swirls back down around my knees, and I'm left gasping.

He circles around behind me, tugs down the zipper of the skirt, and it falls to the floor, leaving me naked from the waist down. He pulls the white button down off my shoulders, letting it fall around my wrists. And then, in a series of movements too fast and complicated for me follow, he tied the ends of the shirt around my wrists, binding my hands behind my back.

"Wait, what?" I tug, but I'm helpless. "Let me go, Duke. What are you doing?"

He didn't answer. Just stalked back around in front of me, and slid one index finger underneath the elastic band of my bralette, tugging it up over my tits bit by bit until I was bared, the skimpy maroon lace rolled up across the top of my chest. My tits hung free, and my nipples hardened under his gaze.

"What—what did you mean, I'm not pretty?" Stupid, I know, but I still felt unreasoning panic at the idea that he thought I was ugly.

Of course he didn't think that. The look in his eyes, the way he was staring at me, eyeing me head to toe, the way his cock, which I just sucked dry, twitched and hardened a little—he thought I was hot. He'd already said as much. He was playing me for a drawn out compliment, I know it. But when you hear a man say those words:

you're not pretty…it just kind of automatically hits some nerve inside you, hits your confidence and makes you doubt what you know to be true.

"You're fucking…" he trailed off, hunting for the right word, standing a foot away from me, not touching, just staring at my tits, "—You're…perfect."

"Perfect?" Stupid—I'm so stupid. Why did my voice sound so breathless and eager and hopeful, and…unsure? "You're crazy."

"Eh, that's debatable," he said. "Irrelevant to the fact that you're a perfect woman. Like, completely perfect looking."

He was behind me again, whispering in my ear, his voice hot and low against my earlobe; his hands appeared around front of me, sliding up my ribcage to cup my breasts from beneath.

"These? Perfect."

Then slid his hands down, one hand gripping my hipbone and the other delving between my thighs to cup my pussy. "This? Perfect. I can't *wait* to get on my knees and see what your beautiful, perfect little cunt tastes like."

Oh fuck. Oh my fuck. The things he was saying, the dirty, filthy words seared through me, sending desire dripping out of said *beautiful, perfect little cunt.* Perfect? I've been called a lot of things in my life—hot, sexy, lovely even, cute, beautiful, fuckable, dumb blonde, vapid airhead, no-talent reality star, bitch, slut, whore, 'ten out of ten body, but needs a bag over her head,'—in all my life, nobody has ever called me…*perfect.*

He w'asnt done, though. His hands moved around behind me, clutching a double handful of my ass. "This? *More* than perfect. This ass right here, Fancy? This thing is…mmm. Goddamn. It's fucking *incredible.*"

My throat closed, tightened, went hot and thick. I swallowed hard, then, blinking. God, I'm such a dumbass, letting his words get to me. He didn't mean them. He wanted to fuck me, and figured he was more likely to get what he wanted if he buttered me up.

"I'm already a sure thing for at least one fuck, Duke." I endeavored to sound casual, and mostly succeeded. "You don't have to blow smoke up my ass."

He sidled around front again. His palm completely missed my tits, for some reason, and landed on my chin; weird, I thought he'd have better aim, being a commando.

Duke cupped the side of my face with his big rough stupid beautiful bear paw of a hand. "But *this*..."

His thumb brushed over my cheekbone, just beneath my eye. I had to meet his gaze then, and those eyes of his, good god, those eyes...they burned into me. They seemed able to see my secrets and insecurities, which I work so hard to hide.

"This, Temple Kennedy. This face of yours?" That big thumb, sliding again over my lips, then my cheekbone. "Your face is the most beautiful part of you."

"Bullshit." Now...why did I whisper that?

And why did I sound so...like I was obviously lying? Or maybe I just sounded desperate to believe him, but afraid to.

He ignored me yet again. Remained in front of me, cupping my face, but his other hand slid around to find my ass again. "And let me tell you something, Fancy. If I blow anything up your ass, it sure as hell won't be smoke." His long middle finger teased up and down the crack of my butt.

Oh.

Oh.

Oh my god.

Did he just?

"Is that a hint at fucking me in the ass?" I demanded.

His teeth sank into my earlobe, and then his whisper huffed hot on my ear. "Not a hint, sweetheart. A promise." He cupped my ass cheek, lifted, pulled it aside, and then let it bounce free. "This ass? It was made to be fucked. Slowly, over the course of hours, until you're begging me to just fuck you and come inside you. And, when I do? You'll come so hard for so long it'll hurt. You'll squirt everywhere."

His other hand cupped my pussy, a fingertip teasing my clit.

"You ever come so hard you squirt?"

I shook my head. "N-no."

"Oh yeah, this is gonna be fun, Fancy."

I was dripping with desire; I felt it sliding down my thighs. I needed him to touch me. I needed him to make me come; Duke has me worked up, has me twitching and gasping and desperate.

"Stop teasing me, goddammit," I said.

He slid a finger against my clit. "Wanna come, huh?"

"Yeah," I whispered.

"How bad?" He pressed that fingertip against my clit in a light, teasing touch.

I thrusted against his finger. "Really bad."

Duke's finger circled slowly, touching gently. The contact had me writhing, pushing my hips forward in an attempt to get more, but he easily thwarted my efforts, continuing to tease me. "I don't know if I believe you, Fancy."

His chest was hard against my back, his cock a thick, semi-erect ridge between us. I leaned my head back against his shoulder, struggling against the shirt binding my wrists together behind my back. Tried again to thrust against his fingertip.

"Please, Duke," I whispered.

"I like that," he growled in response. "Hearing you beg."

I hissed in irritation. "Oh yeah? It makes you hot and horny to hear me beg, huh? You get off on power trips? Fine, I'll beg."

I pivoted away from him, stood facing him, hands bound behind my back, naked except for the rolled-up lace of my bralette. I felt the fire sparking in my eyes as I spoke, putting the lie to my plea.

"Please, Duke. Please," I said, my voice monotone, uninflected. "I'm begging you, make me come. I'm desperate. Oh please."

His mouth curved in an amused grin. "You're a saucy little minx, aren't you?"

"What the hell's that supposed to mean?"

He blinked slowly, erotic promise in his eyes, that wild, amused grin on his lips. "It means that wasn't begging." He gripped me at the waist, lifted me effortlessly; my legs went around his body instinctively, and now I felt his cock nudging my entrance, not quite hard yet, but getting there. Enough to tease.

"No?" I was utterly helpless, hands bound behind my back. I had only my legs to cling to him with and, in all honesty, I liked the way he held me, the way his hands felt on my ass, keeping me aloft without so much as a tremor of effort. "Then what was it?"

He didn't answer me. Again. Instead, he pivoted and walked out of the room, carrying me into the kitchen. Set me on the counter beside the refrigerator, then pulled me to the edge of the counter. Then…just stood there, staring at me.

Duke should have looked dumb, standing half naked like he was, wearing a tight T-shirt, his guns still in place in that double shoulder-holster harness, and combat boots but no pants. Like for real, he should look stupid and silly, but he didn't. He looked hot. His cock was almost erect now, and his thighs were thick and heavy with muscle and dusted with reddish hair, and his shirt was tight against his chest and showed off hints of his abs, and just…damn. So damn sexy. I've never really admired a man's legs before, honestly. Like, you look at a buff dude, you don't really look at his legs. You look at his chest, his arms, his abs….his cock. But his legs? Nah. Duke, though, half undressed as he was, I couldn't help but admire his legs, how strong they were, how beautifully, masculine, how muscular they were.

He didn't look stupid at all. He looked like I wanted him to put that big fat beautiful cock inside me, is what he looked like.

Which irritated me. I didn't *want* to want him, as I've already pointed out. Wanting him as much as I did frustrated me—I was annoyed at and disgusted with myself for being so stupid, for being so powerless to fight the desires of my pussy. Do you have any idea how annoying it is to be annoyed at yourself? No, probably not. But there I was, sitting completely naked on a counter, legs open, pussy throbbing, a non-stop pulse of need; the throb of my pussy was saying *fuck me, lick me, touch me.* Wanting him. Staring at his huge cock, now all but fully erect within minutes of blowing his load into my mouth. I hadn't even touched him, which was the shocking part. Was he really that virile? Or was he actually that attracted to me? Both? I hoped for both. It'd be my luck that he'd just be that virile and it had nothing to do with me, which would be a blow to my ego…which wasn't as iron-clad as most people assumed. Far less so, TBH.

And he just looked at me.

"I thought you were going to give me an orgasm?" I asked.

He stroked his cock with his fist. "Oh, I will."

"When? Because it seems like you're stalling, maybe hoping I'll just let you fuck me instead of holding you to your end of our bargain."

"I'm waiting for you to beg, Fancy." He said this with a leer, his fist sliding slowly up and down his impressive length.

"You agreed, Duke. I blow you, you go down on me. That was the deal. Why would I beg you for something you agreed to? Especially when you, as you said, always keep your promises?"

He sidled closer, fist gliding on his cock. "Because it's more fun when you beg."

"More fun for who?" I whispered, hating myself for losing my voice at his proximity.

"Both of us."

"You already got your fun," I said. "I swallowed your fun about two minutes ago."

He stood between my thighs, gripping his cock at the root, and teased the lips of my pussy with the head of his dick. And damn, damn, damn…it felt *amazing* when he did that.

"Babe," he said, "I don't think you understand how this is going to work."

He pushed into my pussy, splitting the labia open millimeter by millimeter, sliding into me in torturous, aching, delicious increments.

"Oh fuck," I whispered, the expletive yanked out of me by the glorious feel of him inside me. "What don't I understand?"

"Me." He pushed all the way in, taking all of thirty seconds to fully penetrate me. "How I work. What I do, and how I do it."

"Oh god." Another gasping curse jerked out of my mouth, beyond my control as he pulled back. "Obviously not. You should—oh *Jesus*—maybe you should explain."

"I'm good at a lot of things," he said, beginning slow, deep, rhythmic thrusts, "but there's two things I'm a goddamn master of."

"And that would be what?" I even managed to sound sarcastic; go me.

"Fighting," he murmured, pushing into me slowly. "And fucking," he said this on the withdrawal.

"I see."

His hands, up until this moment, had been braced on the counter on either side of me. Now, he slid them up my body to cup my breasts. With his cock inside me and his deep, powerful voice resonating in my ear, every last part of me was hypersensitive, so the brush of his rough palms over my breasts left me quivering and gasping.

The gasps turned into a sudden, surprised shriek as he pulled back in the same slow rhythm and then, without warning, slammed into me hard and fast. I was bounced backward on the counter, my tits jiggling as he drilled home hard enough to lift me off the counter.

"I don't think you do see," he said. "I bet you think I'm fucking you right now."

His cock drove in, pulled back, drove in, and with each thrust I wobbled and toppled closer and closer to orgasm, each drive of his dick pushing me higher and higher.

There was no mistaking how close I was to orgasm. I mean, it's not hard; I'm not a difficult woman to read in that regard. I get all flushed, my cheeks turn bright red, my skin breaks out in a sweat, my pussy tightens, and I lose all ability to not make stupid porn star sounds—*ohhhh, oh yeah, fuck yeah, oh my god, oh god fuck me harder*, breathy erotic crap like that. Plus I'm a whimperer. I don't usually scream, but I do a lot of gasping and shrieking and whimpering. Funny thing is, out of the dozens of men I've fucked, only three have ever made me come during actual intercourse, and I think all three instances were flukes.

This?

This was intentional. Duke knew *exactly* what he was doing. Each thrust was designed to push me closer. He changed his angle, the force and speed, the depth, so I never knew what I'd get, how he'd thrust into me, and the not knowing was driving me mad, in the best possible way. And then his hands cupped my tits, and his fingers pinched my nipples, and his breath blew warm on my neck, his waist gliding against my thighs.

I'd had my eyes closed as he fucked me to orgasm, but now, now I had to open my eyes. I had to watch as his cock pushed into me. My pussy was stretched so tight, and his cock was so huge, disappearing into me and pulling out. It seemed impossible that I could take all of it, but I did. And it was unbearably hot watching his cock slide into my pussy, watching his face shift expressions as he fucked me.

"You're…oh god…you're not fucking me?" I asked.

His grin was feral. "Not even close. I'm just getting you ready."

"It looks like you're fucking me, and it feels like you're fucking me."

"This isn't fucking, Fancy."

"Then what is it?"

"I just said. I'm getting you ready."

"Ready?" I gasped as he thrust in three times in quick succession, short sharp battering thrusts that knocked me to the shuddering brink of climax. "Ready for what?"

He leaned closer, his face inches from mine, his eyes hot and fierce and wild, arrogance and lust warring in his gaze. "For this."

Duke's mouth crashed against mine with sudden, bruising force, his tongue claiming my mouth as his with ferocious dominance. I had no chance of resisting the kiss. All I could do was succumb, give in, be kissed senseless. His fingers found the elastic band holding my hair in place and tugged it free, yanking the bobby pins out, and then my hair was falling loose around my shoulders in a blonde cascade.

The moment my hair was free, he wrapped it around his fist to control my head, and with my hands bound behind my back and his cock driving into me, I was…utterly helpless. I should have hated it. I should have been furious, or terrified. Instead, the helplessness, the fury and the mastery of his kiss…drove me over the edge.

I broke the kiss to throw my head back and shriek on a gasping intake of breath, the climax starting low and deep.

He pulled out of me as I began coming, leaving me aching and crazed and desperate. "NO! Duke, no! Please, please, god please keep fucking me!"

There was no sarcasm that time, no attitude, only raw desperation, genuine begging.

The climax lost its edge as I lost the stretching fullness of his cock inside me, as I lost the stimulation.

Duke dropped to his knees between my thighs, grinning up at me. "Beg harder, Fancy." He touched his tongue to my clit, and a zing of heat blasted through me.

"Fuck—oh *fuck*, Duke, please." I met his gaze, let him see how real I was. "Give it to me, Duke. I—I need to come. Please, *please*."

As I breathed the final plea, he buried his face between my thighs and drove his tongue into my pussy and dragged it up to my clit, and I arched my back and gasped.

"Like that?" He breathed.

"Yeah, except shut up and keeping going."

He laughed, but dove back in, and this time slid three fingers into my slit as he latched onto my clit. Two quick thrusts of his fingers, one hard suck around my clit, and I was gone. My feet planted on his shoulders, my head and neck braced against the cabinet behind me, my thighs falling apart, my head tipping back, a stacatto series of shrieks ripping out of me as he worked my exploding orgasm into a frenzy. His fingers pumped in and out of my channel, and his tongue lashed my clit in a furious onslaught of side-to-side movements, drawing my shrieks into breathless gasps. He shifted tactics then, slowing his fingers, curling them against me high inside, massing some point just behind my clit inside my pussy, his mouth suctioning around my clit, his tongue moving in slow circles.

The abrupt change of pace and tactic should have ruined the orgasm, but somehow it didn't, instead made me come all the harder. I was struggling against the shirt binding my wrists, thrashing against him, hips pumping, shrieking and gasping as he ate my pussy with such skill that I couldn't seem to stop coming, could only continue thrashing, orgasming, wave after wave wrenched out of me.

"Untie me," I whispered, as soon as I was capable of speech. "Please. Let me touch you."

"If you can talk, you're not coming hard enough."

He stood up, lifted me off the counter with one arm under my knees and the other around my shoulders. Half a dozen steps, and we were at the futon. I was tipped backward, his face over mine, his lips glistening with my essence. He set me down and then stood in front of me, his cock erect and still wet from being inside me.

"Lick me," he ordered. "Taste your pussy on my cock."

And, like the desperate slut I was, I obeyed him. I leaned forward, hands still bound behind me, and licked up the side of his cock, tasting my pussy mingling with the salt of his skin.

"You want me to untie you?" he asked.

"Yeah."

My orgasm was subsiding now, aftershocks shuddering though me.

"Lay down on the futon."

I moved to lie down as instructed, head by one armrest, feet at the other. He wedged one of his legs between me and the back of the futon and kept the other on the floor, then bent over me, tugged my leg aside, and licked my pussy, once, slowly. His cock was over my face, hard, sticky from my pussy, begging for me.

"Suck my cock, Temple." Another command.

And, yet again, I did what he told me. I wanted to, though. That was the only reason. I'm not the type to let myself be ordered around by anyone. I've walked out on executive producers who thought they could order me around. Some guy thinks he can tell me what to do? Hell no. But Duke...I had no control over my reactions. He commanded me to take his cock into my mouth, and so....

I lifted up and captured his cock with my mouth, took him to the back of my throat, and then sank back down, tilting him away from his body so I could slide my mouth up his cock from tip to root. His mouth was on my pussy, his tongue moving, his lips kissing, as if he was making out with my vagina. Slow, thorough. Pushing me from subsiding aftershocks to writhing as another climax welled up inside me, and this time the hums and moans and gasps were muffled by the thick salty musky tang of his cock in my mouth, nudging the back of my throat as I lifted my face up toward his body, taking him deeper each time.

Whatever magic it was he had over my body worked again, bringing me to orgasm within a couple minutes, making me shudder and writhe, struggling to free my hands, orgasming, and sucking his cock all at the same time. I was lost to the experience, totally committed. No holding back. I felt him push past the back of my throat as I lifted up, groaning around him as I shuddered and writhed and came, and then I had to open my throat as he went deeper, my breath snorting out of my nose he filled my throat. Too much, too much— and then he was gone, pulling out of my mouth as if sensing what I needed before I even had a chance to make a sound.

I felt his hand under me, moving, pulling at the shirt, and then my wrists were free and he was tossing the shirt across the room. Instantly, my hands flew out to clutch his cock, stroking, plunging, caressing, feeling my own saliva slick on his shaft, still moaning as wave after wave of my second climax shattered through me, rendering me helpless to do anything then except hold onto his erection and shriek and gasp and come.

He devoured me through it, licking and suckling every last shred of orgasm out of me, until I was limp and gasping.

And then he stood up. "That's two orgasms in ten minutes, princess."

I was still panting, shuddering, thighs trembling from after-shocks. "What?"

"Our deal?"

My brain wasn't firing on all cylinders just yet. "Deal?"

He leaned down over me, and I smelled my pussy on his breath. I didn't mind it—my pussy smelled pretty good, if I say so myself, and when he kissed me earlier, I tasted myself on his mouth, which also wasn't unpleasant. "You go down on me, I go down on you. If you come more than once, I decide what we do next."

"Oh." I stared up at him. "So…what are we doing next?"

I wasn't sure what to expect. Anal? Another BJ? I wasn't even sure what I wanted.

"Stand up." His voice was low and quiet, but still a very clear command.

One which, yet again, I was powerless to refuse. So I stood up, and Duke took my place on the futon.

"Fuck me," he ordered. "Ride me until we both come."

"Condom?"

He quirked an eyebrow and reached for me, pulled me closer. "I was just bare inside you."

"That was a mistake," I said, resisting his pull, both literal and metaphorical.

He shook his head. "Fancy, you think I'd have done that if I wasn't clean?"

"How do you know I'm clean and protected?"

"I don't."

I shook my head. "Then you're an idiot."

"A very, very careful idiot," he said. "You're the only girl I've done anything like this with, ever. I'm safe, always. But you…you make me crazy. This whole thing…it's fucking crazy."

"I'm always safe too, but…"

"My boss makes us all get tested for just about everything, STD and otherwise, on a regular basis, since we're overseas so much. I've got years worth of clean reports I can show you."

"I believe you," I said. "But still…condom?"

"Tell me why. The truth."

I blinked at him for a moment, and then felt the truth bubbling out of me. "I don't want to deal with the mess, for one."

"And?"

I sighed. "And…you feel too good bare inside me."

"So what?" I hesitated, and he reached out, grabbed me by the hips, and pulled me closer. "Tell me why that matters."

"I don't *want* to like you. I don't want this to feel so fucking good. This whole thing, it's…it's nuts." I resisted his efforts to pull me closer yet. "Yeah, I may do one night stands, but I'm usually tipsy enough to not care. I don't do…this, not sober. I don't—everything we've done, it's crazy, and it's not me. You're breaking all my rules, and letting you fuck me bare…that's too far."

He eyed me for a long moment. I was standing between his thighs, his cock standing flat against his belly, my hands on his knees. I was seconds from betraying myself, from saying fuck it and climbing on him, sliding that fantastic, talented cock of his inside me and fucking him until we both came.

I even had images of that dancing in my head, his hands on my hips lifting me, pulling me down on him, his bare cock sheathing into my core, my tits bouncing, hair flying.

He nodded, breaking my mental fantasy. "I can respect that." He stood up, pushed past me. "Then I guess we wait."

I blinked, stunned. "Wait…what?" I turned and watched him disappear into the gun room and return with his shorts in hand. "That's a deal breaker for you? Are you for real?"

He stepped into his shorts, his massive erection making it difficult for him to zip and button. "No, it's not a deal-breaker, I just don't keep condoms here."

I frowned. "You…you don't?"

He shook his head. "Nope. This is a stash spot and safe house. I've never brought anyone here. Not even my boss knows this place exists." His gaze met mine. "So, no condom, no sex. I get it, and I respect it."

"But, I—"

He moved to stand in front of me. "Unless you're changing your mind?"

I wavered, and then mentally cursed myself for being stupid. "No." I forced the word out. "No, I'm not changing my mind."

"Then we'll wait." He cupped the back of my neck, pulled me close; he was still hard as a rock inside his shorts. "When we finally do get to fuck…it's gonna be intense, Fancy. You better believe that."

"Isn't that uncomfortable?" I glanced down at his erection, tenting his shorts.

"Yep. But it'll go away eventually." He ground himself against me. "Unless you're volunteering to help me out?"

I shouldn't. I'd get carried away. But I knew what frustration felt like, what it felt like to be aroused and horny and have no way of alleviating it.

His erection looked painful.

And he had given me not one but two orgasms in a row, which was more than any man had given me in one day…well…ever, probably.

"You're not saying no." He sounded bemused. "Means you're considering it."

"Would you stop me?"

He snorted. "Hell no. Princess, if you want to help me out with this monster hard-on, I sure as fuck ain't gonna stop you. I won't ask you to, but I won't stop you either."

"It would only be fair. You did make me come twice."

He laughed. "Babe, ain't no such thing as fair in this life. I don't give a shit about fair." He lost all trace of humor then. "I don't keep track, and I don't do things to be fair or equal. We get a hold of some condoms, Fancy, honey, I plan on fucking you into a stupor. I plan on making you come so many times you'll lose count, and I won't expect you to do shit in return. That's not what sex is about. It's not about things being fair, or who gets off first, or most, or hardest. It's about making each other feel good. That's how this works, for me. So don't make this about shit being fair or whatever."

"I just—"

"Be honest with yourself about why you'd be helping me out."

Why would I do this?

Because he makes me horny, that's why. Because his cock is a thing of beauty, and I can't get enough. I'd had him in my mouth, had him in my hands, even had him in pussy for a far too short amount of time. And I wanted more. I didn't care if it was fair. I didn't want to help him out with his erection because I really cared about him being uncomfortable, although it did look painful to be so hard. I also knew it would go away after awhile…he'd even said so himself. No, the reason I wanted to help him out was for me. It would be for me. Because I wanted it. Because I wanted *him*—damn his stupid gorgeous self.

I groaned, and then hooked my finger in the waistband of his shorts and led him toward the bathroom. I shoved him in ahead of me.

"Sit," I commanded.

He quirked an eyebrow at me. "Oooh, getting bossy. I like it." He sat on the closed lid of the toilet. "Now what, mistress Temple?"

I glared at him. "Now *you* shut up." I reached for him, unzipped his shorts, flipped open the button, and his cock sprang free. "No talking, no moving, no touching. Just sit there and watch."

"Yes ma'am." His grin was eager, arrogant, and willing.

5

BLOOD ON YOUR HANDS

WELL GOOD GOD AND HOT DAMN, THIS GIRL WAS INSATIABLE Like…holy motherfucking hell, she's such a complicated, gorgeous, insatiable, difficult, wild little piece of ass.

But no, she's not just a piece of ass—don't be a dick, Duke: she's way more. She's class, but she's also open about the fact that she likes sex, and that she has a lot of it. I like that. I get judged a lot for being a self-proclaimed manwhore, even some the guys on the team—except Thresh—sort of shoot me side-eye sometimes when they watch me bang a different chick every night of the week, and sometimes more than one in a night. Temple would get that. She wouldn't judge me for it, just like I don't judge her for it.

She's fucking difficult, though. Like, I want to assume she's just another rich spoiled celebrity chick with more looks and money than sense or personality. I also want to assume she's down for just about anything, that we can just bang and be done, like we're both used to. But it's obvious both of those assumptions would be wrong. The blowjob she gave me earlier was, as I told her, the hottest I'd ever gotten, but it was because it was unpracticed, a little clumsy. She wasn't sure of what she was doing, obviously didn't do it a lot, as she admitted. But she took care of my cock with an eagerness and even an affection that I hadn't expected and didn't know how to handle. She *enjoyed* it. Not because I was so delusional to think she got some kind of weird sexual rush from it, but because she liked doing it, for reasons I couldn't begin to fathom. It was…fucking hot. Everything she did was fucking hot as hell, and it drove me nuts. Like, I just don't get her. Why she does what she does, why she says the things she says. I don't get her resistance to this. All we're doing is fucking. Neither of us expected anything more than casual sex, good old no-strings-attached fucking.

But then she did things I didn't expect, looked at me in ways I couldn't fathom, and it threw me for a loop, and I was left trying to figure out what was going on in that gorgeous head of hers.

She held her ground on not having sex if I wasn't wearing a condom, which I totally respect. The fact that I'd been about to drill her without one was honestly freaking me the fuck out, because that's a hard and fast rule of mine which I've never broken, not ever, no matter what, no matter who. And I didn't even stop to think about it. I don't know this chick. Like, at all. We just met. Yet I put my dick in her bare, and never even stopped to think about bagging my shit. Weirder yet was that neither did she, and I get the impression that's as abnormal for her as it is for me. I honestly had to pull out and switch tactics because I was about to blow inside her from just a few thrusts, which is insanely fast for me. She just…does something to me. Bare, skin to skin…god, it felt incredible. Too good, way, *way* too good. So good I needed more, but was a little wary of doing that again, for fear of embarrassing myself in a way I hadn't since the first time a girl put her hands down my pants. But Temple, the way she felt, the way she touched me…she drove me nuts. And I couldn't figure it out.

Like right now, after denying us the sex we were building up to, instead of taking the out I was offering, no pressure, no big deal, figuring we'd fuck all the harder for it later, she shoved me into the bathroom, ordered me to sit down, and now seems to be working up the courage to do something. Or figuring out what she wants. I don't know. I can't read the girl. I just don't know what she's planning.

I liked that. It made me nervous, but I liked it.

She reached out, wrapped those slim, small, pale fingers around my cock and stroked me, top to bottom. At first, that was all she did, and I was fine with it. More than fine. If I could hold off coming indefinitely, I'd be content to sit here and just let her touch me like that, just watch her hand slide up and down, watch her thumb caress over the top. It was incredible, how good just her hand felt. I leaned back against the tank of the toilet, laced my hands behind my head, and watched.

And she just stroked me. One hand, then the other. And after a while, both, hand over hand, the way I liked it best.

"Goddamn, Temple," I growled.

She'd told me to shut up and hold still, but sometimes that was just impossible. Like right then, there was no way I could keep still, no way I could shut up.

I was on the edge, riding the cusp of climax and holding it back as hard as I could. My eyes flew open so I could watch what she did when I came.

"Don't warn me," she said.

I did my best to hold still, and just watched as she switched back to one hand sliding up and down my cock, going fast now, and obviously recognizing how close I was to losing it. Kept the quick strokes going, staring at my cock with fascination.

Then she glanced up at me, as if gauging my reaction.

And then, seconds before I was about to come, she bent over me. Her hair draped across my belly obscured her face, so I reached out and brushed her hair aside, holding it out of the way so I could watch my cock slide between her lips, watch the way her eyes slid closed.

"Jesus," I grunted.

She had her hand around me still, and resumed stroking, going faster than ever, and I was flexing my hips, grunting, cursing under my breath from the effort to hold back, to not fuck her mouth like I wanted to so damn badly. God, her mouth was wet and warm, and it felt like fucking ecstasy as she slid her mouth down my shaft and back up, fist sliding hard and fast.

No warning, she'd said, so I gritted my teeth and flexed hard, one hand in her hair, the other clenched behind my head.

She was sucking hard, fist grinding in a blur. Her tongue swirled around my cock, licking away the cum as it seeped out of me, and she kept going, sucking and jerking, until I was arched fully off the seat, groaning helpless curses, both fists buried in her long sun-blonde hair, gripping the shimmery, silky locks with all my strength and trying desperately to not crush her against me.

And, at that exact moment, still coming so hard I was dizzy and breathless, Temple's mouth halfway down my throbbing shaft, the soft globes of her tits draped against my thighs—

A tall male form appeared in the hallway, holding a suppressed 9mm. He stopped as he came to the open doorway of the bathroom, pistol swinging to cover the opening.

Temple, head down, eyes closed, utterly focused on giving me the single most erotic moment of my entire motherfucking life, never even saw him.

I reacted instantly, instincts and training kicking in faster than thought. My pistol cleared my holster faster than it ever had before.

It's funny how time slows down in those moments—I had time, somehow, between drawing my Beretta and pulling the trigger, for a thought to flash through my head: *please don't bite me, Jesus fuck, Temple, please don't bite me—*

I pulled the trigger twice, aiming for center mass, the concussions coming one after the other so fast they sounded like one report.

Temple screamed and fell backward, hands over her ears and, thank fuck, she didn't bite down in shock.

My rounds hit dead center, two red circles spreading across the intruder's chest, right over his heart.

The silence was sudden and deafening. Or maybe it was the ringing of my ears from two gunshots in a tiny, tiled-in bathroom that had me momentarily deaf.

And then Temple's voice, soft, fearful. "Um, Duke? What—what the hell?"

I blinked, glanced down at her. She was sitting naked on the floor of the bathroom, huddled back against the corner where the tub met the wall. She had a string of my come dribbling down the side of her chin, about to drip off. I holstered the pistol and reached out slowly, carefully, aware that she might freak after the sudden violence. She flinched, brows drawing down, jaw hardening, but she didn't cringe out of reach. I slid my thumb down from the corner of her mouth, wiping my come away. Only, the last droplet dangling from the edge of her jaw dripped free and landed on the upper swell of her breast. We both glanced down at it, and then I used my index finger to wipe that away too, lingering a little, just because.

And then her gaze went to the body slumped on the floor in the hallway, leaking a pool of blood. "Who's that?"

I shrugged, following her gaze. "No idea. One of Cain's assholes, I'm assuming. Real question is how they found this place, and how many more there are."

At least I had toilet paper in this bathroom; I unrolled a huge wad and cleaned the mess off my stomach.

"What do we do?" she asked, rubbing at her ears in an attempt to clear the ringing.

"Get the fuck out of here, that's what we do," I said, standing up. Or rather, *tried* to stand up; my legs were still so weak and shaky I didn't quite make it to my feet, and had to sit back down for a moment. "Good goddamn, Temple, that was…I swear to god I don't have words for how fucking incredible that was."

She blushed. "I don't know what came over me—"

"You better not apologize," I interrupted.

She managed a small grin. "Not apologizing. It was hot, watching you lose it like that." And then her gaze went back to that stupid dead guy, ruining the moment. "I'm gonna be sick," she said, twisting her head to one side and making a retching sound.

I made it to my feet, then reached down and lifted her to her feet. "Don't look down, and don't think about it."

"Easy for you to say," she murmured.

I pivoted us, so her back was to the hallway. "Just look at me, yeah? Think happy thoughts."

"You just shot someone while I was sucking you off. What happy thoughts am I supposed to think?" She was shaking all over, and not in a good way; I had to keep her distracted.

"Think about how we sixty-nined. That was pretty fuckin' hot, wasn't it?" I pulled her against my body, pressing her face into my shoulder. "Think about that."

I lifted her up, and her legs went around my waist. We were both still naked, and I knew there was no way anything else was happening now, but holy shit, she felt perfect like this wrapped around me. I stepped over the dead guy, glancing down to make sure he really was dead—his eyes were staring unseeing at the ceiling, so yeah, he was gone.

I moved into the weapons rooms where our clothes were, kicked the door shut with my foot, and then set Temple down. She was still shaking and shuddering, breathing hard, desperately trying to keep it together and doing damn good job. Her skirt was in a pile on the ground, so I snagged it, oriented it so the zipper was facing her back, and knelt in front of her. Lifted her heel, helped her step in.

"You don't—I can—"

"Just step in, Fancy." I helped her get her other foot into the opening of the skirt and then lifted it up around her waist, zipping it closed. Sad to cover such a gorgeous ass, but it was go time. "Just breathe, and think about whatever will distract you."

"You distract me," she said.

"I do? How so?" I stood up and rolled the lace of her bralette down over her breasts, then reached inside the material and pulled her breasts fully inside, like I'd seen done in the past.

"You're too damn pretty for your own good. More accurately, you're too damn pretty for *my* good." She just stood there and let me dress her, which was a little worrying, but she was still talking, so that was good. "I look at you, and my brain goes dumb. You touch me, get near me, and I just…go loony."

I helped her slide her arms into the sleeves of her blouse, and then made quick work of buttoning it. I found her shoes where she'd kicked them off at some point, though I had no memory of when she'd done that.

"So, think about me," I said, finding my shorts and putting them on, then sliding the belt through the loops. "Think about how it felt when I was inside you."

Her eyes fixed on mine. "That's a bad idea."

The air between us went thick and tense. I held her gaze, and in those blue eyes I saw a lot of the same things I saw inside myself—mainly uncertainty regarding what the hell to do about these weirdly intense emotions we seemed to share.

"You ever like something so much it scared you?" she asked.

"I do now."

"That's why I shouldn't think about us like that," she responded.

"That's why you *should* think about it." I caught her hips in my hands, pulled her close. "Because sweetheart, that's happening. You and me, bare, nothing between us."

"I can't."

"Why not?"

"Because—because it's a terrible idea."

"It's a fantastic idea."

"Which is why it's stupid," she breathed. "So good it's bad, and I don't know how to do that."

"Temple—"

"Plus," she said, babbling right over me, "it breaks every single one of my rules."

"Temple—"

"And my rules keep me safe. They keep all you asshole men in your place. My rules make sense for me." Her eyes went down, to where my shorts were still open, unzipped, held up cock in one of my hands. "Doesn't matter how beautiful your dick is, or how perfect it feels, that can't happen. It'll break all my rules."

"You're gonna have to explain these rules to me, Princess," I said. "Because I don't get 'em. But right now, we gotta go, okay? Those shots will have drawn attention, and we don't need that. So you're gonna hang out in here for a hot second while I get rid of our friend out there, and then we're gonna book it out of here. Okay? Just…stay here."

She nodded, and I cupped her nape, pulled her close, then grabbed a handful of her hair and tipped her head back. Our lips were millimeters apart. Her breath was warm and sweet and smelled like my cum, which was hotter than it should have been, for some reason. Temple stopped breathing as I lowered my lips to hers, and honestly, I don't think I was breathing either. Usually a kiss doesn't mean shit to me, it's just part of fucking. Chicks dig a hot kiss, it turns 'em on, gets 'em ready, sort of puts 'em in the mood, know what I mean? But for me, normally, a kiss wasn't anything to get all excited about.

Temple Kennedy, as she had in literally everything else so far, proved that to be a lie. Her lips on mine…fuck. I was gone, man. My heart started pounding like I'd just humped five miles uphill in full gear at a run. My hand shook on the back of her neck. The wet warmth of her mouth, the way she leaned up into the kiss, melting into me, melting into the kiss…

Goddamn it.

God fucking damn it.

Tearing myself out of that kiss was like ripping duct tape off my skin. I staggered backward, jaw clenched hard, a frown tightening my face, chest heaving.

"You're fucking dangerous, Temple."

I left the room as fast as I could, because if I didn't I'd kiss her again, and we didn't have time for that shit, and also because I didn't know how to handle that shit.

I took a second to zip, button, buckle, and tuck the front of my shirt behind the buckle of my belt, and then leaned back against the closed door, wiping my face with both hands. I wasn't sure what was coming over me when I was around Temple, but it was seriously fucking with my mojo. I had to get my shit together. I had way too much to worry about to be getting caught up in some rich bitch's web of complications. Getting my dick wet wasn't worth it, no matter how perfect she was.

Yeah, I didn't believe myself either, but I had to try, right?

I tugged my hair free of the ponytail holder, shook it out, scrubbed my fingers through it a few times, and then tied it back once more, this time putting it up in a topknot. Harris called it a man-bun, but those fucking things were stupid. Only girly little millennial hipster twinks wore man-buns, if you asked me. A topknot was different; if samurai wore topknots, then I could wear a topknot. Those dudes were badasses. Not always the honorable, upright, holy warriors mythology tends to make them out to be, but they were certainly badasses.

Hair out of the way, shorts fixed, cock under control—and feeling drained, let me tell you—breathing normal, hands steady, heart no longer hammering…yeah. I was good to go.

I grabbed the dead dude by the ankles, hauled him into the bathroom, and heaved him into the tub, keeping his pistol.

No point in covering the bloodstain on the carpet, so I left that alone. I went into the kitchen, then over to the fridge. It was off, unplugged, and chained and padlocked. Weird, but it served a purpose. The padlock was biometric, like all the other important locks in this place—I couldn't put a fancy lock on the front door, and there wasn't a point anyway, because even if they got in, they weren't leaving with anything valuable. I put my thumb to the pad, which flashed green, and the hasp popped open. Inside the fridge, instead of shelving and food, there were six black duffel bags stacked on top of each other, each containing stacks of cash.

Yeah, I had a bank account, but I only kept enough in there to pay bills and look legit to anyone who might go sniffing after me. My real bank was kept here, in this fridge, which wasn't a normal fridge. Old school, heavy as fuck, lead insulated, solid steel, and just about indestructible. Even if this entire building burned down, my cash stash would survive.

I snagged one of the bags, unzipped it just to appreciate the stacks of green, and then re-zipped it. Closed and locked the fridge, hoping against hope that if this place got raided by the boys in blue they wouldn't think to check the strange, out of place, heavily locked refrigerator. But that was a faint hope, especially if they got a look at my weapons collection.

At that moment, there was a knock on the door. "Dan? I heard—I heard...it sounded like gunshots, and—"

Old Bruce, doing his job, damn him.

I cracked open the door. "Had the TV on too loud, buddy. Nothing to worry about."

He tried to peer past me. "You sure? It sounded like—"

"New surround sound system," I explained. "Didn't realize how loud it was, I guess."

Bruce eyed me suspiciously. "Well, all right. Keep it down, yeah? I had a couple complaints." His expression knowing, then. "The complaints mentioned some screaming, too."

I winked at him. "Yeah, well, you know how it is."

He snorted. "Not so much anymore, unfortunately." He grinned at me, then, and ambled away. "Just keep it down, Dan."

"You got it," I said, and closed the door.

I carried the duffel bag into the bedroom, where Temple was wandering from case to case, examining my guns.

She picked up the stuffed tiger and examined it. "This seems oddly sentimental for a guy like you, Duke."

I took it from her, a little brusquely, and shoved it into the duffel bag. "It was a foster brother's. Good kid." I fingered the button eye. "Leukemia. Didn't make it."

Temple didn't comment, but I saw her realizing that I might be more than just a hard-ass fuckboy commando. Like, hey, I might just have real feelings in me, somewhere. Weird, right?

I grabbed the HK and stuffed it into the duffel and transferred all the magazines I had in my pockets, which lightened things considerably. I added an extra pair of Berettas and extra mags for those, and fuck it, may as well toss in a flashbang or two—you never knew when those would come in handy.

I hefted the bag, testing the weight of it, and decided I'd better call it good.

Temple was staring at me. "Um."

I stared back. "What?"

"You have an actual duffel bag full of cash?"

I shrugged. "I have several. Why? Is that weird?"

She quirked an eyebrow. "Yes. Most people…oh I don't know… use banks?"

I snorted. "Fuck the banks. Banks are bullshit. I don't trust any institution, let alone ones who handle other people's money for profit. My money is my money, and I don't want to have to deal with asshole bankers to get at it. Plus, there's just something satisfying about a bag full of hundos, know what I mean? Also, who's gonna rob me?"

She bobbled her head side to side. "I see your point." A sarcastic eye roll then. "Do you have a stack of fake passports too?"

"Holy shit! I can't believe I almost forgot those!" I dropped the bag and pointed at her. "Good call, Fancy."

I left the door open and ducked across the hall and into the bathroom, lifted the lid off the toilet and fished out the triple-bagged, sealed, and waterproof bundle of IDs, went back into the bedroom, shaking excess water off the bundle before wiping it dry on the front of my shorts.

Temple had three fingertips pressed against her forehead, staring at me in disbelief. "That was sarcasm, actually."

I laughed. "Yeah, well, a high-end fake passport is expensive as fuck and hard as hell to get hold of, so I ain't about to leave these here for the cops to find. The guns, my cash, I can deal with the loss. It's gonna hurt, but I can deal. My fakes? Oh hell no. Cost me several hundred grand and a bunch of favors to procure these, and they're always useful."

Temple just sighed. "You're a piece of work, Duke."

I just winked. "You think this place is something? You should see my pad at Harris's compound."

With that I led her out of the bedroom, careful to make sure she didn't glance into the bathroom on the way. I paused at the door of the apartment, watching out the peephole. When I was reasonably sure it was clear, I toed open the door and pivoted out, scanning the hallway, the stolen pistol in hand.

Empty, for now.

I gestured for Temple to follow me to the stairwell, putting a finger over my lips to make sure she stayed quiet. I nudged open the door to the stairwell, inched in far enough to peek down the stairs, listening and watching.

I heard voices below, chatting in low, gruff tones in a language I didn't speak, probably Ukrainian or Russian. Damn. I glanced back at Temple, shushed her again, and then put my mouth to her ear so I could whisper.

"Stay here, and stay low," I hissed as quietly as I could, setting the duffel bag at her feet. "Don't move from this spot until you're sure it's me coming up for you."

"If it's not you?" she asked, sounding more than a little panicked.

I grinned and winked. "It'll be me, sweetpea. No worries."

Down the stairs then, in a low tactical crouch, back to the wall, aiming at the stairs below me. I got down to the first floor and then I crouched on a landing and waited. The voices grew louder as they ascended the steps, clearly unhurried and unworried. Which was stupid, on their part.

If you're hunting Duke Silver you'd better be worried, motherfucker.

I waited until the first one cleared the landing completely, the second right behind him. I drew a bead on the second dude's forehead and squeezed off a round. The *snap* of the suppressed report echoed in the stairwell, and there was a spray of red and a thumping as he fell backward. The guy in the lead burst into motion, throwing himself to one side as he hit the stairs on his belly, Tec-9 whipping up.

I scrambled to my right just in time, his semi-automatic chattering. Half a dozen rounds smacked into the drywall where I'd been, and four more strafed across, following me. I hit the landing hard on my right side, rolled, and popped off two fast shots at the shooter. Only one hit, but one was all it took. The round splattered through the top of his head and exited near his shoulder blade, making a godawful mess of the stairwell.

I held my position for a moment, waiting for a third dickhead to pop up. When half a minute passed without anyone shooting at me, I shifted to a crouch and inched toward the stairs, not taking anything for granted. I counted one dead guy and a second corpse on the landing below him, and a third standing in the corner—

Fuck.

CRACKCRACKCRACK!

Three rounds buzzed past my head, the last one nicking my earlobe, missing my neck by gnat's whisker. I slammed against the wall to one side, pistol whipping up, cracked off two rounds one handed. Again, it looks cool in the movies when the hero does that whole one-handed, arm extended shooting thing, but in real life that's liable to get you killed, as you're likely to miss even if you're as highly trained as I am. You just don't have the stability to aim accurately one-handed. I mean, if you're a gunslinger in the Old West and you're drawing and firing in one motion, aiming for center mass, sure, you've got a decent chance of hitting someone, *if* you're ten or fifteen paces away at most. Further than that? Forget it.

So yeah, my stupid ass missed. But my shots got close enough to make the guy duck, which bought me a few more seconds. And in a firefight, seconds are all you get. I used those seconds to slap my left hand up against my right in a nice, clean two-hand grip.

SNAPSNAP—

The suppressed pistol bucked in my hands, time once again slowing down as it does in those situations. I saw the shooter at the bottom of the stairs, tucked into a corner, crouched, both hands on his pistol in a professional grip, barrel aiming at me. I saw his finger squeeze the trigger once, twice, saw the weapon buck. My own was barking just a hair ahead of his, and then I was moving, throwing myself to the opposite wall. Something hot and sharp sliced my left bicep, and then a bee buzzed angrily past my ear, and then my foot was slipping in the gore on the stairs and I was flying, momentarily weightless.

I hit the stairs hard enough to knock the wind out of me, stars dancing behind my eyes, and then I was rolling down them. I reached the landing dizzy and disoriented and gasping, thudding up against a bleeding corpse, with the third shooter still standing, clutching his gut, shakily drawing bead down on me.

I was on my back, and he was behind me, and I couldn't breathe and my head was spinning and throbbing from the topple down the stairs, but I got my piece up and a round squeezed off before rolling twice to one side, away from the dead guy. A bullet hit the concrete of the landing centimeters from my face, spattering me with sharp shards of spraying concrete dust, and then a second one hit an inch from my leg, and I had to roll again, but there was nowhere to go except down the stairs again and the asshole still wasn't dead, despite a bullet in his gut and another in his chest.

"Fucking die, motherfucker!" I growled, and shot him twice more before throwing myself down the next flight of stairs.

I was ready that time, though, going down feet first on my back, my ass and shoulders taking the brunt of the initial impact, and then I twisted to my stomach, sliding down two more steps, my pistol aiming upward.

The soon-to-be-dead asshole staggered into view, torso now dotted with spreading stains. Tough sonofabitch, I'll give him that.

"You first," he ground out in a thick Eastern Bloc accent, arm rising limp, aiming at me.

"Yeah, I don't think so," I said, and ended the discussion via the expedient method of a well-aimed bullet to the brainpan.

Gore painted the wall behind him, his head yanking backward as the round exited the back of his skull.

A sound below me had me rolling to my back and aiming down the stairwell, finger tightening on the trigger. Until I saw that it was Bruce, pepper spray in hand, eyes wide.

I groaned in relief, and lowered my gun. "Ain't you ever been told not to roll up to a gunfight with pepper spray, Bruce?"

He stopped, nearly dropping the can. "What—what in the Sam Hill is going on, Dan?"

I let my head thud against the stair. "Ran into some trouble, my man."

Bruce's gaze went to the red mess on the wall of the landing above me. "Heard shooting, figured I'd best come investigate."

I met his fearful gaze. "You don't want any of this mess, Bruce. Go home. Say you got sick, had to run home before you shit in your boxers. Hell, say you got drunk on lunch break. Just…go home. *Now*. You never saw me, or my girlfriend, okay? We were never here. You've never even met me, matter of fact." I lifted an eyebrow. "It's for your own good, buddy. Now go on, git."

Bruce hesitated, and then his gaze flicked up to the red dripping down the wall. "Yeah. My wife has been sick. Best go home and take care of her."

"You do that, Bruce."

He turned and lumbered back down the stairs and out of view. I heard the door at the bottom of the stairs slam closed, and then I finally relaxed, but only for a moment.

I had to get out of here.

The one thing that was really bugging me, though, was that they'd found me here. Harris didn't even know about this place, and four of Cain's mercs had found me? How? I'm not sloppy. I know I hadn't been followed here, because I'd been watching. So…how in the ever loving *fuck* did they manage to find me? Not luck, that's for damn sure.

I couldn't figure it out, and that was a serious problem.

I scrambled to my feet and jogged up the stairs to Temple.

As soon as I came into view, she rushed over to me. "Duke! There was so much shooting, I was sure you'd—shit, you're bleeding!"

Awareness was returning, now that the high adrenaline of the shootout was receding. I touched my earlobe, and found the lower half of it missing, blood dripping onto my shoulder. "Guess I won't be getting that earring I was thinking about, huh?"

Temple gaped at me. "You're cracking jokes?"

I shrugged. "It's just an earlobe, princess, I barely even feel it." That was a lie—it stung like a motherfucker, but compared to a full-on gunshot wound, it was a minor inconvenience.

I checked the magazine of the suppressed pistol and found it empty. It didn't use the same kind of rounds as any of the firearms I had, and the suppressor wouldn't fit any of them either, since I was carrying all 9mm pistols and this one was a 5.56. Which sucked, but whatever. I stuffed the empty firearm into the duffel bag—since I wasn't the type to leave a perfectly good gun behind, especially if it had my fingerprints on it and had been used to kill more than one someone. Then I threaded my arms through the cloth handles of the duffel bag so I was carrying it backpack style.

I pulled Temple face to face with me. "Got a bit of a mess going on down there, princess, so you may want to close your eyes and let me lead you down, okay?"

"Is this how it's going to be?"

"What do you mean?"

She gestured at the stairwell. "People shooting, you bleeding, dead dudes everywhere…"

I shrugged and nodded at the same time. "Yeah, probably."

She sagged against me, her head buried against my chest. "Yay."

I tipped her chin up. "Come on now, Fancy, where's that sass?"

She jerked her chin away and re-buried her face into my shoulder. "It's gone," she drawled, "I lost it. Bye-bye."

"Listen, kitten, I've kept you safe thus far, yeah?" I nudged her chin up when she didn't reply. "Yeah?"

She nodded. "Yeah, but—"

"Well, I'll continue keeping you safe." I gave her my cockiest grin. "You're with Duke Silver, babe. Ain't no half-ass wanna-be two-bit thugs gonna get anywhere near you, and that's a promise."

What I wasn't saying was that these guys hadn't been half-ass, wanna-be, two-bit thugs. They'd had training, decent training at that, they'd just underestimated me and I'd gotten the drop on them. That last asshole had sent a few rounds my way, which had nearly had my name on them.

Temple frowned at me, but it was an amused frown, which didn't make any sense, but there it was. "You really think highly of yourself, don't you?"

"When you've been through the shit I have, not much will faze you. A few thugs trying to kill me? Meh."

"What would faze you?" she asked.

I thought for a moment. "Me and my unit, back when I was with Delta Force, we were pinned down, surrounded, outnumbered, and running out of ammo. And *then* the fuckers went and tried to crash a goddamn helicopter into the location where we were hunkered down. Well, they didn't *try* to, they *did*. Only the L-T saw it coming, so we had to make a break for it." I hesitated, realizing she probably wouldn't want to hear the rest of that particular story, "That wasn't fun. Or, the time the helo I was in got shot down over enemy territory, and me and four other guys had to fight our way out. That was also severely lacking in chill."

Temple stared at me. "That all really happened to you?"

I shrugged. "Well, yeah. Why?"

"And you survived it all?"

I laughed. "Clearly, since I'm standing here looking all sexy and shit." I tapped her nose. "Babe, I grew up on the streets running in gangs. First time I saw a dude get shot I wasn't even old enough to jerk off. Going into the Army just meant I got three squares a day and got *paid* to do gnarly shit, instead of risking arrest for just trying to scrape by."

Her expression went soft. "You were homeless?"

I felt my walls wanting to slam up, my expression tightening, my natural tendency to tell her to fuck off with her questions and sympathy rising up inside me. "Something like that, yeah." That was as nice an answer to that question as she was gonna get.

I slipped my hand over her eyes. "We gotta go. I hear the fuzz."

It was long past time for the cops to get here, actually. The first shot had been five minutes ago, although it felt more like twenty—the shootout in the stairwell had only taken two or three minutes at most, despite how it had felt.

"Fuzz?"

"Cops," I explained. "And I ain't stickin' around for questions."

I led her down the first flight of stairs, guided her around the first dead guy, lifted her over the second, and skirted close against the wall to avoid the third.

"Something smells funny," she remarked, hands outstretched, as if I'd let her run into a wall or something.

"That's the smell of death, princess. Or, more accurately, the smell of a gut shot."

"Why does a gut shot smell so bad?"

I debated on the best way of putting it. "Um…you open up the belly, what's inside? Guts, right? Perforate those with slugs, well… you're in for a bit of a stench."

She gagged. "Oh. I'm sorry I asked." We made it down another flight, away from the corpses, before I uncovered her eyes. "How many were there?"

"Three," I said. "Well, four, including the guy upstairs."

"Is that all of them, you think?"

"Of this group, probably."

"How many are there, like, total?"

I shrugged. "No clue. Countless, would be my guess. He doesn't pay them all directly, like, on a payroll. They live their lives, run their product, and keep their cut of the profits. Situation like this, they'll get a call from one of Cain's lieutenants giving 'em instructions with a promise of a reward if they catch me. So it's not like he has this army of mercenaries sitting around waiting to his bidding, not like that at all. This is a drugs and guns and prostitution ring, these guys are mostly just your average criminals who happen to work on his behalf." I gestured back up the stairs. "The more of those guys I take out, though, the more pissed Cain is gonna get. Eventually he's gonna send some of his real-deal trained mercenaries, ex-Spetznaz and KSK and whatever. That's when this shit is really gonna get fun."

"We must have drastically different notions of fun, Duke," Temple said. "My idea of fun is spending an afternoon shopping on Rodeo Drive, or having a long brunch with my girlfriends. Running for my life and getting shot at is *not* fun."

I paused at the entrance of the building, peering outside. It looked safe, so I grabbed the door handle, but Temple stopped me.

"Um, are you going out there like that?" she asked.

I stared at her. "Like what?"

She gestured at my shoulder holsters. "The guns? Isn't it…a little obvious? I mean, the police take one look at you, think, huh, we just got a call about a shooting, and that guy is wearing guns right out in the open, so—"

"Okay, okay, I get your point," I cut in. "Hold on a second."

I jogged back up the stairs to where the three corpses were; the first guy I'd shot had been a single round to the forehead, and he'd been wearing a windbreaker, which hopefully wasn't too messy. I found the guy in question, head hanging backward off of a stair tread, dripping nasty on the step below. And bingo, his windbreaker was brain-matter free, thank god. I stripped him of it, slid the duffel off my shoulders, and shrugged into the jacket—the dead guy was a bit smaller than me, so it was a tight fit but it disguised the holsters. I snagged the duffel and hustled back downstairs.

Temple stared at me as I led her outside. "Is that…from one of the guys you killed?" she asked as I led her out of the building and away from it as fast as possible without looking obvious.

I nodded. "Yeah. Most expedient way of solving the problem, as I don't keep clothes at this place either, and we don't have the time for me to go back up even if I did." I gestured at the crowed around us, people milling, chatting, checking cell phones to see if there was news on what was going on. The first cruisers were just starting to arrive and were setting up a cordon, but hadn't started blocking access yet. Cops scrambled out of the cars, weapons drawn, chins dipped to report into radio mics

"What do you do at a long brunch?" I asked, trying to sound casual as we pushed through the crowd of onlookers. .

"Um, well? We drink a lot of mimosas and eat finger food and talk about boys and gossip, basically. Girl stuff." She was keeping up the charade like a champ, bless the girl.

I laughed. "Oh. And a long brunch is what? An hour?"

Her turn to laugh. "An hour? Hardly. If you're not still there at, like, three or four, you're an amateur. We brunch until dinner on a regular."

I goggled at her. "And you literally just sit around and get wasted and gossip? Like, all day?"

We were away from the bulk of the crowd by now, and had reached an intersection; I turned at random, my main priority now being to just get us away from the scene, ASAP.

She shrugged, sticking close to my side as we rounded the corner. "That's the point of brunching. It's a social activity." She glanced up at me. "Don't you and your buddies go out drinking?"

I nodded. "Well, yeah."

"Same thing. We just start out late morning and go all day."

"Damn, that's actually kinda hardcore," I said. "And you're drinking the whole time?"

She bobbed her head side to side. "Sort of? We start out with mimosas or screw drivers usually, and then once we've had lunch we switch to white wine. So, I mean, it's not like we're drinking to get black-out drunk. You're brunching all day, so you have to pace yourself. You can't be falling down drunk by like two or we won't invite you back. You have to be able to keep up and hold your liquor."

"Sounds competitive." I was keeping her busy so she wouldn't notice me scanning our surroundings.

"Oh it is. Getting invited to one of my brunches is a big deal. It can make or break your social standing. And if you get drunk and we have to ask you to leave because you're embarrassing us? Forget it. You're done. You can kiss your reputation goodbye."

"Has that ever happened?"

She nodded. "Oh, yeah, all the time. It's like the first couple episodes of *The Bachelor*, there's always someone who gets obliterated and makes a fool of themselves."

"*The Bachelor*?"

She rolled her eyes. "You've never seen that?"

I frowned at her. "Do I seem like a guy who watches *The Bachelor*?"

"I guess not. What do you watch?"

"I don't watch TV," I said. "Never got into the habit."

"What do you mean, you never got into the habit? It's television."

We'd been walking in a straight line for too long, so we turned the corner. I wasn't going anywhere specifically yet, more just trying to see if anyone was following us. Once I'd determined that we weren't being tailed, I'd catch a cab to the airport and try to figure out some way of hooking up with the guys. Times like this, I wished payphones hadn't gone extinct—it'd make it easier.

"Like I said, I grew up on the streets. Not much opportunity to sit around staring at a TV screen. Gotta run the hustle, you know?"

"Not really, no."

I let out a soft, irritated breath. I hadn't meant to let the conversation go back to this topic. "I crashed on a lot of couches when I could, and slept in alleys when I couldn't. And during the day I was hustling."

"What does that mean?"

"Dealing, Princess. Slinging dime-bags. Scrapping with rival gangs. That kinda shit."

"Oh." Her voice was…small, and tight. Disapproving. Which only pissed me off more, and I was already antsy from talking about this in the first place.

"Listen up, Fancy. Not everyone was born with a silver spoon, okay?" I stopped and faced her. "I didn't have a famous mom and dad to put everything in my hands. I never knew my dad, and my mom was literally a crack-whore. Meaning I was born addicted to crack and shouldn't have survived, but I did. You know who didn't survive? My mom. I found her OD'd when I was six. Came home from school one day and there she was, passed out on the couch like usual. Only, she wasn't just passed out, she was fuckin' dead. That's how *my* life started. So yeah, I was a drug dealer by the time I was ten, pimping by fourteen, and pushing kilos by the time I was seventeen. A *criminal*. I was dirty, and violent, and mean. I was a piece of shit, is what I was. Is that what you wanted to hear, Fancy?"

I was in her face, fuming, teeth gritted. And she was cowering away, frightened.

"No," she whispered. "I didn't—I mean…I didn't mean—"

I pivoted away, scrubbing the side of my jaw. "I know you didn't."

I grabbed her arm and hauled her back into a fast walk. And she let me, for all of a hundred steps, and then she yanked her arm free, and then it was her turn to stop facing me.

"You what? Fuck you." She stabbed her finger into my chest. "I didn't ask to be born to rich parents. I didn't ask for the life I have. It's all I know—all I've *ever* known. And what, I'm supposed to apologize for my easy life because yours has been shitty? *Fuck* you."

"No, you don't choose the life you're born into, and no, you don't have to apologize for yours. But you don't get to give me that look, the one that's all pitying and *disapproving* because I spent the first half of my life surviving the only way I knew how."

"It wasn't pity!" Temple shot back. "Or disapproval."

"The fuck it wasn't. I know what that shit looks and sounds like, okay? Someone finds out how I grew up, they give me that same look."

"Compassion and pity aren't the same thing, Duke," Temple said.

"Yeah, well…I don't need either." I pushed past her, stomping back into an angry walk. "Not from you, not from anyone."

Stupid shit was, I didn't even really know why I was so pissed. I hated talking about my life pre-Army, hated telling anyone about it because I always got the same sappy bullshit pity. But this, the blind, unreasoning anger I was feeling, it was more than that—I just wasn't sure what it was. I didn't like it, though. I didn't like emotions I didn't understand, which is why I avoided situations that might involve emotions, because I didn't understand most emotions.

Emotions were hard. Fucking, fighting, drinking, breaking down doors and clearing rooms and rescuing people, I understood that. It was easy.

This…wasn't. Temple wasn't easy, and I didn't mean easy as in loose, easy to get into bed, but rather…she was just…difficult. She was hard to understand, and worse, she made me feel like shit and I wasn't sure how or why she did it, but she did and it pissed me off.

But even all that wasn't why I was so pissed off.

I kept walking, stopping to glance back at Temple now and again, making sure she was still behind me. She was staying a few paces, power walking to keep up with my long legs, and looking equal parts pissed off, confused, and hurt.

Which didn't help.

I was trying to push all this emotional horseshit away so I could focus on the real problem at hand: getting away from Cain's dickheads, and getting in touch with Harris and Thresh and the boys. I'd been out of communication for a while, which was unusual for me, especially when it came to Thresh. He and I were always in contact, so I knew if he didn't hear from me soon, he'd start to worry.

Then, being mentally preoccupied, I nearly got us both killed.

A big black Tahoe zipped past us, which wasn't a big deal; they were a common kind of truck. When the SUV hit the brakes and swung a smoking-tire U-turn, that was a big deal. Problem came when I was too caught up in my own mental bullshit to register that maybe they were making a U-turn because of me. I missed that little signal.

The Tahoe burned rubber, bolted back the way they'd come, and then cut in toward the sidewalk.

Toward Temple.

And that was when my head cleared enough for me to jump into action.

"Temple! Duck!" I shouted.

I hauled at the Beretta, palm slapping over my trigger hand to brace myself. I cracked off two shots, one round fragmenting the rear driver's side window and the other plugging into the door beneath it. The truck kept going, hitting the brakes and sliding to a halt a dozen feet away from Temple, who had, as I'd instructed, hit the sidewalk and was hunkering with her hands over her head. I probably should have told her to run, but I'd been more worried about accidentally shooting her if she moved the wrong direction.

And now the driver's door was opening, as were the doors on the passenger side. The rear driver's side door stayed closed, which meant I'd probably taken out at least one. Still, I had a feeling I was about to be outnumbered and outgunned, and Temple was in the middle, a good fifteen feet away.

I popped off a shot at the body emerging from the driver's door; I hit him I wasn't sure where, but I knew I'd hit him because blood spattered and his feet slipped and he slumped to the ground. Not dead, but out of the fight. I was running, obviously, and ten feet hadn't ever felt so far. It felt like I was running in place, not quite able to cross the distance between me and Temple, not quite able to put myself between her and the bad guys.

Fuck, fuck, fuck.

I let my pistol do the talking, cracking off another two shots at the partially broken rear window, shattering it completely and breaking the window on the other side, making way for the second round, which—through sheer luck, found a target. The dumbass was just standing there, as if the window was going to stop a bullet. My round caught him in the shoulder, sent him spinning and clutching the wound, and I sent another bullet his way, which hit him in the face and dropped him. Two down.

I reached Temple, crouched in front of her, waiting. "Stay down," I hissed, and she nodded under her hands.

"How do they keep finding us?" she asked, her voice muffled and shrill with hysteria.

"Fuck if I know. These guys probably knew we were on foot somewhere near the apartment and just went in widening circles until they found us." I hoped that was the case, because this was becoming intensely distressing, the way they kept showing up. It was twice now. Twice could be luck, or coincidence…but my gut instinct was suggesting otherwise.

I saw a pair of feet underneath the overhanging back end of the SUV, wearing black sneakers, creeping toward us, crouched to take advantage of the body of the truck. I heard voices muttering low, heard the *snick-click* of slides being pulled and released. At least two more, maybe three or four. I glanced around quickly, hoping to find somewhere for Temple to take better cover, but there wasn't much except doorways. Which, I supposed, were better than being in the open.

I tapped Temple on the shoulder. "You're gonna run for cover," I said, pointing at the doorway of an office building twenty feet behind us; at the first bark of gunfire, the few people there'd been on this side street had vanished, but it wouldn't be long before black-and-whites started showing up here, too—time was at a premium once again. "When I say three, you're gonna run fast as you can for that doorway and you're gonna hunker there till I finish this shit off. Ready?"

Temple's gaze went to the dead body half in and half out the driver's door, the shattered rear window, the blood splattered on the black leather interior, and then she glanced back at me and nodded.

"Ready," she said.

I cut a look at her feet. "Shoes?" I said, ejecting the partially used magazine.

She wiggled her toes in her wedge heels, and then slipped them off and held one in each hand. "Okay, I'm ready for real this time."

I slid a fresh magazine into the Beretta and pulled the slide. "One…two…" I fired two rounds at the rear of the vehicle, and then shouted "THREE!"

Temple took off running, and I was impressed. She was faster than I thought she'd be—the doorway was twenty some feet away, and she was halfway there before I'd finished the shout. I brought the Beretta to bear on the front of the SUV as I moved to put my shoulder against the wall, caught a bit of black hair and the top of an ear. Sent two rounds at the head, aiming a little high for the first one and lower for the second. Red sprayed, and I bolted forward to lean against the hood of the Tahoe, paused, and then rolled out to the other side. Two bodies. Made that four down, and at least one more to go.

I straightened into a Weaver stance. "Hey, asshole. Over here."

Stupid bag of dicks fell for it, too. He popped from behind the Tahoe, but at least he came out firing. He missed, but points for the effort. Four banging concussions, yet none of his shots came close enough for me to even notice, and then my pistol bucked in my hands and he fell backward. No tricks or waiting, this time. I swung sideways all the way around the back of the SUV, and then peeked in the back window.

That was all of them, then. I jerked open the rear driver's side door and let the dead body fall to the ground; thank god I'd popped this asshole first, since he'd been packing an AR-15. The trunk of the Tahoe was filled with firepower—two more AR-15s, two small rectangular cases which I assumed contained more handguns, several boxes of assorted bullets, a Mossberg 500…these boys had been packing the right firepower to take me on, they'd just made the stupid mistake of not using it the second they saw me.

I yanked the corpse out of the driver's door and kicked him aside, noted with relief that most of the mess from my round hitting him had been contained to the side of the driver's seat and the metal of the A-pillar between front seat and rear. Meaning, the seat wasn't all nasty. I tossed the duffel bag behind the driver's seat, kicked the back door shut, then hopped behind the wheel, keyed the ignition, and hauled the driver's door closed.

I pulled even with Temple and grinned at her from behind the wheel. "Good news is, we got us a ride."

"But there's—there was—"

"Yeah, well beggars can't be choosers. No mess on your seat, so just don't look back if it bugs you." I reached across and shoved open the passenger door. "Now let's go, sweetcheeks!" I heard sirens close.

She hopped in, and looked back. "Oh my god. There's blood everywhere! And the windows are gone!"

"I told you not to look. At least the dead guys aren't in here with us, right?"

She shuddered. "Yeah, I guess that's a bonus."

I gunned the gas pedal and we took off. "Need you do to me a favor."

She eyed me warily. "I'm not giving you road-head."

I snickered. "Well damn, how'd you know what I was gonna say?"

She rolled her eyes. "You're a typical guy, so all you think about is getting your dick sucked."

I shrugged and pulled a *well yeah* face. "I mean, it is pretty much the best thing ever." I jerked my thumb at the rear of the truck. "But actually I was gonna ask you to climb back there and grab the shotgun for me."

She glanced back. "Shotgun?"

"In the trunk. Big fuck-off black thing, like an assault rifle only bigger. It's got red shells stuffed into these little loops on the side."

Temple sighed and climbed over the console into the backseat. Which...unfortunately, *was* a little messy. "OH MY GOD that's so *gross!*" She toppled sideways into the footwell. "I've got blood all over my hands and skirt."

"Um. Ooops? Forgot about that, sorry."

She popped up between the seats. "You *forgot* about a giant pool of blood?"

I glanced back. "That's not a giant pool. That's a bit of splatter. If I'd nailed him in the head, there'd be a lot more of a mess. That's nothing to worry about. It'll wash right off your hands."

"And my skirt?"

I growled. "Once I sort this bullshit out and get you safely back to Malibu, I'll personally take you shopping to buy you a new fucking skirt." I eyed her. "Now please…get me the shotgun."

Temple groaned in disgust, but climbed gingerly onto the seat and leaned over the back, reappearing with an AR-15 in her hands. "This?"

"No, honey, that's an assault rifle."

"So that's not it?"

"Nope. Try again. Big. Black. Red shells on one side."

"This is big and black." At my sigh of irritation. "Hey, what do I know about guns?"

She leaned over the seatback once more, the wind whipping through the broken rear windows, ruffling her hair and skirt. I was watching the through the rearview mirror because, come on, the view was to die for. That tight round ass of hers was all framed and spread out, bulging against the fabric of the skirt, which was inching up bit by bit as the wind blew it around. She leaned further over the seat, reaching, tiptoes pressing against the floor, and then…oh hell yes—the wind tossed her skirt up completely as she stretched to reach the shotgun, showing me that bare, delectable, perfect ass for a brief but beautiful moment.

She squealed as the wind blew her skirt up, tugging it back down and twisting to sit on the bench. She shoved the shotgun through the opening. "Here's the stupid gun." She stuck her tongue out at me. "Enjoy your free peep show?"

I took the shotgun from her and stuffed the barrel down near my left foot, leaning the stock against the side of my seat. "Hell yeah,

I did." I grinned at her as she climbed back over the console into the passenger seat. "I told you already, Fancy, you've got the most gorgeous ass I've ever seen. I could stare at it all damn day and never get tired of looking at it."

She rolled her eyes at me, but couldn't quite hide her flattered, pleased smile. Then she glanced at her hands, and lost the grin. "So gross, for real." She wiped her hands on the front of her skirt, which helped only marginally.

"Your hands are just gonna be sticky for a bit, I'm afraid to say," I told her. "Blood can be hard to get off your hands."

She didn't answer right away, staring at the tacky redness on her palms. "Do you mean that literally, or metaphorically?" She asked, after a while.

I sighed. "Wow, going right for the hard shit, huh?" On a whim, I dug into the console storage compartment between our seats, and found a bottle of hand sanitizer. "Here, squirt that on, rub your hands together, and then wipe them on your skirt, should get some of the blood off."

I watched her squirt a ridiculous amount of sanitizer onto her hands, and then returned my attention to the road.

"Well," I said, "I guess I mean it both ways. Or maybe I mean it literally because I know it to be true metaphorically, as well." I thought for a moment. "Literally speaking, blood is an incredibly damn hard substance to deal with. It stains, it hardens, goes all tacky. Get it in your hair? Forget about it. You'll be shampooing that shit for twenty minutes. Metaphorically speaking, the first few kills tend to stick with you. You never forget those. Then, after awhile, you just… learn to deal with it. You don't think about it, because if you do you won't be able to do your job. But sometimes when my insomnia gets bad, yeah, the metaphorical blood on my hands can be pretty fucking hard to wash off. "

She was obsessively squirting sanitizer onto her hands and rubbing it off, even though her hands were mostly clean by that point. Eventually, she tossed the now half-empty bottle into the little cubby beneath the infotainment center.

Her eyes went to mine, blue streaked with green and brown, her expression unreadable. "Do you…do you enjoy it? Killing people?"

I narrowed my eyes at her sidelong. "That's a shitty question to ask, Temple."

"It's an honest question. I want to know what kind of person I'm with." She stared unblinking at me, until I looked away first.

I spent a good long time thinking as I drove us out of Denver, keeping an eye on the road behind us. "Do I enjoy it? No. I'm not a serial killer or a sociopath. I don't do this job because I get some sick pleasure watching motherfuckers bleed out, okay? I do it because I'm damn good at it. I'd never shoot an innocent person on purpose, and I do my fucking damnedest to keep collateral damage as minimal as I can." I fiddled with the A/C settings just to have something to do with my hand. "I'm good at what I do. I was a good soldier, a better special forces operative, and I'm one of the best goddamn security contractors in the game. I've got zero problem dropping some asshole who's shooting at me, and even less problem taking out someone who's done violence to someone innocent. But I don't do it because I enjoy killing. Does that answer your question?"

"I suppose." She picked at her fingers, scraping underneath one fingernail with her thumbnail. "Have you ever killed an innocent person?"

I eyed her. "Well, good goddamn, woman. Any other deep dark secrets you plan on ripping out of me?" I gripped the steering wheel with my right hand and used my left thumb to flip the safety button on the top of the shotgun from safe to fire and back again. "Yes. That's the short answer."

She waited a moment before following up with the next question, which I was expecting, but was hoping she might not ask. "And the long version?"

"Why do you want to hear this shit?"

"I told you, I'm trying to figure you out."

"You do realize this is the kind of thing you're not really supposed to just come right out and ask a guy?"

Temple just shrugged. "I've never played by anyone's rules but my own."

"Fair enough. But if I answer your questions, you have to answer mine." She nodded, and I took a minute to put together my thoughts. "You have to understand the scenario. We were in Africa, the Congo. Part of that nasty business that's been going on there for so fucking long. Can't really say much, except that my unit was part of a larger offensive. It was urban warfare, in an occupied city. Innocent people everywhere, and damn near impossible to tell who was the enemy until they shot at you. Absolute fucking hell is what it was. Our orders were to push the bad guys out of that city entirely, which was like playing whack-a-mole at best, suicide at worst. Well, I was around the corner of a building with the other guys from my unit. We'd been chasing this group for several blocks in this back and forth sort of battle. They had us pinned down, and the L-T had tapped me to roll out and try to draw their fire while laying down some suppression." I focused on just retelling the story without thinking about it too much. "So, I rolled out. Put down suppressing fire, drew theirs. It was all well and good until I saw this body peek out from behind the side of a building. I shot half a dozen rounds at him and it turned out to be this…it was a woman. Hiding, just trying to figure out how to get to safety. Hers is blood on my hands that'll never wash off."

She reached out and slipped her hand under mine, palm to palm, and gave my hand a squeeze. "I'm sorry."

"Yeah, well, now you know." I glanced at her. "My turn."

She sighed. "Let me guess…you want to know about my rules."

"You've mentioned them a few times. So, yeah, I'm curious."

6

RAPUNZEL

I WASN'T EVEN SURE WHERE TO START, HONESTLY. MY RULES WERE complicated, and had arisen from more than one situation. I'd never explained them to anyone. Which was weird, considering how many girlfriends I had, and how often we talked about boys. But then…none of those girlfriends were really…*friends*. Not close friends, not the kind I'd unburden this kind of thing to. This was deep, and hard to talk about, and real. Which begged the question… why was I telling Duke? If I didn't trust my inner circle of friends with this, then why was I trusting Duke with it?

Because even those dozen girls that formed my inner circle…I still didn't totally trust them. They were wealthy, beyond wealthy, like me, but…they weren't on my level socially. They didn't have famous parents. My mom had been, and still was, one of the most famous actresses in the world, and my dad was a rock god, on the scale of Stephen Tyler and Mick Jagger. Some of the girls actually came from more money than me, so it wasn't about money. It was about status. It was about the red carpet that got rolled out whenever the Kennedy name was mentioned, the constant press around my parents' every move, and then add to that the fame I'd earned on my own with *Temple*, my reality show…everyone wanted to be close to me. I didn't trust anyone to care about me for *me*. No one. I'd learned this hard way. I'd had too many so called "friends" sell stories about me, tip off my whereabouts to paparazzi so they'd be photographed with me, or invite themselves on vacations, or try to finagle their way into my house when they knew the cameras were running.

Duke? He didn't give a shit about any of that. If anything, he was derisive of it.

I trusted Duke, literally with my life at this point, and I just didn't see him being capable of trying to cash in on knowing me, or having fucked me.

"Fancy?" Duke asked. "You in there?"

"Yeah, sorry. Just...thinking." We were on the freeway at this point, cruising at a steady seventy-five.

"About?"

"How weird it is that I'm talking to you like this."

"Why's it weird?" He asked, his thumb still constantly flipping that button back and forth on the scary-big shotgun.

"Because I don't talk about myself with my girlfriends." I twisted a lock of hair between my fingers. "I talk about boys, or gossip about who's fucking who, or fashion, or pretty much anything else. But...I never talk about this shit with my girlfriends."

"Why not?"

"Well, that's what I was just trying to figure out."

"And?" He prompted.

"You don't seem impressed by who my parents are, or how much I'm worth, and you don't seem too keen on getting your fifteen minutes of fame out of me. If you're gonna use me for anything, it's gonna be my body, and—I'm more okay with that than I am with you trying to use me to get fame or favors or money." I paused, but then kept going to keep him from saying anything. "I guess it's just weird, because I've known a lot of the girls in my inner circle of friends for eight or ten years. I've known most them since we were little. Our parents are friends, and a lot of us have traded boyfriends back and forth. But...we're not the kind of friends that confide in each other, because none of us trust each other. Especially me. I don't really, truly trust any of them."

He frowned, and scrubbed the scruff on his jaw. "Doesn't seem like much of a friendship, if that's the case."

"It's how things are, the way I grew up. Famous parents and more money than god? Everyone wants a piece. I've been sold out and betrayed more times than I can count, so my cynicism is well-earned, I'd have to say." I sighed. "But you're different. And again, it's weird because I barely know you. It's been what, a few hours? But I'm literally trusting you with my life, so it doesn't seem like that much of a stretch to trust you with some dirty history."

Duke didn't answer right away. I'd noticed that about him—if the answer was especially important he thought about his response before he spoke; it was a rare and unexpected quality. "I've got no use for your money, and even less for your fame. Shit, I don't even like being photographed for passport pictures, much less want to be have some picture of me out there in magazines with a bunch of bullshit speculation about my life or whatever the fuck." He glanced at me. "Plus, I take trust *very* seriously, Temple. If I say you can trust me, you're getting the full force of everything I am as a man behind my word. I don't say that to many people. I mean, professionally, my word is my bond—if I say I'll get your kid back, or shut down a blackmail attempt, then it's as good as done. But personally, I trust about as easily as you do. Which is to say not at all."

I realized we'd been holding hands for several minutes now, and for some reason that made my heart beat harder. I swallowed and stared at our joined hands, mine underneath his big paw, his fingers curled down to enclose my smaller hand. It felt…natural—not at all weird.

And that was weird.

"So," Duke prompted. "Your rules."

"When I was nineteen, I met a guy named Lane."

"Sounds like a pretentious goof-tard."

I laughed. "Yeah, he kind of was," I admitted. "But he was…

good-looking, in a pretentious, Beverly Hills goof-tard sort of way. And he came from serious, serious money. Like, Bill Gates, Koch Brothers, Warren Buffet sort of money."

"I know a guy like that," Duke said. "He's actually a really good dude."

"There aren't that many people out there with that much money," I said. "Who is it? Maybe I know him."

"Valentine Roth."

I gaped. "You know Valentine Roth? He's, like, one of the most mysterious people in the world. He lives this wild, mysterious, Phantom of the Opera sort of life. Everyone I know was always going to Manhattan hoping to be seen with him. He's a seriously big deal." I grabbed Duke's arm. "What's he like?"

Duke shrugged. "He's a good dude. Rich as all fuck, but cool. Not stuck up. Just…he's cool. I don't know him very well personally, but my boss, Harris, he worked for Roth for years and Harris's girlfriend is best friends with Valentine's wife. We get invited out to the Roth's private island down in the Caribbean for Christmas parties every year. Those parties, man…they're nuts."

Temple made a disgusted noise. "I can't believe you know Valentine freaking Roth. Until he up and left Manhattan with that girl he obviously ended up marrying, he was the most eligible bachelor like, anywhere. I know some girls who managed to score a hook-up with him a long time ago, but they said he was…difficult. Not very nice, but hot and rough and *amazing* in bed."

Duke shook his head at me. "Well I don't know about any of that shit, but I can see it being true. Miss Roth…Kyrie, she sort of turned him around. Gave him something in life worth being nice about." He laughed. "Aside from billions of dollars, I guess."

I tipped my head to one side. "Well, I can say from experience that money really doesn't always make people nice, or happy. I mean, having money is awesome, and I don't mind admitting my worst fear—until all this happened, at least—is being poor. But money doesn't make you happy. If that was true, I should be happier than I am."

Duke's gaze shot to mine, and I regretted that last admission. "You're not happy?"

"That's not necessarily what I meant."

"Sounded like the truth, especially now that you're trying to walk it back."

I slid down in the seat, put my feet up on the dash, and stretched my skirt over my knees. "I'm not trying to walk it back, I'm just—" I groaned in irritation, and started over. "Look, I'm stupidly lucky, and I know it. I'm spoiled rotten. I've never had to do a day's work in my life, and I could have gone on that way forever. I didn't want to, though, I wanted something of my own. I'm not an actress like Mom, or a musician like Dad, so I had to use what I have, which was instant recognition. Everyone knows the Kennedys. Mom and Dad have been married for twenty years and together for twenty-five, which is absolutely unheard of for people in their stratosphere. We're just... well, we're the Kennedys. And as their oldest and their only daughter, I've always been...sort of...just famous for being me, I guess. So I capitalized on that. I pitched the idea of a show to my agent, and he went bananas, because it meant a shitload of money for him, of course. So, I made my own fortune on the show. Then I started a bunch of product lines, clothes, makeup, perfume, branded accessories, jewelry, girly things like that.

"I'm not famous for nothing, though, and it bugs the shit out of me when people say that. I work my ass off. I design all the products myself, and I find distributors and do commercials. I'm a multi-million dollar company all by myself, and it's a full-time job running it all, which is something I do myself. That's not to mention the need for a constant social media presence, the sponsored posts and whatever? It's a lot. It takes a shitload of work maintaining a constant level of presence in our society, which, can I just say, is crazy hard because as a society we're pretty much Captain Distracto. We're always looking for the next new thing, the next new fad, the next new Instagram or YouTube celebrity, so remaining relevant is damn hard."

Duke glanced at me, looking amused. "You're avoiding my question, Fancy. Don't think I didn't notice."

I huffed. "I am not. I'm setting it up." I glared at him. "Plus, you distracted me."

"You mentioned some asshat named Lane?"

I lean my head back against the seat and sighed. "Yeah. When I was nineteen, I met an asshat named Lane. Only, I was young and naive and thinking with my hoo-ha, so I didn't realize he was an asshat. He was hot, and he came from money. I thought that was a good thing, because I'd hoped it would mean he wouldn't be interested in me for my parents' money seeing as his were worth billions to my parents' hundred and twenty mil or whatever it is."

I thought back, warily letting my mind delve into the memories, and even more warily letting my frozen, walled-up heart feel some of the old pain. "He was hot, he was filthy rich, he was just…cool. He had a business degree from Stanford, and he was on track to inherit not just his father's fortune, but also the reins of the company. He wasn't just some lazy playboy, he was making tracks as a businessman in his own right, and he was only twenty…twenty-one, I think? Maybe twenty-two. It seemed like love. He wasn't my first, but he was my first real boyfriend. I'd had enough friends lose their V-cards before me to know the first time wouldn't be amazing, so I gave mine the year before, to a sexy asshole nobody at a party when I was half-drunk. It was…okay. A little ouchy, at first, but the asshole—James, I think his name was—he knew what he was doing. I don't think I was his first virgin which, looking back, makes him even more of a dick, but whatever. It worked for me. Lost my virginity to some jackass I'd never see again and didn't really care about. I cried a little the next day, felt a little buyer's remorse or whatever you want to call it, but I don't regret it now.

"I could claim honestly I wasn't a virgin, but I was inexperienced enough that Lane could teach me. He liked that, I think. That I wasn't a virgin, that he didn't have to worry about that, but that I was so inexperienced he could show me how he liked things."

"He sounds like a real winner," Duke put in.

I shook my head. "Oh, just wait. It gets better." I let out another breath, and kept going. "So things were fairly normal for the first year. We dated, we had a lot of sex, whatever. He'd take me to his family's estates in Italy and Greece, we'd go to A-list parties in Manhattan or LA, it was classic rich assholes of Instagram bullshit. Lavish parties on mega-yachts, rolling up the PCH in his drop-top Rolls Royce—which, by the way, had crushed-diamond white paint, like several million dollars worth of actual diamonds crushed and mixed into the paint job. We'd fly to Antigua in his G6 on a whim."

"Seems like you guys had it made."

I nodded. "Everyone thought we did. Hell, *I* thought we did. The tabloids followed us everywhere, called us the *it*-couple of the decade. That was when I really started to get media and social media attention on my own right, and not just for being my parents' oldest kid. It seemed like everything was gorgeous and perfect. I was in love, and he loved me. We talked about it, said it to each other, and he'd even dropped hints about a wedding."

"Hmmm, I wonder what could have possibly gone wrong?" Duke deadpanned.

"If you're assuming he cheated on me, that'd be a smart assumption, but wrong." Now came the hard part. "The first sign I should have broken up with him was when a sex tape of us got leaked."

Duke glanced at me. "The motherfucker leaked a sex tape?" He sounded...*pissed*. "And you *stayed* with him?"

I shrugged. "It wasn't immediately obvious it was him that leaked it. We'd taken the video with my phone, so the initial assumption was that I'd been hacked. I was devastated, of course. I mean, that was *private*, right? I was livid, and mortified. My parents' press team did spin and damage control, and I mean, it's not like I'm the first celeb to have a tape leaked, but it still messed me up. And Lane played the understanding, supportive boyfriend to a T, in private and to the press. And that was kind of the second thing that should have been a warning sign. You have to understand that Lane's dad isn't high profile. Most people haven't even heard of him, honestly, even though he's one of the richest people in the country. And Lane, he was even less high profile. He was a young businessman, working his ass off to take over his dad's company the hard way, earning it rather than just inheriting it. But he wasn't famous. Unless you were part of the elite business world, you wouldn't have heard of Lane Behr.

"So when the tape got leaked, I went into hiding. Natural enough, right? I didn't have the show yet, didn't have the brand to worry about, so I just kind of went into seclusion. Stopped going out, declined party invitations, refused to go on vacations, wouldn't even leave my room for the most part., stayed off social media. Lane sort of took over for my parents, in terms of dealing with the press on my behalf. He'd spin things into positive stories, talk about how I was rebuilding myself, and reassessing my future in light of the leak, bullshit like that. He was good at it. I appreciated it, my parents appreciated it—"

"And Lane appreciated it, because it was the spark that set his star to rising?" Duke ventured.

I nodded. "Exactly. The media realized Lane was magnetic and photogenic and charming, and that he was this up-and-coming young businessman from an elite family—everything the press loves to shove down our throats. He played it cool, though. Didn't immediately start grabbing all the attention he could. No, Lane is way more devious than that, thinks more long-term than that. He set himself up as my spokesperson, sort of, coaxed me into posting selfies now and then with pithy captions that made it seem like everything was great."

I paused for a moment, wishing I could skip this part. "He was the reason I decided to pitch the show. It was his idea. I had to use the attention caused by the tape to my benefit. Turn it into something good for myself. People loved the little hints they'd been getting of my life—me and Lane at home, Lane with my parents on the deck at sunset, opening a bottle of wine, all that stuff. He was so fucking good at it. These cute, intriguing hints at our beautiful, perfect life. It was a great contrast to what we'd been posting before that, the extravagance, the lavishness, the drama and excitement. These were just little hints, and people wanted more. So he convinced me to put the embarrassment of the tape behind me, to embrace the attention. 'Kim had a tape, and look how successful she is,' right? So I pitched the show.

"We got it approved, the crews showed up and started filming, and then the first episode aired, and…Lane was a star. He was funny, he was in every scene, he was hot and rich and just…perfect, and everyone loved him. That whole first season was all about Lane. It solidified his status as a celebrity. Lane was the star of *Temple* even though it was my name on the title card, even though it was supposed to be about me."

I paused again. "He accused me of cheating on him at the end of the third season," I had to stop again, because this was where things got really gnarly. "He'd gone behind my back and convinced the editors to cut footage so it looked like I'd cheated on him. My best friend Holly's boyfriend had appeared on a few episodes, and they'd been fighting, and I'd had this whispered argument with Paris, Holly's boyfriend, and Lane had them edit it so it seemed like I'd been hooking up with Paris behind Lane and Holly's backs. My bikini top was pretty skimpy so it looked like I might have been topless, and with some creative editing, it looked like Paris and I had a thing. I'd actually been telling Paris what a jackass he was for hurting Holly—I'd been sticking up for my friend, and Lane turned it into this cheating scandal. All it took was some footage and some rumors."

I scratched a patch of drying blood on my skirt. "He managed to make sure Holly saw the edited footage first, so Holly bought it, and she and I had this massive blow-out fight, and Lane was acting all hurt, giving these clips acting all heartbroken, how he loved me and didn't understand how I could do this to him…blah-blah-blah. I didn't realize what he'd done at first, and then one of the producers had a conversation with one of the editors, and got the story of what

Lane had done, how he'd gotten the footage edited and then leaked it to Holly and the tabloids and everywhere, and the producer told me." I blinked again, but I wasn't crying. Nope. "Holly was my best friend. We'd been friends since we were ten. And she believed *him*. She believed the footage. Paris told her nothing had happened, I told her nothing had happened, we all tried to tell her there was zero evidence of anything happening between Paris and I except that one piece of footage even the network admitted had been doctored. She didn't care. I lost my best friend, and the whole thing happened on camera. The network ate it up, the tabloids loved it, the bloggers loved it. And Lane loved it, because it put him in the spotlight more than ever. When he started doing magazine and blog interviews and going on *Watch What Happens Live* talking about us and the scandal…that was when I realized what he was doing, really realized it."

Another deep breath. "So then I hired my own investigators, and they came back with definitive evidence that Lane had sent the sex tape from my phone to his, and then had someone else anonymously leak it to 4Chan, where it went viral…" my voice quavered. "The evidence my team brought me was incontrovertible. So I confronted him in private. He got all pissed and tried to pivot back to the cheating thing…it got ugly. We both screamed a lot, and eventually my dad made Lane leave. The cameras were taping the next day, so they caught the really juicy fall-out, when I confronted him about it again, and told him about having the footage doctored to fake the cheating scandal…it nearly turned into a fistfight. It turns out Lane had been manipulating all of us, and we realized it all at once, on camera."

"Jesus, what a mess." Duke's hand laced into mine.

Solid, comforting presence, his hand warm, his body huge next to mine.

"Yeah, it was a complete disaster." I blinked again, harder this time. "There aren't words for how ugly it got. He…he flat-out told me, *on camera*, that he'd never loved me. That I'd only ever been a cash cow for him, a chance to get famous and even richer than he already was." I made my voice as gruff as I could, which didn't sound like Lane at all, but got across the point that I was quoting him. "'You're hot, but you're a typical dumb blonde. And the really sad part is, you're a lousy fuck.'" I felt a tear trickle down my cheek, and ignored it. "He went on a tirade. Told me I was stupid, told me the only reason he ever even considered fucking me in the first place was because I was kinda famous, and he saw a chance to make something off me. Said I had tight pussy, but that I was a dead fish, and gave shitty BJs. On camera, he said all this. Said the sex tape was the only halfway decent sex we'd ever had."

"Jesus," Duke said. "What a bastard."

"Yeah," I agreed, "he was a bastard, all right."

We drove in silence for a minute or two, and then Duke pulled off the freeway and into one of those gas stations right near the entrance and exit ramps, told me to stay put, and ran inside. He was only gone a minute or two, and then returned with a bag of snack food and a few bottles of water and a pay-as-you go cell phone. After filling up the gas tank, we got back on the freeway.

Once we were underway, Duke's gaze went to mine. "So, what I don't understand is how does everything between you and Lane, as crazy and fucked up and painful as it sounds, explain your rules about sex?"

I laughed. "Of course you bring it back to sex." I'd laughed, but not with amusement. Was that really all he cared about?

Duke took my hand, squeezed it, and made sure I was looking at him before he spoke. "It's not about sex, it's about the rules. I want to know how you decided a bunch of rules was the best way to fix your life."

"I was lonely. I just...I was heartbroken and angry and confused. I just...I hated everyone. I argued with my parents and my brother and literally everyone, because I was miserable. I hadn't just been dumped or cheated on—I'd been made a fool of in front of millions of people. And I didn't know how to deal." I closed my eyes. "It wasn't...it wasn't the same. I didn't have Lane, and I felt like...who could I trust? I couldn't trust anyone."

"Still not—"

"Oh just shut up and let me talk," I said. "I've never told anyone this before, so I'm gonna tell it my way."

Duke held up his hands. "Okay, shutting up and listening."

"Good plan." I tapped his knuckles with a fingertip, tracing the scars on the knuckles from a lifetime of fighting. "Like I said, I was lonely. But…I needed sex. It came down to that. I was horny and it was making me miserable, because I wasn't getting any release or satisfaction. Also, I didn't see how I could possibly trust anyone enough to date them. So I decided not to. I figured if all I really wanted was the sex, then why not just…take what I wanted? It started with one of my younger brother's friends. We were taping a family vacation to Greece, and Quinn brought a couple friends, and I hooked up with one of them." I laughed. "Yeah, that didn't go well."

Duke was warily silent, lifting an eyebrow in query.

I shook my head, laughing again. "Quinn went apeshit and the guy I hooked up with told everyone all the dirty details…more good TV that was bad for my heart and pride. The next guy was a random, someone off-camera, not part of the show, just some guy I met at a club one night. That was…better. I got what I needed, and it seemed like he'd respect my privacy."

"Not so much?"

I shook my head. "Not so much, no. He didn't, like, sell the story, but he told his friends, and the rumor got spread around, picked up, and put the paparazzi on my heels. So then the next time I tried to hook up with a guy I met at a bar, it got photographed. The stories went viral, and the next few hook-ups got made into this big thing—Temple Kennedy is rebounding by hooking up with as many guys as she can, that sort of thing, half-truth, half-fiction. It wasn't a rebound; it was just me…me finally going after what I wanted. I couldn't avoid the press, couldn't avoid the photogs and whatever, so I started trying to be more discreet about it, going to less high-profile Hollywood sort of bars. But even then, I couldn't win."

"How so?"

I shrugged. "If the press didn't find me, the guys would inevitably tell someone, and it would get out, and there'd be another story. And I just...all I wanted was to be able to have sex without it being a major news cycle story. Didn't seem like much to ask."

"Wouldn't think so, no."

"People say oh, it's the price of fame, but that's bullshit. I signed up to have *parts* of my life televised, parts I *chose* to have taped...not every last detail. People think they're entitled to know everything about me, every detail, every little thing I do, everywhere I go, every guy I so much as look at. And the guys, they're just as bad. They all seem to think that just because we fucked once or twice, that they're gonna be on the show and that I'm gonna buy them a Ferrari and take them skiing in Switzerland or whatever. Or if they don't think that, they feel like it's no big deal to take a picture of us together and sell it. Before I came up with my rules, there'd be stories and photos and whatever, and it always came from the guy. Like...how fucking hard is it to realize I just want things kept private? I didn't go to a bar in Rancho Palos Verde because I wanted everyone to know who I was hooking up with. Just because I took my clothes off for him doesn't automatically mean he can take picture of me naked or half naked and fucking sell it to TMZ. Yet they kept doing it."

I glanced at Duke. "So that's when I made up my rules. Now every guy signs a non-disclosure agreement. You don't get so much as a look at my cleavage without signing that NDA. And the NDA covers pretty much all the other rules. No photos. No selling stories. No telling your friends, no telling your family. Not a single word about anything we did to anyone, ever. That's the first rule, and it's legally binding. It protects my privacy, and it ensures the guy knows I'm dead serious. Anyone can break a promise not to talk, but they're a lot more likely to keep that promise if they've signed a legally binding document, which also means they can't tell anyone about the NDA itself, which is a super clever piece of legalese, if I do say so myself.

"The second rule is no contact once you leave. You don't get my phone number, I won't be texting you, and you won't be texting me. No stalking me on Facebook and sending me PMs or Tweeting me, nothing."

Duke did the eyebrow thing. "That's pretty clear cut, I'd say." He hesitated, a moment. "And you tell them this in so many words?"

I nod. "Yup. I have a speech."

Duke clapped his hands together once. "Let's hear it."

I sighed. "Okay, fine. Here it is." I crossed my arms under my chest to prop up my cleavage, which is part of the spiel. "'Listen, Duke'—and here obviously I say their name—'I think you're sexy, and I'm looking forward to getting to the good stuff. But, there's a little thing we have to discuss first.' And here I'd bring out the NDA and a pen. 'So, obviously you know who I am, and I hope you understand that I'm only doing this to protect my privacy, but…I'm going to need you to sign this non-disclosure agreement. This is non-negotiable, I'm afraid. You can read it for yourself, but it basically says you won't tell anyone, *ever*, *any*thing about what we do together. That includes your buddies, the paparazzi, bloggers, tabloids, your closest bro, nobody. Ever. You also can't tell anyone about the NDA itself.

"'There's one other thing you're agreeing to, if you sign that, and let me assure you that if you don't sign it, then you'll be leaving. You don't contact me after we're done. No phone calls or texts, no PMs, DMs, or Tweets, nothing, ever. That's not what we're doing here. So, Duke, if you agree to all that, then sign and date the document, and we can move on to the fun part.'" I shrug. "That's pretty much how it goes, more or less."

Duke was quiet for a while. "And they agree?"

I nod. "Ninety-nine point nine percent of the time. I've had a couple guys back out, but yeah, most of the time they agree to it, and they sign it." I glance at him. "Why do you sound so…skeptical?"

He bobs his head to one side. "Well, because I wouldn't agree to that shit. My word is my bond, at the risk of sounding archaic or whatever. That shit is...crazy. I'd never sign a legally binding document just for a chance to bone a chick, no matter how hot or famous she might be." He glanced at me, making an *oops* face. "That came out kind of harsh, maybe. I just mean—"

I shrank against the door, away from him, staring out the window. "You've made yourself very clear, I'd say."

He reached for me. "I didn't mean it like that..." he trailed off, lowered his hand. "Well, maybe I did. But it's not about you, necessarily. Like, It's not about you not being worth the trouble or some shit. It's just...that whole process, it's just...cold, I guess. Takes the fun out of it. Part of the rush of casual sex is the risk, the mystery. You never know who you're hooking up with, which is why you gotta be safe about things, obviously, but I just mean...shit, I don't know how to put it."

He took a deep breath and let it out, then continued. "The excitement, the fun, the passion—it's about the mystery, not knowing the other person, sharing something intimate with a total stranger."

Duke pauses then looks at me with a very serious expression on his face. "Putting a legal element to it, banning all future contact, putting this big legal disclaimer in front things, like hey, we're gonna fuck, but you can't ever tell anyone about it, you can't talk about it, you just have to keep this thing that happened secret. I mean, I get why you do it, but it seems like it takes something away from the whole thing."

"You don't get what it's like—" I started.

"No, I don't," Duke interrupted. "But that's not the point. Yeah, you got burned, hard. And then you kept getting burned. But even for me, a committed bachelor, an expert at the random hook-up, it seems like you've made a logistical science out of the one-nighter. You've turned it into this—this...cold, passionless...*thing*."

He glanced at me, and I hated the look in his eyes almost as much as I hated the precise, brutal accuracy of his assessment. "It's just about the sex, at that point. And honey, plain old sex, if that's all that's happening, well goddamn, that shit is boring. That's where things *end*. That's the culmination of all the fun parts. If you're just taking these guys home and climbing on and riding their dicks and then kicking 'em out…where's the fun? Where's the—the juicy, messy craziness? Where's the part where you rip each other's clothes off and fuck like animals because you need the *fuck*, and I mean the tongues and the hands and the devouring each other, the teasing, the edging, the hardcore, rough and rabid, animal *fucking*?

"You make a guy sign some stupid paper, yeah it binds him legally, but he's thinking about *that* shit, not about how hard he's gonna make you come, not about how he can get you to lose your fucking mind. Especially if he knows going in that all he ever gets is one shot? He gets to hook up with *the* Temple Kennedy, but he can't tell anyone and he only gets one lukewarm fuck? There's no reason to up his game. It's bullshit, is what it is. Yeah, it protects your privacy, but it also puts you up in this unbreachable tower like some kind of fucking Rapunzel. Sex isn't about putting the dick in the pussy, Princess. It's about a whole hell of a lot more than just…*fucking*.

"And I'm saying this as someone who rarely taps the same honey twice, okay? But when I do hook up with a girl, I make sure there's…*passion* in it. I don't know dick about love—I don't mean that kind of passion. I don't even know if that shit exists. I told you where I came from—some asshole paid my mom for a quick fuck with a bag of crack rocks. There ain't ever been love in my life, unless you mean the guys I served with and fought next to—I can say I love those guys, but most of them are fuckin' dead. So I don't mean this is about the love kind of passion, like they put in those stupid Hollywood movies. That shit is for fairy tales and saps and fools, and I don't buy it. So don't mistake me, all right?"

He stabbed a finger at me, vivid, piercing blue eyes blazing at me before looking back at the road. "But sex, *good* sex, even with a random, you gotta put a little bit of yourself into it. I've had chicks who think they can make me believe in love try to tell me, oh, Duke, you're giving away part of yourself every time you have causal sex with someone you don't intend to ever see again. But the way I see it, yeah, I'm giving part of myself away, but shit, I'm getting that same thing in return from the girl. That's how it works. If she's acting like I'm just some dick for her to ride and it don't mean shit, it's just gonna be some quick fluid-swapping, belly slapping fuck...and I'll shut that shit down with extreme prejudice.

"Be *real*, that's all I ask—be *into* it. I'm real; I'm a straight-up kind of dude. I'll say it like it is, no bullshit. I'll tell you it ain't gonna be love because that shit doesn't exist, but I'll also promise it'll be the best damn night of your life, and I'll give it everything I've got to make that promise a reality." He met my gaze again. "And what you're doing, Fancy? That shit ain't real. It ain't even fucking. It's just...sex. And, Honey, that's sad, if you ask me."

My head was spinning, my heart aching, my eyes stinging. "You're a bastard, Duke Silver," I said, my voice thick, breaking.

"Dammit, all I meant was—"

My voice was a hissing whisper. "Do *not* fucking talk to me. Don't call me Fancy, or Princess, or any of that shit. You want to rip my life apart? Okay, fine, whatever. But you don't get to keep talking to me, or acting like you know me. You don't know me. So *fuck... you.*"

"Temple, calm down a second."

"Fuck YOU!" I shouted. "I tell you things I've never told *anyone*, I *finally* open up to a man because I think maybe I've found the one guy who could understand me, just a little, or at least accept me, and what do you do? You tear me apart and make me feel like shit. Like I'm just some slutty ice queen." I can't help a sniffle, a tear, but then I clamp down on it and focus on pushing the emotions back down where they belong—under the surface, deep down, never to be seen again. "God, just when I thought I couldn't get hurt any more, along comes Duke fucking Silver and his pompous, arrogant ass, proving me wrong, proving to me that, yes, there really is yet another way a man can hurt me."

Duke opened his mouth to speak, but then the world ended in a deafening crash, and then the universe was spinning and twisting

and flipping and something white exploded in my face and something crushed into my chest and something else sliced across my
face and lanced past my breast and there was another crash and
noise and pain—

7

YOU DON'T KNOW SHIT

WELL...FUCK.

Again.

I felt myself coming to, but this time it happened all at once, and in a blinding flash of pain. Then I was hit with the sudden realization that I was upside down, and that something was wrong.

Everything was wrong, but something big and important and specific was very, very wrong.

I forced my eyes open, struggling to focus past the crushing pain in my skull and the blood rushing to my head and the blood dripping down my chin and into my eyes and off my nose. Glancing to my right, I could see Temple, dangling limp, suspended by her seatbelt, passed out. She was a mess. Blood was matted in her hair from a cut along her hairline and another dripping slice across her chest, right across that perfect cleavage of hers.

What happened?

I was in pain, but nothing felt too fucked up. A headache, whiplash, aches and bruises—

I glanced to the left, out the window. We'd been knockoff the highway and had rolled down a steep embankment, through a fence, and were upside down in a field. This was the middle of nowhere, a desolate stretch of highway that saw little traffic, which made it not an accident.

Confirming my suspicions I saw, a quarter mile away, the hoods of two big black Wranglers parked side by side, angled in toward each other. They were kitted for off-road duty with big knobby tires, heavy duty brush guards, LED light bars, winches, and snorkels. Each Jeep was in the process of disgorging four men each armed with HK MP5s, and what looked like body armor. They were walking, single file, in our direction in a neat, precise line, all eight of them. Submachine guns up, butts to shoulders, laser sights on me.

Shit, shit, shit, shit, shit.

I braced my hand against the roof below me, and popped open the seatbelt buckle. I toppled clumsily to the floor...ceiling, whatever. The shotgun, thank god, had stayed in the vehicle with me, so I grabbed that and tossed it out the window on the opposite side of the car. Positioning myself beneath Temple, I unbuckled her, caught her as best I could, which meant letting her lower half hit the floor/ceiling and catching her head and shoulders with one arm. I checked for shards of glass in the shattered passenger window, kicked out a few remaining jagged spots, heaved Temple's limp weight out as far as I could, then scrambled out the rear window, already broken in the previous firefight. I pulled Temple the rest of the way out, and left her passed out behind the crumpled wreckage of the SUV. Peeking over the Tahoe, I could see that the mercenaries were only a couple hundred feet away.

I snagged the strap of the Mossberg, leaned into the trunk compartment and snagged a box of shells and one of the AR-15s. I dumped the shotgun shells in a pocket, tossed the box aside, and pumped the charging handle of the AR-15. Checked the magazine—full.

I glanced around me, looking for alternate cover, and saw nothing but the wreckage of the Tahoe and a stand of Aspen a good two hundred yards behind me. Plus a passed-out, bleeding Temple.

And eight professional badasses coming my way, with proper firepower.

Good thing I'm more badass than most professional badasses, right?

My duffel bag was inside the SUV. I hooked a foot into the strap and tugged it toward me, and yanked open the zipper. Where are they? Shit, shit…there they were: two flashbangs, buried under the cash.

I peeked up over the top of the upside down SUV and saw I was shit out of time.

I pulled the pin and tossed the flashbang, ducked back down behind the bulk of the vehicle, counted to three—

BANG!

This close, the detonation was deafening, as it was meant to be. The second I heard the bang, I sprang up, laid the barrel of the Mossberg over the top of the Tahoe, and squeezed off a blind shot into the smoke pall left by the flashbang, the butt kicking against my shoulder like a mule, then swiveled to the right and fired again, swiveled back the other way and fired again, then ducked down, thumbed fresh shells in to replace the spent rounds, and set the shotgun aside, bringing the rifle up.

I waited a ten count, and then rolled out around the back end of the Tahoe. The smoke was clearing, and two of the mercs were down, one writhing in pain and one motionless. The other six—

Shit. One of them was nearly on top of me, firing as he trotted smoothly in my direction. His shots thunked into the body of the SUV, and I returned fire before ducking back behind cover. More bullets were plugging into the SUV, now, from the remaining six men. The racket of gunfire was deafening, and I knew it was only a matter of time before they started punching though and getting lucky.

As the lead guy was rounding the tail end of the Tahoe, I had no choice but to fire from a crouched position, my rounds crunching through his throat and sending up a spray of blood. I grabbed him by the vest and pivoted behind him, feeling his blood rivuleting warm down my side as I pressed my shoulder into his back, felt him groaning, heard him gulping wetly, and then he was jerking as his companions' rounds slammed into his armored chest. I moved sideways with him, using him as a shield to absorb the fusillade of bullets, and then threw him forward as I reached the back end of the Tahoe. They'd flanked me from the right, coming around the hood.

Which meant Temple was between us.

Rage blasted through me, which I couldn't afford to give into. I had to keep cool, keep my head, and fight smart.

But fuck, they might hit her, or I might hit her, or they might just snatch her and run—

I rolled back out, rifle sweeping in a horizontal arc as I side-stepped into the open.

They had Temple.

One in front, holding her limp form across his body as a shield, the rest of his buddies clustered behind him. He was assuming I wouldn't shoot, that I wasn't willing to risk hitting Temple.

Never call my bluff, motherfucker.

I put three rounds through the face shield of the man holding Temple, since he didn't have a gun to her head. He dropped her to the grass, and fell backward, and then I was opening fire, strafing round after round as I hurled myself sideways. Hit the ground rolling, left the rifle on the ground and whipped up the shotgun as I came to my knees a few feet away.

Temple was still out, but she was moving and moaning now. The mercs were backpedaling, finally realizing exactly who the fuck they were dealing with.

A bullet creased my shoulder, another sliced my side open, and a third tugged at the loose fabric of my shorts, burning my thigh as it seared past me. Good thing close doesn't count. I aimed high, let loose with that sexy fuckin' twelve gauge, blast after blast, driving them backward and scattering them. One fell, then a second. Another bullet plucked at my shirt, a second scraped the outside of my ribcage, and a third buzzed past my ear. This was getting too close for comfort. One thing about luck is it always runs out. The trick is, know when to fold your hand before luck runs out on you.

I burst into a run, right at them, thumbing shells into the chamber before unloading more slugs their way. I was aiming more *toward* them than at them, trying to scatter them, suppress their fire and make 'em run. Which is what they did, the two that were left on their feet.

They were hauling ass across the field, and making damn good time, too. With the rifle I could've dropped 'em, but with a shotgun, at this distance? I didn't even try. Just let 'em run.

They reached their Jeep, and I stepped out into the open after them. "TELL CAIN TO FUCKIN' BRING IT!" I shouted. "I'LL TAKE ON EVERY LAST ONE OF YOU MOTHERFUCKERS!"

One of them answered with his HK, sending half a dozen rounds in two bursts at me. He missed by a mile, but got his point across. I ducked back behind the SUV, letting them get away, especially since Temple was starting to sit up.

There were groans coming from most of the guys on the ground, but I was too relieved to see Temple sitting up on her own to worry about them.

Once I was sure the two survivors had driven away, I scrambled to her side. "Hey there, Fancy. How do you feel?"

She moaned, clutching her head. "Hurt." She dabbed at her face, glanced down at her chest. "What happened?"

I unbuttoned her shirt, pulled it off, and used it to gently wipe at the cut across her chest, which was long and messy but not deep. "We got knocked off the road."

She hissed. "How do they keep finding us?"

I wiped at the cut to her face, which was even more minor, a little nick across her forehead. "That's what I want to fucking know. You're gonna be okay. A couple cuts, and you'll ache for awhile, but nothing damaged that I can see."

She eyed me. "You're bleeding too."

I thumbed more shells into the chamber of the shotgun. "Yeah, well, nothing to worry about. Cuts and bruises like you." I stood up.

"Stay here a minute."

I trotted over to the nearest guy moaning on the ground and put my foot into his shoulder. I kicked him over onto his back, and then stuck the gun barrel in his face. "You speak English, dickhead?"

He'd taken the shotgun slug to the chest. His vest had absorbed some of the impact, but he was still in a bad way—those vests will stop a lot, but not a twelve-gauge from close range.

He glared up at me, spat at me. "Fuck you, fuckhead," he said in a Bronx accent.

"Guess that's a yes." I knelt beside him, drew my KA-Bar from the sheath and stuck the point under his chin. "Listen, I really don't wanna do this in front of the lady, but I will if I have to, yeah? All you gotta do is tell me how you fuckers keep finding us."

He laughed, wheezing, coughing blood. "You must be dense." He laughed again. "You think you're winning? You don't know shit. You can't get away. You can kill some of us, but trust me when I say Cain is just playing with you. He'll find you. And he'll make you pay."

I pushed a little harder. "Save the tough talk, numbnuts. How's he finding me? Talk, or I'll gut you like a fish."

I could feel Temple watching. That tempered me, just a little.

The guy laughed again. "Do what you want. I don't give a shit. He'll find you."

"He's a piece of shit gangster. What's he gonna do? Feed me to the fishes?"

Another derisive, wet, sucking laugh. "You don't know shit," he repeated. "You think this is about that rich bitch over there? You must be dumber than you look. Cain is more than you'll ever know."

"Ooh…ominous." I sheathed the KA-Bar, wishing Temple wasn't here so I could just pop the fucker in the head and be done with it. "Let me guess, he has a secret lab on a secret island, and he's got a nefarious plan to take over the world."

That fucking laugh again. "If ignorance is bliss, you must be the happiest shithead on the planet."

I gave a disgusted huff, and then left him to bleed out; it wouldn't be long. I went back to Temple and helped her to her feet then got her back into her shirt. I snagged the duffel bag from the ground, grabbed one of the AR-15s and some magazines from the back of the Tahoe, and led Temple to the remaining Jeep.

"HE'LL FIND YOU!" Came a shout, with another of those wet, gurgling laughs.

Temple tried to look back, but I hauled her in a near run to the Jeep. "What did he mean by that?" She asked, clearly trying not to sound hysterical.

"Nothing."

Temple whacked me on the arm, which stung, because that was the arm that had been opened earlier. "Don't bullshit me, Duke."

I shoved her into the passenger seat and rounded the hood to hop behind the wheel. Thankfully the keys were still in the ignition. The engine started with a burly rumble, and I peeled out in a wide arc, bumping up the incline and back onto the empty highway.

"He's full of shit. Talking some nonsense about how Cain will find us, he's playing with us, blah blah fucking blah."

Temple's frown was worried. "Normally I'd call that bullshit too, but it does seem like they just…know where we are, or where we're going. They just keep showing up out of the blue. It doesn't make any sense."

I scratched my jaw, and then shifted my torso, testing the sting of the various cuts and aches. "Yeah, you've got a point. And I've been pretty damn lucky the last couple times they've showed up. They underestimate me, and I pull out the win by the skin of my teeth. But my luck's gonna run out sooner or later. You can only get into so many outnumbered gunfights before someone gets in a lucky shot, and it only takes one."

"That's what I'm afraid of." She craned her head to look back at the scene we were leaving, the overturned SUV, the bodies scattered around it. "How many were there this time?"

"Eight." I rubbed the back of my neck. "And they're getting better every time."

"But you're the best, right?"

I wasn't sure if she was joking or not; I shrugged. "In most situations, yeah. But there's always someone better, somebody luckier. And it don't matter how lucky or how good you are, they send enough guys, catch me with no cover and no backup, it won't matter what I do. This shit is becoming a lot more serious than I assumed at first."

"So what do we do?"

I sighed. "Same plan as before. I've got to connect with my guys. This is too much for me to deal with solo. There's shit going on I'm not smart enough to figure out—I just don't have all the information. I need Lear and Anselm and Puck. I need Thresh, goddammit. With that motherfucker by my side I can fuckin' wreck the world. These jackasses won't stand a chance. But on my own…trying to keep you safe? My options are limited."

"So where do we go?" she asked. "How do you reach them?"

"Harris has his main compound not too far from here. Couple hours drive at most. I'm gonna head there. If he's not there Layla should be, and she can reach him."

I dialled Harris's personal cell phone number, but it went straight to voicemail—unsurprising given that he only used his encrypted satellite phone when he was on assignment. Problem was, I didn't have that number memorized.

I dialled Thresh, got his voicemail. Dialled Anselm, got his voicemail.

"Goddammit, nobody is fucking answering!" I shouted in frustration.

Finally, I tried Lear. He never answered his damn phone, although he'd usually call back if you left a message.

It rang half a dozen times, and then, thank god, he answered. "Hello? Who's this?"

"Lear, it's Duke. What the fuck is going on, man? Nobody is answering their damn phones."

"Duke? Shit, man, it's good to hear from you. You went AWOL, we've all been trying to find you."

"Yeah, well, things are completely FUBAR, Lear—"

"You're telling me," he interrupted. "I've been scrambling for days, trying to find you, trying to dig up intel on Cain, trying to track down Thresh—it's nuts, man. Look, I gotta go. Harris is waiting for my call."

"Lear, wait a second. I'm in deep shit, still, I need—"

"Can you get to the compound?"

"I'm on the way there already, but—"

"Anselm is at the compound. He can sort you out. I really gotta go, man. Harris is the air circling, waiting for this intel. Get to the compound and talk to Anselm."

And then the fucker hung up. I wondered what the chances were he'd even tell Harris he talked to me; when Lear was in hyper mode, he's completely one-track, and forgets pretty much everything except what he was working on. I tossed the phone aside in frustration.

"Stupid tech monkey," I growled.

We drove in tense, awkward silence, and then finally, after almost an hour of that, Temple swiveled her head to look at me.

"Duke, about earlier—" she started.

I took her hand. "We can talk later. Try to rest, yeah? It's been an awful few hours."

She eyed me levelly, and then nodded. "Fine. But I have things to say to you."

I grinned. "I'd be disappointed if you didn't."

Temple rolled her eyes at me, and then reclined the seat and was soon snoring softly.

I was glad she could sleep; she seemed to be dealing with this mess better than anyone had a right to. I wasn't sure I'd be sleeping any time soon, but that was a little different.

She was taking up a lot of my headspace, and even more worryingly, heart-space….something I hadn't thought I even possessed. Yet she was digging in there and rearranging all my ideas, setting up shop somewhere inside my chest.

I just had to keep us both alive long enough to figure this shit out.

We reached Harris's compound two and a half hours later. The main gate was closed, as always, but there was a keypad, and every A1S employee had a personal keycode. The gate was a good ten feet high, made of solid black iron, connected to an eight foot high stone wall extending to either side into the thick stand of pine trees surrounding the compound. You couldn't see the buildings from the gate, and the stone wall continued a good hundred feet into the woods in both directions, where it transitioned from there to a fifteen foot high steel prison fence topped with razor wire. The entire compound was surrounded by fencing, with the gate as the only way in and the only way out, and it was heavily fortified, electrified, monitored, and alarmed.

Beyond the gate, the narrow dirt road wound away out of view, disappearing into the trees. Eventually the woods gave way to open space around the house and various other buildings of the compound, but even that was under constant watch. The compound encompassed a good portion of the foothills in which this place was nestled, and from several points in those hills a sniper could settle in and keep a hawkish eye on the whole compound—which I knew for a fact was something Anselm often took upon himself to do quite frequently, his big old Barrett fifty cal rifle in hand.

But I was nervous. This wasn't my car, which meant Anselm was likely to shoot first and worry about wondering how I got past that gate later; Anselm didn't take well to unannounced visitors.

I took a deep breath and hoped for the best, then entered my keycode. The gate swung open on silent hinges admitting the Jeep, and then closed again seconds after I was through. The cameras didn't follow me, I noticed, which meant they were recording but were not necessarily being actively monitored—not good news, because someone watching the camera would see me and alert Anselm not to send a fifty caliber slug through my skull.

I pulled carefully through the woods, emerging into the opening holding my breath. I made it twenty feet, fifty...a hundred...

And then a fountain of dirt exploded ten feet in front of the hood, and second five feet away—a clear message to halt. Those bursts of dirt were HUGE, and definitely from Anselm's Barrett. A fifty caliber slug from a Barrett would go straight through the engine block like a hot knife through melted butter from a thousand yards; I've seen what it does to a human, and that's a nasty, nauseating image I know I'll never forget. I tapped the brakes to stop the Jeep, exited the Jeep slowly, hands up, standing in the open door where I'd be visible.

"It's me, numbnuts!" I shouted.

I heard a distant, shrill, two-note whistle, an acknowledgment from Anselm. Thank fuck. I got back behind the wheel and pulled forward again, Temple still snoring. Five minutes later, I was braking outside Harris and Layla's house. It was a sprawling, custom-built ranch, single story, and it looked deceptively ordinary. It wasn't ordinary, though, at *all*—Harris didn't do anything in half measures. The main, visible level consisted of maybe three thousand square feet, enough to be roomy yet small enough to be cozy, considering it was just the two of them. Really, the house looked like any old Colorado ranch home, and the main level supported that illusion. It was what was hidden underneath that was unusual: a massive underground bunker, literally fortified against nuclear warfare, coded to Harris and Layla's palm and voiceprints alone. The bunker contained enough weapons and ammo to take on a medium-sized third world country's army, plus extra living quarters and enough rations to last seven or eight people for a year. Outside the house, there was a huge, custom-built barn.

Well...*barn* is a misleading term. We called it a barn but it was, in fact, an airplane hangar capable of housing several full-sized aircraft, and it usually housed at least one plane in it at any given time.

Aircraft were Harris's hobby and, like everything else, he didn't do it half-assed. He had WWI biplanes, WWII fighters, a MiG, an F-4 Phantom, and a Huey all from the Vietnam era, and several generic, less exciting single and double engine private prop planes, plus his six-person Gulfstream.

Some guys restored hot rods or bought vacation properties; Nick Harris restored fighter jets and bought heavy weaponry.

He'd personally restored each one of the vintage aircraft, and was licensed to fly anything that would go up in the air, from passenger jets to fighter jets, from helos to prop planes. Not only licensed, but one of the most talented pilots I've ever met. A little known fact about those fighters he owned: he'd procured, somehow, machine gun ammunition and rockets for all them. As in, if he wanted to, he could carry out his own goddamn airstrike. I wasn't sure even Layla knew he had another bunker underneath the larger, more nondescript hangar by the runway, which contained his stock of heavy duty ordinance—rockets, grenades, fifty and thirty-eight caliber machine gun ammo, a few crates of SAMs, and that was just what I'd personally inventoried.

The man was legitimately ready for war.

I kicked open the door of the Jeep, checked to see that Temple was still out, and decided to leave her be for the moment. Let her sleep, she needed it. I had a feeling shit was about to get seriously wicked.

I expected Layla to burst out the front door and holler some funny shit at me from the wraparound porch, and I even had a few good comebacks chambered, but she never appeared.

"What the hell?" I muttered to myself. "Layla! Where you at, bitch?" I bellowed.

The buzzing rattle of a powerful dirt bike echoed up in the hills, the noise getting louder as it approached. I assumed it was Anselm, but I wasn't about to take any chances. I fetched one of the rifles from the backseat, tracking the incoming dirt bike from across the hood of the Jeep. It appeared after a minute or two, and even though the figure on the bike was wearing all black BDUs and a full-coverage helmet, I knew it was Anselm by the sight of the fucking enormous rifle strapped across his back.

He braked to a dramatic, arcing rear-tire skid, planted one boot in the dirt and stood up to let the dirt bike lean against his thigh. Tugging off the helmet, he passed a hand through his messy brownish blond hair, smoothing it back across his scalp.

"Everyone has been searching for you, Duke," Anselm said, by way of greeting. He spoke English more fluently than I did, though he spoke it with a thick German accent, and sometimes he rearranged the grammar in quirky ways.

"Yeah, well, I ran into some trouble."

He peered into the passenger window. "And still managed to procure a lady friend."

"She's not my usual brand of lady friend," I said, tossing the barrel of the rifle onto my shoulder. "And she's part of the trouble."

Anselm's eyebrow lifted upward which was, for him, kind of like shouting a question. "Meaning?"

"Meaning, someone whacked me across the back of the head, shot me full of sleepy time drugs, and stuffed me in some shitty ghetto basement in the Denver suburbs. I'd been about to chat up this chick outside the bar, so I guess they decided to not take any chances and just grabbed her too."

Anselm nodded. "I have much to fill you in with, and we must also call our mutual employer. Thresh is rather worried about you, I should mention."

"You know what's going on?" I asked.

"To a degree," he answered. "Cain is making a play for his vengeance."

"I thought Harris said Cain was a low-level kingpin with more ambition than sense or some shit like that?" I lifted the rifle. "The guys I've been cleaning out haven't been amateurs, man. The last bunch were pro mercs, eight of 'em, well armed and decently trained."

"They chased Thresh and a...a friend of his all the way into the

Everglades, and he barely made it out alive himself. Puck had a run-in of his own, and Lear is hiding somewhere digging for information. We are scattered, my friend. It seems Harris greatly underestimated this Cain individual."

"Yeah, I talked to Lear, and he hung up on me." What he'd said about Thresh registered, then, belatedly. "Is Thresh okay?"

"He was wounded in one arm, but nothing life-threatening."

"But this is serious."

Anselm nodded. "*Ja*. Very serious, in my estimation."

I circled the Jeep to stand nearer Anselm, leaning back against the hood. "I tried questioning one of the mercs but he wouldn't tell me shit, except that Cain isn't what we thought, that we don't know anything and we can't get away. He said Cain will find us. Normally I'd have made him talk, but with Temple watching...?" I shrugged. "Chicks don't dig watching torture, yeah?"

Anselm chuckled. "No, indeed not."

"What worries me is how they keep finding us. These guys just... show up, like they know where we are."

Anselm's features tightened. "That is worrying. You are not ignorant in the art of throwing a shadow."

"It's really fucking weird, is what it is. We got out of the basement they had us in, and I didn't leave any survivors. Then they found us at my stash house, which *nobody* knows about—that shit is under an alias, man, and you *know* I'm careful about keeping those clean and separate. Four guys came after me, and again, I didn't leave any survivors. They found us on the open road, Anselm, on the highway heading this way. Middle of nowhere, just fucking...*poof*, they appeared and knocked us off the road."

"And you fought off all eight by yourself? Without sustaining any major injuries?"

I shrugged. "Got lucky. It was close though. Couple shots nearly had my number, dude, and that shit is starting to fuck with my head."

Anselm was staring at me. "That is quite worrying, Duke. They should not be able to just find you no matter where you go." He toed down the kickstand and sidled toward me. "It seems too sophisticated and high tech for me to believe this, but…it almost seems as if they put into you a tracker."

"Like…a tracer? *Inside* me?"

"It would explain how they are able to keep finding you." He tipped his head to one side. "But that is an expensive proposition. That technology is not so easy to procure, even if you have the requisite funds. And it seems to be a lot of effort to expend merely for revenge. If he could kidnap you, he could have easily put a bullet into your head and be done. The mystery of his tactics worries me. There is something we are missing, I think."

I hissed. "And now I led them here, to Harris's compound."

"It is only conjecture on my part," Anselm said. "I do not know for a certainty if you have been implanted with this tracker. We should be safe here for a time."

"Still, we should get contact Harris."

Anselm nodded. "Perhaps bring your friend into the house." His action suited his words and he headed inside, where I noticed the front door had a new biometric lock.

In fact, the windows seemed reinforced, and the door looked heavy…

"Hey, Anselm…looks like you've been busy up in here." I opened the passenger door of the Jeep as I shouted to Anselm.

He nodded. "Harris has been wanting to improve the quality of physical security, so I did that while covering the compound."

I looked down at Temple and shook her gently. "Hey, babe. We're here."

She blinked awake, twisting in the reclined seat, peering at me as she stretched. And goddamn, that stretch…arching her back, pushing her tits out, looking sleepy and sexy and fucking temping as hell.

"Where are we?"

"My boss's compound." I couldn't help brushing a flyaway lock of hair out her eyes. "Safe, for now."

"That's what you said about your stash house."

I grimaced. "Yeah, well…this place is fortified. Plus," I gestured at Anselm, visible through the open doorway of Harris's house, "now we've got some back up."

"Who's that?" Temple asked, pulling the seatback forward and yanking her hair out of the ponytail holder to rearrange it.

"That's Anselm."

"The scary German dude?"

"That's him. But he's on our side, and be glad of that. We should be okay here for a while."

I grabbed the duffel bag out of the back seat, along with the other rifle and the Mossberg. No sense being caught unarmed, right? Temple and I went into the house, and I closed the door behind us. The lock clunked home, a solid and reassuring sound.

The inside of Harris and Layla's house was as nice and unassuming as the exterior. Cozy, country, and comfortable, is how I'd describe it. Lots of wood, exposed beam ceilings, hardwood floors with hand-woven rugs on top, and artfully, intentionally mismatched furniture. It had an open central floor plan, with the master bedroom on one side of the house, and a set of guest rooms on the other, and a spacious study for Harris off the living room. I'd only been inside a few times, as the HQ for the crew was housed in a separate building over by the runway and the barn, and that's where we A1S guys spent the bulk of our time when at the compound. This was Harris and Layla's personal full-time residence, and thus seemed a little… off-limits, I guess.

"The doorway can withstand a sustained automatic weapons fire," Anselm said from the foyer area, "and the windows are all bulletproof. Additionally, there are now motion sensors along the perimeter, and extra cameras in key locations. I have installed sniper's nests in several places up in the hills as well, each with its own rifle, ammunition, and range finder, as well other hideout locations with backup weapons and food."

"You've been a busy boy, buddy," I said, laughing.

Anselm nodded. "I do not enjoy idle time. And I do not ever

underestimate my enemy. I am prepared to defend the compound against any who wish to try their luck." He unslung the mammoth rifle and set it butt-down on the floor, leaning it against the doorframe. "If they wish to take this place, however, they should better be ready to dance with the devil."

Temple was eyeing the rifle. "Holy shit, that is the biggest gun I've ever seen."

Anselm patted the barrel. "*Ja,* the Barrett, she is my very best friend." He held out his hand to shake Temple's. "I am Anselm See." He pronounced his last name *zay,* rhyming with *weigh,* or *hay.*

Temple seemed wary. "I'm Temple Kennedy. Nice to meet you."

Anselm gave a small, but charming grin. "I think Duke has been telling stories again. He and Thresh, they like to make anyone who meets me think I am some kind of Boogie-Man." It was obvious from his lack of reaction that Anselm hadn't heard of Temple, which wasn't surprising; he wasn't really the pop-culture sort of guy.

"Motherfucker, you *are* the Boogie-Man," I said, clapping him on the shoulder. "You're just *our* Boogie-Man."

Anselm shrugged one shoulder. "I will accept that." He shot me a look. "And you know, Duke, you curse more than anyone I've ever known. A foul mouth is the sign of a weak mind, my father used to say."

"Yeah, well, my father used to say people who swear a lot are smarter."

Anselm cocked his head in confusion. "You did not know your father. I am sure of this."

"And *you* don't *have* a father," I retorted.

"Everyone has a father."

"Except you. I've always assumed you were created fully-grown in some super secret spy laboratory."

"Spies do not work in laboratories," Anselm said, deadpan serious. "That is scientists."

I laughed. "You gotta get a sense of humor, my man." I hesitated, and then figured I'd just ask and see what he said. "Where *did* you grow up?"

As far as I knew, none of us had ever dared ask him anything about his past, under the assumption he wouldn't answer, or would get pissed at the invasion of his privacy—and nobody wanted to risk a pissed off Anselm.

Anselm was quiet a long moment. "I was born in Berlin, Germany, April 30th, nineteen seventy-nine." He hesitated another long moment. "My father was a government official, and my mother was a homemaker. My childhood was unremarkable in every way. It is my adult life which is…more difficult to explain."

"Well, I hate to interrupt such a riveting conversation," Temple said, "but I'm hungry. Is there anything I can eat?"

Anselm nodded. "I will fix you something. Do you have any allergies to food?"

"Nope."

"Well then, I shall see what there is. Please, be at home." Anselm moseyed into the kitchen, and I heard the sounds of cabinets opening and closing.

We moved into the living room and sat down on the couch, which was a deep, thick leather monstrosity, well worn and stupid comfortable, the kind of couch that liked to eat you and never let you get up. Temple curled up with her feet under her legs, sitting closer to me than I'd assumed she would, after that last conversation we'd had.

When Anselm was busy and out of earshot, Temple eyed me skeptically. "He seems nice. You made me think he was some kind of vicious assassin."

I laughed. "Oh, he is. He's also super nice. That's what makes him scary. He's never anything but nice and polite and calm. He doesn't get excited, doesn't yell, doesn't curse. I'm not sure he even drinks booze. He's just…utterly calm, *all…the…time*. It's unnerving. We'll be in the middle of a shootout, bullets flying every which way, people dying, screaming, fucking rockets exploding, and Anselm will be in my earpiece acting all cool and collected, like it's just a day at the fucking beach. Or whatever it is that freak does for fun. If he even knows what fun *is*." I leaned backward over the couch. "Hey, Anselm!"

He was at the island in the kitchen, making sandwiches. "*Ja?*"

"What do you do for fun?"

He finished one sandwich and started on another, answering without looking up. "Practice at the shooting range. Read books. Track down my enemies and eat their hearts." He glanced up and winked at Temple. "The usual."

I boggled at him for an entire half-minute. "Holy shit, was that a joke?"

"I don't know, was it?" His grin was subtle, but it was there. "That is the Boogie-man, *ja*? He eats the hearts of his victims?"

I laughed at that. "Fuck me, Anselm, what kind of Boogie-Man stories did *you* grow up with?"

His grin vanished abruptly. "I was sent to a private military school when I was fourteen, so, for me, the Boogie-Man was the *kommandant*. He was the most frightening and unpleasant man I have ever known, and I have been acquainted with professional torturers. Children who infracted the rules would go to his office and never return. Some of the children at the school whispered rumors that he ate the rule-breakers, and others said that he did things far less savory than mere cannibalism to them."

"Well that's...fun," Temple said. "Aren't you just a ray of sunshine?"

"I have never been accused of being jovial," Anselm said, and went back to making sandwiches.

"Yeah, I guess not," Temple said.

"I think you're getting a little too much me-time, Anselm," I said. "You're going stir-crazy. This is the most I've heard you talk about yourself in the entire time we've known each other."

Anselm brought two paper plates with cold cut sandwiches and corn chips, carrying those in one hand and two cans of light beer in the other.

"Harris does not believe in soda, it appears," Anselm said. "So you drink beer."

I cracked open the beer and crammed half the sandwich into my mouth. "Soda is bullshit," I said, around a mouthful of food. "Cancer juice. I never drink soda."

"Why not?" Temple asked, biting into her sandwich with a little more delicacy than I was displaying.

I nodded. "Had this buddy in the Army, he was a mechanic, worked on the deuce-and-a-halfs. He'd clean parts with Coke. Like, he'd scrub dirt and rust and shit off the metal with Coca-Cola, and it'd be shinier than new. If it does *that* to fucking steel? Hell if I'll drink that shit."

We all ate in silence then. Anselm finished his food first, somehow, and went about making more sandwiches, bringing me another and one for himself. When we were finished, he took our plates and disposed of them.

"I must return to the nest. Your information is worrisome." He indicated a large, blocky cell phone on the island counter. "A sat-phone, with Harris's terminal number programmed into it. Call him, tell him you are alive and what you told me about Cain."

Temple stood up. "Is there a chance I could shower? Things have been…yucky."

Anselm nodded, his eyes going to the bloodstain on her skirt. "Of course. I think Layla has some clothing to possibly fit you, if you would like."

"That would fantastic."

Anselm went into Harris and Layla's room, and emerged a minute later with a pair of black yoga pants, a T-shirt, a hoodie, and a pair of flip-flops.

"I do not know if the sandals will fit, but they might be more appropriate under the circumstances than your current footwear," he said.

"Better than nothing," Temple answered. "Thank you."

He nodded and then from a counter in the kitchen, he grabbed a military grade long-range two way radio with an earpiece and throat mic and handed the set to me. "Keep in contact and be alert. I'll be watching, but at this point in the game, I think perhaps anything is possible."

"I might try to pop over to the HQ. I've got some spare gear over there."

Anselm shook his head. "*Nein*. You stay here. This is the safest place on the compound, and you have *Frau* Kennedy to worry about. You need BDUs, I assume, *ja*?"

I nodded. "Yeah, and some extra hardware. All I've got is those scrounged pieces, my HK, and a couple of pistols."

"I will raid your quarters and bring you what I find."

"Great."

Anselm gestured at the sat phone. "Now call Harris. We have to be coordinated."

"Yes sir," I said, mocking a salute.

He shook his head on the way out the door, slinging his Barrett over his shoulder. "You are too irreverent for your own good."

"It's like you know me," I joked.

When he was gone, I showed Temple the spare bathroom. "Take your shower while I make a call."

After the water was running, I sat down on a stool at the island, the Mossberg leaning against the side of the counter and the rifle on top of it, and dialled the single number programmed into the satellite phone.

"Anselm, what's going on?" came Harris's voice.

"It's me, boss. Heard you guys were missing me."

"I've got Duke," I heard Harris say, his voice muffled, speaking to someone on the other end. "Where the fuck have you been, jackass?"

"Well, you see, I took up ballet. I was working on my pirouette and lost track of time."

His voice was razor sharp. "This isn't the time for fucking jokes, Duke. Where—the *fuck*—have you been?"

I let a sliver of my irritation show through in my voice. "I got snatched, dude. Like, cracked across the head, drugged, and stuck in a basement somewhere in Denver."

"You got out, obviously."

"Well, no shit. That's not the point."

"What is the point, then?"

"They snatched someone with me."

"Who?" Harris asked; I heard voices in the background—sounded like Puck, Thresh, and a female voice I wasn't familiar with.

"Temple Kennedy," I answered.

"Temple Kennedy? Why does that name ring a bell?"

The female voice in the background spoke up. "Her mom is Jane Kennedy, and her dad is Craig Kennedy, like from Suicide Cult. She's got her own reality show."

"Oh yeah, I think Layla watches that," Harris said. "So…they kidnapped you *and* this Temple Kennedy chick?"

"Sure did."

"And what were you doing with Temple Kennedy in the first place?"

"Nothing…yet, at least. I was setting up to talk to her, and *wham*, next thing I know I'm bound hand and foot and I'm in a shitty basement, and this chick is bound and gagged beside me. Bunch of Cain's Eastern Bloc gangster types came down talking shit, kicked me, and left again. Dumbasses tied me up with zipties—"

Harris snorted. "Amateurs."

"Yeah, that's what I said. I took 'em out, and hightailed it out of there with Temple."

I filled him in on the rest of the events of the day, leading up to showing up at his compound, including what Anselm had said about the possibility of me having been implanted with a tracer.

There was a long, tense silence on the other end. "Fuck, fuck, fuck." Another pause. "This changes things."

"I think you might have underestimated your guy Cain."

"Yeah," Harris agreed. "I mean, I never said he was stupid, just that he wasn't a great tactician. He's definitely not stupid. This doesn't feel like Cain, though. That's the problem. He doesn't snatch, and he doesn't go in for elaborate revenge plots. He goes in and kills you and your family and your friends and anyone you ever spoke to, and he does it brutally, bloodily, and publicly."

"So maybe he's got a tactical advisor or something?" I suggested.

"Possibly, but I don't know. Something about this doesn't feel right."

"Well, all I know is that I barely got us out the last time, and if Anselm is right and the pattern holds, they're gonna show up here eventually. So...I guess I'm just saying sorry in advance for what might happen to your compound."

"Yeah, well, it's all just stuff. Keep yourself and this Temple of yours alive until we can get there. Stuff can be replaced, you can't."

"Awww, you're makin' me all mushy inside, boss," I said. "Hey, is Thresh with you? I heard he had some fun. And who was that girl I heard talking? It didn't sound like Layla."

"Yeah, Thresh is with me, and no that wasn't Layla. That's Thresh's new girlfriend. Her name's Lola."

I was stunned silent. "Thresh's new who-the-what-now?"

Harris laughed. "Yeah, that was my reaction, too. She's cool, though."

"Huh. Weird." I decided I couldn't handle the idea of Thresh with a girlfriend, so I just wouldn't think about it. "Where's Layla, then?"

"I sent her and Sasha down to stay with Roth and Kyrie while this whole thing is going on. After what Thresh went through, I wasn't taking any chances. She's probably not gonna talk to me for a month, but better that than Cain getting his hands on her. Roth's place in the Caribbean is a fortress, and I hired a bunch of extra guys to keep an eye the place."

"She let you send her packing to safety?" I asked, incredulous.

Layla wasn't exactly known for her practicality when it came to being safe; she preferred to be in the thick of the action, wherever Harris was, no matter the risk, and got...pissy, let's say...when

Harris tried to put her somewhere out of the way.

"It was a fight, but she went," Harris said, and the tone of his voice told me how serious that fight must have been. "She hadn't seen Kyrie in a while anyway, so I think that was what convinced her more than anything I said."

"So what's the plan, boss?"

"We're in the air right now, headed your way. I've got Thresh and Puck with me, Lear is who knows where, and Anselm is there on the compound. I think you need to hang tight."

"Have you thought about bringing Lear in?" I asked. "He can do okay, but the guys I've been tangling with are no slouches, Harris. I barely got away, and that's with a shitload of fucking luck and experience." I laughed. "I called him awhile ago from a non-secure line, and he hung up on me. He's a space cadet when he's working. Not sure he'd even hear the bad guys coming, Boss."

"Don't underestimate Lear," Harris said. "He's tougher than you think. But, yeah, I've been in contact with him, and he's better off out there, wherever the fuck he is. What he lacks in combat experience, he makes up for in the ability to run and hide while still making himself useful. He's digging for intel right now, so hopefully he'll come back with something that'll give us a plan of attack."

"Sounds good," I said. "Can I talk to Thresh?"

"Sure." I heard muffled sounds on the line, and then Harris's voice, distant. "Yo, Thresh. Your boyfriend's on the phone for you."

Thresh came on, then. "You worried me, fucker."

"Did you cry?"

"Nearly."

I toyed with the charging handle of the rifle on the counter. "Heard you got yourself a girlfriend."

"And I heard you like it in the ass, you twinkie."

"You wish." I hesitated a beat. "But for real. I thought we didn't believe in that shit."

"The right chick comes along..." Thresh trailed off for a moment. "I don't know, man. I know it sounds like that sappy bullshit we've always made fun of, but dude, it's real, and it's no fucking joke. This shit just…changes you."

"I think I might be tracking that myself, brother."

"No shit?"

"It's confusing, man. Like, the things I think, the shit I find myself doing and saying when I'm around her…it's been literally a matter of hours, and she's…"

"Under your skin, but not in an annoying way? Like suddenly everything seems to just revolve around her?" It was weird hearing Thresh talk like that. It was like…Ellen DeGeneres's voice come out of Jerry Seinfeld's mouth. Just…fucking weird. But goddamn if he wasn't right.

I groaned. "Exactly."

"Can I offer some advice? I'm going through the same thing, just a little further ahead than you are, it seems like."

"Let me have it, bro."

"Just go with it," he said. "Don't fight it. There's no point. Once you stop resisting it and just sort of let the mushy romantic lovey-dovey bullshit suck you in…I don't know. It's not so bad."

"Who the fuck are you, and what have you done with my best friend?"

"Shut up, cock-knocker," Thresh said, with a laugh. "I know it's weird. You think like it'd be emasculating or some shit, but…it's not. I swear. The right girl, she'll make you feel like *more* of a man, not less. I've been forced to realize something, brother: we don't know shit."

"That's second time I've been told that today," I said. "And you just used 'emasculating' in a sentence—now I know you've been brainwashed."

"Shut up, ass-face. I can still pound your skull in."

"Yeah, again…you wish."

"I gotta go. Harris is giving me the wrap it up signal."

"This shit isn't a joke, Thresh, and I'm not talking about girls anymore."

"I'm well aware. I've been busy myself." Another pause. "Okay so I guess I really have to go. Harris wants the line free. Watch your six, brother."

"You too."

I hung up, left the phone on the counter, and brought the shot-gun with me as I went to check on Temple. She'd been in the shower for quite a while at that point.

The bathroom door was cracked, steam billowing out. I heard Temple's voice, but she was…moaning. Low, quiet. Erotic.

"Duke…" she whispered.

Shit…she was thinking about me? Moaning like that…

Ten to one she was fingering herself.

I pushed the door open slowly and stepped in as quietly as I could.

And yeah, there she was in all her naked glory. Sprawled out in the tub, water up to her neck, hand between her thighs moving fast and splashing water everywhere, back arched, head thrown back. Tits breasting the surface of the water, nipples hard, her whispering voice saying my name…

I wondered if Harris and Layla kept any rubbers around? I backed out of the bathroom as quietly as I'd snuck in, trotted to Harris and Layla's bedroom, muttering an apology for being nosy as I rifled through the bedside table drawers. Bingo. I found their stash: several vibrators of varying sizes and styles, a shitload of con-doms, fur-lined handcuffs, a cock ring, anal beads…I pushed any possible mental images far, far, far away and tore off half a dozen condoms and stuffed them into my pockets, and then trotted back to the bathroom, hoping I hadn't taken too long.

Thank god, she was still going. Her hips were flexing, now, her left hand holding her pussy open, her right splashing in circles un-der the water. Her eyes were closed, tits bouncing and splashing, hair wet and sticking to her face and neck. Still gasping my name—"Duke! Oh god, Duke!"

I shucked my clothes in record time, making sure the Mossberg was readily available, just in case.

Tiptoeing closer to the tub, I ripped open a condom wrapper and left it on the sink for when I was ready.

Then I reached for Temple…

8

SO MUCH MORE

A SHOWER HAD SOUNDED LIKE THE BEST IDEA ON THE PLANET, until I saw the oversized claw foot tub, and decided a scalding bath was an even better plan. So I ran the bath and sank into it, luxuriating in the piping hot water, my exhausted, stressed muscles soaking up the heat even though it stung the cut on my chest and the nick at my hairline. Neither were anything to worry about, but they still stung.

The thing about a bath is that it leaves a lot of time to think—which, usually, is the point, right? Take half an hour or an hour to just soak and let my mind wander, sort through the events of the day and how I felt about them? But under these circumstances, I wasn't so sure letting my mind wander was the best idea. There was a lot of nastiness I was actively working at suppressing: heads bashed in, faces shot away, sucking chest wounds, dead bodies. So many dead bodies. So much gunfire. This was all brand new to me; I'd never even seen a real gun up close or heard one shot, much less seen a dead body. I mean, I'd gone to my great-grandma's funeral, but that's different—she'd been in a casket, at peace, already dead from natural causes. Watching someone get shot? Watching Duke smash a head in like a watermelon? How was I supposed to feel about it? How do you deal with that? I didn't know how, so I was trying to just pretend it wasn't real, that I was watching a Bruce Willis movie. It wasn't real. I hadn't really seen...how many was it?...a dozen men die? Nope. Fake. Fake blood. Fake bullets. Fake deaths. This wasn't happening to me.

Denial was working okay, for the most part. It let me continue operating on something like a normal level instead of collapsing into a quivering, sobbing pile of uselessness. Some instinct deep down kept telling me that I couldn't afford to panic, yet. I couldn't afford to give in to the nervous breakdown I felt building up inside me. I had to focus, had to keep my emotions in check...which meant pretending I was fine, pretending all this was fine, cool, great, normal. No problem here. It's just me, Temple Kennedy, trapped in a Robert Ludlum novel. No big deal, happens all the time.

Only, the longer I lay here in the tub, the more the reality of my situation started to seep through my carefully constructed game of pretend.

I had to distract myself. I needed to relax and not think about the yucky stuff.

Duke was the perfect distraction.

I pictured him naked, which was a mental image hot enough to make my thighs clench together. But if I thought about his cock? His fingers? The things his tongue had done to me?

God.

I pictured him standing in front of me in the kitchen of that apartment of his, cock in his hand, fist sliding down his shaft...teasing me into begging him to fuck me. I've never begged for a damn thing in my life, but I had begged him. And I'd do it again, for a chance to feel that massive dick sliding into my pussy just once more. I could probably come all over him, reach the orgasm while he was inside me—shit, he'd probably make me come twice or even three times before we were done.

But other thoughts bubbled up inside my head, unwelcome thoughts—his judgement of the way I lived my life, his accurate and brutal assessment of my sad sex life. It *was* sad, wasn't it? There was no joy in it, no passion. I couldn't remember most of the guys I'd fucked. They all ran together, blurred into a flickering montage of half-drunk fucking, the guy finishing before I did, getting out of the bed, dressing, and leaving while I watched, frustrated, from the bed. As soon as he was gone, I'd pull out my Lelo and finish myself off.

And that was that.

I'd never had anyone look at me the way Duke looked at me. I'd never had anyone touch me the way he did either, or kiss me that way. The orgasms he'd given me…? They were the most intense I'd ever felt.

I wanted him.

Goddammit, I wanted him.

I wanted to be in bed with him, a string of condoms on the side table, and an entire weekend with nothing to do, nowhere to go, just Duke and me naked together, fucking until neither of us could move.

My fingers drifted down between my thighs, almost of their own volition. I pictured his eight-pack abs, his pecs, his brawny arms and burly shoulders, the dusting of ginger pubes around his heavy balls, his enormous, cock standing flat against his belly, thick as my wrist and just begging for my fingers to wrap around it, begging for my lips, for my tongue to taste it, begging for my pussy to swallow it deep.

I could almost feel him, smell him, and sense him. My fingers were flying, the orgasm reaching critical mass.

"God, Duke," I whispered. "I'm gonna come…"

And then, as the orgasm rolled through me, I felt his lips on mine, felt his hand join mine, and felt his fingers take over. My eyes flew open, and there he was, leaning over the tub, naked and real, touching me, fingering me to orgasm and kissing me senseless. I couldn't possibly fight it, could only fly off the face of the world as his tongue scoured my mouth and tangled with my tongue, could only gasp helplessly as the climax tore through me, my hips flying, water splashing everywhere. Pleasure was a wildfire inside me, and the heat in his eyes made it even better, the feel of his fingers swirling around my clit intensifying the ecstatic rush of bliss.

I came, and I came, and I came.

My eyes didn't leave Duke's as I whimpered through the orgasm.

"Say my name again," he growled.

"Duke," I whispered.

His expression was dark and hot and hungry. "Can you stand?"

I shook my head, still trembling head to toe. "Not—not yet."

He snagged the towel I'd set out on the toilet lid. Reached down, scooped me up and wrapped me in the towel in a single adroit maneuver. Carried me into the bedroom to which the bathroom was attached and tossed me onto the bed. I bounced, and the towel flew open. He lingered for a moment, staring at me.

"So goddamn beautiful," he murmured. Then, louder: "Stay there."

"Where would I go?" I asked, not all sarcastic. "And besides, my legs are still shaking too much to walk."

His smile was pleased, and then he pivoted, vanished into the bathroom, and returned with condoms in one hand and the shotgun in the other. The gun he leaned near the bed, and the condoms he tossed on a bedside table, keeping one square packet in his hand, which I saw he'd already ripped open. This he tossed onto my belly as he climbed onto the bed.

"Open your legs for me, sweetheart," he ordered, his voice an irresistible snarl.

"I—I already came," I protested. "I just want you."

"You'll have all of me you can take," he answered, "and then some. But I need another taste of your pussy first. So open up."

I had no idea what came over me then, but I snapped my thighs together and smirked at him. "No," I whispered.

He stopped on all fours, and then reared back on his knees. "No?" He sounded genuinely puzzled.

I was breathless, then. "Make me."

He laughed, then, a predatory sound. "You sure that's how you wanna play it, Princess?"

"I'm sure," I answered, only lying a tiny little bit.

"I'm not a gentle man, Temple," he bit out. "I've been keeping the beast in check for your sake."

"The beast? Is that what you call your dick?"

His laugh was one of amusement, this time. "My cock doesn't have a name, but if that's what you wanna call it, go for it." He prowled toward me on all fours once more. "It was just a reference to how I like to fuck: rough, wild, and fierce."

I shivered at the fire in his pale blue gaze. "That's what I want. Show me how to fuck like that, Duke."

"You're sure?" He put a hand on one of my knees. "I don't wanna hurt you or scare you."

"Duke?" I said, instead of answering.

"What?"

"Shut up and fuck me." I snagged the condom wrapper off my belly and prepared to tug the thin latex circle out.

"Not yet," he said, taking it away and tossing it back onto my stomach. "First, you come again."

He yanked my thighs apart, and this time he didn't do it gently or sweetly, but roughly. Brusquely. He grabbed me by the hips, laying down on his belly half on and half off the bed, and then jerked me to the edge of the mattress. He lifted my ass into the air, smashing his mouth onto my pussy. His tongue assaulted my clit with immediate ferocity, no build up or teasing, just immediate oral stimulation, sending me from still quivery to gasping in three seconds. He didn't slow, didn't vary, no fingers, no sucking or licking, just that tongue slashing in wild circles around my clit until I was heaving, whimpering, hips flexing involuntarily.

He kept it going until I was moaning his name nonstop— "Duke, Duke, Duke...ohmygod, Duke..."

He seemed to know exactly when I was about to come, because that was when he stopped, slid two fingers into my channel, and started moving them in and out of me. He began slowly, giving me time to warm up to the sensation, curling his fingers just so, exploring the interior of my pussy with his fingers, scissoring them apart, curling, stroking, moving them faster and faster until I was groaning with the slick pressure of his touch inside me, and snarling with frustration because I couldn't come like this, not without clitoral stimulation…

The bastard knew my body like he'd designed it himself. He finger-fucked me until I was a writhing mess of arousal and frustration, and then he pushed me past that point, into something like madness.

"I need your tongue, Duke," I gasped.

"Yeah?"

"God, *please*, Duke. Please. I need to come, and I can't. Not without—" A moan ripped through me as he brushed my G-spot, cutting off my words.

"Not without what, Temple?"

"Lick my clit," I begged. "Or touch it. Something, anything. I just…I need…I need to come, and I can't unless you lick my clit."

He slowed the thrusting of his fingers until I was lifting my hips off the bed, slowly grinding, rolling, bucking, begging him with the movements of my body to finish me, to give me what I need. I watched him slowly, teasingly, extend his thumb toward my clit, and I lifted my hips, trying to close the distance, to get that final touch.

"God, Duke! Stop fucking teasing me!" I shouted.

"No."

He moved his thumb away and resumed the thrusting of his fingers, this time letting the heel of his palm brush my clit ever so gently, and then he increased the pace, and each time his fingers buried into my channel, his hand bumped against my clit, providing the tiniest amount of stimulation, so I was roiling, grinding, groaning, hips flexing wildly, desperately seeking the pressure and stimulation I needed.

"Fuck, Duke. *Please*."

"Take what you want," he said. So I slid my hand down my body and touched my clit with two fingertips, immediately gasping in relief—until his hand latched onto mine like a vise and prevented me from touching myself enough to matter. "Not like that."

I wrapped my hand around the back of his head and jerked him toward my pussy, lifting my hips to push myself against him. "Eat me, Duke," I demanded. "Make me come. *Now*."

His laugh was feral with desire and rife with amusement. "Thatta girl," he murmured, the words vibrating against my flesh.

And then I was gone, screaming out loud as the long-denied, pent-up orgasm rippled through me like a shockwave, just from a mere brush of his tongue against my clit but he wasn't satisfied with that, oh no. He added a third finger inside me and fucked my channel with those thick fingers of his and his mouth suctioned around my clit and his tongue thrashed against me. The orgasm was nuclear, ripping me into a million pieces.

He pushed me through the orgasm into paroxysms of shuddering release, gasping, shrieking.

And then he bent over me, kissed me, and pressed the condom into my shaking hands. "Put it on me," he ordered.

My eyes flew open. I sat up, slid the condom out of the wrapper, gripped his cock in one hand and rolled the condom down over his shaft with the other. He stood at the foot of the bed, staring at me, his cock straining, now sheathed in thin, studded latex. His jaw flexed, his chest heaving as if he was the one who'd just come instead of me.

And then he moved with the speed of a striking serpent, flipping me onto my belly so fast I wasn't sure what had happened until I felt the comforter under my cheek and his hands on my hips. I wasn't afraid, exactly, but he did say he wasn't gentle and that he liked it rough, and I'd never exactly done rough before. So yeah, I was a little nervous.

Okay, fine, I was afraid.

I didn't like pain, and I was afraid of what I'd asked for, that he'd want to, like, choke me or spank me until I cried or something. Or that he'd start just fucking me so hard it hurt—

Instead, he just caressed my ass.

Slowly, gently, reverently, with both hands, massaging and

kneading as I descended from the orgasm.

And then he slid his hand between my thighs and found my pussy, teased it with a fingertip…god, then finally I felt him touch the tip of his dick to my entrance, but didn't put it in, just teased, rubbed, pressed.

"Duke, what are you doing?"

"Taking my time," he answered, "and enjoying your body."

"I thought you liked it rough." I tried to hide the quaver of nerves and anticipation in my voice.

"You that eager?" he asked, leaning over me to put his mouth to my ear. "Or are you nervous?"

"Both," I answered.

"Good." He nudged his cock between the lips of my pussy. "You should be a little nervous."

"Why? What are you gonna do?"

He didn't answer. His hands smoothed over my ass again, and then went to the swell of my hips, dimpling the flesh, gripping hard—

No warning, no gentle slide in, just a sudden slap of flesh against flesh, his cock penetrating me until his hips clapped against my ass cheeks, and I couldn't help crying out from the unexpected fullness. Oh god…oh my god…he was so big, his cock stretching me apart, filling me until I was gasping breathlessly and clawing at the comforter, legs scything in an attempt to get purchase on the bed, to find a position that allowed me to adjust.

He didn't let me.

I was on my stomach on the bed, the edge of the mattress just at my navel. The bed frame was high enough and I was short enough that this position kept my feet off the floor, kept me off balance and at Duke's mercy. Just the way he liked it, I imagined. He held me up by my hips, keeping my feet from touching the floor. Withdrawing slowly, he paused when just the tip of his cock was left inside me, fluttered there for a moment or two, teasing us both. He adjusted his grip on my hips, lifted me so my hips were off the bed entirely.

And then he slammed into me again, another hard, unexpected

thrust, the slap of our bodies loud in the bedroom.

This time, he didn't slow down when he reached full penetration. I cried out as he slid deep, and then he was fucking me so hard I couldn't catch my breath, his cock driving into me hard and rough and fast. I couldn't keep up, couldn't breathe, couldn't scream, could only claw at the blanket with shaking hands and take his fucking. Never in my life have I felt anything like the way Duke took me, then. I realized that all the guys I'd been with before had been nervous or drunk, usually both, and always hesitant. Because it was *me* they were with, and they wanted to impress and didn't want to assume too much or push things too far, or risk pissing me off; they weren't fucking me, the woman, they were fucking Temple Kennedy, the celebrity.

Duke didn't care. He took me the way he wanted me, hard and fast and rough, and he didn't hesitate, didn't worry about how I'd feel about it. He knew he'd already made me come, and knew he could get me to orgasm again so fast it was kind of stupid…

He took what he wanted, how he wanted it.

In this case, it was me.

And, oh god, it was incredible.

It hurt, but not in a way that made me want to stop. If anything, it made me want more. The way his massive cock split me open and slammed hard all the way into me, pounding my pussy relentlessly… it made something inside me crack open, took the nascent desire I'd always felt, the constant need for sex that I could never quite satisfy, and set fire to it.

And then, just as I was starting to feel the bubble of orgasm, despite the lack of clitoral stimulation, he stopped, buried deep.

"Duke—"

His name was all I managed to get out, and then one of his hands smoothed in a caressing circle over my ass cheek…

Crack!

His palm smacked against my ass with sudden force, spanking me so hard my entire body rocked to the side, my ass quivering and on fire.

"What the fuck!" I gasped, shocked, outraged, and secretly turned on.

He didn't answer, only gripped my hip again and released with the other hand, caressed the opposite cheek.

"Duke, *wait!*" I cried out, but he ignored me.

Crack!

My other ass cheek was now throbbing. He plunged his cock into me once, hard, and I whimpered with the pleasure of his huge, perfect cock sliding into me, and then he spanked my right butt cheek again, fucked into me, spanked the left, fucked...and set a rhythm, a single hard thrust, a spank, a thrust, a spank, until my ass was throbbing and on fire and I was gasping from the breathless ache of it, near tears from the fierce, piercing pain of it, but I couldn't quite bring myself to ask him to stop because it was naughty, it was dirty. What he was doing to me was something I'd never dared do, never thought I'd like, something I'd always been too scared to try. Fuck, I'd never trusted anyone enough to let them do this to me. But I just *knew,* as surely as I knew my own name, that the second Duke sensed I really needed him to stop, he'd stop. No questions asked, no hesitation, no judgement. I didn't even need to test him on it, I just knew.

I lost track of everything except the burning aching throbbing sting of my ass and the pounding thrust of Duke's cock, the crack of his hand across my ass cheeks—

He stopped abruptly.

"Duke, did you—"

He cut me off, once again without words. He lifted me effortlessly, tossed me forward onto the bed, literally tossing me as easily as if I weighed nothing. I hit the mattress, bounced, and rolled to my back, caught sight of him prowling onto the bed after me, huge and powerful and feral, thick cock jutting, slick and wet from my pussy.

"Duke...god, you still haven't come yet?"

He grinned, self-assured, pleased, the grin of a predator with soft, easy prey in sight. "Just gettin' started, Fancy."

"Jesus."

"How's that ass?"

"Stings."

"Good." He lifted up onto his knees. "All fours, babe. Lemme see how red your ass is."

I scrambled away from him—now that I was out of the heat of the moment, my ass was stinging like hell and I wasn't sure I wanted to be spanked any more.

He lifted an eyebrow at me. "You gotta trust me to know what you can take, honey. Now...you gonna do what I'm telling you, or do I have to manhandle you again?"

"Don't spank me anymore," I said.

"I'll do what I want, and you'll like it. If I didn't know you'd like it, I wouldn't do it." He grabbed my ankle and hauled me toward him.

"Duke, I—"

"Get on your hands and knees, Temple." He released my ankle, his expression now unreadable. "Show me your ass."

Normally, I adamantly refused to do anything if it sounded like an order. I did *not* take instructions, I gave them. No one told me what to do. Spoiled brat? That's me. The producers learned early on the best way to get me to work with what they wanted was to ask nicely, to butter me up. Not even my parents could order me around. My boy-toys? Yeah, that's a joke. I told them what to do, got what I wanted from them, and kicked them out. The slightest hint of...well, the exact dominating, macho, me-Tarzan-you-Jane attitude Duke was flashing me right then...and the guy was history.

No one gave me orders, *ever*.

Yet here I was, rolling to my hands and knees, obeying Duke. Presenting my ass to him, baring myself for him, vulnerable, eager to please him.

I watched over my shoulder as he slid his palm against my ass cheek—I flinched in anticipation, and he shot me a shit-eating grin.

"Relax and trust me, Fancy."

I forced myself to remain still as he palmed my ass again. His touch was gentle, in juxtaposition to the merciless spanking he'd administered just moments ago.

"Jesus, Temple. You're...fucking perfect. Have I said that yet?" He used both hands, now, caressing my ass as he had at the very beginning. "Your ass is all red now...even more perfect."

"You've really got a thing for my ass, don't you?"

His lip curled in a snarl. "You have no clue."

Duke shuffled on his knees closer to me. Palmed my ass yet again, caressing from side to the other with one hand, and then sliding his palm up my spine. He gathered my loose, wet hair in his fist. At first, he just gathered it up in a knot, and then released it to slide hand down my spine. He fitted the head of his cock to my slit, using both hands to spread my ass apart, and then slid into me in a smooth, slow glide.

I cried out from the gentle bliss of it. "God, Duke. Your cock feels so good.

"Being inside you...Temple, honey—" he stopped, as if at a loss, gathering my hair into a ponytail, and then wrapped it around his fist. "Fucking you is...god, I'm never tongue-tied. I just don't have words for how good your pussy feels squeezing around my cock."

I felt him tug on my hair, and I shifted backward toward him, taking him deeper, and then I felt him pull out almost all the way, leaving just the tip in, and then with a grunt he fucked into me and yanked my hair to pull me backward. His grip shifted, twisting so his fist was buried against my scalp, tilting my head back. He pushed me down so my face and tits were pressed against the bed, my ass in the air, my pussy impaled on his cock.

He fucked me breathless.

Each jerk of my hair, each slap of his hips against my ass, each drive of his dick into me, and I lost more of my ability to breathe, to function, to think, to do anything except cry out in ecstasy. He fucked me, and he fucked me, and he fucked me, pulling my hair to yank me back into each thrust.

I felt something hot and crazy welling up inside me, something powerful, something enormous. And the harder he fucked me, the hotter and harder it got, spreading through me until I was a wild thing, desperate to reach whatever it was Duke was building inside me with this rough, hair-pulling, spank-my-ass brand of sex.

"Duke…" I breathed. I wasn't sure what I was asking.

He just grunted at me, a feral, brutish snarl of inquisition.

"Please."

"Please what, Princess?"

"I need—" I didn't know what I needed.

"What do you need, honey? Tell me."

"I don't know," I admitted, beginning to writhe back into him, to give in to the need for madness, my fingers clawing into the blanket, slamming back into his thrusts, crying out between desperate gasps. "More of…you…god, I don't know!"

I felt his breath on my ear. "You're perfect, Temple Kennedy," he whispered. "And I know exactly what you need."

"You do?"

"Yeah, babe." He slowed his thrusting, then, skimming both hands down my spine to rest on my ass; I was afraid he was going to spank me again, but all he did was caress me possessively, affectionately. "Touch your pussy for me, gorgeous. I wanna feel you come around my cock."

"I—I want *you* to come," I breathed.

"Oh, I will," he said. "I'll come when you do."

"At the same time?"

"That's the plan," he said. "You ever have a mutual orgasm with anyone?"

"No," I whispered. "Have you?"

"Only once," he admitted, "and finding that again has been a fantasy of mine for a long-ass time."

"And you think we can do that?"

"Fancy, I have absolutely zero doubt."

"Why?"

"Because…" he started, trailing off. He leaned over my back,

JASINDA WILDER

pressing his lips to my ear again. "Because our chemistry is off the fucking charts, Temple. For reasons I can't explain and in ways I don't even understand myself...I just...I *know* you. I know your body. I know what you want when even you don't."

I couldn't deny what he was saying. "We're...there's a connection here, isn't there? That's what you're saying."

Duke's hesitation, then, spoke volumes. He pulled his hips back, paused at the apex of his withdrawal, and then slid back into me, but slowly. Gently. Reverently, almost. Groaning deep in his chest.

"Yes, Temple," he murmured as he filled me. He pulled back again, slowly this time, and when he pushed back in, he did it leaning over me, whispering into my ear, intimate, his voice a rough, ragged and raw. "There's a connection between us. A fucking intense one."

"It scares me," I murmured.

"Me too." Duke's voice was almost inaudible as he whispered this admission. "I've been through a dozen different kinds of hell, so there ain't much that scares me anymore. But babe, this shit between us scares me."

"God, Duke—what's it mean?"

"It means start touching your pussy."

I pressed my cheek into the mattress, letting my head, shoulders, and chest take my weight, and slipped my fingers between my thighs. Found my clit and gave it a hesitant touch; I've never touched myself *during* sex before, only after. That single touch made me flinch hard as searing pleasure shot through me.

"Oh...*fuck*," I grunted.

"You never touch your pussy during sex?" I shook my head, and Duke laughed. "Babe, you've seriously been doing sex all wrong."

"I think I'm starting to agree with you."

"I ain't a facts and trivia sort of dude," Duke said, "but I happen to know that at least eighty percent of women find it difficult if not impossible to reach orgasm without direct clitoral stimulation."

I couldn't help a laugh at hearing Duke—big, muscular, über-macho, all testosterone and guns and protein shakes Duke

Silver—spouting a factoid about female orgasm like some kind of sex nerd.

"It's true," he insisted.

"I'm not laughing because I think you're wrong, I just—it's funny, hearing you say that."

"Why?"

"Because like you said, you're not a random facts kind of guy." I laughed again, but it was breathless, because Duke was thrusting rythmically, slowly and gently, and my fingers were finding the rhythm I needed to reach climax.

"Maybe not, but I am a sex kind of guy, and that's a handy fact to know," he murmured. "Maybe I'm weird about this, but I get off harder when my partner is losing her damn mind. The harder I can make you come, the harder I'll come. So if you're not getting all the pleasure possible when we're fucking, then I'm doing it wrong. Porn's got it all wrong, is what I've learned. That shit is stupid. Women ain't gonna get off just by pounding into 'em like a damn jackhammer."

I realized something else that was weird about having sex with Duke: all the talking. I'm the first to admit that most of the time, I'm a stereotypical motor-mouth blonde, but get me naked and put a dick in me, and I clam up. I just don't know what to say, and don't see the point of all the talking; just fuck me and go away, already.

But, as Duke said, I've been doing sex all wrong, I was realizing.

The problem is, I'm relatively certain at this point that I'll never find anyone equal to Duke in terms of doing it right.

Because HOLY SHIT, this was intense.

I don't have the word to capture what Duke was making me feel, what he was doing to me.

He was fucking me, his cock sliding slowly into my pussy and withdrawing, each wet inch driving raw ecstasy through me filling me, stretching me apart, pushing the ecstasy into something so virulently, violently potent there wasn't really a word for it. Add in the touch of my own fingers on my clit, circling with the precision and rhythm you can only give yourself, and the orgasm slammed through me hard and fast, an abrupt, unstoppable tsunami of spastic bliss.

"Oh fuck, Duke—Jesus, Jesus, I'm coming so hard—" I lost my voice, then, had it stolen by the violence of the climax.

I dissolved into screaming, thrashing madness, slamming back into Duke, and then as I called out my impending orgasm, he started fucking me hard and fast, my fingers a blur on my clit the whole time.

"Duke, I—fuck, ohmyfuckingod—I want you to come with me."

In another of his lightning fast snake-strike moves, he pulled out of me and flipped me to my back. I was left gaping, gasping, curled into a quivering, thigh-trembling mess, mouth open as I fought for breath, pussy clenching at the sudden loss of Duke inside me

"Duke, please, god…please—" I whimpered, reaching for him, not caring how pathetic and desperate and breathy and porn-star whimpery I sounded—that was exactly how I felt.

Duke planted a hand into the mattress beside me, his massive bulk levered over me. His chest blocked out everything, his abs were rippling ridges of iron-hard muscle, his cock was a long, thick, jutting monster, his arms bulging, his hips trim and narrow. His eyes blazed, intense and virile and fiery.

And that was when I realized something that left me shaking: everything up to that point, up until he flipped me to my back, had been the build up.

What was about to happen now…this was the main event.

He was breathing hard, but not just from exertion. His brows were furrowed, his jaw clenched, his expression fierce and primal and possessive and promising dark and dirty and beautiful things I couldn't begin to fathom.

He was on top of me, over me, staring down at me, just breathing, just staring into my eyes for a moment out of time, and I felt the connection we'd both acknowledged snapping and sparking between us, felt it as real and physical as an electric shock; that moment, no part of our bodies touching, just our eyes meeting…

It felt like gripping a live power cable, it felt like a million joules coursing through me.

"Duke," I whispered.

And then he pounced.

He stroked my slit, guiding himself into me, and then bracing himself with both hands. I cried out in relief as he filled me, and this time I had his eyes, had his open, unguarded expression to go with the physical sensation, and I knew then that I'd never feel anything like this singular moment ever again, his eyes spearing into me, his cock sliding deep, gliding into me, the real and undeniable emotional or psychological or whatever it was connection crackling between us.

But I was wrong.

It got even more intense:

He kissed me.

Good god, he kissed me like I've never been kissed before.

And now he was inside me, and he was kissing me. He was moving, thrusting, filling me and withdrawing and pushing in and dragging out and his tongue was tangling with mine and he was moaning into my mouth as he moved, as we moved together.

Because this was…

Something totally other than sex.

More.

So much *more*.

I wrapped my legs around his waist, discovering that I had hands, and that I wanted to touch him. My hands scoured his skin, clawed down his shoulders and raked his sides. I ripped his topknot out and ran my fingers through his soft silk hair and cupped the back of his head and grabbed his ass and dug my fingers into the hard muscle around his spine, and all the while I was discovering as well that my hips had a mind of their own.

I was utterly wild.

We couldn't sustain the kiss any longer, then, and I was the first to break away, gasping on a sob. I promptly bit his shoulder and cried out, teeth latched onto the thick trapezius muscles.

"Temple—" he snarled, sounding as stunned and breathless as I was.

"Don't—don't ever stop, Duke," I said, and then kissed him where my teeth had left red marks on his pale skin. "God, please don't stop."

I forced my gaze up to his, and found what I was looking for, what I'd always been looking for, without ever realizing it: A man, powerful, confident—arrogant, even—completely focused on me without being intimidated by me…who could fuck me senseless and push me out of my boundaries, and yet, in that moment, he was completely vulnerable.

I saw his fear at how intense this was, and I knew it was everything to him that it was to me. I saw his need…for *me*. I saw his desire for me, which was a separate thing from the need.

I reached up, clutched the back of his neck, and pulled his face down to mine. Touched my lips to the shell of his ear. Cupped his pumping, pulsing ass in my other hand, heels hooking around the backs of his thighs just beneath his buttocks.

I whispered in his ear: "Let go, Duke."

I felt another orgasm boiling up deep inside me. I let go of his butt and wedged that hand between our bodies, touched my clit, felt the white-hot lightning slice through me at my touch, spasms seizing my belly and my legs and my core. My thighs trembled and my hand clamped down on Duke's neck, clutching as hard as I could.

"Duke—let go, baby." I bit his lower lip, writhing my hips against his, taking his cock as deep as it would with each slow thrust. "Let go with me. I'm gonna come again. Come with me."

"Temple—" he growled, and one of his hands brushed across my breasts and then found my free hand and our fingers tangled together stretched out over our heads. "Fuck, fuck. Temple—Jesus."

I squeezed his hand, clamping down as we ground our bodies together, the room echoing with the sound of our grunts and sighs and the wet sucking slapping.

I felt him begin to lose control, then. His fucking thrusts lost their machine-like rhythm and his breathing went ragged and he was grunting and groaning. Each thrust was magic, filling me, stretching me, and my fingers were crazy on my clit and he was slamming hard and fast now.

"Yes, Duke, Duke, god, keep fucking me. Come with me, Duke."

I felt the orgasm rip apart inside me, felt my pussy squeeze around his cock, and I wrapped around him, yanked my hand free of his and curled my legs around his waist and clawed my fingernails down his back as I came with such intensity that tears started in my eyes and the waves of climax physically wracked me and my voice was hoarse from shrill breathless screams.

"Holy shit, Temple—*Temple*," Duke gasped, awed, reverent, stunned.

"Oh god, oh god, oh god, oh god!" I cried out, "come with me, Duke, now, come with me *now!*"

"Now, Temple. Do you feel me?" He wedged a hand under my head and jerked me up, his lips smashing against mine, his mouth trembling, his breath coming ragged.

He wrapped his other hand under my ass and lifted me up bodily so he was upright on his knees and I was impaled on his cock and he was holding me clenched against his body, his face buried in the side of my neck, his hips swiveling, his cock drilling up into me. I clung to him and hooked my feet together behind his back, lifting myself up and letting myself fall onto him, my lips at his ear, my teeth scraping, breath stuttering in gasping whimpers.

"I feel you," I whispered. "I feel *us*."

"Us," he repeated.

"Us."

He pulled his head back far enough that he could meet my eyes. And that was when he came. He released with a bellow, an animal growl, and even through the condom I felt the power of his orgasm. He slammed up into me hard, hard, so fucking hard, his hips slapping up against my ass, his hands clutching my buttocks and spreading them apart so his thrusts drove deeper than ever, fucking as deep as he could go, and now as he came his thrusts went staccato, more powerful then ever but arrhythmic.

"Temple—Temple—*Temple*—" he chanted my name as he fucked me, but I knew this was so much more than fucking, infinitely more, because neither of us dared look away.

He poured himself into me with his eyes open and boring into mine, and I came around him, quaking and shuddering and gasping and whimpering and sobbing, feeling my tits bounce with each powerful thrust.

He finally finished his orgasm, and allowed us to fall to the bed, me on my back, and him above me.

I buried my hands in his hair, tangling my fingers tight against his scalp and yanked him down to me and kissed him, biting his lip and demanding his tongue, my pussy spasming around his cock. He shuddered, hips still flexing out of involuntary reflex, and his moan as I kissed him came from the depths of his soul, as did the sob from me.

A long moment spent kissing and shuddering and shivering together, and then he flopped to one side, pulling out of me, and then cradling me in his arms. I curled against him automatically, as if it was the most natural thing in the world to snuggle against his chest, my thigh across his, my hand on his belly, low, just above the slackening, condom-sheathed length of his cock. The tip of the condom was heavy with his come, and his breath came in ragged heaves.

"Jesus," he gasped, after a moment. "That was…"

"I had no idea," I said.

He swiveled his head to look at me. "Me either."

"So the one mutual orgasm you had—"

"Was a firecracker in comparison to what we just did together," he finished for me. "That was…nuclear. I don't know any other word for it."

"It's not just that I've never felt anything like that before," I said. "Which is true, but everything I've done with you so far is just…new, and different, and better. This was…fuck. I don't even know how to

say it. It was just...I didn't even know it was possible for sex to be...
just—"

"So much *more*, in every single way?"

I nodded, and then, for some reason, kissed his chest. Once my
lips found his skin, I couldn't quite stop them from exploring. First
I kissed his chest, the flat hard bulge of his pec, and then across between them, leaning over him, pressing against him.

"Temple?" He seemed as confused as I was by what I was doing.

I looked up at him. "I don't know what I'm doing. Not with any
of this."

"Me either," he answered, "but...keep going."

9

TAKEN

Holy shit. Just…holy fucking shit. We'd *cuddled*. I'd never done that. Never. Once the chick and I were finished, I wouldn't necessarily just bounce out of there or kick her out, but I sure as hell didn't fucking *snuggle*. But with Temple, it just felt like the easiest, most natural thing in the world to snug her into my arms against my chest and hold here there. And the weirdest fucking part was that it didn't feel weird at all.

And then she started kissing my chest. Like, what the fuck? But it felt…incredible. Not sexual, but…affectionate. Still erotic, but in a tender way. And I *liked* it. I wanted her to keep doing it. So I touched her wherever I could reach her as she moved over me, kissing my skin. I caressed her shoulder, her hair, her waist, as she gradually moved closer and closer to me, moving more and more on top of me, her mouth exploring my body. She started at my chest, and then moved to my ribs, then up to my opposite shoulder, and by that point she was basically laying on top of me. Her hands were busy too, just sliding and touching and clutching. Her lips found my neck, my throat, underneath my chin—and god, that, her lips kissing the soft underside of my jaw, it was so crazy intensely personal and just so…*much*—for lack of a better word—that I couldn't breathe. Then,

Jesus, then her lips stuttered and jumped and flicked over my jawline and up to my cheek, kissing, cheek to cheekbone and then to just this side of my ear, her breath loud and hot on my ear. I had a double handful of her ass, clutching and kneading, and then as her kisses went up to my face and my hands slid, of their volition, up to her back and into her hair.

Temple kept going, her lips touching delicately to my eyes, down the side of my nose, to my mouth. Her breasts were flattened against my chest, her stomach on my waist, her body diagonal to mine. And her hands? One was on my chest, just resting, and the other was stroking my thighs and exploring my abs, deliberately ignoring my cock in a way which told me that was exactly what she was thinking about.

She finally pressed her mouth to mine, her breath warm on my lips, and then her teeth clacked against mine and her tongue slid between my teeth and the kiss was slow and hesitant and taut with so much intensity both of us shook from the potency of it.

And then Temple broke the kiss and looked down my body. She sat up, glanced at me, and then back to my cock. With two fingers she angled my still-slack dick away from my body, circled those two fingers around me at the root, and with her other hand she carefully and slowly peeled the condom off of me. Sliding off the bed, she went into the adjoining bathroom with the condom, her beautiful, pale, juicy round ass swaying and jiggling with each step. The view as she walked back toward me was just as incredible: her tits bouncing and swaying, her pussy playing peekaboo at each step, her body trim and strong and lithe, yet with enough flesh and curves and bounce to make my mouth water and my cock sit up and take notice…and her face, goddamn, her face. Those eyes, bright blue streaked with brown and green, fierce and wild and intense and playful, her features so perfect, so fucking beautiful, so lovely. There was a reason she was as famous as she was—Temple Kennedy was the most beautiful woman I'd ever seen, even just from the shoulders up…include the erotic perfection of her goddess body, and she became every man's fantasy.

And she was with me, naked for me. Climbing into bed with *me*.

She'd come all over me, clung to me, chanted my name as we fucked—

Not fucked. It wasn't just fucking. It was—god, I wish I had a word for it.

Except for the obvious word, of course, the word I've never said, never heard spoken to me, a concept I've never believed in. Was it that? I refused to even think the word, but I could skirt around it mentally as I watched Temple sway and bounce from the bathroom back to the bed.

Was it *that* word?

Fuck…it was. I mean, as far as I could tell, that's what this was. The most cliché shit in the world: one amazing fuck with the right woman, and I was falling for her. And yeah, I was acutely aware that she was falling for me.

Just go with it, Thresh had said. *Don't fight it. There's no point.*

The right girl, she'll make you feel like more of a man, not less.

Just go with it.

But…how? I couldn't even think the L-word, much less say it. Plus, it was fucking nuts. I just met the woman. It's not possible. Insta-love isn't real. You don't just meet someone and fall in love that same day—even after a day like the one we've had.

You don't know shit.

Temple was on the bed, crawling for me on all fours. Breasts swaying beneath her, hair falling in blonde waves on either side of her gorgeous face. When she reached my thighs, she stopped.

"Now…where was I?" she asked.

I swallowed hard. "Kissing me."

"Where?"

I tapped my lips. "Here."

She grinned. "Oh…yeah. That's right." She ran her palms up my thighs. "I'm thinking maybe I'll start over…down here."

And she kissed my thigh, just above my kneecap. And then higher. She pushed my other leg aside, and kissed around toward the inside of my thigh, her hands on either side of her mouth, fingernails gently scraping as she slid upward, kissing. It was hard to breathe when she did that, when she kissed me like that. Made it hard to think.

"Temple—what are you doing to me?" I heard myself say.

"Kissing you," she answered, the words huffing against my inner thigh, inches from my balls. "Kissing you everywhere."

"You're making me crazy."

"Good. I like it when you're crazy."

"But I don't—I don't know how to handle it. It's—fuck. It's crazy." I gasped helplessly as she breathed a hot breath across my balls and then kissed my opposite thigh mere millimeters away. "It's too much."

One hand on each thigh, lips traipsing and teasing and kissing toward my hip, she paused when she reached my hipbone, glancing up at me. "Too much, huh?"

"Yeah. I don't know—It's fucking crazy."

She laughed. "So you've said."

"It's—it's the *way* you're kissing me. It's not just the teasing, it's—"

Her eyes found mine, knife sharp and intense and fierce. "It's *us*, Duke. That's what you can't handle. The way I'm kissing you? It's because I'm kissing you like I…" she trailed off, swallowing hard.

"Don't say it, Temple."

"But that's what it is, isn't it?"

"Yeah, but…fuck. That's what it is, and I know it, you know it, we both know it. But that doesn't mean we have to say it. We can acknowledge it, but we don't have to say it."

I was worried she'd take it the wrong way, thinking I was afraid of her, or of the word, or of commitment. And really, that's what it was, that's exactly what it was, all of it, and as soon as the words left my mouth, I felt panic hit, fear that she'd miss the deeper truth of what I was saying.

"I know you're afraid of this—"

"One thing you should know about me is that I never back down from a challenge," I said, interrupting her. "If I discover something I'm afraid of, I face it. I take it on, and I defeat it."

"I wasn't doubting—"

I brushed my thumb across her cheekbone. "My point is that fear doesn't stop me. It doesn't rule me, doesn't own me." I made sure she saw my eyes; saw the truth in my gaze. "Yeah, this shit between us scares me. But that won't hold me back, Temple. I just—I'm not quite ready yet, even if I see things for what they are."

Temple's eyes watered, and she blinked hard. "Duke, I—"

"You don't have to say anything, Temple. I just wanted to clarify."

She laughed. "You need to learn to let me get a word in edgewise every now and then."

Her hands resumed their exploratory caressing of my thighs, sliding up to cup the sides of my hips and brush the outsides of my buttocks and then tracing back down toward my knees, and then up again, her hands brushing inches from my cock, which was beginning to regain feeling, blood pumping through me and into my eager-for-more dick.

I held still, letting Temple do what she wanted, curious to see where she'd take this.

When I didn't say anything else, she pressed a slow, damp kiss to the inside of my left thigh, so close to my groin now that her cheek brushed my balls as she kissed my leg. "What I was going to say, before you interrupted me, was that I know you're afraid of this thing we've got, and so am I. And I agree. We don't have to make it...*that*. It's more than just fucking, but it doesn't have to be labeled. Not yet. I'm not ready for that, either."

I let out a sigh of relief. "Thank god."

"It's crazy," she said, "but it's real, too, and I'm not going to pretend otherwise."

I gasped again as she slid her mouth over my flesh up from inner thigh along my balls and the root of my cock to my belly, her cheek brushing me, her mouth leaving a wet trail along my skin. My cock was hardening, now, but she ignored it even though it was thickening and straightening against the side of her face. She kissed my belly just above the root of my cock, nudging my shaft out of the way with her cheek, and her hands caressed my abs, then slid down to follow the progress of her mouth, a hand on either side of her face. My cock was resting on top of the back of her hand, and now her mouth lifted and crossed over my dick and landed on my belly on the other side, kissing across to my hip, down to my thigh, and then back across to press light, wet, teasing, tongue-flicking kisses at the tender, sensitive crease where my balls met my body.

"Temple—" I wasn't sure what her game was, but it felt incredible.

I was fully hard now, and she'd only touched my cock incidentally.

"Hush." She slid up my body to lean over me, tips of her tits grazing my chest, and pressed two fingers to my lips. "Just…hold still and shut up."

I tucked my hands behind my head. "You got it, Fancy."

She kissed her way back down and then she glanced up at me, and then back to my cock, a smile spreading across her lips. Inching closer, she moved upward and opened her mouth, glancing up at me, so close to taking me in her mouth now that I was tensed, abs drawn inward in anticipation.

"That's what you want?" she breathed.

"Fuck yeah," I growled.

She slid downward again; still so close I could feel her breath on my skin. Her hands scraped over my flesh on either side of my dick, and her mouth was opening and her tongue was snaking out to flick against the taut, sensitive flesh of my testicle. "How about that?"

"God. Yeah, Princess. That too. Anything. Jesus, anything."

"You want this?" She flattened her hand palm down and rubbed it up the length of my cock. "Want me to touch you?"

I couldn't help flexing my hips. "Fuck—*fuck*…yeah."

Her tongue flickered out again, and then her lips pressed an almost-kiss to the outside of my sac. "You want me to take your balls in my mouth?"

I was beyond words already, incapable of much more than an

unintelligible grunt. "Unh…yeah…just like that—"

She scraped the length of my cock from tip to root with a finger-nail, and kissed my sac again, a slow, wet, full kiss. "I think I might like a little begging. You made me beg, well…how's that phrase go? Turnabout is fair play?"

I laughed, and the laugh turned to a groan as she teased another not quite touch along my cock and flicked her tongue against my sac yet again. "Fuck, Temple."

I didn't beg. I'd never begged anyone for anything in my life.

But when I hesitated, she took her hand away from my dick and moved her mouth away, went back to teasing, sliding her hand over my abs, close to my cock but not touching it, kissing just *this* close to my balls, but not quite there.

And just like that, I realized I really would do anything for this girl. I'd cross every line I'd never been willing to cross for anyone else.

Her eyes were on me, watching me process through it; she had a small, secret smile curving the perfect cupid's bow of her lips. "Well?" She moved her mouth over me, breathing on my balls, up my shaft, then pressed her cheek to my belly so her mouth was in position to take me in, teasing, tongue flicking out against my tip. She made her voice deep, *"Please, Temple, I'm begging you. Take my balls in your mouth. Please, please, put your hands on my big monster cock."*

I laughed, struggling to keep still, fighting the urge to pounce on her and make *her* beg. I wanted to pin her against the wall and fuck her senseless, wanted to pin her hands over her head and fuck her so slowly she'd beg me to let her come. Instead, I listened to Thresh's advice: I went with it.

"Temple, please. Touch me. Lick me, suck me, fuck me. Do whatever you want, just…please touch me." I wasn't faking it, wasn't pretending, wasn't just saying what she wanted to hear; I genuinely, deeply wanted to know what *she* wanted to do to me, wanted to feel what she wanted to give me. "I'm begging you Temple. Please, *please* touch me."

Her grin was ear-to-ear, pleased, thrilled, and still erotic. She took my cock in her mouth, and then immediately backed away, making a face. "Mmm—yuck...you taste like condom."

"Shit, I guess I would, huh?"

Temple wrapped both hands around my shaft and stroked me tip to root, slowly. "That's okay, because I can still do this..." and she twisted her hands slowly in opposite directions as she stroked me, over and over. "And this..." and then she took my sac into her mouth, bit by bit at first, just one side, kissing the flesh, tonguing me.

Then, as her fists slid up my cock and plunged back down, she took more of my balls into her mouth and then back out. One of her hands cupped them, lifting them, caressing, and kept kissing and tonguing and taking the taut sensitive sac into her mouth; all the while her other hand was squeezing my cock, twisting around the head, brushing her thumb over the tip and then plunging down.

It didn't take long before I was fighting the urge to flex my hips, to fuck her hand, to make the push for orgasm.

Only...Temple knew. She felt it, felt me tensing, felt something less tangible.

The moment I felt that urge, she was crawling up toward the head of the bed, snagging a condom from the string and tearing it open. Kneeling beside me, she rolled it down my shaft,.

"I need you inside me again, Duke," she murmured. "But I want to do it my way, this time."

"This is all you," I said. "Whatever you want, anything you want."

"Don't move. Don't touch me. Just...lay there."

I couldn't help a grin. "Won't work, sweetheart."

She frowned in confusion. "What won't?"

"Sex won't ever be the same, now," I said. "You won't be able to just fuck me and be done. It's gonna end up being more, just like it was before."

The smile that spread across her face then was sultry and secretive. "Oh, that's not what I'm gonna do."

"No?"

She shook her head, blond waves swaying. "Nope. I just want to make you…crazy. You like to be in control, you like to make sure I know who's the boss. Well, I want *you* to know the same thing. You might be Mr. Big Macho Commando guy, but I'm Temple Kennedy. And you're gonna let me take you *my* way."

There was no guile or falseness in my next words. "I'm yours to take, Temple. Show me your way."

She swung astride me like I was a horse, her hands bracing on my chest. Lifting up, she glided her pussy against my cock, grinding against me lightly, hips pivoting back and forth over me. Up, then, leaning over me, draping her breasts against my chest, pussy writhing against my abs. Higher, higher, fists in the pillow and her pussy on my diaphragm, dragging her big, round, silk-soft tits against my face, brushing me with them, rubbing one nipple against my mouth, over my lips, then the other.

God*damn*, I wanted those tits in my hands, wanted to suckle those thick nipples into my mouth. I even let my hands come out from beneath my head, reaching for her.

"Ah-ah," she scolded, backing out of reach. "No touching. Not till I say you can."

I laced my fingers together beneath my head and forced myself to lay still. She pressed her slit along my shaft, ground herself against me, sliding the length of me through her damp opening. And again, instinct and need crashed through me, driving me to lift my hips, to try and get my cock inside her, to grab her hips and push into her—but I force myself into stillness with great difficulty.

"Fuck, Temple. You're killing me."

She leaned over me, face inches from mine, eyes on me, hot and sultry and fiercely erotic—her mouth drifted close to mine, and her tongue flicked over my lips, and then she teased a kiss to my lips. But before I could appreciate the softness of her mouth, the warmth of her breath, she was moving away, not quite kissing the corner of my mouth, and all the while her hips were driving back and forth, teasing, and grinding the length of my shaft between the plump damp lips of her pussy.

A moan left her, and I realized then that this was as much tease and torture for her as it was me; somehow that made it easier to bear, and it was more erotic than ever, knowing how badly she wanted me and yet was still denying us both. The thrill was heightened; the intensity ramped up to insanity.

She ground hard against me, pressing her pussy against my cock, rocking, seeking the perfect angle. Her hands were on my chest, her head hanging, eyes closed, mouth partially open, lips quivering. Her thighs quaked, and her tits shook. She kept rocking against me, shifting angles now and then, leaning forward then backward, tilting her hips. She was looking for the angle that would let her grind my cock against her clit so she could come, I realized.

"Why don't you just—" I started, but she had other ideas that didn't include me talking.

When I started talking, she lifted up and leaned forward to drape her breast against my face, dragging her erect nipple from my forehead my down to my lips, pressing her tit into my mouth to shut me up. I moaned in sheer bliss at the taste of her flesh, at the feel of all that soft, generous skin against my face…and then I moaned again because she'd taken my cock at the base and pulled it away from my body and was using me as a dildo. She pulled my cock in circles, rubbing the head against her clit, and immediately her moans turned to whimpers and her hips began gyrating as she toppled toward climax. I gritted my teeth and held everything back as hard as I could, focusing on lavishing worship on her tits. She let me suck and nip and lick at her left breast for a few moments and then slid her right tit into my mouth, arching her spine to press herself against me, both of her hands braced on my shoulders, fingernails digging into flesh and muscle sharply enough that I knew I'd have marks later—which I'd wear with pride.

"Duke—" she gasped, hips pivoting back and forth wildly, her fist around my cock grinding the head against her clit faster and faster.

It took everything I had to keep still, to hold back my own

impending orgasm, to stop myself from crushing into her and taking her the way I wanted.

This was better. She was moaning breathlessly, head hanging, hair a damp blond curtain obscuring her features as she writhed on top of me, using me to get herself off. She was seconds from coming—I could tell by the way she moved, the jerky, uncontrolled gyrations of her hips, the way her moans were turning to those high-pitched, out of breath shrieks.

"Oh god, Duke, I'm gonna come. Fuck, I'm coming, I'm coming—oh god, oh god, oh my god...*Duke*!"

At the moment of her orgasm, as she shrieked my name, she impaled herself on my cock, slamming her ass down onto me and collapsing forward onto my chest, her lips crushed against my cheek, her hands sliding under my head to clasp her arms around me in a desperate, trembling embrace. I couldn't help it, then; I grabbed a double handful of her ass and bit her earlobe and groaned as I felt her tight pussy clamp down around me, hot and wet and pulsating as she orgasmed above me. She clung to me for a moment, just like that, my cock buried deep, her face against mine, her breath ragged, her whole body trembling on top of mine.

"Don't come yet, Duke," she murmured. "I'm not done with you yet."

"You're making it damn near impossible," I said.

She pulled back from me, took my hands and pressed them over my head once more. "That's the point," she said, lifting up so I flopped out of her slit and slapped against my belly. She pivoted on me, so she was facing my feet, now, rose up on her knees and braced her hands on my thighs, pulled my cock away from my belly and slid me into her pussy. Starting slowly, Temple began to ride me, lifting up, pausing, and then slamming her ass down on me; I was utterly hypnotized by the way her ass moved, watching my cock disappear inside her as she lowered herself onto me, and then the way the generous flesh rippled and jiggled as her beautiful ass slapped against my hips.

"So fucking gorgeous," I said, unable to help myself.

Temple didn't respond with words, but the way she whimpered and started riding me harder told me she'd heard me, and what those words meant to her.

"I need to move, baby," I said, helpless to stop my hips from pumping with her sensual rhythm.

"No," she gasped. "Don't move."

"Fuck." I grabbed a double fistful of the pillow under my head, gritted my teeth, and held still.

Her pace was frantic, and it took every last ounce of control and restraint I possessed to hold back my orgasm as Temple rode me. She leaned back so she was sitting up on top of me with her shins beneath her, rolling her hips in wide, exaggerated circles. Her hands went to her pussy, one hand spreading those plump pink lips apart, the other tapping her clit a few times before rubbing in circles. This was when I discovered something I hadn't noticed until just then: there was a mirror on the bureau opposite the bed, giving me a perfect view of the front of Temple as she rode and masturbated herself to another climax.

Fuck—I could see *everything*, her tits jouncing as she began bouncing on me, her pussy stretched out to accommodate my cock, the way my shaft slid into her and reappeared, her fingers a blur on her clit…

Heat boiled inside me, a violent pressure aching in my balls, a fierce desperation pounding through my cock.

"I have to come, Temple. I can't hold it anymore," I said, "I just can't."

"Not yet, Duke," she gasped. "Wait for me."

"Fuck, honey, I'm trying."

"I'm almost there," she murmured, riding me hard and fast, her fingers circling crazily.

It hurt, fuck, it hurt to keep holding back like this. My balls were about to explode, the pressure inside too much to bear, the need to come too powerful.

I felt my hips begin to move on their own. "I can't, baby, I can't wait anymore. I gotta—Jesus, Temple, fuck, I need to come."

"Wait for me, Duke, I'm almost there!"

I was clamping down with everything I had, every muscle tensed, head thrown back, spine arched, even my toes were curling and my jaw was grinding so hard I worried I was gonna crack a tooth.

"Oh fuck—fuck!" Temple screamed, falling backward onto me, her back to my front. "*Now*, Duke! Ohmygod I'm coming! I'm coming!" The last words were a sob as she reached back to find my hands with one of hers, her other still flicking back and forth across her clit as fast as she could.

"Watch us in the mirror, Temple," I said through clenched teeth. "Watch us come together."

I saw her eyes flick open, meeting mine in the mirror, and now we both watched as we came apart in unison.

My fingers tangled with hers, and I bellowed in pure relief and utter euphoria as I let myself go. I fucked her with everything I possessed, then, my hips slamming up to meet hers as she bounced down onto me. Her face was beside mine, then, and her mouth slid across my cheek and I turned to meet her mouth, our lips and teeth clashing in a frantic, gasping kiss.

I came within three thrusts. Our kiss became a mutual, shared groan, teeth clicking together, breath mingling and moans echoing as I fucked through my orgasm, feeling her pussy squeeze around me with impossible, unbelievable force.

I poured myself into her, into the condom, one hand tangled with hers, my other roaming her body, cupping her tits and gripping a rough handful of her hip, then knocking her hand away to take over flicking her clit, my orgasm still powering through me in wave after wrenching wave.

After a long minute or two of spasming, gasping ecstasy, Temple finally went limp on top of me, my cock still throbbing inside her, our synched breathing coming in ragged gasps.

There was a world of thought and emotion barreling though me, then. "Temple, I—" I started, intending to put some of it into words.

She shifted up my body so I slipped out of her, and then rolled to lie on top of me once more, her breasts flattened against my chest, her hair cascading over one shoulder.

Searching my eyes, she cupped my face in both hands, her brows drawn down in a frown of deep, emotive, intensity. Her mouth opened, which is why I stopped, thinking she had something to say. Instead, she claimed my mouth with hers, and this was the first kiss we'd shared outside the fury of sex.

For the first time in my life, I finally understood what real, true, soul-deep passion was; I found it in that kiss.

As earth shaking, soul-shattering as the sex had been, that kiss was more. I wanted the kiss to last forever. I buried my hand in her hair at the back of her head and kept her locked into the kiss, pulled her closer, deepening the kiss until it was all consuming, until it felt like something inside me was melting and seeping into her and merging with her. It became something more than just a kiss, then.

The whole "becoming one flesh" thing from the Bible? Yeah, I finally got it. Hey, when you do things I've done, seen the things I've seen, you look for absolution anywhere you can find it. I've spent my fair share of between-ops downtime in the chapel, talking to the chaplain and leafing through an old Bible, wondering if it really had useful answers in it. I can't say I really found what I was looking for, but then, I'm not sure it exists.

Shit, I'm getting off-topic. My point is, when Temple kissed me, there in Harris and Layla's extra bedroom, I finally understood what it meant to become one flesh. I always assumed it was a reference to fucking, right? Dick goes in the pussy, and bam, you're "united", and you two have technically merged, sort of. Kind of dramatic, but whatever, it was a less explicit way of talking about sex.

But no, that's not it at all. Not even close.

Sex, fucking, banging—it's just body parts and a few minutes of feeling great with someone sexy. Of all the women I've ever banged—and that number is higher than I care to think about—I've never felt like she and I were…*one*, like we'd become something more than just the sum of our two bodies and souls. Shit, I rarely ever even thought about souls. Sex was just sex. I loved women, I loved their bodies, their curves, the softness of their flesh and the way they look beneath me or above me, I love watching them squirm and hearing them scream when I eat them out, and I love feeling them come apart in my hands.

But souls? Becoming one? Passion? Nah, man, I'm good.

And then Temple Kennedy kissed me, and I just got it. Fancy-shit writers would probably say I'd had an epiphany, and they wouldn't be wrong. That's what it was.

Becoming one flesh? It's when something inside you opens up and reaches out and becomes part of the other person. It's when sex and kissing and touching and holding each other just aren't enough, like you want to somehow just…fuck, I don't know how to put it. It's…it's when no matter how deep you are inside her, no matter how hard you kiss her, it's not enough. It's when you feel her heart, her metaphysical heart, the very essence of who she is, becoming inextricably interwoven into who you are, just from the kissing, the fucking, the touching, the holding and moving together and breathing each other's breath.

That's what it is, and that's what I discovered when Temple kissed me.

The moment was broken by the sound of an explosion—

BOOM!

The explosion was a thin, distant crumping of explosives.

And then I heard Anselm firing—***BOOM!***—the report a deep, shaking, shuddering, echoing roll of fifty-caliber thunder. I knew the sound of that Barrett as well as I knew my own reflection in the mirror; once you've heard that big fucking rifle, you never forget it.

"Fuck." I broke the kiss, whispering the epithet. "Sounds like we've got company."

BOOM! BOOM!…BOOM!

I rolled to set Temple aside, scrambling out of bed as fast as

I could. I'd discarded the condom and was dressed in thirty seconds flat, stomping into my boots and tying the laces in a blur of movement.

The walkie crackled from my hip pocket where I'd stuffed it in my hurry to get naked. "*Sie sind hier,*" Anselm said, reverting to German—*they're here.*

"How many?" I asked, shrugging into the double shoulder holster harness and buckling it in place.

"*Zu viele.*" His Barrett cracked twice more—*too many,* that meant. That was six shots, which meant six kills—Anselm never missed, ever.

"How fucking many, goddammit?"

"I don't know!" Anselm actually shouted back at me, which stunned me motionless. "A fucking shit load of them, *mein Freund.* Twenty? Thirty?"

I was out the bedroom door with the Mossberg, and then stopped abruptly. Temple was dressed by then—wearing the clothes borrowed from Layla—and was hustling after me. I shoved the shotgun into her hands.

"Hide in the bathroom and lock the door." I guided her toward the bathroom, gave her the walkie talkie, and emptied my pockets of shotgun shells. "Shoot first and ask questions later. If it's me or Anselm, we'll identify ourselves. Anyone else, blast 'em."

"I don't know how to shoot a gun!"

I was already backing out of the bathroom. "Keep a good grip on it, that fucker kicks like a howitzer. Tuck the butt tight against your shoulder and squeeze the trigger. Don't close your eyes, don't try to aim. Just go for the belly and you'll get close enough."

"But...but, Duke! I—I can't—don't leave me!"

I leaned back in and kissed her quickly. "You can. You have to. There's too many of them out there for me to have the luxury of thinking about you. You're safe in here. I'll have a radio too, but don't contact me unless you have to. Okay? You'll be fine, I'll be fine, everything will be fine. But I gotta go."

Anselm's Barrett was blasting nonstop, and I heard return fire, small arms, mostly. There was the sharp crack of a .308, which worried me.

Anselm was too good to be caught in a sniper's crosshairs, but it meant they'd seen the muzzle flash and had a lock on his position. Which meant I really had to move—I'd already wasted too much time.

I cursed myself for getting so caught up in Temple that I missed their arrival, but really, deep down, I couldn't regret it, not after what we'd shared.

I scrambled for the AR-15, then ripped open the duffel bag and slung the HK MP7 over my shoulder. I had magazines in my pockets for both and another flash bang. I wish I had my body armor, which was back at HQ—I thought Anselm had gone to grab it, but I guess he got sidetracked. I grabbed a radio from the rack and set up the earpiece and throat mic, then peeked out one of the front windows, using the frame as cover. A Suburban was hauling ass toward the house, still a good half-mile away, just emerging from the shroud of trees that lined the fence, followed by one of the big tricked out Wranglers like I'd stolen, plus what looked like a Hummer. There were more vehicles behind those, but I couldn't make out what they were, and it didn't really matter.

I heard the Barrett, and the hood of the lead Suburban crumpled, the front end slamming down into the dirt road. The Wrangler behind it gunned its engine and veered around it adroitly. The Suburban flipped, twisted, and rolled to one side, glass shattering.

"I need your backup now, Duke," Anselm said over the radio. "The fun is about to begin."

"How the fuck did they get here so fast?" I demanded. "And how'd they get in the gate?"

"It's been an hour," Anselm said, a note of amusement in his voice. "I left your gear by the kitchen door."

"An hour?" I exclaimed. "I had no idea. I didn't hear you come in," I said, running for the kitchen.

"It is not so surprising you couldn't hear me. You and the lovely Miss Kennedy were rather…occupied." A pause, and then another blast of his rifle, and then his voice in my earpiece. "They brought explosives, blasted the gate open."

That explained the first explosion I heard.

He'd brought my body armor, a bandolier of grenades, and my favorite personal weapon, an M4 carbine with the M203 grenade launcher attached to the rail. Fuck yeah. I tossed the AR-15 aside and checked my rifle—loaded, grenade in the chamber, charged, plus a stack of pre-loaded magazines. I geared up in record time. My armor had double handgun holsters already attached, so it was a matter of stuffing the nines from holster to holster, and then I was out the kitchen door.

Anselm was still cracking off shots. I trotted around to the front corner, took a knee, and scanned the scene with the optical scope. Anselm was picking off the survivors crawling out of the Suburban, and he'd also taken out the Wrangler, but there were still two…no, three…shit, *four* more vehicles behind that. The Suburban held eight, most of the others four or five…Anselm's estimation of twenty or thirty was on the nose.

The four remaining undamaged vehicles skidded to a halt three hundred meters from the house forming a U with the opening facing the road. The doors opened and operatives in full gear poured out, each armed with carbines or HKs. I still heard that .308 cracking, but couldn't see where it was coming from.

"You have a lock on that rifle?" I asked, the throat mic keying to pick up the vibrations when I spoke.

"*Nein*," Anselm answered. "But he is only guessing at my location, and I am in motion. He is no worry—I will find him. You worry about evening the odds."

I tilted the rifle and squeezed the trigger of the 203—the carbine gave a hefty kick and there was a hollow metallic *thunk* as the round left the chamber, then a pause of a few seconds, and then the center-most vehicle, a Hummer, exploded with a deafening *crump*. Orange flames billowed and the vehicle rocked skyward then crashed back down. Men shouted and screamed, scattering—making my job easier. I pinned the optics on a running operative, squeezed off a few rounds, and then shifted aim, fired again.

Anselm had set a pattern: fire three times, move positions, and fire three times. I knew his patterns, and knew he wouldn't be moving in any predictable patterns, sometimes running a hundred meters to a new spot, and sometimes just shifting half a dozen or so meters. We worked in synch, then, Anselm plugging operative after operative, one shot one kill, then going silent as he moved to a new position. While he was moving, I'd open fire, picking a target and firing in three-round bursts.

It took nearly a minute for Cain's mercenaries to figure out my location—and then they opened fire on the house almost as one man, rifles chattering, rounds smacking into the wood siding. Sloppy bastards, taking that long to peg my location. I ducked back out of view, switched mags, loaded another round into the launcher, and scanned for a secondary firing position. Harris had cleared the area around the house, so there wasn't much; this was intentional, meant to put anyone approaching the house from any direction out in the open, but it also meant there wasn't much cover for me either.

Nothing for it. I'd have to just make do with what I had.

I edged to the corner again, peeked, and then rolled out to squeeze off a couple bursts, rolled back behind the corner. Rounds thunked and whizzed and buzzed, plunked into the grass under foot, smashed a window. The Barrett barked, the .308 cracked twice, and then I heard the wood siding splintering, which meant their shots would start to punch through soon. Time to move.

I broke into a run, circling around behind the house to the opposite corner. I hadn't made it even halfway when I heard Anselm over the radio.

"They are going into the house," he said. "If your girlfriend is in there, she is in trouble."

"She's got a radio," I said. "Temple, you hearing this?"

"Y-yeah." Her voice was shaky and quiet. "I hear them."

"Don't hesitate, don't think, just shoot. I'll be there in five seconds."

"She may not have that long, Duke. *Mach schnell.*"

I skidded to a stop, scrambled up onto the back deck and yanked open the sliding glass door. The open plan of the house meant I had a clear view of the front door, catching the tail end of a quartet of mercs filing in. My carbine spat and the rearmost operative dropped, writhing, a round in his throat between armor and helmet. I trotted after the rest, slamming my shoulder into the wall to halt my progress and then rolled out into the hallway.

I was thrown backward by a hard punch to the chest, a round slugging into the body armor. I hit the floor on my back, sliding, gasping, chest aching, throat closed and burning as I struggled to breathe. Even in pain and unable to breathe, my training kicked in. Still on my back, I fired from the hip, four rounds, then three, then four more. The merc I'd dropped was behind me, the other four spread out in the hallway, two in front, one in back, the other pivoting to search the other rooms.

The nice thing about throat mics is that they can pick up a whisper in the middle of a firefight; I whispered as I fired, hoping they wouldn't know who I was talking to.

"Anyone gets near that bathroom, you shoot and don't stop."

"O-okay."

I rolled to one side and fired again, but my rounds hit the ceiling. My first bursts had founds targets, though, dropping one of the mercs and sent the others scrambling for cover.

"You have incoming," Anselm said. "*Zu viele, zu viele*. I cannot help you in there."

I'd found my feet now, and the hallway was empty. I switched mags again, stuffing the partially empty one into a pocket with the other. Crept toward the nearest doorway, swung out to the opposite side of the frame, carbine sweeping the interior of the room, Harris's study. The operative was in the far left corner, hoping to get the drop on me as I rolled in—dumbass, thinking he could get me with that trick. When you clear a room, you always start at the corners, exactly where that fucker was hiding. I was firing before I even fully registered his presence, ducking into the room to use the doorway as cover.

I heard the Mossberg's sharp belch, and then a second shot, and then Temple screaming.

Thought and training and caution bled out of me instantly, and I darted out of the room at full speed. I heard an HK chatter behind me as I passed the half-bath adjacent to the study, felt a round whisper past my neck. I hit the far wall of the hallway, twisted in place, fired a handful of rounds to push the shooter back under cover, and then scrambled into the spare bedroom.

Two bodies dressed in tactical black were on the ground in front of the open en suite bathroom door, blood pooling beneath them.

"It's me," I shouted, "It's Duke."

I heard scrambling on the tile, and then Temple rushed out and slammed into me full force. She was coated in blood spray, but seemed unhurt.

"You got 'em, babe," I cooed. "You got 'em. Good shooting."

"He—he yanked the door open so fast I didn't know what had happened. He just stared at me for a second, and I—I froze, I froze. But then the shotgun, it just—went off. I wasn't holding it right, I didn't have it against my shoulder like you said, and it almost jumped out of my hands when I shot it. The guy—the shot—" she shuddered, convulsing in my arms. "His head, it's—"

I glanced down, and realized that she'd shot him at an upward angle, the slug going under his helmet and up through his skull, splashing gore soup all over him, and thus all over Temple who must have been less than a foot away.

"Yeah, a twelve gauge slug will do that."

Temple gazed over my shoulder, her eyes widening, and I reacted instantly. I threw us both to one side, shoving Temple back into the bathroom as I hit the floor outside it. I fired lying down, took out his knee, adjusted my aim and put two rounds through his facemask. Red sprayed, and he dropped.

It wasn't over, though. Not by a long shot. I heard footsteps in the hallways, boots on hardwood.

The carbine was too big for close quarters, so I switched out for the HK MP7, a much smaller firearm. The steps were close, now.

I crept toward the doorway, whispering into the throat mic— "Stay there, Temple."

I took a deep breath, and then rolled out into the doorway, opening fire. The hallway was black with mercenaries. How many? A dozen? Jesus. Fuck, fuck, fuck. My initial burst took down the lead, my second dropped the guy behind, and then they were firing back and I had to crouch and keep firing, feeling bullets whine overhead to smash into the wall behind me, peppering the window and the floor and the bed.

A bullet bit into the floor between my feet, and then splintered the doorframe by my face—time to retreat. Good thing about such numbers in a small space is that they can't all fire at once, or I'd be dead. I had the last flashbang hanging from my pocket—I pulled the pin and tossed it into the hallway, waited till I heard the *whump* and saw the flash, then pivoted out into the doorway, firing into the pall of smoke.

I heard a thump as a body hit the ground, heard shouting, stepped out into the hallway and pressed against the right hand wall—just in time, as bullets raked the doorway from several rifles. I darted forward, strafing the hallway with a long burst, then let the HK hang by its strap and drew my Glock.

The smoke was still skirling in the hallway, concealing everyone, but I saw a body in tactical black and grabbed him by the front, stuffed the pistol under his helmet and fired, saw another body, fired into the face mask, and then everything was a whirling scrum of chaos, guns going off, cursing and screaming. I was a devil, then, unstoppable, a tornado of death.

Ever see *John Wick*? I could give that chump lessons.

I yanked a body in front of me, felt him flinch and jerk as bullets hit him, then I fired around him. Threw him into the weltering chaos of moving bodies, and then went in after him. I moved like lightning, then, breaking arms, snapping kneecaps, putting rounds through soft skulls.

Within thirty seconds, the hallway was void of living bodies.

On a quick scan, I counted thirteen, plus the two Temple took out, back in the bedroom.

My face stung, and there was a dull hot throb in my left leg, but I didn't have time for pain. I heard Anselm firing still, but the sharp crack of the .308 was absent, so I assumed he'd taken the sniper out.

I jogged back into the bedroom to snag my carbine. "Temple, stay here, babe. Same rules as before—lock the door and stay put, and if I don't say it's me, you shoot. Got it?"

"Got it." A brief pause. "Duke? I lo—"

"Don't say it," I cut in, leaning into the bathroom doorway to look at Temple. "When you say that to me, we're gonna be naked and I'm gonna be balls deep in that tight pussy. Until then, don't say it."

"Okay, Duke." Her eyes were wide with fear, her lips trembling, sweat on her forehead, chest heaving.

"You're fine."

"I killed them."

"You did what you had to."

Anselm cut in over the radio. "Apologies, but this is not yet over."

I heard a helicopter overhead, low, close, and loud.

"They've got a fucking helo?" I shouted. "Motherfucker!"

"They are remarkably well equipped, but unprepared for an encounter with operatives of our caliber."

I hustled to the front door. Bodies littered the gravel driveway and the front lawn, the Suburban was smoking and on its roof, the Hummer still burning. And yet there were still mercs behind the Wrangler and another Suburban, and now a helicopter was descending, two descent lines dangling from each side.

I angled out the front door, which had been blasted open.

Black-clad figures with rifles on their backs slid down the descent lines—I heard the Barrett speak, and one of the bodies went flying. I fired at another and watched him drop. Carbines and HKs chattered from the line of vehicles, rounds smashing into the front porch and the wall and the door, forcing me to duck back under cover.

I heard a truly terrifying sound, then: the chainsaw buzz of a door-mounted SAW.

"You have *got* to be fucking kidding me," I groaned, throwing myself away from the doorway.

The SAW rounds disintegrated the front wall of the house, shredding the door and the porch and the roof, punching holes to reveal spears of daylight.

I heard the Barrett again as I scrambled for the kitchen door. The SAW went silent momentarily, and then started up again, the massive rounds chewing up the house. I threw myself out the kitchen door and came face to face with a stunned merc who'd been trying to do an end-run in through the door I was exiting—my trigger finger was faster, and he fell backward, choking on the hole in his throat. Once again I found myself at the front left corner of the house, staring down a numerically superior force—which now included a fucking helicopter and a goddamned SAW.

The helo was hovering a good two hundred meters away, less than fifty feet off the ground—well within range of my 203, right? I took a knee, calculated the trajectory best I could, and squeezed the trigger.

Kick—*thunk*—silence—*crumpBOOM*!

Apparently I'd calculated the trajectory pretty damn accurately, since the grenade smashed into the side of the helo's engine just beneath the rotor, belching yellow-orange flame, the rotor shredding and tangling. It hit the ground behind the line of vehicles in a blinding, deafening explosion, sending shrapnel flying in every direction. A jagged chunk of metal spun past my head, barely missing my face, to bury in the trunk of a tree several hundred meters away.

I sprinted across open ground, carbine barking three-round

bursts, target after target dropping. I deked and juked side to side, throwing off their aim, and even then rounds whined past me, one snapping so close to my ear I felt the sting as it burned past me. I hit the side of the Suburban, hunkering behind it.

"That was an amazing shot, *mein Freund*," Anselm said over the radio. "But you have a problem."

I leaned around the front of the overturned Suburban and poured fire on the operatives. "What's that?"

"Look behind you."

I slid to my haunches with my back to the SUV, and my heart sank. A line of mercs were emerging from the woods, having circled wide to flank me. They had the drop on me, ten of them all with rifles trained on me; they were holding their fire as they jogged toward me, which meant they wanted me alive, even after the number of corpses I'd created.

"Can you take 'em out?" I asked.

"*Nein*. My angle is no good. I might hit you. By the time I move to a better angle, they will have you."

"Fuck."

"*Ja*." There was a pause. "But I have a line on the interior of the house, so I can see the doorway where *Frau* Kennedy is hiding. I can protect her from here."

I raised my hands over my head, the carbine in one hand. "Take care of her, buddy."

"What are you going to do?"

"Go with 'em."

"They will kill you."

"Maybe, maybe not." I watched them approach with my heart in my throat. "I got away once, so I'm gambling I can again."

"Duke?" Temple's voice in my earpiece. "What's going on?"

"Hit a snag, sweetheart," I said.

"What's happening?" She was shrill, panicked.

"Stay where you are." They were ten feet away at that point, and closing in fast, rifles trained on me, fingers ready to pull the triggers, ready to drop me if needed—they wanted me alive, but would settle for me dead if necessary, clearly. "Anselm will take care of you. Don't worry, baby. I'll be fine."

"Duke? No! No—don't…don't let them take you!"

"No choice, honey. Only way to keep breathing at this point. I'll get away, okay? I promise. Just stay where you are. Swear to me."

"I swear. But—"

"No buts. Stay put. Wait for Anselm." I switched off the radio, ripped off the headset and throat mic off, and then tossed the radio aside.

The ten operatives were in front of me, then. A rifle butt smashed into my gut, knocking the air out of me, and another cracked against my skull, dropping me to the ground, agony firing through me, my breath gone, head pounding, stars flashing behind my eyes. I could have fought, but I didn't. Maybe if they took me, they'd leave Temple.

It was a gamble, but I really didn't have a choice. Surrender, and live to fight another day. It galled me, though.

I felt the cold **O** of a rifle barrel against my temple. "You're a hard man to bring down, Duke Silver," said a rasping, guttural voice.

"You have no idea," I growled.

He laughed. "Get him up."

I was hauled to my feet and stripped of weapons and body armor, a gun to my head the whole time.

The man who'd spoken, the one with the gun to my head, was the ugliest motherfucker I'd ever seen. He was short, squat, and powerfully built, with a jaw so square he looked like a cartoon character. His face was acne-pocked and ribboned with a knife scar from beneath his left eye across his mouth, with deep-set, beady brown eyes and a huge nose. He'd removed his helmet, revealing lank black hair and oversized Dumbo ears.

Ugly stared up at me, standing a good foot shorter than me. "I'm Rayburn, Cain's second in command."

"And I'm Duke Silver, the man who's going to kill every last one of you motherfuckers." I jutted my chin at him. "You first, you ugly fucking piece of shit troll."

He just laughed again, that hoarse, raspy voice of his like sandpaper over stone. "Big words, my friend. Big words." He stepped close to me, his expression dead, cold, hard. "Big, but empty. Like you."

He swung his rifle at me so hard and fast I had no chance of ducking, dodging, or blocking. Not that it would have done any good, but still, my pride's on the line, so I have to point out that I couldn't have dodged even I'd wanted to. The butt smashed against my kidney, causing such fierce sudden pain that I dropped to my hands and knees, dry heaving from the agony of it. Rayburn kicked me, his foot slamming into my gut, tossing me onto my back. I tried to curl in, instincts forcing me to try and protect my core, but before I could, he lashed out with the rifle again, bashing the butt against my left forearm. I heard the *crack* first, then felt the fiery razors of excruciating pain searing through me, centered on my broken forearm.

"You suck," I growled. "But I'm still gonna kill you."

"You're even dumber than you look," Rayburn said. "Cain wants you alive, so if I were you I'd shut your damn mouth. Because trust me, I'd be happier to leave you dead."

He crouched, drawing a knife from a sheath on his armored vest. Rayburn reached up, snagged the sloppy ponytail I'd made of my hair in my rush to get dressed, and sliced it off, then showed me the stump of my hair.

I laughed in his face. "Ooooh, scary. You cut off my hair. Whatever will I do?" I was still having trouble breathing past the pain from my broken forearm; I could see white points of bone stabbing through the skin, so I knew it wasn't a minor break, but I had to keep playing tough. Well, I wasn't playing, I *am* tough, but you know what I mean.

"Why taunt me?" Rayburn asked.

"Why cut off my fucking ponytail? It's just hair. What's that prove, other than your lack of imagination?"

"I could cut off your ear. Is that creative enough for you?" He dragged the tip of the knife along my skin where my ear met the side of my head, sending blood trickling down my neck. "Maybe cut out your tongue." He slid the blade flat between my teeth, grabbed my jaw where it hinged and forced it open.

I just stared at him until he let me go, wiping the blade on my arm. When he stood up and backed away, I rolled to my back and sat up. "Quit the games, Rayburn. Cain wants to use me as bait? Fine, but get on with it. Kill me, don't kill me, torture me, don't torture me. I don't give a fuck. Just quit your goddamn yapping." I stood up, cradling my fractured arm against my belly. "Let's go, Quasimodo."

This earned me a laugh from Rayburn. "You've got balls, I'll give you that." He sheathed his blade and stood behind me, the barrel of his rifle to the back of my head. "To the vehicle. And if your friend with the Barrett out there pulls that trigger, you die."

I'd tossed the radio, so I couldn't tell Anselm to hold fire, but I hoped—and was gambling with my life—that he'd correctly read the situation.

I was marched across the yard to an undamaged vehicle, shoved in hard enough that I toppled across the seat, landing hard on my broken arm; the sudden lance of agony sucked the light out of the world, sent dizziness rushing through me, shoving me under the surface of consciousness.

The last thing I heard was Rayburn's voice, speaking to someone else. "Yeah, it's me. I got him. I'm down to maybe a dozen guys, but I got him....yeah, that many of us. Told you it'd be costly, Cain...the girl? No, just Silver, no sign of the girl. Yeah, well, you weren't here, boss. It was a fuckin' bloodbath. I hope this is worth it, that's all I'm gonna say..."

I passed out, then, the pain too blinding to ignore, the darkness too powerful to resist.

10

NEW FRIENDS

I SAT HUDDLED IN THE CORNER BETWEEN THE TOILET AND THE tub, clutching the huge, heavy, cold shotgun in shaking hands, my breath in my throat. The gunfire had stopped, and Duke had gone radio silent. Fear and worry boiled in my throat, warring for supremacy. I heard engines roar, the sound fading.

After a moment, I keyed the radio. "Anselm? What's—what's going on?"

"They have taken Duke, and are now exiting the compound."

"Did they hurt him?"

The hesitation told me everything. "He is an extraordinarily tough and resourceful person, Miss Kennedy. If anyone can survive this situation, it is Duke."

"Where are they taking him?"

"I do not know."

"Are you going to rescue him?"

Another hesitation. "I am going to contact my employer first. This rescue will require more than just me, I believe." Silence, then, for a minute, almost two, in which I tried to exert some control over my breathing. Anselm's voice startled me. "I am entering the house, now. Please, do not fire your weapon."

I stood up slowly, gingerly, shakily, and warily pulled open the bathroom door. Mistake, big mistake—the two men I'd shot were laying on the ground in a huge pool of blood. Nausea shot through me; I dropped the shotgun at my feet, barely making it to the toilet in time to empty my stomach, tears trickling down my cheeks.

I heard footsteps. "It's me, Miss Kennedy," I heard Anselm say from behind me.

His hand gathered my hair and held it aside. "It's all right."

I shook my head, coughing bile and spitting. "It's not. He's gone, they took him. And I just—we just—Duke and I—"

"I understand. I know things are not okay. I meant it is no shame to be sick the first time you end a life."

"I couldn't—I didn't have a choice."

"You did exactly the correct thing, Miss Kennedy. Kill or be killed is the rule of law in the world in which Duke and I live. They would have killed you or worse. It was unpleasant, but necessary."

"His head—god, I'll never be able to forget the way his entire head just—" I heaved again as the image burned through me.

"Would you care to hear my advice?"

"Yeah, please," I said, finally feeling like the vomiting was over. I sank to my butt on the floor, wiping at my mouth.

Anselm left and returned with a new, sealed toothbrush and a tube of toothpaste, handing it to me. I stood up and began brushing my teeth while Anselm sat on the edge of the tub and watched, his huge rifle cradled easily in his arms.

He let out a breath and then began speaking. "To kill, it is not an easy thing. It should never be easy. But when you are faced with a situation in which you have no choice, well…you must constantly remind yourself that you did what you had to do to remain alive. When your mind attempts to remind you of the events, showing you what you did—then you must force the images away. Refuse to think about them. Do not give the event power over you. You did not choose it, you did not do it out of malice. You must not allow guilt to enter you."

"How do you deal with it? When you do it for a living?"

"For us who make war professionally, it is different. It is still never easy, but I think we have learned to…separate ourselves from it, in a way." Anselm passed his hand through his hair, ruffling it. "When we work, when we fight, we are a different person than when we are idle, or at play. But sometimes, for me at least, things have a way of coming back to me in the quiet hours of the night. This will happen to you, I should say. Expect it, deal with it as well as you can, and know that you will be okay, in time."

I rinsed my mouth, washed my hands, and finger-combed through my hair. "What do we do now?"

"Now? I call Harris, and we formulate a plan to retrieve our comrade." He moved out of the bathroom, and I followed him, doing my best to not step in anything messy while keeping my eyes off the yucky stuff.

The hallway was…there weren't words. Bodies were piled on the floor, blocking the way forward, bullet holes pocking the walls, blood everywhere.

I stumbled to a stop, hand over my mouth. "Jesus. What…? What the hell happened here?"

Anselm grabbed me around the waist and lifted me past the worst of it, then set me down facing away from the ruin of battle. "Duke Silver happened."

"He did this?" I glanced behind me, trying to fathom how it was even possible; there had to be at least ten or twelve dead men in that hallway. "By himself?"

Anselm nodded. "In less than a minute, with his bare hands and a single pistol." He gestured at the front of the house, which I now realized was… essentially gone, shredded by that machine gun. "There is no way to shield you from the unpleasantness, I'm afraid. There is more out there."

I nodded and followed Anselm through the wreckage that was the front end of Harris's house and out into the yard. What I saw made me feel faint. The wooden porch we stood on was so full of holes it was a wonder it still stood. An SUV sat upside down, full of bullet holes. Another vehicle was burning several yards away, the flames flickering orange, sending black smoke into the sky. Behind that was another heap of burning wreckage, along with the remains of the helicopter. There was a bit of rotor hanging limp, the end broken and dangling, flames crackling and leaping, the skeleton of the aircraft blackening.

There were bodies everywhere.

I saw more smoke skirling skyward from the direction of the gate.

I leaned against Anselm. "You and Duke…you did—all this?"

"Mostly Duke," Anselm said. "I contributed to a portion of the body count, and that burning vehicle by the gate, but the rest of what you see was caused by Duke."

"Why is all this happening? What do they want?"

"I am not sure anymore."

An electronic trilling sound came from inside the house, a phone ringing. Anselm trotted in and retrieved the ringing device and answered it.

"*Ja*, Harris, *was geht ab*?" He paused to listen, then answered in English. "Things are not so good on this end. They came in force. We held them off, but they managed to take Duke….No, they captured him alive." He glanced up at the sky, and that was when I heard the sound of a jet overhead. "You have some rebuilding ahead of you, let's just say that, *ja*? You will see what I mean. No, she is with me. *Ja*, see you shortly."

I took a seat on the step of the porch while Anselm spoke to Harris, and finally had a moment to get a good look at the man.

At first glance, Anselm seemed average and unremarkable. He wasn't overly tall or muscular, not like Duke, and nor was he as stunningly, classically handsome in the face like Duke was, but once you took a closer look, it became obvious that Anselm was anything but average, and far, far from unattractive. His attractiveness was understated, is how I'd put it. He had a strong, angular jaw shadowed with stubble, vivid, dark brown eyes, clean, symmetrical features, and an artfully messy crop of brownish blonde hair. He was clearly in incredible shape, as well, judging by the way he filled out the black para-military clothing.

Made me wonder what the rest of Duke's…friends…were like.

I'd soon find out, I realized, when the sound of the jet approached, the aircraft appearing on the horizon, flying low and fast. It was a private passenger jet, but it was being flown more like a fighter jet, skimming the treetops at breakneck speed, and then when it neared the clearing it slowed and began a lazy bank, tilting and circling—so the pilot could get a look at the mess, probably. It made a partial arc around the clearing where the house sat, and then the jet took off at an angle, skirting wide before banking back around far in the distance. There was a landing strip out there somewhere, I assumed, since the jet was now approaching from the opposite direction, landing gear down, nose up, speed slacking off as it descended. It vanished under the trees, and then the sound of the engines faded. A few minutes later, I heard a different engine approaching, this one smaller and thinner; it sounded kind of like an off-road vehicle.

When it appeared, it was exactly what I thought, an off-road utility vehicle. It had no doors, only a roof supported by black bars, and a green body with yellow trim—something made by John Deere, though I knew nothing of that kind of vehicle, obviously. It was occupied by four people, one of them head and shoulders taller than the rest and nearly twice as broad, so big he had to sit in the pickup truck-like bed, and was big enough that his weight made the entire back end dip significantly. That must be Thresh, Duke's monster of a best friend. The other three were two men and a woman.

The utility vehicle braked to a halt a dozen feet away and the four occupants got out. Thresh, the big one, was indeed a literal giant of a man, standing seven feet tall and so packed with muscle I'd believe him capable of lifting this entire house off its foundation with his bare hands, if he wanted to. His hair was white-blond and spiked in a three-inch wide mohawk, the sides of his head shaved to the scalp, although he obviously hadn't had an opportunity to shave it recently, judging by the short stubble growing there. He had an arm in a sling and cast, held close to his body, and his eyes were so pale blue they were almost white. Those eyes were piercing, frighteningly intense and cold and hard as they scanned the battlefield wreckage.

The woman hopped out of the UTV and went to Thresh's side, and his arm went around her, tucking her against him. She was stunningly gorgeous, with flawless caramel skin and thick inky-black hair done in a loose braid. She was tall, too, nearly six feet herself, and looked seriously buff as well as stupidly well-endowed in both boobs and butt while still maintaining a trim physique; I was a little jealous, if I'm being honest.

The other two men circled the front of the vehicle to stand by Thresh, shaking their heads and staring at the ruin. One was tall and thin and hard, with messy brown hair and a short beard, both shot through with hints of gray, wearing an all black paramilitary uniform; the other was shorter but nearly as broad and heavily muscled as Duke and Thresh were, though he stood maybe five-nine at most, and had an epic beard, his head shaved bald, the beard thick and black and braided to hang down to mid-chest—he wore a pair of black military pants with sagging-open cargo pockets and a black T-shirt with the sleeves cut off, some kind of gory, scary looking symbol on the front, probably advertising a heavy metal band, tattoos covering one arm. Each man looked hard, deadly, and dangerous in his own unique way—although, if you asked me, none of them could match Duke.

Duke was dangerous, obviously, but he was just gorgeous—pure, unadulterated sex appeal, sharpened by the fact that you couldn't miss how rough, rugged, and dangerous he was, which only made him sexier.

But god, thinking about Duke brought tears to my eyes. Before that rifle went off, breaking the moment, Duke and I had shared something. We'd…gone beyond just sex, although now I wasn't really sure it had ever *been* just sex between us, even from the very first time I'd touched him.

My head was spinning as everything started crashing in on me, mentally, emotionally, and physically. I mean, it was early evening at this point—six? Maybe seven?—and I'd been through more trauma and emotional rollercoasters in the last ten or twelve hours than in my entire life up until now.

Kidnapped, waking up in a strange place, handcuffed and gagged with a man I didn't know—the escape, the sudden and gory violence of Duke killing those men…and then realizing I was attracted to Duke more intensely than I'd ever been attracted to anyone, and that he returned it in spades…followed by a series of mind-altering orgasms and giving Duke not one but *two* blow jobs within the span of a few minutes…god, what was wrong with me? This was, as my kid brother might say, batshit crazy. Duke had killed so many men—I couldn't even begin thinking about the number, and that was just *today*. But he'd done it all in self-defense, and in defense of me. He'd protected me. Taken care of me. Showed me that he had a tender side, that he did have a big heart, but it was buried deep beneath his arrogance and machismo.

But…*more than just sex*? How could I be thinking that, feeling that? What the fuck was wrong with me? You didn't just meet a guy and fall in love on the same day.

Except that's what was happening, and it was fucking stupid, fucking crazy, and fucking scary.

I could go home, right now. I know these men around me would take me home and have someone watching in case this Cain guy tried to come after me. I didn't ever have to see Duke or these guys again. I could forget this whole thing. Accept that I'd had the best, most life-changing sex of my entire life, and just go home.

Go back to my life, to my rules.

I could go back to picking up losers at shitty dive bars, go back to quick, passionless sex, devoid of emotion or meaning.

I could go back to my show, my infinity pool, my Bentley, my fifteen-thousand square-foot Malibu beach-front mansion, my rich, fake, shallow bitchy friends and their rotating roster of rich, fake, shallow, douchebag Beverly Hills boyfriends.

I didn't want to go back. Not to any of that.

I wanted to get Duke back. And I discovered, as I searched myself, that I was willing to pick up that shotgun again, if I had to, if it meant getting Duke back in one piece.

I felt someone sit down beside me. "You look shell-shocked, sister." It was the exotic-looking woman, Thresh's girlfriend.

"Yeah, that's about right." I picked up a brass shell casing from the ground and stared at it. "Less than twenty-four hours ago my life was neat, normal, predictable, and safe. Today?" I waved at the mess around us. "This."

The woman sighed dramatically. "Yeah, I can identify. Not even seventy-two hours ago, I was doing rounds in the ICU and, like you said, my life was as normal and predictable as you could ask for. And then that big beautiful bastard showed up asking for me. Next thing you know, people were chasing us and shooting at us and Thresh was killing people like it was the most normal thing in the world, when it's just fucking *not*, right? It's not, but he makes it look easy. And not only that, but Thresh is—well, look at him." Our gazes met, and an embarrassed but salacious grin crossed her face. "And yeah, the rest of him is just as big, if you know what I mean."

I stole a glance at Thresh, did some quick mental measurements, and shot her a look that meant something like *holy shit, woman, how are you able to walk right now?* And she shot me a look back that meant *sister, you have NO idea,* and then we were both giggling like women who'd known each other for ten years.

"Temple Kennedy." I stuck out my hand, and she shook it, her grip punishingly strong.

"Lola Reed." She took her hand back, but the look on her face told me what was coming. "So, I promise I won't say another word, but I have to say that I *love* your show. I watch it after work, like, every day. And I hope it's not too forward of me to say, but I really like the show a lot better now that Lane's not in it. And—yeah. So I'm kind of a fan."

I started laughing and couldn't stop laughing until I was out of breath. Lola and everyone else was staring at me by the time I got myself together. "Sorry," I breathed, "Sorry. I just—after everything I've been through today, I don't even feel like the same person I was yesterday. The show, Lane, everything, none of it feels real, after Duke and all the shooting and everything." I felt myself shudder, the aftershocks of laughter threatening to become sobs. "I think I might be cracking up a little."

Lola leaned into me. "Now *that* I can identify with. I'm not sure my life will ever go back to the normal I used to know, and honestly, I'm not sure that's a bad thing." She eyed me with curiosity in her eyes. "What's Duke like? Thresh talks about him like he's...I don't know, some kind of demigod or something."

I chuckled. "He kind of is, honestly. He's huge—not as big as Thresh, but huge." I leaned closer and whispered confidentially to her. "And by *huge*, yeah, I mean *huge*."

Lola tried to stifle her laughter, but couldn't quite manage it. "So you and Duke—"

"Oh yeah." Images of Duke and me flashed through my head. "Yeah. Which is...part of what's got me shell-shocked, I think."

Lola nodded. "Same here. It all happened so fast, but it just seemed..." she trailed off, hunting for the right word.

"Inevitable?" I supplied.

"Yeah, exactly," Lola said. "So...aside from having a monster cock, what's he like?"

"Complicated," I said. "Arrogant, sarcastic, funny...sexy, even sweet when he wants to be...and really, really scary."

"Sounds like Thresh."

We sat side by side in silence, then, watching Thresh, Harris, the bald bearded guy, and Anselm conferring. None of them seemed especially bothered by the fact that there were dozens of dead bodies everywhere, and Harris had barely given his house a second glance.

"What do you think they're going to do?" I asked.

Lola shrugged. "Hell if I know. Some kind of fancy commando shit, probably."

Harris sidled over to Lola and me. "Ladies, we have to get moving." He extended his hand to me. "My name is Harris. Sorry to be meeting you under these circumstances, but nonetheless, it's a pleasure to meet you, Miss Kennedy."

I shook his hand. "Call me Temple. And yeah, despite the weird and scary circumstances, it's nice to meet you." I stood up, brushing off the seat of my pants. "I'm sorry about your house."

Harris waved it off like it was nothing. "It's just a house. I can rebuild it. I'm just glad you weren't hurt."

"They took Duke, though."

Harris's shrug wasn't dismissive, but a little more nonchalant than I would have liked. "It's Duke. I won't say I'm not worried, but... it's Duke. He's unstoppable." He waved a hand around us. "Look around. He'll be fine."

"But you do plan on rescuing him, don't you?"

"Of course. That's where we're going now."

"Which would be where?"

"Anselm got a look at a few license plates as Cain's guys left, fed them to Lear, our computer expert, and he's tracking them via satellite. It looks like they're planning on taking him to an airfield an hour and a half from here. We're getting into my helicopter and we're going after them. If we can't catch up in time, Lear will keep track of their flight and we'll regroup."

Thresh came over, then. "And we're doing all this with a couple of civilian women along for the ride?" He glanced at Lola apologetically. "No offense, babe, but—"

She raised her hands. "Hey, I don't want any part of the action. That's your thing, not mine. You gotta go get your buddy back, I'm happy to be left out of it. I'll be on the ground waiting if you need stitching up."

"I'm with her. I've already shot two people today—I'm not exactly itching to do it again, like ever. So, if there's somewhere safe we can hide out, that's totally fine with me."

"Problem is, you're both on Cain's radar now," the bearded guy said, swaggering up to join the conversation, with Anselm close behind. He shook my hand. "Name's Puck, and if hot women like you and Lola here are gonna keep popping up in this little adventure we're having, I volunteer to be next."

I gaped at him. "You call this an *adventure*?"

"It's a hell of a lot more fun than sitting around with my thumb up my ass." He examined his thumb suspiciously. "Tried that once. Do *not* recommend it."

I looked at Lola for help, and she just shrugged. "Don't look at me, sister, I just met him myself."

Harris laughed. "Puck, can you rein in the weird just a little? You're creeping out the new girls."

Puck dug the stump of a cigar out of a pocket, examined it, picked lint off the charred tip, and then lit it with an electric lighter he'd produced from nowhere. "Boss, the weird cannot be contained. The weird abides, man." He puffed a noxious cloud of smoke skyward, eyeing us all expectantly, as if he'd made a point we were all missing. "No? The Dude? Nothing? Okay, whatever. Point I was making is, we need all hands on deck to go after our boy Duke. Not sure who we can spare to escort them somewhere safe, and where safe even is at this point. If they're capable of this bullshit? Your compound *was* the safe spot, Boss."

Harris stole the cigar from Puck and sucked in a mouthful of smoke before handing it back; he held the smoke in for a moment and then blew a concentric series of smoke rings. "You have a point, there. But it's not like they can just sit and wait in the helicopter while we infiltrate Cain's hide out or wherever. Ideas, anyone?"

Puck chewed on the end of his cigar for a moment. "I got one."

Harris eyed the shorter man skeptically. "If it involves hookers, I don't want to hear it."

Puck let out a long-suffering sigh. "Not *all* my ideas involve hookers, you know." Dramatic pause. "Strippers also feature prominently."

"Puck—" Harris barked.

"But in this case, my idea contains zero percent naked women…" he eyed both Lola and me as if he was mentally undressing us, "unless you two wanna go skinny dipping with me, that is."

"PUCK!" Harris shouted, drawing a pistol from a belt holster and aiming it at Puck's foot. "I swear to fuck if you don't make your goddamn point I'll shoot you in the fucking foot, you creepy, lecherous little nymphomaniacal douchebag!"

Puck didn't seem fazed. "I'm not an addict, I can quit any time I want," he quipped. "What I was gonna say before you so rudely interrupted me with your empty threats, *Boss*, was that I got a place over in the Ozarks. Been in my family for going on a two hundred years now, and the only deed that exists is a crumbly old piece of paper in a dusty archive somewhere. Meaning, unless you know about it there ain't no way to find it, and you ain't gonna know about it unless I tell you."

He took another puff of the cigar, rolling it and tapping it at the same time.

"This place is *remote*, like way the fuck out there in the middle of damn nowhere. It's an old hunting shack way up in the hills, don't look like much, and hell, it *ain't* much, but it *is* private, and as unfindable as anything you can think of." He gestured at Harris with his cigar. "You fly us near it in the helo and let us down as close as you can. I'll get these two set up nice and cozy, and then we'll bug out, rescue Cain from Duke, and find some strippers and blow to celebrate."

Harris shook his head. "Is there a word stronger than incorrigible? 'Cause whatever it is, you're it, Puck." He nodded, thinking. "But the idea has merit."

Thresh spoke up. "This the place you took me? The one you mentioned on the phone the other day?"

Puck nodded. "Yep. Where we went after that Moyers-Andersen debacle."

Thresh frowned. "That place is a fucking dump, Puck. *I* wouldn't want to stay there for more than five minutes, and you're gonna stick a couple high class women in there for who knows how long?"

Lola kicked Thresh's shin. "Who're you calling high class, asshole?"

"I mean, it *is* a little rustic, I admit, but—" Puck started.

"Rustic?" Thresh echoed. "Rustic is a campground with a communal bathroom, your so-called *hunting shack* is a two hundred year old log cabin with an actual outhouse, and by outhouse, I mean a hole in the ground with a hut on top of it."

Lola cut in. "Look, normally what you're describing sounds like my idea of hell, but if we have to hide out for a while, then I'll go with it." She glanced at me. "But I can't speak for Temple, obviously."

I hesitated. "My idea of rustic is a four star hotel, so this sounds… positively primeval." I swallowed hard, realizing I didn't have much choice. "But if it's a choice between a hunting shack and more shooting, I'll take the hunting shack."

Harris nodded. "Then we're agreed." He clapped his hands together once, sharply. "Thresh, get the women to the helo and start her up. Puck and Anselm, we're gonna go down to the bunker and gear up."

Which was how I found myself buckled into a seat in the back of a Vietnam-era ex-military helicopter, complete with the machine gun and a complicated system of winches and cables meant to let people rappel from the hovering aircraft to the ground. Thresh had driven a tank truck over to the helicopter, fueled it up, re-parked the truck, and then went through an extensive checklist for starting up the helicopter, fumbling through each step, especially since he only had one working arm.

Another few minutes, and the other men arrived in a battered, rusted pickup truck. The bed of the truck was full of black bags, each of which looked heavy, meaning they were full of guns and ammunition and other such unpleasant things these men liked to play with. They also had a huge white YETI cooler and a smaller, less heavy duffel bag, which they tossed to us.

I unzipped it, and discovered it to be full of what appeared to be Layla's clothing.

Harris shrugged when I glanced at him in curiosity. "You're all of similar size and build as Layla. Might not fit exactly right, but I figured it's better to have extra clothes that don't quite fit, and Layla has so much clothing she'll never miss that shit anyway." He gestured at the cooler. "That's got food in it, as Puck wasn't sure what was at the cabin. Sit tight for now, we'll be underway shortly."

By underway, I discovered, he meant skimming the treeline at speeds that made my stomach queasy, the side doors hauled open so the ground whizzed beneath us mere feet away, only the seatbelt keeping me inside the aircraft. Anselm, for his part, had his rifle on the floor beside him and was sitting half out of the helicopter, one foot on the landing strut, not even holding on to anything, looking absolutely at ease.

Once I got used to the speed and the open doors, though, the flight proved boring, and I felt myself nodding off.

Eventually, I gave in and let myself fall asleep.

11

THE BEAST

MOTHERFUCKERS WEREN'T PLAYING AROUND, THIS TIME.

I spent a good hour and a half in the back of that Wrangler, broken arm throbbing like a bitch. I wasn't bound in anyway, but the Wrangler was doing eighty-five on a freeway, and there were two other SUVs full of Cain's guys behind us, so there wasn't much I could do just yet.

We pulled into the private aircraft section of a rural airport and parked by a waiting Gulfstream. The line of vehicles maneuvered to a stop around the rolling stairs leading up to the jet, positioned in such a way that I had nowhere to go but up and into the jet. Rayburn yanked open the back door, grabbed me by the collar, and hauled me out of the back of the Wrangler fast enough that I had to scramble to avoid hitting the tarmac. A quick glance around told me that my escape wasn't happening now, either, as I was surrounded by HKs and M-16s, each one trained on me; I counted a dozen.

Guess they were finally starting to feel a bit of respect for my abilities, huh?

Rayburn gestured at the jet. "Get up there, or die on the tarmac. Your choice."

Knowing when to cut the bullshit is an important skill to have, and one I've not exactly mastered, but in this situation I was prudent enough to know I'd pushed Rayburn as far as I could. If I wanted to keep my body free of unnecessary holes, I'd keep my mouth shut and watch for the lowest-risk opportunity to escape.

Thus, I walked my ass up the stairs and into the Gulfstream. It wasn't as nice as Harris's, and certainly not as swank as Roth's, but it was a nice jet.

It was also stuffed full of more mercs with assault rifles and submachine guns.

I shot a look at Rayburn, who had come up behind me. "Seriously, how many of you fuckers are there?"

Rayburn quirked a grin at me. "More than you know."

I rolled my eyes as I took an empty seat. "You know, this whole Cain-is-so-mysterious, Cain-is-more-than-you-know bullshit is seriously over the top. Like, dial it back a few notches, ya'll. This ain't a Clive Cussler novel, and Cain sure as shit ain't some super villain."

Rayburn laughed. "You know, under different circumstances, I think you and I might have gotten along, Duke." The humor drained out of him, and he stuck the barrel of a pistol against my forehead. "But the circumstances being what they are, you need to shut the fuck up. I'm under orders to bring you in alive, but you keep running that mouth of yours and I'll put a bullet in your pretty fucking head."

"Aww, Rayburn, you think I'm pretty?" I winked at him. "I don't swing that way, but I'm flattered."

Rayburn thumbed back the hammer of his pistol with an ominous *click*. "One more joke, Silver—watch what happens."

I leaned back in the comfy leather seat and buckled up. "All right, all right. I'm shutting up. Don't get your panties in a rumple, Stiltskin."

The door was closed from the outside, and then after a couple seconds I felt the engines spool up; a minute later I was pushed back in my seat as we launched skyward.

I've always been a restless, active kind of guy; if I'd gone to school regularly past, like, seventh grade, I'm guessing I would have been diagnosed with ADD or ADHD, because I just can't sit still, can't be inactive, can't just sit and do nothing, and focusing on boring shit like reading is an act of will—which makes my university degree one of the greatest accomplishments of my life, because that shit was *hard*. I don't sit still well, which means flights are fucking torture for me. My knee bounces on its own like a motor-driven piston, my hands find something to fidget with, be it a pen I click or a seatbelt latch, or paper I can shred; if there's just nothing to do, I can get…annoying, let's just say. The guys in my unit, when we took long flights to deployment or an insertion or something, discovered the best way to keep the peace with me on the flight was to keep me entertained. We'd arm wrestle, play cards, prank each other, immature guy shit like that. It helped that we were usually in the back of a military cargo jet or something like that, maybe an Osprey if it was an in-country insertion, meaning there was more room for me to move around.

This shit? A fancy ass jet with leather seats and no legroom and nothing for me to fidget with?

I suffered in stillness and silence for about fifteen minutes before my restlessness kicked in. Plus, my arm was killing me—well, not literally, maybe that was a poor choice of phrasing…but I needed a distraction or I was gonna get cranky.

"Yo, Rayburn. I'm bored as shit, dude." He was sitting in front of me, so I emphasized my point with a kick to the back of his seat.

He twisted in place. "I can break your other arm. That'll give you something to focus on."

"Nah, that'll just piss me off." I nodded at the wood paneled wall at the front of the cabin. "This thing have a TV?"

That earned me a chuckle from one of the operatives in the back of the jet, which was quickly stifled behind a cough as Rayburn shot a glare back that way.

"Maybe you don't fully understand the gravity of your situation, Silver. You are only alive right now because Cain has plans for you which are best carried out with you still breathing." He rested the barrel of his pistol on the top of his seat back, aiming it at me. "This isn't a social call. You are a prisoner. So no, there is no fucking *TV*, you fucking twat."

"Okay, well, I'm just saying, when I get bored, I get annoying. How long is this flight, anyway?"

A long, irritated sigh. "You're like a goddamn child, you know that?" He rubbed his forehead with a knuckle. "Couple of hours."

"And you expect me to just sit here doing dick that whole time?" I groaned. "I'm so gonna get shot before we get there."

Rayburn dug through a compartment hidden next to his seat and tossed me a stack of magazines: *Wine Enthusiast*, *Cigar Afficionado*, *Ultimate Homes*, *Luxury Real Estate*...the kind of boring shit only rich pretentious douche-lickers subscribe to.

But then an idea hit me.

I still had my belt on, with the empty kydex sheath threaded through it. And I had a decent sized magazine...

I whipped my belt off, zipped the sheath off, chose what seemed to be the best magazine from the selection I had, and then stuck the sheath between my jaws. After examining my broken forearm, I summoned every ounce of badass tough guy macho I-don't-feel-pain courage I possessed, and tugged at my wrist until the shard of bone slipped back under my skin—that was part one. I managed not to scream, but there was a lot of clenched-jaw heavy breathing, which drew the attention of pretty much everyone. Rayburn, for his part, pivoted in his chair to watch, but didn't make a move to either help or hinder me.

Part two—I prodded at my forearm, which felt super fucking awesome, trying to ascertain how the break was aligned without the benefit of an X-ray. A deep breath, repositioned the sheath in my jaws, braced my shoulder against the seat back, extended my arm out straight—I was already snarling in pain and hadn't actually set it yet...this was going to be fun. Another bracing breath, got a good grip on my wrist with my good hand...and pulled my wrist away from my body. The pain that lanced through me then was unlike anything I've ever felt, including that time I was pushed off the third story of a parking garage and broke pretty much everything. I didn't set my bones then, and when it was done to me, I was under anesthetic so I didn't feel it. This was just...utter blinding agony so fierce I nearly passed out.

When the worst of it passed, I wiped the sweat off my forehead, took another few moments to breathe through the waves of pain, and then set the *Wine Enthusiast* magazine underneath my forearm and wrapped it upward around the set bone fracture. I then wrapped the belt around the magazine several times—the belt was just a knock-off para-military web piece, so I was able to tug the it tight enough that I was sure it would function to cinch the magazine tight as a makeshift brace, and then looped the excess belt material between the magazine and the belt so I could pass the bitter end through the loop to make a knot.

By time I was finished, I was breathing hard, feeling faint, and was in so much pain I felt my temper flaring.

The thing about me that might become relevant at this point is that I have a vicious bitch of a temper, but it's one I keep tightly caged at all times, because once it's been let loose, it's pretty much impossible to contain my appetite for destruction until I'm either tranquilized or my rage burns itself out. The funny thing is, I'm hot headed, quick to irritation, but just as quick to let it go. I'll throw myself into a bar brawl without a second thought, but I'll turn around and buy the poor bloody bastards a round. That's not my temper, that's just my basic, essential personality. I run hot, but it cools off quickly, and my overall good humor returns. No hard feelings, kumbaya, what the fuck ever. Someone nails me in the jaw, yeah I'm gonna kick and shout and curse and then beat the ever loving hell out of the dumb motherfucker, but I haven't lost my temper, I just don't like being punched.

Me losing my temper is a whole different beast.

Thresh is the only person who's ever seen me go truly berserker. Without going into detail, let's just say I don't deal well with two kinds of people: rapists, and those hurt kids. Well, Thresh and I got sort of involved in a scenario where there was guy who'd done both to this little girl. Nasty, vile, evil shit, and he thought we'd laugh with him when he described what he'd done. My memory of what followed is hazy at best, because I saw black. Thresh tried to haul me off, but even he couldn't control me—he got a black eye and three teeth knocked out for his trouble. The piece of shit wasn't recognizable as a human by the time I finished with him. Thresh hasn't spoken of it since, and neither have I, and nor will we ever. But the knowledge is there, that the beast inside me is something that should never be let out.

But I felt it boiling, now.

The trouble I'd been through, being yanked away from Temple after what we'd shared together, the fact that the fuckers had destroyed my boss's house, the humiliation and helplessness of being captured, and now the pain? Yeah, Evil Duke was rearing his ugly head.

I focused on breathing, then, focused on building mental bricks around the Beast's cage, deep down inside me where he lived.

Something to focus on, at least, right?

I built those walls high and thick, focused on the pain, breathed through it.

When that stopped helping, I re-lived everything Temple and I had done together, but that started giving me wood, so that wasn't going to work, not in a plane full of men, all of whom would kill me soon as they look at me.

Eventually, I settled into a light doze. It wasn't really sleep, because the seething anger was still on simmer just beneath the surface, but pretending to be napping worked as well anything in terms of keeping myself from yanking one of those submachine guns away and going apeshit on this jet. Which would be a bad plan, since we were at cruising altitude and I didn't have a 'chute.

So thus, I napped.

But make no mistake: the Beast was awake.

12

TRANKED

Puck went down first. He stepped into a harness and just sort of swung out of the side of the helicopter like he was climbing over the side of a boat for a swim. Anselm was working the controls and lowering Puck to the ground. When he was down, Anselm drew the cable back up, worked it in a complicated series of knots and loops around the cooler and lowered that to Puck, and then it was my turn. I'm not afraid of heights, but getting into a stupid harness and dangling out the side of a stupid helicopter just seemed ridiculous. Did I mention this was stupid? But yet I got into the harness, let Anselm clip the carabiner to the harness, and then I climbed carefully out onto the strut, my heart in my throat, my stomach doing backflips and pirouettes, my palms sweating.

"You must slide off of the strut, Temple," Anselm called to me. "You will be safe, I swear to you. I have done this countless times."

I should point out that a hovering helicopter doesn't just sort of float there like a balloon. It moves this way and that as the pilot—in this case, Harris—feathers the controls. So it's not, like, steady. Harris was a talented pilot, I'd been told, but this was terrifying. Sitting on the strut of a helicopter a hundred feet off the ground, trees looking small beneath my feet, nothing to stop me from falling except some material around my hips and waist and a thin cable? Yeah, it's not exactly mimosas for brunch, which was, up until I woke up in that basement next to Duke, the most demanding thing I'd ever done in my short, stupid life.

"If you do not move," Anselm shouted down to me, "Harris will tip you out. Believe me on this, *bitte*."

So…I swallowed hard, closed my eyes and said a prayer to whoever or whatever was out there, and angled myself forward so the thick cold metal of the strut slid out from beneath my butt. And then I was dangling in open space, twisting this way and that, the downblast of the rotors battering and buffeting me, the noise deafening, the ground hurling up at me. Yeah, I know, I was actually descending at a slow, measured pace, but when it's *your* ass hanging out over nothing, you tell me it feels slow.

I squeezed my eyes shut for a moment, and then I felt ground beneath my feet and Puck was helping me to my feet and deftly freeing me from the harness—without copping a feel, which kind of surprised me. Honestly, he just seemed like the type who would "accidentally" brush his hand across my ass.

The cable retracted, and a few short minutes later Lola was descending. She was whooping the whole time and laughing, and trying to get Anselm to let her down faster. Because of course she would, the bitch. Just kidding, Lola was awesome, and we were going to be BFFs, I was pretty sure. But it was annoying that she loved it when I was so relieved just to be on the ground.

Puck reached to help Lola out of the harness, and she slapped his arm.

"What was that for?" Puck asked, staring at her.

"That was for grabbing my ass when you take the harness off," Lola replied, quirking an eyebrow.

Puck frowned at her. "But I haven't even done anything yet."

"Yeah, well you were going to."

Puck shook his head, grumbling under his breath as he undid the harness without touching her and then jerked the cable to tell

Anselm he could retract it.

The cable spooled back where it belonged, Harris tipped the helicopter to one side and drifted away.

I nudged Lola. "I expected him cop a feel, myself, actually. But he didn't."

Puck clapped a hand over his heart. "You wound me, ladies. I do have *some* honor, I'll have you know. You two are my buddies' girlfriends. There's a code about that shit, all right?" He seemed genuinely affronted. "I'd never make a move on you. If you two were single ladies I was helping out of a harness, yeah, my hands would be all over you. But you're with Duke and Thresh, so that means that my hands stay to themselves, and that you're as safe with me as you would be the rest of the guys."

"Puck, I was just—" Lola started.

"I may be—what was it Harris called me?—a creepy, lecherous, nymphomaniacal douchebag, but I do have *some* standards."

"Puck, I'm sorry," Lola said. "I was kidding."

He pointed at her. "Never bullshit a bullshitter, sweetheart. You weren't kidding."

She shrugged. "No, but I misjudged you, so I *am* sorry."

He grinned, then. "Eh, no hard feelings. None of us are exactly the types you'd want to bring home to mama, and I'm the worst of us." He fished a cigar from a pocket, this one fresh, unclipped, and full-size; a cigar clipper appeared in his hands— he clipped the end and stuck it unlit between his teeth. "Now, if we're done with the judgmental portion of the program, I'd like to get moving." He crouched, swung the YETI cooler up onto his shoulder, and set off marching up a hill.

Lola and I trotted after him. He seemed to know exactly where we were going, even though Harris had let us down in what seemed to be a random clearing in the middle of a seemingly endless forest in the Arkansas Ozarks. We followed Puck up the side of the hill for a good ten or fifteen minutes, until he stopped, again somewhat randomly, peering around at the trees, all of which seemed identical.

"Are we lost, Puck?" I asked.

He chewed on the cigar for a moment, and then glanced back at me. "Nah, I just ain't been back here in a spell. Always takes me a minute to get my bearings." He peered around a bit longer, and then set off marching again, reaching up to tap a weathered symbol carved deep into the trunk of a tall, thick, ancient tree as he passed it. "See? My great-great-great grandpappy's mark, right there. Cabin's just over the rise."

"Puck?" Lola said, trotting to catch up to him. "I didn't meant to be judgmental, I just—"

"I give off a certain…aura," Puck cut in. "I know that. I'm rough around the edges, and that's puttin' it lightly. Manners ain't ever been my strong suit, and won't never be, I don't guess. I like naked women, and I like booze, and I like poker, and I like shootin' guns—the bigger the better. Maybe it's the redneck in me, I dunno. So…it's easy to cut a quick judgment on me, and I get that. I ain't gonna hold nothin' against you, because I get it. But I got honor. I live by a code. I'm good at gettin' bitches naked and on their knees, but I wouldn't ever pull that shit on a woman claimed by someone I've spilled blood with. 'Specially those two—Duke and Thresh are just about the only family I got. The whole crew is family, but those two are my boys. They get me in a way Harris, Anselm, and Lear just don't."

"Well, I think you're sweet," Lola said.

Puck snorted. "Honey, I'm about as sweet as salt. But thanks all the same, and I think you're pretty all right myself." He rolled the cigar from one side of his mouth to the other. "Now, the sooner we quit gabbing, the sooner we get to the cabin. This cooler ain't exactly light." He hiked the YETI higher on his shoulder and set off up the slope again, heading on an angle rather than directly upward.

Lola and I followed him at a distance of a few feet.

I nudged Lola again. "You ever notice his southern accent comes and goes?"

Lola nodded. "Yeah, I have. I get the feeling he's super smart, but he likes people to hear the drawl and underestimate him. Or maybe he just likes to mess with people? I don't know."

"Or maybe I'm just self-conscious about it and can't ever quite get rid of it," Puck said from ahead of. "By the way, I have excellent hearing."

We reached the verge, then, where the hill leveled out a little. The mountainside angled off to our right and left, descending downward head of us. Puck plucked the cigar from his mouth and pointed with it: on our left and down the slope about a quarter of a mile, another hill rose up to form a nook where one mountainside met another, and tucked into that crevice was a tiny log cabin which looked every single minute of the hundred and fifty years Puck claimed it was. It was surrounded by trees, so that it was nearly invisible, and even after Puck pointed it out, I had a hard time keeping track of exactly where the little cabin was located. The age of the wood, the obscuring foliage, and the mountains rising up on either side all worked to create almost perfect camouflage.

We descended toward the cabin, Puck taking long, bouncing strides downward, the cooler swaying precariously on his shoulder, Lola and me not far behind. We reached the porch, which was just big enough to stand on, and accessible from the ground by a set of steps made from crumbling cinder blocks. The cabin itself looked snug enough, the logs thick and weathered, set closely together and sealed somehow. The roof had been re-shingled in the recent past, but the rest of the cabin, as in my initial estimation, looked exactly as old as it was. It didn't even have a real doorknob, only the kind of lever you'd see in *Little House on the Prairie*, or maybe old westerns. And, as Thresh had claimed, there was an actual outhouse. It was... well, I guess you'd call it a hut, just barely large enough to allow a grown man room to stand up in. It was down the hill a ways, and nestled against the side of the mountain.

Puck lifted the lever and kicked the door open with his toe, peering inside briefly before going in and setting the cooler down with a grunt. The interior, when I ducked in, was maybe a total of a hundred square feet, maximum. There was a fireplace on one wall, a wood-framed cot to left of that, a low table opposite the cot, sitting on a round, aged, hand-woven rug in the middle of the room. That was, quite literally, it. Well, except for a stack of milk cartons near the table, which contained some canned goods and bottles of liquor.

I stared at Puck. "A little rustic?"

He shrugged. "I come here to sleep on hunting trips, don't need much else."

"Is there even electricity?"

"Nope." He waved his cigar in the direction of the outhouse. "There is a well pump down thataway, though."

Lola just blinked, glancing around. "Well, for me, it won't be much different than Dad's place in the 'Glades. No water and different trees, but…the same basic lifestyle."

I shot her a look. "The primitive kind?"

Lola shrugged. "Yeah, basically. My dad has lived off the land down in the deep Everglades since I was little girl, so I'm used to sleeping rough. This place has walls and a door, my dad's *fale* doesn't."

"FAH-lay?" I asked. "What's that?"

"The Samoan word for our traditional home, which is a roof and some upright poles, and that's it."

The radio on Puck's belt crackled. "Puck, you about ready for extract?"

Puck lifted the radio to his mouth. "Affirmative. Give me ten minutes."

"Make it eight. Lear has updated intel."

Puck hooked the radio back on his belt and exited the cabin, slapping the doorframe on the way out. "Well, lovely ladies, assuming all goes well, I'll be seeing you in twenty-four hours or less."

Lola and I had taken seats at the table—we waved goodbye, expecting him to leave.

Only he didn't.

He just stood there, looking suddenly tense. "Now how the hell…?" he murmured.

"What is it?" I asked, not like the sudden tension in Puck's shoulders.

Lola was closer to the doorway; she lifted up out of her chair and leaned to one side, peering around Puck's shoulder, and then sank back into the chair, wiping her face with both hands. "Well fuck."

"What? What is it?" There were no windows, so without looking out the door, I had no way of knowing what they'd seen.

Puck's hand, resting on the doorframe, slid upward toward the lintel. Resting on a set of hooks over the door was a shotgun, but not a matte black tactical new one like Duke had used, but rather one of those with a wood-stock and a long metal barrel with a pump slide under the barrel. Probably used for hunting. Old, worn, but well-cared for, if I was any judge of such things, which I wasn't.

"Oh," I said, understanding what it meant when Puck reached for a gun.

Puck glanced at me. "See that box of shells on the table by your left hand?" he asked. "Hand 'em to me." I gave him the box of shells, and he dumped the entire contents into the cargo pocket of his pants.

"Get down, stay down, and stay put," he ordered, his voice quiet, all trace of a drawl gone.

Lola and I both slid underneath the table and huddled together while Puck cracked open the shotgun, checked it, and slammed it closed again, but held it out of view of those beyond the door.

"That's far enough, boys," he called out, his voice once again the gruff, genial drawl. "Ya'll are trespassing on my private property. Best get on."

"The girl," came a muffled male voice. "Hand her over, and we'll leave."

"If I had a girl here, I sure as shit wouldn't be sharing," Puck said. "Now one last time I'll tell ya'll: get the fuck off my land."

"We know she's in there," the voice returned. "You have thirty seconds. It's ten on one...be smart."

"I got a better idea. I'll bust out the Wild Turkey and we can have ourselves a party." Puck put himself fully in the doorway, lifting the shotgun into view and pumped the slide. "Or, I can start putting some buckshot in ya'll's asses and we can have ourselves a different kinda party."

There was a moment of tense silence, and then several things happened at once.

Puck leapt into motion, throwing himself to one side and blasting with the shotgun, firing and pumping and firing three times in rapid succession before he hit the ground on the far side of the porch. The next thing that happened was a small silver canister landed with a hollow thunk on the floor of the cabin. It sat spinning for a moment, and then began spitting a dense cloud of thick white fog, which quickly filled the entire cabin, forcing Lola and I to stumble choking and coughing outside. The next thing that happened was a crackle of gunfire, the blasting of Puck's shotgun, his shouts of rage, and then a cry of pain.

"He's down, sir," I heard someone say, as I tried to breathe and see, but I couldn't manage either due to the blinding chemical sting and burn in my eyes and mouth and throat.

"Dead?" Another voice asked.

"Negative, sir. I think he was wearing a vest."

"Grab 'em," the first voice said, "and trank 'em. The blonde kicked up a hell of a fight last time."

The blonde, meaning me. So, I kicked up a hell of a fight as I felt bodies around me. I heard Lola screaming, heard thrashing and male grunts of effort, and then a pair of strong arms wrapped around me, pinning my arms to my sides. Something sharp poked the side of my neck, and darkness reached up to swallow me.

"Got two for one, sir," I heard the second voice say. "I think this is that bitch from the swamp."

"Good work. Let's move before that helo circles around."

And then the darkness swallowed me, sucking me under.

13

GOOD NEWS, BAD NEWS

I WOKE UP WITH MY HEAD THROBBING LIKE A MOTHERFUCKER AND my arm throbbing like a double motherfucker. Everything was hazy, dim, difficult to grasp.

I worked myself to a sitting position, blinking against the blinding pain, and tried to force some clarity through my foggy, cotton-stuffed head.

The realization that I'd been drugged again was the first thought to ripple through me.

The second was that I wasn't alone.

I was in the center of a small, dark, dim room, lit by a naked light bulb hanging from the ceiling. The walls were bare concrete, the ceiling corrugated iron and crossbeams. There was a single heavy door, no window, no handle on the inside—a prison cell, or close enough. Huddled around me were women, about thirty of them, all clustered together as close to each other and as far from me as they could get. I had to blink a few times to be sure I was seeing what I thought I was seeing, but then, as the chemical haze faded, understanding started washing through me.

The women were all young, under thirty, most of them, and if I had to assume, I'd say most of them spoke English as a second language, if at all. Mexican, Middle Eastern, South or Central American, Indian—I wasn't sure who was which, but that's what I was seeing. Most of them were clothed in rags, literal rags, scraps of clothing. Most sported bruises on their bodies, but not on their faces. One woman sitting nearest me was clutching her waist in a way that made me suspect a cracked or bruised rib.

I'd been taken by Cain, which meant these women were in Cain's possession.

The Beast was fully awake now, and rattling his chains—enough of the metaphors, though. I was feeling the black rage come over me.

These women were sex slaves.

"English?" I asked, remaining on my butt on the floor.

Most shrank away from me, but one raised her hand, near the back of the room. "I…speak a little English." She spoke barely above a whisper, and it was obvious she was close to hysterics.

"My name's Duke," I said, keeping my voice low. "I'm not going to hurt any of you, okay? Can you tell them that?"

"I…they…we—we are not all the same speaking—the same… language."

"You guys, you're—why are you here?" I asked.

"Slaves. To be sold for—for…sex," the girl answered. She couldn't have been more than eighteen at most, and I saw a few who were younger than that, thirteen or fourteen.

"Yeah, well, not any more," I growled, and the raw rage in my voice had the women around me scrabbling away from me in fear.

"But—they—they are many." She blinked at me as if I'd spoken incomprehensible nonsense. "They will kill you."

I focused on containing my rage and when I was calm enough to speak, I glanced at the girl. "They'll try," I snarled. "And they'll fail."

I heard footsteps beyond the door, faint voices. "…Be awake by now. Last time, we gave him enough for three men and he was awake within hours."

I stood up and shooed the women away from the door, herding them into the farthest corner. I held my finger over my lips and crept to stand by the door. A key rasped in the lock, the knob turned, and the door swung open, away from me. A man entered, carrying a shotgun in both hands, a second behind him, also carrying a shotgun.

I pivoted away from the wall, grabbed the man in front by the shirt and smashed my forehead against his nose, kicking out with my foot at the same time to launch the second merc flying. My forehead crunched cartilage, blood squirting. I grabbed at the shotgun while the guy was dazed, snatching it away, stepping backward and to the side, and then fired one-handed. Which isn't as easy as Arnie makes it look in *Terminator*. Outside of point blank range, I would have missed, but as it was I was close enough to send the lead merc sailing backward with a ragged hole in his chest. The shotgun was a tactical model, thankfully, so I didn't have to pump it. I hurled myself through the door the second I'd fired, smashed the barrel into the chest of the second merc, who'd landed against the far wall opposite the doorway. I pulled the trigger, turning my head away from the spattering gore. Fucking messy, Jesus. There was a third man, standing outside the door holding a submachine gun and looking stunned. He didn't get a chance to get over his surprise: I laid the barrel over the elbow of my injured arm and fired again. The kick sent a spear of agony through me, but I didn't stop to let it take hold. I scooped up the submachine gun, an HK MP5, and rifled the body for magazines. The women were standing in the doorway, looking fearful and tentative; one of the bodies on the floor, the first man I'd shot, had a key ring in his hands.

"Get the keys," I said, pointing at the ring. "Start letting people out."

I kicked a shotgun across the floor to them. "Use that, if you're so inclined."

There was a moment of silence, and then a girl of maybe twenty or so stepped forward; she had dark hair and dark skin and a bindi in the middle of her forehead, making her from India. She caught up the shotgun, examined it, then bent and scooped up the key ring.

She nodded at me, and then moved down the hallway to another door, tried half a dozen keys, and found the one that fit the lock. She threw it open, waved, and went to the next door.

I didn't stick around for the reunions, though. I stuffed the spare magazines in my pockets and jogged for the open door at the end of the hallway. I heard shouting, and knew my not so subtle escape technique had alerted the rest of the compound, or whatever this place was.

Reaching the doorway, I leaned my shoulder against it and peered around the frame and up the stairs; light from above cast long, distorted shadows that were moving down the stairs toward me. I hesitated, considering letting them come down to me, but then decided I didn't really have the patience for tactics. I jogged up the stairs, twisted to aim the submachine gun upward. As soon as I saw a flash of black BDUs, I fired a burst, and then leapt up the stairs three at a time, hitting a landing, aiming upward, and firing again. There were more coming down the stairs, a lot of them. In this scenario, though, I had the advantage. No one behind me, no one in my way. A rifle barked and a round pinged off the railing to my left, then ricocheted off the wall. I ducked away, leaning against the wall to find the best upward vantage point, firing another burst at the scraps of black I saw on the stairs above.

I worked my way upward like that, ducking the occasional close round, but these operatives were clearly not well trained in the art of stairway warfare. It's all about angles, and being an accurate shot. You see a scrap of cloth or a hint of a body, you have to make the shot instantly and accurately, or your round will hit the stairs or the railings, which most of theirs did and a good number of mine as well, seeing as I was firing with a handicap. Fortunately the MP5 is small enough and packs little enough of a kick that I was able to fire across my elbow, even though each burst sent jolts of pain through me. All I could do was grit my teeth and keep going.

I reached the top of the stairs eventually, climbing over bodies, and kicked open the door, hesitated to one side, then took a peek.

Fuck.

The door led outside to a nook between wings of the building, and surrounding the door at a distance of twenty feet or so was a semi-circle of mercenaries waiting for me, their rifles trained on me.

In the center of the group was a single, unarmed figure. Tall, broad-shouldered, dressed in the same paramilitary black as the others. He was rocking a bit of a gut, with side-swept blond hair and brown eyes. He held himself erect with the bearing of a career military man, his hands behind his back.

"Mr. Duke Silver. Thank you for joining us." He spoke with an Eastern European accent.

"Cain."

He nodded. "That is one of my aliases, yes." He gestured to me. "Come, lower the rifle. We have to talk."

"So talk," I snarled, not leaving the doorway.

"I would prefer to do it somewhere more…amenable."

"Yeah, well, I'm not feeling particularly amenable."

Cain shrugged. "You're probably wondering why I brought you here."

I groaned. "Is this where you monologue like a James Bond villain?"

"Aren't you at all curious?"

I shrugged. "To kill me slowly, I assume, and send the video to Harris."

"Oh my, how unoriginal. No, not at all." He brought his hands around front, revealing a tablet computer, an iPad or something, which he set on the ground and slid over to me. "Press the home button, and then play the video."

I snagged the pad with my injured hand, and then ducked back inside the doorway. I hit the home button as he'd instructed, which brought the screen to life, showing a stilled, blurry image of blond hair and pale skin.

"Fuck," I snarled. "Fuck, fuck, fuck."

I touched the play icon at the center of the screen, and the blurry image began moving, resolving into Temple, handcuffed and gagged, eyes wide and fearful.

She tried to talk past the gag, and a gloved hand reached out and yanked the gag down. "Duke, they got Puck, at that cabin. I don't think he's dead, but—baby, I—"

She was cut off by the gag being shoved back into place. In the background, beside Temple, was another woman, darker skinned with long black hair, gagged and bound as well.

A hand reached for the screen, and the images went still and blurry again.

"You see, Mr. Silver? It is in your best interest to cooperate."

Outside I heard a helicopter in the distance. Rage was seething inside me, then, black and thick and all consuming.

"It was never you, you see. I knew who Temple was the whole time. She was the target all along, as a matter of fact, you were just a bonus addition." A pause. "You met some of my...chattel, I believe the word is, down below, yes? Well, your new friend Miss Temple Kennedy, and the other woman, Lola Reed, who is associated with your large comrade Thresh, I think...they are going to join my operation. I know several wealthy gentlemen who will pay a rather staggering sum of money to possess a beautiful, and famous, woman like Miss Kennedy."

"People aren't for sale, you bastard," I shouted.

"Of course they are," Cain answered, his voice smooth and unperturbed. "It's an ancient, time-honored business, the sale of woman flesh. And rather lucrative, I might add."

I took another peek outside the door, and saw that the helicopter was getting closer, approaching over the horizon. I could make out the tail markings, now: N10043Z.

Harris.

How was Harris here?

What about Puck, and the girls?

What the fuck was going on?

I took a breath as I swung back behind the doorframe, switching mags.

I prepared to roll out and face the firing squad—

And then I heard Anselm's Barrett belching thunder, and that fifty cal machine gun started ripsawing, and chaos erupted.

I heard small arms fire from the mercs, and the Barrett, and the fifty cal, and a lot of screaming and shouting, followed by silence.

"Yo, dumbass get out here," Thresh called.

I stepped out; the mercs were all dead, but I didn't see Cain anywhere as I jogged through the mess toward the helo, which was hovering a couple feet off the ground.

I reached the strut, and Thresh reached down with his right hand, grasped mine, and yanked me up and in. I found my footing, and faced my best friend, noticing he was sporting a similar busted left arm—although that was no news to me, I'd just forgotten. The scene in Nevada seemed ages ago, now, although it had only been a matter of a week, if that.

"Thresh, you big bastard. How are you?"

He clapped me into a one-armed hug, and then backed away, as Harris brought us skyward. "They've got our girls, buddy."

I nodded. "Yeah, Cain showed me a video." I glanced around, saw Anselm with his rifle in a seat, and Harris in the pilot's seat, but no Puck. "In the video, Temple said Puck had gotten shot or something. Where is he? What the fuck happened?"

Thresh winced. "Yeah, um, well…we heard shooting so we hauled ass back to Puck's cabin—"

"Wait, back up," I interrupted. "How did you get there? And why?"

"We were stashing the girls there. Puck said nobody knew where it was, that it would be safe. We figured they'd chill there while we came and got you." A shrug of his huge shoulders, though his dark, angry expression belied the casualness of the gesture. "They were on the ground less than fifteen minutes and they got ambushed. Puck laid into 'em, but they popped some tear gas on the girls, snatched 'em, laid Puck out, and took off."

"So where's Puck?"

Another shrug. "We don't know. He wasn't there. Saw a little bit of blood where he'd been, but he was nowhere to be seen, nor were the girls. There were a bunch of tire tracks near the base of the mountain not far from the cabin, but…" Thresh lifted his good hand in a helpless gesture. "They vanished."

"Puck keeps a dirt bike near the cabin. Think he went after 'em?"

"It's the only idea that makes sense. He wouldn't just vanish, not when he knew we were there waiting. But if he had a bike and thought he could catch up to the fuckers? Yeah, he wouldn't hesitate." Thresh held up a radio. "He had a radio, but it was on the ground where we found the blood."

"So…you said fuck the girls, let's get Duke?" I demanded, feeing the anger bubble up. "Forget me, I can take care of myself!"

Anselm stepped forward, holding a hand up in placation. "We assumed it was you they had put a tracer into," he said. "But it was not. It was—"

"Temple," I bit out. "Yeah, I figured that out myself too. Cain said before you showed up that it wasn't about me, it was about her." I rubbed my temple. "All this time I've been assuming Cain's guys were after me, following me, tracking me."

"Meaning what?" Anselm asked.

"Meaning this whole fucking thing has been about Temple! He's gonna sell her to someone as a sex slave." I glanced at Thresh. "So how do we find her?"

Thresh answered. "With the help of our good buddy Lear." He gestured outside, to the compound we were flying away from. "He's hacked into their system. He says he can find the signal they're receiving and send us to it."

"And Puck?"

Anselm answered. "Would you want to be on the receiving end of a very angry Puck?"

I pulled a face. "Hell no."

"We go after the girls, and assume Puck will make his presence known along the way."

Harris twisted in the pilot's seat, his expression grim. "More bad news, boys." He tapped his headset. "Just got a call from Roth. Apparently Cain's guys hit the island too. He's got Layla and Kyrie, too."

"Shit," Thresh, Anselm, and I all said at once.

"He's planning an auction," Thresh said.

I met Harris's gaze. "I think we're going to need more friends."

Harris nodded. "Already done. I've got Sasha and the rest of the Caribbean crew headed this way, along with a very, very pissed off Valentine Roth."

Everyone went silent at that news; Roth was intimidating when he was in a *good* mood.

Harris turned back to the controls, and we flew in silence for a few minutes. After a bit, Harris sat up straighter, listening to something in his headset.

He turned back to face us. "The good news is, Lear has the signal."

"And the bad news?" I asked.

"They're over the Atlantic, heading to Europe." Harris reached out and clapped my shoulder.

"What about Puck?" I asked again.

Harris chuckled darkly. "Something tells me he's on that plane."

Keep reading for a sneak preview of:

PUCK

AN ALPHA ONE SECURITY NOVEL

By
JASINDA WILDER

1

99 PROBLEMS

Now, I've been in some hairy situations before, but this one? This was a hell of a pickle.

I'd followed the Hummer with the girls in it for something like a hundred miles, keeping off the road and following from just inside the tree line, staying as far back as I dared when the tree line ran out. Which was a difficult job in and of itself on a dirt bike, but considering I'd taken half a dozen NATO rounds to the center of my chest, and another one that had claimed the upper half of my favorite finger—the middle one on my left hand—I was not happy.

I was wearing a vest, so the rounds to the chest had just left gnarly bruises and hurt like a bitch, but weren't anything to worry about. The finger was a bit of a problem, though. How the hell was I going to flip people off, now? One full birdie and a stump? Fuck that. And yeah, it didn't tickle, having a finger shot off. There hadn't exactly been a lot of time in which to do triage, so I'd lit my cigar, puffed till it was nice and hot, and then used the nice bright orange cinder to cauterize the end.

Sounds fun, right?

Yeah, it wasn't.

Problem was, a cigar cherry ain't nowhere near hot enough to really truly cauterize something, so the stump was getting bloody again.

Which was number…like, fifty, on my list of problems.

Ninety-nine problems, but a bitch ain't one—the Jay-Z line went through my head, which was funny, because it wasn't one bitch that was the problem, it was *two*. And don't get your panties in a cinch. I just meant "bitch" as a generic term for woman, and in this case, I meant it as a term of endearment—I like those girls, Lola and Temple, which is why I'm here in the first fucking place.

Significantly higher up the list was the fact that I was in the cargo compartment of a privately-owned 727, and we were way, way up there, which meant it was cold as fuck in here; they hadn't bothered warming it, since it was empty…except for little old me.

Also a problem was that I had no weapons, since I'd had to leave the shotgun behind in order to ride the dirt bike.

Furthermore, I had no plan for what to when we got wherever the hell we were going—the lack of knowledge was yet another problem on the list.

Additionally, Harris and the gang, as far as I knew, had no idea what was going on, although I trusted them to find out eventually. Which meant, for the moment, I was on my own.

In the hold of an airliner at cruising altitude.

Without a weapon.

Responsible for the lives of two beautiful women, who happened to be the girlfriends of my two closest brothers-in-arms.

And have I mentioned the twenty-some armed men a few feet above me in the passenger cabin?

Going in my favor, though, are two facts: I'm a stone-cold, hard-ass motherfucker, and I'm *really* pissed off.

Good thing I like to party hard.

Puck: Alpha One Security: Book 3
COMING SOON

JASINDA WILDER

Visit me at my website: **www.jasindawilder.com**
Email me: **jasindawilder@gmail.com**

If you enjoyed this book, you can help others enjoy it as well by recommending it to friends and family, or by mentioning it in reading and discussion groups and online forums. You can also review it on the site from which you purchased it. But, whether you recommend it to anyone else or not, thank you *so much* for taking the time to read my book! Your support means the world to me!

My other titles:

The Preacher's Son:
Unbound
Unleashed
Unbroken

Biker Billionaire:
Wild Ride

Delilah's Diary:
A Sexy Journey

A Sexy Surrender

Big Girls Do It:
Boxed Set
Married
Pregnant

Rock Stars Do It:
Harder
Dirty
Forever
Omnibus

From the world of *Big Girls* and *Rock Stars*:
Big Love Abroad

The Falling Series:
Falling Into You
Falling Into Us
Falling Under
Falling Away
Falling for Colton

The Ever Trilogy:
Forever & Always
After Forever
Saving Forever

From the world of *Wounded*:
Wounded
Captured

From the world of *Stripped*:
Stripped
Trashed

From the world of *Alpha*:
Alpha
Beta
Omega
Harris: Alpha One Security Book 1

Thresh: Alpha One Security Book 2

The Houri Legends:
Jack and Djinn
Djinn and Tonic

The Madame X Series:
Madame X
Exposed
Exiled

Badd Brothers:
Badd Motherf*cker

The Black Room
(With Jade London):
Door One
Door Two
Door Three
Door Four
Door Five
Door Six
Door Seven
Door Eight
The Deleted Door

Standalone titles:
Yours

Non-Fiction titles:
Big Girls Do It Running

Jack Wilder Titles:
The Missionary

To be informed of new releases and special offers, sign up for Jasinda's email newsletter.